BY WESLEY CHU

The Art of Prophecy

The Art of Destiny

THE ART OF DESTINY

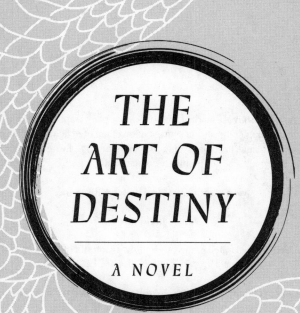

THE ART OF DESTINY

A NOVEL

THE WAR ARTS SAGA: BOOK TWO

WESLEY CHU

NEW YORK

Published in the United States by Del Rey, an imprint of Random House, a division of Penguin Random House LLC, New York.

Del Rey and the Circle colophon are registered trademarks of Penguin Random House LLC.

Map on pages viii–ix by Sunga Park was originally published in the paperback edition of *The Art of Prophecy* by Wesley Chu (New York: Del Rey, 2023).

Hardback ISBN 978-0-593-23766-3
International edition ISBN 978-0-593-72419-4
Ebook ISBN 978-0-593-23767-0

Printed in Canada on acid-free paper

randomhousebooks.com

2 4 6 8 9 7 5 3 1

First Edition

Book design by Jo Anne Metsch

To those searching for their way,
and to those guiding them

To Tricia

WHITE GHOST
LANDS

DIYU
MOUNTAIN

CLOUD
PILLARS

VAUZAN

YUKIAN RIVER

WUGOH

MANJING

NGYN OCEAN

TRUE FREEZE

HRUSHA

MT. SHETTY

ALLANTO

SHINGYONG
MOUNTAINS

JIAYF

DANZIYI

CELESTIAL
PALACE

SEA OF
FLOWERS

SÁNBA

XUSAN

BLUE
SEA

SAND SNAKE

THE ORIGINAL TEMPLE
OF THE TIANDI

DRAMATIS PERSONAE

THE TIANDI

Bhasani, Narwani Master of the Drowned Fist.

Chown, Wu Master mapmaker in Sanba. Father to Zofi. Deceased.

Dongshi Duke of Lawkan. Former whisperlord of the empire. Leader of the Ten Hounds.

Faaru Palacelord of the Celestial Palace. Father figure to Jian. Deceased.

Fausan, Noon also God of Gamblers. Master of the Whipfinger Style Song Family Ho Lineage.

Guanshi also Guanshi Kanyu. Master of the Longxian Northern Fist School of War in Jiayi. Killed by Sali.

Hachi Heir to the Whipfinger Style Song Family Ho Lineage. Close friend to Jian.

Horashi Bodyguard to Jian at the Celestial Palace. Spared by Taishi.

Jian, Wen also Lu Hiro. Champion of the Five Under Heaven. The Prophesied Hero of the Tiandi. Heir to the Windwhispering School of the Zhang Lineage. #1 Most Wanted Fugitive in the Enlightened States.

Kaiyu, Hwang Heir of the Houtou style Third Lin Lineage. Close friend to Jian.

Kasa, Hwang also the Sky Monkey. Master of the Houtou style Third Lin Lineage. Father to Kaiyu.

Keiro, Zhu Senior of the Southern Cross in Jiayi. Former rival to Xinde.

Kua Naifun also the Black Night of Xing. Tea Master of the Hazy Dreams Tea House in Bahngtown. Adviser to Taishi.

Kui Master acupuncturist. Doctor in Jiayi. Teacher to Meehae.

Li also Auntie Li. Former cook at the Longxian Northern Fist School of War.

Liuman Hansoo monk. Twelve rings. Pahm's former master. Killed by Qisami.

Meehae Apprentice acupuncturist. Close friend to Jian in Sanba.

Mori, Lee Templeabbot of the Temple of the Tiandi in Vauzan. Former lover to Taishi.

Pahm Hansoo war monk. Four rings. Close friend to Xinde and Jian.

Riga Bodyguard to Jian at the Celestial Palace. Betrayed Jian. Not spared by Taishi.

Saan also the Painted Tiger. Duke of Shulan. Former Emperor Xuanshing's second son. Former student to Taishi.

Sanu Templeabbot of the Original Temple of the Tiandi. Killed by Qisami.

Sohn, Soa Master of the Eternal Bright Light Fist Pan Family Pan Lineage. Lost heir to the family's schools. Formerly nicknamed Pan's Pillaging Playboy. Wanted Fugitive.

Sonaya, Ras Daughter of the Drowned Fist. Bhasani's heir.

Sunri also the Desert Lioness. Duchess of Caobiu. Former concubine to Emperor Xuanshing.

Taishi, Ling also Nai Roha. Grandmaster of the Windwhispering School of the Zhang Lineage; Windwhispering School of the Zhang Lineage of the Ling Family Branch. Distant #2 Most Wanted Fugitive in the Enlightened States.

Urwan, Psy Horselord of Gyian. Horse breeder residing in the Cloud Pillars. Friend to Taishi.

Waylin Duke of Xing. Cousin to the Emperor Xuanshing.

Xinde Captain of the Caobiu Stone Watchers long eyes unit. Former First Senior of the Longxian War Art Academy. Close friend to Jian from back in Jiayi.

Yanso Duke of Gyian. Former purselord to Emperor Xuanshing.

Zofi, Wu Taishi's close confidant and assistant. Best friend and tutor to Jian.

THE SHADOW

Akiana, Aki Lady of Aki household. Twin to Akiya. Youngest daughter of Lord Aki Niam. Under the care of Qisami as Child Companion Kiki.

Akiya, Aki Lady of Aki household. Twin to Akiana. Youngest daughter of Lord Aki Niam. Under the care of Qisami as Child Companion Kiki.

Burandin Shadowkill in Qisami's cell. Husband to Koteuni.

Chiafana also Firstwife. The Minister of Critical Purpose. Adviser to Duchess Sunri of Caobiu.

Cyyk, Quan also Cyknan. Lord in the Quan family of Caobiu. Son of Highlord General Quan Sah. Former student of the Longxian School. Grunt in Qisami's cell.

Eifan also the Black Widow. Silkspinner. Weblord of Jiayi. Cousin to Qisami.

Haaren Shadowkill in Qisami's cell. Opera. Killed by Taishi.

Hari Estatekeeper on Duke Yanso's estate. Boss to Qisami.

Hilao Palacemaiden to Duke Yanso's estate in Gyian. Best friend to Qisami on the estate.

Koteuni Shadowkill in Qisami's cell. Second in command. Wife to Burandin. Close adviser to Qisami.

Niam, Aki High Lord of the Aki House of Gyian. Lord of the Fine Blades. Close friend and adviser to Duke Yanso. Father to Akiya and Akiana.

Porla Scullerymaiden on Duke Yanso's estate. Roommate to Qisami.

Qisami, Maza also Kiki. Copper tier Shadowkill from the Bo Po Mo Fo training pool. Former diamond tier operative under demotion and garnishment from the Consortium.

Ruli Palacemaiden to Duke Yanso's estate in Gyian. Roommate to Qisami.

Yoshi, Sabana Senior Account Executive with the Central Orb. Silkspinner.

Zwei also Zweilang. Shadowkill in Qisami's cell. Opera. A Yiyang.

THE KATUIA

Ariun Defensechief of Nezra. Former Council member of Nezra. Adviser to Sali. Deceased.

Batu Clan chief of Sheetan.

Daewon Master tinker (unofficial). Council member of the Nezra clan. Husband to Mali.

Hampa Viperstrike. Neophyte to Salminde.

Jhamsa Elder Spirit Shaman of Katuia. Council member of Chaqra, the Black City. Former heart-father to Sali.

Jiamin also The Eternal Khan of Katuia. The Lord of the Grass Sea. Childhood friend of Sali. Deceased.

Lehuangxi Thiraput Cungle Captain of the *Hana Iceberg*. Friend to Sali.

Mali also Malinde the Master Tinker (unofficial). Sectchief to Nezra tinker sect. Council member of the Nezra clan. Sister to Sali.

Marhi also Hoisannisi Jayngnaga Marhi. Rumblerlead of Hightop cluster. Friend to Hampa.

Quasa Custodian of the Viperstrike. Former viperstrike.

Raydan also Raydan the Stormchaser. The Stormchaser. Former raidbrother to Sali.

Sali also Salminde the Viperstrike. The Viperstrike. Will of the Khan. Council member of the Nezra clan.

Shobansa Nezra Supplychief. Trader and wealthiest person in Nezra.

Suriptika also Conchitsha Abu Suriptika. Happan ritualist. Cobbler in Hrusha. Healer to Sali.

Yuraki also Rich Man Yuraki. Elder of Hightop cluster. Important politician in Hrusha.

ACT I

CHAPTER ONE

THE MAIL

The caravan of covered wagons snaked along the craggy face of a mountain range known as the Five Ugly Brothers. They were three quarters of the way up the fourth Ugly Brother, and running late. Jai Janus had hoped they would reach the mail post before nightfall, but he wasn't sure if the oxen had enough pull in them to clear the final stretch. To be honest, he wasn't having an easy time keeping his own eyelids open either. Fortunately, his side-seat driver was excellent at keeping him awake.

Besides being able to navigate routes and flash signal codes, Aimei was incredibly adept at talking for hours on end, pausing only occasionally to breathe. She had been prating on about her latest drama since dawn, when they had set off from the peak of the second Ugly Brother. "He's out every night with his gross, mangy friends, skulking on the streets, and then creeps home in the morning, stinking of sweat and piss. All my bed sheets are ruined!"

Janus bit his lip and swallowed another sigh. "Why don't you just—"

Aimei finished taking a breath. "The worst part is he always brings home a midnight snack and insists on eating it right on the bed. There's gross leftovers scattered all over the sheets every morning. And my mattress is woven from loose straw, so you know I can't just wipe it off. To clean up all the bits of food—can't have crumbs, mind you. It'll attract sludge beetles—I have to comb through the straw and individually pick every piece out." She gesticulated with conviction. "Don't get me started on his breath. It's like death. Like if I just mouth-kissed a ten-day-old corpse."

"You did what?"

Aimei's eyes brimmed. "He used to be so affectionate, so much fun. Now he ignores me and pretends I don't exist unless he needs something, like I'm just a servant or cook or some occasional plaything when he's bored. It's really unfair. I'm always so nice to him."

"Just lock the door at night. Teach him a lesson. Don't let him push— Hold." Janus scanned the horizon. Night had swept in quicker than expected with both the Queen and Prince hidden behind a thick blanket of dark rolling rain clouds. It might get wet soon. He yanked on the reins to urge the oxen forward. "We're losing visibility, even with the forward lantern's spotlights. The road will soon tilt to the right up ahead. Signal a warning to the rest of the team."

Aimei lived to chatter, but that didn't take away from her being an otherwise skilled and well-trained side-seat. She grabbed hold of a lantern swaying off the side of the wagon, sliding the cover in and out to flash a long blink, a pause, and then two more. A row of single flashes, one for each wagon behind them, confirmed receipt of Janus's order.

"Prep the spotlights," he added.

Aimei slipped off her perch to light the two lanterns hanging off each side of the wagon. Two strong beams of yellow light shone straight into the night haze and the darkened tree lines. Two more on the other side lit up shortly after. She returned to her perch a moment later to yank at a long lever near her feet, releasing two poles out along the sides of the wagon, each with a lantern at its end. The other wagons soon followed suit, extending their own antennae two at a time until the caravan looked like a giant centipede skittering up the side of the dark mountain on glowing feet.

Once all of the antennae had fanned opened, Aimei picked up where she had left off. "How could you say such a thing? I can't just lock Mop out of the house. He won't last one night by himself."

"Maybe you should just get a new cat then," Janus muttered. Before she could sputter her outrage, he pointed forward. "Check the road up ahead."

Aimei obeyed, grabbing the handle of a large forward-facing spotlight and directing it just ahead of the team of oxen. She swept it back and forth along the ground, each time aiming just a little bit farther out. It wasn't long before she found something: a pair of knee-high brown boots. The spotlight continued to climb upward, revealing a colorful, garish, and slightly oversize merchant's travel cloak and settling on the pale face of a young man below a fountain of black hair.

The man waggled his fingers in a wave. "Ho, honorable friend. It is such a great fortune to see your arrival." There was an insecure smugness to his smirk, unearned bravado.

Janus gnashed his teeth. "I actually thought we were going to finish this leg without incident."

Aimei leaned close. "Maybe we should just run him over."

He shook his head. "Nah, that's rude. It would violate the commerce codes anyway. I'm not paying a fine on his account."

"My horse, my poor horse has fallen lame. I am left stranded." The stranger in the spotlight launched into a well-rehearsed monologue, raising one arm toward the sky and cupping his heart with the other. "Could I beseech you, noble sir, for some assistance?" The young man couldn't have been more than twenty. His skin was too milky for a peasant, and his words too flowery, reflecting an education. He also couldn't act his way out of a burlap sack.

Janus snapped his fingers twice and waved him off. "First of all, that's a terrible delivery. You weren't even looking at me. Why are you talking to the sky? Who are you serenading, the Queen? My face is down here. Look at the person you're talking to, me, the person you're trying to rob. Second of all, your tone is all over the place. I can't tell if you're trying to swindle me or bed me. Pick a motive and stick to the lane, son, because it's late, and my back is quivering from having to hunch forward all day. We have a full wagon of ducal post to sort tomorrow, and my eyes are burning from a long day on the haul." He gestured for the stranger to hurry up. "So skip to the epilogue, yeah?"

The stranger did not seem to mind the interruption. "Very well." He raised his arms dramatically and clapped three times. Several figures emerged from the shadows. He continued orating. "You have the privilege of being robbed by the Righteous Raiders, the crew of a hundred scores."

"Really?" Aimei's eyes widened. She had been taken in by the bandit's presentation. She was usually easily impressed.

"Righteous Raiders, eh? Stupid name." Janus got a better look at the stranger. "You look a little too much of a small dumpling to have earned a hundred scores."

"It's more of a goal," the young man admitted.

Aimei's eyes narrowed, and she folded her arms. "How many robberies have you *actually* pulled off?"

Janus elbowed her in the shoulder lightly.

His side-seat elbowed him back. "What? I want to know."

"Five, but three were in the past few weeks."

Janus didn't bother stifling his laugh. "Five? No wonder your scabbard's tied on wrong. You bunch of muddied pig feet flee your lord and suddenly think you're all real bandits now, yeah? That's a nice blade. Where did you steal it?"

The stranger stayed in character. "Earned in a duel with a master war artist off the Tyk Coast."

"It's pronounced Tyk Coast, third accent," Janus retorted. "Get it right."

"Are you in charge?" asked the orator.

"I'm the headguard. Are you the leader of this band of dirt-wallowing peasants?" he shot back.

"I am the legendary Tuhan the Woo."

"Never heard of you." Janus actually had, but he wasn't going to give the boy any cred. He rose to his feet and crossed his arms. His back really was aching. He couldn't wait until he could hand the reins over to Aimei.

She just needed a little more seasoning. "Wait, you're that runaway monk. Brother Big Brother."

"He doesn't look that big to me," scoffed Aimei. "Why do they call you that?"

Tuhan shrugged. "I go by many titles, but that's a new one." He turned to those standing nearby. "Boys, anyone ever hear me referred to as that?"

A smattering chorus of "No, Big Brother, never, Big Brother" followed. More bodies emerged from the tree line. The lead wagon was now completely surrounded.

"Let's get this over with." Janus nudged Aimei, but the girl was already prepared, one hand resting on the shaft of a holstered short spear. Janus grabbed a mallet the size of his palm and banged the small gong hanging off the side of his perch. The ringing passed from wagon to wagon all the way down the line. Then he jumped off the wagon and drew the mallet's much larger sibling, which rivaled Janus's height. The rest of the caravan guards emerged from their wagons and began making their way to the front. The last few coming up from the far back were still strapping on their armor.

The two sides sized each other up. Janus didn't get an accurate count of how many, but he knew at a glance the numbers were skewed enough that it didn't matter.

Tuhan looked smug. "Twelve guards against forty Righteous."

"Closer to thirty," replied Janus.

"I have more in the woods as backup."

"Sure you do."

The monk flashed a bright smile as if he were giving a sermon on Tenth Day Prayer. "A word of advice, my good senior sir, you should just take the loss. It's better for everyone."

Janus considered the odds for a moment. Then he considered all the other financial implications involved. He shook his head. "Nah, we'll fight it out."

The leader of the Righteous Raiders momentarily broke character. "Are you sure, headguard?"

"Let's see what you have, double brother runaway monk."

The guards and bandits lined up politely. One never knew when the person across from them may end up on the same side one day. After a few last-minute armor adjustments and drawing of weapons, Janus raised an arm and stomped his feet three times. Tuhan mirrored the movements.

The two sides came together in a messy, dull crash. It had been a long day, and everyone was tired. A lazy ax met a half-hearted swung sword. A mace dinged against a shield when it really should have been a louder dong. Even the grunts and yells sounded forced. It was also quickly obvious that these mud-slipping, doe-faced peasants were just that, not experienced soldiers or bandits. You could put these peasants in the finest armor wielding the sharpest swords and riding the fiercest steeds. It didn't matter. Regardless of how you dress them, a peasant will always be a peasant. Arrow fodder was all they were good for.

No one was fighting particularly hard, except for perhaps Aimei, who was obviously working for a fight bonus. She always did. Apparently, feeding that cat was expensive. Janus's side-seat fought in the thick of the battle, clashing with several bandits at once and finding the mark in several, which was good enough to earn the first blood payout.

Janus wished the girl didn't always give her full effort. It was exhausting just to be close to her sometimes, but as the only woman in his crew, she worked twice as hard as everyone on everything, and as his apprentice, she was twice as hard on everyone else as well. He had been meaning to have a talk with her about that. There were many times when a crew should give it their all. Right now wasn't one of them.

In any case, Janus had no intention of letting this play out any more than necessary. After a brief series of hits and blows, his people holding their own but slowly getting overwhelmed by sheer numbers, he decided to call it.

Janus raised his mallet over his head, slightly disappointed he hadn't even gotten to use it. "All right, that's enough. The caravan is yours, Brother Big Brother."

Tuhan, who also hadn't drawn his saber yet, was standing on the opposite side of the small field, and frowned. "Are you sure? The stoppage feels early."

Janus shrugged. "Long enough for my crew to earn fight pay. Not worth it to go for the win bonus." He had to pull Aimei back from still trying to paw at her opponent, and then hauled Enja and Pio off the ground. Pio *may* actually have broken a leg, which looked like the worst of the injuries. "Surrender formation, boys. Back to the wagon and let the good raiders finish their work." Once his people had retreated, Janus turned over a sand clock to start the count and turned back to Tuhan. "As agreed by the commerce code, you're allocated fifteen minutes. Try to keep it neat, will you?"

Tuhan the Woo was too preoccupied to listen, however. He had picked up Aimei's dropped short sword and was busy asking her to tea, which she was clearly enjoying. Janus reluctantly admitted the bandit-lord came across like a rogue straight out of a Burning Hearts romance. The man was a jackass, but at least a dashing one.

Janus hauled her back to the surrender formation before the two could set a date. "Act professional, will you?"

The Righteous Raiders began to pick through the caravan like ants on a rotting melon. What they lacked in skill and organization, they made up for in numbers. Janus was surprised to count that there really were forty or so of them. With so many mouths to feed, it was no wonder they had to hit so many caravans.

The bandits were midway through ransacking the third wagon when the door to the riding carriage in the rear banged open. A stout, fleshy man with neatly combed hair stumbled out still wearing a sleep sack. He looked aghast at the bandits crawling all over the wagons and stormed up to the front of the caravan.

He shook a fist at Janus. "What's going on? What is the meaning of this? Why aren't you stopping these brigands from absconding with the merchandise? They're robbing me!"

"We tried, Boss Izun. Battle's over. You lost." Janus shook his head. "I *did* tell you twelve was too few for a caravan this size, but you didn't want to bring on my second unit. You wanted to save the liang."

"Battle's already over?" Izun looked the guards over. "There's barely a mark on any of you!"

Everyone looked offended. "Of course not," huffed Enja, who was one of the ones wearing only half of his armor. "We're professionals. We don't chop people up every fight. Who can do business like that?"

Janus hurried to calm Izun's nerves. "Worry not, Boss. Everyone's operating under the lunar court commerce rules. These fine gentlemen won't take more than a quarter, and it'll be merchandise only. No personal belongings or extracurricular killings. On their good word."

"A quarter? On a bandit's good word?" The caravan boss paled. "What am I paying you miserable dogs for?" He turned abruptly and took two steps toward the leader of the Righteous Raiders. "And you, I don't know who you think you—"

"I'm surrounded by amateurs these days," Janus complained. Before his employer made it a third of the way, Janus hooked the shaft of his mallet around his weedy neck in a choke hold and dragged him back to the rest of the guards. "Don't mind him, banditlord. He's new, just like you, and needs to learn the rules."

"Traitor, traitor!" Izun screeched, pawing ineffectually at Janus's face. "You're all in on this vile scam, you backstabbing goats."

Janus jerked the mallet sharply sideways and thunked the boss across the head, just hard enough to shut him up. "Stop squirming or I'll throw you into a trunk until this is over. I just saved your life." He handed the quivering Izun over to Aimei once the man settled down. "Stay on him. No one gets paid if he dies."

The merchant struggled weakly in her grasp. "You . . . traitors . . ."

Janus held up his hands apologetically. "Sorry about that disturbance, banditlord. Fresh fish from Lawkan. Hasn't learned the local commerce rules yet." His voice trailed off. He looked up. "Do you hear that?"

The Righteous Raiders boss frowned. "Hear what?"

Then they all did, a faint wailing over the high-pitched whistle of the stiff breeze.

Tuhan glanced back at his crew and at the rest of the raiders. No, the sound was bouncing across the mountain range, but it was coming from farther away. Janus looked up the road and squinted, noticing for the first time a lone figure running toward them from up the road, wildly flapping arms.

Tuhan by now had noticed as well. He cupped his palms around his eyes. "Who interrupts a robbery?"

"One of yours?" asked Janus.

"Don't think so. We've been lying in wait all day. Maybe someone from the delivery post?"

The yelling became more coherent as the intruder neared. "Wait, don't leave yet."

The two men exchanged glances.

"Who is leaving?" asked Tuhan.

"Certainly not us." Janus checked the sand clock. "Not for another seven minutes."

"Thanks for the reminder." Tuhan raised his voice. "Wrap it up, my righteous brothers!"

The stranger reached the edge of the crowd near the first wagon. He slowed to a labored jog and then hung his head low, his chest heaving as he rested his hands on his knees. "Thanks . . . thanks for waiting. I got to the drop post late, thought I'd missed the wagon. Then I saw your lanterns in the distance and tried to catch up. I have a package to pick up . . ."

The newcomer was young, with long hair pulled back at the nape of his neck. His face was youthful, with a sparse patch of hair on his chin. The rest of his face needed tweezers more than a blade. His skin was tanned, wind-whipped and beaten by the King. His plain, coarse tunic and dirty trousers were of livestock quality, soaked with sweat and caked to his body, revealing a surprisingly lean and muscular figure. He was also completely oblivious to the situation. Janus recognized him after a few moments. It was one of the local boys who had moved into the region the past few cycles. It took him a bit longer to put a name to that face.

Janus raised a hand. "Hello, Hiro. You should probably go back to the delivery post. We'll be along shortly."

Hiro waved back and then appeared to realize that he was surrounded by armed men with their weapons drawn. "Is this a bad time?"

"Who is this guppy?" asked Tuhan.

"Just a local kid," he told Tuhan. "Don't mind him."

"Are your wagons stuck here? I can help push." Hiro offered a weak smile. "Hey!"

One of the bandits had grabbed him by the collar and was shoving him off to the side.

"Just hang still, Hiro," shouted Janus. "We'll get to you after this business is done."

A commotion at the back of the caravan drew Janus's attention. One of his guards was quarreling with four bandits. "Headguard," called his man, "they're trying to break into the mail wagon."

The merchant Izun's eyes bulged, and he temporarily escaped Aimei's grasp. "That's an official postal wagon, you ball-licking dog. It's ducal insured and off-limits, you mud-faced, stone-brained ass-bottom!"

This time, the flat of Janus's mallet knocked him out cold. That didn't mean the trader was wrong, though. Janus snapped at the banditlord. "What are you little minnows doing? Can't you see the imperial purple seal with the bright gold Zhingzhi? You can't be that fresh of a fish to hit up a ducal-backed wagon."

Tuhan did not appear to worry. "The dukes are too embroiled in their civil war, burning their own lands, to worry about a little disruption in the post. They won't care."

Janus knew for a fact they would, on pure principle if nothing else. The dukes of the Enlightened States never let anything slide. Attacking anything ducal-marked was an attack on their power. Still, if these dumb carcasses wanted to wrap their mouths around this hook, he would let them. He signaled to his man to step aside and let the righteous fools gleefully tear into the ducal wagon. He shook his head in disbelief and disgust as people's mail packages, crates, and personal belongings were haphazardly tossed onto the muddy road.

"Hey," Hiro protested, squirming in a bandit's grasp as one of the raiders pulled out a package neatly wrapped in bright-orange rice paper and sniffed it curiously. "That's my aunt's delivery. She really needs it."

The bandit holding him pressed a blade to his throat. "Your auntie needs that package like you need a hole in your neck, swine."

"I'm not the one who smells like I bathe in a trough," Hiro shot back, earning him a punch in the gut. Interestingly, it didn't fold him over. Either the boy was made of tougher stuff, or the bandit didn't know how to punch. The boy's protest, however, caught Tuhan's attention.

The runaway monk walked over to the discarded crate with the expensive orange wrapping paper. He nudged it lightly with his boot. "What do you have in here that's so important, son?"

Hiro must have realized his mistake too late. "Nothing."

"Right." Tuhan flourished his expensive-looking saber, used it like the ignorant peasant that he was to crack open the crate. The saber was obviously a nobleman's toy, probably not suited for battle, and definitely not suitable for packages.

A pained cry drew Janus's attention back to Hiro, who had somehow acquired a knife from one of the bandits. The young man, with an arm around the bandit's neck, dragged him toward the crate while leveling the knife at any nearby bandits. "I don't want any trouble. I just want to get my package and go. My aunt's been expecting it. If I don't get it to her, there will be trouble. And I'm honestly not in the mood for that tonight, or any night, really, so let me just get my stuff, and you all can keep"—he motioned at everyone—"doing whatever it is you guys are doing."

Tuhan pointed his blade at him. "Get this dog!"

Janus tried to defuse the situation. A commoner getting gutted during a robbery was bad business for both sides. "Come on, this is embarrassing. Let's not kill each other over the mail."

It was too late, however.

The rest of the raiders converged on him. The nearest bandit, a large, brawny man wearing a wok as a breastplate, tried to knock the boy over with a metal-gloved fist. Hiro turned aside sharply and sent the raider flying onto his belly. The boy twisted and turned through the onslaught, impressively avoiding fists, thrusts, and tackles coming at him from every direction while mucking around in ankle-deep mud. He ducked the swing of a mace that would have exploded his head like a melon. He dodged the slash of a rusty ax that would have taken his arm off. Within a matter of seconds, four of the bandits were groaning on the ground. Two others were unconscious.

Janus's jaw dropped. All this time, he had thought the boy weak and hollow-headed, always averting his gaze from meeting theirs. No one would have suspected he had this war artistry in him.

Then Tuhan the Woo found himself alone with the young man. The bandit's face was sheet-white and his eyes wide like moons, but still he continued the bravado. "You're begging for a messy death, guppy!"

Hiro pointed unhelpfully at Tuhan's tight two-handed grip on his saber. "You're holding it wrong."

"Shut your dirty mouth!" Tuhan lunged forward.

The weapon seemed to pass through Hiro's body with no effect. The boy had trapped the blade in his armpit. He spun around, whipping the saber out of Tuhan's grip. This was skill, but nothing special. Janus himself had had to use that technique back when he had been employed at a gambling hall. That meant the boy had high-level training, though. Janus wondered from whom; he couldn't quite make out the fighting style. It certainly wasn't from any of the mainstream schools.

Hiro released the blade from his arm and caught it with his other hand, all in one fluid flourish, bringing the edge of the saber to rest on Tuhan's shoulder, with just enough pressure to drive him down to his knees. The runaway monk froze, terrified. A few moments later, Hiro tossed the blade aside. "I don't want any more trouble. I just want my package."

"Fine," cried Tuhan the Woo. "Take it. Get out of here."

The rest of the raiders had learned their lesson and backed away. Hiro carefully put the lid of the crate back on, then hefted it onto his back. He rummaged through the container of letters, pulling out several, then looked over at Janus. "Are you going to be all right, Headguard Janus?"

It took him a moment to process that. He nodded. "Sure, Hiro. Don't worry about us. We're all covered under the commerce codes here. Assuming these fools don't break those too." Breaking ducal laws was stupid enough, but no one messed around with lunar court decrees.

Hiro nodded and then retreated into the now-black woods, heading the direction of the fifth Ugly Brother. A quiet settled over the area. Janus looked over at Aimei, nodding. "I did not expect that."

"Does that mean we get a victory bonus, boss?"

"It doesn't work that way, girl. You can't surrender and then try to win."

She frowned. "Why not?"

"Because then no one will ever let anyone surrender ever again, and that creates problems for everyone."

"I see." Aimei didn't look as if she did see the point.

Tuhan scrambled to his feet and grabbed onto Janus, yelling, "What was that about? You said he was harmless!"

"I mean, he *looked* harmless." Janus barely noticed Tuhan's limp grip shaking his tunic.

Eventually, Tuhan realized he wasn't paying any attention. His outrage sputtered, and the runaway monk named Tuhan the Woo, or Brother Big Brother, quieted as his gaze followed Janus's into the mountainous forest where the boy had disappeared. The banditlord furrowed his brow. "What was that boy's name again?"

CHAPTER TWO

A LONG DAY

Wen Jian, Prophesied Hero of the Tiandi, the Champion of the Five Under Heaven, the Savior of the Zhuun, and also probably the most wanted man in all the Enlightened States, felt like the hopping dead by the time he dragged his feet up the long, winding stairs that coiled around the pillar up to the plateau he called home. Even before he arrived, he was already exhausted, hungry, wet, and completely miserable. Home was a small cluster of stone-and-clay hovels framed by a crumbling wall that rested upon the giant stone pillar that made up part of the Piranha Peaks nestled deep within the Cloud Pillars on the other side of the valley opposite the Ugly Brothers.

Zofi was waiting when he finally made it to the top of the stairs. She enjoyed reading by moonlight on the balcony jutting over the cliff's edge and had probably seen his lantern on the way up. The young woman, a former mapmaker's daughter Taishi had picked up during her travels through the city of Sanba on her way to the original Temple of the Tiandi, had accompanied Taishi to the Cloud Pillars, and ended up staying to offer the "softer" and quite possibly more important portion of Jian's education. She tutored him in language, geography, politics, and mathematics. Jian was by all accounts a mediocre student on his best days, and an embarrassing fool on most others.

Her eyes widened when he walked into the glow of her lantern. "What happened to you? Did you get into a tussle with a hippopotamus?" She had recently discovered these creatures' existence, and they were now her favorite thing in the world.

Jian slumped his shoulders. "It's been a long day."

Half of his body was caked with mud, and a great welt, shaped like a purple flower and the size of a dragon fruit, had blossomed on his cheek. The rest of his body was marked with scratches and cuts, several visible through his shredded robe. He also may or may not have broken a toe.

Zofi held out a hand. "Hand over the fish you bartered for with Kasa. Get cleaned up first before you set foot in the main house."

"About that." Jian's shoulders clenched. "I lost it."

"Lost what, the fish?" Her eyes grew intense. More intense than usual. "I had to trade two jars of truffles that I dug up with my two bare hands for that fish!"

"Technically, we dug those up together." Jian regretted the words the moment they left his lips.

Zofi shook both hands at him. "How did this happen?"

He shrank under her gaze. "I slipped off a current while riding toward Bahngtown and dropped the sack of fish into the river."

"Couldn't you just have swooped down and picked it back up again?"

"I sort of fell in with it." His face turned red. "A passing flock of geese startled me. They came out of nowhere!"

Zofi buried her face in her hands. "A goose scared you? That's why you dropped a week's worth of meat?"

"It gets worse," he muttered.

"Oh, glorious. I guess we're eating rice and spiced vegetables for the next month." She fixed him with a stern look. "You did get the spices, right?"

"Like I said, worse." He offered her a weak, guilty smile. "The Yukian's currents were rough today. I almost drowned. I really should learn how to swim one of these days." He paused. "Anyway, by the time I made it back to shore, I was too far downstream from Bahngtown to make it back. I had to head to the delivery post instead."

"Rice and unseasoned vegetables. That's great." Zofi scoffed. "Did you get the mail at least? Taishi is going to have one of these depictions of you on the wall come true if you didn't get her shipment."

He held up a small bundle of letters and turned around so she could see the crate strapped to his back. "More or less."

"At least you didn't screw that up." She squinted. "What happened to the container?"

Jian wasn't in the mood. "Can we go inside first? I'm cold and tired, and I haven't eaten since that terrible breakfast you made."

"This morning was not my finest work," she conceded. "Come on, I left you a plate of scallion pancakes."

They passed through the courtyard gates and made their way to the kitchen, which was a small building adjacent to the main house. This property had once belonged to the Temple of the Diyu Red Lanterns, a fringe Tiandi sect convinced that their high priest was destined to consume the Prophesied Hero of the Tiandi's flesh and assume his place within the prophecy. The members of the Diyu Red Lanterns had interpreted their doctrine very literally and enthusiastically, which had become a serious problem for the neighboring settlements.

Taishi had been hired to investigate these disappearances several decades ago and ended up dismantling the cult entirely. She had liked the view from the plateau so much, however, that she had moved in soon afterward and turned it into a second home. Many of the cult beliefs were painted and carved in excruciating detail on the temple walls and remained to this day. It was a daily reminder to Jian that an entire sect of the Tiandi religion wanted to eat him, usually in soup or over a barbecue spit. So that was fun and not creepy at all. Fortunately, he had gotten used to it by now.

They passed under an awning with a depiction of the high priest drinking a bowl of noodles with Jian's hand sticking out, and proceeded into the kitchen. Hanging from hooks off several low rafters right above the table was a colorful assortment of dented pots and woks. On the near side was a row of water barrels. All were empty. Next to the other door leading back to the courtyard was a square dining table, currently occupied by only one empty plate. A trail of flaky crumbs ran from the table down the hallway toward Taishi's private quarters.

"I was expecting you back this afternoon," said a hoarse, raspy voice as soon as the pair walked in.

Taishi was sitting at the table next to the hearth in the middle of the room. She sniffed the air. "You fell into the swamp again?"

"The river, actually." He slung the crate off his back. No sooner had he placed it on the counter than Taishi flicked her wrist toward herself, and the crate flew effortlessly across the room and landed on the table in front of her. His master looked indignant. "What happened to the package? The paper is ripped, and it's caked with filth."

"I had some problems during the pickup," he said.

"What sort of problems?"

Jian tried to look nonchalant. "I took care of it."

Taishi looked ready to pry further, but Zofi jumped in to save him. "You have letters too, Taishi." She held up one of the letters and sliced it open. "Master Fausan sent a reminder that it's your turn to host in ten days' time. He also reminds you that you've backed out the last three times you were supposed to host."

Taishi considered. "Fine, I'll host. Better check our wine stores. What else?"

Zofi held up a dark red envelope with a wax seal. "It's Master Hoon. He's politely but insistently asking for a reply to any of his last three letters."

"No. No, I don't want a seat on his master war artists community council. No, I don't want to have tea with him, and no, I definitely don't want to join his stupid cricket fighting league."

"This is a new request. He requests the pleasure of your company to fly kites—"

"I'm just going to have to kill the man next time I see him. It's the only way to stop him from pestering me."

Jian stared at the empty plate on the table. "What happened to the scallion pancakes?"

"Oh, were they for you? I got hungry," said Taishi.

Jian's stomach grumbled. He had been looking forward to those pancakes.

Zofi glanced at the box curiously. "What's in the package?"

"Oh, yes." Taishi returned to the table. She tore the lid off with a hard yank, then slowly, gleefully, pulled out a plain but finely crafted chest. She placed it on the table, unlatched the lock, and then swung open the lid. Inside was a stack of round, pink objects.

Taishi plucked one from the pile and sank her teeth into it with a satisfying crunch. She closed her eyes. "Straight from the peachlord's estates. Amazing." She took another bite and turned to leave the room. "I'm using all the hot water."

Jian called after her, his voice noticeably softer. "Taishi, how is Uncle Faaru doing?"

She hesitated at the doorway. "His family is well." And then she disappeared into her chambers.

Jian wasn't sure what that meant. He didn't remember much about the day he last saw the palacelord, the man who had treated Jian like a son at the Celestial Palace. Jian hoped he was all right. Then his stomach grumbled, reminding him once again that food had not passed through his mouth since dawn. His body instinctively reached for the nearest edible item, which was one of the peaches in the chest.

Zofi slapped his hand away. "Not if you know what's good for you. I'll boil some eggs."

That would have to do. "I'll start the fire."

"Oh no you don't." She hooked his elbow and changed his direction. "You smell like you just came out from between an ox's cheeks. You're not allowed in the main house until you've bathed."

"Is there any water left?" While a bath sounded tempting, he didn't want one badly enough to make the trek to the water hole at the far end of the pillar.

Zofi pointed to a bucket she had left for him near the door. He hefted it in both hands and staggered to the far corner of the property to a small structure that consisted of four corner posts and a circular roof. The Pagoda of Death was so named because this was where the Diyu Red Lanterns had performed their ritual killings. The altar under the pagoda was a water-tight stone depression dug several feet into the dirt. Jian didn't even want to guess what it had been for. It was now primarily used as a holding pen to bathe their animals. The roof was a small dome with depictions running all along the inner band of Jian getting chopped into pieces and served on several platters.

It did not take long for Jian to bathe. Freezing water made for a quick bath. He emerged from his bath, more or less clean, and found Zofi at the fire pit behind the kitchen, stirring a pot of boiled eggs over a small fire. She picked one out with a pair of cooking chopsticks and offered it to him. Jian, famished, cracked and stripped the shell expertly with the tips of his fingers and wolfed it down whole even as he panted from the heat.

"More?" she asked.

He nodded, juggling another between his fingers like hot charcoal. A dozen eggs vanished just as quickly as they came out of the pot. He sprawled into a couch of hay and loosed a long breath, the work from the long day finally draining out of him. Zofi tossed a few more tied batches of dried grass into the fire, sending a fresh snow of embers floating up into the sky. She used the long chopsticks to fish out a few more of the boiling eggs and placed them in a waiting bowl. Zofi let him have four; he gave her the two largest eggs.

She offered him half of her blanket, which he accepted. They huddled closer together, shivering at the midnight breeze running its fingers through their hair as they stared up at the star-freckled sky. It was as if the curtain had been pulled aside to reveal the celestial world in its pure splendor. The thunderclouds, after rinsing the Cloud Pillars for weeks, had finally passed. The land would be green and lively for the next few days where dozens of pillars would release waterfalls to dry themselves out. The blooms would take advantage, and with it the prey, the predators, and then the hunters.

Zofi pointed toward the night sky. "You see that sharp orange glimmer there? It's the Monsoon Star. Never trust it."

"What is so untrustworthy about a star?"

"It dances ever so slightly every cycle, moving just enough that someone relying on it for guidance ends up somewhere else. It also changes its color as if seeing if each shade is to its liking, and then sometimes it just disappears."

"Sounds very unreliable." He yawned.

"Hey." She nudged him, their shoulders touching. "Are you going to tell me how you got beat up like that? Did you try to hug a wild cat again?" She smirked when he hesitated. "Why so mysterious, Savior of the Zhuun? It must be really embarrassing."

"Now you're just blowing things out of proportion," he muttered.

"Come on. I'm stuck on this rock all day." She elbowed him in the ribs. "Let me live vicariously through your blunders. I could use a good story."

"Fine." He peered toward the house looking for signs of movement. When he was sure Taishi wasn't going to just appear behind him out of nowhere, he confessed. "I walked in on the caravan getting robbed."

"Is that how you got your injuries? You fought them?"

He nodded.

"Why would you do a fool thing like that?" She looked bewildered. "Let them play it out under commerce rules."

"I couldn't." He lowered his voice. "They were breaking into the mail wagon."

"They attacked a ducal-insured wagon? That's idiocy." Zofi slapped the top of her head with both hands and closed her eyes. "Oh, no no no, Jian, you're literally one of the most wanted fugitives in the Enlightened States. The bounty on your head is so large *I* almost want to turn you in. And you decide to intervene in an event that will most definitely warrant a magistrate's investigation? Was that smart, or not smart?"

"They were going to steal Taishi's peaches!"

"Who cares about stupid fruit!" She jabbed his forehead with her finger. "You could have blown your cover. Someone could have recognized you." She took in a deep breath. "Maybe I'm getting ahead of myself. Maybe it's not so bad. How badly did you win?"

"I knocked down a couple of people."

His master's eyes narrowed. "How many is a couple? One, two?"

"Maybe more, eight or ten?" He felt the need to explain further. "These guys were so incompetent they were practically impaling themselves at my feet. Anyone remotely competent could have beaten them. You know, the Cloud Pillars could really use a better class of banditry."

"Jian, ten?" Zofi's disbelief made her hoarse. "Are you *trying* to get caught?"

"They were armed and trying to kill me. What did you expect me to do?" he explained defensively. "Let them crack me over the head?"

"Yes, Jian. Yes, you should have let them club you over the head. For being so stupid!" She was nearly shouting. "Or better yet, don't get into a brawl with bandits while they're in the middle of robbing someone else."

"I'm sure neither the bandits nor the guards will remember." He paused. "Oh, the headguard knows me."

Zofi slapped her head. "Of course they'll remember the person who beat them to a pulp. Not only that, but they'll also remember a man who bears a striking resemblance to the missing Prophesied Hero of the Ti-andi, who looks about the same age as that missing hero, and who to-night took out ten men in an ambush. That's what they're going to remember, and they're going to gossip. What possessed you to take this risk? What were you thinking?"

Jian stared into the fire. His voice was small. "I didn't want to come home empty-handed. Everything was such a mess today. I just wanted one thing to go right." A long silence passed between them, interrupted only by the crackling flames and the occasional chitter and hoots of nature around them.

"I understand that." Zofi loosed a resigned sigh and patted him on the shoulder. "It was still egg-headed, though. Taishi is not going to be happy. She's going to flay you into next week."

He looked momentarily panicked. "Don't tell her, please! She doesn't need to know."

"Jian, this is serious. You could have magistrates here within days. We need to be ready."

He pleaded. "What's the big deal? It's just a stupid postal caravan! What's a missing shipment or two? Mail gets lost all the time."

"Don't talk like that in front of the old lady. She'll grouse and blame me for neglecting your civics. By the way, make her dress more warmly. Her cough came back."

"What's a civics?" He tried switching tactics. "I don't care. Look, if she finds out, she'll forbid me from leaving the pillar for at least until the next cycle. If I'm grounded, that means you'll have to do all the supply runs and carry everything yourself."

Zofi made a gesture as if strangling air. "Why do you think I'm so pissed!"

CHAPTER THREE

THE MASTER

Ling Taishi awoke to two roosters competing for one job. She reluctantly opened her eyes and stared at the soot-marked ceiling of her bedroom. The small hearth in the corner had gone cold during the night, but a light haze still hung in the air. That meant the chimney was clogged again. That boy was falling behind on his chores, which wasn't surprising. Taishi had stepped up his lessons from two to three—sometimes four—times a day, which was grueling by any measure.

More crowing pierced the morning quiet. The older rooster, his voice scratchy and low, stuttered as if he had run out of breath or had choked on a kernel of corn. The younger one, on the other hand, was loud, shrill to the point of cutting. The eager cockerel had a set of lungs that could go on all day.

The wily old rooster had done an admirable job keeping his coop safe from weasels, badgers, and chi dragons over the years. While Taishi always valued experience, she was also distinctly aware of the dangers of someone operating well past their prime. Maybe it *was* time to retire the battle-worn bird and pass the reins. Then again, young meat was much more tender, especially when drizzled with sesame oil.

Taishi rose from her marble slab bed, feeling the chill in her joints. She waved off the lingering smoke trails and wrapped her favorite llama-fur robe over her shoulders. She padded out of her chambers in her matching fuzzy llama mittens and slippers, and continued through the covered archway connecting the main house to the kitchen, where she was warmly greeted by the pleasant aroma of deep-fried dough and hot soy milk.

Her favorite teapot with matching cup sat on the small, round table just outside the door. On an oval plate were one sweet white bun and one peach. Several wax-stamped scrolls were neatly fanned out in front of her breakfast. Half were likely fan or hate mail; who could tell the difference anymore? The others were probably bills. One had to honor one's debts, even when in hiding, sometimes especially so.

Taishi was about to cut open the first letter when she noticed a body slumped by the fire pit outside the kitchen. More curious than alarmed, she stepped out to check. The cool mountain winds raised the hairs on the brown-and-white llama fur, swaying it north. She peeled off a mitten and hovered her hand over the hanging pot, feeling no heat. Inside were two boiled eggs sitting in a puddle of milky white soup. The ash in the hearth still emanated heat.

She walked up to the slumbering Jian, who was wrapped up in a horse blanket like a spring roll and snoring long, labored breaths. His legs sprawled out from under the blanket, one elevated over a hay bale, the other sticking straight out, a potential tripping hazard right next to the fire. His neck was bent forward in an unnatural way to make a pillow of the wall of the hay bale. He was going to feel that when he woke up.

Taishi didn't blame the two children for staying up late. She didn't mind that they made mistakes. Better to do it here under her guardianship than out there in the world, where a poorly considered mistake could mean death. Young people were social creatures; Jian and Zofi were orphaned puppies who had somehow found themselves under her guardianship. More important, they had found each other and formed a close bond that could only come from shared trauma and circumstance, especially here in this lonely corner of the world. They now leaned on each other for support, especially since there was no one else around . . .

Zofi appeared from around the sunflower garden carrying a basket of daikon radishes. She hefted it onto the wooden table next to the hearth. "I let him sleep in," the mapmaker's daughter said. "He needs it."

"Prophecies don't take days off." Taishi was about to flick his nose with a pop of air when she reconsidered. She noted his many blemishes and bruises. He did look more haggard than usual.

"You've been running him ragged lately," said the mapmaker's daughter. "How has his training been coming along?"

Taishi's gaze lingered on her sleeping disciple. "Physically, he can pass the test tomorrow if I allow it. The Test of the Lineage is about raw power and talent, both of which he has in abundance." She tapped her head. "It's here that he needs seasoning, but it's impossible to expose that experience to him without increasing the risk of someone identifying him."

Taishi decided to allow her ward to sleep a little longer. As the scripture of the wise Goramh taught: one rested day was worth three weary ones. Jian had come a long way in the three years he had lived here under her tutelage. He might one day be worthy to succeed her as the master of the windwhispering Zhang lineage, but that wouldn't be enough. The succession of her family line had never been her goal. Jian was meant for greater things. His destiny was to slay the Eternal Khan of the Katuia, and there was no telling when the prophecy would call. It could be tomorrow, a decade from today, or possibly never if the Khan was actually dead. All Taishi knew was that she had to prepare the boy to the best of her ability, and time was running short. The candle was burning on both ends.

Taishi joined Zofi at the long wooden table, where the daikons were now arrayed in neat, straight rows. Zofi was peeling the radishes with a paring knife, stripping each bare with seven or eight inefficient slow strokes, then soaking them in a water basin.

It looked easy enough. Taishi took position opposite the girl and hiked up her llama-fur sleeve on her good arm. Zofi snorted but slid a spare knife across the table to her. Taishi picked it up and twirled the blade between her fingers. The weight was off, the handle loose, and the blade was as dull as a duke's dinner party, but it was rare for a war artist to wield the perfect weapon for a fight.

"I'm sick of radish soup." She raised her blade in salute, and then she attacked, lobbing the daikon into the air and making four perfect slashes, two vertical and two horizontal. Then she caught it in her good hand and spun it ninety degrees before bouncing it back up and repeating the exercise again with two vertical slices. Taishi then slapped the radish cube in midair with the blade, bouncing it into the water basin.

Zofi did not look impressed, but she did begin to peel them a little faster. By the time the girl had peeled three more radishes, Taishi had finished five. It wasn't a fair competition, even with Taishi one-handed, but it was amusing how much the girl hated losing.

"One expert hand was far superior to two untrained ones." There was a Goramh quote for everything, even if much of his wisdom was just variations of the same thing.

The girl's jing, her life force and the energy swirling from her soul, was her intelligence. She was a clever and ambitious young woman with a sharp and expansive mind. She was also brash with little appetite for imperfections. Taishi appreciated that most about her. Zofi, however, was also as agile as a duck on land. She fell into the pond at least three times a year. She once broke her nose missing the doorway and running into the wall. Earlier this year, she had given herself a concussion running into the only tree on the entire plateau.

Finally, the two had whittled through half of the basket, with Taishi paring double what Zofi was managing, not that anyone was keeping track. Zofi suddenly flinched, and the knife flew from her grasp. A burst of crimson appeared at the tip of her finger and ran down her palm. She cursed and squeezed it with a rag.

Taishi caught the knife in midair and gently placed it on the table. "Your fingers always follow your eyes. Remember that, girl."

"Yours don't."

"You're not me."

Zofi wiped her bloody finger with the rag. "Something on your mind, Taishi?"

"Why can't I just be here to help?"

The mapmaker's daughter put on the air she reserved for mocking and imitating Taishi. "Grandmaster Ling Taishi does not lower herself to help in the kitchen. She's far too important to dawdle with the help." The girl raised her bloodied finger dramatically. "Except when Grandmaster Ling Taishi either wants something or is hungry for my twice-cooked crispy barbecue pork with a honey glaze. Then she is all of a sudden immensely helpful."

Smart girl with a smart mouth, although her self-assessment of her culinary skills was overly generous. In so many ways, Zofi reminded Taishi of another mouthy girl trying to find her way in the world, except the young Taishi was twice as confident but only half as clever.

"What happened to him last night?" she asked.

Zofi's gaze darted over to the still snoring Jian. "He asked to keep it a secret."

Taishi shrugged. "Sure, it's a secret. Go on."

The mapmaker's daughter loosed a breath. "Jian stumbled upon an ambush on the caravan last night. He broke it up when the bandits began robbing the mail wagon."

Taishi's fist clenched. "What!"

"Go light on him. He's had a few difficult days."

"Who cares about Jian getting into a fistfight with a bunch of low-grade ruffians? That's what boys do," Taishi raged, feeling insulted. "What type of unpatriotic, low-life pigeon-brain robs the postal caravan?"

"These are desperate times. There's famine in the south and pestilence in the north," said Zofi. "Wars everywhere in every duchy. Fields are burning. Respect for tradition and unity is the first thing to fall by the wayside. Peasant bandit groups are popping up like dandelions on the border. There's been word that some Katuia clans have reneged on the armistice, breaking the indentured servitude contract, and are re-arming their people."

"And the dukes are too busy fighting one another to do anything about it," Taishi muttered. "It's about time the warmongering western duchies feel war on their lands, Shulan especially. The greater the devotion, the greater the warmongering. Most of them live too far from the Great Sea's edge. They heard about war only from afar. Feels different when it's in the ruined fields of your potato crop."

"We might get lucky," said Zofi. "Maybe Saan will be too busy fighting the war to investigate the attack. Maybe they never come."

"Oh, they'll come, without a doubt." Taishi shook her head. "An attack on the ducal-marked is an attack on the dukes themselves. Disrupting the mail is a direct attack on the Zhuun people. Saan *has* to respond. If he lets even one offense slide, then others will follow. A duke is not a duke if his word is not law. Besides, their egos would never allow it."

"You're not mad at Jian?" Zofi pointed at their topic of conversation. "I thought it was pretty stupid."

"Oh, idiotic, completely," said Taishi, throwing her arm up in resignation. "Stupid and naive. Don't misunderstand. I appreciate his dedication to my peaches, but it's a dog-piss piece of fruit. I'm not that unhinged." She had to take a moment to consider that. "Am I? As for getting into a fight, well, that's what boys with too much war arts training and too much boredom do. They find trouble, even inadvertently. I'm not angry. I'm just going to pretend I am until he finally fixes that blasted roof."

"Last week's rain soaked three of my books," Zofi agreed. She stared poignantly at Taishi. "This conversation stays here?"

"Of course." One of the first things Taishi did after they moved to the temple was make Zofi a spy. She was just looking out for Jian's best interest. Taishi could not afford to make a mistake with him. As the Prophesied Hero of the Tiandi, his life was of paramount importance to the Zhuun. His death, however, would be just as important to others. Taishi had to be prepared for any potentially dangerous situation. Moreover, Zofi was living in *her* house.

That didn't stop the girl from driving a hard bargain, negotiating a weekly stipend, final say on the menu, and a vow upon Taishi's honor to one day avenge her father and murder those underworld thugs in Sanba.

The young woman could be surprisingly bloodthirsty at times. She also wanted the largest spare bedroom. Taishi didn't have the heart to tell the girl that the bedroom had once served as the temple morgue, so she didn't. Zofi was irrationally fearful of corpses, ghosts especially.

"It's only a matter of time before the magistrates arrive," said Taishi. "Jian stays on the pillar until then."

"You can't do that," Zofi protested. "It could be months."

"I just did."

Zofi crossed her arms. "You'll cut the web if you do that."

Taishi snorted. The girl had been reading too many romantic fables at the teahouse. Her threat, on the other hand, was very real. The last condition Zofi had arranged for her services was that she would cease spying for Taishi the moment she thought Taishi's actions would betray Jian's trust. It was at *her* discretion. Those were her terms. The girl wasn't wrong about the dukes either. They *did* have their hands full wrapping them around one another's necks. It could be months before they sent an investigation. Jian couldn't do half of his chores if he couldn't leave the pillar.

"Fine," Taishi said. "We'll go about like everything is normal, but you do every delivery post pickup from now on. Jian also does not head into the outpost unaccompanied. I want you with him every trip. Understand?"

Zofi crossed her arms. "He's the one who messed up. Why am I being the one punished?"

"That, unfortunately," said Taishi, "is what happens far too frequently in life, and I'm sorry for it. You deserve better, but here we are." Taishi wiped both sides of the paring blade on a rag before putting the knife down. "If there's nothing else."

"There is one more thing." Zofi considered her words carefully. "I need help with Jian's education. He's falling behind."

"Like what, more paper and ink, books? I'm not spilling coins out of my robes here. Carve it out of bark if you must."

"That's not it." Zofi tossed a daikon into the basin, splashing water over the sides. Taishi noted it was also only half-peeled. The mapmaker's daughter admitted, "I'm not qualified. I can teach Jian to read and write, but I can't explain the context behind Goramh's Ten Tenets of War. I can teach him to do math past his fingers and toes, but Gyian rice tariffs still look like imagined nonsense." She became more animated. "I only attended two years of university. You're asking me to teach him things I still have to learn myself." She gesticulated to her surroundings. "Especially in this backwater nowhere. The teahouse is the only place to check out books, and most of their selection is tawdry."

"What's wrong with that?" said Taishi.

"Nothing. I love Burning Hearts romance too," admitted Zofi, "but I need help. I can't take him any further."

"You're doing a fine job so far." That was supposed to be reassuring. The girl had actually surpassed expectations. "I couldn't ask for—or afford—a better tutor."

"It's not good enough." Zofi, as always, was being too hard on herself. "He's not understanding everything, and I'm not qualified to teach him. Jian may know basic geography, but nobody knows why Lawkan houses never face north, why the people in the Shulan and Lawkan duchies don't like the number three, and why the Xing kneel only on one knee while in court. I taught him as much as I know about history, but there are so many things I can't explain. Why do two armies throw a party the night before a battle? Why does everyone hate Caobiu? And what is the three-hundred-year cold war with the White Ghosts? What even *is* a cold war? Why are they even fighting?"

"It was over a misunderstanding," explained Taishi. "When the Zhuun first encountered their people, the White Ghosts envoy did not take his shoes off when he entered the palace."

Zofi recoiled. "They walk around indoors with their shoes on? That's gross and barbaric!"

She agreed. "It appears the White Ghosts believe that undressing in public is unseemly, which includes shoes. When their envoy still refused to take off his shoes when he entered court, the emperor had him beheaded. Things went downhill from there."

"Serves them right." Zofi looked properly offended for a Zhuun. "What about the Shulan and number three?"

Taishi shrugged. "The Shulan always pray in pairs. To be the third is considered ill fortune."

"And the one-knee thing with the Xing?"

"The current duke's father took an arrow to the knee in his youth. He was unable to properly kneel ever since, and then it became a thing at court."

"Maybe you should teach his classes then."

Taishi harumphed. "I'm too busy trying to make sure he doesn't crash into a tree to teach him about silly customs. I'll see what I can do to get you some help, but don't expect too much. Like you said, we live in a backwater nowhere, and we're fugitives. It's not like I can just put out a call for a tutor." She glanced down at the water flowing over the edge of the full basin. "That's a lot of radishes."

Zofi sighed. "Jian gave the fish back to the Yukian yesterday when he fell off an air current and into the river, so it's radish every day every which way for the next ten days." She began sweeping the peeled skin off the table into a waiting basket on the ground. Those bits would get mashed up for the pigs' slop.

Taishi picked up a misshapen radish still dressed in half its skin. "You got sloppy on the last few. Long, even strokes. More wrists, less forearm."

Zofi bristled. "Okay, ma'am. Whatever."

The girl's flippant remark, complete with a sigh and eye roll, touched a nerve. No, a memory. Annoyance turned to an amused chuckle. Taishi had never wanted a daughter, after having been one. Her relationship with her mother had always been complicated. Hui Yinshi was once a songmistress in the Xing court, a prestigious posting at any level of the choir. She had ambitions one day to start her own opera house. That was until the day a young, brash, and dashing Ling Munnam had walked into court to collect the notorious Slitherhead bounty. It had been love at first sight, a whirlwind romance and marriage, and then it had become all about him.

Taishi had witnessed from an early age her mother shriveling with every passing day, hidden in the shadow of her overbearing husband, and Taishi hated her for it. It wasn't until years later as she tried to make a name for herself that Taishi realized how much she had misjudged Yinshi. By then, it was too late. Her mother had passed away during one of Taishi's campaigns in the White Ghost lands. It would be another three years before she returned to visit Hui Yinshi's grave site.

". . . war is completely wrecking commerce," Zofi was saying. "We're low on just about everything, especially cooking oils and salt. Our garden is going to spoil if I can't pickle most of it. All these problems to soothe the ego of five bulls rampaging the countryside."

Taishi's mind returned to the present. "Four."

Zofi picked up the water basin and hugged it close to her chest. "Four what?"

"Four bulls," she repeated. "The dukes only have four cocks between them, so four bulls. Sunri stands on her own. Listen closely, girl. Men tend to erase women from history. We do not do that for them." She had snapped back harsher than she intended, but a mental visit to her family tended to have that effect on her.

"I just lumped all of those worthless dukes together. Who cares?" The mapmaker's daughter looked taken aback by Taishi's stern retort. "I thought you hate Sunri. You called her a callous, bloodthirsty, murderous bitch just the other day."

Taishi picked up a paring knife, flipped it around her fingers expertly until it slipped into her grasp, and then she slammed it down, embedding the entire length of the blade into the wood. "Duchess Sunri of Caobiu, the Desert Lioness, is a genocidal, psychotic cunt. She's as rotten an evil egg as they come, *but* she is also one of the five dukes of the Enlightened States and the only woman to have ever earned this title, and she did so as a lowly concubine crushing every weak man that stood in her way. I will happily spit on her grave after she is rot and fungus, but until then she more than deserves her place alongside those entitled men. Do you understand?"

Zofi failed to mask her youthful annoyance. "Fine. Four bulls and a cow rampaging through the countryside with their silly civil war. Happy now?"

"Yes, quite." Taishi turned her attention back to her sleeping heir, who had already wasted half of the morning. "Speaking of entitled bulls, wake up the savior of the Zhuun. It's nearly noon, and I've just tacked on three more chores to his list."

Zofi plucked a daikon from the basin and lobbed it at Jian in a way that revealed that no one had ever taught her how to throw anything. The radish flew well over Jian's head, as did the next three.

"Stop muscling it with your arms." Taishi stepped next to the girl and picked out her own radish. "The secret to a good throw is to remain relaxed and supple. Brute strength is not the key. Next time Fausan comes to game night, watch his arm when he throws dice. The God of Gamblers is a one-trick dog, but it's an awfully good trick." Just as she was about to make the throw, Taishi's shoulder spasmed, and the radish flew straight into the dirt.

"Just like that?" Zofi covered her smirk with her hand. Her amusement quickly washed away to worry. "Are you all right?"

"I'm fine." Taishi gritted her teeth and stuffed her hand into her robes. The tremors were still crawling up her arm. She stomped over to the sleeping Jian and nudged him with a fuzzy slipper. "Wake up, lazy boy."

"What? What happened?" Jian startled and then groaned, rocking side to side like a turtle on its shell. At least he woke easily. "What time is it?"

"The day's already half over," she replied. "Help Zofi with the slop for the pigs, and then meet me at the edge of the Headless Forest. I heard you fell into the river and lost our fish. We're going to do nothing but work on riding until you no longer land like a pregnant hen."

Jian blanched. "The Headless Forest? You ordered me to never ride the currents there. The crosswinds will cleave my head off."

"I have faith in you," said Taishi.

"I don't," he muttered.

Zofi looked equally concerned. "Maybe we should talk this out, because I don't either."

CHAPTER FOUR

BAD REVIEWS

Maza Qisami fiddled with the wooden reed sticking out of her cup of rice wine, swirling the piss-colored liquid until it formed a funnel. Bored to near death, she rested her head on her other hand as she tugged on an ear. It was past time for a bath, but tub fees in Wugoh were tripled due to war and drought. That explained why everyone in the desert settlement stunk.

She glanced across the street into a dress shop and caught sight of her mark, a tall, twiggy woman with dragon eyelashes and paper-thin skin pulled tightly against her husk-like face. Her mark had wandered inside two hours ago and had still not emerged. How long could it possibly take to buy a stupid dress? She wore an outrageous bright orange robe and a gem-encrusted hair piece that wrapped around her nest of hair like a coiled snake. She looked like the stereotypical wicked firstwife pulled directly out of a bad countryside opera production. Qisami was admittedly very taken by the headdress and planned to swipe it as a bonus to her contract.

Qisami leaned back and slurped her drink, her left foot nudging the wicker basket containing the pig head soaking in a bed of salt. Her instructions were specific: gut the mark from neck to groin, put on the piggy as a helm, and splay the body on the lord's bed in all her naked glory. It was a tale as old as time. Boy meets girl. Boy marries girl. Boy is a pig and marries another. The two girls try to kill each other.

Qisami blew a raspberry and picked at her bowl of sweet gelatin. If someone had accused her two years ago of taking street-level jobs worthy of only grunts and footpads, she would have taken these chopsticks and rammed them through both eye sockets. Being hired by the secondwife to kill the first was so, *so* beneath a shadowkill, yet here she was, earning silvers to settle a domestic squabble.

A shrill whistle escaped from behind her pursed lips. Life had taken a hard downturn over the last few years, specifically since she had last been in Jiayi and had failed to capture the Prophesied Hero of the Tiandi. He had slipped through her fingers, and with him the juicy contract she had been promised. Not only did she not earn her fat retirement payday, but the Central Orb had also filed a complaint with the Consortium for negligence, demanding reparations for her broken contract. The silkspinners and dukes were probably the only groups the Consortium trod carefully around, so of course they threw her to the jackals.

To rub salt into the wound, they penalized and fined her for taking on an unsanctioned contract. That was ridiculous, because every shadowkill took off-book work all the time. Unfortunately, so-what-everyone-else-does-it was not a good defense. Now she was banned from taking top-tier contracts for the next five years while at the same time half of her earnings were garnished as restitution to the silkspinners.

That left Qisami and her cell—she glanced into the shop and caught sight of that wonderful headdress—having to take on marital counseling jobs, or worse. Their previous job before this had been to hunt down a man having sexual relations with a farmer's sheep. The one before that from a spoiled nobleman to stage a robbery so he could fight them off, all in order to impress a young lady.

Qisami was still stewing over the bowl of gelatin when Firstwife finally emerged from the shop. She sneered. Three hours, and the old rag hadn't even bought anything. She swallowed the last few gulps of gelatin and snuck out behind the woman.

Qisami slid her right hand up her other sleeve and cut her nail into her forearm. *Mark is moving.*

Finally, came the first reply right away. *I overheard the accountant talking to the tax collector. He says rice prices are at an all-time high. Want to get into the rice business?*

The only thing Qisami wanted was for Koteuni to report in. Her second-in-command had become such a bored grandmam lately. Qisami never realized how much the former court brat cared about their finances until they had none. She was starting to actually believe that Koteuni was doing shadowkill work for the money, not fun.

Mark not moved since he arrived. Burandin was keeping an eye on the lord and husband. Both were currently lounging on opposite ends of a salon.

I hope you're having a good time. Koteuni had a knack for displaying sarcasm through blood scrawl.

Thanks. Burandin could barely read, let alone notice the inflection accents in her words. The two had been quarreling more lately. They had all been on edge.

A wall of incoherent slashes next came across her forearm. That was probably Cyyk, their grunt, who still needed a lot of practice blood scrawling. She didn't even bother to try to decipher his scratching. The idiot could still barely cut three words after all this time in training. She should do him a favor and slash his throat. Save him the embarrassment of washing out of the Consortium training pools.

Cut it out, Broodbaby. General Quan Sah, a high-ranking Caobiu lord and general of the world's largest army, had indentured his fifth son, Cyyk, to fulfill his brood atonement as a security payment to stay all assassinations for a ten-year span. There were dozens of ways a nobleman could ward off assassination. The brood atonement was the easiest and most effective. Indenturing one's child guaranteed a mark shield that was insurance not only from the Consortium, but from all other organizations of assassins as well. Anyone who crossed a mark shield risked the Consortium's wrath, which usually meant death.

Qisami was always quick to remind Cyyk that his rich and powerful father chose to sell his youngest son into indentured servitude rather than put in the effort to buy off individual contracts or just boost his personal security. It amused her to see anguish paint his face. It was also a necessary lesson. It would soon be time for Cyyk to apply to a training pool. It was her duty to prepare her grunt for the hard road ahead. His success and failure would reflect directly on her cell. She would never live it down if he didn't get accepted by at least one pool.

Qisami turned her attention to the one who didn't answer the roll call. They sometimes got too deep into character and forget to pay attention to the blood scrawls. *Zwei, converge on Happy Fortune Street.*

She trailed after Firstwife for a few blocks, keeping her distance and staying on the opposite side of the street. The woman was heading west, toward this tiny backwater settlement's noble district, which was nothing more than a cul-de-sac at the end of Golden Echo Street. Qisami matched her mark's pace, slowing to a crawl when the woman paused to admire a warbling songbird on the shoulder of an old man strumming a lute. She found herself humming along until an ox-pulled wagon obstructed her line of sight. By the time it cleared, there was no sign of Firstwife.

Qisami sped up, hiking her pants up as she crossed the muddy street, weaving between the oncoming bodies. She craned her head side to side, trying to catch a glimpse of a glittering snake headdress. Qisami had been blessed with many incredible talents, but height was unfortunately not one of them. It wasn't long before she found herself completely turned around. This was embarrassing. How had Firstwife slipped away so quickly?

Qisami was about to break into a sprint when a gentle arm wrapped around her shoulder. A hot perfumed breath tickled her ear. "Mark just turned the corner, boss. Heading straight toward the estate."

Zweilang was the newest member of the cell, having only joined last year to replace Haaren, who had retired via the tip of Ling Taishi's sword. They were tall, with narrow shoulders and long limbs, and a striking but unusual face, with a strong, delicate bone structure, high cheeks, and long silvery hair hanging over both shoulders. They were a yiyang, someone gendered both ways. That trait allowed Zwei to excel in roles with either gender, giving them great versatility.

It had taken two years to find Haaren's replacement. With the tier blacklist and garnishment in place, few reputable free agents even considered joining her cell. Qisami had been suspicious when Zweilang had agreed, especially since they had graduated high in their litter. It didn't take long before Qisami found out why.

Zwei touched Qisami's shoulder again. "Firstwife turned again onto Happy Fortune Street. Is it me or does every town have a Happy Fortune Street?"

"It's not you. There's a Happy Fortune and Great Wealth street in every settlement." Qisami scrawled on her arm. *Burandin, close back to first position. Koteuni, kill the ears.*

They strolled casually down Happy Fortune Street, acting like two old friends deep in thought. A pair of guards passed by, barely giving them a second glance. It was best they didn't draw any attention. Qisami would have a difficult time explaining what she was doing with a decapitated pig with the name of a local lord's firstwife cut into its forehead.

They reached the nobleman's estate after a short walk. Calling Wugoh a town was being a bit generous, just like calling this small compound an estate. It was more a string of squat buildings enclosed by a leaning clay wall that looked like it was slowly melting.

Qisami eyed a dirty young man with a pudgy nose and permed curly hair sitting lazily against a lamppost. He looked convincingly asleep, or drunk. "You're supposed to watch the gate."

Cyyk pried one eye open and looked over at the bright orange gate across the street. "What do you think I'm doing?"

"In disguise, as in without bringing attention to yourself."

The grunt whined. "I am in my disguise as a beggar. I certainly dress like one. Certainly smell like one too."

Zwei agreed. "You do stink."

Qisami pointed at his taut, bare shoulders and arms. "What sort of beggar packs this much muscle?"

"You do look like a street thug scoping out a hit," agreed Zwei. "The estate probably doubled their security because of you."

Someone whistled behind them. All three turned to look. The garish orange door was slightly ajar, and Koteuni's head was sticking out. They hurried across the street.

"Two guards. I took care of them," she said.

"Are they alive?" Secondwife had offered a small bonus if they didn't kill any of the staff.

"I think so. One might bleed out." Koteuni shrugged. The no-collateral-death clause of their contract was a large enough bonus to consider, but not large enough to go out of their way to get inconvenienced. "Firstwife returned a few minutes earlier and went straight through the main building to the back. She has a workshop. Fancies herself a calligrapher."

"How many other guards?" asked Qisami.

"Three others. Two patrolling, one with the lady."

Qisami frowned. "Five for the entire estate? He's a lord."

"Technically yes," conceded Koteuni. "But he's only a fablelord in this backwater court. No matter how good his court status, he's just still a writer scribbling children's stories. He's barely compensated better than the court clowns."

"Still rich enough to have two wives and an estate," said Zweilang. "I read some of his work. He isn't that good." Zwei sniffed. "This estate probably came with Firstwife's dowry."

"And now she's going to get murdered for it." Koteuni threw a look at Burandin. "Men are terrible."

The four followed the perimeter path that ran along the side wall, their soft padded shoes making no noise along the wooden beams, save for an occasional creak under Cyyk's weight. Qisami felt a tickle in her ear. The place was too quiet, bereft of other souls. Even a modest estate should have at least a servant, a cook, and a maid. Maybe a stable boy and gardener.

Koteuni must have sensed it too. "I've only seen a few souls wandering the grounds. Could be on account of the rain, or maybe he really doesn't have two gold liangs to rub together."

Zwei mused. "How does a man have two wives but no servants?"

"Maybe he married her to avoid having to pay her to clean," said Cyyk.

The cell entered the main building and found something better than coins. A small library just past the main foyer had a sprawling wall of floor-to-ceiling shelves filled with books of all sizes. Placed on a pedestal in the center of the room was an open copy of Goramh's *Unabridged Classics*. Zwei, who was a voracious reader, squealed and began to browse the contents. They took a large book off a shelf and buried it in their satchel. *"The Interpretations of Tiandi Mosaics, Cooking Rice Spiritually Three Ways,* oooh, Goramh's *Poetry to Recite While under Duress!"* They pocketed that one too.

Qisami grabbed Zwei by the belt and dragged them out of the room. If left to their own, they would stay in here for the next cycle. She looked over to see Koteuni swiping a complete set of opera romances. "We're shadow*kills*, not shadow*steals*! We don't rob marks." She remembered Firstwife's headdress. "Unless they're dead."

Koteuni was defiant. "I don't care. Selling these books would cover bathtub fees for an entire cycle. I can't live smelling like camel turd anymore. I'm so pissed and desperate for coin these days I would go beg my father if I hadn't killed him already."

That *was* desperate. Qisami honestly didn't mind a little theft on the job—everyone did it—but she usually stole something because she wanted it, not because she wanted to sell it. That just felt wrong. Still, Koteuni did have a point. "I'm going to look this way. You do what you—"

A silhouette passed a window just outside. Qisami raked her middle nail along her forearm, and the rest of the cell immediately retreated into cover, hiding behind furniture or blending into the shadows.

Qisami was back to business. *I need ten minutes with the firstwife to gut her properly and put on that pig head. Koteuni, clear the outside. Burandin, keep the escape route open. Cyyk, watch the front door.*

"But—" he protested.

"One more word and I'll break your pretty nose again, Broodbaby." She turned to Zwei. "You're with me on Firstwife."

Zwei protested as well. "Can I help Koteuni instead?"

Qisami glared. "I'm not asking for your opinion on job assignments. I need you to hold Firstwife down while I disembowel. The client's instructions were very specific."

Zwei sulked. "Fine."

Koteuni stepped into a shadow while Cyyk hoofed it back to the front door. Qisami drew a black dagger and continued down the corridor toward Firstwife's suite, the tip of the blade slicing and parting the paper walls. Zwei drew their emei claws, three long prongs protruding from their gloves, and did the same with the opposite wall.

They reached the door to the firstwife's antechambers, a small room with cushioned benches on both sides. On the other side was a tall mahogany door with a carving of a spectacles-wearing dragon reading a book while curled around a pond. Qisami tapped it lightly with her pinky nail: solid core, heavy, dense. It would muffle the woman's screams well.

The door squealed as it swung open. The dimly lit room on the other side was dark around the edges. A lone lamp at the far end of the room offered light over a face-painting table. *Firstwife sat on a cushioned seat, with her back to the door, fussing with her hair in front of the mirror, pulling out hairpins and letting her hair fall over her shoulders. The snake headdress was placed on a small pedestal nearby, just begging to get stolen.*

The two shadowkills split, moving like their namesakes and blending into the darkness. Firstwife placed the brush down and began to tweeze her eyebrows.

Zwei had made it to the far corner and was approaching the opposite side of the ornate wedding bed next to the vanity table. They paused and looked over at Qisami. *Kiki, Firstwife is overacting.*

Zwei would know a thing or two about overacting, but their point was made. That was when she felt it: a blind claustrophobia. Qisami eyed the shadows nearby. Something was filling up space in the shadows. She drew a second black dagger and waited, sensing the darkness shift around her.

Zwei yelled and fell from behind the wedding bed. Their arms swiped in several directions as two hooded figures emerged from the darkness to surround Zwei. All of their swings missed by a good arm's length, at least. Zwei was a polished and talented shadowkill, a versatile operative, and an expert on poison, but they were the worst war artist Qisami had ever seen. Zwei flailed around like an injured fowl.

Qisami left the clumsy duckling to fend for themself as she noticed the four silhouettes converging on her, each wearing matte black leather armor with short cloaks flapping off their shoulders. Qisami's nerves turned cold: Mute Men. What could they possibly be doing here? It was unlikely that some backwater fablelord in this ass-crack peasant settlement could afford the service of the Quiet Death, on a writer's income no less.

Several pairs of black-gloved hands reached for her. Qisami slashed and spun away, using the depth of darkness to guide her. More hands pawed at her. They were trying to take her alive. Qisami took advantage of that, pressing forward and slicing open a forearm. She danced away and then stepped into a shadow, reappearing at the edge of the light beaming down on the face-painting table.

Several more Mute Men appeared, surrounding her. Qisami couldn't believe it. "Six Mute Men? He must be the best damn fablelord this side of the Grass Sea."

There was no winning this. A shadowkill was rarely a match for a Mute Man in open combat. Fighting a cluster of them was just stupid. Considering they were obviously trying to take her alive, Qisami's decision was easy.

"All right, cheaters. You got me." Her knives disappeared, and she extended her hands over her head. "Zwei, stand down. No need to die ugly."

That, however, appeared to be unnecessary. Qisami looked over to see Zwei already on their belly trussed up like a chicken about to get bled. They squirmed and thrashed ineffectively, snarling and biting at the feet of the Mute Man standing next to them.

It was getting a little embarrassing. "Surrender like a pro," Qisami hissed. She shrugged at the Mute Man cranking her arm behind her back. "Excuse my friend there. Their first time getting captured."

A loud clap reverberated through the room. "That will be enough. They are our guests, after all."

Being considered a guest was welcome news. It was clear by now this was a trap, but why? More importantly, who? Which powerful noble-man could Qisami possibly have pissed off enough to send an entire crew of Mute Men? It was flattering, but complete overkill.

Firstwife stood from her seat and turned to face them. Gone was her affectless gaze, her tight skin cracking with the slight upturned ends of her lips. She glided closer with the assuredness of someone familiar with command. Her movements were slow, but measured.

The woman knelt next to Qisami and raised her chin with a long, bony finger. "Maza Qisami, my mistress requires your audience."

The number of women who wanted Qisami's head was, unfortu-nately, likely higher than the number of men. "My cell is in high de-mand." That was a lie. "Perhaps she can schedule something next cycle, unless whoever needs killing needs to be killed quickly."

"My mistress waits for no one under the Tiandi."

Before Qisami could utter a retort, a hand holding a handkerchief smothered her. She caught the strong whiff of slumberweed. Her nostrils briefly burned with mint, and the world suddenly felt very heavy.

CHAPTER FIVE

HOUTOU

For as long as Jian had known his master, Taishi had been a woman of her word, to a fault. When she had informed him that they were going to focus only on windslipping until he no longer looked like a clipped chicken, she meant exactly that. Two weeks later, Jian was still struggling at it, crashing into trees, walls, and earth, eating more dirt than he cared to think about, and nearly splattering his brains on several occasions. He was improving, though, sort of, slowly.

"Once you get the feel for it," she explained, "it will become second nature, assuming you survive that long."

That provided little comfort. Jian was currently perched on top of a cluster of bamboo trees with their tops sheared off. Bamboo leaves were the main source of nutrients for many species of animals in the Cloud Pillars, including several giant leathery-winged birds. Jian glanced at one such bird gliding on the breeze overhead. Its beak was as long as Jian was tall.

Taishi's hoarse voice barked from below. "I don't have all day here. I could be painting a self-portrait or sewing a beautiful wedding dress instead of standing in the rain waiting for you to grow a pair of eggs."

"You don't know how to sew," he grumbled. The wind was strong today, but chaotic, some currents weaving through the bamboo stems while others meandered in random directions. A few had even gotten themselves tied up in swirling vortexes that kicked up funnels of leaves and branches.

Most of the currents were too thin, weak, or slow to hold his weight. The strong ones along the wider corridors, however, were blowing by too quickly for his comfort. That meant the only way Jian could windslip to the ground was to pick his way down carefully, like putting together a puzzle, and then navigate down like running an obstacle course.

After he had plotted his route, Jian swallowed the bile collecting in his mouth, exhaled, and then stepped out onto open air. The attempt started out . . . fine. He balanced atop a fat current angling downward in a spiral that was moving a little faster than he was comfortable with as it curved around an open space. He stepped off right before the current broke apart against a tightly knit cluster of bamboo trees, his feet pedaling in small steps on several smaller currents. He minced his way across a dozen more closer to the ground, becoming more sure of himself with every step.

He had nearly made it halfway down when his confidence outgrew his caution, and he misstepped and slipped off the side. Control, once lost, was difficult to regain. Jian yelped and pawed the air as he plummeted headfirst, the ground racing toward him. He was a breath from crashing when a strong force yanked him sideways, sending him tumbling along the earth and brush until he finally skidded to a stop. He groaned and blinked, looking up at the towering green stems buffered by the clear blue sky.

Taishi appeared over him. "Another ugly landing." She nudged his feet with hers. "You rushed again. The moment you get cocky, you get careless."

He sat up and wiped his mouth of grime and mud, then raised his arms to take in a full breath. He touched the part of his shoulder where he had torn off the top layer of his skin. Nothing felt broken—thanks to Taishi saving him at the last second, again—but this crash was going to linger for a few days. "I can't seem to recover from a fall no matter how much I stay calm."

"Because you didn't stay calm, and it took you too long to regain control." Taishi hauled him to his feet and brushed the rotting leaves off his back. "Here's a trick. When you're falling out of control, latch on to two opposite currents and pull to cross them." Taishi's voice took on a different tone when she was actually teaching and not just being derisive. Jian listened attentively as she demonstrated, weaving the air around her as if she were an artist painting.

He nodded after she finished. "I understand."

"Prove it. Do it again, and this time drop directly from the trunk. Take what's given to you. Stop hesitating like a frightened field mouse. We'll do this with the Celestial Family watching if we have to."

Zofi emerged from the brush at the edge of the clearing a moment later, just as Jian was about to climb back up to the top of the bamboo tree. She wore her travel sack and was carrying a basket. "Is this a good time? I brought lunch."

Lunch was, unfortunately, again, radishes every which way. Today's meal was cold daikon soup and a side of pickled radishes with sweetened daikon chips for dessert. Jian was impressed with the many ways Zofi could dress up one vegetable.

"I need a few things from town as well," said Taishi as she raised her bowl and slurped her soup. She dictated to the mapmaker's daughter a long list of items.

Zofi's eyes narrowed as she scribbled them down. "My shopping list is already too long. We're low on everything. Spare me Jian for a day or two?"

Taishi's eyes narrowed. "He needs to train. His windslipping still borders on suicidal, and his Grand Supreme Punch technique is pitiful. He's sloppy like a five-gourd drunk whenever he practices it."

"It's a stupid skill! There's nothing grand or supreme about it. It's not even really a punch, more like an awkward palm slap on the chest," he complained. "Not to mention it's practically impossible to land. The setup requires a stationary target, and the windup requires focusing all of my jing into one punch, which takes an hour of meditation."

"That's because you suck at it."

Zofi crossed her arms. "Taishi, if you want everything here, I'm going to need help."

"Fine, but be back in two days. The boy needs to train. Don't let Jian pick the melons. He wouldn't know ripe if it split over his head." She gave Jian a side-eye. "You get a small reprieve, but we'll start again the morning after you return."

"Yes, master. Thank you, master." Jian could barely contain his glee. Anything to escape this torture."

"Bye, mistress." Zofi waved, pulling Jian along. They weren't far from the clearing when Zofi broke into a run.

He limped behind her a few steps, working out the kinks from his hard fall. "Hang on. Slow down. I just fell off a tree."

"Yes. I saw. It was spectacular." She smirked. "Why do you keep landing on your face? Is it a new technique?"

"Very funny." He grunted. "Thanks for making up an excuse to get me out of training."

"Who said it was an excuse? I was hoping you would volunteer to go by yourself. How's the flying coming along?"

Terrible. Painful. Impossible. "It's fine."

"That bad, huh?" Zofi didn't look worried. "You'll get it, eventually. You better, Great Savior of the Zhuun, or we're all in deep dung."

He grumbled. "We better learn to speak Katuia then."

She clutched his shoulder. "Hey, don't worry about it. You'll be fine. You'll either fulfill the prophecy and slay the Eternal Khan of Katuia, or he'll rip you limb from limb."

Jian scowled, kicked a stone, and watched it bounce and tumble down the path. "Do you think Kaiyu will come with us?"

Hwang Kaiyu was Hwang Kasa's son and disciple, and the closest thing to a friend Jian and Zofi had in the Cloud Pillars. He was a few years younger, brash and innocent, with the disposition of a happy puppy.

Contrary to their supposed isolation, the Cloud Pillars was home to a teeming community of war artists. Most kept to themselves. Some were older masters who had retreated from the world to live out their last days. Others, like Kasa, had returned here to raise and train their heirs. More than a few were hiding from the law or the wrath of some noble, or in Jian's case both.

The two continued picking their way down the rough, winding trail. With so much rain, thick forests of bamboo trees grew quickly and often rearranged the ways they traveled. They reached a narrow rope bridge connecting two mountains several hundred feet above the ground. The long way down through the valley would take an extra hour to traverse.

"I hate this part the most," she muttered, staring at the two fraying ropes serving as railings.

"I can carry you on a current if you'd like," he offered.

She blew a raspberry. "No thank you. I just saw you land on your face."

Jian and Zofi crossed the rickety bridge one plank at a time, feeling each one skate beneath their feet. They crossed without incident, as they had a hundred times before, and continued along the path as it wound down the side of the mountain until it ended at the base of a tall, plump waterfall.

Kaiyu was fishing in the waterfall's basin when they arrived, wearing nothing but a pair of trousers rolled up to his knees. The boy was small for his age, his body not yet filled out. His head was shaved at the crown, but the hair along the sides hung down over his face like a curtain. He wielded a fishing spear in one hand and a knife in the other. The spear hovered overhead for several seconds before darting into the water. It came up empty. Kaiyu waded a few steps deeper into the murky green pool, then reset again.

Without taking his eyes off the water, he whistled. "Hi, Zofi, Jian. Need something?"

Taishi never bothered to hide Jian's identity from the other master war artists. There was no use, she had said. Both of them were too notorious under the lunar court. She trusted that the small brotherhood of master war artists, as a courtesy, would not give her up. So far that theory had held true. It also didn't hurt that every master knew that Taishi would murder their entire lineage if they betrayed her.

Zofi waved back. "Just the wagon, Kaiyu."

"Bahngtown or the lion farm?"

"Supplies," said Zofi.

"Ah, too bad. Go on ahead to the houseboat. Ba's mending nets."

"What's too bad?" asked Jian. But Kaiyu was already focused back on the water near his feet, the spear still held high and ready.

"Come on." Zofi dragged him by the collar and waved back at Kaiyu. "We'll see you at the boat, yeah?"

Kaiyu's arm snapped downward, and this time the spear tip came out with a large blue-and-yellow toad, its legs kicking weakly into the air. Kaiyu wasted no time putting the creature out of its misery and dropping its body into a satchel hanging at his waist, then he reset again.

Jian and Zofi continued down a short way along a babbling stream that eventually drained into the Yukian River. They passed several fenced pens with assorted livestock, and a pair of oxen grazing ankle-deep in water. To the left, a little farther from shore, was parked a long covered wagon.

The two approached a wiry man manually patching a broken fishing net hanging from a stand. The top of his bald head reflected sunlight like a mirror while long white hair hung from the sides down to his shoulders. He wore a loose oversize shirt, which hung off his scrawny shoulders like a dress. One could have easily mistaken the man for a homeless vagrant.

Jian and Zofi touched their closed right fists to their open left palms and bowed. Hwang Kasa, known throughout the Enlightened States as the Sky Monkey, had been a moderately renowned war artist for the better part of the last century. He was the head of the Houtou style Third Lin lineage and had earned a sterling reputation throughout his career. His list of slain named enemies was impressive, and his eccentricities had earned him a niche but fervent fan base under the lunar court. For whatever reason, Kasa still could never break into the highest echelon of war arts masters, though he was certainly worthy.

Though Taishi and Kasa tended to campaign on the same side, there were times when they found themselves on opposing fields. As one would expect from professionals, there were rarely ever hard feelings. This was fortunate, because Kasa had moved into Taishi's neighborhood over on the next mountain two years ago when he decided to retire from the world and settle down to raise his son in peace. The masters enjoyed a healthy and respectful relationship. As a bonus, Kasa had a nice wagon, which he generously lent anytime they needed it.

Master Kasa looked as if he were strumming a harp as his fingers passed over the fishing net, untangling knots and tying loose strings together. The Houtou style emphasized trickery, agility, and evasion, traits both the master and his son exhibited with ample abundance. Jian had sparred with Kaiyu many times, both serving as their respective master's proxy.

The two boys were evenly matched in open hands. What advantage Jian had in height and reach, Kaiyu made up for in quickness. They paired similarly well with weapons, with the exception of Kaiyu's bound staff, to which Jian had no answer, much to Taishi's chagrin. It was beneath both masters to duel for honor and prestige at this late point in their careers, but it didn't mean they couldn't duel vicariously through their heirs.

"How is my good friend Ling Taishi?" Kasa asked, his eyes fluttering alongside the blur of his fingers.

"My master is well and sends her regards, Master Hwang," Jian replied, bowing stiffly and formally. Kasa couldn't care less if Jian squatted in front of him and relieved himself, but Zofi insisted he practice presenting protocol whenever possible.

The two waited a few seconds longer as Kasa completed the section and tied off the net. He patted the white resin off his dusty robes and turned to face them. He eyed Zofi up and down. "You need to eat."

"You need to mind your own business," she shot back. "I'm the perfect size."

"I have smoked salmon hanging off the rack, fresh raw salmon, and fried salmon with chives."

Zofi held up her satchel at her waist. "I have daikon radishes, pickled daikon radishes, and daikon radish chips."

Kasa grunted. "Always radishes. Taishi needs to diversify."

"Master Taishi has not stepped foot into the garden since when we moved in. *I* grow daikons because they're hardy, versatile, and tasty." Jian didn't want to break it to her that all her radish dishes tasted exactly the same, and none of them were tasty.

The master grinned. "Any time Taishi no longer needs your services, I'll steal you away on the spot."

"You can't afford to employ me, master."

He scratched his bristled cheeks. "I was thinking more of you and Kaiyu matching well together."

That was when Zofi broke character and guffawed. She covered her mouth with a hand, and her body convulsed as she tried to swallow her laughter. One or two outbursts escaped her lips before she regained her serenity. She bowed. "You are too generous to consider me, master."

"You wouldn't consider it, would you?" he probed.

"Not a chance in the twelfth depth of hell."

"There're only ten," Jian added unhelpfully.

"I stand by what I said." She turned to Kasa. "I am honored, though, master."

Kasa was unfazed. He stepped onto the ramp and waved at them to follow him onto the boat. "Bah, you're both young. You'll have time to reconsider. Come, stay for dinner. You can leave in the morning."

The houseboat was an old pleasure barge converted into a homestead. Kasa had figured it was easier to pull a boat upriver than it was to build a house from scratch. The main living quarters were a canopied tent lashed together with bamboo and canvas, forming a curved arch covering the middle of the boat. Underneath the tarp were a large table and six chairs, two beds, and a strange array of structures of hanging bars, handles, and wobbly platforms.

Kasa opened the door to the smokehouse. "Come, you're welcome to dinner."

What the scrawny old goat actually meant was he was welcoming them to cook *him* dinner, but Jian and Zofi were happy to oblige. Their meals were often at the mercy of what was available, so having as much fish as they could eat was always a treat. Kaiyu returned from the lake just as Zofi brought out salmon and radishes three ways. Zofi pursed her lips for a few moments before the giggles burst through into fresh laughter, to the boy's confusion.

Afterward, they joined Kasa in meditative stretching as they con-

torted their bodies into awkward poses while listening to his calming instructions. They had varying success. Zofi promptly sprained her ankle,
and everyone retired shortly after, with Kasa disappearing below deck
while Kaiyu climbed into a hammock hanging between the two masts.

Jian found a lumpy, torn daybed on the upper deck and declared it
their camp for the night. He and Zofi spent the rest of the night drinking
radish juice and staring at the Queen, the Prince, and the rest of the stars
that made up the Celestial Court.

He nudged her with an elbow. "Let me ask you something. I think it's
time for me to ask Taishi to get my own guardian lion. What do you think
of that?"

Zofi elbowed him back. "I think you're a dumb egg. Don't even think
about asking."

"Why not?"

"Because guardian lions eat four chickens a day, have rancid breath,
and their fur smells like wet dog."

"But Kaiyu says he might get one soon!"

She turned her back to him. "Go to sleep."

Jian lay wide awake well after she began snoring. Zofi did not say no,
and his birthday was approaching. Taishi had even mentioned in passing
once or twice about beginning his training for the final test. That had to
mean he was almost ready. Jian relished that thought and took it with him
into his dreams where he imagined himself becoming the new grandmaster of the Windwhispering School of the Zhang lineage family style,
all while riding a giant red guardian lion that smelled like wet fur.

CHAPTER SIX

DESERT LIONESS

Qisami raised one eyelid but couldn't quite muster the energy to open the other one. Her head was heavy as a brick and felt like it had been stuffed with gravel. Her skin itched as if she had been wrapped in a blanket of low-quality wool. Her head lolled to one side, and she found her face half buried in a smelly bed of dirty straw. A beam of sunlight drew her attention to an all-too-familiar view of a small window on the other side of several thin metal bars.

Great. She was in jail. Again. It wasn't a big deal. This wasn't the first—or even the tenth—time she had woken up in one. Qisami didn't mind being imprisoned that much either, because there were few cells that could hold a shadowkill.

It took her several attempts to sit up. She couldn't feel her arms and legs past the joints, and nothing seemed to be working. Her eyesight was still fuzzy, and all she could hear was a muffled hissing sound, as if someone were whispering words she could not make out. At least her neck still worked, sort of. Qisami rolled her head back to the center and stared curiously at the ceiling. Why would there be bars overhead as well? In fact, was there another jail cell above her? Then the entire room shook, jostled, more like it.

Where was she? How many hours had she been out? The diffused light from the frosted windowpane made it difficult to tell. Had she been out a few hours, or was it the next day? The last thing she remembered was Firstwife smothering her with slumberweed, then darkness. Something was different, though. Qisami used to take slumberweed for fun, but she had never awoken to such a headache and body weakness. She couldn't understand it. What crazed maniac could she have angered so badly that they sent all those Mute Men and then went through the effort of locking her up? Who even kidnaps a shadowkill?

It took a while before any sensation returned, first to her head and body, then to her limbs. Her lips were dried and cracked, and her belly growled badly. Her one opened eye kept wanting to droop shut, but she forced it to stay open, which required much more effort than she thought possible.

Moving sluggishly, Qisami pushed herself up and banged her head on the cell, her red hair pressing against the metal bars. She opened her mouth to groan and tasted blood on her dried, cracked lips. She made it into a sitting position, but toppled over. Only another wall of bars to the side kept her from falling flat. Something sharp jabbed into her side as she tried to roll onto her back again.

Qisami noticed several small needles clustered around her elbows and wrists. She found more on her shoulders and neck. She touched her porcupined face. These needles were everywhere. A realization struck her. If an acupuncturist had put her to sleep, then she could have been out for days, maybe weeks.

She ran her hand over her body, swiping away most of the needles. Feeling returned shortly. It was little wonder; an acupuncture-induced sleep was rarely restful. The stinky, lumpy straw bed under her didn't help matters either. She had been locked up many times, but this was the first time she had found herself in what appeared to be some sort of dog cage.

Wait an egg-cracking moment . . .

Qisami scanned the rest of the room. The other side was just a wall of cages five wide and four tall, each with a bed of straw and a bowl. A narrow path divided the two walls of cages. One end had a small unlit lantern hanging off a hook, while the other had a tall, narrow wooden door.

"This is *actually* a dog cage!" Qisami hollered, more insulted than anything else. She kicked the bars on the other end and rattled the side with what appeared to be a door.

The entire room shook again, rattling the metal bits and throwing Qisami against the bars. She snarled and curled her fingers around the gate. Vibrations were crawling up and down the metal bars, and two lanterns at both ends swayed with a steady cadence. Then Qisami heard a grinding noise, like heavy wood against stone. She looked back at the window with the thick frosted glass. She was in a wagon of some sort, and it was moving.

Something moved out of the corner of her eye. She focused on it, studying the faint outline in the darkness. Someone groaned, and then a familiar voice spoke. "Ow, are there ants all over me? Get them off! Get them off!"

"Koteuni," Qisami whispered, although she didn't know why she bothered keeping quiet.

"Kiki?" she whispered back. "Is that you? What are we doing here? Where are we?" She sniffed. "Why does it smell like an old pimp's crotch in here?"

"Jailed, in a dog cage on a kennel wagon." Qisami sniffed. Her full sense of smell had returned, unfortunately. "Can you believe that?"

"Someone's definitely getting fined for this." The outline of Koteuni's face appeared near the bars. "Seriously, why does it smell like my grandbaba's pants in here?"

"I didn't know your grandfather was a pimp."

"I'll have you know my grandbaba was a great man and a learned noble in the Lawkan Court. He just happened to always smell like pee." Dirty straw began to rain out of Koteuni's cage. "Where are the others?"

Qisami scanned the room, first sighting Zwei curled in a fetal position in the top corner cage. Burandin was in a bottom one just below one of the lanterns. Cyyk was directly opposite her one row down.

"Everyone's here," she said, wondering. "Even the stupid baby Broodbaby. They must want the cell intact, but why?"

"Maybe it's a job." Koteuni couldn't hide the tinge of desperation in her voice.

"Charging them triple under the table if so," muttered Qisami. "Considering they blew up our last job."

"They were waiting for us. We were ambushed. How?" her second said thoughtfully. "One moment I'm poking holes in those two guards like drunk Ling Taishi during her ill-tempered years, and the next two Mute Men jump me. I'm not going to lie; I was flattered whoever sent them thought fit to send two. Still, I was going to escape and leave you to your fates, but then someone bull's-eyed my forehead with a needle. Has to be a highly skilled acupuncturist. Next thing I know, I have piss-soaked pieces of straw sticking into my mouth."

"Wait," Qisami interjected. "You fantasized about being Ling Taishi? How could you do that?"

"She was always my favorite," Koteuni admitted. "Ever since I was a little girl. I've seen all the street operas about her."

"She killed Haaren, and she almost killed you!"

"It would have been a pretty neat way to die, Kiki." Koteuni took a breath. "Speaking of death, how did the Quiet Death capture you?"

"Are you kidding? I'm not stupid. I surrendered." Qisami snorted. "The entire thing was a setup. No wonder the pay and bonuses felt too sickly sweet to be true. I should have sniffed something was off." If she hadn't been so impoverished and desperate for a decent contract, she *would* have done proper—or even any—due diligence on this job. The pay was too good, though, which in hindsight was probably the point. "Mute Men means it's nobility, and that many at once means someone high in court."

"Hopefully not the Gyian court." Zwei had awoken and joined the conversation. "I have a little matter of a death sentence there."

"Look at that," Qisami remarked, impressed. "So young and already a death sentence."

"Feels like overkill for just five shadowkills," huffed Koteuni.

"Counting Cyyk is generous," said Qisami.

The wagon rocked again, more violently this time, and then gravity shifted toward the left wall. They were rounding a bend and descending, possibly down a windy mountain pass? It felt colder outside, or perhaps it was just disgustingly humid in here.

"How long have we been out?" asked Zwei.

Qisami squinted at the opaque glass window. "With needle sleep, it could be a while."

"So we could be anywhere."

"Even Gyian," added Koteuni.

"Drat."

Burandin had awoken during the conversation, but as usual was more content to listen than participate. His wife did enough talking for both of them. That left Cyyk, who was still snoring in his cage. Qisami grimaced. Koteuni was right; they should have pushed harder for a girl grunt instead of getting assigned this useless Broodbaby. Well, she could worry about addressing that regret later.

Right now she had more pressing matters to figure out, first of which was finding some food. Qisami wrapped her fingers around the metal bars and surveyed the shadows and darkened corners. Most were too shallow and small to shadowstep through, at least for now. The two lanterns hanging at both ends of the room did a decent job warding back the shadows, but they presented an opportunity when they swayed.

Qisami bided her time, watching and counting the beats, as the lanterns jostled back and forth. They were swinging in unison, and the shadows they created lasted moments. She had to be careful not to get lost in the shadowstep, or get cut in two as she stepped out. Qisami had always been fascinated with dying that way. It had been a popular topic of conversation back at the training pool, but it had never actually happened to any shadowkill in living memory. At least it was not something anyone was willing to admit.

Qisami's moment came on a sharp left turn. Gravity shifted again. The two lanterns leaned sharply to one side, creating a large enough black spot right next to Burandin's cage. She went for it, pushing herself toward the back of the cage into the shadows. A ripple passed through her, like she was being enveloped by a thousand bubbles that tickled her as they passed.

She emerged an instant later, bounding out of the darkened corner just as it closed. She surveyed herself, patting away the straw clinging to her shoulders. "There is still not a cage that can hold a shadowkill."

Careless, stupid jailers, practically begging the shadowkills to escape. Anyone with half a chicken brain would know that, contrary to popular mythology, light was a shadowkill's friend. A smidgen of light was needed to give darkness dimensions, form, and structure. The only way to truly contain one of their kind was to shroud them in complete dark.

Qisami rattled her knuckles along the bars as she walked down the aisle to the door in the back. "All right, pudding peas, time to go."

Zwei reached her first. They had picked the latch with a wire and unlocked it from the inside. Koteuni shadowstepped next to her a moment later. Burandin just kicked his gate open. Cyyk they had to let out.

Qisami grabbed the door handle and pushed slowly. Sharp beams of white light, temporarily blinding, shot through the crack. The sound of travel grew much louder: the large wheels rolling on the paved road, the oxen mooing, and the sounds of shouting and footsteps. Many of them. Qisami readied for a fight, and then swung the door all the way.

This particular wagon had a peacock's tail, a small balcony attached to the back that fanned out for several feet. Qisami's eyes widened. Sitting on the tail was Firstwife, looking like she was expecting company. The woman looked over at Qisami and stood. "About time you woke. Follow me. The rest of you stay."

Qisami began to plan her escape. She was happy to play along for a while mainly out of curiosity. The King was setting on the horizon, his rays burning rust upon the landscape. Dusk was approaching, and with it a blanket of darkness. A shadowkill was a slippery eel at night, difficult to capture and nearly impossible to contain. All Qisami had to do was bide her time.

The rest of her cell, however, were on their own and would have to find their own way out. She blood scrawled on her forearm. *Go back in your cages. I'll be back, maybe. If you can escape, do. But remember, no one gets paid if I don't make it out alive.*

A cool, crisp blast of wind slammed into Qisami the moment she stepped away from the safety of the wagon doorway. Many war artists, especially the younger fools, tried to act tough and pretend the weather didn't affect them. Qisami had no such hang-ups. She shivered and jumped up and down. She blew a raspberry and pulled her long sleeves over her hands. She almost asked a nearby guard to give her his cloak.

The change in climate also meant the wagon had been heading in a northerly direction. By the looks of the tall hills around them, Qisami guessed they must be heading northeast, deeper into Caobiu lands. West would have taken them to the humid river lands of Lawkan. East would have been the arid Xing.

Qisami wasn't thrilled with being back in the duchy. She hadn't worked here since Jiayi. There was also the matter of the civil war. If she were lucky, they would maybe be taking her to a rural place far from the conflict and fighting.

"I just have to figure out where we are." She followed Firstwife to the front of this long, slow line of wagons.

The guard escort chuckled. "Look to your right, you caged dog."

Qisami scowled and shook a finger at him. "I'll remember that. I've memorized your face. One day, poof. Watch the shadows. I'll be right there, stabbing your eyeball." She looked to the right anyway, and she felt a sudden intense need to eat a lot of sweets. "Oh, pig feet."

Sitting on a plateau halfway up a mountain down a long, winding cliffside road was the unmistakable and imposing capital city of Caobiu, Danziyi. Her captors had literally dragged her from the safe anonymity of a backwater settlement to the very beating, slaying heart of the War of the Five Dukes. More fortress than city, Danziyi was the center of Sunri's extremely centralized seat of power, from which every aspect of her government flowed up and down through her extensive chains of command. There was no delegating. Danziyi also housed the largest standing army in the world, which made it the focal point of every other duke's war plans. It was well known that whoever controlled Danziyi controlled the Celestial Palace.

Qisami stayed just a few steps behind Firstwife as they continued up the wagon line, her stare glued to the giant, ugly fortress. Sunri's stupid hideous city on a hill. It was the last place Qisami should be. She glanced to her other side. In the valley below Danziyi were several expansive terraced rice fields with half-submerged green sprouts in neat rows. The water in the fields was higher than normal, courtesy of a healthy Spring this cycle. There were so many places she could shadowstep away to; it was almost too easy.

They skipped the turn that would have led them into the city and continued northward. A spark of hope kindled inside. "We're not heading into the city?"

"Our business lies elsewhere."

This was a good sign. A wise shadowkill avoided ducal gold. Although they paid handsomely, it was almost never worth the hassle. The Caobiu court's bureaucracy was particularly dangerous. They crested the hill, and Qisami's optimism dissipated. She squeezed her eyes shut, but she had already seen a vast flat plain below, where a sea of red and yellow was arrayed in neat marching squares that crawled as far as the eyes could see. Qisami had not only been brought into the heart of the Zhuun civil war, but it also appeared she was smack-dab in the middle of an invasion, and by the direction everything was moving, of Gyian. They continued down the road, merging with the heavy traffic of wagons punctuated by the rumbling of a thousand boots marching.

The heavy congestion on the road slowed them to a crawl. Firstwife did not slow, however. She grabbed Qisami by the elbow, digging her sharp claws into Qisami's joint, and dragged her along, breaking away from the wagon. By the strength of her grip, the woman must either have trained in the war arts or have been a schoolteacher. The surrounding soldiers took one look at Firstwife and parted, forming a clear path before them. The woman had to also hold some position of authority.

It soon became obvious where Qisami was heading. Near the middle of the long line of soldiers in red armor was a line of four massive wagons, each draped with yellow flags. Large war wagons were common enough. They came in all shapes and sizes, with differing levels of armaments and mounted weapons. A well-supported war wagon was a fortress that could advance and gash a deep wound into an enemy's ranks, or defend a position for days.

These new monstrosities on wheels, however, were on another level. Each was three times taller than any wagon had a right to be, and so wide it took up the entire width of the road. Plated with thick slabs of yellow-painted armor, the wagons were protected by lines of murder holes on the sides and archers' nests on each upper corner. Each wagon had eight large wheels taller than a man, complete with spikes. Two ballista on the roof completed these armaments, leaving no doubt as to these wagons' function.

Qisami was admittedly intrigued. "I've never been captured by a general before."

Firstwife stepped up to the giant wagon's long tail, which led up to a set of wide double doors through which she ushered Qisami. The doors shut behind them with a loud clang.

Inside was dark, save for the hint of a lantern on the other side of a beaded curtain. Qisami could tell with a glance by how the yellow light refracted off the beads that they were crystal. Also, not one bit of light came through from the outside. The interior here was sealed shut. Qisami always appreciated fine craftsmanship. It really showed dedication to the craft. Still, a little light would have been nice.

It took a few moments for her eyes to adjust. As much as her kind operated in darkness, shadowkills could not see in the dark. It would certainly have been useful, but no war arts style had yet created this particular ability. There were rumors that the Katis had achieved a way to work around seeing in the darkness, some dog-piss fantasy about training their eyes to see heat or something equally outlandish.

That was the thing about the war arts. Most of it was rubbish and lies, a game of one-upmanship between competing styles, or in the case of empires, a cold war between two people. A country's superior war arts could be a decisive advantage in war and diplomacy, so there was always an aggressive push to develop more powerful and deadly styles and techniques, or at the very least lie about it to frighten enemies.

The rest of the room came into focus. Qisami appeared to be standing in a small foyer. To the right was a half-table leaning into the wall. A pot of tea and cups were waiting there, inviting her to sit. The left side of the room had a row of cushioned chairs, possibly swan down. Very nice. The quality of the crystal beads on the curtain was a nice touch as well. This general had good taste and a fat wallet.

Qisami slid through the crystal-beaded curtains into a large room that stretched almost to the other end of the wagon. There was a raised dais at the far end flanked by columns. It was almost like a miniature court. It was dark except for a light at the far end, and the ceilings were low, which gave the room a claustrophobic feel, but then again they *were* in a wagon.

It was then Qisami heard the voices. Two men warbling forcefully at each other. They were soon joined by a third, higher pitched, and then another. The chatter grew heated and chaotic.

"That's enough." A woman with a firm voice cut through the chatter. All the other voices died instantly. She continued a moment later. "We'll cede the Celu Mountain passes to Xing. No point in prolonging it at this cost. Once they spill in, however, I want them battled to the ground. Delaying action only. Show me the map of our supply lines. There, we break the Jii Dam, which should flood the entire south plains into a sea."

"The collateral damage will be high."

"What do I care? It's their territory now. Let them pay for repairs."

"Forfeiting those holdings betrays weakness."

"That's because we are weak!" she roared. The room was dead silent after that.

A figure moved forward from the shadow into the light at the far end of the room. Cloaked in yellow, complete with peacock headdress, there could be no mistaking her jet-black hair hanging over half of her porcelain-white face. Her visage was stamped on half the coins in the Enlightened States. A red-robed attendant, a young girl, flanked her, holding Duchess Sunri of Caobiu's infamous straight sword, the Blood Dancer, offering it at the ready for her grace's draw.

Qisami gave an audible gasp. "Oh, pig feet."

CHAPTER SEVEN

THE TROOP

Jian awoke the next morning to the heady aroma of fried trout sizzling in a pan. Zofi, who once more had stolen most of the blanket, was curled in a fetal position with her back to him, edging him off the mattress. Jian rolled off and sat up, his bare feet feeling the cold sting of the damp wooden planks.

Kasa appeared a few moments later, carrying a tray of fried mangoes and a whole fish over a bed of brown rice. "Good morning, my boy."

"I didn't know masters served students," he said, a little in awe.

"Bah," the man said, placing the tray next to a small table. "You're not my student. You're my guest. Come, come, eat."

It felt wonderful to sit with the Houtou master and just chat about a range of things small and personal. Kasa had grown up a whaler's son in a small fishing settlement at the western edge of the Sea of Flowers. They had lived in a small cabin on stilts due to flooding from the rains every third cycle. He had had eight cats, named One to Nine, with the exception of the number Three because of the bad luck. His mother once beat a shark to death with her bare hands when it tried to eat his sister. Jian even learned that the final test for every Houtou master was to climb the bell tower of the Temple of the Tiandi in Allanto and ring the Gong as Large as the World three times.

"Did you really do that?" Jian asked.

Kasa nodded. "Twice. My master disqualified me on the first run because I took advantage of some workers' scaffolding."

Considering the Zhang lineage windwhispering final test required the student to shatter their master's body to absorb their jing, the Houtou test felt extremely lenient.

"I don't get it, master," said Jian, troubled. "I don't understand how that final test is a test at all. How does that prove an heir is ready to take the mantle of your lineage?"

"Ah, that's because you assume too much." Kasa grinned with his wooden teeth. "For most styles, the final test is a test, a challenge to prove the heir's worth, but for the Houtou, it's a celebration. By the time the master offers the test to the heir, the master already knows that they are worthy. One test should not change that."

Jian would have much rather he climb a temple than kill Taishi. That inevitability frequently haunted his waking thoughts Every time he had brought it up to Taishi, she had brushed him aside, calling him a yolk trying to peck his way out of his eggshell. But how could he not dwell on it?

"Are you all right, Jian?"

Jian gave a start, realizing he had blanked away, lost in his thoughts. "Forgive me, master. My mind has been heavy."

Kasa patted his shoulder. "Given your place in the prophecy, son, I'm not surprised."

Jian nodded. It was nice to feel heard by an empathetic ear. It felt as if Taishi had been distancing herself from him lately. He couldn't figure out why.

Kasa picked up a severed fish head and ate it whole. "I cannot begin to understand the weight Taishi must carry, like a mountain on her back."

"What?" Jian said. "What about *me*?"

"What *about* you?" Kasa leaned over and offered Jian a second helping of sweet mango. "You, Wen Jian, Champion of the Five Under

Heaven, Prophesied Hero of the Tiandi, will try your best regardless. You will do what needs to be done, or you will die. What else is there to say? It is as simple as that.

"Master Ling Taishi, on the other hand," Kasa continued, "carries the burden of our people on her shoulders. She is charged with training and preparing you for the battle against the Eternal Khan of the Katuia. That is a responsibility that I would not wish on anyone."

"Doesn't seem so simple to me," he grumbled. "I feel like I'm still the one that has to do the hard work."

"Ah, but no one will blame you if you fail. You tried your best and died for it. But Taishi, her they would absolutely blame for your failure, considering everyone believes she had kidnapped you. She'll have to deal with the humiliation for the rest of history."

"I'm still the one who has to kill the Khan."

"There's also the small matter of his immortality. And of his death." Kasa stood up and stacked the used plates. "In any case, Jian, bring Kaiyu along to Bahngtown. We also have need for supplies, and that will save me the trip. If I let him go alone, he will end up chasing dragonflies off a cliff." He looked over at the still snoozing Zofi. "It would be good if those two spent some time together. Let the boy show her his good heart."

A cough came from where Zofi lay. Jian kept a straight face. "We would love for young Kaiyu to accompany us. He's like a little brother to me."

She stopped pretending and sat up after Kasa had left. "You're not helping. We're going to pretend he never said that and never speak of this again."

"It's sweet, though, and Kaiyu *does* have a good—"

"Never again, Wen Jian, if you wish to live long enough to get butchered into small pieces by the Khan."

Kaiyu was ready and waiting by the time they had gathered their belongings and walked off the planks of the houseboat. A team of two old mares were hitched to the wagon, and Kasa was dictating his shopping list for Kaiyu to memorize and repeat.

They set off with Kaiyu at the reins and Zofi next to him—Jian insisted—while Jian sat in the back. The first part of the journey up the Yukian River was calm and relaxing. Zofi spent most of the trip avoiding conversation and reading a cooking manual on potatoes. She'd been on a culinary kick lately. Jian passed the time stretching his legs along the bed of the wagon and chewing on dried seaweed while staring at the empty blue sky. It was nice to finally have a bit of a respite from Taishi's training sessions.

The light from the King poked through the forest canopy, swaying in a dancing kaleidoscope as a strong breeze ran down the length of the gushing Yukian River.

Kaiyu turned from the driver's seat and grinned while resting his elbow on the back. "Guess what, Jian? I'm getting a cat!"

Zofi nudged him. "Shouldn't you be watching the road?"

The boy shrugged. "These horses have made so many runs to Bahngtown, they know the way."

"Your ba said you can have a shishi?" Jian melted with envy. He was really hoping Taishi would soften to the idea of a riding lion too.

"He says as long as I take care and clean up after it, and if I have all the Houtou scriptures memorized by my next birthday. I finished that two weeks ago, so ba brought me to the ranch. Master Urwan let me pick out my egg. I'm hoping for a boy. They're smaller and not as fierce, but quicker."

"How is he doing, by the way? Your father, not the guardian lion." Zofi liked her animals stuffed.

"He is as strong as ever." Kaiyu did not sound convinced of his own words. "Last third winter was hard. It took him an entire cycle to shake off his pneumonia, but his health is much improved now."

Kasa was from a generation of war artists older even than Taishi. Under the lunar court, he was ancient. He had so far been blessed with a long life and a fruitful career, but age eventually catches up with everyone. The Houtou master was content to spend the rest of his days in the Cloud Pillars with his adopted son. He had found the three-year-old running alone on the dirty streets of Manjing. The boy had been days from death, rail-thin, his ribs protruding through taut dark skin, with contusions and blemishes all over him. The old master, never married and without an heir, had taken pity on the street rat and taken him in.

Kasa told everyone who listened that it was actually Kaiyu who had saved *him*, that adopting the boy was the finest achievement of his life. Not only did raising him give Kasa purpose and joy, but it also allowed him to train an heir and carry on the Houtou Third Lin lineage. But really all that mattered to the two was that Kasa had Kaiyu in his life, and Kaiyu had Kasa. Jian couldn't help but feel a bit wistful every time he saw the father and son together.

Kaiyu continued, his words tumbling over one another. "My ba thinks I will be ready to announce to the lunar court in two years. Then I can really take over the mantle of the Houtou. I hope the people who admire him will admire me too. It'll be a great weight off his shoulders." He faltered. "I hope he makes it that long." It wasn't unusual for him to run through an entire spectrum of emotions in one breath.

Zofi put an arm around him. "Don't you worry. The great Sky Monkey is as old and strong as these mountains and will be flying through these trees long after we're gone."

That did not seem to lighten the boy's mood. Jian poked Zofi in the back with a finger before she could make it worse. He pushed between them. "Tell us about your egg."

Kaiyu brightened again and bobbed his head, his concern washed away by excitement. "Yes! My egg is super pretty. It's green with specks of silver on top and dark purple swirls at the bottom. It's one of the bigger ones. Master Urwan said it was a fine choice. It should hatch very soon. Did you know it takes guardian lions two years before they grow to full size?"

Jian actually did, since he was the one who'd taught Kaiyu about that. The boy couldn't read, so Jian had spent hours meticulously reading books and brochures about guardian lions to him. It was interesting that neither Kaiyu nor his father knew how to read. How was the knowledge of their war arts passed down from generation to generation? Taishi owned six fat volumes of windwhisper instruction that were the only worldly possessions she ever cared about. If it had come down to a choice of saving Jian or those manuals, he was fairly sure she would make the right decision, but she'd be awfully conflicted.

They spent the rest of the journey listening to the Houtou heir detail every color, texture, and sound of his lion egg. He followed that up with lion hygiene and care, and then the stories of all the adventures the two planned to take.

For most of the way toward Bahngtown, Jian sulked with jealousy.

CHAPTER EIGHT

THE PROGNOSIS

The three knocks on the door were polite but insistent, measured and just loud enough to make out over the fury of the rain outside. The rocking chair came to a rest, and the hermit looked up from his work, his busy hands still moving, scraping the carving knife against the dense block of petrified onyx wood. For a moment, he wondered if he had imagined the noise. It wouldn't be the first time. After a few beats of peace, the rocking chair started moving again, and the hermit picked up where he had left off humming the second act of his favorite opera, *The Sea Mistress with the Long Beard*.

The knocking continued, three beats growing louder and more insistent. The hermit wasn't curious enough about the visitor to make the trek across the room to the front door. He hadn't moved from his seat in three days and didn't feel like budging now, and certainly not on account of uninvited visitors. He continued his work carving a new set of Siege game pieces, using his gnarled fingers to make a decisive stroke with each rocking of his chair. If whoever was out there really wanted to see him, they would find a way.

After about two minutes, whoever was outside finally lost their patience. The door swung open, splintering the wooden bolt. A gust of frigid wind and wet air intruded into his underground home, annoying him greatly. Two cloaked figures stepped inside, dripping all over his floors.

"Close the door behind you." The hermit did not look up from his work. He was old and dying, and there was nothing here worth stealing. The only thing of value that he treasured now was his comfort. "You let out all my warmth."

"Sorry," one said, immediately obeying the order. That was always a good sign. Bandits didn't usually take orders from their victims.

"If you're lost, Nee Outpost is three days to the west. If you need a place to stay for the night, my dog passed away a few years back. You can sleep in his kennel. If you're hungry, I have flavored water broth. If you're here to burgle, then you're idiots." The hermit glanced up from his work. The second individual stepped into the light. The hermit squinted and held up a hand. "That's close enough, lass. You look awful. Are you diseased?"

"It's not leprosy." Her annoyed scowl informed the hermit she probably got asked that quite a bit.

The young man had come in first, wielding a mace in one hand and an ax in the other. He scanned the room and settled on the hermit, speaking in a steady but youthful voice. "Are you, old one, known as Subatai the Carpenter?"

The hermit bristled, involuntarily yanking at his long, scraggly beard. "Subatai the Carver."

"What?"

"I do not work in construction, lad. I don't frame houses, fix fences, nor do I build wagons. I don't fabricate, and I don't work with gear. I revive the spirits of dead trees and make them into beautiful things." Subatai sighed. "I'm an artist, you nit."

The uncouth peasant looked confused. "So you *are* the one known as Subatai? Were you also known at one point as Sakurai, Chaqra's Keeper of Legends?"

Now that was a name he hadn't heard in years. Very few living still remembered his past with the shamans even though he had never shied away from it. The tattoos on his face were a dead giveaway. "In a previous life perhaps. Who is asking?"

The woman stepped forward. "Sakurai formerly of the council exiled for heresy?"

"I mean, if you want to only highlight the bad parts of my career," he muttered. That was all anyone remembered of him anymore. "Technically, I retired to pursue my artwork, but yes, it was a messy breakup." Subatai switched his grip on his knife. These weren't mere bandits or lost travelers. He crossed his arms and his carving knife. "State your business unless you wish a taste of my blade."

The woman pulled her hood back. "Will you share your hearth with us, honored custodian?" By her tone this one was obviously in charge.

"You look like the dead, woman." To Subatai's credit, he didn't flinch when he got a clear look at her face. "My hearth offers little warmth, but I give it freely to those in need. Next time you want to ask for the traveler's gratitude, tell your boy to keep his hands off his weapons. He's fondling them like he would a lover."

"I was not!" the young man protested. "I was just being prepared."

"I bet you sleep with them every night." Subatai rolled his eyes. He caught the woman doing so as well. She was definitely the boy's master. He gestured for them to make themselves at home. The woman accepted his invitation while the man stayed near the door. She moved with the gracefulness of someone with martial training, while her demeanor revealed her to be of high caste, and high-mannered.

The woman was also very obviously dying. Her eyes were sunken, her cheeks were gaunt, and her skin was deathly pale. Her hair was flat and peppered white, and there was a greenish pall about her. Her gaze, however, was still sharp. Whatever sickness plagued her had not yet reached her mind.

Subatai held out his hand. "Show me your palm."

The woman offered it. Her knuckles were bony and calloused, and the skin pulled tight. The flesh was tinted with green and brown. Her grip was still strong. "How long?"

"Since the Eternal Khan passed."

The implication was clear. "Impossible. That was five years ago. No one survives that long. Besides, that would make you . . ." His voice trailed off. She certainly looked the part. "What are you, a justice, wisdom, consort?"

"A Will of the Khan," said the woman.

Subatai was impressed. "Ooh, very high in the Khan's Sacred Cohort, eh? Your closeness to the source explains your condition, yet you are strong enough to endure it? Fascinating." That was when he put it together. "You're Salminde the Viperstrike, the oathbreaker and betrayer!"

A small smile cracked on her face. "Sure, if you only want to highlight the bad parts of my career."

Subatai chuckled. "I may be exiled, but I still hear well enough."

"We met a long time ago, spirit shaman."

A memory joggled Subatai's mind. "Wait. Viperstrikes are Nezra. You're Faalan's little runt. You sat next to him during my trial. I remember at the time what that gangly sprout was doing there. What were you, fourteen?"

"I was ten at the time. Chief Faalan was my uncle."

"Look at you now, Salminde. I wager your uncle is proud of how high you've climbed, viperstrike. How is that self-serving hyena?"

"He died in defense of the city."

"Ah yes, the infamous Battle of the Recovered. Your city destroyed and your clan enslaved, and yet somehow, you miraculously brought everyone home safely from the Zhuun only to have your entire clan exiled for your efforts." He pointed at his cauliflower ears. "I'm old and nearly deaf, but I still enjoy juicy gossip. Couldn't have happened to a more arrogant clan."

The woman's eyes flashed. "Are you really still holding a grudge against my family?"

"I was in the clergy. All we do is hold grudges." He chortled. "Being exiled is terrible, isn't it? Severed from everyone and everything you ever knew. Cast adrift with no past or future. And now you're leading a rebellion against the spirit shamans."

"That isn't what happened. If there is a rebellion, I am not involved."

"Those are the whispers on the wind throughout the Grass Sea.

You've roused many slumbering discontented." Subatai leaned back in his rocking chair. "What brings you all the way out here to see me, exiled orphan of Nezra?"

"You're a former Keeper of Legends," said the viperstrike. "It is said you know all. I am suffering from the sickness of the Pull of the Khan." Her voice went hoarse. "No one knew more about the Eternal Khan than you. I need a cure or treatment, anything to combat this disease."

"Let me look into your mouth." Subatai gripped her chin and moved her face side to side. "The part of the Khan's soul inside you is rotting and poisoning your body. Five years of your body being ravaged by rot. It's unheard of. You should have been dead by now."

"I don't care about what I should be. I only care about what needs to be done. How do I remove this sickness?"

Subatai shook his head. "Sorry, lass. The only cure is to march straight back to the Sanctuary of the Eternal Moore in Chaqra, lie on a death slab, and fulfill your duty as Will of the Khan by releasing that decaying remnant of his soul back to the Whole. That's how you cure yourself. You die."

"That is death either way. Give me something else."

"There is nothing else. Sometimes a dead end is just that. You can choose to face the inevitable, or not. You knew what you were receiving when you accepted the Khan's *blessing*." Subatai couldn't mask his sarcasm. "Come now, you've lived a noble and glorious life, Salminde the Viperstrike. Better than most. The time you spent this life cycle has brought your eternal soul ever closer to enlightenment. Be content with that and die with honor."

Salminde leaned forward. The weakness in her voice was temporarily gone. "I will not give those shamans that satisfaction. I have people to protect."

It had been many decades since Subatai had to think about other people. The idea of it felt strange. Foreign, even. Considering this woman was the niece of the man who had him exiled to this dirt hut, he was not inclined to help. However, Subatai also despised the spirit shamans of Chaqra, probably even more than she did, so any way for an old man to fan a grudge one last time was worth considering.

Finally, he said, "I don't have any answers for you, Salminde, but there is one place that may. Your odds are slim, but it's your only one."

"What is this place?"

"Hrusha, birthplace of the Eternal Khan. The people in that village have long studied the type of spirits that have possessed our khans over the centuries. If there is anyone who may know how to cleanse what ails you, it would be them."

The viperstrike looked curious. "Possess. Cleanse. Those are unusually strong words for a holy man to utter about their god king. You must be out of practice, shaman."

"I never said those heresy charges weren't true." Subatai's shoulder slumped. He felt every one of his eighty years. "When you serve as a spirit shaman for as long as I have, you start to see how the strings are pulled. How the system grooms everyone to fulfill their expected roles and play into this corruption. I, as Keeper of Legends, was responsible for documenting and understanding everything about the Katuia, and passing it along to my successor." Subatai looked at the wall. "Once you know too much, however, you realize that everything is a game. If there is a place that can get you the answers you need to sever the Khan's will from your own, Hrusha in the Sun Under Lagoon will be your best chance. Your only chance."

"Hrusha," said Salminde, as if committing it to memory. "This is within the Grass Sea?"

"Far northeastern border, near the top of the world. Find Joguan outpost and keep going for three days. I suggest you go quickly, viperstrike. Your time in this life grows short. You might want to dress warmly too."

Salminde stood and placed a fist over her heart. "Thank you, wise custodian. Your wisdom brings insight and closure." She joined the young man and stopped at the doorway. "He didn't have a choice, you know. My uncle Faalan, that is, when he passed judgment on you. The spirit shamans wanted your head. As the great chief, he did what he could to keep it attached to your shoulders. The exile saved your life. If it's any solace, he always thought you were handed an unjust sentence."

Subatai thought about it and then shook his head. "That does not make me feel better."

The young man stopped at the door after Salminde left the hovel. "Could you really have taken me with just a knife?"

Subatai held up the carving knife and closed his eyes. It took an embarrassing moment; he was out of practice, but some things you never forget. The former spirit shaman and now artist flicked his wrist. The knife momentarily disappeared, and then blinked back in his hand. The young man suddenly flinched and grasped his left palm. A long gash had appeared on the back of his hand dripping down his middle finger, further staining the floor.

Now especially annoyed, Subatai waved them off. "I would wish you luck, but I really don't care. Now, get out."

CHAPTER NINE

NEW JOB

Qisami had thought she had been brought to Sunri's court to speak with the duchess. Instead, nothing happened. She had sat in the back room for the entire day until Firstwife came to bring her back to the kennel wagon. Qisami was brought back the second day to the same room to repeat the experience. Other people came and went, sitting there in holding, but they all eventually left, save for Qisami. It was as if she were the last crispy duck hanging at the butcher shop. Firstwife had just come to collect her once more when a tall, thin woman with a white mask over her face wearing a matching leather robe swept before them.

Firstwife nodded expectantly. "Voice of the Court."

"Minister, you've returned at last," came the voice's reply in a strong, ringing voice. "She expected you weeks ago."

"She only cares about results."

"This delay has consequences."

"I caught a shadowkill, not a fish."

The two appeared closely acquainted, but as rivals, playing the game in Sunri's court. The veiled Voice of the Court turned to Qisami. "You have been summoned. Follow."

Two Mute Men women—that even sounded awkward in her head—fell in next to her. Firstwife and the veiled woman walked side by side up a set of narrow stairs to the upper level. They were met at a set of large sliding doors by even yet another stern-looking veiled woman, this time in red: the Mistress of Etiquette.

The mistress held her ground between Qisami and the doors. "Bow."

"No, you bow," Qisami shot back.

She returned a flat stare. "Show me how you will bow when you're in the duchess's presence."

Qisami didn't know there was more than one way to bow. She lackadaisically placed her right fist to her left opened palm, and bent forward slightly at the waist.

"This isn't a street war arts school," the stern-faced woman tsked. "Palms down, right hand over left. Never close your hands into a fist in front of the duchess. Bow low, slowly, hinging at the waist. Acknowledge Her Grace with your eyes, and then lower them. Do not raise them again. Do you understand?"

Qisami didn't really, but she nodded, and did as she was instructed.

The hateful woman smacked her hand with her fan. "Palms down, not facing you, wretch. You are *not* the duchess's equal."

"I'll make you equal," she muttered, but turned her wrist to reflect the Mistress of Etiquette's instruction.

"When we enter the chambers, stand behind me within arm's reach with your head bowed and your fingers laced together at your navel. To my left, mind you. You are not a man."

What did that even mean? Qisami nodded anyway. Not that she cared.

The Mistress of Etiquette rattled off several more instructions: eyes lowered. No eye contact. Slow half-steps. Walk with dignity, but submissively. Never address a question to the duchess. Never turn your back to her. Leave the room walking backward, again in shuffling steps. Do not breathe excessively around Her Grace. Take long, deep breaths.

Qisami wasn't even sure how half of that was possible, but she agreed to it. What's the worst the shriveled, stone-faced woman could do? The Mistress of Etiquette nodded to the two Mute Men. Qisami nearly giggled when she saw that the dukes were using Mute Men, the most feared war artists in the Enlightened States, as doormen. Even the Quiet Death needed their own version of grunts, she surmised. The doors slid open.

Firstwife and the Voice entered together, with Qisami trailing in the center between them, just as instructed. An assassin did not remain one for long if she could not follow simple instructions. The duchess's quarters was exactly as one would expect from one of the most powerful people throughout the Enlightened States. It was one large, expansive room that spanned the entire floor of the wagon. Qisami didn't much care for this open floor plan environment. She liked the rooms and hallways filled with nooks and crannies.

Displayed prominently in front of the entrance was a large mannequin wearing what could only be described as duchess robes: yellow with red trimming, like veins, which crawled all over the cloak. Her famed Ten Star Phoenix headdress with its glimmering metal plumes fanned out directly above the ducal dress. Blood Dancer sat in another stand next to the dress, easily within arm's reach if Qisami had wished for it, either to sell for a fat payday or use to escape to freedom. She wasn't sure what to wish for at this time.

A large, extravagant wedding bed the size of a wading pool was the star of the room. It was large enough to sleep an entire retinue, which perhaps, from some of the more lurid tales about Sunri, was the purpose. Qisami liked the woman already. The right side had a desk, a map table, and a small liquor bar. On the far side past the mannequin was a training area abutted by several large wooden curtains.

"Chiafana, the Minister of Critical Purpose, has returned, Your Grace," announced the Voice of the Court.

"Honor to the Desert Lioness," Chiafana, the minister, Firstwife, replicated the Voice's bow perfectly. So many titles. "Maza Qisami, the shadowkill, has received and accepted your summons, Your Grace." As if she had a choice.

Qisami's bow wasn't nearly as smooth as those of the others, but it was adequate. She kept her eyes on the rich mahogany floors. Whoever eventually destroyed this thing could make a fortune off the salvage.

"Good. Clear the room. All eyes."

The Voice hesitated. "She's an assassin. At least keep some Mute Men for your security."

"Now. Out."

Both Chiafana and the Voice bowed in perfect unison, as if they were partners in a dance. It was the Voice's turn to whisper as she retreated out the door. "Remember your place, shadowkill. Your life depends on it."

Qisami was finally locked in with Sunri, or was it the other way around? She still had no clue how she could have earned the duchess's attention, let alone wrath. Shadowkills tried to avoid ducal politics like they tried to avoid syphilis. Wait, that was a bad analogy. They didn't try very hard.

Blood Dancer resting on its stand was just sitting there begging for Qisami to draw. It could be in her hands in just a few steps. Whatever it took to secure her escape. A duchess bled as freely as a peasant. It was a last resort, of course. Killing one of the dukes was definitely the sort of life-altering event that a person really couldn't walk back.

Qisami risked a peek and got a rare close-up look at the Duchess of Caobiu. Sunri in every way lived up to her legend. She was beautiful, with sharp features, a pointed nose, and piercing seafoam eyes. She was tall, with narrow shoulders and a perfect face. Her dark hair flowed from her perfect head down past one shoulder to her perfect body, covering one of her perfect breasts. The bathing robe she had donned, while plain, accentuated her figure to every possible advantage, covering and wrapping tightly around her body while opening up like a tulip in bloom to expose the sharp lines of her shoulders.

None of this was surprising. Sunri's beauty was often the topic of songs, operas, and bawdy tales. Her image was on paintings, sculptures, and tapestries all over her duchy. Every silver-minted liang in the Enlightened States displayed her profile on its side, the good half, it was called. That honor was the wedding gift of Duke Yanso of Gyian back when he was just a coin-fingering purselord.

But, if Qisami were to be perfectly honest, all of those descriptions she had just run through of Sunri sounded like a ten-year-old brochure about the duchess. Upon closer inspection, it was apparent that those grand compliments no longer pertained to her, but one could see why they had once said those things.

Sunri's perfectly groomed raven hair was peppered with strands of gray. Thin but pronounced lines now spiderwebbed around her eyes. Her famed high cheekbones had sunk, giving her a slight gauntness, and her skin, without powder and paint, revealed the usual stains of time and experience. The idea that Duchess Sunri could grow old had never occurred to Qisami, so great and terrible was the woman's reputation. Regardless of her slight physical blemishes, Sunri still looked mostly perfect: tall, beautiful, and always exuding confidence. She was still the patron saint of little bloodthirsty girls everywhere. She was often spoken of as simultaneously the most admired and most hated person in the Enlightened States.

The duchess approached and studied her. "You're smaller than I imagined."

"You look older than I imagined." Qisami quickly bit her tongue. That had been a mistake.

"You look older than I imagined, *Your Grace*." The duchess did not seem offended by her retort. "It's far easier for the masses to fear and obey a reputation than an old woman." She pointed at the table with the pot of tea. "It's rare Red Robe tea. Join me, sit."

Perhaps everyone was wrong about the legendarily cruel Duchess Sunri of Caobiu. Qisami did as she was ordered, bowing and making the Mistress of Etiquette proud as she shuffled in half-steps across the room. The way this woman controlled the room made her whole body clench. It was curious how unconcerned Sunri was about being in such close proximity to an assassin. No servants, guards, or Mute Men in sight. If she had been the mark, Qisami could have reached over and snapped her neck.

Sunri surprised Qisami again by pouring both their teas, and then gestured to Qisami to join her. "My face is up here. You will not inspect your toes in my presence."

Qisami remembered the Mistress of Etiquette's words clearly. She looked off just over the duchess's shoulder. "Yes, Your Grace."

Sunri loosed a long sigh. "You can look at me, shadowkill. I promise I won't have your eyes gouged out."

That wasn't reassuring, but Qisami did as she was told. "Yes, Your Grace."

Sunri sipped her tea and held the cup out. "You may also address me as Sunri."

Qisami's jaws dropped. This was unheard of. She blurted, "This sounds like a trap."

"My Voice of the Court really needs to lighten up. You have my permission to speak my name in the privacy of my chambers." The duchess placed her cup on the table and studied Qisami as if appraising a prized pet. "Maza Qisami, formerly diamond-tier operative of the Consortium, trained in the prestigious Bo Po Mo Fo training pool. Graduated near the bottom quartile of your graduating litter, but far and away the highest earner of your group and once even placed fourth on the overall Board of Highest Earners."

Qisami's eyes narrowed. "You know a lot about Consortium operations."

"I'm a duchess. Everything is *my* business," she replied. "You were a rising star, that is until three years ago when you were very publicly and unceremoniously stripped of your diamond status and demoted to copper." She even sounded sympathetic. "It must be difficult being denied access to top-tier assignments and relegated to street-level jobs reserved for first-year freshies and rotted retirees." She sat back in her chair. "That's quite a fall. Care to explain?"

"Not really," Qisami replied. "But then you already know, don't you?"

"I do." Sunri poured herself another cup. "That wage garnish is quite oppressive. One so heavy I can't see how you can ever repay the debt."

Qisami glowered, crossing her arms. "Did you kidnap me just to gloat, because that feels really beneath you." She had forgotten her place again. "Your Grace."

"On the contrary. Come with me." The duchess walked to the front of the wagon. Qisami didn't have any choice but to follow. The woman had exposed her back. Sunri must be confident in her skill, although her body language so far had not given away any hint of war arts skill or training.

The duchess pulled on a rope, and the wooden curtains parted, revealing several large windows overlooking the army marching around them. Qisami saw four lines of war mammoths pulling the fortress wagon along a straight road. Marching in front of the mammoths were double their lines of heavy cavalry that spanned halfway to the horizon. The infantry, thousands upon thousands of tiny red and yellow fire ants, scurried up the winding and hilly road as far as the eyes could see.

"What do you see?" asked Sunri.

Qisami shrugged. "I see a bunch of corpses walking to their graves."

"This is the Caobiu Crimson Nu Gui. This army was formed nearly two centuries ago after the greatest leader the Zhuun had ever witnessed, the War Empress Huasanyi, fell during the Fourth Battle of Shinyong. The Zhuun forces had been annihilated and forced into a full retreat. The remnants of that army, warriors and heroes from all eight ends of the Enlightened States, gathered together in Jiayi. In an attempt to cleanse their shame, the survivors banded together and raised the crimson flag of the Nu Gui as a means to carry the great war empress's spirit. Every emperor since Huasanyi's successor had called the Crimson Nu Gui their personal retinue. They are the greatest army the world has ever witnessed, and the symbol of the Zhuun's pride and might."

"That's nice." Qisami had never even bothered to learn her grandparent's name, let alone ancient history. "What about it?"

Sunri's voice grew rich with pride. "When Tsunshing, my husband and emperor, passed, the Crimson Nu Gui rallied to the Caobiu banner, to me. That, above all else, should have determined whom the rightful empress should be."

Qisami had heard it differently, but now wasn't a time to quibble. "If you need one of those lobsters down there dead, I'm your girl. Otherwise, what does this have to do with me?"

Sunri stared outside. "The Nu Gui has never felt the sting of defeat under my command. Since this war began, Caobiu has won every single major battle against every enemy on every side. Yet we are losing the war. I've run roughshod over every Xing army, yet their forces now are massing on my borders. I annihilated Lawkan's only legitimate army, and still their navy starves my supply lines. The Gyian melt away every time we take the field, but stay close enough to swoop in for the kill and pick at my corpses like the vultures they are."

"What about Duke Saan's boys?" asked Qisami. Only the Duchy of Shulan could muster anything resembling a challenge against the Caobiu.

"My stepson put up a fight," was all she said.

"We had a saying back at the training pool," Qisami drawled. "The only time you want to be stuck in the middle—"

"—is if it's an orgy. Yes, I know."

Sunri pointed at the map table. "Taking the center of the empire had been a calculated decision. My bid for succession was more indirect than the others," stated Sunri. "They thought I did not belong, and did not have enough support to make a claim. I needed the support of the Nu Gui, and taking the Celestial Palace was a condition to their fealty."

"It looks risky."

"I had the advantage and would have won the original succession if it were not for the coming of the Horde. They invaded our lands like locusts, and the dukes were forced to a poor truce, which gave the others time to rebuild from their defeats. Now that the Katuia have been subjugated, the other duchies have all reconstituted. I am beset on all sides."

Qisami was more impressed the duchess knew the quote. Orgies were probably popular among the nobility as well. "I love a good army origin story as well as the next killer, but what does this have to do with why you kidnapped me?"

Sunri ran her finger north along Kyubi Road. "In one cycle's time, my army will arrive at the gates of Allanto. I will meet with Duke Saan of Shulan and Duke Yanso of Gyian to discuss an alliance, with Caobiu in third position. I am to wed Yanso."

"Uh, congratulations on your upcoming nuptials?"

The Duchess of Caobiu looked anything but pleased. "Even a pack of jackals can take down a lioness, but survival sometimes requires sacrifices. There are many who would not wish to see this alliance formed and will do anything to prevent this marriage from being consummated. My spy network has uncovered plans of nefarious assassins and saboteurs. I need a skilled assassin to protect me from the shadows."

"You want to *hire* me?" Qisami sputtered. "Is this a joke? That's impossible. The Consortium will never sanction anyone, especially a copper tier, to work in ducal politics." That's when the realization dawned upon her. "You want this off-book!"

Sunri did not deny her statement. "The Consortium has already authorized a contract to mark me. They cannot be trusted."

Qisami was shocked. She had never heard of the Consortium targeting a duke before. She was liking this job even less. Two cells operating on opposite sides of a contract was strictly forbidden. The Consortium did not tolerate shadowkill-on-shadowkill violence. If caught, her people would hang.

She had to figure a way to weasel out. "I'm really booked right now, and my rates are exorbitant."

"I assure you, Maza Qisami, your schedule is pretty open, and you are very affordable. I've drunk bottles of wine more expensive than you."

The duchess must have had access to a Consortium bookkeeper. "Why not leverage your spy network, or hire a teahouse or protection outfit who specializes in this sort of work?"

Sunri shook her head. "My people are not up to the task of shielding me right now. I need someone who thinks and operates like a shadow-kill."

"What's the pay?"

"If I survive these negotiations, then consider your debt to the silk-spinners covered. You will be free and clear. I will also ensure you are returned to the diamond tier."

It was a generous offer, but not nearly as tempting as the duchess thought. The risk of getting caught running an off-book job against another cell was far too great. "What if I refuse?"

Sunri paused, as if the thought of rejection had never crossed her mind. "It is your choice. I'm not holding a crossbow to your head. I would never want to force anyone to work for me. It is within your right to choose your own employment."

That was surprisingly easy. "Great. Thank you, Your Grace, for the generous offer, but my cell is not suitable for this job." She bowed formally and began to mince backward toward the door, as the Mistress of Etiquette had taught her.

A taut twang echoed through the room, and then a metal crossbolt punched into the wall in front of Qisami's face, nicking the skin off the tip of her nose. With her mouth agape she stared at the short black bolt sticking into the nearby beam. A carving of a faceless head was etched into the shaft.

The duchess returned to her tea table and refreshed her cup. "I actually *am* holding a crossbow to your head, several actually. Consider your next few words carefully, shadowkill. The next bolt goes through your skull, and then I'll set fire to the kennel wagon."

"Sounds like a waste of a good wagon." Qisami sighed. "What happened to it being my choice?"

"It still is." Sunri raised her cup. "More Red Robe tea?"

Apparently, everyone was *not* wrong about Sunri.

CHAPTER TEN

BAHNGTOWN

Jian, Zofi, and Kaiyu arrived at Bahngtown by late afternoon. The King was just beginning to dip into the jagged mountains in the distance, and the Prince was beginning his climb from the northern edge of the forest. The Queen was nowhere in sight. It was a rare night for the Prince and Princess to be away from their mother. It happened only in the first half of the second cycle on every eighth and fifteenth year. This was one such, which probably also explained the early temperamental weather.

Bahngtown was a trading post nestled in the palm of the Five Ugly Brothers near the southern end of the Cloud Pillars on the shore of the mighty Yukian. The settlement was just one long, winding street sandwiched by buildings. The two ends of the settlement had tall, decrepit, and mostly ineffective wooden gates. A century ago, a forward-thinking entrepreneur had envisioned a trading post at the basin of the valley being ideal for the miners, loggers, fugitives, and everyone else in the area.

Over the years, more buildings had sprung up along both sides of the dirt road, and for a while the settlement flirted with the possibility of growing into a fully fledged commandery officially operating under ducal rule with its own lord, taxing administration, and garrison. That proved overly ambitious, and the trading post eventually simmered into a settlement that was just large enough to warrant marking on a map, but little more. That suited the residents of the Cloud Pillars just fine.

Kaiyu guided the wagon past the opened gates and then parked at the first available hitch a few hundred feet south. The three jumped out, leaving the horses at a trough. Horse and wagon theft were uncommon and deeply frowned upon in these parts. To suffer being called a horse thief required either a duel to the death or an admission of guilt.

They stopped first at the butcher's shop, passing glistening red barbecue-roasted ducks hanging in columns from the ceiling. A giant of a man with arms like stone posts, almost as large as a Hansoo, with long gray whiskers for eyebrows, stood behind a counter. Two apprentices were slowly turning a line of ducks on a rotisserie.

The white-aproned man wielded an unusually giant cleaver and used a large tree stump as his cutting board. He must have been a powerful war artist in his day. He minced four ducks with six clean cleaves, then arranged them adroitly in neat little squares to place in small wooden boxes. He pushed a small stack of boxes to a young girl. "The first is to the garbage crew. The second to the tanner. The magistrates' order will be ready by the time you return, so hurry."

Jian and his friends waited quietly in line as the butcher continued his work. He cut up the hind of a pig and wrapped it in paper. He chatted amiably with the customer before handing it across the counter. "Next." He glanced up, and his shoulders deflated. "Oh, it's you."

"Hi, Suma." Jian wasn't sure why the man seemed displeased to see them.

Zofi's hands were on her hips. "Where's my meat, Suma? You promised me the turkey back in spring. I paid in full."

Suma rolled his eyes. This was apparently a recurrent topic between the two. "It takes time, girl. Pestering me isn't going to make it quicker. I had to source it from the ass end of the Enlightened States. There's also the matter of a war going on."

"Don't make promises you can't keep then," she shot back. "I want a refund."

The butcher sputtered. "Refund? The order's already out. I can't just recall it. It's probably halfway here by now. Be reasonable."

Telling Zofi to be reasonable was the last thing anyone should do. She rolled up the sleeves of her robes and double-palmed her hips like the grandest of snotty dowagers. "Reasonable was a season ago. If you couldn't come through when you promised, you shouldn't have accepted my coin then. In fact, you owe me interest since it appears to have been a loan."

"That's not how this works, lass. I'll sooner go vegetarian than return one liang." Suma brought his massive cleaver downward, sticking it into the stump. "How about this? I'll throw in a crispy duck. Just to tide you over. No hard feelings."

"I paid you a duke's sum a whole cycle ago, and you want to appease me with a cheap, over-seasoned duck, and *you* say no hard feelings to *me*?"

Jian couldn't hold back his gasp. Suma spoke in a low, quiet voice, his voice sounding as if thunder were rolling from his throat. "What did you say about my twice-fried in duck fat rotisserie duck?"

Zofi had really crossed the line, but she held her ground. "You've been putting too much salt on your fried duck, probably because you're trying to cover over the fact that the quality of your birds has declined. It's gotten a lot more gamy lately."

Suma's face turned red. His chest heaved twice, and then he leaned in toward Zofi. "You can tell?"

"I can, but that's because I actually have a palate. Most of the miners here can't tell duck from rabbit." She considered. "Give me three ducks."

"Three!"

Jian put his arms around Kaiyu and pulled him away. "Come on, she's going to be a while. We'll meet back at the wagon."

Zofi called after them before they left the shop. "Make sure the cactus tea is freshly ground. Don't bother going to the market. I don't trust you picking melons, Jian."

"I know how to pick melons," he shot back.

"You also keep picking parsley instead of cilantro."

"Fine. You can do it." He waved her off and stepped out onto the streets.

"What are they quarreling about?" asked Kaiyu.

"Zofi's been a little homesick. The butcher claimed he had a contact for some desert turkey and a jug of tzatziki. He's failed on both counts so far."

He made a face. "Turkeys are gross."

Jian chuckled. "What Zofi is owed, Zofi expects, no exceptions."

The pair hurried next door to the Hazy Dreams Tea House attached to the butcher shop. They entered through an earthy, purple-colored door with bright green trim. The entire building was swirled with orange and blue, the only colorful unit in this otherwise drab and gray outpost. A bell tinkled when they came in through the front door.

"Hi, Auntie Naifun," waved Kaiyu. He was everyone's unofficial nephew.

An older woman with long sheet-white hair hanging over one shoulder greeted him with a bright smile, one she was rarely seen without. "Kaiyu, my child. How is your father? The two of you up to good trouble, I hope." Naifun wore a gaudy, bright yellow robe that was accented with pink-and-green flowers. There was a lot going on with her look.

Jian placed Taishi's order for tea leaves, and Naifun continued to dote on both of them. "How is your aunt Roha, Hiro?" she asked, weighing his pouch of purchased tea on a scale. She also smelled like a mixture of age and freshly cut grass.

"She's well, mistress." Jian kept his gaze averted. He waited until the tea master finished scribbling their added tab into her ledger, then stepped aside quickly so Naifun and Kaiyu could continue where they left off.

Jian passed the time pretending to study the dozens of jars of tea leaves in neat rows alongside both walls of the store. Unlike Kaiyu, Jian did not make friends easily. At first he thought it was because he had to be guarded as the Prophesied Hero of the Tiandi, but then he realized no one cared or bothered to recognize him. Jian just wasn't good at making friends. Everyone wanted to be his friend at the Celestial Palace because he was their people's savior. Everyone had to be his friend at the Long-xian school because they were his brothers and sisters. But here, out in the wild, Jian was no one of note.

Jian moved on to the tea master's small library. It was the only one in the settlement and had an extensive collection of Burning Hearts ro-mances, often called upon by both Zofi and Taishi. It wasn't long before one of Naifun's apprentices, a graceful, pretty girl with plump cheeks and long, straight black hair brought out his package boxed with rope and a wax seal. The tea master had several apprentices, which was strange for a tea shop in such a remote part of the Enlightened States. How hard could it be to prepare tea?

"Hi," he tried. "I'm Hiro."

"We've met three times now," she replied. "You introduce yourself to me every time."

"Oh." He fumbled for a response. "Can I get your name one more time?"

"I don't think so." She shook her head and walked away.

The front door jingled, and another customer coming in saved Jian from further embarrassment. He grabbed Kaiyu by the elbow and dragged him outside. The two continued with their errands, pausing to poke at the latest weapons on the blacksmith's rack and stopping to ad-mire an impeccably dressed bounty hunter war artist passing through the outpost on horseback. The trading post was busier than usual this time of the year. This was around the time most of the locals would come to stockpile before the weather turned.

"Hey, look, it's Master Urwan." Kaiyu broke away before Jian could respond. He darted across the street to a large holding pen filled with horses, giant Komodo iguanas, and shishis preparing for auction. Kaiyu had Urwan's attention by the time Jian caught up with them and was peppering the man with questions.

Master Psy Urwan was another retired war artist. Once the horselord of Gyian, he had spent a decorated career training and leading Duke Yanso's mounted cavalry into battle. Now, long having sheathed his saber, he enjoyed retirement as the finest breeder in all of the Cloud Pil-lars.

"How are you, my boy?" Urwan asked, cutting Kaiyu's question short. "How is your master?"

Jian's fist touched his palm. "My master is well and sends her regards."

"Will she need help soon building a cat pen?" He winked.

Jian bit his lips. "I'm working on it."

"She'll come around." Urwan patted Jian on the shoulder and turned his attention back to Kaiyu, who picked up where he left off.

The two boys hung around for a while longer ogling the colorful iguanas and furry lions frolicking like puppies. But Jian remembered his errands. Watching only fed his jealousy anyway.

He left Kaiyu and hurried farther down the long, curvy street, passing several shops on his list. He'd hit them up on his way back. The bakery at the southern end of the outpost was the priority. They usually sold out of their entire day's inventory by sundown. Jian prayed he wasn't too late. He would rather stay an extra day and sleep in the wagon than return to Taishi empty-handed. Jian was halfway across the settlement when a blank storefront where Wi Wi's Slippery Piggy Grease shop used to sit caught his eye.

"Please another bakery, a bookstore, or a noodle shop," he prayed aloud. "Or better yet, a delivery post inside the settlement." Anything not to have to trudge all the way to the Fourth Ugly Brother to get the mail.

The storefront had only Zhingzhi to indicate its purpose, which only piqued his interest more. Two sawhorses sat outside to the left of the entrance, and a mound of broken pieces of wood and debris was piled to the right. The door was slightly ajar, emanating a golden yellow light from inside. Jian pressed his face against the dirty windowpane and searched for clues. A large piece of parchment hanging over the window from the inside obscured the view, but he could make out the rough outline of the counter in the back and a shelf on the near wall that once was used to hold oil barrels.

A shadow passed by the window, startling Jian, and then footsteps crossed the window toward the door. He scrambled to run away and tripped over the rimmed frame of a broken oil barrel. None of Jian's war arts training saved him as his foot skated on the greasy surface, and he toppled onto his backside with a heavy crash.

A bald man a few years older than Jian, with painted eyebrows, appeared at the doorway. "Can I help you, friend?"

Jian struggled to get back up with his greased-up hands and feet. "I'm sorry to disturb you," he mumbled. "I was just curious about your shop."

The man stepped out onto the walkway. He was plainly dressed in red-and-white robes that draped over his shoulders and tied around his waist. His feet were bound by rope and cloth, and he carried an unusually long broom in one hand. He offered his other hand.

Jian stared suspiciously at first, and then quickly realized he had taken too long to consider it and that it would look strange if he didn't accept the help. He was pulled quickly to his feet. "My thanks. I'll be going now. I didn't mean to snoop."

The well-groomed bald man looked down the street both ways. "It's all right. Everyone who has passed by the past few days has stopped in to take a look." He offered a friendly smile. "Would you like to come in, young sir?"

Jian probably shouldn't. Taishi had impressed upon him the importance of keeping his distance, especially from strangers. "You never know if a cute girl at the night market batting her lashes at you is a spy or silk-spinner looking to sell you out to one of the dukes," she had said.

He was about to apologize and hurry on his way to the bakery when his curiosity got the better of him. "What are you selling?"

The young man looked pleased. "I'm not selling anything. We're offering salvation and a way forward, free of charge. Come in, come in."

Jian didn't understand what that meant but followed the bald man into the shop anyway. Inside was mostly empty except for the shelves and counter on the sides, and several small copper urns lined up just under the front window. A few held colored incense sticks. Hanging on the back wall was a painting of some sort.

Then Jian recognized the picture. The orange-and-yellow skies with the King's light tanning the tops of clouds. The blue-and-green–tiled landscape with the mountains and snaking rivers forming the figure of a naked woman. The burrow of underground tunnels filled with walking flames with horned heads. This was a Mosaic of the Tiandi. Every temple hung one of some sort over its altar. Jian hadn't seen one in years, having avoided anything to do with the Tiandi religion since fleeing the Celestial Palace. He hadn't even given it much thought, although he probably should have since he was technically its centerpiece.

"You're a monk," he blurted.

The monk bowed. "I am Brother Hu Lao from the Temple of Manjing of Lawkan, serving Heaven and Hell and all the creatures who reside in the middle kingdom. And who are you, friend?"

Jian was at a loss for words. It took him a moment to remember his name. "Hiro, just Hiro."

Then the disappointment hit him. The first new store to come to Bahngtown in over a year was a lame temple of the Tiandi.

"Definitely not a bakery," he muttered.

"What was that?" Lao asked.

"Nothing."

Jian studied Hu Lao closely for the first time. His garb was a step nicer than what was usual around these parts, but that was a fairly low bar. The way his eyebrows were shaved and painted marked him as a westerner. A necklace of large wooden beads hung off his neck and disappeared into his robes.

"Forgive the state of the temple, Just Hiro." Lao's smile was disarming. Jian could feel his shoulders relax. "There's not much for now, but soon it will be a holy place of worship to rekindle the flames of the devout. The rest of the sacraments won't come until the next caravan."

Jian was surprised the religion was still limping along. He had thought it had withered away after he had disappeared. On the one hand, it would be nice if Jian was no longer a wanted fugitive, but on the other, he secretly enjoyed still being important. His curiosity got the best of him. "Forgive me, but I'm a bit confused. I thought the prophecy had broken. What is there left to worship?"

The young monk's face brightened. He must have been waiting for someone to ask just that very question. "Absolutely not, friend. The prophecy is a living thing. The events on this Earth are but a ripple within the celestial mosaic. The choices of man, no matter how false or misguided, cannot change the will of the heavens any more than they can alter the course of a raging river."

Technically, they could. Zofi had taught him about how the engineers of Sanba, her home city, had altered the river to harness its power. He kept that detail to himself. The last thing he needed was for one of the devout to guess his identity. Curiosity again won out. "What do you mean a living thing? Has the prophecy changed?"

"Oh, no," said the monk hastily. "The prophecy is infallible. Only our interpretation of its events have changed. Our noble abbots have acquired new insight regarding the will of the heavens."

That sounded like they had changed it. "What does it say now?"

"If you have a moment, I can explain." The monk set his broom aside and beckoned Jian to join him at a small table at a far corner of the room. "Allow me to share our wisdom. Tell me, have you ever walked under the light of the stars in the heavens?"

Jian hesitated. Taishi's voice was barking in his head to get out. So was Zofi's. So was his own, for that matter. He took several steps into the shop—er, temple. "I know all about the Tiandi scripture," he said. "Well, sort of. I'm not an expert like you or anything."

"Excellent." Lao appeared genuinely pleased. "That saves us time. As you may know there have been some unfortunate incidents which have affected the Tiandi religion over the past few years."

Jian did his best to act dumb, which wasn't difficult.

"With the reported death of the Eternal Khan of the Katuia and the Zhuun villain vanishing from the Celestial Palace, the world was in upheaval."

Villain? He nodded anyway.

"While many believed the prophecy broken, our wise templeabbots revisited and delved deeper into the mosaic than ever before. It was then revealed that this was all indeed still part of the grand plan of the Celestial Kingdom."

Another nod, just to keep things going.

"The templeabbots entered the Great Chamber of Divine Thinking and communed with the celestial skies for five hundred days, without food or water, until they received a holy message. The all-wise holy men decreed then that the Prophecy of the Tiandi was indeed still alive, still strong and true, but it was the hero who was weak, was wicked, and it was *he* who had betrayed the people."

Jian startled. "Wait, what?"

Lao, having mistaken the cause of his surprise, put a reassuring hand on Jian's shoulder. "It is sadly true, my friend. All of us in the Tiandi were saddened, and shocked by this news. How could this be? Why would the Prophesied Hero of the Tiandi turn his back and betray his own people? The devout were despondent, as you must have also felt yourself."

Jian looked back toward the door. "Are we talking about the same religion? The hero is supposed to save the Zhuun from the Eternal Khan of Katuia."

"That was the original interpretation, yes," the monk replied. He sounded *so* patient. "Recent revelations, however, show that the figure in the prophecy is indeed a precursor to the final death of the Eternal Khan and our victory over the savage Katuia horde. What was mistaken in our interpretation was this prophesied figure's role. He is actually no hero, but a villain, a fallen prophet who is a cautionary tale to all of our people who stray from the path of the Tiandi."

Jian's face froze. "This is outrageous."

Lao continued to misread his reactions. "Outrageous indeed, Hiro. I too was shocked and angered by this. However, the wisdom of the templeabbots is vast, and they have foreseen a new path for the devout. It is now our solemn, sacred duty to hunt down this villain of the Tiandi and bring him to justice. His capture and his eventual redemption is what will also redeem the Zhuun." The monk paused dramatically. "The people need the Tiandi more than ever."

Jian had stopped listening to the monk's pitch. He couldn't wrap his head around the idea that he, the Prophesied Hero of the Tiandi, the Champion of the Five Under Heaven, was now the bad guy, the villain and some fallen prophet? Was there any truth in it? Had he had it wrong all along? Had his entire life been an even bigger lie?

"I . . ." Jian stammered. He felt numb. "I have to go. My aunt is expecting me."

Lao didn't miss a beat. He put his palms together and bowed. "Of course, I have already taken up too much of your time. May the blessings of the Tiandi shield you from evil." He dropped the preaching tone. "As a newcomer to this settlement, I would appreciate a true friend."

"I would like that." Jian even meant it. He couldn't help but like this young monk.

As he turned to leave, Jian noticed again the paper nailed to the wall next to the door. The blood immediately rushed to his head. His hands balled, and the veins in his neck bulged and threatened to pop. He pointed. "What is that?"

Lao became more animated. "Yes, yes, please take one. You would be doing the Tiandi a great service. Be vigilant!"

Jian couldn't look the monk in the eye. He stormed out of the temple and rushed back to the animal pens. His hands shook so furiously he was afraid they would attract attention.

Kaiyu was still where Jian had left him, leaning over the fence, his eyes glued to the many lion cubs crawling over one another.

Jian grabbed a fistful of the boy's collar. "We have to go."

"Already? We just got here. Master Urwan said he'd teach me how to feed—"

Jian shoved the paper in front of the boy's face. He repeated. "We have to go now."

"Oh. Wow." Kaiyu's mouth dropped, and he broke away from the fence. "Get Zofi. I'll hitch the wagon."

CHAPTER ELEVEN

GAME NIGHT

Taishi missed having the house to herself. The past two days had been serene without her two wards ambling about, their teenage voices always loud and urgent. She couldn't remember the last time she could close her eyes and listen to the evening without the two yelling at each other across the courtyard, their footsteps hammering on the creaking wooden floor, or their shrieks of glee emanating from the next room.

Taishi didn't mind the latter that much. Laughter had returned to the temple. The old house felt revitalized again with youth and energy. Best of all, it provided Taishi with a source of cheap labor. Taishi hadn't realized how much she'd missed that—the laughter *and* the cheap labor—until the two children had come to live with her. Of course, the sounds often brought back memories of the life and family she had once had. There was no bringing Sanso, her long dead son, back, but it was still good to hear joy in the old walls.

With all that, it was still lovely to have the house all to herself for at least a few days. She enjoyed the break from being someone's master. She spent the first day and most of the second lounging about, in the tub, in bed, on the lounge chair, and next to an unnecessarily large fire at the hearth, reading a steamy Burning Hearts romance she had borrowed from Naifun's teahouse. She had devoured the first six volumes in the series, only to discover that there were eighteen more waiting for her. Who knew sex could come in so many forms? Taishi had obviously not used her years efficiently.

Taishi spent the second night hosting and gambling with friends. She leaned back in her chair, put her feet up on the table, and took a swig of plum wine. "Come on, Sohn, we don't have all night. I was young and beautiful when your turn began."

Sohn was frozen in place for several more seconds before picking a green tile from his stash and placed it delicately on the game board adjacent to another green tile. He splashed a handful of copper liang into the betting pot and looked over at Taishi with a solemn face. "Your beauty perseveres through the ravages of time, Ling Taishi."

"It's better to have been beautiful once than to have never been at all." She cracked a salted watermelon seed between her teeth and flicked a shell off Sohn's forehead.

Soa Sohn had once been known as the missing heir of the Eternal Bright Light Fist Pan Family Pan lineage. Once a dominant style in the southern duchies, it had fallen into disrepute and out of favor the past few decades, incidentally right about the time Sohn, who was known as the Pan's Pillaging Playboy, had taken over the family business. A breathtakingly talented war artist in his prime, his skill and prowess was overshadowed only by his incompetence and corruption in business. Young Sohn had simply enjoyed pillaging, playing dice, and tainting his family name for personal gain.

The irony now was that Sohn no longer used his surname. According to the family's ancestry book, young noble and brave Pan Sohn had drowned fighting Dew Drop pirates while protecting the important Xing ducal water canals. The truth was that Sohn had accumulated so much gambling debt that the Desert Whale Underworld had threatened to murder his entire family line and burn all of their schools to the ground. By his father's order, Sohn had faked his own death and had hidden out in the Cloud Pillars ever since. That had been more than forty years ago.

Taishi and Sohn had crossed paths while hunting the same wild boar in the forests around Allanto during their youths. After the initial chest-puffing and feather-ruffling, they had teamed up and killed the boar together, becoming friends and remaining so ever since.

Fausan, the player to Sohn's left, chuckled as he picked a blue tile from a pile and arranged it in front of him. A handsome man with short salt-and-pepper hair, a long rectangular jaw, and a hooked nose, Fausan was easily the most recognizable person at this table, although not particularly for his war arts skill. In fact, most of his worshipers—quite literally—didn't even know he was an accomplished war artist.

Noon Fausan was renowned throughout the gambling halls of the Enlightened States as the legendary God of Gamblers, the Man with Twelve Fingers, and sometimes less flatteringly the Cheater's Saint, although never to his face. Many gambling establishments still had statues or depictions of a bare-chested Fausan twisting the ends of his comically long catfish mustache. Players would rub his generous belly for luck as they entered the establishments, and rubbed it again to pass the luck on to the next player when they left. It made for a very dirty belly on every stone statue, tiled mural, or woven tapestry. Most gamblers still invoked his name for luck.

Fausan was also the master of the Whipfinger Style Song Family Ho lineage, an ancient and obscure style that happened to be the key to his gambling success and legend. Basically, Fausan wasn't some divine god of gambling and luck, but just a really good cheat. He was the reason they could never play any games requiring dice or sticks. The whipfinger master finished his turn with a flourish, and gestured with a long, delicate hand to Taishi. Contrary to legend, Fausan also had only ten fingers. While Sohn was painstakingly deliberate with every move, Fausan gambled with reckless abandon, barely looking at his stacks while flinging and pulling tiles on and off the board with quick, fluid motions. His turns often happened so fast the other players couldn't follow them, which was exactly his intent.

"Why couldn't Kasa join us today?" he asked as Taishi began her turn.

"You know how he gets when he's smoking fish and game. He turns into a mad dead-carcass-whisperer, basting, rubbing, petting, singing to them." She swigged her plum wine and picked through her purple tiles, not liking what she saw. "It's a little troubling."

Fausan leaned in, as if speaking conspiratorially. "I hear he gives the animals acupuncture to relax them right before he kills them in order to make their flesh more tender."

Sohn almost spat out his drink. "I've seen him do it. He treats those dead animals better than I've treated any of my wives. That man values his meat."

"And you lament why you can't keep a woman or student." Taishi chuckled. "Sohn, you're a good friend, but a terrible person."

"It's been a while since we gamed under your roof again," said Fausan. "You've canceled on us so many times we almost invited Bhasani to take your place."

"How dare you think that backstabbing rice ball could take my place," she shot back. "She's nowhere as good company as me."

"Half of being good is being available," he replied.

Taishi grudgingly conceded his point before pulling out another gourd of wine.

The three masters continued their game of Sparrow, the tiles clicking and clacking on her dining table. Taishi had known Kasa and Sohn for many years, and Fausan for a few less. He had moved to the opposite face of her mountain a few years back, but the four were just a small part of a few dozen master war artists who call the Cloud Pillars home.

"My student quit again," Sohn was complaining. "Said he was homesick, wanted to propose to this girl in his village. Can you believe that? Rather make babies and take over his father's shoe shop than become a bold adventuring war artist. The nerve of young people these days."

"Don't these spoiled children know serving you hand and foot is the greatest honor of their lives?" She spoke with a straight face.

"How long did this one last for?" asked Fausan. "Two cycles?"

"Children used to be made of far sturdier stuff." Sohn huffed. "I'm getting too old to keep starting over. Lupai was my last chance to defeat my younger brother's lineage and regain my place."

"Everyone knows you're better than him," said Fausan. "You're still technically both Pan. Just pretend you're *that* Pan."

Sohn touched his chest. "I know it in here."

Taishi rolled her eyes. She refreshed each of their cups. "Enough talking. Next round."

Sohn looked defeated. "I'm running out of villages to scour for talent, especially since I can't advertise, on account of being dead. All the potential students have already left to join the war."

"Speaking of this fool's war." Taishi picked up several new tiles and organized them in front of her, careful to keep the characters away from Fausan's cheating eyes. "Any news near our doorstep?"

"The Shulan Blizzard Hawks are encamped at the north bank of the Yukian River, while the Fist Navy of Lawkan patrols from here all the way to the Caobiu border. The Blizzard Hawks tried to cross twice, but got their noses bloodied by the patrols. For now they're at an impasse." Sohn tossed a tile to the side. "Saan's dogs can't do anything but sit on their spears. That's what happens when you don't bother investing in a navy."

"Not three years after beating the Horde, the dukes go at it full tilt." Fausan shook his head and sighed. "I would have thought they'd wait . . . five at least. I was being generous."

Sohn shrugged. "It was inevitable. Half of the Enlightened States is built for waging war, and the other half is built for supporting it. The entire country would tumble into financial ruin if they didn't find someone to fight."

The games continued well into the evening. Taishi had suffered a losing streak earlier in the day, but was rallying late, winning four of the last six. If she won this next match by at least three tiles, then she could claw her way past Sohn, which meant he would have to host the next game night.

"I heard from a lady friend in Souk settlement the other day," began Fausan. "Someone hit a mail wagon."

Taishi frowned. "Jian interrupted an attack on a caravan a few days ago. Those bandits hit the mail wagon as well." Taishi frowned. "The lunar court better stamp this out. Nobody wants ducal heat in the Cloud Pillars."

"How is the Prophesied Hero of the Tiandi's training coming along?" asked Sohn slyly. "Any chance he'll wash out?"

"Not even if I'm dead, Sohn."

"Come on, Taishi," he complained as he splashed the pot. "You have two students. Offer one to me."

"You don't want Zofi as an heir, trust me," she scoffed. "And the boy carries more baggage than Duke Yanso on holiday. Go find your own sucker."

"How *is* the Hero of the Tiandi's training coming along?" asked Fausan.

"It's as well as can be expected," she said. "It's not like I was ever good with children anyway."

"He'll be ready to kill the Khan, should he somehow return?" the whipfinger master pressed.

"It depends on when he returns, if ever," she replied. Her head bobbed slightly. "Coin flip, probably, at best."

Fausan broke into a pained laugh and slapped his thigh even as his face involuntarily contorted with worry. Taishi thought that was the right response to the situation. "Coin flips are not the odds anyone should choose to walk into battle."

"It only goes downhill after 'at best,' Fausan."

"Guess he's lucky the prophecy is piss then," Sohn interjected. His face turned thoughtful. "On second thought, it must be miserable preparing for something that never comes. Talk about unfulfilled purpose." He turned gloomy.

Fausan picked up two tiles and returned two to the stacks. "Bright Light here has a point. A lifetime of training and no conclusion, no closure. How can a man live like that?"

Taishi took a deep gulp of her cup and forcibly swallowed with the lump crawling down her neck. She shrugged with exaggeration. "If the prophecy proves useless, then Jian becomes a master war artist. He will possess rare skill and walk a prestigious lineage. He can find his own purpose in life instead of being led by a leash. Life continues even after destiny ends."

"You also know what needs to happen for him to assume that mantle," the whipfinger master said in a softer tone. "It's not just about him."

A flood of memories suddenly swept through Taishi when she least expected, and like a blind punch it hit her hardest. She saw Sanso right there on the other side of the kitchen, her young pink-skinned babe when he took his first step. The first time he picked up a sword. When he rode an air current. His first successful bounty. When he was poised to step out of her shadow. Then the test. His shattered lifeless body in her arms. She turned away. "It doesn't matter. I'm already living on borrowed time."

Taishi stayed distracted, and Fausan won the next three rounds. The man gave no quarter and chuckled as he reached out with his two beefy arms and swept the large stack of coins in the middle of the table toward himself. That's what Taishi and Sohn got for playing against the God of Gamblers. It was a good thing he was a good friend who didn't care too much about money or debt collection. Fausan just liked winning.

A loud, slightly grating voice reached them from somewhere outside. "Taishi, Taishi, where are you?" It sounded strangely urgent.

She sighed. "I wasn't expecting them until tomorrow."

Fausan looked up from his tiles. "Sounds like trouble."

"In here!" Taishi bellowed, and then muttered in a more even voice, "I hope those stupid chicklings didn't accidentally kill someone."

"At least someone who didn't deserve it." Sohn shook his head.

Jian and Zofi appeared at the doorway a moment later. They looked disheveled and exhausted, as if they'd been running all day. Someone following them here would be worse than an unjustified death.

"We have a problem," said Zofi.

Jian walked up and slapped a piece of paper on the middle of the table, sending tiles and coin scattering in all directions. He seemed more angry than anything else. "Look."

"We were in the middle of a match, son," growled Fausan.

Sohn, the usual biggest loser of the night, quickly cleared his tiles. "Well, I guess it's a draw then. Oh, well."

"Like the ten hells it's a draw." Fausan pointed at his large stack. "I'm pummeling you both. You can't—"

Jian stabbed the paper on the wooden table repeatedly. "Look! Look!"

Taishi did, whipping it from under his finger and studying it. It was a wanted notice with a large, sketched face in the middle of the page. Tai-shi couldn't put a name on the face at first. It appeared to be a man in his mid-thirties. He had a wide face like he carried extra weight, and his nose was upturned as if he were a snorting pig. His eyes were squinted, and coupled with the curved sneer on his face, he had a menacing brigand-like appearance.

Beneath the picture on the bottom of the page were these words in blocky black *Zhingzhi*:

WANTED: THE EVIL PROPHESIED VILLAIN OF THE TIANDI

Last sighted this cycle on the Five Ugly Brothers mountain range to the east of the Yukian River within the Cloud Pillars

"They're talking about me! They called me evil and a villain and made my face all bloated and sinister! They think I look like that. I don't look like that. I look nothing like that!" His emotions pivoted once more. "Do I look like that?"

Taishi took another look. The man on the paper's hair was shaved on the sides with a loose and messy ponytail on top. She glanced over at Jian, with his also loosely pulled ponytail leaning to one side, a mirror image. There was also the matter of the image's single eyebrow. Jian had accidentally singed his left eyebrow off a few weeks back.

"What's a Villain of the Tiandi even?" asked Fausan. "Is that a different person or just rebranding?"

"That's what the prophecy calls me now!" Jian pounded his own chest with his hands. He was taking his religious demotion rather personally. "Look at this drawing. They drew blood dripping from my chin. I look like I eat babies! I'm all of a sudden the bad guy!"

"Well, do you?" Sohn chuckled, which earned him an incensed glare. It was very inappropriate for her disciple to treat the other masters like this, but no one seemed offended. "I don't get it. How could the Tiandi religion, after five hundred years, suddenly turn their Prophesied Hero into the villain? The word 'hero' is literally in his title. He's the reason they exist."

"Looks like they're changing the narrative," said Taishi. "Now that the prophecy broke, the Tiandi religion is trying to reframe itself by declaring Jian the enemy. Everyone loves someone to hate."

Fausan agreed. "It's brilliant, really. Some might question the change, but repeat it enough times, hammer it into their heads enough times, and the truth will be what you say. Within a generation, it will be as if it has always been that way." He whistled. "The Tiandi temples were always very skilled at publicity."

Taishi couldn't agree more. She secretly adored their outrageously colorfully decorated and intricate robes, and always thought it had made Mori flamboyant and sexy. The templeabbots in Allanto looked like fluffed peacocks, and she enjoyed watching their constantly changing styles. Who would have thought it would be the clergy who were the most fashionable.

Jian looked aghast. "But you can't change history."

"Of course you can, boy," said the whipfinger master. "It's one of the biggest perks of winning wars."

Jian turned to Zofi. "Are the history books you taught me full of lies?"

She shrugged. "Probably."

"Doesn't it matter?" he asked.

She shrugged again. "Probably."

"This new development changes nothing," Taishi announced. "We continue as planned."

"How can you say that?" Jian demanded. "How can it not matter that I'm now the villain of our people?"

"Because what they think doesn't matter, boy," she snapped. "You already topped the most-wanted list. Who cares if those secular-minded Tiandi templeabbots decide to sell fast-track tickets to Heaven for whoever turns you in?"

Zofi mused. "What's the price for an automatic ticket to Heaven?"

"Depends on how you've lived life so far. If you're worthy, it means little. But if you've been bad . . ." Fausan shook his head. "Then I reckon it's worth more than all the liang in the Enlightened States."

Jian scowled. "This feels like cheating."

"None of this is relevant," Taishi repeated. She stood from her seat.

"Now that you're back early, catch up on some of your chores. We go back to the Headless Forest at first light. Wash up first. You smell like cat piss."

Jian and Zofi bowed, retreating from the room.

"Wait." Taishi held out a hand. "My pastries. Hand them over."

The girl blinked and looked momentarily panicked, then she pointed at Jian. "He was supposed to get them." And then she fled.

Jian looked after her and then became deeply interested in the rug. "I . . ."

"Did you forget?" Taishi wasn't asking a question.

"I tried. I was on my way." Jian slumped his shoulders. "Then that nice monk distracted me, and then I saw my wanted poster."

"Nice monks are the most dangerous ones." Taishi got over the disappointment about the pastries quickly, but she would let him stew on it overnight. Ignoring the master's orders—especially in regard to desserts—was not a habit she would encourage.

The other two masters were finishing for the evening. Sohn drained the last of his drink while Fausan gathered his winnings.

"Actually, brothers, a moment. I . . ." She made a face like she was sucking on a sour plum. ". . . need to ask the two of you for a favor."

Both looked as enthused as she felt and regarded her warily.

Sohn was already backing into the doorway. "The last time you asked me for a favor, I ended up in prison for three weeks."

"And I woke up from a terrible hangover married to a barmaid," added Fausan.

"I had forgotten that. She was pretty." Taishi chuckled, pointing at her old friend. She turned to Sohn. "This is important."

Sohn sniffed and sighed. "Oh, fine. I just hope it won't be as bad this time around."

Taishi wasn't one to mince words. "Worse, probably. Definitely."

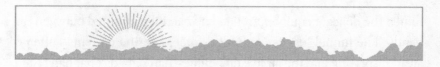

CHAPTER TWELVE

THE MOTLEY CREW

It was early morning, predawn. The King was just a glimmering band on the horizon, and the two roosters were already trying to out-rooster each other.

Jian had been up for more than an hour already, his face and body perfectly still as he sat cross-legged on the bench atop the rickety balcony hanging over the cliff's edge. He was babying a small wind funnel swirling between his outstretched hands. It required all of his concentration to channel his jing and manipulate the small strands of air moving in a steady, circular pattern. Contrary to what he had assumed when Taishi had first introduced this lesson, coaxing the air to do as he wanted was far more difficult than simply latching on to a current and letting it take him for a ride.

This exercise wasn't made any easier by Jian practicing on a rickety platform shuddering against the wind blasting up the sheer face of the pillar. His friend Meehae had called it the Deck of Faith for Fools, which was apt. He missed his old friend dearly.

Eventually, one of the small gusts leaking upward through the cracks between the wooden planks seeped into his bundle of swirling air and ruined the delicate equilibrium Jian had carefully nurtured between his hands. The funnel lost its centrifugal force, and the currents fluttered away, dispersing into the air like dragonflies. Jian sighed. That had lasted a little more than two hundred heartbeats, a slight improvement over his last attempt, but still far behind where he should be. It had taken him an entire year to get even this far.

Jian wiped off the sweat on his face. Staying relaxed to channel his jing was physically taxing. He had to be doing something wrong. He had another hour of practice before breakfast, and then he would have to warm up for his morning lesson. Jian shook his shoulders and arms out, drank from a cup on the ground, and tried again.

Taishi had been pushing him extra hard lately, ever since they had returned from Bahngtown two weeks ago. Their sessions had become substantially more punishing. She was much more generous with the stick if he dawdled or lost focus, and talked about adding another session to his evenings. Considering it was *he* who usually woke up the roosters every morning, Jian had no idea when he was supposed to sleep. What had gotten into Taishi lately?

He worked on the wind-in-his-hands exercise several more times before moving on to the last and most difficult exercise in his warm-up routine: juggling. He placed a bucket of water in front of himself and dipped his right hand inside until the water touched his wrist. He drew it out quickly, dragging a stream into the air. His left hand curled underneath his right, and in one smooth motion, bundled and wrapped the water together in a cushion of air until it took the form of a sphere the size of a child's fist.

He nearly lost control for an instant, but recovered in time to keep the ball of water spinning and churning just above his outstretched left hand. When he was sure the first ball was steady, he dipped his right hand back into the bucket. This was the tricky part. It took him six tries before he managed a second ball of water. Now was the really hard part. He counted down from three, and was about to go for a third ball when a stench like rotting meat and wet hair tickled his nose.

It was followed by "Hey, Jian! That's a neat trick."

Jian's singular focus crumpled as he lost control of one and then both balls. The small ball fell to one side while the larger tipped over into him, drenching his face and shirt.

"I was *so* close." He wiped his face and shook his fists toward the sky, and then rounded on the intruder. "Next time, show a little . . ."

There was Kaiyu, riding atop a brownish yellow guardian lion. It was a large and beautiful creature with a fierce face and long, jagged fangs protruding from its bottom jaw. Its mane was rich and curly, flowing loosely in these high winds. The magnificent creature's chest was wide and deep, and its legs short and stubby, but muscular. The creature opened its mouth, revealing several rows of twisted sharp teeth as its forked tongue flicked the air. It gave off an off-key squeak that sounded like a giggling donkey being tickled to death.

Jealousy punched Jian in the gut. "Is this your new shishi? It's so beautiful!"

"Oh, no," said the boy. "This is Master Psy's trainer lion. He wants me to learn how to ride and care for Forty-Two so I'll be ready when mine hatches."

"Forty-Two?"

"Master Psy doesn't bother with names on his farm. Every animal is named a number based on their roles. In this case, the forties were for trainers and Forty-Two is the second."

Something streaked into the air, and then Kasa landed silently next to Kaiyu. It wasn't lost on Jian that Kasa was holding the Strength Bends, his family lineage's weapon, an incredibly long flexible staff etched with strange markings along its shaft with the ends tipped in silver.

Jian bowed. "Master Hwang, this is a surprise. I didn't see you arrive. What brings you here today?"

"Fetch your master, young Jian," was the only reply.

A new voice added, "Bring a cup of oolong tea as well."

Jian noticed for the first time a woman riding behind Kaiyu on the lion. How had he not noticed her earlier? She was striking, older, with pale skin and long, flowing midnight hair fluttering in the wind. Her eyes were two colors, one yellow, one green, and her gaze had a soothing effect on Jian, as if she were tucking him into bed. "Make it strong, brewed twice and steeped long, be generous with the agave, and add a dash of chia seeds. Now go, young one."

"Yes, Mistress," Jian bowed several times before taking off in a full sprint back to the house.

"Is that him?" asked the woman as he was leaving.

"That's the Zhuun's savior, yes," said Kasa.

"He doesn't look like much."

"That's part of the problem."

"But he's really nice," added Kaiyu.

"Even worse," the woman replied.

Jian was out of earshot as he hurried to the kitchen, focused on his task at hand. He added water to the kettle and tossed a handful of spark-stones into the small fire of the cooking oven. Next, he began to swing open the cupboard doors, pushing the assorted jars and packages to the side. "Oolong, oolong. Where are you, oolong?"

He grabbed a tin that might have been what the mistress requested and sniffed the bitter odor of the dark green leaves. "Think that's right," he muttered. "What else? Chia seeds and agave." Jian wasn't even sure what they were, but he was intent on finding them. He rummaged through the shelves, pulling down jars and twisting open lids. His search became more frantic. "I need chia seeds."

"Poppies or flax seeds would do in a pinch if you're out of chia, sweetie," a voice purred behind him.

Jian startled and turned to see a girl sitting at the table resting her chin on her elbow. She was pretty, about his age, with deep amber skin, dark, luminous eyes, and thick black hair pulled back into large knots just behind her ears. A bright blue gem rested on the center of her forehead, right above the eyes. "You better have agave, however, or there's going to be trouble."

"Who are you?" he asked.

"Don't mind me, sweetie," the girl purred. He stopped minding her.

"Wait, the dry closet." He snapped his fingers and ran to the opposite end of the room, flinging open the closet where they stored all the dry goods. He emerged a few moments later, triumphant. "I think I found them." By then the girl had disappeared. Had she actually been there? He kept not minding her as he, whistling merrily, took the pot off the heat and poured it into their finest glass cup.

Jian was busy, intent on making the finest cup of oolong tea the Enlightened States had ever tasted, when Zofi walked in. The mapmaker's daughter looked around the disheveled kitchen, her jaw dropping. "What happened in here? Why is every drawer and pantry door open?"

"I'm making oolong tea for mistress." He remained focused, slowly steeping the leaves.

Zofi looked confused. "Taishi hates oolong."

"Not for her." He was completely focused on his task. "For ..." What was that woman's name?

"You're acting funny. What is wrong with you?" Zofi crossed her arms. "Did you get into her liquor *again*?"

"No, I just need to make tea for mistress." He tried to pull away.

"Taishi," called Zofi. "An oolong-loving evil spirit has possessed your heir."

"That makes no sense. Everyone knows spirits can only drink plum wine." Taishi appeared a few seconds later. She glared at the table. "What is this mess?" She took one look at Jian, and her eyes narrowed. A disapproving growl grew from deep in her throat. She walked up to him and jabbed him in the left temple with her index finger, and then again on the crown of his forehead. Before Jian could register the pain, she spun him around and jabbed her finger again into the back of the head where it met his neck.

All of a sudden, Jian's focused train of thought dissolved, like sand blowing away in the wind. He blinked his eyes shut and looked around. "What was I doing? Where was that pretty girl?"

Zofi's eyes narrowed. "What girl?"

"That evil fox!" Taishi stormed outside. "Bhasani! You are begging for death coming here and brain-tainting my simpleminded disciple's simple mind."

"What just happened?" he asked.

Zofi yanked Jian by the wrist and dragged him after Taishi. They were met with a long forked tongue as Kaiyu rode Forty-Two into the courtyard and paraded around the well. The smell of rotten meat and spoiled egg tickled their noses.

"What is this raggedy stink doing in my house?" demanded Taishi.

"It's mine, Master Taishi," beamed Kaiyu. "I'm a lion-rider-in-training."

A tepid smile was all she could muster. "Good for you, boy. Now get this guardian lion out of my house. You can hole her up in the barn, but stay away from the chicken coop. If this cat so much as looks at one of my chickens, I'm going to make a coat of her."

"Yes, Master Taishi."

The striking woman with the ghost-like black hair swept in through the front gates next, with Kasa and the pretty girl with the gem on her forehead at her sides. Jian breathed a sigh of relief; he had begun to think he had imagined her. The woman approached Taishi with her arms wide open. "Dear sister. I'm so glad to see you well. It's been years."

"For good reason, Bhasani." There was an edge in Taishi's voice. She pointed back at Jian. "Don't try that again."

"Oh, relax. I just wanted to assess his mental mettle. He failed, by the way, completely. Like, negative points." Bhasani waggled a finger at him. "Melted like an ice cube during the third summer in Xing. Do you have my tea, little one?"

"I do!" Jian perked up. "Here you go, Mistress."

Taishi held up a hand. "Don't take another step."

Her words pierced through the fog in Jian's head. He furrowed his brow at the teacup in his hands. He shrugged and took a sip. He wrinkled his nose. "This tastes awful."

"Don't be mad at her," said Kasa. "She came to help with your problem."

Jian leaned into Zofi. "What problem?"

She subtly nudged him away. "Hush."

"I'm going to murder those two idiots," Taishi raged. "I gave them a list of acceptable names."

"I made the call," said Kasa. "Bhasani owed me a favor, and she'll cover several needs. You know what's at stake, and so does Bhasani, so swallow your pride and play nice."

Jian had never heard anyone talk to Taishi that way.

Taishi rolled her eyes at the other woman. "What did he do for you?"

Bhasani shrugged. "He fixed my plumbing last year." She looked over at Jian. "It's a good thing he asked for help. You didn't steel and fortify the boy's trap. The spirit shamans are going to churn his mind to butter."

"I have a lot on my plate." Taishi closed her eyes. Her chest visibly expanded and contracted. She opened them again and then pointed at the house. "I'll have Zofi serve tea for three."

"Fausan and Sohn should be here soon as well."

"Saves me the hassle of hunting those two stink eggs down."

The courtyard quickly emptied. Zofi hurried off to the kitchen to pre-pare tea and refreshments, leaving Jian standing with the dark-skinned girl.

He offered a chest-level wave. "Hi. I'm Jian. Wen Jian."

She made a show of sizing him up, her eyes twinkling with mischief. "I read up on you. The rest I learned from reading you. And seeing your wanted poster. You look a lot less menacing in person, Champion of the Five Under Heaven." She pursed her lips. "That's a mouthful. I'm going to call you 'Five Champ' from now on."

He had no idea what that meant, but he rolled with it. "Are you a war arts disciple?"

The girl raised her chin. "Ras Sonaya, daughter and heir of Master Narwani Bhasani, direct family single lineage of the drowned fist."

"Bhasani is your mother?" he asked. "You two couldn't look more dif-ferent."

"The disciple is always called the daughter."

"What if the disciple is a boy?"

That earned him a flat, barely tolerating look. "Mother requires quar-ters in the main house."

"We don't really have a guest room," he said. "The main house only has two bedrooms. Taishi has the main wing, and Zofi and I share the other. There's a store room we can probably use. It's damp in there, but it is spacious. I think you're better off taking the loft in the barn . . ."

Sonaya's expression hadn't changed.

Jian sighed. "I'll pack my belongings."

"Wise choice. Mother will not allow visitors into her quarters once she claims them."

Her quarters. "Do you need a sleep sack for the barn as well?"

"I'll be staying with my mother."

"Of course you will." The girl somehow got him to give up his own bed without even asking. Not only that, but he had given up Zofi's bed too. She was going to kill him.

He picked up her woven travel trunk and led Sonaya into the house. "What brings you to our end of the Cloud Pillars?"

"Didn't your master just have an entire conversation about it with mine?"

"She didn't even know you were coming." Jian looked at the luxurious and intricately decorated travel cloak she wore. "You didn't know either, did you?"

Sonaya's smug confidence cracked just a smidgen. "Mother told me about it while I was pouring her morning bath."

"Do you take more than one bath a day?"

She ignored him. "She told me we were going on holiday. It was a surprise." Sonaya's voice took on an edge. "I thought we were going to Vauzan, or the ice slopes near Kyung. Instead I'm here, wherever here is." She looked around. "At least the architecture is creative, albeit a little dire."

"It used to be a cannibal temple," he replied with exaggerated casualness. He would have enjoyed seeing her lose her cool facade, except she didn't.

After they dragged Bhasani's trunk off, and Jian had gathered his and Zofi's own meager belongings, Sonaya offered to help carry it all to the barn. It was the least she could do, she had declared.

"I've never heard of the drowned fist," he said, struggling with all of the bedding. When she had offered to help, she had really meant only the pillows. "I would enjoy seeing a demonstration sometime. Maybe we can train or spar together. Not like it's a challenge or anything," he said hastily. "Master Taishi always says it's important I experience many different flavors of war arts."

"You've already seen it," she replied. "When my master ordered the tea."

Jian stopped in his tracks. "How is that a war art?"

"Jing manifests differently in every skill." Sonaya poked him in the chest. "You can attack the body." She then leaned in and spoke softly close to his ear. "Or you can hit something softer."

"I don't understand," he said.

"There's no puddle." Her words were barely a whisper.

There actually was. Jian had seen it while they were walking across the field, and somehow stepped in it anyway. He cursed as his bound shoes sank into the mud. "What was that?"

"Exactly." The mischief returned to her eyes. "I will enjoy taking you up on your challenge, Five Champ."

CHAPTER THIRTEEN

OLD FRIENDS, NEW ENEMIES

Sohn and Fausan arrived later that evening with Hachi, Fausan's heir, trailing in their wake with a large bag slung over each shoulder. They were accompanied by a new face, a young girl, who trailed behind the rest of the group. Apparently the cannibal temple was about to see its third incarnation as a retired war artist encampment.

"About time, you rotted melons." Taishi picked up two short cups of zuijo with her long chopsticks and flung them across the room. The God of Gamblers caught his deftly and set it spinning on the tip of his finger. He bounced it along from finger to finger before dropping it into his palm to take a sip. Show-off. Sohn, on the other hand, took his right to the chest, good alcohol drenching his stained shirt.

"Forgive the tardiness," Fausan responded without missing a beat. He offered Bhasani a quick wave across the table. "Hey."

"How's your shoulder?" she asked.

"Only aches when it rains," he quipped, rolling it. "How's Floof?"

"Dead ten years now, idiot. Dogs don't live that long." The two shared a long and complicated on-and-off history, mostly off.

Taishi had to get something off her chest before they began. "I gave you a specific list of names: Dong, Meisan, Hamraki, Loong, Xuan—the ugly one—Pabin, the Mapo sisters, or anyone in the Sarang clan."

Sohn ticked off his responses on his fingers. "Dead, dead, opiumed out of his gourd, and adamantly refused because he secretly hates you with the passion of a thousand spears. The others were either happily retired or wanted nothing to do with you or Jian, mostly you."

"The two of you are poison right now," said Fausan. "I think it's all worked out for the best. Bhasani easily tops that sad list of yours."

That much was true, but there were principles to consider. "Bhasani isn't getting within a hundred paces of my disciple."

Bhasani shrugged at Kasa. "See, I told you."

"Be reasonable, Taishi," he replied, which earned him an even sterner glare.

"She can stay for a few days, but I want her gone back to whatever backstabbing hole she crawled out of by cycle's end."

Taishi signaled to her two wards. Jian pulled up two sets of chairs and made room at the table for the new arrivals while Zofi brought in several small dishes. Then they retreated outside along with the other newly arrived disciples, closing the doors. Not that it mattered. The framed wooden sliding doors were literally paper.

"Before we begin." Kasa filled his zuijo cup to the brim and held it up. "It is a rare privilege to share wine with so many esteemed masters. May you still experience many more dreams than memories."

"Little chance with this wrinkled, gray-haired lot," chuckled Sohn.

Fausan raised his cup with both hands. "May your lineages be forever fertile across all of time."

As the host, Taishi downed hers first. "Dry cups to all."

"Dry cups," the rest echoed.

Kasa wasn't wrong. The caliber of war arts skill in this room exceeded most courts. The five of them together could probably take out an entire city garrison. They were also, however, well past their prime. Sohn was practically blind after sundown. Fausan hadn't had stamina even during his prime. The only thing he loved more than rolling the dice was fried pork belly. And Kasa, well, Kasa was just old. As for Bhasani, she didn't count.

"Why were the two of you late?" asked Taishi.

"Got held up at Mapetown," said Sohn. "Another caravan got hit, Head Boss Vu's route this time, mail wagon included."

"Another one?" Kasa shook his head. "Terrible business."

The rest of the table muttered their agreement. Amateur banditry made for bad banditry, and bad banditry attracted the worst sort of attention, which was bad for the lunar court. Good banditry followed rules and stayed below the magistrates' attention, and was a win for all parties involved. All the right people got paid, everyone profited, no one went to jail, and no one died.

Kasa drained his cup and wiped his chin with his forearm. He waved for quiet. "They keep this up and we'll have the Cloud Pillars swarmed by Lawkan White Tigers or Shulan Meat Cleavers soon enough."

Sohn shook his head. "A ducal garrison is like weevils on rice. Once they infest a settlement, they're nearly impossible to clean out."

"Don't be so dramatic," Bhasani scoffed. "It's a bunch of dumb, desperate, runaway peasants who don't know the rules. They're probably sitting in the forest right now drinking piss soup and eating tree bark. Just have a local lunar court enforcer bust some sense into the rabble. They'll learn the rules quickly enough. If they don't, round them up and sell their services to the army. Every vanguard these days could use replenishment. Anyone dumb enough to rob ducal-backed wagons is dumb enough to soak up some arrows."

Taishi raised her voice. "We have greater things to deal with right now. I asked you here to help complete the Prophesied Hero of the Tiandi's education. If my job were only to train him to become the greatest war artist in the world, then it wouldn't matter. He needs to be more than that, though. He also needs to be a leader, a diplomat, a general, and a politician. Jian needs to know how to inspire and command."

"He needs perspectives, and opposing viewpoints," added Bhasani.

Taishi grudgingly nodded. "Some of which I cannot teach."

"What he really needs is to get his face bloodied," said Sohn. "Knock some of those baby teeth out. Season him up a bit."

"Wen Jian is a good lad," said Kasa. "It is our responsibility as a brotherhood of masters to shepherd his path."

"Sisterhood," Bhasani grumbled.

"Peoplehood," Taishi snapped at the same time. "I originally intended to have Jian travel to each of your homes for his education, but now with these wanted posters showing up everywhere and the mail wagon robberies, it may be best to do everything here."

"Prudent." The eternal bright light master picked up the zuijo pitcher and helped himself to another pour. "I was at the Zahn's gambling hall in Bahngtown last night when a ducal emissary rolled in. White flags marked with gray fangs."

Taishi scowled. "A Lawkan white owl, magistrate administrator. He's going to take over the settlement."

"Wait until Saan learns that Dongshi moved on his western flank," chortled Bhasani. "The handsome lad's going to throw a fit."

Fausan shook his head. "Saan won't even notice. He's too busy being paddled by Sunri. What is it, four battles, four routs now?"

Sohn grunted. "Probably more. We'd know more if the mail wagons weren't getting attacked and sacked."

Bhasani gestured to Fausan to refresh her drink. He obliged. "I heard the Third Golden Retinue managed a draw and was able to retreat back over Big Head Mountain. That's sort of a win."

Taishi shook her head. "Poor Saan must be furious. That boy hated losing, especially to his stepmother." The Duke of Shulan had trained under her briefly. He had modest potential as a war artist and was very pretty to look at, but he was as stupid as the King was bright.

"It's surprising how badly he's getting thrashed, isn't it?" Bhasani was saying.

"I'm not surprised in the slightest." Kasa chuckled. He leaned in. "I was there when Sunri arrived at the emperor's Jade Court. Right away, you could tell the concubine was ambitious, always conspiring. A couple of the court bookies had her prospects as high as fourth or even third wife. Little did anyone know. She was first concubine in a year. Fourth wife in three. Now she's a warlord." Kasa shrugged. "One of five who will sit on the throne."

The masters spent the rest of the evening working out arrangements and schedules. Taishi made it clear she was the headmaster. She would take charge. Jian was *her* student and *her* responsibility. Taishi had no intention of muddling his instincts and muscle memory. It would be her voice that sang loudest in his head in the midst of battle. Everyone was bleary-eyed by the end, in Sohn's case because of the five gourds of wine and zuijo.

Kasa, who usually went to bed right after dinner, was the first to retreat. He rose unsteadily and yawned. "I'm retiring for the night. Is the hammock in the grove still there?"

Taishi nodded. "We have beds in the main house, Kasa. I'll kick my wards out."

Bhasani shook her head. "I already moved in there. Sorry."

"What happened to elders first?" said Taishi.

"We're all elders now," the drowned fist master replied. "What's a difference of a few years at our age? If big brother Kasa wishes it, I will happily concede the bed to him."

"You stay," he replied. "I enjoy sleeping under the stars."

"Where do I sleep, Taishi?" Fausan stood up next and stretched his arms and generous midsection, his left arm struggling to rise past his shoulder. The God of Phoenix had tortured him for the location of the Goddess of Willow, and his shoulder had never recovered. There had been a trend a few decades back when every war artist with any sort of reputation would attempt to deify themselves. Taishi was more than happy to have ignored that tacky and obnoxious phase of the lunar court. Only Fausan's well-earned title had lasted over the years.

"I'm not an inn," Taishi retorted. "Find your own bed."

Jian and the rest of the students sat outside around the fire pit. It wasn't often he gathered with all of his counterparts like this. He looked across the fire at Sonaya. Their acquaintance was probably short-lived. Their masters did not appear to get along very well. Hachi and Kasa were at the pens playing with Forty-Two. The whipfinger disciple had been so taken with the guardian lion that he may have caught the shishi bug and would try to acquire one for himself. All three boys were of the age when most in this region got their own lion. They were not only loyal pets and fierce protectors, but their ability to scale the pillars meant freedom and movement throughout the Cloud Pillars.

The door to the kitchen opened, and Sohn and his new disciple walked out. The eternal bright light master said a few words to her and sent her to sit near the burning fire. He beckoned to Jian.

"Yes, Master Soa," he said politely. Chances were the master was going to tell him to fetch more gourds of wine.

"Listen, Jian." Sohn pointed at the departing girl. "That's Wyn, my new disciple. She's only been with me a short while. Really short, like fresh raw catch from the coast short."

"I'll make sure that she feels welcome," said Jian, bowing his head slightly.

"Oh, no, I don't care about that. She could feel as welcome or ostracized as you like." Sohn put his arms around Jian's shoulders. "My new student. Let's just say we need to go through a bit of a trial period before we know she's, um, you know, if she's trustworthy. So it might be a good idea to keep your real identity on the low until we know Wyn over there is on the up?"

Jian stiffened. "You don't trust your own disciple?"

"I'm just being careful, son," said Sohn hastily. "You're a very important secret."

"Why did you even bring her here then?"

The eternal bright light master looked slightly abashed. "I didn't want to leave her alone in my place. I didn't rule out the possibility that she might clean me out by the time I returned."

Jian lost his composure. "And you brought her here? Taishi is going to murder you!"

"She is the one who told me to speak with you after I informed her about my concerns regarding Wyn." He paused. "There were some threats of murdering earlier when we spoke, but we're both in full, complete agreement."

"Wait," said Jian. "Wouldn't she recognize Taishi too?"

Sohn shrugged. "Do you know how many Taishis there are in the world? There was a time during your master's career when women would make pilgrimage to the Shulan court just to ask Taishi to bless their newborn daughter, Taishi."

Jian did not realize that was a thing that happened. "Wait, so there are possibly hundreds of Wen Jians out there in the world too."

"Why would anyone name their child after the Prophesied Hero? That would be stupid."

Jian wasn't sure why it would be stupid for any parent to name their child after him. "I think my name is nice."

The eternal bright light master shook his head and then raised his voice. "Anyway, Hiro, treat my new disciple well. Really make her feel like part of the family."

"Yes, master," said Jian.

"Don't trust her one bit," said Sohn as he passed Jian and headed back into the kitchen.

Jian watched him go and then went to introduce himself to the new eternal bright light heir. Wyn was a small, sharp-faced girl who looked younger than Jian, but had far older eyes and a wary disposition. She had kept mostly to herself this evening, choosing to spend most of the evening by herself in the foyer rather than with the rest of the students in the kitchen. Even now she studied him with distrusting eyes as he approached her next to the fire. Jian was intent on making her feel welcome, though. It was a lesson he had learned back at Longxian, when Xinde, someone he considered a big brother, had gone out of his way to be his friend. Jian hoped to continue that tradition.

He placed his fist to his palm. "I'm Hiro. Master Soa said you're from the Tyk Coast. Welcome to Cloud Pillars. How long have you been here?"

"Since last week."

Jian wasn't great at math. "That means you've only been studying under Master Soa for . . ."

"Nine days," she said.

Jian had had relationships with cold sores for longer than that. "Where did you train previously?"

"I've never trained before." The new eternal bright light heir spoke with pride. "I was the best brawler in my village. When Master Soa came to my village, I thought it was my chance to escape the farm and see the world. I sought him out and challenged him to a duel."

"How did that go?" he asked.

"He threw me face-first into the mud."

"And you got back up and challenged him again?" Jian nodded. "Well done. Resiliency is the backbone of all war artists and often can't be taught. It's important to pick yourself up if you get knocked down."

"Twenty-six."

"What?"

"Master Soa knocked me down twenty-six times," said Wyn matter-of-factly. "Then he tired and told me to fetch him a cup of water from the stream, which I did. I didn't even know who he was or what style he rep-resented. I just wanted out of my village. Now I'm the true heir to the Eternal Bright Light Fist, and the rightful owner of its vast network of schools."

That last bit did not sound innocent at all.

Jian looked up and waved at Hachi and Kaiyu coming from the pens. Kaiyu went to go talk to Zofi, who was working on something at the table, while Hachi came to the fire and sat next to Jian. The whipfinger heir had been the first friend Jian made at the Cloud Pillars. Jian had been so lonely after Xinde and Meehae left that Taishi made a point to invite Fausan and Hachi over. For a children's playdate, she had said. The whipfinger heir was a few years older than Jian. Tall, lanky, and bookish, he looked nothing like a war artist, but the two matched up well when sparring.

"Check this out. I have a business idea, Ji—" began Hachi.

"The stars are waning tonight," Jian said quickly.

All the masters and students—the ones who could be trusted—were well aware of the protocols that Taishi had put in place around Jian with regard to his safety. One of the main rules was to always keep his cover, which meant everyone around him had to know the codes.

"—iro," Hachi finished smoothly.

"What's the idea?"

"Once you master riding currents, let's start a courier company to deliver throughout the Cloud Pillars, especially with the recent rash of caravan thefts. Fast guaranteed delivery under the protection of a skilled war artist, all for a slight premium." Hachi was always trying to get rich quickly.

"That sounds like a lot of work. For me."

"That's why I'm happy to be equal partners." Hachi grinned. "What do you think?"

"I think it's a terrible idea."

Zofi appeared out of the main house, carrying a bucket in one hand and a stack of wooden cups in the crook of her other elbow. She placed the bucket on the nearby table and handed a cup each to Sonaya and Wyn. She looked over at Jian and lobbed one to him, flinging it at least to the second story and into the weeds.

Jian craned his head around to see where it had landed. "What kind of throw was that?"

"Just go pick it up."

Jian knew better than to argue. By the time he retrieved the cup from the dirt and wiped it clean, she had served the entire group. She offered him a ladle of mahogany brown liquid with the tiny bits of fiber and gooey suds floating on top. "The masters took all the good stuff, but I managed to scrounge together some old rice wine we're supposed to use for cooking."

"Not that it matters one bit. They all taste the same anyway," he said, raising it to his lips. "All gross."

Jian swigged his cup in one gulp and immediately regretted it. He was wrong; bad liquor *did* make a difference. It was much worse than he had imagined. His eyes burned and his stomach clenched, and it was a struggle to keep whatever it was from coming back up. Fortunately, he wasn't the only one struggling with his drink. Sonaya had a hand over her mouth, looking green and unsteady. Hachi's lips were pursed as he hissed out a long breath. Kaiyu was leaning over the side letting it back out.

The only one who didn't react poorly was Wyn, who smacked her lips. "It could use a few weeks more to ferment."

The group settled in for the evening. The wind was calm and the sky bare of any clouds. The Queen had returned to the sky, and she and the

Prince were now bathing the landscape with a shimmering aqua-colored haze, making it feel like they were at the bottom of a crystal-clear lake. Kaiyu was getting up every so often to check on Forty-Two, announcing every time that he intended to sleep with his pet. That was fine with everyone else, since that left only the barn to sleep in, and it wasn't a big barn.

The door to the kitchen creaked open, and Masters Taishi, Sohn, and Bhasani spilled out, all looking like they had taken advantage of the temple's liquor stores. Sohn could barely stand. The students rose to their feet as Taishi addressed them. "Everyone is staying for a small while. The rules are simple. Clean up after yourselves, don't be a nuisance, and do your chores."

Kaiyu raised his hand. "What about our training?"

"You will all train together," said Taishi. "A little cross-pollination will do you all some good."

"What will we be doing here?" asked Sonaya.

"Whatever we tell you to," she snapped. "From now on, every master here is your master, understand?"

"Yes, master," they intoned.

"Now that's settled," Sohn burped, leaning on Wyn for support, "I'm off to bed. Which way is the barn again, boy?"

"But we're sleeping . . ." Jian stammered. He dropped his head and held out an arm. "This way, Master Soa."

CHAPTER FOURTEEN

THE RETURN

Salminde the Viperstrike was a child of the Grass Sea. She had been born in the midst of a sweltering hurricane during a world-splitting third cycle summer. The land had surged into a massive tidal wave, tearing and uprooting the very ground in its wake. She killed her first hyena at the age of five when a pack tried to steal a kid from the goats she was shepherding. Sali had nearly given that life back to the Grass Sea two years later when a pride of lionesses attacked that same herd. As soon as she was of age, Sali became a raider to earn glory, honor, and rich bounties for her clan. She became a viperstrike at eighteen, and a Will of the Khan three years later. Then, from her exalted perch, she fell from grace, returning home to find the Eternal Khan slain, her city sunk beneath the Grass Sea, and her clan indentured to the Zhuun.

Sali became a lowly soul seeker and left the Grass Sea to search for her sister, spent a cycle in the hated land-chained city Jiayi, and somehow returned a leader, a rebel, and a traitor. Now, she had the burden of her entire clan on her shoulders. It was a responsibility she accepted willingly, but it was still heavy. She couldn't help but smile at life's strange turns. The circle of reincarnation was taking some unusually strange directions during this cycle's spin.

She sat on her mare at the rim of the caldera surrounding the narrow but impossibly towering Mount Shetty, which cut quite an imposing figure with its fang-like peaks. A crown of thick clouds perpetually encircled the jagged mountaintops. Many legends surrounded Shetty Mountain. It had earned a reputation for sinking pods, drowning armies, and swallowing entire cultures. The soggy, soft ground beneath their feet was supposedly rife with sunken treasure and buried cities. Entire armies, settlements, and even civilizations had disappeared into the dense jungle within the bowl of the caldera. There were dozens of tales and poems set inside Shetty Caldera. Most were sad. All ended tragically.

The Happan and Tsunarcos people to the north and east considered the caldera cursed. The Katuia were generally not as superstitious, but most avoided this region altogether. Sali and the Nezrans, however, had little choice in the matter.

"You go to where the treasure is buried," Mali had insisted to anyone who would listen last year when they were considering their next steps. Six months later, her baby sister's intuition had so far been correct. Following that lead to find buried city pods had been the right move, if an uncomfortable one, and now Mount Shetty was the longest Nezra had stayed in one place since their exodus from Jiayi.

Now, several weeks after visiting Sakurai, it was good to return to Shetty Caldera and to her people. It felt like home, almost. Sali had spent the better part of the past year tracking down the former Chaqra Keeper of Legend. She had gone to that brief visit hoping for a cure, or at least answers. Now she had to settle once again for another lead, and it wasn't one she was sure she wanted to pursue. Sali was not willing to risk Nezra's safety for her quixotic quest for a cure. She was needed here.

It was still a half day's ride from the rim of the caldera to the base of Mount Shetty, and then another half hour deeper into its gut. The wind blew against them from the north. A column of smoke to the east drifted to the sky, merging with Mount Shetty's larger funnel. It could be anything, but best to just avoid if possible.

"Mentor," said Hampa. "It's nearly nightfall, and a storm is moving in. Should we encamp?"

The cool weather was aggravating Sali's illness, exacerbating her chills and making the hot flashes feel even hotter. The weeks of constant travel during the wet seasons did not help either. Sali looked into the distance. The sun was setting, and the blue light of the first moon was just beginning to crawl across the far horizon. The clouds were rolling closer and should reach them within the hour.

"We press on. It will be good to practice your nighteye." She blinked once, and her eyes flared a faint green. Hampa followed suit, although it took seven or eight attempts before his eyes illuminated. Her neophyte needed more practice.

The two continued down the rim of the caldera following the roughly hewn gyre that carved through the jungle. The land beneath their feet was not as lively here in the cold north. Here, it seesawed, was more lilting, slow, and subtle. If she had lain at one end of the tent at the beginning of the night, she could very well end up on the opposite side by morning, even though she swore she hadn't budged.

The steep, straight path of the gyre quickly took them to the jungle floor as it carved deeper into the layers of hardened vegetation in the ground. The gyre was now wide enough it could fit several city pods side by side. As soon as they reached the basin, Sali broke away from the main road and led Hampa to the narrow path next to the outer lip of the gyre. She preferred keeping their traveling along these back ways as much as possible. As easy as the gyres were for travel, they also were too commonly traveled, which often led to undesirable run-ins. Along with the heavier traffic came other dangers: robberies and skirmishes abounded. Warring factions often chose to meet on the gyre to settle armed conflict. It wasn't unusual for travelers to ride their horses past duels or pitched battles.

They eventually turned away off the gyre and continued to hack and forge their way toward Mount Shetty. The two viperstrikes briefly took shelter under the umbrella of a nest of fronds when a brief rainstorm passed by, as they were wont to do, and then they were pushing on again, pressing along the narrow and windy path, picking their way through thick clusters of frigid bamboo shoots.

Sali and Hampa were nearing the base of the mountain when a loud, sputtering sound erupted somewhere in the distance. She stopped moving, raised an open palm to her ear and listened. Hampa, probably daydreaming or dozing off again, was a beat late to react and nearly rode his dun into her. Sali had long resigned herself to knowing that her neophyte was not an exceptional or disciplined talent, nor even a particularly good one.

He had just completed his third-year training under Sali, which was two years longer than she had expected him to last. Soon, it would be time to decide if his name was worthy to inscribe on the viperstrike sect totem. That is, if Sali ever got around to carving a new one. Their previous totem, spanning fifteen generations, had burned down with the rest of their city. It was also assuming Hampa actually finished his training, which wasn't a certainty.

The young man had many positives: he was a proficient hunter, a loyal and considerate clan mate, and was generally well regarded and well liked. Unfortunately, none of those positive attributes were necessary to forge a good war artist. Hampa wasn't naturally physically gifted, and no amount of training or tutelage would ever change that fact. His skill was modest, and his potential limited, and he was not the brightest star in the night sky. In the past, she would never have considered taking someone with his limits or washed him out after a few months. His saving attributes were that he deeply revered the viperstrike sect, was loyal to a fault, and trained harder than anyone else. Everyone also adored him, Sali included.

Sali kept her hand raised, then she pulled her elbow down sharply. Her mare immediately lay down. Sali rolled off and hunched next to her leopard appaloosa with a hand on the handle of her tongue, her personal weapon of choice currently in its roped coil form. Hampa followed close behind, making a little too much noise in the process.

This is not the time to correct him. Sali heard those words in her mother's voice. She brushed off the criticism and focused on the sputtering noises coming from the direction of the main travel gyre. She crept through the thick brush, wading chest-deep among purple fronds and dragon tulips. She reached a small ledge just as a Liqusa patrol passed by, its steam engine warsled sputtering and popping like a dying man gasping for his last breath.

The spirit shamans back at Chaqra weren't satisfied with just punishing Nezra with exile, so they also sent Clan Liqusa with their Necro Citadel to wipe their clan out once and for all. Liqusa, the Bone Clan, known for their obsession with death, had chased them throughout the Grass Sea. The Nezrans finally eluded the enemy several months back and had since relocated to this caldera as they continued searching feverishly for city pods to rebuild Nezra.

Fortunately, the jungle of the Shetty Caldera proved a good hiding place. The vegetation in this region was dense and wild and ran from the ground to the jungle canopy. The Nezrans had managed to cut a system of passages and tunnels near the treetops as a method of travel, burrowing through branches and tangled vegetation.

Their clan could almost hide in the caldera forever, but it was only a matter of time before their luck ran out. One of the Liqusa patrols was bound to eventually stumble upon and capture a Nezra hunter, forager, trader, or surveyor. The people in their clan were loyal, but most were not trained war artists nor were their minds fortified, and the Liqusans were skilled torturers. Sali would never fault anyone from her clan for betraying them under duress.

Instead of trying to war against an enemy capital city far above her clan's abilities, Sali had recruited and installed a network of scouts surrounding Mount Shetty to give their people an early warning. A full tenth of their population, including many of the older children, served as watchers known as howler monkeys. There was even talk among many of their watchleads to form their own howler sect. Sali was lukewarm on that idea.

Speaking of being watched, Sali sensed new attention focused on them the moment the Liqusa patrol disappeared around the bend. She whirled around and loosed her tongue speeding toward an invisible lurker hidden near the top of the jungle canopy. This was Sali's signature weapon, and her specialty with it was unmatched. The tongue was a whip with a spearhead—known as its bite—attached to its end. Its flexible portion was composed of thousands of tiny diamond-shaped metallic links that could stiffen the shaft to form a spear.

She just caught the look of a startled child's face, and immediately yanked the rope, snapping back the attack. She caught the bite in her hand and holstered the tongue in one smooth motion. She waved the girl down. "You observe too intensely, Wani."

"That's because I admire you so much."

Good answer. Wani was an older howler, and one of the group leaders. Sali had had her eyes on the girl for a while now. The clan would need bright young people to build a new future if they were to survive.

Hampa approached from behind. He signaled at the brush, and two more howlers popped out. Hampa touched fists with each as they approached. He was good with children. "Nanka, Wani, Boop. How long have you had eyes on us?"

"We were following that pat-pat when Boop blinked you." Wani grinned. The howlers already had their own language. "You were pretty loud back there, chief."

Hampa, a skilled tracker, had trained most of the children, and was considered their unofficial sectchief. If Sali was honest, he had far greater potential as a hunter than a viperstrike and could serve the clan much better in that capacity. Hampa knew that too, but the heart was not a practical organ.

"Who has eyes on the pat-pat now?" He feigned offense and gave Wani a playful shove that almost knocked her into the nearby water hole. He sometimes misjudged his own strength.

Sali caught the girl's arm before she fell in. "Watch your step, lass."

Wani blushed. She was always flustered around Sali. It was annoying. The girl pointed into the thicket. "Rulari is still on them. Her call is the bad hippopotamus."

"Is there such a thing as a good hippopotamus?" asked Sali.

"Her hippopotamus impression stinks."

Hampa grinned. "We'll have to work on that. That lass always had a clumsy tongue."

The small group continued their journey home with Nanka running ahead to inform the clan of their return as well as with specific instructions to have a hot bath drawn and ready. After weeks of constant travel, Sali longed to soak in a hot bath and melt in a soft bed. Near-scalding water was one of the few remedies that allowed the constant painful churn of the Pull of the Khan, like getting raked over hot coals, to be bearable.

They reached the base of Shetty just ahead of nightfall, which was fortunate. The trek to the lava tunnel was a quarter of the way up the mountain, on a winding slope across fairly jagged terrain. The way up was filled with thousands of stalagmites protruding from the ground like the maw of a giant crocodile. She could feel every step on the blackened, polished-onyx glass ground through the soles of her boots.

They reached the mouth of the lava tunnel, which was a circular hole in the ground just tall enough for her not to have to duck her head as she rode through. Hampa and the children took the short route and skied on the scree down the steep slope while Sali led the horses down the roundabout path off to the side, which the children called the retirement trail. The longer path was shallow and winding, but eventually led her to the others at the bottom of the slope.

They regrouped and continued farther down the lava tunnel. The temperature changes down here were sometimes instant and strange. One part of a tunnel could have icecaps growing, while just a few meters away, puddles might be simmering from an unknown heat source. The four followed the tube as it descended, twisting in different directions several times before emptying into a large chamber. This room was a cold one with sheets of ice blanketing obsidian rock underneath. The ice caps were weeping, dribbling steadily into puddles, plinking like bells.

"We've rerouted part of it for a water trap," said Wani.

Sali nodded. "Did Daewon get that filtration boiler working?"

Boop, the youngest at barely ten, bobbed his head. "It breaks a lot, and the water tastes like dirt, but it drinks clean."

They continued down the left path of the next fork. The tunnel they followed split two more times before merging again. It had taken their people weeks to map out these tunnels. Obsidian rock gave way to soft earth, which then gave way to ice, and then finally back to soft earth.

Several spears were waiting for them when they arrived at the ramp up toward their encampment, and they raised their spears as they passed. The three freshies were more boys than men and were a long way from being ready to take the shield of a towerspear, but even the mightiest tree once began as a seed. Only a handful of warriors had survived Nezra's fall, mostly because, like Sali, they weren't there. Many of the young were rising to fill those ranks, but it would take time.

Their camp at the top of the ramp opened to a large but awkwardly maze-like network of tunnels and small caverns, which the clan had converted into residences due to the proximity to a hot spring. Several familiar faces greeted Sali as she entered the main communal space serving as the clan's central hearth.

A gray-haired older man with a wiry frame was in the middle of a group directing people on how to fill burlap sacks with flour and then how to stack them. He noticed Sali and immediately broke away from the group and headed toward her.

Shobansa was one of the clan's six council members and served as the clan's supply chief. Alongside Mali, he was the most important person in the clan, who kept everything running. The former wealthiest man in the clan had built a fortune as a traveling merchant before losing it all with the fall of Nezra. Now, he wielded his considerable business savvy and experience to keep the clan from starving during the summers and freezing to death during the winters. He wielded an ironclad accounting of every sack of grain, jar of oil, bolt of cloth, cord of wood that passed through the clan. The man was a tyrant with supplies, especially their cooking spices. Sali missed flavored foods.

"Salminde, you're back. Just in time. I have something important to discuss with you." Shobansa was never one for idle chatter, or greetings for that matter.

"I just arrived," she replied. "It's been hard travels. I'd like to see Mali first."

"It's urgent and has to do with her."

Sali pursed her lips. Mali and Shobansa were the two most important people in the council. The two had been butting heads for a while now, forcing Sali to often play peacemaker between them. It was not a job she was well suited for.

Shobansa recoiled when he neared and covered his nose. "By the Khan's hairy pits, you smell awful, Salminde. Worse than usual."

Sali raised a shoulder and sniffed. It wasn't good.

"It's really bad," little Nanka giggled. "We were just being nice."

"We can pick this up later after you've refreshed," said the supply chief.

"What happened to the urgent matters?"

"It and your sister can survive you taking a bath first. The rest of us won't if you don't take one. Now, get out of here."

CHAPTER FIFTEEN

THE CHALLENGE

Jian woke up the next morning to a string of delicate black pearls brushing against the bridge of his nose. He blinked, his eyes first focusing on a shapely neck, and then continued up it until he saw the attached face. "Can I help you?"

Sonaya, her face hovering just above his, cooed. "Five Champ, I'm here to accept your offer."

What offer? Had he made an offer? What offer had he made? Their little group of students had stayed long after their masters had turned in for the night, and that vile concoction Zofi had served had a delayed and heady reaction, so much so that Jian did not remember anything after cheering on Hachi when he picked up the bucket and poured the dregs of that drink down his throat.

"I hope he's not dead," he muttered. His head felt like someone had staked his skull. His stomach was nauseated and his throat was begging for water. The very thought of drinking anything made his stomach churn. At least they had made it to the barn all right.

Jian sat up and felt icy water beneath him. This wasn't the barn. He looked stupidly at the hay scattered all over the ground. Kaiyu was snuggled up with Forty-Two, the two snoring in unison. Wyn and Zofi were sleeping on top of each other, competing for a small horse blanket. Hachi was lying facedown next to Jian. For a second, Jian thought his morbid prediction had come true.

He nudged the whipfinger heir. "Are you dead?"

Hachi rewarded him with a groan and a twitch of his shoulder. Jian breathed a sigh of relief and sat up. "Why are we in the pens?"

"You don't remember?" Why did Sonaya look perfectly fine and chipper this morning? It was aggravating. "You and the rest of the wildlings thought it would be great fun to sleep with the guardian lion."

"How do you look so good?" he asked.

"Why thank you, I always look good." She then admitted, "I actually went to bed before you lot turned into a pack of raving roosters."

Jian rubbed his temples. He remembered that. "What did I promise you again?"

"A challenge." Sonaya grabbed Jian by the hand and yanked him to his feet. She slipped on the wet ground, and they both almost ended up in the mud.

Jian's head was pounding so hard he didn't think Sonaya punching him would make any difference. He didn't put up much resistance as she dragged him through the small path dividing the sunflowers and the radishes. "I didn't mean first thing in the morning. Can we do this another time?"

"Five Champ, it's already noon."

"What do you mean?" He looked up. It was early afternoon. "Taishi's going to kill me."

His master chortled loudly from off to the side. "No, someone else is going to do it for me."

They had reached the edge of the training field to find all five masters enjoying tea courtside. They had been expecting him. He pulled his hand away from Sonaya. She shrugged apologetically. *Orders were orders.* She still could have warned him.

"What are the rules?" asked Sohn. "First to three falls? On points? How many rounds? Open hand, free draw, mix of both?"

"This isn't a stupid tournament," said Taishi. "How about they fight until one of them loses."

"Savage." The eternal bright light master exchanged an intense stare with the whipfinger master sitting across the small table. The two threw a quick hand of Frog, Slug, and Snake with Fausan coming out on top. The whipfinger master scrutinized the two students, and then the men touched thumbs. Jian wondered who had bet on whom.

"This should be entertaining," said Bhasani. "Care to make it interesting as well?"

"Hardly fair. Sonaya's been with you since she was in diapers. I've had stray pets longer than I've trained this boy." Taishi grunted. "What do you have in mind?"

Bhasani craned her neck around. "I like your goat, or one of those fat pigs. I'll wager three bolts of blackworm silk."

"What am I going to do with frilly clothing anymore?" Taishi hesitated. "How soft?"

"Cool and dark like a gown of thunderstorms."

Jian watched as the two masters hammered out the details of their wager. Now he felt like there were actual stakes in this fight, notably Rockbrain, their goat, of whom Jian was actually quite fond.

Sonaya stretched on the other end of the circular dirt arena. He asked, "Are you sure you want to do this?" Jian honestly wasn't trying to be snide or arrogant. He had observed her practice her forms from a distance yesterday and had come away decidedly unimpressed. Sonaya's war artistry had been average. Her open hand was competent, but nothing special. The forms she practiced with her two bladed fans were pretty but limited. Her reflexes and fluidity were good, but no better than many of the more senior students at Longxian. Yet this was someone who, as Taishi said, had trained with her master since she was in diapers. He hadn't seen any manifestation of jing from her at all.

The skill gap between them, in his opinion, was vast. A student's performance was always reflective of the master. He would hate to embarrass Master Bhasani by making Sonaya look bad, but it would also be insulting to hold back. This made Jian all the more suspicious. The drowned fist couldn't be a weak style or a poor lineage. Taishi didn't tolerate fools or incompetence. She would rather drown herself than compliment mediocrity, much less invite it to her home. So why match the two of them?

Jian and Sonaya got ready to spar. They touched fist to palm, and bowed at the waist.

"Honor is the way," intoned Bhasani formally.

"It is the only way," both Jian and Sonaya replied.

"A pig, the goat, two barrels of zuijo, and your sleep slab, Jian," added Taishi unhelpfully.

Why would Master Bhasani want his bed?

Jian's and Sonaya's faces were close as they held the bow. Both silently mouthed "sorry" at the same time.

"Why are you sorry?" he asked.

"I didn't want you to feel like you were set up. I had no choice." She frowned "Why are *you* sorry?"

Because I'm about to beat your ass. "It's nothing. I don't want you to get hurt and take it personally."

"That's absurd. Of course I'm going to take it personally."

"Can we get on with this?" Bhasani called out.

By now, Hachi and Zofi had come up to enjoy the spectacle. Hachi's face was tinged green, and he looked mostly dead on his feet, but Fausan didn't even blink at his heir's state. Zofi didn't miss a beat collecting Taishi and Bhasani's empty tea kettle and refreshing it, not acting at all as if she had been howling at the moon a few hours back.

Sonaya assumed her guard stance, with one arm hanging forward while the other floated near her face, her weight on her back leg. It was a defensive posture. He would have to go to her. Well, if she really wanted a challenge, so be it.

Jian bounded onto a current and launched himself at her. She brushed aside his initial strikes, guiding each blow to the side. Starlings Flight at Dusk met a modified version of Maiden's Wrath Both Ways. He met her strength with his and felt it crumble. Yet when he tried to grab onto her, Sonaya somehow slipped away. It was like trying to grab a fistful of sand.

Two low sweeps followed by a sneaky looping high kick missed their marks, but only by a hair's breadth. He made her pay when Sonaya was forced to raise her guard. Their clashes went in his favor. As much as she tried to sway his blows, his superior strength, mass, and speed were undeniable. Finally, her arms buckled under the weight of Moon Crashes to Earth. Jian clipped her shoulder and sent her reeling backward.

He was surprised she managed to stay on her feet. Just when she thought she had pulled out of the fall, he unleashed a bolt of air that tipped her over. He sneaked a peek over at Taishi, hoping for a hint of approval. She did not appear impressed in the slightest.

That small distraction proved costly. When he looked back, Sonaya was gone. How? He heard soft footsteps behind him and turned. He found nothing.

Jian turned back just in time to taste a foot on his mouth. Sonaya didn't hit particularly hard, but she didn't need to. His jaw absorbed most of the damage, but he managed to turn with the kick just enough to stay on his feet. He spun low and lashed out, sending them both staggering back. He rubbed his jaw as they paced the outer circle. Sonaya nursed her shoulder.

Jian heard an unusual whisper, as if a voice were inside his head. "The earth rolls beneath your soles."

The ground shifted, tilting back and forth like a teeter-totter. Jian struggled to maintain his equilibrium as if he were still deep in the throes of the previous night's binge. He tried to regain his balance, stumbling side to side. Before he could recover, Sonaya was in his face, slipping under his guard and sweeping his legs out from under him, sending him onto his backside.

"Are you still sorry?" she said breathily.

"What did you just do?"

"What do you mean?" Sonaya said innocently, following up with a head stomp.

He managed to roll away, the heel of her foot clipping his ear. Jian was a little shocked by the viciousness of her attack. The drowned fist was not fooling around. Sonaya was on him as soon as he scampered to his feet, launching short punches that, if he hadn't been disoriented, would have not been a challenge. Unfortunately, he could barely stand with the ground trying to buck him off his feet. The exchange put him on the defensive as he ate half of that flurry. The two reset again.

"You underestimated me," she said.

"I did," he admitted. "Perhaps we should—"

Sonaya became the aggressor, launching quick pinpoint punches in rapid succession. Her speed was impressive and her technique flawless. Her power was still just all right. Where had this been at the beginning of the melee? The two continued fighting close. He could smell lilac and citrus on her skin. Jian, on the other hand, was sweating like a hosed-down pig, and he could still smell the stink from a night sleeping in a pen. He really wished he had had the chance to wash up.

Their limbs became entangled in a series of arm-and-leg traps and locks. Their faces drew closer together. Sonaya's lips were curled, just slightly, the only indication of her intense effort and focus. Jian was still bigger and heavier, and he used that advantage to push her back.

Jian was battering through her defenses when he heard the soft voice again: "Watch for the low leg kick."

He hunched forward and lowered his guard, blocking a kick that never came. Sonaya instead went high and clipped him cleanly across the side of his head. The world snapped sideways, and he pulled away. She gave him no reprieve, however, edging him backward with more pitter-patter attacks.

The voice came again. "Careful with that branch near your foot."

What branch? He sneaked a peek at his feet and met an elbow to the nose. The whispers came in a cascade now, distracting him with bad advice.

"A takedown would be a good idea." Jian attempted one and ended up falling into the mud as Sonaya leaped over him.

"Watch for that head kick." That was followed by a knee to his groin.

"Why is Taishi staring like that?" Jian couldn't help but glance to see if his master was paying attention. She was, and she did not look thrilled. Sonaya made him pay for that distraction with a tightly wound push-kick that sent him flying through the air and skidding to the edge of the circle.

Jian was a little longer to get up this time. As expected, Sonaya maintained the pressure.

He needed to put some space between them and regroup. Someplace where Sonaya couldn't follow to keep him off-balance. Jian disengaged from their latest exchange and shot himself up into the air, stepping onto a twisted mesh of air currents swirling overhead.

"Which way is the sky?"

What? Jian momentarily lost track. Once his focus wavered, so did his balance and control. Arms flailing, he desperately sought to recenter himself as he twisted one way and then the other until he slipped off the current and pitched headfirst toward the earth, landing on his bruised neck with his body curled into a ball and legs hanging over his face. He opened his mouth, but no sound escaped. He tried again. No words came out.

"The boy's landing needs work, sister," remarked Bhasani dryly.

"You don't say." Taishi did not sound amused.

Jian struggled to coax air back into his lungs as a buzzing numbness washed over him. He wasn't in pain, but he couldn't feel his limbs. He tried to speak, but the only sound that leaked from his mouth was a weak, unsteady hiss. His mouth opened and closed like a carp out of water.

Zofi and Sonaya hurried to his side. Both seemed more curious than worried. "Are you all right?" asked the drowned fist heir.

"Is anything broken?" asked Zofi.

Still he couldn't say anything.

"He's fine." Zofi turned away. "Come on. I'm frying some dough with soy milk."

Sonaya helped him up. "It was a good match."

Jian ached all over. "I don't know what happened, but I couldn't get you out of my head."

That earned him a small grin. "I have that effect on men." Her tone became more serious and sincere. "I can help you steel your mind. It's just a muscle, like any other."

Fausan and Sohn were exchanging coins off to the side. It made him feel a little better that the whipfinger master had bet on him. It made Jian feel much worse, however, that he had let Fausan down.

Taishi and Bhasani met them at the center of the arena. The drowned fist master hovered a hand just over his skin from his shoulders to his navel. "Nothing broken."

Taishi placed two fingers on the inside of his wrist. "His jing isn't disrupted, although there's some blockage at his conception meridian."

The two masters made quick eye contact, and then both grabbed a leg and pulled him out flat. Jian didn't have the chance to scream in pain before they each stabbed at several pressure points in his neck and checked with their two fingers. Burning pain momentarily overwhelmed him and then subsided just as quickly, leaving him with a heavy soreness all over.

"Ow," he finally managed to get the sound out.

Bhasani rounded on Sonaya. "By the Tiandi, foolish doll, I told you not to hurt the Prophesied Hero of the Tiandi. That included killing him. Where would we be if he had broken his neck?"

"Apologies, master." The playful tone was gone. "But he was trying *so* hard."

Taishi helped him to his feet. "Off to the sidelines, boy."

Jian hobbled off and sat on the bench. He rubbed his achy neck and watched as Taishi spoke heatedly with Bhasani and Sonaya, glowering his way every few seconds. He couldn't help but feel her disappointment, and that hurt much worse than the fall.

CHAPTER SIXTEEN

UNWANTED ASSISTANCE

Taishi flowed through the Third Old Frame Straight Sword Form Number Nine Sixth Frame at the tip of a tall bamboo tree. She hailed from a long line of fairly unimaginative men when it came to naming just about anything. She guessed she was lucky they didn't name the Swallow Dances "Big Pointy Stick" or something equally uncreative.

A stiff breeze passed through the forest, rustling the leaves and swaying her side to side. Taishi stayed one with the branch, bobbing up and down as she continued her form. A comfortable sweat glistened on her face and neck. The Third Old Frame was a complete set of forms Taishi had mastered by the time she was nine, but one she was still striving to perfect even now. That was always the case in the war arts. Achieving perfection wasn't the goal. It was striving toward it that was the war artist's journey.

Overhead Swirl transitioned to Snake in the Grass before she spun softly on the ball of one foot, clearing the way with a sweep before coming to rest in a bow stance, the blade having made a long journey from high to low and then angling upward, preferably into the soft neck of an enemy. Or their belly below the ribs, or their groin. These were all killing blows when using a blade as fine and with jing as powerful as hers. Her wrist inched downward, guiding her blade to the side, before suddenly snapping to a high block.

Taishi was just following through the last sequence when a metal chopstick streaked toward her from somewhere on the ground. She didn't bother reacting as it flew past her head.

She glanced down at her would-be assailant. "You missed."

Bhasani offered an exaggerated shrug. "I was being careful. It's been years since I've measured your skill."

"That and you're more near-sighted than a tunnel worm." Taishi added, "Right, Double Spectacle Girl?"

Bhasani's body froze, and she shot Taishi a flat stare. Then her smooth skin broke into creases as she pointed back at Taishi and smirked. "That one stung. You dug far back there."

Taishi snorted. "Considering your history, I could have called you far worse."

"It was always business, Taishi. Just know that." Bhasani's arm flew outward, sending up another chopstick. This time its trajectory was true, directly between Taishi's eyes. Taishi grudgingly credited her rival; it wasn't an easy throw this high up using a cooking utensil. She had all the time in the world to react, pushing down on the bamboo tree, lowering herself until the chopstick flew harmlessly over her head.

A whisper tickled her ear.

"Don't move. You have a poisonous spider on your leg, Duckface."

Taishi went still. Speaking of digging far back: the drowned fist master's tremendously weighty compulsion draped a memory over her eyes, using the taunt as a catalyst to drag Taishi far into forgotten bits of her past. It had been more than half a century since the last time someone had dared call her Duckface, back when Taishi and her confidence were still fragile creatures.

Bhasani was playing a deep game. The drowned fist master used to claim that she knew her opponents better than they knew themselves. Everyone had tells, she'd boast, from the stride of their footsteps to the cadence of their breath to the small gesture of their fingers when they spoke. All of these slivers of information were clues a skilled drowned fist practitioner could use against their opponents. These abilities were even more pronounced due to their shared history. Bhasani simply had more useful information to analyze and to break Taishi down using an array of sensory points—sounds, smell, touches—to anchor her mind to a memory.

For a moment, Taishi was transported back to when she was just a scrawny and deeply insecure girl wearing gray student-scholar robes at a children's war arts summer camp in Allanto. War arts students of all ages gathered from all parts of the Zhuun lands. Some who were already part of a family would attend to practice and compete, using the diverse experience to hone their skills. Others without a lineage came with the hope of matching with a master.

Taishi remembered being terrified on her first trip to the Glittering City. She had entered the war arts camp grounds and looked back at her mother standing by the gates. Yinshi had tears in her eyes as she waved at her only surviving child, before Munnam had put his arms around her shoulder and led her away. Little Taishi had tried to run after them, only to bowl over another girl with sheet-white skin and long black hair.

Taishi had offered to help her up. "Sorry."

Bhasani had accepted it. "You better be."

The two had become inseparable for the rest of the summer war arts camp and beyond, fighting side by side in many campaigns and quests. Until the betrayal.

The world blinked, and then this old reality began to waver. The sky was too blue, the buildings too tall. The streets of Allanto were never this clean. The clouds above seemed to slither across the sky like snakes while the King hidden behind appeared to be pulsing. Then she looked off to the side of the park and witnessed a tree uproot itself and stomp away, shaking the ground with every step.

That was when Taishi realized that Bhasani was hallucinating.

Just like the windwhisper's final test, the drowned fist style's final ascension was a ritual that included drinking a glowing blue tea steeped from a rare mushroom indigenous to the Sour Swamp just beyond the western borders of the Enlightened States. The drowned fist believed that the psychedelic effects opened and expanded the mind. Most practitioners usually partook of the tea occasionally, but Bhasani was an active fan and drank it regularly. While it may have opened her mind, it definitely gave her hallucinations, which bled over whenever she projected her will onto someone.

Then, the spider bit Taishi in the arm, snapping her out of this lucid dream. She cursed, feeling the sting and poison spread through her body. She snapped back to the present just in time to duck a chopstick that came close to piercing flesh. Taishi snarled and dove downward, the Swallow Dances leading the way. Bhasani fanned out the Sisters, her iron fans individually named Truth of Dreams and Truth of Lies.

The Sisters clashed with the Swallow Dances as Taishi pressed forward. The melee would have ended quickly if not for Bhasani's compulsions continually tickling her ears, trying to trick her into a bad move or incite a bad decision. Taishi's mind was well steeled, but the drowned fist's skill was significant. Taishi slowly gained ground, increasingly able to brush off the mental attack, which freed her to hammer the outmatched Bhasani blow for blow.

The end came abruptly. The edge of the Swallow Dances drew blood along the webspace between the woman's right thumb and index finger. Her hand spasmed, causing her to drop the Truth of Lies. Taishi seized her victory, knocking the other fan to the side, kicking one of Bhasani's legs from under her, sending her to one knee, and then resting her blade against the base of the drowned fist master's neck.

Taishi was surprised she was breathing heavily. "I think we're settled now."

Bhasani held her arms loosely up. "A draw then."

"You're such a goat piss." Taishi snorted, offering a hand.

Bhasani accepted it, rising to her feet. She brushed her fine green silk dress with her hand. "Your will is still as strong as a thunderclap, and you're still the best there is, even though you've lost a step."

"I have not—"

Bhasani waved her off dismissively. "There's no shame in admitting that. We all have. The young and dynamic Taishi would have struck me down from a hundred paces before I could worm a thought into her head." She pulled up next to Taishi as they walked up the mossy path. "The way to defeat the great Ling Taishi was never to match blades. That was suicide for most. No, the secret to slaying Taishi lay in her foundation supports: her family, students, and friends." Bhasani leaned in close. "You wobble those, you wobble her."

Taishi glared. "Point made. What does then have to do with now?"

"Nothing at all, apparently, because you're no longer the heroine of the tale. That must sting just a bit."

"Hardly," grunted Taishi. That wasn't entirely true, but she didn't need to say so to Bhasani of all people. She picked up her folded cloak from a nearby boulder and returned the Swallow Dances to its sheath. The two walked back through the bamboo forest and up the side of the stone pillar to the temple. Taishi could technically just ride a current all the way back home, but she had company, however unwanted, and it would be rude to leave Bhasani to walk all the way by herself. As far as Taishi was aware, the drowned fist had never developed a way to travel, other than using compulsion on someone to carry them.

"Hey," asked Bhasani, as they were a quarter way up the path snaking around the pillar. "Don't take this the wrong way, but what is wrong with you?"

Taishi totally took it the wrong way. "You want to go another round and find out?"

"I would tell you to grow up, but you're already an old woman." Bhasani turned and stuck a finger in her face. "Do you remember the last time our paths crossed?"

"No." And then she did. "About fifteen years ago?"

"Closer to twenty. We were both after the bounty on that mushroom lord."

That jogged Taishi's memory. Her face scrunched. "That greasy silk-spinner who sold both of us the same information, right? I swear, it always pays to buy the exclusive."

"Never worth it to penny pinch," Bhasani agreed. "Still, it was quite a shock when we both ended up in that pleasure barge. And then you came straight for me and tried to tear my head off. You wanted to get to me more than you wanted the bounty for a notorious slave trader."

"I remember that." Taishi's eyes darkened. "It was six months after you stabbed your friends in the back. Were you expecting us to just hug it out?"

"All the flavors in the world, and all Taishi ever chooses is salty," the drowned fist snipped back. "I brought you a basket of bao, and you still tried to kill me. How rude."

"They were red bean paste. You know how much I hate that."

"It was the thought that counted!" She admitted, "They were the only pastries left at the bakery."

Taishi sniffed. "For good reason."

Bhasani sniffed back. "I expected you to still be annoyed, but I didn't expect you to try to take my head off."

Taishi couldn't help but feel Bhasani get under her skin. The woman had a natural talent. "We fought like blood sisters for more than a dozen campaigns, and then . . . then, just . . . What, a six way split wasn't good enough? Two strings of gold liang for betraying your friends?"

Bhasani's face clenched. Light lines cut across her otherwise flawless cheeks. "I'm fully aware of my past actions. I have my reasons, but you made my point very well. I was surprised the other day when you didn't go for my head again the moment I stepped foot on your pillar. It's not like Taishi to just let a grudge prance into her home."

Taishi crossed her arms. "First you accuse me of holding a grudge, and now you say I've gone soft. Which is it?"

"Neither," remarked the drowned fist master. "You're still as granite as this stone pillar, and you sure as the ten hells haven't learned forgiveness, so . . ." She studied Taishi with those intense, probing eyes. "Taishi, it's something else, something serious. Something that has altered your perspective." A soft, sympathetic breath left Bhasani's lips. "You're not well."

Damn these mind-reading drowned fists.

Taishi looked away. "I may not be around when he fulfills the prophecy. Jian is going to need all the help he can get."

"How long do you have?"

She shrugged. "A year? A decade? Does it matter?"

"One to ten years is a fairly wide range."

"We will speak of this no more." Taishi picked up her pace. They had almost reached the temple anyway. She passed by the rickety wooden deck hanging off the edge of the sheer cliff, noting the cracked wood rattling in the wind. She remembered building this thing when she had first claimed the temple as her home. Just like her, it was old, rotting, crumbling away.

Her wards were currently tending the melon field. Zofi was picking bitter gourds while Jian was lugging a staff with two large jugs of water hanging off each end. He was also wearing a vest laden with sand. It was leg day. He stopped and bowed at the two masters.

Bhasani smiled and finger waved. He grinned like a dumb egg and waved back. The staff slipped off his shoulders, overturning the buckets and spilling their contents onto the ground.

The drowned fist master spoke to Taishi without moving her mouth. "You've been derelict with his mental fortitude, Taishi. The boy's head is soft clay. I can burrow in without even trying, or smash it like a ripe melon if I choose. Power is nothing without a forged will. The Prophesied Hero of the Tiandi needs to have steel in the head as well as his heart and arms, or the Khan will devour him from the inside out."

The mental game had always been Bhasani's passion. Taishi, who naturally had a strong will, had put a lot less stock in it, although she didn't necessarily disagree with the assessment. She was also stubborn. "I'm prioritizing. The boy's game was leakier than a fisherman's junk after a rainstorm. I had to patch him up to keep him from sinking."

"Building a miniature version of you, a tiny Taishi, are you?"

"If he were only so lucky," Taishi snorted. "But no. This isn't a matter of ego if that's what you think."

"Glad to hear that." Bhasani's tone changed. "So let me help."

"You've been chewing too much fungus if you think that's going to happen."

The drowned fist sniffed. "Don't be so territorial, blood sister. I'm not trying to steal your pet away." She continued to wrap her compulsion around him like a constricting snake, no doubt to drive home her point. She beckoned Jian to approach, which he did instantly, bounding toward them like a puppy eager to play.

Taishi growled. "I will finish what I started this morning if you pet his head."

"He's so adorable." Bhasani was laying it on thick. "Is he housebroken?"

"Cut it out. Now."

Bhasani didn't take her eyes off Jian. "Look at him. He's congee in my hands. You have to let me help. Get over yourself and do what's best for Wen Jian and our people."

Taishi burned at the thought of allowing someone else, her old rival no less, train her heir. It was offensive, enough so to warrant a duel. But Jian needed the training, and Taishi *could* use the support.

"Fine," she said. "Take his morning session today. We'll see how it goes, but stay only on your track. Keep the focus mental. I don't want him confused."

"I'm a professional."

"That's what I'm worried about."

"It's settled then." Bhasani cupped Jian's chin just as he reached them. "My sweet little kumquat, you're in for a treat. I am taking over your lesson today. We're going to have so much fun. Are you excited? You should be. Oh, that's a good boy." Jian was tittering and working himself up into frantic exuberance. Bhasani reached to pet his head.

Taishi hissed. "Don't you dare."

Bhasani pulled back and smirked. "He needs work. I barely tried. You're free to stay and observe if you like."

"That won't be necessary." Taishi turned away and headed toward the house. "Go teach your mind games. I'm going to soak in the tub."

CHAPTER SEVENTEEN

THE CHOICE

After her brief meeting with Shobansa, Sali handed her gear to Hampa and went straight for the bath caves. She was glad she stank up the place. She was usually inundated with important matters to consider the moment she returned from a long trip, so her need for a bath cleared her schedule for the night.

She entered the main chamber of a cavern that connected several diverging tunnels. The entrance to the left tunnel housed most of the clan while the one to the right held their supplies and perishables. The long ramp in front led farther underground to the dig site, which was the reason Mali had dragged the entire clan to this dank pit.

Nezra's purpose since they escaped Jiayi was not just to stay alive, but to also stay together as a family and continue as a clan. To accomplish that, their people needed a home, which meant building a new city. They would need city pods, and many of them, if they were to survive. It became Mali's—and by extension the clan's—new obsession. She had in many ways become the clan's source of inspiration. This had been their singular focus since the spirit shamans exiled them three years ago.

In those years, Mali had scoured the Grass Sea, chasing every rumor and lead for sunken or destroyed pods. They had come up empty the first year, but at the time, surviving was their priority. They managed to scrounge up two smaller lancer pods the second year and purchased two more from the underground markets at the beginning of the third. Then the spirit shamans had unleashed the capital city Liqusa after them, and they had been on the run ever since. That was, until six months ago, when Mali purchased a lead and a rough map from a prospector that led them deep within the bowels of Mount Shetty, where they encountered a small fleet of pods encased in ice. She had sold the entire clan on coming here, and they had been excavating and repairing the pods ever since.

Sali walked past a line of excavated pods—five lancers, a defense, and a homestead—that they had reclaimed so far, which brought their total fleet to ten. She wondered which city these pods used to belong to. Every city wore its own distinction, and the embellishments and flairs on each pod were foreign to her. This particular city styled walls shaped like wings and staircases framed by large talon-like shapes. Once, these pods must have belonged to an old city whose memory had long sunk beneath the seas. Reclaiming these would be a good start, but they would need more if they wished to reclaim their place among the clans. They would need many more if they wished to ever reclaim their former glory. In fact, they had staked everything on this dig. If the tinkers failed, Shobansa had stated that they would not have enough resources to escape the caldera. The cursed Shetty valley would claim one more clan.

Sali was even further delighted, upon arrival to the baths, to learn that one of the stone tubs was already filled with hot water and waiting for her. Wani apparently had the foresight to send Boop ahead to order it drawn. That girl was going to be a chief one day.

The steam rising out of the bubbling waters immediately drew Sali. Her soaked and smeared heavy cloak slipped off her shoulders at the entrance to the bath cave, then her headpiece, pauldrons, armbands, and other assorted pieces of armor. Her scale mail chest piece and skirt dropped to the ground last. Hampa would have to clean them anyway. That task was usually reserved for a master's neophyte, but Hampa had his hands full managing the howlers, especially after being gone for so long.

Sali was soon sitting in the tub soaking neck-deep in simmering water. The near-boil caused her to flush and raked sharp claws across every bit of her body. Most importantly, it eased the twisting deep pain from the Pull of the Khan as if someone were stepping on her stomach and tying her innards into knots. Slowly, the hot water numbed the sharp, stabbing pains and eased them to dull aches and throbs. Sali floated on the salted water, reveling in the delicious but quiet discomfort. During these few burning minutes, she felt pure, clean, almost like her old self again, not the withered husk that she had become. Those days of feeling whole came fewer and further apart these days. The pain and sickness would eventually creep back into her body.

An hour passed. Someone brought more hot water. The older hens in the clan had taken to caring for her. It was simultaneously considerate and annoying. In fact, just about everyone had been treating her like a fragile ornament, often with bated breath as if she were going to fall and shatter at any moment. She heard the whispers, albeit secondhand. The entire clan was keeping tabs on her. If she died in her sleep tonight, no one would be surprised.

Sali was floating in the hot salted bath when Shobansa's head appeared. "Now that you don't smell like a wet jackal anymore, we have matters to attend."

Well, not everyone.

Sali pried one eye open. "Can it wait until morning?"

"Time is a figment of one's imagination, so we might as well do it now."

"I don't know what that means."

The supply chief took that as a signal to continue. "We have enough foodstuffs and supplies to last through the third cycle. Our medicine stores could be better, but they are manageable. I have trade deals with several rim clans, the ones who don't care about the spirit shaman's decrees. Across the board, with careful planning, most of our stores are in excellent shape."

Sali frowned. "That sounds good. What's the problem then?"

"If you note I said *most* of our stores," replied Shobansa. "The rest, which intersects with our tinker and gear needs, are getting sucked dry faster than a waterskin in the Xing desert. In fact, Mali's appetite for supplies has grown so large it's increased the price of ore in the entire region. At the rate we're burning sparkstones we won't last the year. The third cycle winter freeze will kill us long before the enemy will. We can't stay here indefinitely. The caldera floods and becomes a swamp every few years."

"We follow the tinkers' lead on this," Sali said. "Whatever they need, it's theirs. However long they need, they will have."

"I want a home too, Sali," Shobansa muttered, "but city pods aren't going to matter if everyone's dead."

"Make it work." Sali paused. "How much sparkstone have we burned through?"

"A whole year's worth! Not to mention we're out of copper and zinc."

"I'll talk to Mali, but source more. Whatever it takes, Sho. Anything else?" She leaned her head back and closed her eyes.

". . . matter of a giant lizard problem."

She startled. "A what problem?"

Shobansa brought out his pipe and lit it. The pungent smell of the kind bud wafted up her nostrils. "A couple of the girls stumbled upon a chamber of eggs the size of large dogs. Then they met the momma and barely made it back. They said the lizard could swallow a mastodon whole."

He offered the pipe, which she accepted, taking a puff. She held the warm smoke in her lungs for a few moments before releasing it in a thin stream. "Are you asking for permission to lead a hunting party, or are you asking me to do it?"

"I don't need to ask for permission for anything, Sali."

She waved the pipe. "If the lizard is really that big, that's a lot of good meat. The eggs too."

The supply chief's flat stare didn't change. "Excellent. When can we expect you to slay this beast and return shortly after with two good tons of lizard meat?"

"I'm not going to kill your lizard, Sho."

"What about your neophyte? Is he up to the task?"

Sali grunted. "I would not trust him to not get eaten."

"Pity, well, I guess our people are at the giant lizard's mercy until one of our supposed warriors can take it down. In any case, talk to the tinker chief, would you? She's your sister. She'll listen to you. Oh, did you find who you were looking for?"

Sali nodded.

"And the cure?"

She took a deep breath and exhaled. "I was pointed another direction. This time to the True Freeze."

"That sounds dreadful," said Shobansa. "I've run wagons that way before. High margins, but deadly. When do you leave?"

"I don't know. I might not." Sali ran her hands across her face and stared at the now-muddy water she sat in. "I might just let it go and not chase this foolish quest any longer. I can be content sticking around here with my clan until my last breath with my people."

"What happens after that, though?" said Shobansa. "What happens after you are gone?"

Sali looked away. "I trust by then there will be great new leaders and warriors to head our clan. Besides, the Liqusa patrols are getting close. I'm needed here now."

"You certainly are, but you are needed afterward as well. I trust you to make the right choice, not the easier one." Shobansa paused at the entrance to the bath cave before leaving. "Speak to your sister, Salminde. I don't feel like freezing this winter."

Sali closed her eyes and drifted away again, her mind flirting with sleep. It had been an exhausting and harrowing year of travel searching for a cure to the Pull of the Khan, knowing that her time in this life was running short. There was much still to do and even more at stake. Sali had chased false leads all over the Grass Sea, trying herbal remedies and types of meditation and cleanses first. She searched out healers, shamans, and tinkers alike, and tried dozens of supposed miracle cures. Some, like this scalding bath, helped temper the pull's debilitating waves and shocks of hot and cold miseries, but none provided permanent relief.

Sali was tired of travel, of searching, of looking for hope. The idea of accepting the inevitable and embracing what little time remained had grown more appealing of late. At the very least, she could enjoy her last days with the people and things most important to her. She might even complete Hampa's training and promotion, although no small part of her was inclined to let the sect pass into history rather than compromise and dilute their standards.

Sali continued to float in the bath, her body half-submerged in the salt water, rising and falling with each long breath. She had just drifted past consciousness when someone entered the bath cave. Her chest was about to fall once again beneath the water's surface when she sensed the incoming attack.

"You selfish bitch!"

Sali's eyes snapped open, and she sat up just in time to catch a large wooden block flying her way. She caught it in one hand without sloshing a drop of water over the side of the tub. "It's good to see you too, Sprout!"

"Stingy told me you came home without even seeing me!" That was the name Mali referred to Shobansa by when they were at odds, which was practically daily.

"I really needed to bathe."

"Then Stingy told me you've given up searching for a cure even though you still have leads to chase!"

Sali marveled at how authoritative and decisive her little sprout had become. From that shy, bookish little girl buried in her gear manuals who mumbled when she spoke, to an inspiring—and often demanding—revolutionary leader focused on building a new home for their clan. Sali was, frankly, in awe of her little sister.

It didn't mean Malinde wasn't still her little sister.

Sali stood. A chill rippled through her as the cold air stung her naked body. "Hand me that towel."

Mali picked up a neatly folded towel and flung that at Sali as well. She caught it easily and wrapped it around her chest before stepping out of the tub. "You've gained weight. Have you been working through nights again? You snack nonstop when you do that. You also need your rest."

"You really sound like Mother right now."

"Someone has to take care of you, even if you don't take care of yourself. How goes the excavating?"

"The work is steady. Much of the gear and materials deteriorated over the years. All of the gaskets will need to be replaced, and many of the gears will need to be disassembled— Hey, don't change the subject!"

Sali had nearly succeeded. Distracting Sprout had always been stunningly easy, ever since she was a child. Sali slowed her speaking as if she was speaking to one right now. "Listen, Malinde, it's a weak lead, and it would take me all the way to Hrusha on the frozen ass-end of the Grass Sea. I may never return, or maybe it takes me so long you're no longer here when I do." She choked back some words. "I can't tolerate the thought of not being here a second time when our clan needs me most. This time I will be where I belong, to the very end."

"You are needed here tomorrow, next cycle, next year. And the year after that as well. What do you think happens if you die from the pull? Who will be our defensechief? Hampa? Is your head filled with rocks?"

It was a good argument. Mentioning Hampa really brought the reality of the clan's desperate lack of skilled war arts talent home. Sali was undeterred, however. "I will stand with my clan as long as my strength holds up, the breath nourishes my soul, and my brethren stand shields locked with mine. We will not fall."

To her surprise, Sprout shoved her, or at least tried. "Don't you dare, Sali. Don't you dare put your thirst for a glorious death above the needs of the clan. Stop being a selfish, lazy puss and put in the hard work of staying alive!"

Sali's mouth fell. "What. Did. You. Just. Say? How dare you! I gave up *everything* to find you! I moved the heavens and betrayed my religion *and* my honor for you. I sacrificed everything to save you."

"Now it's my fault?"

The conversation devolved into a screaming match with their voices bouncing off the cavern walls for the entire clan to hear. Mali tended to say what she meant but shouldn't have said aloud, while Sali tended to be flippant but would regret it in the aftermath. It was always worst when fights were waged purely out of love.

"All you care about is what others think of you. What songs they'll sing. What stories they'll tell about the great Salminde the Viperstrike. Your greatest fear is dying of old age. You can't bear the thought of being remembered as a shriveled husk."

That hit too close to the truth.

Sali was also quicker to anger the longer she had been ill. "You've never had to make a difficult decision in your life. Ever since we were children, all you thought about was yourself. You always got your way because you were a spoiled weed."

Mali's eyes went large, and she failed to utter a sound after several attempts. Then she burst into tears, which was unfair. Mali's bouts of tears always had a magical effect on their parents. It was too bad for her that they were useless on Sali.

Well, mostly useless.

"I didn't mean that." Sali really didn't. Some things couldn't be unsaid. She had gone too far. Mali froze, and her lips quivered. She looked as if she was teetering between grief and rage. Fat tears streamed down her cheeks.

Finally, after several moments of muted, accusatory glares and sniffles, Mali chuckled. "You dummy. I haven't been eating too much. I'm with sapling. We were going to tell you tonight and ask you to be the child's guardian."

For a moment, Sali was too stunned to respond. The thought of that possibility had never occurred to her. She gasped. "I'm going to be an aunty?" She had always wanted children, but had long assumed it wasn't meant to be. As the older sister, she had always considered Malinde a child, and the thought of Sprout having her own babies never occurred to Sali. Now, the realization of future generations—of actually considering having one—changed everything in her calculus.

Mali streamed a fresh bout of tears as she, nodding, reached over and embraced her. Sali squeezed her sister close. This shouldn't change anything, but it did.

Sali closed her eyes and sighed. "Fine. I'll go to this stupid place and see if they have a stupid cure."

CHAPTER EIGHTEEN

ALLANTO

The city of Allanto came into view at midday. It had taken almost three weeks for Qisami's cell to reach the crown of the hillside where they could see the tops of the city's famous curling glass towers—known as the Five Fingers of Prosperity—spearing the sky like a shimmering trident. Then they saw the squat buildings that formed the city's five wards, and the ridiculously massive four-lane road leading into the sprawling city that cut through a lush field of pink silvergrass. And then beyond the city was the man-made Lake of Bountiful Abundance, with waters so icy clear you couldn't dump a body into it.

The citizens of Allanto called it the Glittering City, and considered it the greatest city in the world, which would have been true if a city's greatness were measured by size and numbers. Allanto was also the heart of commerce and culture of the Enlightened States. It was certainly the wealthiest, the training ground and playground of the Zhuun's young nobility in their simpering games of intrigue and politics. But it was at the same time a hellish landscape for the poor and downtrodden.

Qisami personally didn't care for Allanto, although her opinion of the city varied based on how heavy her purse was. Four years ago, when coin was plentiful, it was one of the most fun places in the world. Now that her purse was empty, she thought the magistrates' presence was too heavy, the climate too chilly, and the entire damn city was far too brightly lit, which made creeping around stealthily cumbersome and annoying.

The citizens of the city were also the most murderous nonviolent terrible people in the world. Allanto was the only place in the States where people valued wealth over all else, including honor, reputation, and skill, where a gold coin was considerably more deadly than a dagger. It was the only place in the world where being rich was considered a form of war art. Just about everything and everyone in the city could be bought, including the magistrates. Especially the magistrates. Because of this, a fool with plentiful coin could wield great power.

To top it off, the food sucked. Northern food generally tended to be aggressively salty and over-seasoned. Like with their opinions on doors, they believed that the more spices the better.

The group stayed at the top of the hill to allow Zwei a moment to gawk and soak in the view of the Glittering City. Zwei's eyes were wet as they touched their heart dramatically. "It's prettier than in my dreams."

Qisami gagged loudly, but she had felt the exact same way the first time she had set eyes on Allanto. To be honest, her breath still caught every time she stood at this entry point leading into the plaza just past the main gates and gazed upon the majestic Five Fingers as well as the kaleidoscope of glass and colors that covered every inch of the city. The cell had been fortunate that the days had been continually cool and perfect as they traveled across the gentle rolling plains of Gyian duchy.

The rest of the cell's opinions on Allanto, having visited often—or in Cyyk's case having gotten a primary education there—were much less influenced by the city's glamorous exterior. No one had been particularly thrilled when she had briefed them about their new job. Burandin and Koteuni had openly scowled at the idea of working for a duke. Cyyk was panicked and embarrassed with the notion of running into one of his childhood acquaintances in Allanto. And Zwei had thrown a fit when they had learned that there was no pay, only a promise to restore their diamond-tier status.

"You could have at least negotiated a stipend, or some sort of advance," they had complained.

That had sounded close to a challenge to her authority. Qisami had let it go with a warning, but only after slapping some sense into the cell's lowest-ranking member, not that their anger was necessarily misplaced. After all their fees, dues, and garnishments, the cell was barely treading water. Restoring their tier wasn't inconsequential, but it didn't replenish their supplies and ammunitions, cover much-needed repairs, nor put food on the table.

The supplies Sunri provided for the trip didn't help matters much. Minister Chiafana had appeared at the entrance to their kennel wagon the next morning with a donkey pulling a cracked rickshaw, a pile of dirty peasant clothes, and a travel voucher to clear all tolls from Danziyi to Allanto with instructions to report to the Caobiu embassy immediately upon arrival. That was it. No food, coin, or any other supplies.

Three weeks later, here they were. It had taken them an extra week because the rickshaw broke down four times. Qisami leaned back in her seat, feeling every itch of the raggedy burlap robe on her body. It stunk too. She was fairly sure someone had died and gotten buried in it.

Qisami snapped the reins on Puddles, which was the name they had given the donkey. "Come on. It's still a half day to the gates. I'm eating barbecue tonight, either duck at a restaurant or one of you on a spit." She couldn't remember the last time she had had a real meal.

The strong breeze at their backs sent shivers throughout the pink fields, churning up flowers and pollen into the air as if snow was falling up into the sky. The fields surrounding Allanto were infamous. Many warlords or Kati raiding parties had sought to sack the wealthiest city in the world, and few had ever even made it to the city gates. Once the support dams were destroyed, the surrounding lowlands flooded easily. And if the city decided not to drown the enemy—the cleanup was always messy, after all—then they could just as easily set the fields aflame. This particular breed of silvergrass was particularly flammable, even when wet, and when set aflame released a paralyzing toxin.

To make matters worse, the cell had the unfortunate luck of reaching

Allanto during rush hour. The capital city of Gyian was infamous for its many checkpoints and tolls. The six gates into the city, the gilded main entrance and five others for each ward, were a sprawling mess of traffic and long queues. Since they did not know where the embassy was located, nor have ward passports, the cell was relegated to the general-access line, which stretched much longer than any line had a right to.

It took them the rest of the afternoon before they finally reached the gate. The entrance tunnel spanned halfway up the very tall walls, and embedded in the side was a little window with iron bars. Behind the bars sat a young man wearing a black soup-bowl hat wrist-wagging a long brush on a half-rolled parchment. The long tail of his queue hairstyle—popular only in this city—and his plain gray robes marked him as an administrative scholar, a lowly paper pusher and scroll sorter. He signaled for them to wait as he finished scribbling on the parchment. Then the scholar made a show of cleaning his brush and refreshing his inkstone. Qisami was tempted to reach over and swat his soup-bowl–shaped hat off his head. The plainest hats often covered the most sensitive egos. She swallowed her natural urge and waited. Finally, with his head still down, he held out a hand.

Qisami slid over the papers the Minister of Critical Purpose supplied them. The young scroll sorter openly scowled but looked them over. For a moment, she thought something was wrong, which would excuse them from having to do the job altogether. But probably not; that just meant they would have to break into the city the hard way over the walls.

"Smitt Bayara?" He squinted at her. "You don't look northern."

"My ba was a slut."

That appeared a good enough reason for him. He stamped part of the paper. "Business?"

"Looking for temporary work. My peaceful and loyal friends and I were told—"

The haughty paper pusher pushed a small pile of documents through the bars to her. "You need to fill out these documents. Now get out of the way. You're wasting people's time."

"Do I just bring these back to you?" she asked.

He nodded. "Back of the line, though."

Qisami looked back. "Over your mam's decapitated head. Look here—"

An old man riding a mule wedged past her. A few coins were passed to the official, and the old man was on his way within seconds. Qisami's blood boiled. Of course. She stomped back up to the window, earning her a glare from a group of ax-wielding nuns whom she had just cut in front of. "How much?"

"No line-cutting, you runt cunt," the administrative scholar snapped.

She pressed. "How much to get in?"

He acknowledged the six outraged nuns brandishing their weapons. "The fees for violence are in effect within eyesight of the city, your holiness. Make sure it's worth your effort." He turned back to Qisami. "Two coppers a head, one per mount. In your case, you'll need to cover the holy ladies as well."

"Why?"

"You cut in front of them."

"I was here first!"

He leaned back. "It's double the next time you show up at my window."

Qisami swore she would return here one day to kill this neutered mutt. She parted with each copper like a bad breakup. "There."

The administrator-scholar offered a toothy grin. "Welcome to the Allanto, street meat."

She flared a pinky. "I'm going to cut your throat one day. It's going to be so much fun."

The soup-bowl scholar waggled a pinky back. "Triple next time, you hear."

The cell proceeded to the next checkpoint, where this time it was a young woman sporting the same queue haircut and drab gray robes pointing at several colorful slips of paper arrayed before her. "Which ward is your troop of circus monkeys heading to?"

Qisami didn't know. That blasted firstwife hadn't bothered to tell them. "Where is the Caobiu embassy?"

That apparently was the wrong answer. "You'll need all of them then. That's one silver liang."

Qisami gaped. "Just to walk around?" This must be what it felt like to get robbed. She obliged, however, and dug out a silver liang from her purse.

"Per head, mudface."

"Per head?" Qisami could count five silver really quickly. She reached for the woman's collar. "Now you see here."

The administrator appeared used to this. She turned to a guard standing nearby. "What's the penalty for touching a city scholar?"

The red tunic soldier answered immediately. He must have been used to this question. "Death and a hereditary fine."

"Think of your poor indentured family, potato brain." The pleasant smile on the woman's face never changed.

Qisami had learned her lesson the last time. She grumbled as she counted out the coins.

The woman's smile fell slightly when she saw the exact change. "Very well. I'll have to process your access. Come back tomorrow morning."

Qisami was really in a murderous mood now. She pried her fists open and laid out two more silvers. When had just entering Allanto become so expensive? That was when she realized that it had always been this way. Back then, her cell had always just sauntered through the Trip Eights Gate reserved for the noble and wealthy, where all of the fees had been squared away ahead of time by the Consortium. The fees for that privilege had been high, but was worth it if you were willing to pay. Entering Allanto poor was a far different experience than entering the city with coin.

The scholar gave her a flat stare, obviously on the fence about the small bribe. Nevertheless, she waved them through to yet another line. She pointed at the rack of knives crisscrossing Qisami's chest. "You're armed so you have to pay the weapons carry fee. Unless, of course, you wish to stow your weapons at the weapons depot. The fee for that is five copper liang to check in, and five more to check out."

Qisami fumed. "Over my dead body."

A beady-eyed spectacled scholar wearing the same gray low-ranked robes charged her a copper a weapon, which tallied up to three silvers by the time the cell was accounted for. He offered a warning as he waved her through. "Remember, it's a silver per injury and five per death. Make sure whoever gets it deserves it."

The most insulting of the lines, however, was the very last, where their cell was charged a foreigner tariff, charged to anyone whose region was embroiled in a conflict with the Gyian Duchy, which in this case was everyone else.

Qisami didn't even bother arguing and slapped the ten coppers down. Her poor purse was starving now.

"That's what you get for going to war against Gyian, Caobiu egg scum," sniffed the ugly official. His bowl-shaped hat was slightly taller than the others. He waved her off. "Now, get out of my face."

That was the last line. No more bribes, fees, or tariffs. Qisami's thoughts lingered on that last exchange. How did he know they were coming from Caobiu? It wasn't as if they had advertised it. Her features gave away nothing about where she came from. The papers gave them access only along Kyubi Road. It did not state where they had traveled from.

The cell joined the throngs of people entering the city. There was an orderliness to traffic that was unusual compared to most cities. It probably had something to do with the fact there was literally a magistrate on every single intersection directing traffic. Allanto was the most heavily policed state of all the entire Enlightened States.

Every building on the main street was at least four stories tall, each with clean and modern pagoda architecture with long, curved arcs running along thick black-and-red wooden beams. The stewards of Allanto were deeply involved in crafting the city's image, so every building on each block was the same height and architectural design so as to create a balanced narrative. Balconies on the upper levels with vector railings and long curved eave roofs seamlessly integrated from building to building, creating a uniform and unified look to each finger of the city. Glowing volcanic red, mountain green, and arctic blue colors painted the walls, stacked on top of one another as if layers on a wedding cake. The roofs all had elongated corner eaves that curled in exaggerated intricate loops, each bright autumn orange that shimmered under the King's light.

Qisami always appreciated the architecture whenever she came to

Allanto. These over-engineered designs always made nightblossom work easy. Zwei was ogling the city like the country melon that they were, their head craned up at the nearest tower, which Qisami believed was the Finger of Fortune. They pointed. "I never knew a building could be built this tall. It must be like eight stories or something. Is it being held up by magic?"

"The magic of indentured labor, maybe." Qisami shoved them forward. "Be a tourist on your own time."

The main street was paved with smooth tiles with a divider down the center for individual lanes. Bright lanterns and signage hung everywhere, illuminating the evening with colored lights and dancing shadows. Vendors on both sides of the street on the first two levels were shouting at the passersby below, offering kumquats and weighted scales and the promise of the best night of their lives. It took a dozen more questions to random passersby, shop owners, and gray-garbed officials, each with a small bribe of a copper liang, before they finally reached their destination. Fortunately, this time around Zwei caught the attention of a group of wealthy university girls. The cell's opera had that effect on puppies. All it took for them to befriend the girls was an arch of an eyebrow and throwing out a smile, and they were able to obtain instructions on where they needed to go. The girls even offered to escort them part of the way, to the end of the Fortune section of the city.

The Caobiu embassy sat under the shadow of the Finger of Splendid Luck. Situated in a place aptly named Embassy Row, this embassy had obviously seen better times. Several rows of wooden barricades were now laid out like a maze in front of the once lavish estate it sat on. Mounds of dirt and broken stone were piled in front of the central entrance, and there were at least twenty archers manning four small towers facing the street. The outer walls, once pure marble white, were now chipped and smoked, with assorted red, green, and brown stains blotting the entire front like an errant canvas. The faint outline of the words "eggface incubators" had recently been burned into the once-glistening facade.

Qisami scanned the neighboring estates. The Lawkan embassy was the next one over. Across the street were Shulan and Xing. Just past them were the embassies for the Northern Tiandi Temple, the Silkspinners

Brokerage, and the Meatpacking and Dairy groups. All of these other estates appeared pristine and orderly. The destruction here was strictly a Caobiu thing. The red army was the only one of the five duchies demolishing every other in battle. Sunri's famous aphorism rang true: too much winning was also a bad thing. They were apparently winning so much that they were now on the cusp of total collapse. Still, the people needed to take out their frustration and anger on something, and the embassy was as apt a place as any.

Eyes right top, scrawled Burandin, his words still barely legible.

Koteuni's mouth barely moved, her voice a faint whisper. "Shifty eyes pruning the bush."

Creeper walking his cat, added Zwei. *Don't think he's a spy but he has a creepy face.*

"We passed the entrance," Cyyk announced loudly, unhelpfully. He was very skilled at announcing the obvious.

Inside voice, Broodbaby, she scrawled, *or I am going to make you eat your left pinky toe.*

It was times like this when Qisami really missed Tsang. The cell's old grunt had completed his apprenticeship and had been accepted into Ji xi qi, a third-tier bottom dweller training pool somewhere in the Xing desert. He was lucky he had gotten in anywhere at all. She hadn't been sure any pool was going to accept him. Last she heard, he was doing well. Not that she was keeping tabs on him or anything.

Too many eyes on the mouth. Head to the backhole, she scrawled, turning down the narrow alley between the Caobiu and Lawkan estates.

The Gyian had a thing for entrances: doors, entryways, gates, archways, tunnels. Anything that involved going in and out of any place. They were all used to show prestige. Closed doors guarded wealth; open doors meant opportunities. For the Gyian, the more doors the merrier, sound architectural design and pragmatic security be damned, which explained why their outer wall had a dozen or so gates. This cultural belief reflected heavily in their buildings, which always had at the very least a front and back gate, known as the mouth and the backhole. Larger estates had more doors and gates, with some ostentatious estates having more doors than walls. It probably made guarding the estate a pain, but someone who could afford that many entrances likely didn't have a problem affording a security retinue.

The backhole entrance was as they expected. There was a short line of commoners up all the way to the corner running parallel to the estate's sewage lines. Most looked like laborers and small-time merchants, likely looking for work or selling services and supplies to the embassy. More than a few looked like displaced refugees, which was expected in the middle of a civil war. Almost all kept their eyes to the ground as they muddled forward under the watchful eye of a squad of soldiers. Qisami bit her lip as they joined the back of the line. After a week of traveling, the indignity of having to wait in a peasant line did not help her mood.

"Name," the captain of the guard mumbled, not looking up.

"Ai Bayara," she repeated for what felt like the sixth time.

He raised his eyebrow, shuffled through a leather notebook, and then pointed to a building with five entrances off to the side. "Second door."

The five of them found themselves in a windowless room barred from the outside. They settled in. Time passed, several hours by the feel of it, before the door finally opened and a familiar face entered the room.

Qisami startled, then glowered. "Firstwife? What are you doing here?"

The stern-faced woman stepped into the middle of the room, flanked by two servants each carrying neatly folded stacks of clothing. She took inventory of the group. "Address me by my title, assassin, not Firstwife. I arrived by carriage three days ago."

Zwei raised a finger. "Wait, you came by carriage? Why couldn't we just ride with you? Why did we have to walk?"

"It's not very discreet to travel with a personal envoy of the Duchess of Caobiu, is it? I am your handler for this assignment. You will do exactly as I order until your mission is completed and you are safely out of Gyian lands. Do you understand?"

Cyyk piped up. "What exactly is the mission?"

"You do not need to know. You just need to do." The minister of so-called critical purpose eyed their grunt up and down. She chose a set of clothing from one of the stacks and tossed it into his lap. "You're a young lords' training field dummy."

He blinked. "I'm a what?"

"Thank the blasted Tiandi." Qisami smirked. "Kids are the worst. I'd rather sit in a pit full of vipers than be a noble brat's target practice."

Chiafana moved on to Zwei. She put the next stack of clothing in their waiting hands. "Stable hand."

They looked nonplussed. "I don't think so. I hate horses. I hate hay."

She continued to ignore them as she moved on to Koteuni. "Rabble-guard."

Koteuni scoffed. "Rabbleguard? Look at me. I'm a tiny woman with short arms and very narrow hips. No one is going to believe I'm on riot control."

"Storyteller's troupe" went to Burandin, who offered a blank look, possibly because he didn't know what that meant.

Chiafana handed the last stack to Qisami. "And you, children's companion."

"Children's . . ." Qisami's urge to kill was rising. "What does that mean? Like some rich little spoiled egg's plaything?"

The minister pursed her lips in a smile. "The last time three or more of the dukes met, the Champion of the Five Under Heaven disappeared under dubious circumstances. I expect this meeting of the three will not produce equally earthshaking consequences, but we must be ready. In preparation for the upcoming negotiations, the Allanto court is bringing in seasonal staff. I've arranged positions for all of you at the palace. The duchess plans to arrive within a cycle, which should give you plenty of time to embed with the rest of the Gyian staff."

"We have to stay in cover as the *help*?" Qisami balked.

Koteuni scoffed. "An entire cycle? Kiki, you said this was a one-off job, not a cock crap honest full-time employment. I enjoy being a free agent."

"We're not even getting paid." Zwei couldn't seem to let that go.

The minister nodded. "You will actually be getting paid. Weekly salary, one string of copper liang for the storyteller, two strings each for the stable hand and the scullery maid, three for the rabbleguard and children's companion."

"That's not what shadowkills do," interrupted Koteuni. "We're terrible spies."

Cyyk raised his head. "Being a practice dummy sounds like an awful thing."

Burandin leaned over. "I hate interpretive dance. Want to trade?"

"Your roles have already been determined and cannot be altered," Chiafana said firmly. "In the meanwhile, you blend into the background, embed with the locals, do your jobs, and wait for activation."

Qisami threw her hands up. "What do you expect us to do while we wait?"

Chiafana nodded. "I expect you to be an excellent rich little spoiled egg's plaything, shadowkill."

ACT II

CHAPTER NINETEEN

NEW OLD FIND

Sali detested the cold.

Along with Hampa and Daewon, she had pressed north for several bloody frigid weeks. The icy winds flayed at her half-exposed face until her skin was raw and bleeding. The constant assault on her senses exacerbated her symptoms, continually drained her already dwindling strength. The sky turned ten shades of gray speckled with white swirls of snow. The wind had grown menacing, lacerating her cheeks until they were chapped and stinging. Sleet turned the ground into a freezing swamp that sank horses to their knees, while never-ending swirling snow flurries continuously layered the landscape. This blasted land couldn't decide if it wanted to freeze or melt, and its indecision just made everything worse.

The landscape in this northern region was simultaneously familiar and alien. Gone were the humidity and heat, replaced now by a cold, biting wind and wet, soggy rain. The abundant and chattering jungle wildlife was replaced by an eerie silence and layered by the constant low whistle of the breeze. Life was still abundant here even if the denizens of the Grass Tundra weren't the most social creatures and tended to keep to themselves, but Sali could still sense their eyes tracking her every step.

They passed the borders of the Grass Sea two days ago and were now plodding slowly, single-file, through icy slush that rose to their horses' knees, making each step as miserable as Sali had anticipated. It was worse, actually. Their small party lost half a day when they had to detour around the Cliff of Moraka, which was a massive hole where the sea waterfalled into a black abyss. Legend had it this was where a giant fiery jewel from beyond the sun had crashed onto this world and broken the crust of the lands that eventually created the Grass Sea. Sali always thought it was a stupid children's story, but having seen it in person she was no longer sure.

They had stopped at Kopacara, a fishing outpost, to resupply before continuing easterly. That was two days ago, and the last time Sali had seen another living person other than her immediate company. It was a miserable trek, and she was thankful that Mali had turned down the offer to come. When they had announced Sali's plan to head to Hrusha, both Shobansa and Daewon insisted they arrange a trade deal while they were there. Hrusha was a volcanic land and a known mining colony, famed to possess copious quantities of high-quality sparkstones. For once, both the tinkers and the supply-side of the clan agreed on something, and Daewon was the council's representative, for better or worse.

Mostly worse.

It didn't matter. Sali wouldn't have allowed Mali to make this journey, not because she was pregnant but because she was indispensable to the excavation. *Her* work was crucial to the clan. Sali's well-being was not nearly as important.

Sali wrapped her cloak around her body and buried herself in her leopard appaloosa's thick mane as they plowed against the wind and waves of snow flurries pummeled into them. The appaloosa pranced and tried to turn away, but Sali squeezed her hips and kept the horse moving forward, gently guiding the appaloosa up the gentle but deceptively dangerous slope. Sali never thought she would miss the sweltering heat and the swarms of flies providing shade from the scorching sun. What she wouldn't give to sleep in a cocoon high in the weeds as the night creatures came alive or listen to the crickets' and cicadas' vibrant nocturnal performances within the Grass Sea while she gazed at the theater of stars.

It took more effort than it should have to reach the top, but she succeeded after dismounting and dragging the horse up the last stretch. Hampa, who had taken point, was waiting at the top. He clasped her forearms and pulled her the final way to the crest. She peered over his shoulder at the vast white plains before them. "What do you see?"

He pointed to their right. "We're close. See that tree line over there? It's right through that passage, between those evergreens and that outcrop of boulders. According to the map from Kopacara, that's the way to the harbor."

Sali's gaze followed his finger. Her neophyte might not have a natural talent for the war arts, but he was a gifted tracker. That narrow path dividing the tree line *did* appear unnatural. The Grass Tundra this far north was barely more than snow and ice, snowcapped peaks along the horizon flanked by white-blanketed trees on all sides. Even the air shimmered white. The only thing breaking up the monotony of this bleak snowfield were the heavy, dark clouds racing overhead. She shouted back down the ravine, "Hurry up, tinker."

Daewon must have gotten turned around, which honestly wasn't too difficult in this flurry. He was shouting in the wrong direction. "I don't see you. Where did these footprints come from?"

"Those are yours, you clownfish!" she shouted back.

Sali growled her irritation as the tinker slipped and pedaled in place, his feet unable to catch against the slippery slope before falling back down to the bottom of the ravine. They didn't have time for this. The traders who had given them these directions had warned that arctic barges did not approach the shore after dusk. If they delayed much longer, they would have to encamp for the night, possibly with limited shelter. Sali slid down to where Daewon had abandoned his horse. The mare stared blankly while munching on a blade of grass it found under the snow. Sali drew her tongue, which was coiled at her hip, and shot to the right of Daewon, puncturing a fallen log inches from his nose.

"Grab on," she yelled over the roar of the wind.

Even then, it took ten minutes before she was able to haul the tinker and his chestnut back up to where Hampa was waiting. Daewon fell to his knees, heaving for breath. Sali didn't know why, considering she was the one who did all the work.

"Are we almost there yet?" he asked for the thirtieth time. She was keeping track.

"You're lucky Sprout is fond of you. Come on, get up."

"Are you sure we're headed the right way?" That was the ninth utterance of that phrase. He did have a point this time.

Sali felt the direction of the wind slicing across her nose. She looked one way and then turned in the opposite. "We go this way."

"How do you know?"

She raised a finger. "Third cycle. Spring. The wind at our back."

Hampa added, "The big Uhna."

"The Star Serpent coiling down the sea," she quoted. "Leading her thousand and one children across the sky to drape over and illuminate the lands our ancestors traveled."

"She always changes directions and blows east this time of the year."

Sali nodded. "And will continue to do so for another three weeks until the second cycle summer, then she blows southwest for another three, her gale softer." Sali paused. "Learning how to read the air could save your life. Otherwise, you won't last a day if you ever get lost, tinker."

Daewon struggled to mount his mare. "Let's be honest, sister-of-my-heart. I can't fight. I can't hunt. I can't build a shelter. I'm allergic to half the berries in the wild and most mushrooms. I think orienteering will be the least of my concerns if I ever get lost." He nudged his horse forward. "Lead on."

Those traits he rambled on about were the least of his problems. Daewon tended to go soft under pressure, like a teenage boy on his first bedding night. There was a saying among the Katuia: "Courage is forged in the mind. Bravery is seared in the soul." That young man didn't have the warrior's fire in him. Most hearts, in fact, were not tempered for battle. Mali had always said that though his heart lacked the sear, it was warm and inviting, and that was what mattered most to her.

The three Katuia continued down the other side of the sloping hill, the hoofprints from their horses the only evidence of disturbed snow. Each step was crunching deeper into the drifts, making it difficult to gauge the depth of the terrain. They crossed over onto ice, and the ground was moving beneath their feet, bobbing slightly. They must be near the coast. The land here, at the far edge of the Grass Sea, moved differently than near its heart, where people lived. There, the ground undulated almost playfully. Here, the land seesawed, tipping to one side and then slowly rolling to the other over the course of hours.

They were closing in on the signal point. Sali hoped the map they had purchased was true to its markings. She glanced at Daewon slumping in his saddle. They didn't have enough rations for the trip back. She would have to take his horse and supplies and leave him behind if one of them were to survive. Mali would be displeased, but that was Mali's problem, not hers.

It was times like this she was glad Hampa was riding at her side. She had almost made him stay home. Like she always said, he served the clan much better in every capacity save a viperstrike, especially now. He had insisted, however, on going with her. He'd begged, threatened, and thrown himself at her feet. His arguments started with, "The neophyte's place is always next to his mentor." Then it was, "You need someone to guard your back." Then, "If you try to leave, I will simply follow." Finally, through blubbery words and fat tears, "Please, mentor! Don't leave. I'm lost without you." He had threatened to go on a hunger strike if she did not change her mind. Like she had said, he was loyal to a fault.

"Go ahead," she'd replied. "Everyone's hungry. One less mouth to feed."

Hampa ended up getting his way, but not for the reasons he believed. Sali signaled to her neophyte to fetch Daewon, who had fallen behind. They reached the upper rim of a sheer cliff that overlooked a small, icy cove not far from the beach. She caught herself holding her breath until she noticed the long wooden pier jutting out into the intense blue waters of the True Freeze.

"There's the signal urn." Daewon pointed at a large stone bowl sitting atop a small pyramid off to the side of the pier.

The small group followed a narrow path that curved along the wall of the cove down to the beach. Daewon swung off his chestnut at the base of the pyramid and began to make his way toward the bowl. Sali swung her leopard appaloosa about and circled the pyramid, scanning the top of the cove and the dense clusters of boulders around the sheltered cover. They hadn't seen another soul in days, but she hadn't survived this many campaigns by being lax.

Daewon soon reached the urn and pulled out a metal rod the length of his forearm. He squeezed the trigger of the tinker's tool, known as a fire twig, until a small flame the size of his fingertip began to burn. Daewon circled the urn and nursed the fire, stoking it until the flames licked the edges of the urn, and then rose above it. A column of smoke soon drifted into the clear blue sky.

Sali slowed her weary leopard appaloosa to a leisurely trot around the pyramid, partially to stay alert for potential attack but mainly to cool down the horse after a hard day's travel. She made it a quarter turn around the structure when she noticed something unusual sticking out of the snow.

At first, it appeared to be two twisted branches, but upon closer inspection, she realized it was two rigid arms. Then she spotted a pair of legs and a half-buried face nearby. Sali found another frozen corpse a few steps past the first, and then still another. A battle must have been waged around here some time back, likely bandits ambushing merchants who were waiting for the barge. Now, the losers were preserved for eternity in the snow.

"Huh, this branch sticking out of the snow looks weird." Hampa peered closer and pulled back. "Ugh, it's a hand!"

She glanced behind her and pointed at his feet. "Stay clear of those limbs and watch where your roan steps. This would be a bad place and time for her to break a—"

It may have been the breeze or a trick of the eyes in this blinding white, but for a moment, Sali thought the hand attached to the end of the frozen arm curled its fingers—and there it was again. She was sure of it this time.

"Hampa, step back." Her hand drifted toward her tongue. She called out. "Daewon."

"Hang on." Daewon was leaning over the side of the urn, nearly tipping inside. "Water got mixed with the oil."

The corpse's eye blinked, and then its body shook, shedding snow as it rose. Sali wasn't ashamed to admit she nearly fell off her horse at the shock of seeing a corpse move. The tinker pulled away from the bowl as a jet of flames abruptly kicked into the air. A slanted plume of smoke grew fatter as it tainted the cloudless sky. "This should do it," he said, waving his fire twig in the air. "If that doesn't get the barge's attention, I don't know what will. I'm coming back down—"

"Stay up there!" she yelled. "Do not take one step."

"Why? What are . . . Oh!" Daewon turned shrill. "You never said anything about the breathing dead up here." The idea of walking, breathing corpses was an old Zhuun superstition told by farmers to their children to keep them close to home. Sali watched the corpse twitch her elbow and neck as if loosening her joints.

"Viperstrike," the woman hissed in a raspy voice as if her mouth had not yet thawed. Short, three-pronged weapons shaped like dagger-sized tridents, known as iron rulers, appeared in both hands. "You've kept us waiting."

Her instincts had not been wrong. This was an ambush. Several more corpses rose from the snow. These assailants wore a camouflaged patchwork of thick white and brown fur held together by links of flame-hardened onyx wood. Their stiff movements and narrow stances shared a common ancestry with most northern Katuia sects. The iron rulers were another giveaway. They were a common weapon and tool among a certain caste of war artists who depended on stealth over battle.

These were not the breathing dead, but something worse: lowly bladethugs lying in ambush.

The bladethug flung her arm, sending an iron ruler streaking toward Sali. She grabbed her coiled tongue and swatted the pronged dagger out of the air, and then bounded off her horse, landing on the step pyramid. She ran across its steps and leaped again, dodging another throw before retaliating, her tongue uncoiling. It snapped at the bladethug, Sali's weapon's spearhead cracking against the buckler on the bladethug's wrist.

Sali landed stuck hip-deep in snow. Three more bodies closed in and blocked her from reaching the pyramid. Hampa fought a bladethug at the bottom of the stairs hoping to tag his quicker opponent. Some of his whiffs were pretty large and embarrassing. The viperstrike training she was putting him through was a little different from the one her family studied. Always cater training toward one's skill sets and talents, as her own mentor, Alyna, often cited, or in this case the lack of them. Sali admittedly wasn't the best teacher, but she tried her best. Hampa's tendency was to batter his enemy like a raging elephant. Sometimes she thought about doing them both a favor and shipping him with a referral to the Bullcrash sect.

Two of the white-clad assailants were climbing up the steps on the other side of the pyramid, and to Sali's dismay, Daewon was heading down to meet them, wielding that stupid fire twig like a weapon.

Sali yelled at the tinker, "Stay with the urn!" She dodged left to avoid a double iron ruler thrust and rewarded her assailant with a kick to the side that disappeared him into a mound of snow.

Daewon picked himself up and fumbled for his dropped fire twig. "I can help!"

"No, you can't. Stay still, you dumb rabbit."

More white-cloaked bladethugs came at her from every direction. Sali's tongue lashed out and kept them at bay, but none of her strikes were slipping past their attackers' defenses. The conditions weren't ideal, but these attackers deserved credit for their skill. The group worked silently yet also in unison, constantly probing and nipping at her like a pack of hyenas trying to down a lioness. Sali was at a disadvantage against a dozen or so bladethugs in these wet and icy conditions, but in this battle, she was still the lioness, and these yippy hyenas were just that.

The tongue's sharp tip found its next mark, its spearhead plunging through the chest of a bladethug and out the man's back. He stiffened mid-swing, his arms raised high and locked in place. Sali loosened the shaft of her weapon until it was once again as supple as silk, and she yanked, extracting the bite violently from his body. Another bladethug hovered too close and suffered when the tip of her tongue gashed his chest open, spraying the white snow with a shower of crimson. Even the blood that exploded from his chest came out like slush. These blade-thugs must have a technique with their jing to adapt their bodies to their environment, similar to reptiles. That explained how they survived these conditions lying in ambush, and why none of their breaths misted.

Sali sent a jolt through her tongue mid-swing, hardening the shaft until it became a spear, and lunged in an unexpected direction at a blade-thug who was positioned farther back, gaining another quick kill. She landed just as Daewon's scream took on a more panicked pitch. The tin-ker had tripped and fallen on his backside as the two bladethugs stalked him up the stairs of the pyramid.

"Hampa," she called. It took long enough, but her neophyte finally finished the bladethug he had been locked in combat with. His hip movement needed work. "Save the rabbit."

"Yes, mentor."

In the near distance, a bell tolled, its tone loud above the sounds of battle.

Sali cut down the remaining bladethugs with a series of quick attacks until only one remained. It was the one who had originally greeted her. Sali pointed the spear of her tongue at the woman. "Submit."

The ringing bell grew louder.

The bladethug reversed one of the iron rulers in her grip and saluted over her heart. "I am Ashah, Fifth of the Coldshatters, a scion of Liqusa. I thought the days of the viperstrike were over. It is a privilege to cross paths with the last of you." Ashah offered an overly formal and reverential—almost pandering—bow.

Sali scowled. A polite and respectful enemy was the worst kind to face when someone was in a hurry. The two coldshatters over the wom-an's shoulders were overwhelming Hampa, forcing him back toward the top of the pyramid.

"Call off your dogs. Submit," Sali barked again.

"There is no ill intention, only duty. The Sacred Braid still binds us." The coldshatter was leveraging the decorum between sects to take ad-vantage of the situation. Tradition demanded a cursory answer.

Sali had no time for that. She sent a jolt through her tongue and shafted it straight through Ashah, Fifth of the Coldshatters' throat. The fact it was a Liqusa sect was just a bonus. She almost preferred killing Liqusa warriors over Zhuun. Still, how did they track Sali all the way here?

Sali speared her tongue into the ground and sent two jolts through its shaft in succession. The first relaxed it into its coil form, and then the second hardened it back up. She held on to the end as the resulting kinetic change vaulted her out of the snowbank. She lashed out with the tongue while in midair, striking one coldshatter in the back and dragging him down the stairs. The second turned to face her and suffered Hampa's boot to his chest, sending him falling after his comrade.

Sali landed at the base of the pyramid next to the two fallen coldshatters and looped the tongue around both of their necks. She squeezed and sank the choke in deeper and tighter, feeling their dying gasps grow quieter, their rough hands pawing frantically at her. Her arms quivered with the strain, but Sali refused to release the pressure. It wasn't until both men's bodies had gone limp that she let go.

She collapsed, her breath labored and heaving with puffs of steam drifting from her mouth. This frost made everything more difficult. The air sapped her energy. She had lost all sensation in her fingers and toes, and her joints were stiff as rusted metal hinges. She looked up to see the neophyte and tinker hurrying to her side.

"I could have helped." Daewon's eyes were wide. He held up his fire twig and promptly bobbled and dropped it.

The bell rang again. For the first time, Sali noticed the large iceberg sailing into the cove. The flat chunk of ice had two sails down its center and steam paddles installed along the sides. The arctic barge had arrived. It bounced against the pier, shedding chunks of ice as it linked up. A gate lowered, and two men in leathery walrus-skin jackets emerged. They stopped at the edge of the plank and stared at the bodies scattered about. Another figure emerged behind them, wearing a full polar bear fur suit. He walked off the plank and stepped over one of the bladethugs without batting an eye. Surveying the carnage, he squinted up at the three sitting on the bottom of the step pyramid.

"Light catch tonight, eh? Where to?"

Sali picked herself up and brushed off her lightly peppered shoulders. "To Hrusha. Just three of us and our mounts."

"The Sun Under Lagoon, then. Are you off on a Kati pilgrimage?" The captain noticed the glint in her eyes and raised his hands. "No disrespect. It's just words, ma'am."

Sali continued leveling her gaze at him. "Can your little paddle boat get us there or not?"

"She's an arctic barge, not some rickety Zhuun fishing junk."

"It's just words, seaman."

It was the captain's turn to glint. He eyed her and then broke into a toothy grin. "It's a nine-day trek, give or take three, the Buran winds permitting, with six stops between here and your final port of call. You three share one tent. You're on your own for food. You can purchase fish from the mess or go hungry. Makes no difference to me. One silver a day regardless of the number of days at sea. No weapons, no fires, no trouble. I'll give exceptions to your mounts, but it's your job to clean up after them. If I catch you pissing on the snow, I'll throw you overboard. Same goes for your animals. Does that flow?"

Sali sealed the terms with a nod.

"Good. I'm Captain Lehuangxi Thiraput Cungle. You may call me Captain Lehuangxi Thiraput Cungle." Sali had once met a Happan trader from the Spotted Chain Isles far in the Ngyn Ocean who also had an unreasonably long name. He too had insisted everyone use his full name. It must be a thing with their people. Captain Lehuangxi Thiraput Cungle turned and proceeded back toward his floating chunk of ice, beckoning for them to follow.

"Welcome to the *Hana Iceberg*."

CHAPTER TWENTY

MONOTONY
THE KILLER

Jian had no idea why he had initially been so thrilled about having the other masters rotate their instruction. Taishi was a creature of habit and repetition, so three years of slow, incremental training in this remote corner of the world had become quite tedious and had worn down his patience. Add the fact that he had been forbidden to leave the temple due to that wanted poster, and the entire second cycle of the year was made all the more unbearable.

When Taishi had first announced that each of these renowned masters would privately train him alongside her, Jian thought they were going to blend their individual styles to form some sort of supreme style, much like what his old masters at the Celestial Palace were doing. He daydreamed about combining all their abilities to become an unbeatable war artist. He would have the agility of the houtou, the trickery of the drowned fist, the range of the whipfinger, and the defensive strength of the eternal bright light all complementing the ultimate power of the windwhisper lineage. All of these pieces would truly make him a war artist worthy of his title as the Prophesied Hero of the Tiandi, the Champion of the Five Under Heaven, the Slayer of the Eternal Khan of Katuia, the Savior of the Zhuun, and any other lofty titles that had been bestowed upon him.

At least that was how Jian imagined things would turn out with his new training regimen. Instead, in her very first lesson, Master Narwani brought Jian to the middle of a clearing in the bamboo forest and told him to be a tree. That was it. Hold his arms limply over his head at an awkward angle and stand still.

Be a stupid tree.

"Feel your roots take hold of the earth. Let the wind sway your branches," she cooed into his ear. "Take in your surroundings and join the forest." Or some other foolish, corny rubbish like that.

Jian spent most of the next several weeks in her class performing other strange nonsensical tasks. He had to stay still as a statue one day, and then the next, she had him run through the bamboo forest in complete darkness until he had nearly passed out from exhaustion, all while trying to have him deepen his emotional landscape to expand his mind. It all felt like a waste of time. It didn't take long before Jian dreaded every single lesson with Bhasani.

Now, nearly a month later, Jian had graduated from posing as a tree to posing as a statue reciting cheek-flaming bawdy poetry.

"What a waste of time," he growled. His stomach growled with him. He was currently in a one-legged heron stance with a knee raised and his arms extended in both directions. Bhasani would sometimes pose him in war art stances, other times like an animal. Sometimes she would place him atop or under a waterfall, or on a slippery boulder, or high on a tree branch, or atop one of the staked poles in the training yard. Other times, she would combine them and make him hold a stance while on top of or under the waterfall or something else. To make matters worse, Bhasani always insisted their lessons begin every morning at sunup.

"He has fairly good balance," Sonaya observed, standing on the other end of the clearing. "But those eyes."

"Dead giveaways," Bhasani agreed. "His gaze telegraphs everything. Stop admiring the scenery." The feather brushed against the back of his neck, sending a shiver down his back. Nothing Bhasani had him do made any sense, and the woman refused to explain anything. He came out of all of her lessons confused, frustrated, and more ticklish than he realized. His skin suddenly crawled all over the moment he settled into a pose. Who knew standing still could be so itchy?

"What's wrong with my eyes?" he whined. "Where am I supposed to look?"

"Statues don't talk, or fidget, for that matter." The end of a feather tickled his ear. That was her way of keeping discipline and pointing out his flaws. It was surprisingly effective. Jian would almost prefer the bamboo switch. Her words also had a way of burrowing through his ear and into his head.

"Look at nothing and everything," Taishi said as she entered the small grove of trees. His master was dressed in her fuzzy robes and holding a cup of steamy tea.

"To see within, one most look far," Bhasani agreed. "Your master and I had the same mind coach when we were young battlemaidens." She repositioned his arms, and the three studied him as if they were critiquing art, or cattle.

"He's steadier," Taishi admitted. "His focus has improved."

"I've been throwing soft compulsions at him all morning," Bhasani agreed. "He's reacted to only half."

"What compulsions?" he asked. "I didn't feel or hear anything."

"Exactly," said Sonaya. "Compulsions are completely mental. Your mind is sharpening and honing its focus. It's starting to passively filter out the noise."

"I am?" He didn't even realize there had been any changes in his thinking or behavior. Hope sprang eternal in his mind. "Does that mean I'm almost done with these horrid lessons?"

Something that felt like a pin prick poked inside Jian's head, sending shivers down his spine, and he felt the sudden urge to clench his bowels. His balance faltered, and he took a step.

"Still a long way to go, Five Champ." Sonaya giggled. "There're few compulsions quite as enticing as delusions."

"All right, stop chatting. This isn't courtship camp. Mirror up. Still Waters. Hold Mischievous Monkey Hangs from Tree until I return." Bhasani turned to Taishi. "Any more tea?"

"Freshly brewed," replied Taishi. "Find me afterward, Jian." Jian and

Sonaya lined up facing each other. Jian sucked in a deep breath, grabbed his right heel and toe with both hands, and raised it straight over his head near his ear. Sonaya did the same but without the use of her hands. She winked, looking only a little smug. As expected, Sonaya was far superior at these exercises, as she should be. She did not take it easy on him in the slightest.

Jian rolled his eyes. Truth was, he was thankful she frequently trained alongside him. Her presence was the one thing that made these terrible lessons a bit more bearable. He shifted slightly, needing a few seconds to stabilize himself. He slowed his breathing and focused looking straight ahead, which was directly at Sonaya. She stared back mischievously, alternating raising one eyebrow at a time, breaking his concentration.

He bit his lip. "Cut it out."

"You need to work on your core," she teased. "You're wobbly as a lamb."

The shaking in his raised leg worsened. "Stop messing with my head."

Sonaya stuck out her pierced tongue, curling it like a horseshoe. It was a trick he could not figure out. The two had spent several evenings trying. He'd come to the conclusion that his tongue just did not bend like that. She had been taunting him with it ever since. Jian had discovered that he couldn't whistle either.

"What's the matter? Can't stand still and talk at the same time?" Her smirk, which may as well be her resting face, grew only wider. The toes on her raised foot next to her head began to waggle. Then her leg, moving with precision, like a dancer, reached over and booped his nose with the tip of her sandal.

"Stop poking me." His fight to stay upright became more desperate. "I'm not doing this all over again just to amuse you." The punishment for breaking form was another session later this evening. He just needed to hold out a little while longer. Sonaya gently nudged him again with her big toe, and then tried to tickle his side and armpits. Jian closed his eyes and did his best to tune out all of these distractions, but he was failing.

"Your legs are aching, aren't they?" she asked. "Mine *sure* are."

"I'm fine. Your evil whispers have no effect on me."

"Is that a mosquito on your leg?"

He felt the itch. The cracks in his focus grew. "It's not going to work, witch."

She blew into his face. That last one did it. Jian smelled strawberries and burnt sugar, and then his connection with the ground broke, as did his balance. He fought against the fall, however, windmilling his hands and thrusting his hips out. It was all for naught. Right before he toppled over, Sonaya grabbed his wrist.

"Got you."

He dangled precariously on the pole, off-balance, her grip the only thing saving him from falling into the frigid, brown water. "Thanks—"

"Did you just call me a witch?"

"What?"

Sonaya let go. Jian squawked and splattered onto the soft, wet ground. His fall had been cushioned by a bed of cold mud that now gunked to his back.

"That was my last clean robe." Jian sighed as he sat up. He was going through a bit of a growth spurt the past few months, so most of his robes, save the one he was wearing, now rode high on his forearm and ankles. Taishi didn't know how to sew, and Zofi refused to, so that left going to Bahngtown to see the tailor, but he was currently forbidden from leaving the temple.

Bhasani returned to the grove just as he was picking himself up. She was holding a cup of tea delicately with both hands. "That was pitiful, Five Champ. I've been gone only five minutes." She turned to Sonaya. "How much method did you apply, daughter?"

"None, Mother. I just blew him a kiss."

"Really? Not a breath of compulsion?"

"Not a squirt." Sonaya yawned and stretched her arms up, ending it in a shrug. "Wasn't necessary."

Bhasani looked annoyed. "So, a pretty girl came close to him and he just fell apart. We have our work cut out for us."

"Wait, that's not what happened." Jian stopped. "Or did it?"

The drowned fist master waved him off dismissively. "Run it again. This time, daughter, don't play with your food for so long."

"Wait, is she here just to mess with me?" Jian scowled as he shook off some of the mud.

"Sonaya isn't practicing the Still Waters exercise for her own benefit," Bhasani remarked. "My daughter had this mastered by the time she was five."

"Traitor." He stripped off his dirtied robes and tossed them onto the grass. He considered stripping it all off, but modesty won the day. He also was out of clean undergarments.

The drowned fist master studied his filthy robes with disdain. "Bah, go clean up and we'll pick it up tomorrow."

Sohn came by that afternoon. He, Fausan, and Kasa came and went since all three lived less than a day's journey away. Bhasani was the only one who had actually moved in since her residence was on the Tyk Coast overlooking the Ngyn Ocean.

The other masters' lessons were worse than Bhasani's. Jian had initially especially been looking forward to his lesson with Master Soa, whose eternal bright light style was peerless with its defensive prowess, which even Taishi often admitted was a weakness in the windwhispering style. That was why he was so chagrined when Sohn came to their first lesson with a stack of books instead of his usual saber and shield.

"Picking up where we left off your education on the proper ways of the court," the eternal bright light master droned. To be fair, he looked as enthusiastic about the topic as Jian felt. He also appeared hungover. "Last week was Shulan. This week I want to focus on the Lawkan court, but more importantly, their underworld organizations. No duchy has more powerful criminal organizations than Lawkan. All the big ones are housed on the coast near Manjing. It has to do with the great weather. Lawkan is the headquarters for the Silkspinners, Consortiums, the Tiandi Religion . . ." He shook his finger. "They're the biggest crooks."

The Soa family were once prominent Xing nobles, whose court was famous for being particularly violent and murderous. Because of that, decorum was specially observed, lest a perceived slight lead to a challenge to the death. There were specific ways to paint one's face depending on the court, specific ways to bow, and specific ways to address each duke. There were strict decorum and rituals to enter and leave the court. Apparently, Yanso of Gyian would cut off the queue of any man who turned his back on him while he was on the dais. Alternatively, Dongshi of Lawkan, reputed to have a sensitive nose, required every person to bathe with rosemary leaves and lemongrass oils before entering his court.

Master Soa was also a noted tactician, having been a battlelord who led Xing forces into the Grass Sea at one point. Jian spent many of his late afternoons with Sohn—the master was a late riser—learning about strategy, tactics, and military maneuvers. Fausan relieved Sohn for their next class, giving Jian only a few minutes to wolf down some food. The whipfinger master's day usually began and ended late, and so did everything else about his schedule.

Surprisingly, Fausan—jovial, funny, pleasant Uncle Fausan, who had always treated Jian like he was family—was the worst instructor of them all. But then, being treated like family within the war arts was often not a great compliment. The whipfinger master had been tasked with teaching Jian about the Zhuun people, which was actually a hotpot of hundreds of different, smaller ethnic groups and tribes clustered under one banner. The legendary God of Gamblers had traveled the entire world, from the distant White Ghost lands to the other side of the Grass Sea. He had returned with tales of bizarre cultures and even more exotic creatures. Most of his stories were so outlandish they could only be true. He had spent years living among the Katuia, even once claiming to be an honorary clansman of the Jomei. Fausan had also once won a pirate ship in a game of dice, and rather than selling it spent three years as its captain in the Ngyn Ocean. He even supposedly spent a year as a sex slave to the Queen of Siamen after losing to her in a game of strip Siege. He had lost on purpose, or so he claimed. All of these diverse experiences had made Fausan uniquely qualified to mentor Jian on the many cultures and customs within and outside of the Enlightened States.

Out of all his grand adventures, one would think Fausan would make a fascinating instructor. However, the moment he became Jian's instructor, Fausan turned into a no-nonsense authoritative bore, lecturing in a slow, flat monotone sometimes for hours. It was through his lessons with Fausan, though, that Jian learned why the ducal-insured wagons were off-limits, why Lawkan house always faced north, and why the Shulan wore undergarments with knee pads, while the Gyian didn't believe in wearing anything underneath at all. Jian never knew the Zhuun could be so complex and varied. Most of the information seemed insignificant and frivolous, but Fausan ruthlessly hammered every bit of it into his head. He also gave written tests, which was why he was the worst.

All this was in addition to the usual lessons Jian had with Taishi and Zofi. His master still made sure he had the same number of lessons, except sometimes she would stack them so he had to endure three or four lessons a day, which amplified an already miserable situation. He didn't understand why she was pushing him so hard. It was all too much.

Jian was weary to the bone and dripping with sweat by the time the King set. The heat had been relentless the past few days. All these individual classes and training left him spent, and this didn't include his usual chores, which he now had to do in the evenings because that was the only time he had left in the day.

Night had crashed, sudden and thick. Dark clouds were rolling and rumbling like ocean waves across the heavens by the time Jian had finished stacking the kitchen's dwindled stack of firewood. He had thought his day had finished when he noticed the six buckets of slop lined just outside the door. He had forgotten to feed the pigs again. Those animals did not take kindly to missing meals and would often break out of their pens in search of food. That was especially bad when Forty-Two was around. As expected, the shishi had a ravenous appetite.

Taishi and Sohn were exchanging heated words just outside the storeroom. Taishi's voice was cutting. "There are already too many mouths to feed, especially with your bottomless appetite. What I don't need is you breaking into the cooking supplies because you can't find booze. For the last time, the rice wine is not for drinking. How are we supposed to cook?"

"You're out of everything else," he complained.

"That doesn't mean you get to drink the cooking wine," she hissed. "You need to take care of this problem before it kills you."

"Why are we talking about *me* at all? You're the one who came begging for favors." He brushed her off. "Besides, it's my problem, not yours. Butt out."

She scowled. "It *is* my problem when I tell everyone else why there's no dinner tonight."

He scowled back. "That's unfair. I'm a guest."

"You're a depraved drunk." She pointed in a seemingly random direction. "Now, figure out how to get three jugs of cooking wine. Send your disciple if you must."

Sohn looked downcast. "I had to let Wyn go."

Taishi feigned being distraught. "It's been over two months since you two became a pair. I thought you two were forever."

The eternal bright light master huffed. "She was stealing from me. You believe that? The youths these days are so ungrateful."

"You've gone through nine disciples in the past two years," said Taishi. "Perhaps it's time for a little self-reflection. What is the common element between all of them?"

"They're ungrateful and lazy," he declared.

"Replace the cooking wine, Soa Sohn, or there will be abyss to pay." Taishi turned away. "Zofi says we have enough for only four or five days."

"I can't do it alone."

Jian couldn't mask his eagerness as he rushed forward, his hand raised. "I'll help."

Taishi sniffed. "Out of the question, Villain of the Tiandi."

"Please, master, let me go to Bahngtown." Jian stopped short of throwing himself at her feet but hadn't ruled it out yet. "I've been stuck here months bored out of my existence. Just let me take one trip to the outpost. I'll be careful. I'll wear a disguise."

"Let the boy go, Taishi," said Sohn. "You can't train a proper war artist by wrapping his fists with pillows. The danger will sharpen him in here." He tapped his right temple.

"You have some shopping to do, Master Soa," she barked. "I suggest you get going." She turned back to Jian and leaned in. The deep crease lines on her forehead grew deeper. "The next time you go to Bahngtown will be over my dead body because you will have shattered my spine and absorbed my jing and become the new Windwhispering School of the Zhang lineage of the Ling family style. And then you will fulfill the Prophecy of the Tiandi and save the Zhuun people. Until then, go clean out the chicken coop."

CHAPTER TWENTY-ONE

THE SUMMONS

That morning, the Diyu Temple became very crowded. More than it had been over the past few months with this ragtag group of over-the-hill and under-the-hill war artists. That was often the pairing because those in between would be adventuring out in the world, fulfilling contracts, earning bounties, and fighting worthy campaigns. Taishi glanced over at the practice yard where Jian and Hachi were quarter-speed sparring. The young and the old.

Taishi felt the quiver in her shoulders. She may have to move up Jian's test. It would be disastrous if her body gave out before she had the chance to administer it. Then he would have no chance against the Eternal Khan, or to fulfill whatever the prophecy required. That was the risk of delaying the test. However, there was also more to being a war artist than raw ability and power. A great war artist must also possess his master's wisdom and insights. It is the mentor who guides and molds their heir to properly shape and temper the blade as well as when to hone or sharpen its edge.

When Jian succeeded her, he would become the grandmaster of the Windwhispering School of the Zhang lineage. The family style would depend on how much he deviated from her teachings. It would also mean Jian had killed her. That would mean he would be alone, without guidance or martial family support. That had always been the weakness of the Zhang lineage. A fatal flaw, really.

The final result of her lineage's narrow hierarchy structure and sacrifices creates incredibly powerful but often mentally immature and ill-prepared war artists. It was a toxic brew, one that could cause terrible decisions ending with terrible results, leaving a lifetime of regrets. It had happened to her father. It had happened to Taishi. Her eyes settled on her disciple. And she was going to willingly pass this curse along to Jian. Live a long, bitter life of remorse or die young and quickly at the Khan's giant rough and beefy hands. Which was worst? She wasn't sure.

Taishi was in the midst of her morning meditation when the old rooster began to hack a raspy crow for all he was worth. He must have been startled since his pipes took a few stuttering cries before it finally reached its proper pitch. The young rooster soon joined in, and soon the two were each doing their best to one-up each other. Taishi opened her eyes and blew out an annoyed sigh. She really needed to eat one of these birds soon.

Then she checked the clock and frowned. It was nearly noon and a peculiar time for the old cock to scream such a fuss. He usually wasn't one to make a stink over trivial matters. Something must have riled him up. The old crow called once more, this time more forcefully. The reigning king wasn't ready to give up the throne just yet.

"Your time has not yet come, young princeling," she muttered, rising to her feet. Taishi was strangely comforted by that. She was rooting for the old bird to hang on.

She better check up on it before whatever it was killed a dozen hens. It was probably nothing, but it could also be a jungle tiger or a giant worm. These predators could kill a dozen chickens in the time it would take her to get dressed, and she was betting on good poultry futures this coming cycle.

Taishi rose from her meditation spot at the pagoda and pawed the ground with her feet until she located her llama slippers. She brushed off the dust and leaves on her lap and crossed the yard toward the coop where the two roosters were still battling it out. Their continued crowing was a good signal that no predator had broken into the coop yet. She hoped it wasn't a giant worm. The slime those things left behind was awful to clean, and she wasn't in the mood to have to draw a cold bath this chilly morning. Maybe it was an edible predator. That would be nice.

Taishi was not surprised to meet Bhasani and Sonaya halfway across the yard. For all her smooth talking and relaxed facade, the drowned fist master had always been a bit of an anxious woman stemming back to their childhood. "I think your roosters are broken," Bhasani remarked. "You should do that old cock a favor and put him down."

"My roosters are doing exactly what they're supposed to do," she replied. "It's probably nothing. Figure out what's riling them up. Be quick about it." It was obviously an order, but there was no chance Bhasani was going to respond to that command. That left . . .

Sonaya hesitated only a moment before bowing. "I will see to it, master."

The two women watched Sonaya slide open the main doors and hurry off to carry out her task.

"She's a good girl," said Taishi. "She'll carry your lineage well."

The drowned fist master barely registered the praise. "Of course she is, and of course she will."

Taishi hid her smirk. The woman had not changed in more than forty years. The roosters went quiet a moment later. An eerie silence filled in the void, interrupted only by the steady cadence of chirping crickets.

Fausan emerged from the main house, his robe half unbuttoned and his carefully combed hair a frazzled mess. He was wearing the infamous red bullet vest that had been synonymous with the God of Gambling since back during his prime. He shivered. "Those birds of yours have some pipes. How much do you want for them?"

"They're not for sale." That was a reflexive answer. Taishi mulled it over again and reconsidered. "Jian is going to need some help with building a smokehouse later this year. Send Hachi over for a few days and I'll give you the younger rooster."

"Done."

"Master Ling," called Sonaya a few moments later. "Visitors at the north end of the pillar on righteous lions."

Taishi frowned. Just in case, she gestured at a club she used to kill rats resting on the garden table and flicked it to her hand. "Let's go say hello."

The pride of shishi arrived at the edge of the plateau. Jian was of course the first to notice them. The boy had been trying to send hints about getting one for weeks. It was never going to happen. Those giant kitties ate more in one meal than any two people in a day. Jian would have to decide who got to eat every day, himself or the shishi. These giant guardian lions certainly fell into the category of being so ugly they're cute for most. To Taishi, they were just ugly.

That was a lot of shishi, however, which could mean only one thing. Taishi shielded her eyes from the King's high-noon glare and waved. "Urwan, you old, seven-legged goat. What are you doing here?"

The former horselord of Gyian cut an imposing and impressive figure as he rode toward them on his magnificent black righteous lion with its flowing, braided mane. Psy Urwan had the look of a horseman if there ever was a look. He was tall, with lanky limbs, and a long, lean body. His face was equally long, sharp, and hard, with a narrow cheek and long chin. His mane of black hair, now peppered with silver, was as lush as ever and hung loosely braided in his wake. The man knew how to make an entrance. There was always something so cocky and self-assured about horsemen. It was an intangible trait that both attracted and annoyed her, but then that was what she could say about most of her love life.

Taishi was fond of Urwan. The two had fought on opposing sides more often than not, although never directly against each other. Urwan usually found himself fighting on the wrong side of history, but his heart was always in the right place. That was what he got for being a general flying Yanso's banner. Taishi was glad she never had to fight her friend. She stared at his long, square jaw. The man was simply too pretty to kill.

The master's guardian lion had been equally as impressive as his master from afar, and even more so up close. It was obviously the head of the pride. The creature's curly mane sprayed in all directions like a water fountain. Its coat, a glowing midnight sheen, and thick muscles rippled underneath its skin. It had large, luminous, round eyes with an intense stare that could shatter the will of lesser creatures. Even facing it Taishi had to suppress the urge to avert her eyes. The shishi was noble, intimidating, and terrible all at the same time.

Taishi looked over at Jian gawking at the guardian lions and Zofi gawking at Urwan. She pointed lazily to the side. "Put your ugly cat in the pen. Make sure it doesn't touch my chickens. Tea? It's too early to get drunk, but for you, I'll make an exception."

"We won't be staying long," said the horselord.

"We'll at least stay long enough for tea," said a strong woman's voice.

Taishi looked over Urwan's shoulders to see Naifun swing off her guardian lion. Taishi's spirits fell slightly. The teahouse master was here. Not that she didn't enjoy the woman's company, but this certainly wasn't a social call. The teahouse master traveled for no one these days. Something serious was afoot.

Naifun was in one of her usual cheerful colorful outfits: a tight floral shirt under checkered robes and several layers of patterned bright small cloaks fluttering at her back alongside her bone white hair. Flanking the tea master were two girls dedicatedly assisting their master with every step. The teahouse master's face was etched with deep lines around her cheeks and forehead. Her eyes were calculating. No one sent this much talent unless there was an important ask. She honestly looked silly. No one would have guessed that this strange old woman once led one of the most decorated teahouses in the realm. There were no finer spies throughout the Enlightened States. Her teahouse entering a contract could alter the outcome of wars. There was no secret safe from her.

That was a long time ago. Naifun, like Kasa, hailed from the last golden age of great heroes, a time when the land was filled plenty with a great number of mighty and noble war artists. Taishi had worshiped many of these heroes when she was a young girl. It had been a grand time to be alive in the lunar court, putting to pen and song and tongue the grand adventures of the heroes of this age.

Taishi offered a deep, reverential bow. "Zofi, prepare a pot of tea."

Naifun held up a small silk pouch. "Here, use my tea leaves. I brought a truffle lychee blend. Great aftertaste and good for your complexion."

She tossed it to Zofi. Taishi could already see the girl's eyes widen, and she held her arms wide as if she were going to hug the pouch. Taishi plucked it out of the air and then handed it to the mapmaker's daughter. "How generous of you, tea master."

"Your tea is always skunk, Taishi. I can't tell if you have a terrible palate or if you're just cheap."

A bit of both. Taishi counted heads and turned to Jian. "Prepare the house for our unexpected but welcome guests. Set a table for four— more—guests." This place was getting awfully crowded. Still, the company of these two was welcome.

"Again, our deepest apologies for intruding unannounced, Taishi," continued Urwan, "but like I said we must depart soon if we are to reach our next stop by nightfall."

"I'll bring the tea out." Zofi bowed and hurried off.

Jian offered a hand to the prettier of Naifun's girls. "Can I take these for you? I'm Jian."

"Fourth time now, Champion of the Five Under Heaven." The girl ignored his offered hand and slipped off the guardian lion gracefully, leaving Jian standing there looking confused. *That poor sot. He'll figure it out one of these days.*

By now word had gotten to the rest of the temple that company had arrived, and they had brought with them an entire pride of shishis. The rest of the boys around the plateau appeared a few moments later.

Taishi watched as those large ugly cats rolled in the dirt and pounced on each other as if kittens. "Urwan," she said, puzzled. "Why did you bring so many guardian lions when there are only four of you?"

"We're picking up some passengers along the way."

Again, with being so cryptic. "Who?" she asked.

"You," he replied matter-of-factly.

"Hah! Good luck with that."

"It's important, Taishi. You know we wouldn't show up like this otherwise." There was a measured pause. "This isn't a request."

She scoffed. "Oh, really? Who's going to enforce it, you?"

Urwan did not look fazed. "Yes, me, because I've been your friend since we were idiot street rats, and have I ever asked anything from you?"

"That doesn't work on me." Taishi shrugged. "So where are you trying to take me?"

Urwan looked as if he were going to tell her and then backed out. "I can't."

"Then," she replied, "by all means, stay for tea, and then safe journeys."

"I'm the one asking," Naifun announced, her usually soothing voice now cutting, leaving little room for disagreement. "But I'm *not* asking. Pack your things. We leave as soon as my teacup is drained."

"I . . ." Taishi had to fight the instinct to stomp her feet.

"My, my. Who dares speak to Ling Taishi in such a brisk manner," chortled Bhasani, arriving with Sonaya. "I'm fond of her already."

Taishi pointed. "This is Narwani Bhasani—"

"Mother of the Drowned Fist," said Naifun, nodding. "Best known for the Betrayal at Eura Gates. That was a terrible thing you did there, lass. You owe Taishi an apology."

Bhasani sighed. "I've tried, a dozen times."

Naifun turned to Taishi. "You should accept her apology."

"Why should I?"

"Because I know why she did it."

"Doesn't matter why. I'm not accepting it until I'm standing over her grave, and perhaps not even then," she replied. "Bhasani, this know-everything is Kua Naifun, tea master of the Hazy Dreams Tea House in Bahngtown."

Bhasani raised an eyebrow. "Naifun the Black Night of Xing?"

"It was a stupid name then, and a stupid name now." Naifun snorted. "When is night not black?"

Well, actually, Master Kua," Fausan interjected, holding up a finger as he arrived from the fields, "I've spent many campaigns in the northern lands, and I can tell you the arctic lights are gorgeous—"

"Go stuff your face, dice god."

"Stuffing my face." Fausan turned and walked out in one smooth motion.

Bhasani was still staring at Naifun. "I always thought you were a man."

"An all too common and foolish assumption." Naifun shrugged. "It doesn't matter anymore. I'm retired, somewhat."

The drowned fist master studied Naifun's swirling robe of bright, clashing colors. "Not so black anymore, I see."

Naifun snorted. "Come to the teahouse sometime, girl. My tea collection rivals the finest houses in the Enlightened States."

Taishi couldn't remember when anyone last called either of them "girl," but generational reverence allowed them great leeway. Respect must always be paid forward because time wins every race.

Taishi was still weighing refusing Naifun's non-request when Fausan barreled into Urwan. "You gray dog, it's been years."

"I saw you just a couple of months back at that Ugly Hom's game night," the horselord replied. "You swept that night if I recall. I can't believe no one has stabbed you for winning so much." The two men's full-throated greeting and embrace concluded with loud slaps on the back. "Good to see you're still alive, God of Gamblers. When was the last time we fought side by side?"

Fausan lowered his voice a notch. "The Madam assassination."

Urwan physically cringed. "Not my finest hour, I admit."

"Not anyone's."

Just like that the two men fell into their usual routine and banter as if not a day had passed. Fausan always took his time with the hellos and goodbyes, treating every greeting with each person like it was the first and last time he'd ever see them. It was a good five minutes before the two men were done catching up.

"How many game nights are you part of?" asked Taishi.

"As many as I'm not banned from." The whipfinger lowered his voice, and the joviality was gone. "I hear you're getting a secret summons to the unknown. Sounds dangerous. Do you need a big brother?"

"That's not necessary," Urwan said hastily. "It's just a sensitive matter we need her to deal with delicately. She'll be back in a day."

Taishi's eyes narrowed. The former Gyian horselord was trustworthy. She would stake her life on it, but games were being played right now. Quite serious ones, by their forced demeanor. Naifun was playing too, for that matter. Who could spook the retired Black Night of the Xing?

"Why, yes," she said. "Company would be appreciated, brother."

Bhasani stepped next to Taishi. "A sister should watch a sister's back."

"Fine." Taishi was secretly glad. "Just don't stab it like you did last time."

The Black Night of Xing did not look impressed. "I don't care who is going. Just you three, however. We don't have enough shishi for your entire entourage. If anything, it gives me an excuse to *not* go."

"I guess I'll join too," said Sohn, strolling to the training yard from the other side of the plateau.

The old woman suddenly moved with alarming speed, her bright, clashing sheer robes fluttering in the breeze like an exotic butterfly. She jabbed a finger in his face. "You dog! How dare you show your face in my presence?" The way she said "dog" was vastly different from the way Fausan had.

Sohn blinked and stammered. "I, um, I'm a guest here."

"What did he do now?" asked Fausan.

The tea master scowled. "I have a list. It's long, and it begins with his tab that is large enough to purchase an estate in Allanto. It continues with the time he tried to poach one of my girls to be his heir. It ends with the time he stumbled into the teahouse stinking of plum wine, passing out in my foyer, and soiling himself on top of my expensive White Ghost rug."

"Oh, come on," said Sohn weakly. "It was an ugly rug."

"The strange abstract one with all those interlinking boxes?" said Fausan. "It was an insulting waste of cloth, in my opinion."

"I know that rug. It *was* hideous," Urwan agreed.

"It was imported spider silk from the other side of the Ngyn Ocean," the tea master snapped. Then she admitted, "Yes, it was ugly, but that's beside the point. It's not a thing for *that* wretched dog to piss and ruin it." An uncomfortable silence occupied the space for a few moments.

"So," Taishi drawled, "does that mean he's coming?"

"Not a chance," snapped Naifun. "I would rather kill him."

"There's a long line for that," grumbled Sohn.

"So why are you involved?" Taishi asked Naifun. "I thought you had bowed out of the lunar court."

"Oh, I'm not," said the Black Night of Xing. "I'm only here to order you to go. Looks like with this many people being added to the party, you will need my shishi anyway. Stop by soon after you return, Taishi. It's been too long since you've visited. Your tab has gotten too large and you have an overdue book."

"Yes, Naifun," Taishi muttered.

"There are enough shishi for each master to bring their disciple," added Urwan. "Pack lightly. Don't worry about rations, and make sure you bring a vomit sack if you're not familiar with riding righteous lions."

Taishi leaned into Zofi. "Make sure you pack one for me."

"I'll pack light." Jian bounced excitedly on his feet. The boy probably couldn't wait to escape the pillar. The fact he thought he was going to ride a guardian lion was just a plus. She almost felt bad breaking this to him. "Jian, I'll be back in a few days. Focus on your training and studies. I want you to be able to move in place on a slow current by the time I return."

"What?" he shrieked. "This is so unfair."

Taishi turned her back to him as if to close the issue. "Zofi, gather your things. Bring parchment and ink. You're only allowed to bring one book."

"Why her?" Jian continued to plead.

"Why me?" she pleaded as well.

"I have insolent wards." There was no need to justify her decision. "Sohn, you're in charge. Make sure nothing happens or I'll flay your skin with ghost peppers. No matter what, keep Jian safe and on the temple grounds. He is not to leave. Understood?"

Sohn pouted, offended at being left out. This was obviously a war artist round-up, and to not be invited could be viewed as a grave insult. He huffed away. "Yes, Master Ling Taishi. Whatever you say. I bet you're going to some boring stupid place anyway."

"We have room for one more," said Urwan.

"Hachi?" said Fausan. "I don't like carrying my own bags."

Taishi nodded.

Bhasani shrugged. "My daughter's allergic to these creatures. Her skin gets irritable and red. Terrible for her complexion."

Taishi turned to leave. "Gather your things. Meet back here in five."

Zofi caught up with her as they headed back to the main house. "Excuse me, Taishi, but why are you asking me to come along? I'm useless in a fight."

Taishi chuckled. "You're traveling with four legitimate master war artists, all renowned. Do you think we need the middling ability of one of our twig-armed disciples?" She tapped the mapmaker's daughter on the forehead. "No, girl, that's precisely why it's you. The five war artists will walk into a room and see the blades and the dangers. I want someone who can see the clues and opportunities."

"I'm deathly afraid of heights." The confession came out hardly louder than a whisper. "I get above a tall branch and the world gets all woozy."

"I don't care," said Taishi. "Remember what you told me when we first set sail on the sand snake and we raced down that first dune?"

Zofi considered. "I told you to get the scream out of your system."

"There you go." Taishi pointed at the water clock. "Four minutes. You better hurry and pack your things."

"Sure, Taishi." She turned back to face Taishi as she walked away. "Why do you call Urwan a seven-legged goat?"

"Figure it out," said Taishi, disappearing into her quarters.

CHAPTER TWENTY-TWO

PALACE LIFE

The morning gong reverberated throughout the two sub-levels of the servants' corridors outside the small, windowless chamber Qisami shared with two other girls. Sleep like a leaf blowing in the breeze, her training pool litter mother used to drone every morning. Qisami was the first out of bed to scrub her face with a damp rag while the water in the basin was still clean. She was already dressed and painting her face by the time the second gong sounded.

Qisami glanced at the bed adjacent to hers. "Porla, dally any longer and you'll get brat duty."

The younger girl, who had just joined the estate staff a few weeks ago, rolled the other way and pulled the sheets over her head. "Just five more minutes. I was having the most wonderful dream."

Qisami was tempted to leave the girl to her hubris, but Estatekeeper Hari was quick to annoyance when someone was late and tended to spray her ire at the rest of the staff. "Come on, get up. I'm not getting yelled at because you can't stop dreaming about the handsome young guard at the second palace's front gates."

Ruli, their other roommate, who was old enough to be their mother, agreed as she buttoned her robes. "Kiki's right, lazy girl. If you're late again, we'll never hear the end of it. A few more tardies and you'll get thrown out onto the streets and end up in a room salon."

Porla sat up and became weepy. She buried her face in her hands. "I want to go home. I miss my mam. Please don't send me back to that awful Tower of Noble Delights. Those concubines are horrid creatures."

They really were, but Qisami kept that to herself. She had already done her stint with those nasty bitches. The ducal mistresses were regarded as just beneath the ducal family while on estate grounds. Every member of the estate staff dreaded working in the Tower of Noble Delights. The concubines waged their own shadowy war against one another in their struggle to climb the standings to become the duke's first concubine. Any servant who wasn't careful would quickly find themselves collateral damage or sucked into their deadly intrigue.

"Be careful, stupid girl," Ruli scolded. "If your opinions get back to any of those ladies, they'll have your tongue."

Qisami moved next to the girl and wrapped her arms around the petite little thing's shoulders. She was barely more than a child. Qisami patted her narrow, freckled face. "There, there, gentle Porla. I feel your pain. Trust me when I say it will get better."

The girl buried her head in Qisami's shoulder and sobbed. "Thank you, Kiki. You're the kindest person in the entire estate."

Qisami kept a straight face. She didn't blame the girl for being so miserable and despondent. Joining the ducal house staff as the lowest servant was usually a poor career choice, and a life very few chose of their own free will. Ruli and Porla both belonged to peasant families who had fallen behind on their taxes and indentured them to Yanso's household. With Karaja, the girl whose bed Porla now slept in, her village had volunteered her indentured servitude in order to buy enough grain and meat to survive a third cycle. There were many servants with comparable stories, and an arrangement unique to Gyian. Ruli had joined the ducal household under Yanso's grandfather. Karaja, on the other hand, had been a servant only a week before catching the duke's fancy. She joined the concubine's tower later that day. Technically, Qisami didn't join the estate staff by choice either, but that was the excuse she used. She was thankful when Porla joined so she was no longer the low woman in the quarters. Everything in their shared quarters was based on seniority. The low woman always had the worst duties and had to bathe last.

Qisami finished buttoning her dress and adorning her servant's hair wrap, and left the room, joining a light rush of servants streaming down the hallway and up the stairs to the main level. Several other servants passed by. The dawn shift was always busy.

"Good morning, Kiki!"

"Hello, little flower."

The waves of servants greeting her continued.

"Good morning to you." She beamed at each greeting and waved back. "Happy mornings to you, dear friends!" Qisami could play the game as well as any. She kept the bright, porcelain frozen smile and greeted at the waves of servants passing by. This estate had an unusually cheerful and friendly bunch of servants. It was deeply annoying.

She only tolerated most of the estate staff and had death-marked a dozen or so of them, but they were unofficial tallies. She actually didn't care enough to officially use her blood to make it serious. This was more for fun.

Someone collided with her and squeezed her hand. "You would not believe what I just heard."

That could only be Hilao, her best friend at the estate. She was a pretty servantborn about the same age as Qisami, with wavy dark hair and a narrow triangular face. She was annoying in the chatty and cheerful sense, but her button nose was keen for gossip, which made her a valuable asset. Not to mention she was a lot of fun. Qisami believed that the only reason a noble hadn't elevated her to concubine yet was because she talked too much. Qisami had even death-marked her once because she never stopped talking—unofficially, of course.

"Oooh, what is it?" Qisami bubbled back, matching the woman's sugary intensity.

"Su told me that Waya, who shares a room with Shinqi, told her that . . ." She made a face and pointed at her belly.

"Nooooo wayyyy!" Shinqi was lovely. Waya and Su not so much, but neither enough to have to go through the hassle of murdering.

"Yaaasssss waaaay!"

Their heads touched as they giggled with mock indignation. "Do you know who the father is?"

"Su wouldn't say. One of the servants in the training field."

It better not be Cyyk. It better not be Cyyk. It better not be Cyyk.

The young nobleman's handsome but roguish face was a popular topic of conversation among the younger staff. Qisami had strictly forbidden him from fishing in this pond. The last thing the cell needed was a paternity problem. It would be catastrophic if it was a nobleman's daughter. It was only a small worry, however. Cyyk was a nobleman's son, albeit a minor one, so he took his lineage and family name quite seriously. No degree of being a shadowkill grunt could wipe off the stink of nobility, although if he ever did accidentally pop a baby, Qisami was sure as hell going to garnish his earnings to take care of it.

The morning staff congregated in their mess room as Estatekeeper Hari, the head of the servants' staff, stood on a small podium at the far end of the room. The woman was a legend among the waitstaff. Wizened, thin, and tall, Hari could throw an imperial stare that could cow a prince. It was said that she was born indentured to the Gyian ducal household. Her grandmother was an indentured servant, her mother was a gardener, and now Hari ran the entire sprawling estate.

"Look sharper, staff. I see too many loose buttons." The estatekeeper's soft, measured voice was just starting to show the signs of her age. She never needed to raise her voice. The room always accommodated her. "Whoever cleaned the guard captain's mess room yesterday did a peasant's job of it. Best rectify that before my next round. Whoever absconded with a half-sack of rice last week, report to the executioner for a lashing." That was all that needed to be said about that. No one dared disobey. The estatekeeper placed the small leather book down and unrolled parchment. "Today, Duke Yanso's schedule will place him in the Shine room, the Diamond Temple, and the Rare Gardens. He'll breakfast in the Flowing Thoughts Garden, lunch at the east pagoda in the life-size Siege game board, and then supper at the Second Palace. If you're a primary at one of these locations, be ready. The rest of you pick up the slack. Lord Hom and family are visiting late in the afternoon. Saba, your team will serve them . . ."

Several more assignments rolled off her tongue in quick succession. Her orders were brief and vague because they needn't be more. Her staff was well trained and loyal. Hari was an exacting woman who ran her large army of servants more tightly than Duchess Sunri with her precious red armies. The estatekeeper would have made a fascinating general in another life.

"Companions," said Hari. "Step forward."

Qisami, along with six other men and women, moved to the forefront of the crowd.

The estatekeeper pointed at the first on the far right. "Hogaan, you're back with Thought Trust Neh's boys. Uana, Lady Qu's daughter." She continued matchmaking until she reached Qisami. "Kiki, Colonel Sya and son are returning to North Pengnin, so you are off that service. However, Lord Aki Niam is arriving with his entire family. He has a large family so the nanny brigade requested help. I'm reassigning you."

Qisami bowed, although she was biting her lips. Sya's son was sixteen and hardly needed a companion other than to prevent him from doing stupid things. Young children, however, were her worst nightmare.

"One last thing," said Hari, closing out the meeting. "As you know, three dukes are gathering at Allanto for important negotiations. It is our job as estate staff to represent Duke Yanso with great honor and impeccable service. Therefore, all lower staff are being assigned double duties to clean and prepare the estate for their arrival. Check the board for your secondary assignments this week. I expect them to be completed in addition to your primary duties. Dismissed."

The last order wasn't surprising. As a lowly companion, Qisami was at the same rank as a scullerymaiden and often assigned the worst dog-piss jobs. Whether it was joining the night brigade or being ordered to stomp grapes or wash laundry, Kiki's name was often called. It was how things were when you start at the bottom. In fact, it happened so frequently early on that she started volunteering for some of the bad jobs just to avoid some of the worse jobs. Good reputation, good latitude, as a shadowkill saying goes. Her ploy so far had not been successful, and she just ended up having to work all the gross jobs.

In many ways, it reminded Qisami of her litter back during the training pools. The girls in her Bo Po Mo Fo training pool were probably the closest thing she had to a family. She also hated all of her pool sisters. The only reason she didn't mark any of them for death was because that meant they would have marked her for death, and then they would spend the rest of their lives expecting someone to jump them from the shadows.

Today Qisami had been assigned to the geese crew. Yanso owned eight large palaces and dozens more guesthouses and administration buildings, all running along the main strip of his estate. The geese crew was a gaggle of five scullerymaidens who would flood into the building to open the drapes, set the water clocks, and light the sconces. They would dust and put on fresh sheets and light the kitchen hearths for whenever the culinary brigade arrived. Qisami detested cleaning, but it was certainly better than washing diapers or prepping food.

Qisami deeply hoped her cell would activate soon. Working as a servant as cover was annoying. She had not heard a peep from Firstwife in a while, and now she was feeling antsy. Things had been quiet for too long, although she surprisingly found herself not hating the life of a servant either. There was something charming about living as estate staff in their own little isolated bubble world here within Yanso's palatial estate. It was fascinating to see the same alliances, betrayals, and burgeoning power struggles that happened in this microcosm, albeit with lower stakes.

After her stint with the geese crew, Qisami rushed back to the Grand Tower of the Blessed Servitude with just enough time to change to a new set of servant robes. Geese duty could get very dusty.

Ruli was sitting on her bed soaking her feet in a salt tub when she hurried in. "Always on the go, girl. Someone wants to be head servant one day."

"You'll rue that day," she quipped, checking herself in the mirror one last time. Being busy all the time also gave her leeway to run her many extracurricular activities here on the estate. "I'm off to be a plaything for the new brats."

"See you at supper, girl."

Qisami departed the servants' tower again and hurried across the campus toward the eastern end of the estate. She had to circle around two quadrants to reach Aki manor. There was a whole hierarchy of real estate along the strip based on the proximity to the first two palaces. This manor was smaller than Qisami imagined a highlord would possess, yet it was certainly luxurious, with an inner archipelago of island buildings in a pond connected by bright red bridges. Also, its proximity to the duke could not be overlooked. Owning the manor on the strip next to the second palace, Duke Yanso's primary residence, was a statement.

She strolled alongside the River of Purity and Richness, which was a shallow man-made stream that crossed diagonally from one corner of the estate to the other. The two main roads in the estate, cutting east to west and north to south, were named Strip of a Thousand Golden Gazes and Path to Eternal Triumph, or simply just Long Strip and Short Strip. They intersected in the middle of the estate at the Grand Imperial Palace of Bountiful Wisdom, or simply First Palace to the rest of the working class. Both strips were lined with opulent buildings, temples, and palaces, and adorned with impeccably manicured gardens and impressive statues and artwork curated from across the known world. Or so Qisami had heard. She hadn't seen it yet. Being treated like a second-class citizen and forced to walk the service tunnels and passages was deeply annoying.

Yanso, much more so than his peers, enjoyed playing the part of a duke. The duke was by far the wealthiest person in the Enlightened States and fancied himself a purveyor and collector of beautiful things. He fancied opulence, showing off impressive feats of construction and beautiful artwork, always presenting a gorgeous facade while the ugly bits got tucked away. Only the nobility, guests, and the affluent were allowed on those strips.

The servants' quarters, guard barracks, storerooms, and other lowly administrative buildings—anything not deemed attractive to the duke's eye—were nestled into the corners of the estate. The servants, guards, and staff were required to take underground tunnels to not blemish the strips' impeccable presentations. Qisami hated walking through those dank passages. They always smelled like sewage. She reached the entrance to one such tunnel and grabbed the lantern hanging on a hook. She proceeded down the wide but low path. Despite her diminutive size, she felt cramped down here. Qisami hummed, slightly off-key, letting her voice carry and echo. She held faint, hazy memories of her mother singing when she was a little girl. The humming was the only thing she remembered.

Once she emerged from the pedway, it was a short jaunt through one of the servants' quarters, weaving through a tight maze of narrow streets and poorly constructed hovels sandwiched together. The cobblestone paths were rough, and the faint odor of urine lingered in the air. She arrived at the servants' entrance to the Aki manor a little later.

The wet nurse, who was part of the powerful nanny brigade, was waiting. The older, plump woman looked Qisami up and down, frowning. "You look like a child yourself. Do you like little ones, Companion Kiki?"

Only to hold for ransom, maybe. Qisami kept her eyes low. "Oh, yes, very much. I hope to have several of my own one day." She may have laid it on a little too thick there.

"Good. Follow."

The wet nurse led Qisami through a pair of bright yellow gates and around back to an inner courtyard where the duke and his family were settling in after their long journey from Shinya, Lord Aki's main city. Qisami heard the bubbly young children laughing and shouting before she saw them. She was already annoyed.

The wet nurse continued up an arched stairway leading to a squat pagoda that seemed to hover over a small waterfall. "The children are enjoying the day here." The wet nurse clapped her hands. "Akiya, Akiana," she said, "Come here, my ladies."

Qisami wasn't sure what to expect. She was apprehensive that she was annoyed, and annoyed that she was apprehensive. Small children set her hair on end. Noble children were worse. Those spoiled yolks were like dumb, untrained dogs, pissing all over the place without consequence. Honestly, Qisami even hated other children when she was a child, long before the Consortium snatched her up and locked her into a training pool. At least she thought she did. Those memories weren't strong.

The first girl appeared from behind the doorway. She was dressed exactly how you would expect a rich brat would dress, in long, silky robes with loose sleeves, a painted face, plump belly, and fingers soft as veal. She was pretty, with big, round eyes and an innocent smile. She held something behind her back. It was probably gross.

"Akiya," said the wet nurse. "This is Kiki. She is watching you and your sister today, by personal request."

"What was that?" asked Qisami. "Whose personal request?"

The little girl walked up to Qisami as if they were equals. "Hi." She whipped out her pink-gloved hand and offered a cut long-stem bright yellow flower.

Qisami hadn't expected that, and she accepted the gift. "Why, thank you."

The girl giggled, as if knowing some inside joke, and fled back into the pagoda structure. The wet nurse shrugged. "Akiya's a shy, slippery one." She added, "That flower is poisonous."

Qisami immediately let it go and scowled. "So that's how it's going to be."

Akiana came next. She was the mirror of Akiya, with the same eyes, pointed nose, and pursed lips. But where the first twin exuded sweetness with her shy smile and gentle demeanor, this smile, Akiana's, was set in a scowl. She carried what appeared to be a tin knife. Many noble children began their war arts training at about this age. This must be the girl's first blade, so it was dull. Not like a child could break the skin anyway, regardless of the blade's edge.

Akiana pointed the weapon at Qisami and stomped her foot. "This is my palace, foul yellow-tooth monster. I, the warrior princess of the green pagoda, will cut you into bits and feed you to my Meow Meow."

"Akiana is the intense one," said the wet nurse. "You're to serve as anything they choose until their bedtime. If there is an emergency, ring the rope bell. Make sure no injury or vice befouls the children. Your life is worth sacrificing for their safety. Understood?"

Qisami nodded. Once she was alone, she carefully stepped to the pagoda and stuck her head inside, and then was promptly pricked in the thigh by the warrior princess. "Ow, you little cunty piglet," she snarled.

Then Qisami remembered her place and covered her mouth, but it was too late. Both girls stared at Qisami, mouths hanging open. This was probably the first time a servant had ever raised their voice to them.

"I mean, my apologies, my lady. Please forgive me." Qisami was throwing herself at the feet of two four-year-olds. Surely this was her new low.

The girls giggled. Akiana roared and charged Qisami once more, trying to draw more blood. Qisami played with the girl a little, turning her around with playful slaps, and then she shoved the little snot face-first into the ground.

"Oops," she muttered.

To her surprise, the girl was tough. She leaped back to her feet and attempted to murder Qisami again. In a way, Akiana endeared herself to Qisami this way.

Meanwhile, Akiya had latched on to Qisami's left leg and was just enjoying the ride as Qisami stomped around. Every once in a while she would try to stick a long goose feather up in her armpit, or tickle-pit, as the little girl liked to call it.

Qisami spent the rest of the time chasing the two little monsters in what ended up being an exhausting and strangely satisfying day. The last thing she learned, however, before the night ended was that, yes, a young child actually *could* break skin with a dull blade if they tried hard enough.

CHAPTER TWENTY-THREE

THE SUN UNDER LAGOON

A harmony of gongs rang over the whistling wind outside Sali's tent. She remained still, sitting cross-legged with her eyes closed, her hands resting on her knees, palms facing up. Her left forefinger closed a circle with her left thumb, while her middle finger did the same on the right. Someone rustled off to the side.

"Sit," she said.

"The chords just called for you," said Hampa. Her neophyte was supposed to be meditating as well.

"Stay." The captain of the *Hana Iceberg* had given Sali her own specific tone as a means to summon her. At first, Sali was offended. She was not some dog to be called with a whistle. By the end of the first day on board the *Hana Iceberg*, she was glad to have been assigned a call and wanted to give Hampa and Daewon tones too. The captain had refused. Only Sali got the dog whistle. She guessed she should feel honored.

Hampa, failing at meditating next to her, was a rule follower with a keen sense of justice. Both were noble traits that would likely get him killed one day. But that could just be Sali's own acrimony more than anything else. She too once dreamed ambitiously with lofty ideals. The descent into cynicism was a rite of passage all war artists must take on their own.

The chord sounded again. Hampa shuffled once more. Breaking the rules made him anxious. It was a cute trait—if he were three years old. A viperstrike must often exist in the gray.

Sali recentered herself. She had been fretting about Hampa lately. There were very few viperstrikes left. It would be up to Hampa, as her neophyte, to rebuild their sect. It was a burden she was not confident he could manage. She felt as if she was failing in training him and in so doing, doomed her viperstrike sect to extinction. It shamed her to think it was she who would be the one to sever their lineage.

The chord rang a third time.

She sensed her neophyte's uneasiness. "Fine. I'll see what the captain wants. You go to the training dummy and work on that combination I taught you, and keep your elbows in, you quacking duck."

Hampa scrambled to his feet and was already halfway out of the tent when she opened her eyes. Sali took her time. It wasn't like he could go on ahead without her. She stood and stretched. She was feeling her age and failing health much more acutely in this wintry weather. Her strength ebbed away here in the True Freeze with each passing day. She donned a seal fur suit one of the crew had sold to her and emerged from the tent a few moments later.

Sali continued down the long wooden path leading to the bow of the *Hana Iceberg*. She had initially been leery of sailing on a large hunk of ice, especially since she could see parts of it break away due to the constant waves battering against it. The captain had assured her that there was no need to worry. Ice barges constantly shed ice.

"What happens when you lose too much ice?" she had asked.

"We dismantle the masts, buildings, and paddlewheels from what's left of the ship, and then reassemble all the pieces on a fresh-cut chunk of iceberg," he said. "Wood is scarce up here, nearer the True Freeze, but ice is the most abundant resource." It was brilliant, really.

Sali had taken ill the moment they lost sight of land and she was suddenly surrounded by this vast emptiness. The clear water seemed as endless as the empty skies above, both equally desolate. She felt like a tiny sliver of grass among an ocean of green. This far north, night had faded until they were traveling in perpetual dawn. The days melded together as the *Hana Iceberg* traveled deeper into the sea at a slow float.

With little else to do, Sali spent most of her time aboard either meditating or training Hampa. Regardless of her skepticism whether he would ever be worthy of the title she bore, Sali trained her neophyte as diligently as if she were training her own blood. They passed the time sparring, running forms, and stretching. Even after three years, the lad was as stiff as an arthritic bull.

She found her neophyte a little ways up the iceberg in the practice yard hacking at a block of ice with his ax and mace. These were his chosen weapons, known as a quarreling couple. It was an unusual choice for a viperstrike, but it catered to his strengths and masked his weaknesses.

He waved them in small circles before suddenly charging forward, swinging and thrusting at the ice block training dummy. Hampa's techniques were hesitant, but fine. His footwork was as shifty as if he were wearing stone shoes, but otherwise fine. His swings weren't crisp or quick, but they were . . . fine. His creativity and originality when flowing with the techniques could be one of those traits where he was less than fine, below average, if you will. Everything about his war arts practice was perfectly adequate. On second glance, his stance was too far forward, his feet were too far apart, and his back too stiff.

"Stop being insufferable," she muttered. Sali still couldn't help but scowl at his elbows. Still flaring out too wide like a flapping duck. It was going to get him smashed one day.

Hampa finally noticed her observing and grinned, waving her over. "How do I look?"

"Fine." She hesitated. No, it wasn't. "I want to glue your elbows to your body."

Sali continued on, past the tents and cargo hold, and then through the kitchen and dining hearth before finally heading up a set of stairs to a large wooden housing that extended past the front of the iceberg. Beneath the platform, churning the water, was a large paddlewheel, along with three others just like it on the sides and back, used to steer the barge.

The captain was waiting for her at the bridge peering through an extended eyepiece, sweeping it slowly from one side to the other.

When Sali wasn't meditating or training Hampa, she spent the rest of her time with the captain and his crew. Sali and Captain Lehuangxi Thiraput Cungle soon became fast friends, each recognizing the other's competence in their respective fields. The captain, along with most of his crew, were Happan, who were considered close cousins to the Katuia.

The Happan were once their own horde, roaming the vast Grass Tundra to the northwest. The two hordes had spent centuries clashing and trading, often raiding each other so frequently they practically became related. The blood feuds between them were legendary, with six-act ballads and poetry accompanied by war drums romanticizing it. At some point, the Katuia grew bored with these skirmishes and turned their attention to unification. It took three generations of khans before the Happan horde's flags were torn down and their people welcomed by the blade into their hearth. Even now, hundreds of years later, relationships remained terse between the rim clans and the primary Katuia clans.

The scars of the gyres cut deep into the earth have long memories, as the saying went.

It was unusual for Sali to see such an eclectic and diverse crew living and working together on the barge. Along with the Happan, there were four Tsunarcos, two Zhuun, and even a White Ghost. These were people, in the past, whom she had viewed only as targets. She had a fresh and interesting perspective now seeing this boiling pot of people from all corners of the world.

Sali moved alongside the captain. "How goes it, Captain Lehuangxi Thiraput Cungle?"

He offered his eyepiece. "See for yourself, landlady."

At first, Sali saw nothing except a wall of thick, gray, roiling haze in the distance rising directly before them for as far as the eye could see. Then she noticed hints of color: red and yellow exploding from within the puffy black smoke. The air around that darkness was also visible: greasy and viscous lines swirling in the breeze. The large wall of smoke loomed larger as they approached, covering the horizon from the water level to the sky, curving into a circle along both sides of the horizon. It was strange to see, as they neared the wall of smoke, that the snowing ash appeared to be drifting upward instead of down.

Sali lowered the scope. "What sort of accursed hell have you brought us to, Captain?"

The captain chuckled. He cupped his mouth and spoke into a curved horn that expanded his voice several decibels louder. "Passing through the smoke ring!"

"Passing through the ring," someone echoed, followed by several more. The large gong on the bridge tolled three times. The starboard pipes and port drums replied immediately, followed by the stern strings a few moments later.

"You might want to hold your breath," said the captain with a knowing glint in his eyes.

The *Hana Iceberg* entered the smoke, and Sali choked as soot and ash filled her lungs. A gust of the ash-colored wind brushed and stained her cheek, flurrying the black specks and roiling dirty air funnels. Sulfur itched her nose while the tip of her tongue tasted like burnt dirt. And then just like that, the curtain of darkness passed.

Sali wiped her stinging eyes and looked back as the barge floated toward clear skies, leaving that poisoned wall of smoke behind. The *Hana Iceberg* was once again sailing into clear skies over blue waters, except the seafloor beneath the ship was a glittering kaleidoscope of yellow, white, and red sparkles. Sali looked forward and noticed, for the first time, the island sitting in the middle of the ring of smoke.

"Passed the ring," Captain Lehuangxi Thiraput Cungle yelled through the curved horn. "Slow to cruise speed. Prepare to maneuver into the channel. Queue up the bellows on the crane. Prepare the cargo for birth." He turned to her. "Welcome to the island city of Hrusha in the Sun Under Lagoon, Salminde the Viperstrike."

"This really is the end of the world," she remarked.

"Your destination is the strangest of places," he replied. The captain wiped the layer of soot caked on his face. "The Sun Under Lagoon is never my preferred destination during any season or cycle, but your silver is as good as your word, Salminde the Viperstrike, so here we are. That wall of rancid ash we passed through is called the Curtain to the Sixth Hell. The smoke is rising from the rim of a massive volcano. We're now in its crater. Not sure why it escapes only around the edges, but it's been that way since the first Happan sailed these waters."

The *Hana Iceberg* slipped into a wide inlet and followed its course as it snaked side to side. Both banks of the channel were steep with sharp, pointed mountains of ice that jutted skyward like the lower jaws of a crocodile. Sali could just make out a wooden pathway running along the length of the western side halfway up the sheer walls of the tall icebergs.

"What an alien place," she murmured.

The captain excused himself to prepare the *Hana Iceberg* for docking in the harbor. Sali continued to look ahead as the arctic barge navigated the hard turns through the channel as it struggled to avoid clipping the jagged cliffs on both sides of the inlet. The channel eventually emptied into a giant lake forming the center of the island.

They had finally arrived at Hrusha, the Holy City. Sali was decidedly underwhelmed. The famed birthplace of the Eternal Khan of Katuia was divided into two parts. The main portion of Hrusha was set on the shores of the lake that expanded in every direction up the slope of the icecap hills surrounding it. White and gray buildings with hundreds of colorfully painted roofs like a quilt lay over the icy landscape.

The second part of the city was floating in the center of the lake. A cluster of large city pods with single- and two-story buildings floated there. A wide wooden bridge stretched from the shore connecting the two sections of the city. More interestingly, these floating city pods shared many of the same design aesthetics and traits as their source, the black city of Chaqra. It had been years since Sali last laid eyes on those lacquered blackwood structures. Even now it made her blood boil.

At first it looked like a trick of the eye, but then Sali noticed that the city was also glowing a burnt orange, and the sky above had taken the color of pink rose, which made for a pretty painting with the blue and green aurora meandering across the sky. The strange effect left a lingering residue that seemed to make the air glow. How could air possibly have color? Strange and eerie indeed.

Sali had been so mesmerized by the sights she didn't hear Daewon join her on the bridge. "Is this Hrusha? Why is everything pee color?"

"If that's the color of your piss, you need to drink more water," she remarked. "You're right, however. Things are unnatural here."

"I've read the shaman texts on Hrusha," the tinker replied. "The island is over the most active point in the volcano, which spits out rich veins of minerals from the bottom of the seafloor up to the surface and then freezes into the ice. The ancient Happans had discovered these deposits some centuries ago and built the settlement here."

Sali grunted. "Did your ancient texts say anything about the Eternal Khan?"

"Only that he's a blessed holy being."

"We'll see about that." Sali grunted. "What do you need while we're here?"

"Just need to make a trade deal on as many tons of sparkstone, iron ingots, and raw rubber as we can get our hands on."

"How are we paying for this?"

Daewon patted a bulging sack tucked beneath his tunic. "Thank goodness one of the richest men in Katuia is keeping us afloat. War is logistics. Empire is wealth, as the saying goes."

The *Hana Iceberg* passed a tall, armored signal tower rising on a small island in the middle of the channel where a dockworker was flagging and directing the many fishing boats, junks, barges, and other crafts of all shapes and sizes flowing in and out of the harbor and lake.

"Busy port for such a remote settlement," she observed.

"Being a mining colony and holy site certainly attracts many merchants and pilgrims. It's a good quarter of my trade route," said Captain Lehuangxi Thiraput Cungle, walking up to them. The captain shouted into his horn ordering the *Hana Iceberg* to steer into one of the larger dock spaces that could hold an arctic barge. The forward paddlewheel swiveled and churned under his guidance as the massive craft bumped its way into its dock, shedding several large chunks of ice in the process. The captain did not seem alarmed by it, so Sali tried not to be either.

Ropes were thrown from the barge to waiting attendants. Once the *Hana Iceberg* was properly moored, several large ramps were extended onto the dock. A tracked loading crane slid onto its rails to the starboard side and began to hoist cargo. A scrawny, bare-chested dockmaster wearing a puffy penguin-fur coat came on board flanked by several dockhands. He met with the captain, and the two were soon haggling over the barge's manifest.

Sali returned to their tent where her two wards were already packing their meager belongings. Hampa traveled light while Daewon brought his entire home wherever he went. Her neophyte went to gather the horses while she used sharp words to tell the tinker to pack more quickly. After they collected their belongings, they regrouped and made their way toward the settlement.

Captain Lehuangxi Thiraput Cungle was still having a heated conversation with the dockmaster when they reached the ramp. Momentarily breaking away, he flourished an elaborate bow. "It appears our journey is coming to an end, landlady. I wish you well on your noble quest for a cure. My great mother suffered from a long lingering illness. I do not wish that end on anyone."

"Thank you, friend," she said. "If your barge is still here when we conclude our business, I would be honored to do business with you again."

"You're my friend for three days." The captain paused, considering. "Maybe a little longer if you flash a little frosting. Three silvers or seven chips a day. I can perhaps drag it out a day or two after that, but you're paying full price then."

"We're obviously not that good of friends."

"If you're aboard the *Hana Iceberg* when we break lips with Hrusha, it's all good. If you're not, it's still all good. Oh, and I need your horses for collateral, see?"

"I see. It's all good, Captain Lehuangxi Thiraput Cungle." Sali didn't love the arrangement, but at least it saved her stable fees. She handed the reins to the captain. "We'll be back for them in five days."

"It's very good," he called after her.

"All good." She turned to leave.

"I treasured our time together." He shouted even louder. "The highlight of my travels, landlady!"

"Goodbye, Captain."

"I shall raise a cup of friendship in your name."

Sali kept looking forward. If she paid the captain more attention, he would go on for another five minutes. Extreme civility was a deeply rooted trait within Happan culture, and getting the last word in every conversation was their national pastime, a game that the captain and his crew played very well. It was amusing at first but quickly grew exhausting.

"What about the horses?" asked Hampa.

Sali collected her ruck and stash of knives and sheathed each weapon where it belonged. Arming herself in such a way had always felt like a ritual, as if she were armoring herself. It was also a stark reminder that Sali had not only returned to a Katuia-controlled place, but the heart and source of their religion. As for the horses, "They stay here."

"Okay." Hampa should have at least asked why.

Sali stopped herself. This wasn't the time to critique. "Let's get some food. I'm going to flip a table if I have to eat more raw fish."

CHAPTER TWENTY-FOUR

DUCAL CONSEQUENCES

It didn't take long for Taishi to determine where their little pride of shishi were heading as they treaded north, deeper toward the center of the Cloud Pillars. Known as the Pit to the First Hell by the locals, the dark heart of the region, officially named Daleh after its lone outpost, was an inhospitable intimidating cluster of crags, mountains, and jungle so densely packed a person would have to excavate through several layers of tree roots and vegetation to even see the ground.

The treacherous terrain was also the least of a person's worries. Giant, nightmarish creatures roamed Daleh. It was said that the legend of dragons originated from the many monstrous lizards that roamed the pits, or perhaps they actually did live here. Others were giant flesh-eating plants that sprang from beneath one's feet to gobble them whole and suck the blood out of their prey. There were also rumors of lost tribes of sub-humans who ambushed travelers in order to invite them to dinner, as the stories went.

Taishi hadn't believed any of those stories until she had encountered a nightmarish buggy-eyed monster while on a treasure hunt for a wealthy Lawkan lord a few decades back. The slithering land monstrosity with its many slimy scaled tentacles and gaping jaws nearly wiped out the entire forty-man hunting party. The glory-seeking lord had still wanted to press on even as the survivors were tending to the wounded. Taishi had no qualms then about leading a mutiny against the foolish young man. She wondered if he ever got out on his own. Probably not.

Still, the memory of her brief excursion into the pit to hell triggered fresh memories. Taishi was not scared of any person, but fear pricked her heart the moment the forest canopy dipped down the long slope leading to the massive hole in the earth, left eons ago by a massive sinkhole. They would pass through to enter Daleh, the Dark Heart of the Cloud Pillars, the Pit to the First Hell.

The air chilled the moment the shishi passed through the entrance, continuing single-file down a set of chiseled and wood-framed steps that curved around the entire opening until it opened up a truly massive cavern where a second jungle had sprung up here underground in the dim light coming in from the mouth of the pit. The fauna down here, however, had grown twisted and alien in this alien environment. The trees were ashen gray with claw-like leaves. Deformed cacti and flowers with long, blackened spikes seemed to float in the air. Taishi glanced up at the top of a tree hanging from the ceiling of the cavern. The vegetation was everywhere: on the ground, the walls, and directly above. Somehow, she would think an upside-down tree would catch her attention, but in this particular case, upside-down trees were the least interesting thing here in the Dark Heart.

This really was not how Taishi had expected to spend the day.

The outpost, fortunately, wasn't too far from the opening, just a few minutes along the tops of the canopies toward the lone beacon of civilization here in this underworld. Taishi's body clenched the entire time as her shishi bounced her on its bony, slithering back. These stupid cats were easily one of the worst modes of transportation imaginable. The righteous lion had a surprisingly supple body and could almost slither like a coiling snake. Its line of protruding spine massaged her backside in the most painful, numbing way possible. Not only that, this mangy creature had coarse, itchy fur.

Taishi's gaze locked onto a silhouette of an impossibly large snake off in the distance hanging from the branches of a nearby massive tree. Its head must have been at least the size of a very fat cow. She watched as its long train of a body uncoiled itself from the branch. A shudder rolled down her spine. She muttered, "A special blend of cray and stupid."

"What was that?" said Urwan. He slowed his lion down and waited for her to catch up.

"This is literally the last place in the world I want to be," she said, re-signed. "I was about to draw a bath when you came."

Urwan looked straight ahead. "We have stood shoulder to shoulder across many campaigns and fields of war. You know I take nothing lightly."

Taishi snorted. That much was true. Which only meant the real reason they were here was probably much worse than she imagined. So why was she here? She glanced over at Urwan. Her only assurance was that the horselord would not dishonor himself so as to betray her.

That was when Taishi noticed the man's tight jaw and focused eyes, and the way he gripped his reins. Urwan was frightened. No, he was worried.

She shook her head. "What have you gotten me into, you ass?"

Daleh was an outpost in the barest sense. It was a jungle settlement, situated high in the trees with platforms and balconies wrapped around massive heartwood trees. These gigantic trees—so large it would take minutes to circle one—were connected in a small network by an intricate series of rope bridges.

The crazed maniacs who call Daleh home—adventure seekers, big game hunters, rare wood loggers, gem miners, and reagent businesspeople among others—did profitable business down here in Daleh. The dangers were high, but the profits justified it, somehow, at least for those who didn't get swallowed up by the Dark Heart. The population fluctuated between a few dozen during mild cycles to a few hundred during third cycle nesting. It was the preferred home to those who wished nothing to do with humanity, or those hiding from the rest of humanity, or people who really loved lumbering or exotic deadly gaming because there was little else to do here. Basically, you had to really hate civilization to live here.

One advantage of being in one of the most inhospitable regions in the world was that it was also one of the best places to take refuge from ever being found. A wanted man, either from the law, the ducal crowns, or the underworld, could usually find safe residence here in Daleh. A wanted person must have really wronged someone badly to have them chase you here.

They stopped at the balcony platform leading down a ramp to the stables a quarter way up a large heartwood tree. Urwan rode his shishi to a graceful stop atop the platform and dismounted first. He led his lion a few steps toward the nearest cabin that doubled as a lighthouse and whistled for the stable hand. Receiving no reply, he ducked into the little hut carved directly into the tree trunk and returned a few moments later with a bleary-eyed young man. The stable hand led their shishis to the cat pen as Urwan rambled off a detailed list of instructions for the care of his animals.

It took some effort for Taishi to peel herself off her smelly cat. On top of their bony spines, guardian lions had enlarged hearts that beat rapidly, which caused their entire bodies to continuously vibrate. After a few hours, Taishi had lost all feeling below her waist. Her knees embarrassingly gave way as they touched the ground, and she almost fell face first. Not exactly a good look for a legendary grand master war artist.

Fortunately, she got a handful of her righteous lion's mane and managed to stay upright. The shishi turned to her and rewarded her with a slobbery lick of its forked tongue. The creature panted heavily in her face, blasting her with a stench of spoiled meat.

The gag reflex twisted in her guts, and then spread inside her, cascading into a fit of coughs that felt like her body had caught fire, reaching deep within her until it felt as if it had cut her soul. Taishi leaned on the Swallow Dances for support like a cane as her body expunged the pain. She sucked in a few deep breaths after it subsided and wiped the blood leaking from the corners of her lips with her sleeve.

Zofi was there by her side. "Are you all right?"

That was one of the reasons Taishi wanted her to accompany them on this trip. The girl would make a good mother. "I'm fine. It's been a while since I've had to ride in such discomfort for so long."

Fausan slid off his cat next to them. He yawned and stretched, already looking for the nearest drink. Somehow, the man had the ability to sleep the entire trip. All they had to do was to tie his wrists to his lion's curly mane. Taishi was envious. It would have spared her so much discomfort.

The four left the stables and crossed a wide wooden bridge heading toward the platform on the next tree over. They passed by a few locals, standing alone, leaning against the roped railing, and looking out into the eerie darkness. None paid them any attention as they crossed toward the other end of the bridge. Most stood by themselves, pondering and staring out into the abyss. Another was sitting on a bench alone reading a book, in the dark. They entered Daleh's center ring, which was the main public square of the settlement. There were just a few shops, and all were closed. Businesses in such small settlements were always open by appointment only.

Urwan caught up a few moments later and squeezed past them to take the lead, with Taishi and Zofi following close behind. Zofi's head tilted toward Taishi. "I'm trying not to stare, but does the horselord have a very defined . . ."

"Ass," said Taishi. "Yes, it's magnificent. His backside is developed from a lifetime of having something between his legs."

"He cuts quite a striking figure." Zofi's eyes were wide and her voice a little breathy. "His unkempt but smoldering hair, layered with white, and that long high ponytail. That chiseled side profile with that cool sharp beard."

Taishi was amused. "Urwan has always been very well put together. You should have seen him trot during his younger days."

"He struts straight out of one of those sordid Burning Hearts," Zofi said, a little breathily. "I mean, did you two ever?"

"I was never his type."

Zofi looked offended for her. "You mean he didn't want to be with another war artist? That's understandable, I guess, but rude."

"A little broader than that, girl," said Taishi with a grin. "I'm going to help you skip a few chapters and save you the heartache. You're not his type either."

Urwan twisted his head back as if to make sure they were still following. He slowed his pace until she was walking alongside him. He looked concerned. The horselord pointed at one of the taller three-story building facades carved into the tree. "This is the main building of the settlement. They are expecting us."

"Who is they?" Taishi's eyes narrowed.

"Taishi, whatever happens next, tread carefully. I want you to know, my friend, that the trust you've placed in our long and well-worn friendship is not misplaced."

His attempted assurance only made her trust him less. Taishi's fingers curled around the hilt of the Swallow Dances as they crossed a wide wooden bridge connecting two of the tree trunks.

The party stopped in front of the doorway. Urwan hesitated. "I'm going to need everyone to disarm."

Fausan crossed his arms. "You're a madman, horsehead. Not a chance."

Taishi's hands stayed where they were. "Trust goes both ways. Brotherhood only goes so far."

"It's not a trust issue, Taishi." He stopped at the door, looking resigned. "Just please, show some prudence." He swung the door open, revealing a dimly lit room inside.

Bhasani stepped to Taishi's other side. Her usually serene face was tense. "The air feels heavy. Something is wrong."

Taishi wrinkled her nose. "What is that soapy smell?"

"Heartwood tree spa smells like durian," said Fausan, stepping next to her. "I quite like it."

"Gross." Taishi made a face and turned to the others. "Disciples, stay outside. Guard the door. Fausan and Bhasani, with me."

Taishi's fingers brushed against the hilt of the Swallow Dances as she entered the dimly lit room. It was an odd shape, long with sharp corners on the far end, and then disjointed walls on the near sides. A long black lacquered table and ten chairs sat in the middle of the room while a covered sparkstone heater on the far end emanated warmth from the fire in its belly. Covered flames were probably a necessity when the building was carved into a tree. A figure sat in a wooden chair next to the orange-

and-red glow of the stove, flanked by three columns near the back. Their back was turned away, but she noticed the fine silk robes and the smooth, bald head. The figure had no reaction when Taishi's group walked in. That usually meant they were sleeping, dead, or . . .

Bhasani stopped at the doorway. "Something is off. There's a strange presence here."

Taishi sucked in her breath. Bhasani was right. Something *was* off. The air around here *did* feel heavy. She cursed. They had clumsily ambled right into a trap.

A metal bullet shot out from behind Taishi, streaking past her ear and into the room. It curved around one of the columns and struck something behind it. Fausan shoved past her, moving more quickly than she thought he was able, and rolled his hands forward in a circular motion, flinging several more bullets into the room. The walls cracked and splintered at the impact. Someone groaned as one hit its mark, and a figure previously hiding in the darkness slumped forward and fell into the light.

The Swallow Dances sang from its scabbard and hummed. "It's an ambush!"

Taishi took stock of the room. They were surrounded by a narrow windowless room with stagnant, almost dead air, and only one way out. Whoever set this trap had done their due diligence. Betrayal was common in the lunar court as long as it was pragmatic and justifiable. Most rarely held a grudge—present company excluded—it was just business, and holding grudges was bad business. It was also considered unethical and dishonorable to betray someone who had retired from the lunar court. Not only that, it was just plain rude.

Bhasani pointed at several figures emerging from the shadows. "Mute Men! Easily ducal show quality by the looks of them."

Taishi cursed. Well, of all the ways she thought she would go, dying in a Mute Men ambush *had* ranked as one of the most interesting and glorious but decidedly unpleasant ways to perish. A silhouette of a figure appeared out of the darkness. The Mute Man flourished his hands upward, revealing two long, curved metal claws extending from both sides of his fist. This must be one of the new generations of Mute Men, always trying to be edgy with stupid new weapon designs.

Taishi normally didn't bother, but if this was her last battle—the odds looked fairly good for that outcome—she intended to fight it with honor and style. She saluted with the Swallow Dances. "Honor is the way."

The Mute Man touched a clawed fist to his chest.

"It is the only way," she finished for him. Taishi touched her fist to her palm. She had never been sure if their tongues had been cut out, or if they had been trained at an early age to never speak.

Their blades came together with a bell-like clash. The Swallow Dances slid into the twin blade's center fist guard. The Mute Man was trying to disarm her. She felt a coldness emanating from his body, his jing at work, suppressing the other jing around it. Taishi curled her sword out of the trap, turned sharply in such a tight space, and was about to score her first Mute Man kill when a woman's voice rang across the room, cutting through the sounds of fighting.

"That is enough!"

Both Taishi and the Mute Man, locked in combat, froze. The tip of the Swallow Dances was lightly pressed against the flesh over his heart, while his right claw in mid-swing was dangerously close to cutting and severing her useless left arm. Not exactly a great loss. Taishi gave herself an even chance of avoiding losing the limb if that exchange had continued.

The figure at the far end of the room stood and turned to face them. It was a tall, statuesque woman with a striking face, raised cheekbones, and a shaven head bereft of all hair. Her travel robes were plain but rich and richly detailed. Most telling, however, were her eyes, which were uniformly gray and glazed over.

The woman glided toward her, anger marking her otherwise smooth and beautiful face. "How dare you. I would think, Taishi, that you would have stayed your blade the moment you recognized the Mute Men. I am disappointed."

Taishi's throat caught. It had been half a lifetime since she last saw a mindseer. They were a rare lineage of war arts whose services were incredibly expensive, so were usually retained only by high nobility or powerful businessmen. The question now was, who sent her?

Then it dawned on her. Taishi sheathed the Swallow Dances in one smooth motion and bowed. Bhasani must have realized the rank of this individual as well. The drowned fist gave a strangled cry and dropped to both knees.

"I would think," the woman continued, "that out of a sense of respect and fealty, you would have done the right thing."

Fealty. Now Taishi knew who was speaking through the mindseer. Taishi looked up. "What exactly is the right thing, my lord?"

"Surrender, of course! What else!" the woman roared. The anger and intensity of her words did not match the serenity on her face.

Taishi's eyes flashed. "There is a bounty on my head that's so large it would probably send the Enlightened States into recession, if it was ever collected, and you want me to surrender to you out of *respect and consideration*?"

Fausan was the only one still standing, looking befuddled. He raised a hand. "I have a question. Who is this pretty bald woman with that gorgeous face? You are an entire package, dear mistress."

Bhasani hissed. "That's a duke, you knob!"

"Duke Saan of Shulan, to be exact," said Taishi.

"That's . . . the Painted Tiger? How is that possible?"

"You've never seen a mindseer before?" said Taishi. "They have the ability to become a vessel for someone to communicate through from a long distance. It's an incredibly rare war art and very much in demand in the courts."

"One was at our wedding, you dung cow," said Bhasani. "My cousin, Surata. She was my swordmaiden at our wedding, you dingus. Why else do you think she's bald?"

"I thought she was just a gorgeous bald woman. She was easily the most beautiful among your friends." He stopped. "Next to you, of course."

"Just because we're no longer together does not mean you get to talk to me like that."

"That was a compliment!" Then the realization struck Fausan. "This is actually a duke standing before us?" He made a sound like a croaking noise and fell to both knees. "Forgive me, Your Grace."

Everyone else in the room followed suit; everyone except for Taishi. Regardless of which duke was currently helming the woman's mind, this woman was still just a mindseer, not the real thing. Besides, Taishi was not in the habit of scraping her forehead on the ground to people who had put bounties on her head.

The ends of the mindseer's lips curled upward. "Is it going to be one of those reunions again, Taishi? Can't we try cordial for once?"

"You tried to have me killed. That pretty much rules out pleasantries."

"That's only half true. I did contribute to the bounty's pot as per my responsibilities as a duke, but I did not order the hit, nor did I advertise it."

"That doesn't make it any better, Your Grace. You put up coin to fund a bounty ordering my capture or death. That's exactly what ordering the hit is, you puffed-up clownfish."

"How does Taishi dare speak to the duke like that?" Fausan was still whispering way too loud.

"Because Saan used to study under her," Bhasani whispered back.

"What? Saan was her student?" the whipfinger master scoffed. "How dare *he* speak to *her* like that? If my apprentice were so mouthy"—he raised his open hand—"I'd give him the meh-meh."

"You would meh-meh the Duke of Shulan?" sneered Bhasani. "Did your mam suffocate you with your umbilical cord when you were in the womb?"

"You know, I can hear every word," said Saan mildly. The mindseer's eyes were still locked on Taishi.

"My deepest apologies, Your Grace," said Bhasani. "I don't know this man. If you intend to execute him, spare me."

The woman chuckled and looked over Taishi's shoulders. "Is he here?"

"No, Saan. He's not, and you'll never get your painted fingernails on him as long as I'm alive."

"Hardly, master," Saan sniffed. "If I had wanted him killed, I would have voted with the others back at the Celestial Palace."

She shook her head. "You could have stopped it if you had committed harder to him."

"True, I could have," admitted Saan. "But it would have required far too much political and material capital to expend. Wen Jian's life simply wasn't worth it." He nodded to Taishi. "I am glad to hear that he is well and thriving. I could not be more pleased with the outcome."

"Fine, what do you want then?" asked Taishi.

Saan glanced at a spray of blood splatter from the fight. "You traveled all night. Go clean up. We'll speak after you're refreshed."

"I don't mind wearing the day's travels a while longer," Taishi pressed further. "What are you doing here, Saan?"

"But I mind that you smell like a wet rat, so I insist. Now, go, by request of a duke's sensitive nostrils." And that was that.

"As you wish, my lord." Taishi bowed and motioned for the others to follow her out.

Fausan whispered too loudly again as they left the chambers. "If anyone who calls me master speaks to me that way, I would for sure give them the meh-meh."

"Like the Ten Hells you would. I've seen you with your students, you soft shell bun." Taishi snorted. "What's a meh-meh, anyway?"

RESPONSIBILITIES

Qisami's new job watching over Lord Aki's four-year-old girls must not have gone too poorly, because she was assigned to the two girls again the next day. Surprisingly, she didn't mind. The high lord's twin four-year-olds had proven to be delightfully chaotic urchins, which were Qisami's preferred type of children, a distant second to having to deal with no children at all.

After running geese crew early the next morning, Qisami found herself again hurrying toward the northeast quadrant of the estates, this time to the training yard. She made a quick detour to one of the large kitchens along the way. She stuck her head in and made eye contact with the person whom she was looking for. Qisami popped back outside and waited until an apprentice from the culinary brigade staggered outside onto the path a few minutes later carrying a large bucket of dishwater.

"Let me help you," she offered, hurrying to hold the door open.

"Much obliged." He winked. The boy was sweet on her. More importantly, however, he was holding a folded parchment between two fingers. Qisami made that disappear quickly and then flicked a copper liang into his shirt pocket.

Working with the geese crew brought her in contact with people working all over the estate. She waited until she was alone continuing through the underground passages before she unfolded the note. It wasn't a secret, but it wouldn't do to flaunt her literacy too much to the rest of the staff. A smirk curled her lips as she scanned its contents. Now she knew how much the head of the culinary brigade was bribing the head of maintenance in order to jump the line with plumbing repairs. This was good leverage to own and useful information to barter.

Qisami reached the training yard by late morning and stayed on the servants' path as she passed armored men and boys swinging swords, flying kites, sparring open-handed, and shooting arrows at flying kites. Those kids were terrible shots. There were also two rows of kids playing board games of Siege off to the side. Most of the children, ranging from eight to twelve, were hilarious with their incompetence. She was sure they would grow up to become worthless adults, which often were the best sort of nobles. Things usually got worse when the nobility got involved in actually doing something.

She sized up several of the lords training as well. Almost all were young, strapping men, dressed in costly robes and light armor, wielding swords and spears that looked as if they had never touched dirt. They wore haughty expressions they couldn't back up with their skills. She could have killed them all without marring her face paint.

"Kiki!" The two little murderous runts screamed. The twins ran up to her, each hugging a leg.

"Lady Akiana, Lady Akiya," she said, patting their heads like stray pets. "Did you girls miss me?"

"Will you come have tea with us?" said Akiya in her squeaky voice.

"You promised you'd teach us how to slay a dragon." Akiana made stabbing motions with her toy sword in the most vicious way a four-year-old could.

Qisami looked around to make sure no one was watching and then lowered herself to a knee. "Look here. See your thumb? If you hold it this way, you're going to hurt it when you stab someone. It's also a weak grip. Here, wrap your thumb around the hilt like this." Qisami demonstrated and helped the girl with a few thrusts. "There you go, my lady."

Akiana's smile grew wider with every jab. "You're the coolest friend in the world, Kiki."

"I know."

That was basically the rest of her day. After stabbing trees with Akiana and picking flowers with Akiya, Qisami spent time slaying dragons, re-enacting a story from the Monkey God's adventures, and having a pre-tend picnic with the girls drinking real hot tea. Akiya burned her tongue while Akiana spilled hers on her fine silk robes. The two then got into a real hair-pulling brawl over whether Qisami was a dog or cat, and which one of the girls owned her.

Afterward, Qisami took them to archery class, and then the noble-men's children's war arts lessons, in which the two were training in the Aki family style known as Far Fist. It was a typical Gyian war art: beauti-ful, elegant, and mostly useless.

By the time Lord Aki's large gaggle of children turned in after a long day out on the training field, Qisami felt worn down like she had just fin-ished an all-night stakeout. The girls were a handful and had many times tried her limited patience, but Qisami had to admit she also enjoyed their time together.

Dusk arrived by the time she was finally released from her duties. Qisami was about to head back to the servants' tower when she realized she was a short jaunt away from where Cyyk was assigned as a training dummy. She detoured across the yard to the groundskeeper quarters and found her grunt polishing a stack of armor next to a washing trough just outside the duke's private yard.

Cyyk saw Qisami approaching and waved at her with a miniature un-sharpened training saber. "Boss."

"Kiki," she corrected. "How's your cover going?"

Cyyk shrugged. "I'm teaching the young lordling Yeenso double saber. He called me his best friend the other day. You hear that? The fu-ture Duke of Gyian said I was his best friend. Me. I'm in the inner circle now!"

Qisami snorted. "He's six years old. Stop trying to leverage a baby for influence, creep." She pointed at the nearby pond. "Besides, Yeenso is fickle. He called a turtle his best friend last week."

"Just wait. One day, he'll be duke and I'll be his right-hand man, then you'll be scraping your forehead to me, Qisami."

"Sure, Broodbaby, whatever. Just know that every male in a duke's inner circle is a eunuch."

Cyyk's eyes widened. He stood a little taller. "I didn't know that."

"Around the duke's wives and mistresses, a handsome little brood-baby lad like you? He'll absolutely cut off your balls. What's more important, your manhood or power?" Qisami didn't think it was a tough question, but he looked conflicted. She tapped his ankle with her toe. "Hey, you're not bedding Shinqi, are you?"

Cyyk looked offended. "She's a peasant. She has a peasant face and peasant hands and her thighs are very peasant-like."

"I think she's pretty." Qisami crossed her arms. "I would absolutely bed her and then leave her the very next day."

"Pretty in a peasant way, I suppose."

It sounded like Cyyk was overdue for a reminder in humility. Qisami *did* enjoy beating the nobility out of him every once in a while. She kicked him in the shin lightly. "You're not that great a catch either, Broodbaby. Shinqi's a nice girl."

"Why don't *you* sleep with her then?" He shrugged. "I mean, I'll do it if that's an order."

She kicked him a little harder.

"Okay, fine." Cyyk bared his teeth. "I'll bed her, if you insist, but we're not getting married."

She knocked him off his seat with the sole of her foot this time. "No! She's pregnant, you cock fungus. I worried it was yours."

"Not me, I don't think." He sat up and mused. "If it's anyone, I bet it's one of those southeast quadrant noble boys. Want me to check?"

Qisami lived for the low-stakes petty drama, but now wasn't the time. "Later. Have you heard from the others?" There were things everyone told the cell's grunt that they would never tell her personally, gossip Cyyk was usually more than happy to spill. The grunt's lips were often too loose.

He shrugged. "Koteuni still has the best fake gig. She's having the time of her life. Her rabbleguard unit was the one that put down that textile factory strike the other day."

"Oh, that was her? Nice. And Burandin?"

"They've relegated him to being inanimate objects when they put on plays. He better figure something out soon or they'll throw him out on the streets." He looked up from the armor he was scrubbing with a mesh rag. "Any word from the client?"

Qisami shook her head. "It's been weeks. She appeared out of thin air at the fish market when the Second Palace head chef ordered me to pick up lobsters from the lake. She scolded me for not being assigned to work closer to the duke." She scrunched her face. "I don't think she realizes how many years it takes to get promoted to ducal staff."

"What did she want?"

"A map of the estate." Qisami grimaced. "I had to volunteer to work extra shifts on scullery duty just to bribe the mapmaker's apprentice with two sacks of sweet barbecue meat for it. I sent it to the embassy and have heard nothing since."

Cyyk set aside a cleaned shoulder pauldron and sighed when he next picked up the armored skirt and then began wiping that down as well.

Qisami sniffed. "Does the young lord still have bowel problems?"

"Pisses himself every time he gets hit with a stiff breeze."

"You're not going to stay a best friend at that rate."

Cyyk put the armor aside and leaned back. "Not a problem. I speak their language. The oldest daughter fancies me. Imagine her surprise when she learns I'm actually a noble."

"You would make a good pair," she agreed. "A good pair of idiots. You better not bed her. Yanso will skin you alive if he finds out his daughter is consorting with a servant, and he would rather skin *her* alive than marry his oldest daughter to the Scorpion General's youngest child. Besides you're just a grunt now, not some noble broodbaby. Right, Broodbaby?"

"One day,"—he nodded at her—"I'm going to thank you for choosing me as the cell's grunt by killing you."

That earned him a smile. If a student wasn't trying to kill their master, then the master wasn't working hard enough. She bowed with attitude. "My blade waits, big broodbaby. Listen up. Your job now is to get closer to the duke's children and gain access to the palace." She stood. "I have to get back. But if you see Koteuni, tell her to rein herself back a bit. Soldiers are exempt from the five-silver murder fee, rabbleguards are not. I can't afford to starve our purse on account she's having too much fun."

"Aye, boss," he replied. "What happens after I get access?"

"I'll tell you then."

Qisami hurried out of the training yard, taking a roundabout way back toward the short strip servant tunnel. The soup had been long gone by the time she returned home yesterday. Qisami had begged the tower cook to set aside some small dragon buns for her for tonight's meal. The cook had initially crossed her arms in a huff, and then winked. "I'll leave a plate for you tonight at the back counter."

"Thanks, sweet uncle." Qisami offered a deep bow. It paid to be nice sometimes, especially when you're not allowed to kill them—yet.

She was about to leave the yard again when one of the guards put his hand out. "Companion Kiki, right?"

Annoyed, she bowed. "Yes?"

He pointed toward the back hall. "Report to the estatekeeper."

She bowed again and hurried toward the armory's rear warehouse. What did the woman want with her now? Was she in trouble? Did she accidentally curse again in front of those little girls? Those little brat snitches.

Hari was speaking to several of the brigade nannies when Qisami entered the estatekeeper's office. The chatter among the six ceased. She bowed and retreated out the door, closing it behind her. She waited outside for what felt like half the night as Hari and those stuck-up nannies had their chat. Qisami began to worry, however. The cook locked up the kitchen at the end of the night. That meant there would not be any dragon buns for her tonight.

Now she was irritated.

Eventually, after what felt like hours, the brigade nannies filed out one by one. Qisami was greeted with a few "Hello, Kiki's" as they passed. She was always well behaved around these women. The best way to get away with murder is if no one believes you are capable of it. That was another training pool lesson.

Hari came out last. She gave Qisami a curt glance. "Follow, child." The estatekeeper led her out through the yard's outer gate. "Are you finished for the day, child?" The woman asked questions like she was making statements.

"How may I serve, estatekeeper?" Qisami executed the perfect bow: graceful and assertive, yet also deferential without being submissive. It was a fine line and she walked it perfectly. Hari detested submissive servants. She slipped her forearms into her oversize sleeves and fell in line flanking the estatekeeper, walking exactly two steps to the side and one step back, as instructed. A shadowkill had to be in tune with spatial awareness.

"The new girl," Hari began as they walked out of the training yard and down the winding paths of the Meditation Onyx Garden. "The one assigned to cleaning the concubine's lounge. What's her name?"

"Porla, estatekeeper." It was not possible the estatekeeper did not know her name.

"How is she doing?"

Qisami considered: which answer was the woman looking for? No, this was a test. Small loyalties versus the greater one. "She is well liked and works hard." Both were lies.

"She's struggling with her role and drawing attention to herself," Hari corrected. "Your allegiance belongs to this duchy, family, and estate. Do you understand? Your loyalty to your friend is commendable, and it is good to know you're not an ambitious rodent, however."

Qisami bowed her head low, partially to hide her smirk. This *was* a test, and the estatekeeper *wanted* the wrong answer. After all, if someone can't be trusted with a friend, how could you trust them with anything more important? What was the right response now? She needed to show some quality humility. Qisami began to lower herself to her knees.

"I don't have time for that girl," Hari snapped. "I need you to set Porla straight. She's failing at her job. The concubines smell blood and are sharpening their claws, and she's the snack. Soon I may have no choice but to throw her out onto the streets. Accompany her one of these days. Show her how to work around those nasty bitches."

"Of course, estatekeeper."

"Not being a snitch is a fine trait as long as you know where your loyalty lies." Hari abruptly changed the subject. They reached the servants' tunnel running under the short strip. Hari slowed her long stride enough for Qisami to hurry down the stairs, grab the waiting lantern, and open the pedway door. Their footsteps clicked loudly against the backdrop of the quiet night before echoing throughout the low, narrow tunnel. The tall woman had to hunch over to avoid scraping her head against the ceiling. How could she be so thin and tall? They were about halfway across when she stopped and faced Qisami.

"Why are you actually here, Kiki? You've been with us only a short while, less than a full cycle, but it's apparent you are not a servant or companion."

Qisami remained calm as her hand floated a little closer to the estatekeeper's reed-thin neck. This tunnel was the perfect cover. No traffic, with no line of sight for witnesses. They were alone. A hard slap to the chest to stun but avoid bruising, then one quick slam against the stone wall to make it look like a head wound from a fall. People would think it was a heart attack or accident, and no magistrate ever looked that hard at a servant.

"I checked your indentured servitude contract. There's no way you're from a small farming settlement in Shulan. You're far too smart and capable for a country fool. You're not only literate, but you're also well read, and your familiarity with an ink quill is not that of a farmer. So what is it? What are you actually doing here?"

Qisami stepped in front of the estatekeeper. One quick blow to the chest should shock her heart . . .

Hari raised her hands, but not because she was trying to protect herself. "Don't tell me. I'm guessing it's an abusive marriage or an unwanted betrothal. Probably the latter with your upbringing. In any case, it doesn't matter. You'll have a safe haven in this household if trouble comes to our door. Your past is yours unless you wish to share, understood?"

Qisami was glad not to have to kill her. It would have been messy. "Thank you, estatekeeper."

Hari clutched Qisami's shoulders with her long-fingered hands. "Your talents were obvious the moment you joined the estate. You're far too competent to remain a child's companion. You learn quickly and make friends easily. You volunteer for the extra jobs. When I assign you a task, you perform like a perfect maiden and you do not speak ill of the rest of the staff."

Qisami had to suppress a snicker.

Hari didn't notice. "You are respectful to the tenured staff, and the younger staff look up to you. You know when to mind your tongue and when to speak with prudence, and your diligence to detail is sincere. Lord Aki's youngest two seem quite taken with you, and the wet nurse has already asked me if I would be willing to trade you to her staff. She even offered me the property rights for the pen next to the servants' tower. It was tempting, but I, of course, refused her. That's the potential I see in you. The question is, do you want to climb to the clouds, Kiki, or do you want to forever wallow here in the mud? Can you see yourself living a life in servitude management?"

That really did not sound appealing. Qisami wasn't sure which way to play this. She stalled for time. "I have never hoped to aspire so high, estatekeeper."

"It's modest but respectable work, and you'll find no greater stability and safety than working under a great duke such as Yanso. Perhaps one day, if you study hard and make the right alliances with the staff, you could take my place as head of the staff. How does that sound to you?"

What was the answer Hari was hoping for? Qisami bowed. "It would be the honor of a lifetime, estatekeeper."

Hari nodded. "Good.

"Niam's estatekeeper has asked for your services for the next few weeks. I went ahead and made the arrangement. Starting next week, however, you will also begin spending your evenings taking instruction on the estate's administration and bookkeeping."

"Every evening?" Qisami blurted. It never occurred to her a promotion came with more work and . . . schooling? That was the opposite of what she was hoping to do. It was too late now. "You shame me with your gracious words, estatekeeper. I will dedicate myself to be worthy of your praise."

Hari snorted. "Don't think I don't know about your side hustle running information brokering, Kiki. I would be careful with running shade operations like that, girl. You'll find it's the relationships you maintain that will be critical to your success. It's time to make friends."

"I'm everyone's friend," was her glib reply.

The estatekeeper paused. "Not professionally."

"What's a professional friend?"

"You'd better find out soon. You're becoming a real player soon."

They reached the other end of the tunnel and walked up a short set of stairs. Hari reached the surface first. She turned and leveled her gaze on Qisami. "Now that you are in management, I would reconsider leveraging any information that could implicate the powerful maintenance brigade with corruption. That would be a terrible mistake. Even worse would be angering the even more powerful culinary brigade, who incidentally are the ones who cook your meals, Companion Kiki. Congratulations on your promotion to palacemaiden. Don't be a failure."

Then the estatekeeper turned and disappeared, leaving Qisami standing there in the middle of the path, stumped, her mouth hanging open. "I can't tell if I just got promoted or shut down. Both obviously. That sneaky old lioness."

Someone began blood scrawling. Qisami pulled the sleeve back and checked the thin cuts moving across her forearm. It was Burandin's rough but concise handwriting.

Sunri.

Has.

Arrived.

CHAPTER TWENTY-SIX

THE LAKE CITY

The residents of Hrusha mainly ate fish, just like those on the *Hana Iceberg*, which shouldn't have been surprising for an isolated island settlement deep in the True Freeze. Sali found this out the hard way after exploring the local food establishments in the village. At least it wasn't raw. The *Hana Iceberg*'s kitchen served only raw fish, which was interesting and tasty the first ten meals, but then quickly got old.

Lunch ended up being a bingsu shop called Salt Fire Ice a few blocks from the lake, about a fifth of the way up a road running from the shore, through the city, and then up one of the nine steep hills surrounding the lake. The restaurant was just a window, booth, and four tables under a garishly painted orange awning lashed together from stalks of bamboo. All the roofs in the settlement appeared to be colorfully painted in this otherwise gray landscape.

Bingsu was the region's local cuisine, which was mostly protein and vegetables over a bed of shaved ice. Their dishes, much to Sali's resignation, were a variety of fish and blubber paired with a plate of anchovies, pickled eel, and fish eggs on the side, or seafood five ways. At least the fish was cooked this time. The meal was also salty but edible, which was the best compliment she was willing to afford Salt Fire Ice. The "Fire," which she had assumed meant spiciness, unfortunately, was nowhere to be found.

"I don't understand this food," said Hampa, picking his teeth with a skewer that had stuck through a fried squid, aptly named Squid on a Stick. He smacked his lips. "It doesn't taste good, but I can't seem to stop eating."

Both Daewon and Sali agreed. The food was chewy, one-note, and over-salted, but all three ended up eating twice what they had initially ordered. At least it was cheap, only a Zhuun copper liang, four Happan chips, or three million Tsunarcos rooples a plate.

The bill arrived as they finished. The total for the food ended up being just nine coppers, which Daewon paid, but he balked when a second bill for the drinks arrived. Hampa's three white drinks, Sali's two zui-jos, and Daewon's four mango lassis, and twelve cups of water between the three of them, amounted to nearly two silvers, or fifty Happan chips.

Daewon, who was in charge of the purse, was outraged. "How dare they scam us?"

He was about to talk to the boss of the establishment when Sali held him back. "Don't attract unwanted attention over a stupid food bill. We also did order a lot of drinks."

"The salty snacks got us," Hampa said. "I couldn't stop drinking that goat milk."

"That wasn't milk," Sali said. "I don't think we got scammed. It's just a sly business. Keep a low profile. Might I remind you this is a Katuia settlement and a holy site, and we're all wanted Nezran fugitives."

Daewon couldn't hide his anger as he glared at the boss behind the counter. The man glared back. "I'm never coming back," the tinker hollered.

"Have a most blessed day, good sir," the boss returned. "Thank you for patronizing my humble establishment."

"Your food tastes terrible," he shouted when they were almost out of eyeshot.

"I love tourists!" the vendor catcalled back.

Sali cuffed him lightly. "When did you get so confrontational?"

It took several moments for the usually low-key tinker to cool down. The lines around his eyes were tight. "I'm sorry. It's just, we're expecting. Mali needs me, and I'm on the other side of the world. My place should be by her side."

For that worry, Sali was deeply sympathetic. It felt like the story of her journey since she returned to find her city sunken into the Grass Sea, her clan destroyed, and her people enslaved. To not be with them now, especially for a selfish quest, was nigh unbearable.

Instead of explaining her sympathy, which was useless, Sali put her arms around Daewon and pulled him close. "You're here now, as am I, brother of my heart."

"I'm here too," piped Hampa.

Sali ignored him. "The only thing we can do is finish our tasks here as quickly as possible so we can return to our people and you can return to your wife and child. Anything else—anger, worry, sadness—is just wasted energy. Do you understand?"

Daewon sniffed and buried his face in his hands. "I can't bear the thought of failing Malinde. I can't let it happen."

It was then that Sali saw a side of the tinker she hadn't noticed before. She eyed him intently and offered her hand. "Then don't. Let's see if you're strong enough to keep your word. Swear it upon your unborn child."

He sniffed, but accepted it, clasping forearms. She noticed his resolve stiffen as his spine straightened, and he rose a bit taller. "I swear it on my boy."

"Girl." She banged him on the chest with a fist, knocking him flat onto his back. No one nearby batted an eye. Sali hauled him to his feet and they continued on, stopping at a crossroads next to the shore. She pointed toward the tallest building in the middle of the cluster of pods. "I'll head over to the city pods to find answers for a possible cure. Daewon, get your supply run figured out. Have it sent to the *Hana Iceberg*. Hampa, find a reputable moneychanger. I don't want to be here longer than necessary. The good captain is leaving in a few days. I plan to be on that barge when they pull out of harbor."

The three joined the light throng heading toward the lake. The two sections of Hrusha, the land and floating portion, were individually smaller than most Katuia capital cities but together formed a fair-size settlement. Sali gave last-minute instructions and then they went off on their ways, moving in different directions. Sali watched Daewon disappear around the corner and then headed for the cluster of pods in the middle of the lake. She pulled her hood overhead and wrapped her travel cloak close, covering as much of her heritage as possible, although there was no mistaking she was both Katuia and a war artist.

The sole bridge connecting the city pods to the rest of Hrusha was manned by two armored squads of black towerspears stationed at the foot of the bridge. A small line of workers and visitors were queued on one side while many Katuia—almost all in shaman garb—were being directed to another line. To Sali's surprise, she was directed to that second line and was immediately waved through while the Happan merchant with a cart behind her was directed to the longer, slower line. On second glance, she noticed that every person in the first line was Happan.

Sali's footsteps clopped across the wooden bridge framed by what appeared to be the bones of giant sea monsters. The strange rose-pink hue was even stronger here and did tricks to her eyes. She stopped halfway across, glanced over the side, and gasped. The water directly beneath her had a strange viscous black churn. Far below was a glowing fiery eye staring back at her from within the depths. Sali marveled at such a sight. What she was witnessing was almost beyond comprehension.

The signage at the end of the bridge marked this cluster of city pods as Masau, which did indeed originate from Chaqra three centuries ago. By her count, there were approximately a hundred city pods, all of which were far larger than their overland counterparts.

Sali followed the small wooden bridges connecting the pods, passing storefronts, warehouses, and several residences. There were many spirit shamans walking about, as if all Masau served them. It made sense, considering Hrusha's exalted status as the birthplace of the Eternal Khan of Katuia. This many spirit shamans walking nearby, however, made her fingers itch for her tongue.

Sali reached a large platform before the main temple dedicated to the

Khan and stopped when she noticed an image of three lightning bolts piercing a dark cloud etched on the side of a nondescript building. Sali recognized the symbol: stormchasers. She had not realized that the spirit shamans' elite war arts sect was based here, although it made sense given the site's importance. The memory of a long-haired war artist who became known only as *the* Stormchaser entered her mind. It was a lifetime ago from a different era, when things were simpler. She wondered if the man was still alive.

Sali pushed those lingering thoughts out of her mind. The fact that the stormchasers had a chapter house in Hrusha meant nothing. Sali was not here to pick a fight with the spirit shamans or with any stormchasers. The cure, or to quickly return home to Nezra, was all that mattered.

She continued past the stormchaser chapter house to the large, central city pod. The massive temple sitting on the pod nearly covered the entire surface. Sali studied the extra-large sign running down the wall next to a set of oversize double doors: "The Grand Monastery of the Dawn Song."

"What a title," she muttered. The monastery certainly was grand, even larger than the Sanctuary of the Eternal Moor back in Chaqra. What it lacked in height, it more than made up for in girth. The temple was a squat, bulky building of geometric octagonal plates linked together to form a half-dome, and easily the largest building Sali had ever seen built atop a city pod, even on water. She wondered if these pods could move from where they were anchored.

Sali sucked in a long breath, touched her gaunt cheeks, and brushed the stray strands of hair from her brow. There was something viscerally unsettling about standing in front of the holiest site of her people. She had been raised deeply reverent of the spirit shamans and the Eternal Khan. It was the religion that made her best friend her god, and the same religion that demanded she join him in death. It was these shamans who had sold her clan into indentured servitude, and the same people who exiled them after her clan escaped and returned to the Grass Sea.

By all accounts, she should hate the spirit shamans. She should hate this temple. And she did, with every fiber of her being. But Sali also couldn't help but wish for the once familiar comfort and love that came from basking in her faith. She had felt truly blessed when Jiamin had been chosen as host to the next life of the Khan, and even more honored when she became one of his Wills of the Khan. She yearned to still worship the Eternal Khan of Katuia, to revere the spirit shamans, and to revere their guiding hand over their people. Even though they, along with all of Katuia, had betrayed Nezra. It was the betrayal that cut the deepest. Now, as she stood before the Grand Monastery of the Dawn Song, all she felt was uncertainty and hesitation, not faith, not reverence, and certainly not love.

Stronger than the fear of facing her old beliefs and broken honor, however, were her people, her clan, her family, her unborn niece or, grudgingly, nephew. Sali needed answers, a cure so she could continue to be with her loved ones and serve her people for many years to come, or if failing to acquire a cure for her illness, then she needed to find out now and return to her clan to protect it until her dying breath.

"Fear is natural. It is your body's armor, preparing for battle. Allow your fear to strengthen you, to hone your mind as well as your mettle." Those were the words Alyna, Sali's mentor, had told her right before Sali fought her first battle. She had pissed herself and had cowered in shame during the lead-up to the clash. Ever since then, Sali had religiously recited those words before every battle, raid, or duel.

Sali stepped up to the large black doors. Her body immediately reacted. Bile crept up her throat and a shudder ran through her stomach, to her spine. It was as if her body rejected entering the temple. The Pull of the Khan, however, throbbed in her chest, reverberating through her limbs, rattling her teeth. Every part of Sali wanted to reject having to go inside. She almost let it win too. For a moment, Sali had wondered if she should listen to what her mind, body, and heart were telling her and flee this accursed place.

Instead, Sali swallowed her bile and clenched her fist. She gritted her teeth and palmed the two black doors. "Fear is the shield that protects me."

If Sali had expected anything spectacular or unusual upon entering this supposed sacred place, she was disappointed. At first, the interior of the Grand Monastery of the Dawn Song looked like most other temples.

It had a circular main area with a sloping ceiling that met in the middle of the room and was shaped to resemble the interior of the ancient yurts their people used before the times of moving cities. Like all spirit shaman temples, there was a large statue of the Eternal Khan of Katuia in the center surrounded by meditation mats. All the glory for that damn guy Jiamin who, before he became Khan, had never prayed a day in his life. Each temple's depictions were different. Sometimes he was holding up an ax while other times he was sitting on a throne. Sali's personal favorite was the Temple of the Mourning Shale in Sheetan depicting the Khan jumping onto a horse. The sculptor who created that statue, unfortunately, wasn't quite up to the task, and it looked like the Khan was taking a wide stance to urinate.

Here at the Grand Monastery of the Dawn Song, the Eternal Khan of Katuia was standing completely naked, facing the heavens with his legs spread and his arms splayed out. Having grown up with Jiamin, she knew for a fact this sculptor had made some flattering artistic choices. Still, it was good to see her friend's face one more time instead of having to rely on a fading memory.

Incense poured from copper pots hanging from the ceiling. Several shamans were praying on padded rugs circling the statue. A steady voice chanted, and a gong sounded at intervals. It was warm, and the air was heavy. The heat from the hundreds of lit candles from the rows of torches on the wall, the lanterns hanging from the dozen or so chandeliers, and dozens of others on individual stands, was suffocating to the lungs. She was also mildly surprised this place hadn't burned down by now.

Sali coughed, wiping a thin stream of blood that leaked from the corner of her lips. Things were worsening; her body, long failing, was shutting down. Her guts twisted but she kept calm and continued walking through the temple as normally as she could. Each step felt like a ten-foot plunge onto stone. She broke into a fever, and sweat drenched her face, but she was also freezing, her teeth chattering. It took Sali several moments to gather herself. She had been closer to vomiting than she was comfortable with. When she was ready, she sucked in a breath and continued deeper into the temple.

Sali continued past the statue and entered another circular room.

The center of the room had a large display with a true-to-life painting of the Eternal Khan of Katuia in all his terrible glory with bulging muscles, long beard, hairy body, and devastating presence. There was a row of paintings of the Khan sitting on his throne throughout the centuries complete with displays of vases, jewelry, weapons, and several armored mannequins. He looked mostly the same in each life, but there were always a few slight differences imprinted by the host.

Lining the walls were several divided booths that spanned the perimeter of the room. Sali walked up to the first and looked inside to see an exhibit of one of the Khan's hosts. The next display was from three centuries ago. His name was Fosai, hailing from the capital city of Jomei. There was a painting of a young bald boy with a high topknot, which was the style then.

"Found when he was nine. Joined when he was fourteen," Sali read aloud. "Known as the explorer, the holy Khan spent little time in Chaqra, but spent his entire reign enriching Katuia by raiding the Zhuun, and beyond, having ventured as far as the White Ghost Lands." A roughly hewn broken lance rested against the wall.

The next exhibit was of a boy named Kira. He was the next in line after Fosai died in battle. It took seven years before the Khan was reborn into a new body. This Khan's reign was marked by philosophical endeavors. He built a code of just law for all people to follow. Sitting atop a small pedestal just below the painting was an open book.

The next was Pompu, and then Shree, and the list continued on. There were more than thirty exhibits, each with a painting of the host and a summary of the Khan's accomplishments during that lifetime, as well as an item belonging to the host.

Sali snorted. This room in the back half of the Grand Monastery of the Dawn Song on Masau was little more than a museum to the Khan. What none of this answered, however, was how the Khan came into being, and if there was a cure for who and what he was. Where was the sacred knowledge? How did the Khan's immortality work? How did he come to be? Where were the holy texts about their faith? What was the ritual for sharing a khan's soul with his Sacred Cohort? Most importantly, was there a way to reverse it without killing her? Where were the holy texts explaining how his powers worked? She didn't travel all the way here for a silly history lesson.

However, as she continued to walk along the exhibits, she became more thankful that something like this did exist. These were the chosen young men before they became the Khan. Each one of them was young, between ten and twenty years old, and carried a certain light in their eyes. No two smiles were alike. Then they became that man whose exhibit sat in the middle of the room: the Eternal Khan of Katuia, and whatever made these children unique was snuffed out by the Khan taking over the body. Without this memorial, these young men and their sacrifices would have been forgotten.

Sali was looking forward to seeing Jiamin's exhibit and was deeply thankful to see a painting of him during his youth, right before he changed into the Khan. Her eyes brimmed when she gazed upon Jiamin's portrait. It had been a long time since she saw his youthful face. It wasn't like she remembered, but it rekindled many fond memories. They were certainly happier times. She remembered the day the painter arrived to draw his portrait. It was considered a great honor not just for him and his family, but for the entire clan. Everyone had been so excited. His mother had been so proud.

Still, Sali couldn't help but mutter, "He should have said no."

Sali read Jiamin's history on his plaque aloud. "Jiamin, born from the hearth of Glassmaster Suryo and Woodshaper Titanish from the Nezra (exiled) clan." Of course they had to add that. "Jiamin was honored at the age of fifteen . . . Blah, blah, blah." The tribute continued about Jiamin's Sacred Cohort, including Salminde as his second Will of the Khan, also with a notation calling her a fugitive and traitor. It listed many of his accomplishments, his raids, putting down the rim clan Choguna uprising, and his successful sacking of North Pengnin, retribution for the slaughter of four hundred of their people by the land-chained savages. Most of the information was correct. Sali would know. She had fought beside him for most of the campaigns.

It was when Sali reached the second part of the tribute that things went sideways. According to the plaque, the enemy had launched a massive attack, throwing the might of the Zhuun empire into a concentrated blitz deep into the Grass Sea aimed at Chaqra. The Eternal Khan single-handedly fought off a Zhuun vanguard until Nezra arrived. Then he and the capital city gloriously fought the enemy to a standstill until Nezra ran out of arrows and their weapons shattered. Still, they fought with their bare hands until the city's sparkstone furnaces were exhausted before the Khan succumbed against the enemy that outnumbered them a hundred to one. It was written here that Jiamin's last stand had saved thousands of Katuia lives.

The last plaque of the exhibit listed that the Khan, through Jiamin, was an accomplished poet and singer. They also said he was an incredible leader with a wondrous harem and that he was singlehandedly responsible for ushering in a new age of arts among the Katuia.

Sali's teeth clenched. While Jiamin did love poetry, he had eclectic and often poor taste. Jiamin also didn't care for sex. He probably had the most unused harem in the history of the khans. Everything else was deeply rose-colored. If the spirit shamans were going to put up an exhibit memorializing all of these young men who became khans, at least they could be truthful to both the good and the bad. Now Sali didn't trust anything that was written here about any of the other men. At the very least, their sacrifice should have earned them the privilege of having their stories told honestly.

Sali scanned for a shaman to berate to correct these lies. She found one speaking to two Happan on the other side of the room. One Happan was dressed in an exceptionally fine puffin-feather fur suit, while the other was a servant holding a broom. The cleaner must work at the monastery, because the shaman was screaming at the man, his voice carrying all the way to Sali. A nearby display of a stuffed stallion, probably one of the previous khan's horses, had fallen over, and one of its legs had broken off. The Happan in the puffin fur suit placed himself between the two, obviously trying to calm the situation.

Sali focused her petty rage at the spirit shaman. Sharp emotions, especially anger, when mixed with the Pull of the Khan, often twisted Sali's stomach in many shades of awful. Her head throbbed while her stomach flipped. The bile began to creep up her throat again. Sali had striven to keep her emotions even-keeled over the past few years. Unfortunately, the lies on Jiamin's display had touched a raw nerve.

Sali marched up to the shaman. "Pardon, holy one, I require words of knowledge and wisdom."

"Yes." The shaman turned to her and recoiled at her unhealthy visage. She was used to it by now. "You are a pilgrim? From where?"

Sali should have prepared an answer. She thought quickly. "Arazraz, Holy One."

"From the southern coast of the Blue Sea? You have traveled far, pilgrim."

She placed a hand over her heart. "I have traveled a long way to be closer to the Khan. Those exhibits, however, contain falsehoods."

The shaman treated her with a haughty and dismissive glance. "Who are you to question the wisdom of the shamans? We are the Eternal Khan of Katuia's stewards. It is our sacred task to guide him into this world and shepherd him when he takes his reprieve from these middle lands. None know his history better than his caretakers."

Caretakers. Sali was about to tell him what she thought of the spirit shaman's caretaking when she remembered her reason for being here. She needed to focus on finding answers for her illness, not pick pointless fights with the people who had the answers.

Sali swallowed her anger. "Of course, holy one. My mistake. I am indeed a pilgrim who has traveled a long journey to bask in the wisdom of the Eternal Khan's ancestral home."

"Of course," said the spirit shaman. "I will be happy to offer you a tour of the Grand Monastery of the Dawn Song."

"No," she said. "I have a . . . friend who suffers from being part of the Khan's gift. He needs a cure—"

"Anything the Khan offers a humble servant is a gift. There is no need to find a *cure* for the Khan's gift. It is not a disease or poison. What it is, blasphemer, is sacrilege. On your knees and beg the spirits for forgiveness," the shaman spat.

Of course the shamans who resided here were the most annoying, fervent fundamentalists. And Sali was not about to drop to a knee for this mouth breather. She tried tact one more time. "I assure you, my friend is very ill. His sickness has spread—"

"The Khan's blessing is healing and power," the shaman insisted. "It's the unworthy body that fails. The Khan's spirit is pure and eternal."

"My friend is dying. I beg you."

"If your friend was truly Sacred Cohort," the shaman sniffed, "which is doubtful, he should let himself die, if he had any honor. His very breath betrays our Khan and impedes the great Khan's return to begin his next cycle."

Sali swallowed the urge to grab that smirking, spitting shaman by the collar and slam his head against the nearby stone pedestal. She was well aware that her control over her emotions had been slipping of late the more her health deteriorated. Sometimes, she couldn't help it. Her hand went as far as to reach for the shaman before her gut failed her. Sali hunched over and spewed fish all over the floor. She shuddered and dropped to a knee. It was so hot in here now. She threw back her hood, her chest heaving before she looked up and met eyes with the Happan servant with the broom. The man's eyes were wide, filled with fear and curiosity.

"Out, out, you diseased wretch. You leper! How dare you soil this holy site with your taint." The haughty long-bearded shaman shoved Sali. She really wanted to hit him back. "Guards, throw this unclean woman out!"

Picking a fight inside the Grand Monastery of the Dawn Song, the holiest site in Katuia, was probably a bad idea. Sali backed away when the guards arrived and allowed them to march her out the door. Sali looked over her shoulder as she walked away. The shaman was already yelling at the two Happan again. He had probably already forgotten about his encounter with her.

Sali glanced back inside and met eyes with the wealthier Happan staring her way just as the front doors slammed shut.

CHAPTER TWENTY-SEVEN

FOSTER TEACHER

Jian grunted as he carried armfuls of firewood to the wall just outside the kitchen. They burned through a lot of fire with this many mouths under one roof. Sometimes, he felt more like Taishi's groundskeeper than her student, let alone heir, let alone Prophesied Hero of the Tiandi.

He passed by Sonaya, who was curled up on a bench reading a book, and deposited his load of cords onto the ground. Jian began to stack them one by one. He looked over at Sonaya. "You know, if you're not doing anything, I could use a hand."

Sonaya licked the tip of her finger and turned the page in her book. "I'm absolutely doing something. I'm reading, which is something you should do more of, Five Champ."

Sohn stumbled out from the kitchen, looking bleary-eyed. His face was red and his eyelids lazy. The man probably hadn't slept yet. He tossed Jian a gourd, who caught it and placed it on the wooden table next to him. "This one's empty. I need another." The eternal bright light master caught Jian's disapproving look and scowled. "What are you looking at?"

Jian averted his eyes and said nothing.

Sohn's scowl deepened. "You have something to say, kid? Is this the part where you dare call me a screwup too? Come on, Champion of the Five Under Heaven. Spit it out, if you have the courage."

That was when Jian realized Soa Sohn was not a stupid man. He was goading Jian, seeing how far he could push him before Jian snapped back. Well, fine, Jian would oblige the eternal bright light master. "If you insist, master. The scholar who teaches my lessons about the Enlightened States and the master war artist who trained me yesterday on the use of shield lock formation is not the same man that loafs around the temple drinking and gambling every day."

Sohn stormed over to Jian and raised a meaty fist, and then he slammed it down onto the wooden table right between them. The thick wood at first splintered loudly, a crack spiderwebbing outward from the direction of his fist. Then the table broke apart in two and collapsed down the center. The hotpot kettle fell onto its side, their breakfast spilled all over the floor. The wine gourd, already down to dregs, leaked what little was left. Sohn's eyes were alight with fury, and for a moment Jian thought the eternal bright light master was going to finish what the Mute Men, assassins, and dukes all failed to do.

The eternal bright light master's hands were clenched into fists, and his chest heaved as he glared into the distance. For some reason, he looked much bigger and more intimidating than he ever had. Finally, he looked down at the spilled wine and yelled at no one in particular, "I need more wine. Someone get me another gourd."

Sonaya, still flipping through her book on the other side of the courtyard, called back. "We're bare, master. You already drank it all."

"What?" Sohn stood abruptly and stormed back into the kitchen. Everyone at the temple could hear his loud grumbling as he stormed outside, his dark green robes fluttering about in the stiff breeze. He disappeared into the storeroom on the other side of the courtyard. A string of loud curses followed the sounds of him rummaging through their dwindling supplies. He stormed back out a few minutes later.

"Aha!" He returned a few moments later with his prize in his hand. "This last one had rolled off the shelf and fallen behind a barrel." The eternal bright light master popped the stopper off the gourd and poured a cup, and to Jian's surprise, offered it to him. "I have a new lesson for you today, kid, and this one can't be taught dry."

Jian stared at the drink. Then he shrugged and accepted it. "Uh, thanks, Master Soa."

"It's just Sohn in this conversation. Walk with me." The master strolled briskly across the courtyard. He stepped over the half-built fence Jian never got around to finishing and then pushed the gates open. He shrugged at a renewed blast of wind and began walking toward the small grove of trees near the southwestern edge of the pillar. "New lesson today, kid. Let's talk about expectations." The master swigged the last few drops of his gourd and tossed it aside. "You're the bloody Prophesied Hero of the Tiandi. I bet that that title means a lot to you."

There was a lengthy pause. "Oh," said Jian. "Were you asking me?"

"Yes, you dumb melon, of course I'm talking to you."

Jian considered the question briefly and then played it safe. "It is a gift, and a burden too, I guess. It does weigh on me a bit."

"There's a saying my ba used to tell me. Every latrine on a ship empties into the sea," said Sohn. "That's what you have to do with those expectations. Let them all go. Don't hold on to that poison, kid. Sure, being called special can get heady, but I bet that burden also drags you down to depths you never realized existed, hasn't it? People have expectations of you. The hero needs to kill this man and unite this empire. The hero needs to be a master war artist and kill the Khan. The hero needs to be tall and strong with a chiseled chin and long, flowing locks of hair. Everyone wants something from the hero, but let me ask you . . ." Sohn's voice dropped into a whisper. "What does the hero want?"

"I want to service my destiny and fulfill the prophecy," said Jian automatically.

"Bah." The eternal bright light master slapped the back of his head. "That's what everyone else wants you to do. What do *you* want?"

"I want to save my people."

A harder slap. "What do *you* want, Wen Jian?"

Jian blinked. "I don't want to disappoint anyone."

The next blow on his back felt more like an open-palmed punch. "I want to talk to Jian, not the Prophesied Hero of the Tiandi, not the Sav-

ior of the Zhuun, or some terror of the hordes and crap. Just Wen Jian."
He rapped the top of Jian's head with his knuckle. "Is Jian still in there
somewhere, or is it all the holy predestined expectations now?"

Jian couldn't take it anymore and batted the master's arms away and
snapped back. "What do you know about expectations? You ran away
from yours." Jian's eyes widened. He gasped and covered his mouth. Behind him, someone else gasped too. Apparently, Sonaya was eavesdrop-
ping.

"Finally, some fire," beamed Sohn, pushing back. "Tell me, kid.
What do you know about me? Tell me all those things children say be-
hind my back that you wouldn't to my face. Go on. I can take it. Go.
On."

Jian averted his eyes. "That you inherited your family's war arts business with over fifty schools. Then you drank and ran it into the ground,
saddled it with gambling debts, and disgraced the family name."

"Hah, if it were only that easy." The master waved his hand. "Blame it
on the drink and addiction. How typical and expected of the first son,
right? Spoiled to incompetence and then to disgrace, right?"

Jian's curiosity was piqued. "You mean, it didn't happen like that?"

"Nah, I was all set to become the new grandmaster of the family upon
my father's death. I was still consolidating my family and supporters. My
franchisees, you know."

Jian really didn't. He nodded.

Sohn continued. "Sohi, my younger brother, approached me shortly
after I became head of the family. He said he had proof that our father
was murdered, but that I was getting framed for it. Of course, he knew it
was a trumped-up lie, he said, but even the accusation would splinter the
family, shatter the war arts lineage, not to mention destroy the business.
Panicked, I asked him what to do, and he recommended I step down to
save the family from shame." He shrugged. "So, I did."

"Wow, that's dumb." Jian covered his mouth again. The zuijo was
making him bold and careless.

"And you wouldn't be wrong," Sohn admitted. "But I was a gullible
seventeen-year-old dumb egg at the time. What did I know?"

Jian frowned. "How old was your brother then?"

"Fourteen," mumbled Sohn. He raised his voice. "But he was a cunning and sneaky fourteen-year-old little piece of dog shit."

Jian stared at his cup and downed the rest. His eyes burned. "So, he takes over the family business and you go into hiding?"

"He said he would concoct a good alibi to explain why I stepped down. Stupid me, I believed him. He told everyone I was a drunk with gambling debts and I was running the war arts business into the ground, so he had no choice but to step up and assume the mantle of grandmaster." Sohn sniffed and kicked a rock down the road. "Not only was I stripped of my home and family, but I was also made a mockery by my only little brother. I should have drowned him in the tub when we were kids."

"Why didn't you challenge him, master?" asked Jian. "Call him out on the lies and reclaim your place in your family."

Sohn bowed his head. "At first, I was too ashamed to speak up. My rat-faced brother convinced me that I had dishonored my family name. Sohi, my little backstabbing brother, had simply embellished my failures. He had even convinced me it was for my own benefit. It was the gambling and drinking addiction that caused my downfall, not my gross incompetence." He chuckled bitterly. "At the time, that somehow was more palatable. With each passing year, those lies turned into reality, not only in the minds and perceptions of those related to us but also in my personal truth. While in hiding, I turned to the drink and the thrill of the dice to numb my shame. Everything else felt dead. I became exactly who Sohi accuses me of being. So, yeah, it's probably too late."

Jian couldn't even imagine that level of betrayal. Mainly because he had no siblings or even knew who his family was, so really, he wasn't that sympathetic, but that did sound like it sucked. "That really sucks."

"It did," said Sohn, without the slightest bit of irony. "Everyone expected me to be something, and I just cratered myself so badly. Head of a lineage to a drunk addict hiding from creditors. How can the lead weight of responsibility and expectations not drag you down, right? But you would know, right? You understand this as well as I do."

"I mean, if I don't achieve what's expected of me and kill an immortal master war artist who may or may not be already dead, then everyone else dies," said Jian slowly. "Don't get me wrong. I understand your point, but the expectations coming from being head of a prominent war arts family aren't quite on the same level as being the center of a failed prophecy."

"Bah, it's not about the scope, kid." He banged on Jian's chest. "It's about how it knifes your heart."

Jian couldn't disagree with that. "How did you deal with the pressure, Master Soa?"

"I hid, and I drank. Don't do that, kid. But here's a piece of advice so you don't end up like me." Sohn was very drunk now. "Forget what everyone wants Wen Jian, the Prophesied Hero of the Tiandi, to do. Ignore all their *expectations*. Find out what you really want deep in your gut and do it. If it feels right, then it probably is. Yeah, kid?" He banged on Jian's chest again. "We need another gourd."

"What happened to every latrine in a ship empties into the sea?" said Jian.

"Exactly," said the eternal bright light master. He looked suddenly sober. "Don't end up like me, kid." Sohn raised his voice. "Someone get me another gourd."

"I told you that was the last one!" Sonaya shouted.

Sohn cursed. "Well, I guess we're going on a booze run, I mean supply run, to the outpost tomorrow."

"I'm not supposed to leave the temple." Jian held on to hope. If there was any master who would flout the rules . . .

"This is a dry emergency, kid," said Sohn. "We need to replenish the cooking wine before they return anyway. It would be irresponsible of me, as the master currently responsible for you. I think it'll season you well to get out a bit. By the way, is Taishi's banking marker still good?"

Jian's head was telling him this was a bad idea, but his excitement spoke otherwise. He nodded. "It is, but I'm only supposed to use it on—"

Sohn brightened. "Excellent then. Where's your sense of adventure, Champion of the Five Under Heaven? Worry not, it'll just be for a day or two, just long enough to replenish our supplies and buy more wine. We'll be back before anyone is the wiser. Go drink some water and get some sleep, kid. We head to the Bahng at first light."

CHAPTER TWENTY-EIGHT

MEETING IN DALEH

Taishi hated to admit that Saan was right. A little rest after the long night's ride did her much good. They were each led to small but adequate personal quarters carved even deeper into the tree trunk. The walls, floors, and ceilings inside had been treated with flames. Disappointingly, no tub, but they were provided a rag and a bucket of lukewarm water. Nevertheless, Taishi put it to good use and emerged from her chambers refreshed as if having awoken from a restful slumber.

A Mute *Woman* was waiting outside her door. She looked younger than the others, likely their pup, which was why she was pulling guard duty. The young lady took her job seriously, however, and shot her a cold stare—obviously trying hard to overcompensate. She pointed outside, back to the outer ring where Urwan, Bhasani, and Fausan were already waiting at the doorway.

Taishi honed her stern gaze on the one among them who organized this expedition. "How much did you know about this ahead of time, Urwan?"

"Don't take it out on me," he replied, undaunted. "The dukes ordered this meeting arranged in complete secrecy. I had assumed he would send a messenger, or even a lord or general. But a mindseer with a full pack of Mute Men?" He shook his head. "They went through some extreme lengths to arrange such a meeting."

The horselord obviously did not understand how Saan thought. "My former pupil never takes chances. He knows that any rank lower than his very presence might not convince me. A mindseer is the next best thing to being here in person. He wants something badly." She joined them at the doorway and continued outside. She admitted, reluctantly, "Still, you're not wrong. Even for a secret meeting involving dukes, scheduling it in such a remote cesspool as the Dark Heart feels excessive."

They crossed two wooden rope bridges between two of the giant trees, walked past the main building they'd been at a few hours earlier, and then proceeded up a suspended spiral staircase made from netting and planks. They continued along the upper platform still not having seen a soul save for the Mute Men lurking about. This particular group was more aggressive than usual for their kind. It could be because they were assigned to the duke, or it could be because they sensed a serious threat.

They entered what could only be considered the mansion of this outpost, a squat five windows wide and three tall facades. Her gaze crept a little above the building and noticed several more Mute Men standing on the branch just above it. Instead of bringing them inside, the Mute Woman led them to a small trail cut into the trunk that curved around the side, zigzagging up to the next branch.

The mindseer was sitting poised and upright on a wooden sofa carved directly into the branch. She lit a cigarette between her elongated fingers and placed it into a tray on a small table next to her.

The woman looked straight at Taishi with a glazed expression, and then her eyes rolled up into the back of her head. Her body went rigid for several moments before her irises finally rolled back. Her posture changed; her shoulders drooped, her body slumped, and then she sank into the cushions of the sofa.

The mindseer looked over to the side at the cigarette burning in the tray and picked it up, this time with her forefinger and thumb. She took a puff and waved them closer. "Splendid. None of you are stinking up around my presence anymore." Saan, now linked to the mindseer, gestured to the Mute Woman standing by. "Gourds and cups all around. Fresh fruit and a plate of sweet fried dough."

Taishi watched the young woman leave. "Don't you have servants for things like that to serve you hand and foot?"

"Not by choice, I promise, but my personal guard detail insist." Saan waved her off dismissively. "I'm not the same pampered boy you trained all those years ago, master, but that's not the ducal way, at least not outside my palace. Trust is a rare commodity in this age of civil war and broken prophecies. Dongshi's sent so many assassins, I'm running out of ditches to toss their corpses into."

"But you're not actually here," said Fausan, frowning. Then he remembered who he was speaking with. He bowed, touched his fist to his palm, and then bowed again. "Your Grace."

"It's annoying," said Saan matter-of-factly, "but if a mindseer dies, anyone linked to them at the time dies as well." He pointed at the many black-cloaked individuals surrounding them. "A duke can never be too careful, thus all these Mute Men. Come, sit, sit."

The four masters sat on the nearby seats in a circle around the duke until it was just Saan and Taishi standing. They studied each other in silence, as much as one could eye a duke. The years had been hard on Saan. During his youth, when he had earned the nickname "Perfect Boy," he had painted his face to bolster that image and good looks. Saan had always understood the value of good publicity.

Now known as the Painted Tiger for his many mostly well-earned victories, his painted face served to mask the flaws in his once strong and confident handsome visage. Still, not even the thick layers could completely mask two deep scars on his cheek and neck. The lines around his eyes cut deep into his face, and there was a tired distant look in his gaze.

Taishi reached over Saan's hand and picked a lychee from the bowl. "How bad is it? Really?"

"Well, we're in the middle of a civil war. We're on the cusp of a famine, and tree bark–chewing morons are robbing mail wagons. Dongshi's snakes are nipping at my ass, and Yanso froze half of my treasury accounts that were kept in Allanto, which I admit now was short-sightedness on my part. He was offering such good interest rates, though." Saan shrugged.

"Not that any of that matters, because my own stepmother is flogging me harder now than when I was a boy. I possess every logistical advantage, and I can't win a battle to save my life."

"You're in the wrong line of work, Saan," said Taishi.

Both Fausan and Bhasani gasped and fell into a heap of coughs.

"What was that?" Saan heard it right the first time. His cool, glib demeanor cracked. "What do you mean by that, Taishi? Speak freely, but I would consider your next few words carefully, master."

"I don't care about your brittle feelings, Saan." She really didn't. "You're not a great administrator. You're not a great general. You're not even a particularly good duke."

"You know, I take that back. Maybe you shouldn't speak so freely anymore," said Saan.

Taishi continued. "But one thing you are extraordinarily talented at is surrounding yourself with good, competent, and loyal people. They're the reason you have the best-equipped standing army in the Enlightened States. It's why your duchy is generally the most boring, the most stable, and why it's where people my age come to die."

"I sound like a fabulous duke then," he protested. "It's the people who make the difference, and I bring the best to my court."

"Your people *do* make you look very good," admitted Taishi, "but you, Duke Saan of Shulan, are flawed and a completely forgettable duke. You love too many women intensely but briefly. You can't be bothered with details, which is ironic considering how many women you love. You also can only focus on one thing at a time, which then you latch on to like a jackal in heat." He was also a touch too sensitive to be an effective ruler. Taishi spared him that. She put her hand on the shoulder of her former pupil. "Saan, it's all right. You're a good man, a middling duke, but a good man. And you would make an awful emperor."

Saan towered in front of her for several moments, temporarily frozen like one of the many statues of him posing in his garden. He spoke loudly to no one in particular. "This is the point when my indignant personal guards draw their weapons."

More than a dozen blades hissed out of their sheaths. The room began to feel suffocatingly closed off. Taishi may have stepped a little over the line, a little. Little Saan had always been a haughty boy, albeit with a good heart. Taishi hoped the others weren't dumb enough to act if Saan actually did order her capture.

Taishi remained unfazed. She might as well get everything off her chest. "Be honest with yourself, Saan. You don't want the job either. You hate being a duke. You hate ruling. You hate making decisions, so why go after the promotion, which is even more of everything you hate, not to mention boring, cumbersome, and incredibly treacherous. You were the handsome auxiliary son, the one without a care in the world. All the rewards of a prince and none of the responsibilities. You sought glory freely at your leisure until your brother choked on a sword. And now the weight of your family, your dynasty, and all of the Enlightened States rests on your weary shoulders. Which sucks for you." Taishi leaned in. "Oh, yes, you're going to have to get married. To one girl!"

Saan growled and curled his lips before his expression turned slowly sheepish. "Except for the part about choking on the sword. It was actually dysentery, but that reflects poorly on the family."

"Did you just say an infection besmirched your family's honor?"

Fausan, who was helping himself to the food the Mute Woman brought over, looked curious. "Wait. If Duke Saan was Taishi's student, then why isn't he the master windwhisper now?"

Bhasani, sitting next to him, hissed. "You're a dumb egg."

"Ooh, is it because he's arrow fodder?" Fausan said the quiet part aloud.

Saan retorted quickly. "My war arts ability serves me well enough." He had always been sensitive about his limited abilities. "I have a duchy to rule and armies to command. I can't spend all of my days training and frolicking like some others."

"What about all those stories about your amazing prowess?" asked Bhasani.

"He made it up," said Taishi.

"I did not make it up!" Saan snapped.

"I've seen you fight. I've trained you. You're not beating Katuia Bullcrash or Tigermaul sect warriors. You didn't walk away surviving an unarmed duel against Diyu Mountain Devils, or however that poem goes.

At least not without an entire personal retinue doing all the fighting for you."

"All great tales required some embellishment," he admitted. "Good publicity is the fourth pillar of power. Public favor is the new third front of war, and it's the only front we are winning at this time." He poured himself a drink and swigged it as if he were in a mess hall with his men. "If I get drubbed anymore, my eastern flank is going to collapse, and then that koala-face Yanso and his pillow-fist army will certainly make a move."

"That right there," Taishi pointed out. "That's what you do best. Stand in the front line and exude charisma and leadership. Look gallant and woo the locals. You're great at that. Your people love you. You are a great figurehead."

"I owe all that to my publicity team," said Saan.

"But you're a mediocre warrior, and worse, an indecisive general," said Taishi. "Which is why you're bogged in the tar while vultures circle overhead. You're considered a competent administrator only because you're charismatic and attract good people. That's the only reason you haven't run the entire duchy into the ground."

The lines around Saan's eyes tightened, and the metal cup began to crumple in his clawed hands. Good, she was getting through to him, finally, assuming he didn't unleash his Mute Men on her first.

Saan plopped back down in his chair. "Remind me never to allow you to be frank again. You were a little rough with me back there, master."

"You're the one who ordered me to investigate the Prophesied Hero of the Tiandi. You're the one who agreed to pitch in on the bounty on my head, sending me scurrying into hiding for the rest of my life. And you're the one who signed my death warrant, so *excuse* me, Duke Saan of Shu-lan, if I hurt your feelings." She poured herself a drink as well. "You don't have the heart for this job, Your Grace, because you're a good man, and good men in these roles either adapt or die. And I know that's something you are incapable of doing. You are a rigid spear. That's also why you're losing to Sunri. You have limits to whatever you are willing to do in a war. She, on the other hand, would sack her own capital if it ensured victory."

"That's something I probably need to hear," he conceded. "No one in court will dare challenge my decisions, even if I command them to."

"Ordering someone to disagree with you is probably sending mixed signals, Saan," she said.

"It was still refreshing. Although you could be much nicer about it." Saan decided to change the subject. He raised his cup. "It's good to see you, master. I'm glad you're alive."

Taishi raised hers as well. "You didn't come all this way to greet your old master. What does my duke command?"

Saan hesitated, and then looked to the side at the nearest Mute Man. "Is the area secure?"

The man nodded.

"Send them in."

The Mute Man bowed and departed. Taishi immediately noticed several more Mute Men closing in on her and the mindseer. She counted more than twenty Mute Men close by now, and that was only those within eyesight. This was far more protection than necessary, all things considered. Everything about this felt strange and wrong.

Another group emerged from a path off to the side. This one had six Mute Men surrounding two large figures, Hansoo by the looks of them. The hair on the back of Taishi's neck rose, and her body tensed as if preparing for battle. The trust and faith she had put in Urwan, and Saan for that matter, went only so far. Had she been betrayed? This wouldn't be the first time it happened, although it might be the last. She considered getting the jump on the Mute Men and alerting the others, but held off. This was a duke she was dealing with, after all, not to mention a former student. She glanced over at Saan, whose eyes were also fixed on the approaching procession. To her surprise, he appeared tense as well. What was happening?

The group stopped just at the edge of the platform where Saan and Taishi stood. The six Mute Men and two Hansoo were at attention, their eyes alert and postures formal. The Quiet Death standing together with war monks was certainly an unusual sight. They all bowed in unison, and then the two Mute Men in front parted to the sides. The Hansoo walked forward together, and then they too parted to the sides.

Standing behind them was a young girl, likely no older than eight or nine, with a once shaved head that was now several weeks old. Her red-

and-white robe and cloak were plain but finely woven wool, but the stains and tears on them exhibited much travel and wear. She was a beautiful child with an ageless look about her, her face glowing with sparkling innocence and calm. The most striking thing about her, however, were her eyes: two islands of blue surrounded by shimmering seas of white that appeared deeply wise and knowledgeable compared to her meager years.

The girl looked nervous. Her voice cracked when she began speaking. She stopped and started anew. "Greetings, Ling Taishi." The child's voice was quiet and innocent. Her light tone bounced around the trees. "It is good to see you again. The mosaic has seen fit for our weaves to cross once more."

"What are you blathering..." Taishi's eyes widened. There were very tangible reasons why a young child escorted by two massive Hansoos would have access to a duke of the Enlightened States. She fell to her knees.

Bhasani, usually the sharpest among the masters, wasn't far behind. The gasp that escaped her sounded as if someone had run her through with a dull blade. She dropped down next to Taishi and went a step further, falling forward and pressing her forehead to the ground.

Taishi's voice quivered like a boy giving a girl a tulip for the first time. "I don't understand. You're dead."

The young girl burst into a grin. "Life and death are just the beginning and ends of different threads. Once you tie them all together . . ." She touched the tips of her forefingers together, and then blushed. Her hands disappeared, and she wiggled as if she had to potty. "I walked your life in my visions, Master Ling Taishi. I'm a big fan of your adventures. Especially when you were just starting off. You were such an inspiration! I want to be just like you when I grow up."

"You should probably aim higher, girl." Taishi harumphed. She wasn't sure what it meant for someone to walk her life, but she didn't doubt the girl's words.

"Can someone tell me what's going on?" asked Fausan.

"On your knees, idiot!" snapped both Taishi and Bhasani at the same time.

"I'm not bowing to someone without knowing who they are," the whipfinger master replied suddenly. "Who is this tiny slip of a girl? I've had dumps bigger than this little dragonfly."

The girl looked puzzled, as if in thought. "That is not true, Noon Fausan, God of Gamblers, the Man with the Twelve Fingers, the Midnight Fox. As for who I am, like you, I have had many names as well. I was called the Beacon of Midnight, the Eternal Loom Mistress, and the Unblinking Blind Eye."

"Well, I never heard of you," said Fausan. "Those names are all terrible, by the way."

Bhasani sucked in her breath. She looked horrified. Since when did the drowned fist master find religion? She never did during her youth.

The little girl did not appear offended. "I especially admired that one time you and six of your fellow war artists defended that village against the Zho Zho Gray Bandit horde. And you took nothing in payment except for rice and a cot to sleep. It was very noble of all of you."

"We were starving and there weren't any jobs to be had at the time," Fausan conceded. "Hey, how did you know this?"

"She's the Oracle of the Tiandi, you lump head," said Saan with a sigh. He turned to Taishi. "Really, master? You always tell me to surround myself with good people, and that's who you band together with?"

"Get out of here. You can't pull one over on me, you rascals," Fausan scoffed. He squinted. A small smile appeared on his face. "All right then. If you are all knowing, can you tell me something, god to god? There's this girl named Ayna I once loved back home. We were promised to each other and were supposed to get married the summer after my first campaign. The war ended up lasting two years. When I returned, she was gone." Fausan looked earnest. "Can you perhaps tell me what happened to her?"

A wine cup flew past him from the direction where Bhasani stood, narrowly missing his head, but drenching him in the process. The drowned fist had her hands on her waist, and her lips were contorted into a snarl. "Again with that girl!"

CHAPTER TWENTY-NINE

THE RICH MAN

"... and then they just tossed me out as if they had caught me smoking incense. The guards not only threw me entirely out of Masau, but I also think I'm banned from even crossing the bridge."

Hampa smiled, holding up his cup. "I smoked the shaman's incense before."

"Everyone has. I'm fairly certain the shamans always kept the good stuff for themselves." Sali grinned. The two touched cups.

Daewon mumbled something.

"What was that?" said Hampa.

"I think that stuff is bad for you."

"I know. After I inhaled it, I thought I could fly so I jumped off the tip of a tall weed. Broke my ankle." Hampa giggled. Sali laughed. They touched cups again. The tinker looked confused.

The three had gathered back at the same restaurant the next day. They had intended to dine at another venue, but by the time Hampa arrived, it was too late, so they decided to eat here again. The vendor had smirked at Daewon when he came to their table to place their order. The food was just as tasty and salty as the last time, but they had wised up to the scam. This time, Daewon insisted everyone drink no more than two glasses of water.

"What happens now, Sali?" Hampa asked as he sprinkled ginger and cumin over his octopus with its tentacles still writhing on top of a bed of salt.

She grimaced. "Nothing else to do here. I'll spend another day searching for other sources of information, but other than that, we go home."

She was surprisingly relieved that her long search was coming to an end. It wasn't that she didn't want to find a cure, but after three years of surviving and searching, Sali was bone weary and growing weaker day by day. She was ready for her struggles to end. All she wanted was to return to her clan, help train their warriors and build their defenses, and spend her last days surrounded by the people she loved. Coming to Hrusha, to the source, had given her a sense of closure that she had needed. Now her conscience was at ease and her soul could finally rest. She glanced over at Daewon. "That is, if your business is concluded, tinker. How goes it?"

Daewon did not look as positive. "The sparkstone quality here is incredible. It's pure and dense and will burn hotter for far longer than anything we've been using. It's also dreadfully expensive."

"More than what Shobansa authorized to spend?"

"By a little." The tinker speared his seared scallop and put it whole into his mouth. "About triple."

Hampa gawked. "The clan will go broke."

"The hunting and foraging isn't sufficient to last the winter. We need to trade for additional food as well," Daewon added.

"Do what we can. We'll figure out options later," Sali said. "Our people can go a little hungry. We can't go without heat, and we certainly cannot operate city pods without sparkstones."

The tinker slumped his shoulders. He looked defeated. "I placed a small order. It's all we can afford."

"Shobansa will kill us if we come back without enough to last the cycle," said Sali.

"He'll kill *me* if I spend three times what I'm allowed," Daewon replied.

"It's an acceptable trade-off." It was meant to be a joke, but the tinker took it rather literally.

"I think so too, to be honest."

It was times like this that Sali regretted being so hard on Daewon. Sometimes, he was almost worthy of Malinde. "Oh, you have to stick around, future father. Can't leave Mali to raise a child alone, can you? That would be inconsiderate. I'd kill you if you let that happen. Figure out how to get a deal done. I'll take care of Shobansa if it comes to that."

"Are you certain?"

"Go double. We can explain double, not triple." Sali was dying, so what did she care if she angered the supply chief. "Do you have any names in mind for the babe?"

Daewon bobbed his head. "We don't have a boy's name yet, but if it's a girl, I'm thinking my great aunt Salmasi."

"What about from Mali's side of the family?" Sali said. "We come from an extensive line of great warriors and famed leaders. Our lineage traces all the way back to our clan's founding centuries before the time of the moving cities. Why not honor one of the many great ones in our blood with the name of your first child?"

Daewon looked abashed. He stared at his plate of scallops on salted ice. "She just took me in when my parents died. Otherwise I would have been an orphan. I owe her everything."

Normally, Sali would have understood and accepted the tinker's simple, heartfelt desire. However, thoughts of mortality tended to change perspectives. Now, there were only two members left in her family. Two women, at that. Sali's cycle in this world would likely not last much longer. That left their entire dynastic lineage that spanned nearly a thousand years on the slim shoulders of Mali, and Daewon wanted to name their firstborn after some unknown because she took him in. Again, not that Sali wasn't understanding, but there were priorities to consider.

"We'll talk about it later, but don't get too married to that name."

"I'm pretty set on it," said Daewon. "You can't negotiate my child's name."

"Just hear me out when we get home, after I sit you and Mali down." She patted his shoulder and took her skewer and speared another scallop. Suddenly, she sensed the silent heat of attention. It was the second time she'd felt it that day. The first was while she was being manhandled out of the Grand Monastery of the Dawn Song. She had felt many stares on her but had brushed them off as curiosity. This time, it was something else; someone was studying her, but who? Sali raised the skewer with the scallop toward her mouth, but instead flung it to the side, in the direction of the attention being heaped on her.

Sali looked over and saw her skewer stuck to a wall of ice. Standing frozen next to it, hunched over with a pale face, failing to stay inconspicuous, was the well-dressed Happan in the fine puffin-feather fur suit she had seen back at the temple. The skewer was just a nose length away from his right eye and would have blinded him if not for the corner of the building. She stood and slowly strutted over to the wall where the well-dressed man with the puffin fur suit was still standing frozen.

Sali pulled the skewer out of the ice and then put the scallop in her mouth. "Why are you following me?"

The Happan looked somewhat concerned by her approach, but he appeared more excited and impressed than anything else. As soon as she walked within range, he reached for her face. Sali almost cut his hand off right there, but she simply stared him down. The man got the hint and pulled his hand back.

His eyes were wide when he studied her. "I have not seen something like this for a long time."

"It's not leprosy, I assure you," she said dryly.

"Oh, much more forbidden than that. I heard that you seek knowledge. You will not find it with the spirit shamans. It was they, your spirit shamans, who have forbidden the Happan to utter the truth, just like they have forbidden the Katuia from hearing it."

The well-dressed man's robes, strange demeanor, and his infuriating smile kept her on guard. "What knowledge do you think I seek?"

"Our history, our secrets, our broken hearts, passed down over many centuries by pipe and smoke." The man continued. "Our ritualists expand their minds by smoking an herb which allows them to memorize our people's history. This is how we pass our wisdom from generation to generation, all hidden while under the heel of the Katuia." Sali imagined if the man spat, he would have done so, if he wasn't so polite.

"Why are you telling me this?" she asked. "I'm just a Kati, right?"

"Because if someone is hated by someone you hate, they may not be such a bad person after all." He smiled. "It, at very least, earned an introduction, especially under your very special circumstances."

"What special circumstances?"

"Your soul rot is far along and indicates you were once closely linked with an old friend dear to the Happan. That makes you interesting and special. I have not seen such an advanced state of soul rot since the times before your last Khan. You must be suffering greatly."

An ember of hope sparked. "What do you know about it?"

"I am not the one to whom you must speak about the wisdom you seek, but I can take you to them." The well-dressed man looked over his shoulder.

Her eyes narrowed. "Why would you go out of your way to help me? What do you want?"

"Just a conversation, for now." The well-dressed Happan placed his hands together and bowed. "Just sharing knowledge. My only request is for you to hear our words, and then you are free to decide if you wish to listen further."

Hampa came up behind her and whispered, "What if we can't trust him?" The Happan heard that. Not that it mattered, except why bother being quiet about it?

Sali considered. On one hand, her instincts believed this man. "What's your name, old one?"

"Yuraki, lady."

"Just Yuraki?"

"I have long since donated my other names. I am now simply Yuraki."

Sali wasn't sure what that meant. "I'm Salminde, just Salminde. That's Hampa, just him too. That one sitting at the table is Daewon."

Daewon looked up from his plate with a tentacle hanging from his mouth. He waved. "Nice to meet you."

Yuraki lowered his voice; his cadence slowed. "Meet tonight up the

Orca Way strong hand sky blue nine down weak side all the way through the end."

"Are you speaking another language?" This person was not serious. Why would he ask for a meeting only to give directions in riddles? What sort of game was he playing? Sali turned away to pour herself a drink. "We're staying at a barge in the harbor. If your people want to meet, they can find us there."

"If you truly seek knowledge, lady, come find me. Perhaps even a cure for what ails your body."

"What?" Sali craned her head around, but then the Happan turned and walked off.

Sali watched the empty space where he had stood moments before. She and Hampa returned to the table and took their seats. "What do you think, mentor?"

Sali closed her eyes. She had just made peace with dying and was looking forward to going home. Now she was annoyed. She was sworn to Malinde and was now honor bound to follow this lead through to its conclusion. A sigh escaped her. "It doesn't matter what I think. We're going."

"What did he mean by those words?"

"I don't know," Sali admitted. "What was that? Orca Way blue strong, strong . . . strong something . . ."

"Orca Way strong hand sky blue nine down weak side through the end," Daewon corrected as he cleaned his plate. "I don't know, but there's a Great White Way three hills over and a Cuttle Way on the other side of the lake."

Sali scanned the lake. For the first time, she noticed the individual paths starting at the lakeshore and running up the slopes forming a sunburst shape outward from the lake. She stood. "Fine. Let's go find this stupid Orca Street."

Searching for this Orca Way ate up the rest of their day, which, of course, happened to be near the opposite side of where they started. They almost passed it due to the path starting a small distance away from the shore because of the dry docks extending far inland. It led to a more rough and derelict part of the city the farther they hiked. The alleys were narrow. Debris and refuse cluttered the paths. People in ratty fur suits huddled around raised fire pits. The temperature continued to drop as they hiked higher up the slope. The ascent was steep, and they were soon standing far above the lake.

"How much farther?" asked Hampa.

"I have no idea," admitted Sali.

Daewon stopped and did a slow pivot in a circle. "Orca Way strong hand sky blue nine down weak side through the end. We're on Orca Way now . . . Wait, I got it. Sali, I figured it out."

Sali was impressed he still remembered the entire phrase. It had escaped her almost as soon as she heard it. "Well, and?"

Daewon pointed several rows down the slope at two roofs on both sides of the road painted an earnest blue. "Sky blue. Strong hand." He raised his right fist.

Sali stared down to the right. "Strong hand facing up the slope means going right, which is that turn down there."

They backtracked a quarter way down and turned east at the sky-blue roof. They moved across the side street down—Daewon counted carefully—nine buildings before arriving at an intersection to an alley. By now, they were far from the lake, and here, on the fringes of the city, every building looked like it was falling apart. The ice block walls were saggy. The roofs and awnings were tattered. Dark figures watched them through shuttered windows. This might not be the best place for three Katuia to be at this moment.

Sali thought about the past part. "Nine buildings down. Weak side through the end." She glanced at her left arm, and then to the alley on the left.

"What if my left is my strong hand?" said Hampa.

"Then you've been holding your quarreling couple the wrong way," she replied.

Daewon looked dubiously at the garbage-strewn narrow alley that also doubled as a sewer. "This feels like a trap."

"One way to find out."

The narrow path continued up the mountain, winding down crooked and sloping paths and around jutting protrusions and sheer escarpments. They passed vendor stalls, homes, and storefronts sandwiched together, with each looking more run-down than the previous. The front facades of the buildings they passed were formed by blocks of ice and stone and framed by bone, with similarly colored roofs and awnings jutting out and hanging over the path they traveled. Several Happans wearing torn fur suits squatted on the sides of the roads alongside piles of junk and debris. The three Katuia came up to an archway cut from bone with a giant whale's rib cage hanging overhead. Just inside was a small town square lined by buildings and iceberg walls. A dilapidated statue of a man stood on a pedestal in the middle of the public space.

No sooner had they passed through the gates than several dark figures swooped in and surrounded them from all sides. Each was wearing a different animal fur suit. A motley menagerie came to mind as two appeared behind them, and then four standing off to the side drew double batons. The middle one of the three in front, the one wearing an arctic fox fur suit, appeared to be their gang leader or whatever this laughable rabble was.

"I was right about this being a trap," said Daewon unhelpfully.

A shadowy figure dropped on top of the tinker's head, throwing him to the ground. Hampa didn't even have time to turn and reach for one of his weapons when a net flew over his head and pulled him off his feet. That left Sali standing alone. The assailants converged on her.

"Be careful with the sickly one," barked the leader. "We don't want to accidentally kill—"

Sali's tongue whipped from its holster and snapped the net falling on her, shredding it into bits that fell harmlessly to the wayside. Her tongue stiffened, and she swung it in several wide arcs. Feathers flew as one man dressed in a chicken fur suit careened through the air and crashed on the ground. Her tongue bit another one on the shoulder, turning him around, and then her third attack leveled the entire wall of the nearby shack. Sali spun, whipping the tongue above her head in a looping circle, and then she went low, sweeping along the ankle and knocking several more of these hooded street rats off their feet. She finished the swings, and raised her left arm, relaxing the shaft and letting the tongue wind against her forearm before catching the bite of it in her waiting palm.

"Be careful, indeed," she remarked. These fools were not warriors.

The remaining assailants who were still standing scampered back, yelling. A cowbell clanged, and then several voices shouted throughout the neighborhood. "Kati coming!"

The busy street went quiet. People sitting at the benches, vendors selling their wares, children playing in the square. All came to a stop as the three Katuia walked into the enclosed neighborhood. Sali could feel all their focus placed upon her, and there were many, and they were terrible. The spirit shamans in Masau may rule the Hrusha, but they certainly did not rule here in this neighborhood. A group of men appeared at the far end of the square. These hefted weapons, but not the sort that worried her. The people in the square scattered. Vendors closed their stalls and fled. Parents picked up their children and herded them into shacks and slammed doors behind them.

"Stop this at once!"

Sali did, as did, to her surprise, the fur suits as well.

Yuraki appeared through the side door and stared, dismayed, at the carnage only a few moments of battle had wrought. He looked down at Daewon still tangled in the net. "I told you to bring them in, as in invite them to you, not try to string them up. When did you lot get so aggressive, Rumblerlead Marhi?"

Their leader, a long-haired young woman with a striking hook nose and intense bushy eyebrows, looked offended. "*Us?* Look at what she did to my crew. Look at Fat Woo's wall!"

"You attacked us first," Daewon said, picking himself up off the dirt.

The woman named Marhi turned to Yuraki. "You didn't warn me they were Kati. The one over there looked like she was sect. My guys panicked, so I improvised."

Hampa finally cut his way through his net. He shot to his feet. "By throwing nets on us?"

"We tried to capture you first. Thought you would appreciate capture over *death*."

"Fair point," Hampa mumbled. "Thanks."

"You're most welcome, handsome." At least they were still polite. Sali watched Hampa's face turn crimson. Or maybe she was just teasing him. She reminded herself to train him on steeling his mind. Hampa had grown quite a bit since he began training under her and was becoming his own man. Several women within the clan, and it appeared outside of it, were beginning to notice as well.

"They are guests." Yuraki turned to her. "Welcome to Hightop Cluster. Excuse our young folks. They're often overzealous with the cluster's safety. There are many dangers, you see."

"Why, what threatens it?" asked Sali.

"Your people do," Marhi sniped matter-of-factly. "But maybe you in particular."

"Why would the Happan have anything to fear from us?" asked Daewon. "We're of the same tribe now."

"Only you think that, Kati," one of the fur suits barked.

"Call us that one more time and you'll taste the bicker of my quarrels," Hampa shot back, taking a step toward the newcomer. The couple slipped into his waiting hands.

"That's enough!" Yuraki stepped between the two groups. "Get your crew under control, Rumblerlead Hoisannisi Jayngnaga Marhi. These Katuia are not here for mischief."

The man taunting Hampa scowled and then flashed dual pinky fingers. "Okay, tough talker. You get a pass. Off you go, then." The rumbler danced out of the way as Marhi playfully kicked at him as he passed.

Sali leaned toward her neophyte when he returned to her side. "The bicker of my quarrels?"

"It's my catchphrase. I've been working on my war arts image. What do you think?"

"I think you need to work harder, or not work at it at all and let it come naturally."

"Easy for Salminde *the* Viperstrike to say."

"Earn the title if you want it, neophyte."

"Is the ritualist at his shop?" asked Yuraki.

Sali perked up. Ritualist? She hadn't seen one of those holy men in years. The spirit shamans disapproved of wildlings.

Marhi nodded. "Yes, Rich Man."

Yuraki beckoned to Sali. "Come with me."

"Where are you taking us?" asked Sali.

"You go to answers. Answers do not come to you."

"The man just recited Goramh's stupid tenets back to me. The nerve," she groused. Sali had a deep love for the adventures of the amazing warrior shaman ever since she was a sprout swinging her first twig staff. The Caretaker, the spirit shaman charged with watching the council children, would recite tales around the evening hearth, especially when their parents' meetings ran late.

Sali had been deeply offended the first time she heard a Zhuun refer to Goramh not only as a priest, but as an old man. Not only that, but those stupid land-chained thought these stories were real. She had laughed for a week. How stupid could those strange foreign folk be?

The rumblerlead led them across the square, past a crude wooden statue of a figure she couldn't quite make out, and down a narrow and dirty side street. The rumblerlead was a few steps in front of Sali, chatting with Hampa and batting her eyes at him. "I don't mind if you just call me Marhi." Hampa, of course, only stammered and wilted under her obvious intentions.

The group continued deeper into the cluster. This place could only be called a slum with its many shacks, broken streets, and worn-down people. Every pair of tired eyes glared as they passed. Blades hissed out of their sheaths while people in torn fur suits hefted sticks and clubs. An old grandmother even shook a pot at them.

They finally stopped at a rickety storefront sculpted by an igloo of ice where a shirtless, bearded older man was hunched over a rusty anvil. He had several small nails in his pursed lips and was busy tapping away with a small hammer on a piece of walrus hide.

"Excuse me, Blessed Elder," said Marhi. "Rich Man Yuraki's friends have arrived."

"Who on the island isn't that man's friend?" The old man glanced up. He did not seem fazed by the dozen people crowding close. His eyes immediately shifted to Sali. "Cobbler Conchitsha Abu Suriptika, at your service." He glanced at her feet. "Lady, your boots are a mess."

"It's been a hard few cycles," she replied.

"Bad shoes means bad roots, which means everything above goes rotten." He swept his finger up the length of her body. The cobbler looked at Hampa and Daewon. "These two as well. I can cut the three of you a deal."

"Another time, perhaps. We're short on coin."

"What brings a Kati way up here to the Happan-inhabited slum of Hightop Cluster?"

"I'm told you have someone who may have knowledge about the Pull of the Khan."

"Hah, is that what you Kati call it?"

Hampa growled again. Sali stayed his hands.

The cobbler was a short, gaunt man, barely coming up to her chin, but was obviously a person of authority. The young ones looked to him to make decisions. He studied her face. "Your soul rot is impressive. You look like the dead walking."

"People keep telling me that. Can your man help us or what?"

"Perhaps. Your soul may be poisoned, but I think your feet are under greater threat at the moment."

"How much will it cost us?" asked Daewon.

"Sometimes, the good deed is payment enough, even for a Kati. Your pain must be terrible, lady." The cobbler put his tools down and wiped his hands on his apron. He pointed at Sali. "Come with me. The others stay."

Hampa tried to argue, but Sali cut him off with a look. The sooner she got this over with, the sooner she could honor her word to Sprout and conclude this search. Then she could go home.

The cobbler led her into his shop and around the counter into a back room. It smelled even worse in there than it did out in the square. The smell of hot oil and sulfur burned Sali's nose as she passed through the cobbler's workshop and into a small yard behind it. They passed through what could only be described as a junkyard full of broken wagons, wheels, and random fragments of wood, bone, and stone on one side, and torn-up shoes on the other.

The two eventually came upon what looked like a roughly hewn facade of a building in the back. It looked like an ancient temple entrance with a hewn statue of a horse on one side and a falcon on the other.

"Is this where the ritualist lives?" asked Sali.

"Ritualist Conchitsha Abu Suriptika, at your service." The cobbler placed his hands together and bowed. "We'd better get started. You may have come just in time. You look like you're about to melt and turn into goo."

Sali made a face. "That's unsettling imagery."

He grinned and wrinkled his nose. "Trust me, you smell worse than you look."

Sali leaned down and sniffed. She hated to say it, but the guy was right. The question was whether the stink was because of travel, or something else inside her.

CHAPTER THIRTY

THE DAY JOB

Several days had passed since Sunri had first arrived in Allanto to much pomp and fanfare. The massive Caobiu army of red and yellow had encamped and surrounded the southern countryside like flames in the green-and-white lotus fields about the city. It almost appeared as if the Gyian capital was under siege. Duchess Sunri of Caobiu, the Desert Lioness herself, had ridden into the city in full public view, and had nearly sent the city into a panic as a result. Half of the mob wanted to lynch her, the other half wanted to surrender to her.

Sunri had entered Duke Yanso's estate and hadn't emerged since, leaving all of Allanto simmering with dread and anticipation. Two dukes together usually meant scheming or war, likely both. Some of the servants who witnessed their interaction at the First Palace said the two dukes were cordial, friendly, even flirtatious. Another round of gossip erupted that spread past the estate walls and to every other part of the city.

Yet for Qisami, still nothing. Not a summons, not a note, not even a checkup from that hag Chiafana. That annoyed Qisami to no end. She was sure they would have received an update on their assignment by now and was beginning to wonder if she had become a forgotten asset left dangling in the breeze.

To make matters worse, Estatekeeper Hari had been serious about enrolling her in lessons. The day after her promotion, a narrow-eyed, big-waisted, gray-haired walking bitter melon with beady eyes knocked on her door after supper and began to drone boring instruction on math. It had been like that every night since. Between that, the morning head staff meeting, *and* watching over Niam's very energetic brats, Qisami had suddenly become swamped with work.

When she had broached her problem with such a heavy workload to Hari on the fourth day, the estatekeeper only shrugged. "Are you a whale, or are you cull?"

The worst part was, even though she was being groomed on the housekeeping leadership track, Qisami still had to sweep the floors, light the candles, and do all the other menial tasks required of her back when she occupied a lowly position. What was the point of a promotion then? Being promoted and put on the management track did not change her responsibilities. She wasn't even getting paid more!

It was the worst of both worlds. Qisami stewed on this every single day for seven straight days.

This morning, Lady Aki was taking her children horseback riding, so Qisami was assigned to prepare the Palace of the Gracious Guest, or the Window Palace, as it was referred to by the nobles. The servants simply called it the Fourth Palace. It was considered Yanso's least favorite palace, and one he rarely visited. Only Yanso was rich enough to have a guest palace. Rumor had it the duke was so displeased with the final product that he had the architect, a nobleman's son named Leeang, switched and stripped of his titles and sent to work on the palace's grounds for the rest of his life. Qisami didn't know if that story was true, but the gardener's name, incidentally, was Leeang.

Qisami spent the entire morning taking out her aggression by beating the dust out of tapestries and rugs with a broomstick. The tapestries hung off a clothesline in a narrow hallway leading to the rear gardens and next to a curtain of chrysanthemums. She cursed with every whack of the broom, and with every whack she executed a high-level war arts move, twirling the blade over her head or throwing two-handed combos.

The broomstick-turned-staff, or anything longer than her forearm, was rarely her weapon of choice. Qisami preferred killing up close and personal, where she could admire the terror in their eyes and smell the fear exuding from their pores. She reveled in the moment of realization as their life leaked out. Mostly, though, she thought killing from afar with a ranged weapon or indirectly with poison a weakling's game. Staffs were also a little too pacifist a weapon for her taste.

Qisami continued beating the rugs. She imagined that the long, ugly hallway runner with the mud stains that wouldn't wash out was her terrible, fat, beardo, slob father. That dainty flowerpot coaster was Yoshi, the accursed silkspinner back in Jiayi who made that terrible off-book contract that got her in trouble in the first place. The once beautiful but now raggedy rug from the rarely used third-floor balcony was that old witch bag Ling Taishi, and the one stupid circular rug around the piss basin was that stupidhead Hero of the Tiandi. The list went on for quite a while, which wasn't a problem because this very drafty and echoey building needed a lot of rugs. Qisami slowly worked up her fury with every blow until the broomstick was a blur. *Bap, bap, bap, bap!* If she had been striking flesh instead of woven fabric, this hallway would have been splattered with blood.

At last, she hit the runner so hard she put a hole through it. That was going to be hard to explain. Qisami didn't care. She could always blame it on that overcooked egg Leeang. The man was a klutz with his tools whenever he tended to the plants inside the palace.

Qisami was so engaged in murdering these rugs that she almost didn't hear the commotion behind her. She stopped mid-swing, spun around, and hid the broom behind her back in time to see five Fine Blades, the duke's personal guards, spilling into the hallway. Her cover must have been blown! How did they find her?

She found herself facing five heavily armored white-clad soldiers with subtle but very pretty swan wings on their shoulder pauldrons. They were quite dashing. This would be a stupid fight, especially since she was unarmed and wearing a constricting and heavy servant's robe and apron. What kind of an army wore white anyway? Such a terrible color for soldiers. War was a grimy affair. Nothing stayed clean in battle, and anyone wearing white at dawn would end up looking like a patch of poop stains by dusk.

Qisami had only a moment to engage with them when she pulled back and instead tried to play dumb and subservient. "Honored Walls of Gyian, how may I assist?"

One walked past her and stopped at the entrance to the back garden. Several more white-clads spilled into the room. Was Duke Yanso paying a surprise visit to this rarely used palace? That would be a first. None of the duke's families ever visited the Palace of the Gracious Guest.

Instead of the duke, however, a very disappointing Lord Aki Niam strolled down the hallway. Niam was a stout middle-aged man who stood high in the Gyian Court. Some say only Yanso and the Light General stood higher. Niam was politically well connected and had a reputation throughout all Five Fingers as an honorable man of wisdom. One of the few in the city, they said.

After accompanying the twins and spending much of her time at the Aki manor in the long strip, Qisami had been both impressed and mildly nauseated by how wholesome and good the family was. It obviously came not from decree, but by example. Those nine stupid kids even formed a choir.

More importantly, Aki Niam had been Yanso's most trusted adviser since the day their noble families had arranged a play date and the two toddlers fought over a wooden soldier. Others say it was a doll, but did that really matter? Niam loved to tell that story. It was a good reminder of just how close he was to the duke.

With the way everyone spoke so glowingly of him, Qisami had assumed he would cut a tall, statuesque figure with a sharp, trimmed beard and haughty eyes, very much like Sunri's resting duchess face. Instead, the mighty and renowned Lord Aki looked like he picked potatoes for a living. There couldn't have been a more peasant face. Tanned, with little hair, he had a large, bulbous forehead and a flat nose; Lord Aki could have been a baker working the ovens. There were many stories and examples floating around Allanto about Niam's generosity and kindness. He also carried a well-earned reputation for being an honest and generous lord.

The moment Niam walked into the room, however, Qisami found herself standing a little straighter. She wasn't the only one. Mailo was the grizzled lone guard assigned to the Fourth Palace. The man had retired many years ago after a lifetime of service but had returned to work recently due to boredom. His hunched back seemed to have fixed itself as the lord passed.

"Glorious day, good people," said Niam. "Be at ease."

Qisami felt the ease wash over her, and then she stopped it. Aki Niam's great charisma wasn't just natural charm. There was strong jing involved. Fortunately, as a shadowkill, Qisami's mind was fortified against the bulk of his effects. She still had to play the part, however. If he sensed her resistance, he could grow suspicious.

He spoke briefly with Mailo and patted his shoulder, then the high lord shared a hushed exchange with the lead of the Fine Blades. His eyes met hers briefly as he walked past. She didn't expect him to know her and was glad he didn't. A high lord's recognition was not the sort of acknowledgment a shadowkill wanted. Why would he, anyway? She was just his children's play friend.

"And where is this wonderful garden you promised, Niam?" an unmistakable voice said. Qisami stiffened when Sunri entered the hallway just a step behind him. The duchess was in full ducal garb with an expansive red-and-yellow dress draped over her body, the light chiffon layers fluttering in the breeze, giving her the impression of someone aflame. Her hair was dressed intricately to accentuate her chin, neck, and shoulders, and where the dress hung complemented her figure and impressive assets. Sunri looked every bit her reputation and exalted position.

"Ah, yes, right this way," said Niam, focusing his attention on Sunri. "By the way, regarding the arrangement, I believe it's important that we frame the relationship properly. Consider us equal partners, just that by necessity Duke Yanso will take the lead on ducal matters. For symbolism, of course, and a united front." The lord spoke with both the urgency of a street vendor with vegetables about to spoil and the earnestness of a neighbor. She could tell he laughed easily.

Qisami had already been forgotten as they strolled past her. Sunri didn't even look in her direction. Perhaps the duchess didn't recognize her.

Niam looked back at Sunri, who had lingered to study the line of hung rugs. "Is everything all right, Your Grace?"

Sunri's eyes lingered on each rug as she paced in a deliberate and cautious manner, her many layers of chiffon drifting in her wake. "These are hideous," she remarked as she caught up to the high lord. "Clear out all of your servants, Niam. I shall use my own." She turned away and paused. "On second thought, leave the scullery girl on as part of my service. I'm sure my staff would appreciate someone who understands the complexities of your estate. That one looks useless enough to spare. At the very least, she could fend off any rabid tapestries prowling about."

"Of course, duchess," said Niam, and then the two continued on and disappeared around the corner. "Right this way."

The Voice of the Court glided in next. She studied Qisami without a hint of recognition. "Know this, palacemaiden: the Grand Duchess Sunri of Caobiu is not to be trifled with. When you serve under this roof, *you serve her*. Nothing else will be tolerated." She waved her hand at the rugs. "See that these furnishings are cleaned and returned to their proper locations before Her Grace moves in tomorrow. Report to me every morning for further assignments."

There went the rest of Qisami's day. "I am honored to serve, Voice of the Court."

The voice glanced over her shoulder and pointed at the Yoshi the Silkspinner rug. "Remove that one and have it replaced. Remove every rug with depictions of tulips. The duchess does not tolerate that flower in her sight."

How could anyone have a problem with tulips? More pressing, how was she going to clean and move all of these rugs before the end of the day? And where was she going to find a bloody replacement rug in the next twelve hours? It wasn't like the duke had a gaggle of rug weavers on staff, or did he?

Nevertheless, Qisami maintained a low bow. "The duchess's expectations will be met, Voice of the Court."

She caught a sympathetic look from Mailo. Chiafana trailed into the hallway at the tail end of the duchess's procession. She was wearing high-ranking Caobiu servant robes, brown with yellow trim reminiscent of an estatekeeper. Firstwife, or rather the Minister of Critical Purpose as was her proper title, scanned the line of rugs and pointed at several indiscriminately. "Remove every one of these pathetic pieces. The rest need to be arranged collectively facing south. Is that understood?"

What? That didn't make any sense. What if a room was not facing north-south? Which way was south? Qisami bowed anyway. "It will be as you say, minister, er, estatekeeper."

Chiafana wasn't done. She pointed at a wall. "Every window needs to be draped, no exceptions. No wind or light must pass through. Fully covered and proportionally sized, mind you. Don't think we don't know there are ears lurking around every corner."

"All of them?" Qisami squeaked. There were a *lot* of windows. It was an impossible task.

Chiafana ignored her and continued to rattle off more unreasonable demands. "The flooring needs to be layered as well. The duchess does not tolerate cold stone."

By now, the duchess's procession had exited the palace and was making its way through the stone garden. Firstwife put a hand on Qisami's chest and then shoved her through a narrow servant's hallway. If it was anyone else, that hand would be severed at their wrist. "Someone is leaking information to the Shulan embassy. There is a courier who delivers the notes to a drop point just inside the south gate of the Path to Eternal Triumph. The route is down Sogano Street in the southwest quadrant of the servants' quarters. Embrace your nature and retrieve the contents."

That was simple enough. "Is the courier under ducal ward?"

"Irrelevant."

"Good enough for me."

"Here's the address of the drop." She pressed a folded piece of parchment into Qisami's palm. "Eye it by the light of the fire."

Qisami nodded. "It will be my pleasure."

Chiafana eyed her with disdain. "Make it look natural." She turned away and strolled to catch up with the duchess.

Qisami stood there for several moments watching Firstwife's retreating back. She mimed in disgust. "It will be my pleasure?" She wanted to slap her forehead. "I can't believe I said that. So embarrassing."

It *was* a stupid thing to say, but in this case she actually meant it. Finally, a job suited to her skills that allowed her to embrace her nature, as Firstwife had said. Qisami had been embedded within the estate staff for so long now she was worried her edge was beginning to dull. She sometimes had to remind herself that she wasn't actually a lowly companion or servant, but a top-of-the-heap, diamond-tier killer. "I'm a big deal," she muttered. She needed only a little convincing as she returned to beat more rugs.

"Is everything all right?" asked Mailo. "That parchment-face Caobiu bitch with the drawn eyebrows is a mean one, eh?"

"Terrifying." She thought about all the work Chiafana had just heaped upon her, *and* she wanted Qisami to do a hit. It wasn't very considerate of her.

The rest of the day was spent trying to work through the duchess's extensive list of demands, finishing the rugs, pulling the winter drapes from storage, yelling at the tailoring brigade to sew a few dozen more.

Daylight fell to evening, and then transitioned through all three shades of night. Qisami had badgered fourteen other servants and laborers to pitch in for the work. All of the rugs had been beaten and returned. The windows were wiped. The candles were lit. Most importantly, there was an ugly plain drape next to every window.

Qisami was only half-conscious by the time she dragged herself back to the Grand Tower of Blessed Servitude. She was used to demanding work—no one claimed being an assassin was easy—but having to clean and cater to a bunch of spoiled, arrogant nobles was exhausting. She would much rather get stabbed.

That Minister of Critical Purpose would certainly be death-marked if she weren't so powerful and close to the duchess. Qisami was tempted to tag the woman anyway, but she had always considered herself a person of character who kept her promises, especially when it came to killing people. By the time she dragged herself into her room and undressed, it was nearly time to rise for the day. Qisami washed up quickly before crawling into bed. She blinked, and somehow several hours had passed. Porla's freckled nose hovered over her face. The other girls were already up and about, getting dressed and preparing for the day.

"Wake time, Kiki." This time the tables were turned. Porla shook her gently. "Like you always say, best not to incur Hari's wrath by sleeping so late."

"Get off me, or I'll cut you to bits and rub chili peppers all over your wounds," Qisami mumbled, hiding under her thin wool blanket. It had been too long since she last cut anyone to bits.

"Poor dear," said Ruli, closing her robes over her sagging breasts. "Heard she had a run-in with the duchess's retinue, and now look at her. I hope she doesn't work our girl to death."

"Kiki, the second gong has already sounded," urged Porla. "You promised to come with me to the Tower of Noble Delights today. I'm getting in trouble. I need help."

Qisami had been meaning to get to that, but she hadn't had time. She also needed sleep. Qisami rolled away from the girl. "Sorry, not today. Maybe tomorrow."

"But, you promised . . ." Porla began to sniff. "I don't know what to do." A high-pitched whine escaped her pursed lips. That girl could weep on command.

There was a short knock on the door, and then it swung open. Curly-haired and pointy-nosed Hilao appeared. "Did you hear the latest scouting report?"

Just like that, Qisami was forgotten as Ruli and Porla gathered around Hilao for the latest gossip.

"What is it? Tell us!"

Hilao lowered her voice cryptically. "My brother's girl is a runner for the second palace facemaker who happened to be busy since the dukes have been in their talks. She heard some chatter about a message that came in by dove. It said that Duke Saan had crossed the border into Gyian." She bounced excitedly. "He's on his way here!"

Both Porla and Hilao danced a wiggly jig in excitement. Duke Saan of Shulan was considered the handsome duke, unlike Yanso, who was considered rich-handsome, or Dongshi of Lawkan with his secret police. Sunri's beauty was a reflection of heaven, while Waylin was just ugly. At least this was how they were described among the house staff.

After more gentle coaxing, Qisami's roommates finally roused her and got her dressed. She limply acknowledged the usual morning greetings as they joined the throng of servants, and stood, bleary-eyed, as both Porla and Hilao held her by the elbows, guiding her to the morning assembly. She slept upright even as the estatekeeper gave out the morning instructions and schedules. A cup of black tea helped revive her, but it wasn't enough to escape Hari's notice for dozing during the meeting.

"Kiki, a word," said the estatekeeper as everyone began their day.

Porla gave her a sympathetic squeeze while Hilao whispered in her ear, "It's that sunbaked witch's fault."

Qisami stood by the doorway as the rest of the servants passed until at last, she was alone with the estatekeeper. She fell in beside Hari as they walked, turning the opposite direction, and heading toward the southeast corner. "You had a late night."

Qisami was tempted to explain herself. Instead, she said, "Yes, estatekeeper."

"The Desert Lioness can be a harsh mistress," Hari began as they walked down the path toward the main strip. "It is your duty to serve her grace with as much honor and dedication as you show our beloved duke."

"I hope to prove my worthiness."

"Her favor can be valuable," continued the estatekeeper. "More importantly, if the rumors are true, our two houses may be joining. She may become your liege, so it is prudent to treat the duchess consort like a future dowager."

Hari stopped as they reached the stairs leading to the tunnel below the strip. "However, until Sunri of Caobiu takes on the Huh surname and officially calls Yanso her lord, you are still a loyal servant of Gyian, and Sunri is our enemy. View her as such, but with respect, of course."

They stepped behind a flowered stone wall and into another hidden entrance leading to the tunnels under the strip. Instead of heading down the stairs, however, Hari headed up.

Qisami hesitated at the bottom. "Estatekeeper, this leads to the strip and it is day. I am forbidden—"

"Consider your clearance raised." Hari opened the door at the top of the stairs and proceeded into a busy hallway with dozens of ugly-hatted administrators running about. Some were sitting at desks while others fussed with several wooden pieces on top of a map of the city.

"The headquarters of the duke's personal guard, the Fine Blades," Qisami snorted. What a hideous name. She had to hurry to keep up with the estatekeeper as they ascended another wide flight of stairs that wound through an open garden in the heart of the building. They stopped at the third floor and headed past the black mahogany columns with the matching wood trim. Several intricate stacks of potted plants bound together by a webbed rope hung from the ceiling. Fine wood with gold trim and jade accents framed every room, and some of the vector doors were made from blown glass. Even at work, the former purselord of the empire did not flinch at luxury.

They stopped at a double door on the east side of the building. Two white-clad guards standing at attention flanked the doorway. Interestingly, they were wielding staves, not spears. A younger soldier working at a desk stood and offered Hari a stiff bow. Hers was perfect, as always, even to this young snot.

The white-armored soldier—he was even uglier up close—walked to the doors and slid them open. He bowed and backed away. Qisami dared to raise her head to peek into the room. For the second time in two days she was disappointed to see Lord Aki Niam, this time sitting at a table at the far end of the opulent office.

He looked concerned and thoughtful. His expression didn't change when they walked in. It remained that way when both women sat and the young soldier left the room, closing the door behind him. Finally, Niam spoke, wiggling a finger at Qisami. "This is the house staff that Sunri chose as her estate intermediary?"

"Yes, Highlord."

Lord Aki Niam was lord of the Fine Blades as well. Interesting. She didn't think the man had the hardness in him to head the duke's personal guard.

"Why her?" The warm friendliness in his voice was gone. She suspected she was now seeing the man with his mask off.

"She happened to be cleaning when your tour passed by."

"Yes, I was there, but we saw many maidens scurrying about. Why her?"

"Why not her?"

"She's been under your service less than a year."

"Kiki is a piece of jade in rock, my lord. The duchess couldn't have picked a better staffer." Qisami's cheeks grew hot. Hari was really sticking her neck out for her. Qisami almost felt bad.

"That name." He looked in thought. "Why does that sound familiar?"

"I'm the companion to your twins."

He immediately brightened. "Ah, yes, the new companion those girls have been fighting over all week. They speak highly of you."

"They are a treasure, my lord."

"Yes, they are." He turned on his charm again. "Companion Kiki, your duke requires your service."

Qisami was about to respond when a quick flick of Hari's hands shut her up. Instead, the estatekeeper spoke for her. "She is honored to serve."

Qisami bit her lip and stayed her tongue.

Niam leaned back. "Very well. Tell me how many bodies are there. Where Sunri sleeps, her habits, and patterns." He grunted. "Can the girl read?"

"Yes, she can," said Hari before Qisami could speak.

"Good. Maps, documents, strategies, especially notations. Financial figures if any lay about." Niam leaned back. "We're wading into the deeper negotiations. We need every edge we can find. Can you do that for your duke, girl?"

Qisami blinked. Was she supposed to say something? Hari flashed annoyance.

She took a chance and bowed. "I am honored to serve, my lord."

"Good, you will serve the duke as his eyes and ears. Remember, Duke Yanso is gracious to those who serve and terrible to those who fail him."

Qisami bowed, and then hesitated as she turned to leave.

She knew if she left without standing up for herself, it would bother her forever. For a moment, Qisami forgot her Kiki the sugar-tongue-cleaning-girl act and raised her hand.

"I get paid extra for this, right?"

CHAPTER THIRTY-ONE

BACK TO THE BAHNG

Jian teetered and tapped his toes with excitement at the first sight of the red-and-brown flags fluttering atop Bahngtown's guard tower just as the road turned inland, breaking away from the Yukian River. This little excursion was nice, even if only for a brief time. The temple sitting atop the lonely pillar had sometimes begun to feel like an open-air prison.

"Don't cover your face so much, boy," said Sohn, who was now his official chaperone, much to Jian's chagrin. "And stop staring at your feet. You look like a monk on penance or like you're hiding something. Both draw the wrong kind of attention."

Jian was confused. "Don't I want to keep my face covered so no one notices me?"

The eternal bright light master chuckled. "Take it from someone who has been in hiding for a long, long time. The secret to being invisible is to be"—he pointed at a nearby boulder—"this rock here, or that tree off to the side. Something ordinary, which will not draw any attention."

"What am I supposed to do then?" asked Jian.

"Act like a blinking normal person, kid. Relax your back. Look straight. Look bored." He lightly smacked Jian on the back of the head. "I said bored, not drugged. Didn't Taishi ever teach you the Thousand Mile Stare?"

"What's that?"

"It's an important war arts move where you stare at nothing while you fight."

"That makes no sense."

"You really don't know?" Sohn was incredulous. "The thousand mile stare as to not telegraph your moves. It also makes a war artist look very cool and handsome. Remember, *how* you look while you fight is just as important as how you actually fight. Otherwise, what's the point? What has that woman been teaching you? Remind me to add another lesson to your empty plate when we get back. For now, just raise your head and look ahead, but at nothing in particular."

Whatever that meant. "Whatever you say, master."

Sohn fixed Jian with an amused glance and nudged him with an elbow. "Finally, some insolence. We need more of that too. The Prophesied Hero of the Tiandi needs a little swagger, not acting like some puppy looking to please their master. I had worried that Taishi had beaten the grit out of you." The eternal bright light master turned his head to his other side. "Kaiyu, why are we moving at a turtle's pace? Are we smelling flowers? Let's go."

"Yes, Uncle Sohn." They had stopped by the houseboat on the way to pick up the wagon, and of course Kaiyu had jumped at the chance to accompany Jian. The Houtou disciple had been splitting his time since he lived so close. He always accompanied Kasa, who came by once a week to teach only one lesson, something he called emotional empathy. After four lessons, Jian still wasn't sure what that meant.

"Hey, Shining Star," called Sonaya from the bed of the wagon. That was actually an official title in the Bright Light Fist family.

"What?" said Sohn.

"You told me to remind you to avoid the teahouse."

"All right, and?"

"Avoid the teahouse. I'm going back to sleep."

"Why does Auntie Naifun dislike you so much?" asked Kaiyu.

"Mind your own matters, kid," the eternal bright light master grumbled. "That witch is no auntie."

The first thing Jian noticed when they passed through the front gates was the difference in the guards. They were now uniformed, and fresh faces. The settlement had previously employed only four guards, and everyone knew them by name, so anything as silly as a uniform wasn't necessary. But now, each guard wore an off-white tunic and an ugly brown hat with a string of beads hanging off the side. It looked as if a rat had died and lain across the top of their heads.

This led to Jian's second observation. There were many ugly brown hats about, certainly more than four. What had happened to this place? Jian counted at least six stationed around the north gate, which was the lesser trafficked end of Bahngtown. They were all fresh faces as well.

The wagon pulled into one of the spots just inside the front gates. Sohn threw on his straw hat and popped up his collar. He held out a hand. "You have Taishi's debt marker?"

Jian looked at the hand with suspicion. Still, Taishi *did* tell him to obey every master as if they were his master.

No sooner had he handed the marker over than it disappeared somewhere inside Sohn's robes. "You can pick up the marker from me tonight. Go find lodging and turn in the supply order."

"Where will you be, Uncle Sohn?" asked Kaiyu.

The eternal bright light master was already crossing the street. He turned to face them as he continued to back up. "I'll be at Zhan's. By the way, whatever the order is for plum wine and zuijo, double it."

"But—"

"Just make sure to fetch me before you leave."

Jian and Kaiyu watched the master disappear into the crowd.

"I guess we're on our own," Kaiyu mused. "Uncle Sohn is a lot of fun. He seems like he doesn't care about anything."

"That's because he doesn't." Sonaya jumped off the back of the wagon and began walking in the other direction. "You better pick that marker up from him tonight before he runs it dry on liquor and whores."

"He's gone through a lot." Jian's sympathy for the war arts master had greatly increased with the time they'd spent together the past few days. It frightened him how similar their paths were. He desperately hoped he didn't end up like that, although those odds were slim. Jian either was going to get killed by the Eternal Khan or by the dukes. Or by assassins or bounty hunters or the Tiandi clergy, or any other coin-chasing ruffian or war artists seeking to make a name for themselves.

"Where are you going?" asked Kaiyu.

"Straight for the spa." Sonaya did not look back.

"Shouldn't we, um, meet up?" called Jian.

"Teahouse" was all she said before she disappeared into the crowd.

So much for the help. "Guess we're really on our own," Kaiyu grumbled.

The two boys finished hitching the wagon and then proceeded down the spine of Bahngtown, as it was called. Jian took his time strolling down the street and taking in the activity. He had been gone for only two months, and it felt like everything had already changed.

The harsh weather in the third cycle had brought in people from the outlying areas seeking shelter. So now there were many unfamiliar people walking about, and long steady lines of traffic on the street. Horses, komodos, and people were pulling wagons and carriages, and even a few rickshaws. Zahn's Super Lucky Fortune gambling hall had a line snaking halfway down the block. The room saloon next to it had an even longer line running the opposite direction. There was also a heavier uniformed presence, although none looked like the local magistrates. Jian fought the urge to stare at the ground as he passed the uniformed guards. *Look natural*, Sohn had said.

The two boys began working on the supply list, stopping by several stores to place their orders for the next day. The first order, as always, was to the butcher for two full racks of crispy twice-fried rotisserie barbecue duck fried in duck fat. They continued down the line, ordering a vat of yeast, a pickax, a bag of copper nails, a barrel of sparkstone-crushed black tar, and a chest plate piece from the tanner. Jian had broken his strap during practice. Next, they went to three separate wine shops to place an order for six total barrels of wine and three cases of zuijo. The boys split up at the farmer's market to place orders for five bags of onions, three bags of rice, a crate of watermelons, and three bolts of linen. Jian also placed an order for a spare axle from the wood carver and dropped off a set of pots to be mended. Zofi was not kind to her kitchen tools.

Kaiyu predictably peeled away and went straight for the lion pens the moment they came into view. "I want to watch for a bit. I'll meet you for dinner, yeah?"

Jian waved him off and continued strolling down the street, taking his time looking through the windows, enjoying his temporary freedom. Just like previously when he didn't realize how much he had missed having people around him before they all moved into the temple. Now he relished the best of both worlds, being around people and yet completely alone at the same time.

Jian had just finished placing his last order of the evening and was making his way back to the teahouse when he caught sight of Lao, the Tiandi monk, sweeping the walkway in front of his new temple. He must be open for business now. Lao was wearing his shepherd's cloak, which was fluttering in the wind over his monk robes, but he otherwise seemed to have fit in nicely with the rest of the settlement.

The monk must have sensed Jian staring. He looked up, and their eyes met. Jian quickly ducked and crossed the busy street. He had liked the monk and thought they could have been good friends under different circumstances. Still, no potential friendship was worth the risk of discovery. Besides, he was still angry about being named the "Villain of the Tiandi," not to mention Taishi had threatened to hang him by his ankle over the side of the pillar if he so much as went into the temple again. Jian believed all of Taishi's threats. His master was not one to exaggerate. Jian did keep his eyes to the ground and hurried past the temple as he continued to the teahouse.

Naifun was picking out one of her jars of tea leaves and speaking with a customer when Jian ducked in. The tea master excused herself from her conversation and approached him. "Hiro, what are you doing here?" She leaned in. "I was under the impression you weren't to leave the temple."

"An urgent and necessary matter brought me here today, tea master."

"Urgent" and "necessary" were subjective terms. Jian thought it best not to bring up Sohn.

Naifun held up a hand and looked over at the customer. "Is there anything else you need, Mistress Xuqoo?" The two women exchanged brief pleasantries as the customer left, and then Naifun turned her attention back to him. "Anything of concern, Jian?"

Sohn has run out of booze. Jian shook his head. "Nothing like that. We just needed some supplies." He glanced around the empty shop. "Auntie Naifun, I apologize for the intrusion, but the inns on both sides of the settlement are full, do you by chance have a stable or a storeroom we may sleep in for the night?"

"I think I can do a little better than that. Call it a professional courtesy." The tea master paused. "Who exactly is we, child?"

"Me, Kaiyu, and Sonaya."

The elderly woman with her wrinkled face wrinkled even more. A small sigh parted her lips. "The report said you came in with that scoundrel Soa Sohn. I suppose the sins of the master do not necessarily carry over to his wards. Very well. There's a spare bed in the apprentice's corridor. You three may share it."

"Thank you, tea master."

"Don't thank me. I'm charging Taishi for the service."

Jian winced. He had hoped to keep Taishi from finding out he had disobeyed her orders. It couldn't be helped. Jian bowed and thanked the tea master for her kindness. Another young apprentice appeared in the hallway as if magically summoned. "This way, please," she said.

"I'm positive we haven't met," he said.

The apprentice rolled her eyes and continued down the hallway. "You tried to help me off a shishi just last week."

Jian was stumped. This girl looked fourteen and was a whole head shorter than him. The one who visited the Diyu Temple could look him easily in the eye. How could they all be the same person? He turned to Naifun. "Tea master, I have never met one of your apprentices with silver hair."

"Awareness is an important skill to acquire, Prophesied Hero of the

Tiandi." The tea master spoke with a straight face, but her eyes twinkled with amusement. The apprentice was outright smirking. Everyone apparently was in on some joke, except him.

"But . . ." Jian was confused. He caught up with the girl. "Can you at least give me your name, so I don't get it wrong next time?"

"Why bother if your memory is so slippery?" The apprentice stopped and crossed her arms. "It's Soomi, if you must know."

The apprentice corridor in the back was one long room sectioned off by dividers that didn't quite reach the ceiling. It might be a trick of the eye, but he noticed, for the first time, that the ceiling felt unusually low for such a tall building. At least the bed was free, and it was a whole lot better than finding somewhere to sleep on the streets since the front gates had already closed for the day. He dropped off his meager belongings and then left the teahouse from the back, with Soomi showing him the way out.

He stopped at the doorway. "How do I get back in if the teahouse is closed?"

"The teahouse is already closed, champion," she said. "Come to this door. Knock twice, once, and then three times, and someone will see to you." She closed the door in his face.

Jian scratched his head and glanced back at the alley entrance as he wandered through the small path separating buildings back into the main street. The King had set, and the streets were emptying. Those remaining were now a rougher crowd, with distrusting gazes following his every step.

Jian first stopped by the animal pens, but they had already closed. The animals had already been led back to the stables, and only a few stable hands were around sweeping the grounds. Kaiyu was nowhere in sight. Jian waited for a few minutes before his angry belly made its mood known. He was about to find a noodle shop when he remembered Sohn still had Taishi's pay marker. Grumbling, he hurried the short jaunt to Zahn's Super Lucky Fortune gambling house.

Zahn's was another place Taishi had forbidden Jian ever to step foot into. To be fair, he never had the urge to visit this dark and smelly smoke-filled establishment full of forlorn people, mostly unwashed men. Suspicious gazes followed Jian as he crossed the room, reminding him that he was still a wanted fugitive, and these were the exact sort of people who would hunt him. He went back to staring at the floor as he checked the tables for Master Soa. He found the eternal bright light master on the third floor sitting at the far back table resting his chin on his elbow and looking every bit as gloomy as everyone else. There was a small stack of colored wooden chips piled on the table in front of him.

Jian leaned over Sohn's shoulder as the man played an intricate tile game called Invasion on a large round table placed on an elevated dais referred to as the high-roller's seat. "Master," he whispered. "I'm sorry to disturb you, but I require the pay marker."

Sohn didn't take his eyes off the game. "Come back later. I'm not finished."

The room was so loud and chaotic it was difficult to speak without shouting. Jian attempted to push his voice to Sohn's ears with his jing. "I need it to pay the deposit for some of the supplies. I also need to eat."

Sohn shot him a resigned look and reached into his robe. Instead of pulling out the marker, however, he dropped a handful of coins into Jian's outstretched hand. "I'm going to need the marker a little longer. This should hold you over until tomorrow."

Jian looked at the three copper liang in his palm. That wouldn't even cover one meal. Perhaps giving Sohn Taishi's pay marker was a terrible idea after all. What could he do now? There was no way he could ask for it back without causing a scene.

"Master," he said, his voice squeaking a bit. "Please, this is not enough."

"Just a few more rounds, kid," said Sohn, pointing at the small bulge of his purple tiles. "It's triple windfall if I break through on the next bet. Kismet is coming, I feel it."

Judging by the small stack of colored chips in front of him, Sohn looked way overdue.

"Master . . ."

"Not now!" snapped the eternal bright light master. A moment later, he lost the hand and his already small stack of coins dwindled more.

Sohn's mood darkened even further. Jian's apprehension only grew when Sohn pulled out Taishi's marker to replenish the stack.

"Master," he tried again.

"This is all your fault! My luck only turned once you arrived!" Sohn slammed his fist on the table, shaking it and scattering several stacks of liang. "What did I tell you? Get out before I beat you!"

Stunned, Jian stumbled backward, nearly tripping over a chair leg. The lines running across Sohn's face were etched in deep and the folds around his eyes more pronounced, The master's gaze became intense, beady, and hateful. His mouth was open in a snarl, and his nose was red and bunched up, like a hissing cat.

Jian nearly fled, but he also couldn't look away. Having spoken to Sohn last night and for much of the trip here had brought new light and understanding to the older man's pain. For a moment he could sense the eternal bright light master's rage and agony as well as his sorrow and regret. It felt uncomfortably familiar, even if what Jian himself felt was not nearly as rabid, nor as worn down.

Jian had always assumed Sohn drank and gambled as an escape from reality, that he was self-destructive because it helped him forget his troubles and numbed his pain. Now, staring into Soa Sohn's glowering and furious mental state, Jian realized he had it all wrong. Sohn wasn't here to forget about his troubles and his past, he was here to remember what it felt like to be alive. And Jian coming to take his marker had threatened his ability to continue playing and feeling something, anything.

"Okay, runt," said one of the bouncers, a bald, beefy, cruel-faced man with no eyebrows. "You're ruining everyone's good time." He lifted Jian by the front of his robes and half-dragged, half-carried him across the room. Jian became deeply aware that every pair of eyes was set upon him. The people who likely frequented gambling houses late at night were probably the same type who paid attention to bounties. He had brought the wrong sort of attention in the worst possible place. Jian broke into a sweat and he tried to cover his face. Someone was going to recognize him any moment. Jian cursed, suddenly feeling the walls and crowds closing in. How could he have been so foolish as to put himself into this mess?

"Stop!" Sohn roared. "Let him go. He's with me."

"Maybe you should take a walk too," snarled the bouncer. A shoving match erupted between Sohn, the bouncer, and just about everyone else around them.

The brawl spread throughout the room like a house fire jumping across thatched roofs. Punches were thrown, tables overturned, and their contents were scattered all over the floor. Half of the players here were enthusiastically joining in the melee, while the other half were on their knees scooping up spilled chips.

Jian stood in the middle of the chaos, frozen. Should he try to help Sohn and join in the melee, or should he make a quiet escape while the attention was off of him. He could visualize it now: Taishi storming into the magistrate's office to bail Jian and Sohn out. Yanking them both by the ears out of the cell. She was going to murder them. That thought almost had Jian making a break toward the nearest exit. He nearly convinced himself to flee when he stopped. He couldn't just leave Sohn here. It wouldn't be right. It wouldn't be honorable.

He turned and was about to make his way back toward Sohn again when someone grabbed him from behind. Someone else pushed them both and sent Jian flying. He cracked his head on the wooden floor and then a stampede of feet stepped on him. A boot smashed his hand and another was on the middle of his back. Jian curled up and tried to protect himself as more bodies tripped and fell on top of him. It became difficult to breathe.

Another set of hands grabbed Jian by the back collar and hauled him to his feet. Jian threw several punches blindly, landing one flush on someone's face, before he realized it was Sohn. "Master, I'm sorry!"

The eternal bright light master didn't look like he even felt it. "Get out of here. I'll keep them company, kid. And hey, I'm sorry about that outburst. You caught me while I was in a hole." Jian appreciated the apology. Before he could reply, Sohn shoved him away as the fighting grew more frantic. Then Sohn threw a punch and threw back three men in one blow. One would think such a powerful act would temper the melee, but it only grew more heated.

Jian struggled his way to the door, eating some punches and kicks along the way, but managed to make it to the staircase. He glanced back at Sohn one more time standing in the eye of the storm, and then ran down the stairs. Several more bouncers passed him going up the stairs as Jian fled to the first floor and then out the door.

He hunched over as soon as he escaped. The strong, hot wind still felt cool and refreshing compared to the stink of smoke, sweat, and suffocating sadness at Zahn's. He sucked in a few deep breaths.

"Are you all right, my friend?"

Jian looked up, momentarily spooked. Standing next to the front door just off to the side and holding what looked like pamphlets was the Tiandi monk dressed in robes as if he were attending Tenth Day Prayer.

Jian froze. What should he do? It didn't feel right to just ignore the monk and walk off. Not only was that rude, but it would also likely rouse suspicion. Like Sohn had advised earlier, he should try to act normal. He waved. "Hello, Brother Lao."

Lao pressed his hands together and bowed. "Greetings, Friend Hiro. I am admittedly surprised to see you come out of this gambling establishment."

"I . . ." Jian began. "What are you doing here?"

The Tiandi monk offered a small smile. "Every night, I come here as a symbol of the hope to any lost souls who might need it." Jian's stomach growled. He had forgotten why he had originally come to the gambling house. Now what was he going to do?

Sohn must have heard it as well. "I was about to head to the noodle shop near my temple to grab a late meal. I have become well acquainted with Cook Sau, and he always serves me healthy portions. Would you care to join me?"

"I can't. I have no coin," he mumbled.

"Then, please, be my guest, young Hiro."

Jian really had no choice now. Besides, he was starving. "Thanks."

The two strolled down the main street toward the heart of the settlement. "Do you really stand out there every night handing out flyers?" asked Jian.

"My father frequented these establishments when I was a boy. It made life difficult for my mother, my three sisters, and me. I was never able to turn him toward the Tiandi." He paused. "Or save him. You could say this is my penance."

"That sounds like an unfair burden to place on the shoulders of someone so young." Somehow Jian felt as if he were talking to himself.

"Perhaps," said Lao. "I like to view it like more of a calling. Just as the Mosaic of the Tiandi guides us to heaven, I hope to guide some of those lost souls to the mosaic."

"And you do this every night?"

"Just on the evenings when my feet aren't too tired standing somewhere else," replied the monk. "Sometimes, when I am particularly weary, I may not stand here long, but I try my best."

"But why?" asked Jian. "It feels so thankless."

"On the contrary. Saving a lost soul is one of the most fulfilling experiences." The Tiandi monk waved at a man carrying a tray of dirty dishes to a wash basin in front of a storefront. "It's also a good way to make friends."

And get free food, for that matter. True to his word, Lao was indeed friends with the boss of the Water Snake noodle shop. The portions were generous, if not a little under-seasoned, but it was a satisfying meal, and best of all, it was free. Jian spent the rest of the evening getting to know Lao and treating him as if he were just another man, not a practitioner of the religion that held Jian as its central figure.

Lao was open about his upbringing, how his abusive and drug-addled father had destroyed their family, and how Lao had found a path to the Tiandi as his salvation, eventually becoming a monk.

"Truth is," Lao was saying, "I accidentally became a monk. My ba was in one of his drunken binges and, as the only son, pointed all of his rage at me. He chased me across my town. I stumbled into our local temple and hid. The brothers offered to make me a monk for a few days until things cooled down at home. I shaved my head and donned the robes. Then I realized I loved the embrace and clarity of the Tiandi and enjoyed the simple monk life. Those few days of being a monk turned into a lifetime." He put his palms together and looked up at the night sky. "Best of all, my father was a deeply religious drunk. As a monk and member of the Tiandi Temple, I was able to get him to do what I could not as his son, but could as a member of the clergy. I commanded he pay penance if he ever raised a hand against my mother and sisters again."

"That's amazing," said Jian. "How did you accomplish that?"

"My ba would never listen to his son, but he'd listen to a monk."

"And then what happened?" Jian had never thought being a Tiandi monk had such powerful jing.

Lao bowed his head. "Once he sobered up, he was so ashamed he hung himself from a suicide tree."

Jian was at a loss for words. "Uh, that's awful, Lao. I'm sorry."

"The Mosaic of the Tiandi always steers us true," the monk recited. "The greater the sin, the more treacherous the path is to heaven."

The two finished their evening meal and were walking back to the temple. "I'm glad we had the chance to reconnect. I sense the weight of the world resting on your shoulders. Would you like to light some incense and pray with me? It will lift your soul."

Even the thought of praying gave Jian a sense of peace. "That is kind of you. I would appreciate that."

"Jian!" Kaiyu appeared, running toward him from the north. "Come quick. Uncle Sohn has been arrested."

"I . . ."

"Come on, it's an emergency." Kaiyu tugged on his arm. "Have you seen Sonaya?"

Jian looked helplessly at Lao. "I have to go."

Brother Lao's face fell. He looked truly disappointed and pained but held up a hand. "Of course, friend. There will always be another time. If your friend has been arrested, tell Magistrate Loal that I am personally asking him for leniency as a favor to the Tiandi."

Jian was deeply thankful. Favors were precious, and Lao just offered one to a near stranger. "Thank you again, Brother Lao. I'll make a point to visit soon. I promise." This time, Jian really meant it, Taishi's punishment or not.

CHAPTER THIRTY-TWO

THE PRIMORDIAL MIST

The first thing Ritualist Conchitsha Abu Suriptika did was disarm
Sali, making her strip off her scale armor and weapons and dis-
robe until she was completely naked. He even went as far as to
offer to burn and dispose of her clothing, which she declined. Next, the
ritualist insisted on bathing her in a hot tub of fine red sand over a burning
hearth. As a lifelong raider, Sali had no issues with modesty, although she
did balk at being cooked over an open fire.

The ritualist left her stewing in the tub for several hours, which Sali
found relaxing and comfortable. The red sands simmered almost like
water, and exfoliated and cleansed her skin. It also smelled like cilantro,
turmeric, and mint, which added to her suspicion that she had fallen in
with a group of cannibals, though it did leave her smelling fresh and rejuvenated, and probably very edible.

After Sali took her long bath, Ritualist Conchitsha Abu Suriptika led
her to the temple in the back, past the two guardian spirits and through
the large, black front doors. She discovered, upon passing through, that
the doors were painted with crushed vantam gems, which were the same
material as the Sanctuary of the Eternal Moor back on Chaqra. That felt

like a strange coincidence, considering that meant this door was probably valued more than an entire city pod.

To her surprise, the temple wasn't a temple at all. The entrance was only a facade, but inside, it appeared to be a cave that stretched deeper into the icy mountain. They walked down a narrow slope in near darkness. Sali had to use her nighteye to avoid tripping over rocks or walking into walls. Interestingly, the ritualist had no such problems navigating. He continued to walk confidently while at the same time occasionally barking phrases in some dead Happan tongue and then continuing to lecture Sali about the finer details of low-ankle slippers. The man positively loved his work.

"There's bark from a dragonscorch tree that produces the finest soles in the world. It's soft, supple, yet tough, and it's flameproof." He had spent a good fifteen minutes waxing poetic about this wood. "It will last a lifetime."

"If I ever come across it, I'll be sure to pick some up for you," she offered.

The ritualist brightened. "Now I consider you a friend, Salminde the Viperstrike. May our bond last a lifetime." The man was certainly Happan through and through.

Ritualist Conchitsha Abu Suriptika led her into a round chamber at the end of the long tunnel. It was plain inside, save for a pit in the center filled with orange-and-green goop. Set above the pool of liquid was a small hearth raised atop a platform, which was in line with the Katuia tradition of burning fires upon the ground.

"What is that?" she asked, "and why burn a fire over it?"

"That is the Primordial Pool," explained the ritualist. He brought over a bucket of sparkstones and shaved several fragments of them onto the hearth. "The fumes from the pool contain certain powers. It is the flame that will ignite them."

"And this pool will cure me of this soul rot?"

Suriptika shrugged. "The cure is no more than a choice, Salminde the Viperstrike."

"That makes no sense. How can the cure be a choice? Why wouldn't I want it?"

"You must ask different questions." The ritualist moved to a small, elevated perch on the other side of the pit and sat cross-legged. He pointed at a small rug next to the pool. "Sit."

At least it was warm down here, sweltering even. Sali sat next to the pit and emulated the ritualist's posture, resting her hands on her crossed knees, facing up with her right thumb and forefinger, and left thumb and middle finger touching.

Ritualist Conchitsha Abu Suriptika scowled. "Who taught you to meditate? You have it backward."

"This is the way I was taught since I was a sprout," she shot back.

"Your teachers were terrible. Your spirit shamans were wrong. You will do what's right. Now."

So pushy. Sali didn't care either way. It wasn't like the spirit shamans meant anything to her anymore. She followed the ritualist's instructions, changing her finger placements and even switching the way she crossed her legs.

"Now breathe."

Sali closed her eyes and inhaled, taking the mist in and out with a steady cadence. It burned her nostrils with every breath in and chilled them with every exhale. The ritualist's voice lulled her to relaxation. The air became heady and time meaningless. Sali didn't know how much time was passing, but every inhale sank her deeper into this supernatural, lucid state.

"Let your mind open. Allow your thoughts to drift where they may. Your memories are not your own." Ritualist Conchitsha Abu Suriptika continued to drone. His voice was soothing, almost hypnotic, lulling her into a rhythm not unlike the soul seeker test used to find the next Khan.

Everything was cool and calm until a jolt surged through her, twisting her body into knots. The world around her seemed to burst into a thousand tiny rays of exploding stars. Sali's eyes shot open, and briefly all she could see was a fog of orange-and-green tentacles floating along currents of air. The chamber walls were now hazed over, with only the glow of the burning fire cutting through the orange-and-green mist. Sali felt weightless floating on nothing.

The ritualist's voice continued, sharper, stronger. "There were once six known Xoangiagu, all born from here in the Sun Under Lagoon. Six great spirits rising from the depths to marry and guard wondrous Hrusha, the Oasis of the True Freeze. Each spirit: the beautiful Woman, the pure Child, the wise Scholar, the giant Bull . . ."

Sali blinked. The mist changed into each of the spirit figures. This haze was drugging her somehow. It was strangely comforting. Sali blinked again.

". . . the sharp Owl, and the staunch Warrior."

Sali was barely paying attention to the haze until the shape of the Warrior came into focus.

"No way," Sali muttered. He wasn't quite as large then—that was the work of the spirit shamans—but there was no mistaking that face, that sharp chin, the intense, brooding eyes. The Eternal Khan of Katuia, their great ruler, was one of these six.

"For centuries, the six were the Sun Under Lagoon's protectors, dozens of generations, thousands of cycles."

Sali watched as the Warrior, along with the other spirits, led the Happan to battle, explored the caves with the Owl, and dove to the deep depths of the burning sea with the Bull.

"The six spirits led us through Together, the Sun Under Lagoon prospered for a beautiful, short eternity. The six spirits cherished the lagoon, and the people here cherished them. They were worshiped and revered, living gods walking among people, cherished by all Happan.

"Then, one day, new people crossed spears with the Happan. Katuia raiders had finally found the paradise of the Sun Under Lagoon with its vast wealth in minerals. The raids grew in frequency as more Katuia clans swarmed the island like locusts. Pitched battles on both sea and land erupted between the two peoples. The Xoangiagu over centuries kept the raiders at bay, but the constant battle took its toll. Then, disaster struck. The giant Bull fell in battle, and its cycle shockingly ended. The Child was severed in an ambush thirty years later. The burden of each permanent death put more strain on the remaining spirits. They began to crumble. The Owl and Woman followed a century later, leaving only the

Warrior fighting at last, alone, against the swelling tide of the Katuia clans.

"One day, a new kind of Katuia came onto our shores. They were the spirit shamans of a tiny clan called Chaqra, and they offered peace to the Happan, for a price. The shamans demanded the Warrior's service to Chaqra, and they would guarantee protection against all Katuia. Fearing their deteriorating plight, the Warrior and Hrusha agreed to this subjugation. Over the centuries, the spirit shamans had poisoned the last of the Xoangiagu, casting their dark magics and twisting the Warrior's jing, slowly coercing, manipulating, and mind-washing the once noble being until he became only a shell of who he once was."

Hundreds of images, sounds, and scenes slammed into Sali's mind. With the Warrior fighting alongside them, Chaqra became a powerful clan, destroying their rivals with the Warrior's might and the spirit shamans' magic. They were the first to unite all the clans to raise the khanate banner. The spirit shamans even made him their Khan.

Sali blinked. The Eternal Khan of Katuia ravaged all rivals throughout the Grass Sea until they alone ruled. The last image Sali saw was the Khan standing at the edge of the Grass Sea overlooking Zhuun lands. He faced Sali, as if he somehow knew she was there and spoke in his all-too-familiar low, thundering voice like he was grinding wheat. "Today, we own the Grass Sea. Tomorrow, all lands beneath the vast skies. I will claim my birthright."

Sali began to choke. It was the cilantro stink. It tasted like soap. She awoke with a start and looked around. The fire had dimmed, the colored haze lifted, and the pool covered with a large circular vantam lid. She shivered. "How long have I been out?"

"The better part of the night and day, Salminde the Viperstrike." Ritualist Conchitsha Abu Suriptika still had not moved from his perch. His eyes opened. "Now you know." They brimmed with wet sadness. "They stole our people's son and twisted him to such evil. The Happan find it difficult and painful to bear, but we are helpless to save him."

"What does that have to do with the cure?" she asked, now suspicious.

"Nothing. We are just sharing knowledge. Do you wish to listen further?"

Now Sali knew what the rich man meant by listening more. She nodded.

"We seek the same north star, Salminde the Viperstrike." The ritualist looked down at her. His eyes glowed orange. "What you seek, we can provide, but you need to make a choice," the ritualist continued. "As a Will of the Khan, you hold a large piece of the Khan's soul. Without it, he cannot be reborn into this cycle, and therefore, cannot reenter this world until your death."

"That's good, right?" With the way he said it, Sali wasn't sure. "You want me to live longer so you should cure me of the soul rot, right?" Then she realized. "If you cure the soul rot . . ."

"Cleansing a body of soul rot is an unpleasant but manageable treatment. There are consequences, however. If you cure the soul rot, then the last of the Khan's soul would be returned and he would be free to reenter this world."

"I could die tomorrow anyway," Sali reasoned.

"Or you could still live forty more years," said the ritualist. "Soul rot is unpredictable."

If the Khan returned any time within the next five years, Nezra would be doomed. They needed more time. That left only one option.

"If I hold on to the soul rot, can you help me manage it?"

Ritualist Conchitsha Abu Suriptika nodded. "There are ways to manage the pain, and medicine to prolong your life, but you will still continue to weaken."

"That means the simple act of living will spite the spirit shamans. My very breath will prevent that bastard from returning to the world." That was good enough for Sali. It was a fair trade. Sali rose to her feet and bowed. "Thank you for this knowledge, ritualist. My mind is made up." She turned to go.

"Salminde the Viperstrike," Ritualist Conchitsha Abu Suriptika said. "You are welcome to return if you need treatment. It gives our clan great honor to practice our ancient ways again. I'll even give you a good deal on a pair of shoes. I may brag so eloquently that Salminde the famed Viper-strike is my best customer."

"How about a free pair of shoes for a sponsorship, then?" she asked, half hopeful.

"Not a chance, Kati."

It was worth a try.

CHAPTER THIRTY-THREE

NAMING THE LIVESTOCK

That evening, Qisami wandered outside the estate, down to the Night Block under the shadow of the Finger of Fertile Vigor. This neighborhood housed much of the estate staff who had done well for themselves operating in Yanso's court, but were still insignificant enough to have to reside on the outside of the estate. Many court officials, magistrates, and politically connected businesspeople called the neighborhoods around the Night Block home. The block was full of bars, restaurants, and room salons. Most catered to the nobility and wealthy who wandered off-strip. It was also where three of the largest universities in the Enlightenment States were located, which made the neighborhood lively, fun, but also very snotty.

The last time Qisami had tramped this brightly lit block was with Zwei shortly after they arrived. The cell's opera now was a regular on these streets. They had originally served undercover as a stable hand but then had faked a horsehair allergy to get transferred. They had somehow sung their way into the ducal morning choir and were residing in one of the skilled shared housing towers.

Qisami had initially been annoyed with how Zwei wandered off-book from their assignment, although she understood why they would have wanted to transfer from the stables to the choir. The two had gotten into a heated argument over the assignment swapping. The Minister of Critical Purpose must have placed Zwei there for a reason, and to get themselves moved to the choir because they didn't like bathing horses was unprofessional. Zwei was slippery that way, however.

The argument between the two escalated into insults about each other's singing abilities, which, in turn, escalated into a sizable gold liang bet, which eventually led them to the nearest singing lounge. There was a lot of singing, a lot of zuijo, and a fair amount of stumbling around, and possibly falling off the stage once or twice. Qisami had woken the next morning in the middle of a rice paddy, missing a shoe. She also may have killed someone. She remembered having fun, just not much else.

Qisami reached her destination at the center of some sandwiched buildings. She entered through the bright green doors of an upscale drink lounge called the Golden Chalice of Fantastic Earnings. The lounge was claustrophobic and narrow. Wall to wall it couldn't have been more than ten feet wide, but the building was long, and tall, spanning six narrow stories. Qisami carefully minced up the stairs, which were only a foot wide, hugging the wall. She passed by a darkened floor with tables and booths sectioned off by rice paper walls. The covered lanterns dangling from the ceiling swayed with a slight breeze.

Koteuni and Burandin were already waiting for her at the front of the fourth-floor balcony facing the main street. The paint on Burandin's face had been only haphazardly wiped off. There were still etchings of bark around his neck. He was a favorite among the court children for his impersonations of trees.

The rabbleguard had also brought her work here. Her armor stank, and Qisami was fairly sure there were fragments of bone and loose pieces of flesh stuck in her curly hair. There was already a pitcher of chilled Double Mist zuijo on the table along with three cups, a bowl of salty nuts, and an opium pipe. Qisami didn't realize it was going to be one of those nights.

She slid into the third seat facing the lounge. She would have much preferred to sit on the side overlooking both, but that's what she got for arriving last. It had been weeks since they'd last met. Koteuni looked like she had just been trampled by an ox. Her face was bruised and cut, and she had bandages wrapped around various limbs. She may have lost a tooth as well. Burandin was wearing a frumpy black dress, for whatever reason. Qisami didn't ask.

"You look awful, Kiki," said Koteuni, swigging her zuijo and grinning.

"*I* look awful?" Koteuni had definitely lost a tooth.

"Yeah, your shoulders are slumped. You're moping, and you haven't stopped eating since you sat down." Qisami's second knew her too well. She leaned in. "Are you cleaning latrines again?"

Qisami poured herself a cup of the double mist and sipped. It was strong and immediately went to her head. She panted. "I am always cleaning someone's shit."

The two giggled and touched cups, and the night was on. Qisami pointed at Koteuni's random assortment of armor pieces strung together by badly cut straps of leather. The white tunic under it was so stained there was barely any white left. "Are you enjoying yourself so much you can't find the time to bathe?"

"It's so much fun, Kiki!" Koteuni raved. "I'm assigned to this goon crew, sort of like our cell, but much more pleasant and fun. The pay's better too. Anyway, every day, the bosses give my crew captain an address. We 'skin on,' as we say, and then go to the place, knock the doors down, and bap, bap, bap." She smacked the air. "Then after, we go home and drink. It's almost like being back in the training pool litter again, except everyone is nice. Just not with a bunch of catty rags. You wouldn't understand."

Actually, Qisami did. She felt the same way about the estate staff. "Don't get too comfortable." She downed her drink. Burandin refilled it. "What about you, big lug? Why are you wearing a sleeping gown?"

He grinned and pointed at himself. "I'm a shadow."

Qisami's expression didn't change. "You're a what?"

"His story troupe has this whole scene in the second act where the mighty hero Li Roy enters the ether world and confronts his own shadow, who mimes and then battles him to death. It's brilliant, and the perfect role for Burandin." Koteuni hugged her man. "I'm so proud of him."

He looked pleased. He pointed at himself again. "Good mime."

Qisami finished her drink and buried her face in her hands. "This place is like a really weird dream."

"Heard from Zwei?" asked Burandin.

She nodded. "That little piss just made it to the main choir. I swear, if the choirmaster makes Zwei the lead vocal, I'm going to have to kill them, because they'll never shut up about it."

"And our little baby broodbaby grunt?" said Koteuni.

Qisami snorted. "Cyyk's teaching little ducal ducklings how to use a sword."

"He certainly swings like a newly hatched egg." Koteuni chuckled and sipped her drink. "Any movement on the job? Rabbleguard is a joy but the pay is piss."

"You just said it pays better than what we're making right now." The look on Koteuni's face showed that she meant what she said. Qisami moved on. "The job's a bit messy right now. Lord Aki wants me to spy on Sunri. Sunri may have forgotten about us, and Firstwife wants me to murder someone." She shrugged. "I'm juggling a lot."

Koteuni's eyes shined, and she pounded her leather-gloved hand on the table. "Double agent double cross! How exciting!"

Qisami poured another drink. "Problem is, this is a double cross between two dukes, which could easily end with us dead if we end up on the wrong side. I'm not even sure who we work for anymore. Not gonna lie; I'm a little annoyed."

"When in doubt," said her second, "go with whoever pays more."

"That's another thing! No one is paying us! We are doing this for free," Qisami complained as she crossed her arms and huffed. "No one has given us any reason to stay loyal."

Koteuni looked dubious. "You sound like you regret signing us up for this job, boss." For some reason that sounded almost like criticism.

"I just don't see a compelling reason to stay involved with any of this. It's going to get us sent to a penal colony."

"Stabbing a duchess in the back will get us sent to a penal colony too!" hissed Koteuni, suddenly serious.

"Yanso would do far worse." Qisami shrugged. "Don't forget. Gyian holds a decisive upper hand in these talks. Siding with Sunri could be the losing play."

Burandin's face came between them as he reached for the gourd on the other side of the table. He poured himself a drink and pondered for a moment. "Feels like a terrible choice. Why make one at all?" Then he emptied the cup in one swig.

"That's . . . not a bad idea, my sweet pea," said Koteuni slowly. "Why decide if we don't have to yet? Just play both sides in the meanwhile and see how things unfold."

Qisami didn't love the idea. "It's such a hassle."

"A double agent does double the work." Koteuni stood and donned her weird pock-marked helmet. She looked stupid. "But it's usually more than double the pay!"

Qisami grabbed a handful of seaweed nuts and crunched on them. "In this case, it feels like I'm choosing between getting shot out of a catapult or getting drowned in sewage."

"Sunri has really big catapults," said Burandin, chewing a mouthful. It wasn't lost on her that he had slid the bowl of nuts closer to himself.

"Thanks for the insight," she replied. "How are *you* doing, you big dope? I hear you're the breakout star of the current production. I'm glad you finally found something you're good at."

"I saw one of his shows," Koteuni gushed, placing her hand over his. "He stood still for three hours. It was an amazing performance."

Koteuni got to knock heads in the rabbleguard. Burandin became a famous actor. Zwei sang in the choir, and even Broodbaby at least got to spar in the field. How did Qisami get the worst job in the cell?

She drained her cup and slapped it onto the table. Burandin was about to refresh it when she covered the opening with her hand. Their night was only getting started. She needed to keep a clear head. Tonight's job was delicate.

Koteuni forced her hand by trying to retire for the night. "Well, Kiki, I'm glad to see you still remember how to have an enjoyable time, but it's time for me to walk the dreams a bit. I have an early day tomorrow." She broke into a grin. "We're going to evict a bunch of homes. It's like a surprise in every hovel."

"Actually, I called you two for cover on a quick hit tonight." Qisami spat out the cracked pistachio shells. "Are you geared up?"

Koteuni put a hand on the hilt of her saber. "I'm already ready to make some carcasses."

"Since when did you get so violent?" Qisami replied. "Rabbleguard has gone to your brain."

"Since when did you not?" Koteuni shot back. Her second-in-command had a point.

Burandin tugged at the collar of his black dress and split it down the middle, revealing his leather garb beneath. He patted one of his hand hatchets holstered at his hip and rolled his shoulders.

"Staying limber is important, sugar-face," Koteuni cooed to her husband. "Especially at your age. What's the job, Kiki?"

"Bagging a courier."

"Sounds straightforward. Why do you need us?"

"I want to be quiet on this one. Don't want to piss where I eat," Qisami admitted. She grabbed a last handful of the salty nuts as she stood. The room swayed. Just in case, she grabbed the gourd of water too. "This shouldn't take too long. Let's go. Drop is happening at midnight."

"Where?" asked Burandin.

"Just inside the main gate on the other side of the wall. Why do you think I picked this place?"

The three had to swim against the traffic streaming into Night Block while heading back toward the south entrance of the estate. They merged onto the main road briefly before veering down a ramp that led to a lower-level servant gate. There was a line to get through, even at this hour. This damn city and lines. At least it was moving at a brisk clip. There was a delivery wagon carrying a brass tree with wine gourds hanging from ropes tied to the branches. There had been a lot more parties since the duchess arrived. It was a fun time to be an artisan in Allanto.

Qisami fell in queue, trying to mask her annoyance. She probably shouldn't have drunk that much.

Young Jupsan was working the gate this evening. He was a servant born on the estate. Working the gate allowed him to see as much of the outside world as he'd likely ever see. The boy was nearing sixteen, which meant it would be time for him to decide his path. Qisami was willing to bet Jupsan was an estate lifer. A man who willingly built his own prison. Nice kid, though.

Jupsan waved. "Hey, Kiki. How was the city?"

She shrugged. "Usual trash. Busier than usual." She shrugged as she handed him her painted gray wooden chip. Burandin pulled out his sky-blue chip. Both were allowed to pass through. Koteuni, however, was a different matter. Qisami realized her error too late.

"Unless you are summoned or conducting an investigation, rabble-guard, you are forbidden from entering ducal grounds." He looked her up and down. "Especially dressed like that."

"I'm off duty," she growled.

"Even worse."

He took a small book from her and stamped it.

"This is my friend." Qisami leaned close to Jupsan's face. "I just want to show her around. Help me out this one time, yeah?"

Jupsan looked truly sorrowful. "I would if I could, Kiki. There's no bending rules now that the duchess is here. You understand."

Qisami did indeed. She shifted and placed herself between Koteuni and Jupsan. It was already late, and traffic had slowed to a trickle. It would have been easy to disappear Jupsan. Koteuni was about to pounce when Qisami interrupted the kill.

"Totally understand." She turned back to face Koteuni. "Sorry, friend. I guess I can't give you a tour today. Another time?" Qisami's glower was intense.

"Fine." Koteuni scowled before finally relenting. She turned and stormed off.

"Good night, Jupsan." Qisami turned and strolled past the gate, her finger already clawing at her forearm.

Meet around the gate. West side. Alleyway. Third manor from center.

What was that stupid deal with the gate boy? Koteuni's usually beautiful calligraphy was uneven tonight, rushed and touched with annoyance.

Zero kill night, do you hear? I don't want to wake up to panic tomorrow morning and a lockdown for the rest of the negotiations.

It's just a stupid servant. No one would miss him.

Ruli was Jupsan's godmother. She would be devastated. Then Qisami would never hear the end of the woman's incessant bawling. Jupsan was also betrothed to the kennel cook's apprentice, which was the main reason he never left the premises. Not to mention the entire estate staff got depressingly morose every time someone ended up murdered. Estate staff were a terribly emotional bunch.

Qisami traveled along the back alleys and servant paths. It was near curfew, so the streets were emptying. She stayed in servant garb a while longer. There were ways a palacemaiden could talk her way in that a shadowkill could not. She was still feeling the zuijo, but it certainly wasn't the first time she had finished a job with her head buzzing like a dragonfly. It was part of the fun.

There was a soft pop, and Koteuni appeared next to them. She had shed her clunky rabbleguard uniform and was now dressed in shadowkill black. She looked irritated, or it could just be the alcohol. "I had to sprint all the way back to the middle gate and do a six-step over the walls." She bent over, panting. "Next time, just kill the boy and save me the hassle."

Qisami waved her off. "You need the practice."

She led the other two to a narrow intersection with the northern way being a dead end. "I want you two flanking the east and west blocks. We wait for the drop, and I take care of it. If an alarm is raised, provide cover."

"No witnesses?" asked Koteuni.

Qisami grimaced. "I have to live with these people for a little while longer. I don't want everyone to start acting weird because their friends got killed. Like, if it's between killing someone and taking a spear to the gut, just know I'll get you to a good surgeon."

"No fun," groused Burandin. His wife agreed.

The three shadowkills broke apart, moving in different directions. The drop point was a stone statue of a multi-colored kismet hawk, one of many symbols of luck and fortune. Qisami scrambled under the shelter of a hanging eave. She lay flat and relaxed along the curved wood of the support beams. She took the time to change into her shadowkill garb, covering nearly her entire body. This time she elected to wear a hood and face covering, just in case. She had only two of her black knives on her person, but that should be more than sufficient.

Koteuni and Burandin were having a spirited discussion through blood scrawl about the way she wanted him to cook her eggs tomorrow morning.

Qisami didn't care. She stretched like a cat and curled herself into a comfortable spot. Most people think stakeouts suck, but she liked them. They gave her time to nap. She closed her eyes and slumbered. Her eyes closed, and the world drained away. The sound of footsteps roused her several moments later, a fast, light gait. Qisami's eyes opened. It took a little longer than usual for that switch in her head to go. She was rusty.

The mark appeared a moment later. They were cloaked and carrying a satchel slung over their back. The giveaway, however, was the large white medallion dangling from their neck.

Qisami dropped, landing softly in front of the courier, her legs spread to cushion her landing while she wielded a black knife in each hand very theatrically. Contrary to the derision a dramatic stance often received when running forms, it served a purpose.

The courier gave a startled cry, clutching the ducal ward as a shield, as if it offered any protection. Usually, it would. There were few matters in the world so important one is willing to risk the wrath of a duke's protection. They say a person with the jade ducal ward could walk naked carrying a fat sack of gold, and no one would dare touch them. Unfortunately for the courier, the ward didn't matter this time.

Qisami thrusted both knives toward the courier's neck. One quick thrust and maybe they could get back to their table at the drinking lounge before the hostess gave it to someone else. The courier's hood tipped back and the light spilled onto her, revealing a young, terrified girl with a thin freckled face. The tip of the blade stopped mere inches from drawing blood. Qisami's gut clenched as the dim light from the three moons revealed a familiar face. What was Porla doing running messages to the Shulan? What had that girl gotten herself into?

Qisami cursed under her breath. One of those blasted concubines must have roped her into this. She had been so busy lately she didn't get to help guide her, and now the girl was involved in something way over her head.

Qisami's annoyance at having to deal with the fallout stayed her hand. She lowered her voice and hissed, "Hand over your bag."

"I'm on official duke business!" Porla blinked as a flood of tears streamed down her face. She tried to hold up the ducal ward again. When she realized that small piece of jade would not protect her, she broke into loud, wailing sobs. "Please don't kill me! I'm on duke business! Help!"

This was not going the way Qisami had intended. She had only a moment to decide what to do: finish the kill or abort the job? The professional in her demanded she kill the courier, retrieve the contents of the package, and give it to the client. The servant, mentor, and roommate in her was whispering that killing Porla would cause more problems than it was worth. Both sides weren't wrong.

Qisami was now annoyed with herself. She had let her emotions cloud her professional judgment and named the mark. It was especially bothersome because Qisami had just spent the past few weeks taking the girl under her wing, helping her get settled with the estate staff, and advising her on those treacherous bitch concubines. Now, Qisami had to kill her. How annoying.

She gritted her teeth and tried to thread the needle the only way she knew how. The knives disappeared back into their sheaths, and she slapped Porla hard across the cheeks. The young girl's face was a mask of terror as she froze, stunned, her eyes wide and lips quivering. She opened her mouth just to eat a punch in the gut that doubled her over. The scullerymaiden collapsed onto her knees, gasping.

Qisami pounced on the girl, backhanding her across the side of the face and then kicking her waist. She kept most of her blows light and where they wouldn't be seen. She continued smacking the girl from different angles until she was a pile of whimpering and tears.

The beating finally stopped after a short while. Qisami stood over Porla, her feet straddling the poor girl, and snatched the satchel. She growled in a low, scratchy voice, "Next time I will slit your throat. Understand?" Porla didn't nod quickly enough, so Qisami slapped her one more time. "Are we clear?"

Porla was a gibbering mess moving her head up and down between body-wracking sobs. The girl was traumatized, but at least she was alive. She better take the threat to heart, because there better not be a next time.

Qisami hurried away from the crime scene and blood scrawled in large, bold strokes, cutting through Koteuni and Burandin's constant chatter. *Done.*

Koteuni and Burandin dropped next to her moments later. Koteuni stepped next to her. "Need body removal?"

"Not necessary," Qisami answered. "Hurry. We need to go."

A man's shouts cut through the night, followed by the dull clanging of magistrate bells. Porla's high-pitched whine soon joined in the mix.

Koteuni stopped and looked back the way they came. "Kiki, what the hell? Did you let the courier live? What about—"

Qisami shoved the shadowkills forward. "I said, get going!"

CHAPTER THIRTY-FOUR

BAD TROUBLE

It took most of the night to bail Master Soa Sohn out of the magistrate's holding cell. The only way they were even able to free the eternal bright light master at all was because it seemed Brother Lao's favor was actually worth something. That, and the two boys had to make a special trip to the money lender to get a new pay marker and increase Taishi's—or Nai Roha's, in this case—limits.

They finally released Sohn just as the King's first rays were piercing the forest canopy. Both Jian and Kaiyu were exhausted. Jian, particularly, was dead on his feet. The previous night's excitement and then the stress from worrying about Taishi's wrath had spent him physically as well as emotionally. There was no way he could keep this trip hidden from Taishi. He was fairly certain she was going to skin everyone involved. Well, except for Kaiyu. Everyone loved that kid.

"Thanks for bailing me out of jail. I don't know about you boys, but I'm beat." The man did not sound remorseful. "I take it the marker's no good now."

"I might have to cancel some of my order," Jian admitted. He had already decided to cut the alcohol order in half but didn't feel like arguing about it.

"When will everything be ready?"

"Tonight." Jian yawned. "It depends on whether the blacksmith can get to the pots by then."

The yawn became contagious. Sohn stretched. "We'll leave first thing in the morning. Now if you'll excuse me, I'm going to find a nice bed of moss and some shade under a tree. Get me when you're ready to go."

"We have a bed at the teahouse," said Kaiyu.

"I would rather sleep in jail," Sohn called back.

"How do we find you?" asked Jian.

Sohn didn't look back as he walked away. "I'll find you, somehow."

"So we just wait around for you to come?" Jian threw his arms up when he didn't get an answer. "He can reach us, but we can't reach him?"

"You told me yesterday you thought he was misunderstood," said Kaiyu.

Jian sighed. "That was before he gambled away all of Taishi's coin, incited a riot, got arrested, and then left without even saying thanks." Jian raised his voice and shook his fist. "You could have at least helped load all the booze you're going to drink!"

"It's going to be a big load, isn't it?" asked Kaiyu.

"At least four trips from the houseboat to the temple," said Jian.

"It'll be good conditioning." Kaiyu had an uncanny ability to see the good in every situation.

The two returned to the teahouse. The shop had not opened yet, so they circled around to the back. It took Jian four tries knocking on the door before someone answered. He had mixed up the knock sequence, first knocking three-one-two, then three-two-one, then finally the correct two-one-three, except he became so annoyed, there wasn't a long enough beat between his two and one.

This time, the teahouse apprentice was a young man. At this point, Jian wasn't taking the bait. "Hello again."

"Excuse me?" asked the apprentice.

Jian ground his teeth. "Bah, forget it."

The two were led to the servant's corridor, where they slept in the narrow cot until late morning. Naifun was good enough to serve them a late breakfast, although Jian suspected it was more because of Kaiyu than anything else.

The two split afterward to finish the supply run and load the wagon. They threw a couple games of hands to see who took what task. Jian won more than he lost—Kaiyu was predictable—and chose several of the closer shops to the wagon, though he volunteered to take most of the bulkier supplies—the plum wine and zuijo, specifically—because it probably would have taken Kaiyu the entire day to move some of the heavier loads. Kaiyu was quick and deadly, especially with a staff, but the boy had noodle arms.

Jian's last stop of the day was also the most important. The savory smell of sweet and tangy barbecued meat wafted into his nose the moment he entered the butcher's shop. Suma was in his usual spot behind the tree stump, slicing and dicing a whole pig with his giant cleaver with the pinpoint precision of a scalpel. That man must be an amazing war artist.

He waved. "Hi, Boss Qu Suma."

Suma continued his work. "Your order is ready. Want it now?"

Jian nodded. "As soon as everything is loaded."

"Where to?"

"Hitch five on the left."

Suma pointed at one of his three nephew apprentices, and the large lad scurried off, presumably to fulfill the order. Jian ducked under a raft of ducks hanging by their curved necks on a bamboo pole and offered the pay marker to the butcher.

The butcher offered it back but then held on when Jian tried to take it away. "One more thing. You tell your aunt to put in the request ahead of time. Two days, at least. No more rush jobs after this." He emphasized each word with a delicate tap of the cleaver against the stump.

"Yes, boss," said Jian, dipping extra low as he bowed. Unlike Zofi, he was not brave enough to cross the only decent butcher in the Cloud Pillars who could competently barbecue roast duck.

Jian stepped out and headed for his wagon. Kaiyu should be back soon as well. He didn't know where Sohn or Sonaya were, but at this point he had no qualms about leaving them here. It had just been one of those trips.

He was nearly back to the wagon when he remembered something even more important than the meat. Jian turned around and hurried toward the pastry shop. He hoped he wasn't too late as he maneuvered around oncoming traffic, once hurtling over a small wagon. It was nearly noon and the Super Mighty Sweet Yum closed as soon as they sold all of their inventory. He could not fail Taishi again.

He arrived at the other side of town a few minutes later, panting. Some wet mud had splattered onto one of his pant legs, making a squishing sound with every step. Even worse, and much to his dismay, there was a crowd clustered around the door to the pastry shop. Jian's heart sank. There was no way there was going to be anything good left by the time he got to the counter, but he had to try. Failing once was understandable. Twice would be a betrayal.

Jian pushed his way through the mob of patrons, mostly kids. The sweet smell of jam, sweets, and hot bread washed over Jian as he stepped inside the pastry shop, stopping him in his tracks. He used to eat all the pastries he wanted back at the Celestial Palace. Uncle Faaru made sure whatever he wanted was available. An entire kitchen of chefs catered to his every whim. Jian hadn't realized how much he had taken that perk for granted.

The bakery, as usual, was bustling. Fathers and mothers with their children picking out custard treats for the first time. The older boys there with their friends, hanging around like young ruffians. The shelves on the walls were mostly picked over and bare, as were the three tables arranged in a row against the back wall. Jian grew nervous. Did the bakery already sell out for the day? Had he come too late?

Fortunately, his concerns melted away when the back doors swung open and the baker's three daughters emerged, each with a tray of treats. The excitement in the room crescendoed, and the children clamored and pawed for the treats like little silver piranhas. The forest of candied fruits on a stick was quickly stripped barren, with one stick remaining and only because the candied fruit had fallen apart. The baker's wife brought out a large tray of flaky wife cakes piled into a pyramid. Those disappeared immediately as well. All that remained relatively untouched were the durian custard pies, for good reason.

A new group of people entered the shop behind Jian. A loud voice drowned out the children's clamoring. "Yes, Brother Tuhan the Woo, the Generous, the leader of the Righteous Raiders is here. Hey, bakery boss, treats for all these kids. My tab. Mine, Tuhan the Woo. Remember kids, Tuhan the Woo!"

"Woooooo," the crowd chorused. Apparently, the guy was pretty popular around the settlement. The tiny mob of greedy children surged forward, overwhelming the baker's family and nearly tipping the tables over. Jian took several steps back as the crowd pressed forward even harder.

"Who do you thank?" Woo shouted.

"Thank youuuuu, Tuhan the Wooooo."

The wave of children surged to the counter to collect their free treats, leaving Jian standing alone in the center of the bakery. Tuhan looked over and offered him a piece of candy. "You can have one too, friend. Just say Tuhan the Woo."

Jian was tempted to do just that. Free pastries weren't something any sane person should pass up. He was about to offer Woo that praise for free treats when Tuhan squinted at Jian. His eyebrows shot up to his forehead. "Guppy?"

Jian suffered a similar epiphany at the same time. "Mail bandit?"

Both men pulled away from each other. Jian nearly ran blindly into the wall, while Tuhan tripped over his own man and then barreled through a five-year-old boy. A cascade of crying followed.

"What's the problem, boss?" One of his men helped him stand.

Tuhan fingered Jian, shaking his hands. "That's the guy! He's the one who jumped us at the caravan. Teach him a lesson!"

"What, *me*?" Jian couldn't believe it. It happened again. This was the second time someone had distorted what happened to make him look bad. Well, he wasn't going to tolerate it, not this time. Jian was about to set the record straight with Tuhan when he realized how outnumbered he was. There were eight or so Thieving Raiders in the shop, and he wasn't supposed to exhibit any war arts in public.

"You take a beating if it happens," Taishi had repeatedly warned.

The thought of getting beaten by these really, really bad bandits was insulting. Wait, but there was another option. Just because Jian wasn't allowed to fight or show any ability in Bahngtown didn't mean he couldn't run.

He feinted right and then plowed toward the door, using a current of air to split two of the bandits standing at the doorway apart as he shoved past them and out of the bakery. He took off, heading north, weaving through the crowds and throngs of wagons. He slipped on mud more than a few times and nearly fell and got trampled by a horse. That would have been a terrible way to die.

The Thieving Raiders weren't that far behind. A group of them had been waiting outside the bakery when Tuhan rushed out. He pointed at Jian, and suddenly there were twenty raiders chasing him. This day was not going exactly as planned. In fact, it couldn't get any worse. Taishi was really going to kill him. He could feel the mob bearing down on him. Their shouts were getting louder. Where were the guards? What was the point of having all these ugly dead rat-hat guards if they weren't around to protect someone when something bad happened?

Jian was so distracted he plowed into Lao, the Tiandi monk, who was standing at his usual spot in front of his temple.

Lao held up his hands. "Hiro, what's going on? Are you all right? You look flushed."

Jian tried to avoid a collision by juking left, but Lao slid the same direction when he tried to get out of Jian's way. And then both men slid in the same direction again, and then they collided, Jian's momentum sending them crashing to the ground in a tangle of arms, legs, and broom. The butt of the shaft stabbed painfully into Jian's gut, as he gasped for air. A small crowd gathered around, mostly to help the monk back to his feet. No one cared about Jian. Monks were revered in Shulan; impoverished orphans, not so much.

Instead of standing, Lao leaned into Jian and pointed toward the temple doors. "Go in that way. You'll be safe."

Jian crawled into the temple and then took refuge against the wall beneath the storefront windows. He could hear Lao speaking on the other side. "Nothing to see here. I just stumbled."

The sound of footsteps approached, followed by shouts, one of them, definitely Tuhan the Woo, demanding to know where Jian had gone. Lao's firm but gentle voice quickly eased the charged tension in the air, and then he sent them off, the thunderous sound of their footsteps fading with each passing moment.

"Nothing to see here! Everyone go along with your day. May the Heavens bear you fruit," Lao called. An awkward silence stretched for several moments before the Tiandi monk came inside. He leaned his broom against the wall, barred the door, and closed the drapes. Finally, when he was sure they were alone, he offered Jian a hand. "Are you all right, friend?"

Jian didn't realize he had been holding his breath until he let it all loose just now. "Thank you, Brother Lao."

The monk patted his shoulder. "Of course. I am happy to help. What were those brigands after?"

"I . . ." Then Jian remembered who he was supposed to be and whom he was not supposed to be speaking with. "I'm not sure. I think they were trying to rob me." That made little sense. Jian did not look like a person worth stealing from.

Lao checked him over. "It is a blessing you survived the ordeal unscathed. The Tiandi must favor you. Do you need to rest? Catch your breath?"

Jian took several long, anxious, heavy breaths. "No, you saved me. Many thanks."

"Are you here alone? Can I send a runner to fetch someone?"

Jian was about to ask him to send someone for Master Sohn when he caught himself. He shook his head. "I'm all right, thanks. I should go. My friends are waiting for me at the wagon."

Lao ducked into the back of the temple and appeared a moment later with a pitcher of zuijo and two cups. "This will help calm your nerves."

Jian's throat was parched. He nodded in thanks. They touched cups, and he took a sip, feeling the harsh but cold liquor swill down his throat.

His face immediately flushed. He looked to the side to see his face on the wanted poster right next to him. "I appreciate everything you've done, Brother Lao, but I must go."

"Of course," said the monk, after a slight hesitation. He looked out the window in both directions. "Leave from the back at least. Just in case."

Jian followed Lao around the divider and into the back half of the temple. There were piles of books on tables, wooden statues on their sides, and a row of freshly washed laundry hanging on a line. Priests must go through a lot of undergarments. He carefully stepped around a couple of urns, past a crate of religious texts. Cheap artwork and figurines littered the floor.

Jian was halfway across the room when a wave of heat overwhelmed him. Everything slowed, and his face began to tingle like a hundred acupuncture pricks sweeping across his body. The world swam. Time began to stutter.

Jian blinked a third time, and Lao was standing at the back door. "Safe travels, my friend."

Jian fought for a labored breath and panted. "Thank you again, Brother Lao. I will not forget this."

"I sincerely hope not." Brother Lao opened the door, and Jian came face-to-face with three armored men wearing those ugly, brown dead rat-hats.

Jian startled. "What?" He looked past the shoulder of the guard in the middle and noticed Tuhan the Woo and his gang standing just behind them. "Ah, Jian, you dumb plum," was all he managed to utter before a punch in the gut pushed the air from his lungs and folded him in half. Jian got his revenge by spewing the contents in his stomach all over the nearest guard.

A burlap sack was thrown over his head. A dirty, smelly, gooey one that reeked of rotten eggs and tar.

CHAPTER THIRTY-FIVE

ORACLE OF THE TIANDI

Taishi spent the next two days with the Oracle of the Tiandi. It was an enlightening and strange experience. Taishi had only learned about the oracle's existence a few years back when she had visited the original Temple of the Tiandi and found the former oracle, a disgusting, unwashed, drug-addled old man, passed out sleeping in his own piss-soaked sheets. Three days later, that crazed shadowkill Maza Qisami cut his fingers off and then stuck a knife into his heart.

Taishi looked over to the side at the girl frolicking in the small garden with her pet red fox, with the two Hansoo standing watch on both sides. Apparently, the girl was one of the children who was there that day and witnessed the previous oracle's death, and now she had been chosen to be the next Oracle of the Tiandi.

The girl had a name too, which at first surprised Taishi, to realize that there was actually a little delightful girl behind that exalted holy mantle. Her name was Pei, and her little fox's name was Floppy. She was a precocious, bright young girl, who was at the same time brave and cautious, inquisitive yet guarded. Pei had been orphaned at an early age when her miner parents perished in a cave-in. She had been offered to the Tiandi

Temple in Xusan, and had been raised under their tutelage ever since. The templeabbot of the temple had seen the potential spark in her and had sent her to the original Temple of the Tiandi. And now she was the Oracle of the Tiandi.

Pei skipped to Taishi. "Can we finish reading the story about the singing ox today?"

The girl acted just like any other little girl. She skipped and danced and picked leaves. She read, she giggled, and she threw little fits that all little girls do, and that was marvelous.

"Only if you can promise to keep Floppy off the couches." Taishi really didn't care about the fox one way or another, but she had noticed early on that Pei was at her most natural childlike way when the conversation centered around the creature. She hoped the Hansoo had checked it for rabies.

Pei nodded enthusiastically. "Huouh said he'd give Floppy a bath later on tonight." Apparently, becoming the Oracle of the Tiandi excused you from having to bathe pets. That task was left to the younger of her Hansoo protectors.

"As long as you keep him inside at night, you hear, girl?" said Taishi. "There're many predators out there that will eat that pathetic excuse for a dog in one bite, and then disappear back into the darkness without anyone knowing better."

"Of course. He'll sleep with me!" Pei wore a grin from ear-to-ear as she tussled her red fox's hairy mane. Taishi had a hard time imagining this little girl shouldering the responsibilities of being the oracle for their religion, and having to endure all those many past lives until the strain pushed one to inevitable insanity. It was not a fate Taishi would wish on anyone, let alone someone so young and innocent.

Pei locked eyes with Taishi. She waved, and then she stopped. Her arm dropped, as did that smile on her face, the sides lowering, almost mechanically, bit by bit until her face was neutral, devoid of emotion. "Ling Taishi, your faith in the prophecy is to be commended."

Any sign of the little girl was gone from her eyes. This was the reason Taishi had spent every waking hour with Pei. She was young, so the essence of the prophecy, the Hansoo had explained, manifested at random times and moments. In those brief moments when the essence of the prophecy took over, she became a different person: cooler, colder, and wiser. So far over the past two days, Taishi had managed to have only one other brief conversation with the oracle as she tried to coax a foretelling.

"Especially for an unbeliever." Even her voice carried lower.

"The Tiandi never gave me many reasons to believe," Taishi replied.

"The gentle will of the Tiandi guides with the breeze," the oracle said.

"They never helped me." Talking to the girl was probably the closest Taishi was ever going to get to airing her grievances to those running things in heaven.

"Do you believe your ascent to becoming one of the greatest war artists of your generation did not come with a little divine favor?" asked the oracle.

"Not one bit. It was all hard work and bad luck." And she meant it.

"Well," said the oracle. "Then you will receive this news poorly. Prophecy is probability, and it still holds. The hero's path must touch the Lord of the Grass Sea, or all will be lost."

"How is that possible? He's dead."

"Yet you still train the young hero. Why is that?"

Taishi thought about her past choices. She considered framing them within the context of the prophecy, but then settled on just being honest. Could someone even lie to the Oracle of the Tiandi? "He had no one else. He was a good boy too. You can tell. If he only had a stronger and wiser guiding hand. He could have been great. He could have changed the world." Taishi shook her head. "Perhaps he still can, with or without the prophecy. In any case, even without it, he needed a master. I had no heirs, and the Zhang family line was in danger of dying with me." She shrugged. "In the end, it felt like it was the choice that served the most people. Don't you already know this? You know everything, right?"

The oracle walked over to Taishi and held her good hand in the girl's two little ones. "Truth requires more than thought. Sometimes it needs to be spoken aloud to take shape. Your actions that day in saving Wen Jian's life forever altered the path laid out for your people. Whether it's for better or worse is up to him, and up to you. Just know that the choices you and he make hold weight and consequence."

"What does the Tiandi need from us?" she pressed. "What demands does the prophecy need of him? How can he serve our people? Does the Khan need to die again? How can I prepare for what lies ahead?"

"There is no such thing as preparation for a task," intoned the Oracle of the Tiandi. "There is only preparation for a choice that Wen Jian must soon make, and one that you, Ling Taishi, must soon face. The Prophecy of the Tiandi does not ordain or instruct, it only informs. The decision rests upon those with the will to decide." She broke into a smile. "But you are correct. I did already know your feelings."

"So you already know what I'll do, right?"

"Just because I know what you've done and why you did it doesn't mean I will know what you will decide to do. There is no ability in the cosmos that can determine the future. Free will forbids it. The oracle can only predict where a path may go, but it is never for certain."

Taishi bristled. "Why don't you just tell me what you want to happen then, instead of speaking so cryptically?"

"The role of the oracle is to inform, not to sway," the oracle replied. "Choice matters. Free will matters."

"You sound too wise for your own good," Taishi grumbled.

The oracle blinked, and then the creases from her smile lines returned, followed by her eyes widening with momentary confusion before refocusing back on Taishi. Pei had returned. She nodded vigorously. "Soyo says he has never seen an oracle or girl as bright as me."

As if silently summoned, the older Hansoo appeared just outside the doorway. His large frame required some contorting to come in and out, so he was content to kneel just outside Pei's quarters. Brother Soyo was one of the highest ranking war monks treading outside the Stone Blossom Monastery, and the one responsible for Pei's safety and well-being. The war monk bowed his head. "It is the time for the Oracle of the Tiandi's afternoon nap."

Taishi fell to a knee and clutched her hands. "That story will have to wait. I promise we'll read it tonight."

She stood and left the room, acknowledging the older Hansoo. His wrinkled and gray head was nearly twice the size of hers. He also smelled like flowers. The Tiandi sects were notoriously hygienic folks.

Saan, as the mindseer, was leaning against the opposite post, waiting for her. He was alone, or as alone as a duke could be in a dangerous place. The Mute Men had not relaxed their guard since their arrival. "Any progress?"

"A good five minutes." She accepted a cup from him and drained it in one gulp. He must have brought this good stuff with him, because this was good wine. Which was all the more peculiar considering it was the mindseer drinking it.

"Did she say anything useful?"

"Apparently, my saving Jian was the aberration. He was expected to die back at the Celestial Palace."

"That's rather morbid." He arched one thick, bushy brow. "And now you saved him. Is this a good or bad thing? I can't tell."

She shrugged. "I would do the exact same all over again."

"Fair enough." Saan took a step forward and met her in the middle of the path. "How much longer do you anticipate spending time with the oracle?"

Technically, she could spend months with Pei. There were so many things she could learn. However, things were even more pressing now. She had to return to her responsibilities shortly. "Five or six more days, perhaps, and my time here will be concluded." She considered, and added slowly, "Thank you for arranging this meeting, my lord. This journey must have come at a great cost in manpower and coin to you. I am in your debt."

"Six days, good. I can work with that." Saan nodded. "Speaking of debt, walk with me."

Taishi noticed the smirk on his face. "Damn you, wry weasel."

"I require your counsel, master." The two strolled back down the stairs of the curving branch. Several Mute Men appeared in front and behind, matching the rhythm of their footsteps with theirs. Two more shot on ahead to clear the way, leaving them alone walking down a curved ramp following the circumference of the tree. An entrance at the bottom cut through the tree. "There is an opportunity for peace. Gyian, Shulan, and Caobiu are considering an alliance. I depart soon to Allanto, where we will begin discussions on a treaty and how this partnership will look. The other dukes must realize that I am in the weakest position and will seek to press their advantage. These negotiations are fraught with peril. Yanso is also marrying Sunri, which leaves me the odd wheel out. I need your wisdom to navigate these treacherous waters. After your business is concluded here, I would like you to come to the Gyian capital and serve as my adviser."

"Impossible, I'm a fugitive," said Taishi. "They'll hang me the moment I'm exposed, and then hang you for treason right after. Also, Yanso and Sunri, together, there isn't a pit of deadlier vipers."

"You can be my shadow adviser and operate under my protection the entire time. I swear to you, I will send you back on the fastest steed the moment the treaty is signed. You will be gone no more than half a year. In the meanwhile, I will also assign a full retinue of Mute Men to protect the Prophesied Hero of the Tiandi."

"You want my advice? Don't make this unholy alliance with you three. Instead, stay home and fortify your defenses."

"Taishi." Saan looked uncomfortable. "I'm asking as a friend. I need to have successful negotiations to protect my people. Turtling will only delay the inevitable."

"Don't make it about protecting your people, Saan. The world knows it was the Second Light Ryli Road standoff that started the war. You're a good man most of the time, but you also love glory, and in this case, it got the better of you. Restoring your family line to the Heart of the Tiandi Throne would be the ultimate prize." Taishi shook a finger at him. "You wanted this war, and now it's not going the way you expected. So no, I am not going to travel with you to the glittery ass-end of the Enlightened States to negotiate with two devils to protect your power, influence, and land rights. I'm sorry, Saan. You're on your own."

"I'm no longer asking as a friend. I'm ordering you as your lord." They entered his residence. Saan went to the table and held up a plate. "Moon cake?"

She shook her head. The court's rich flavoring would upset her bowels terribly. "The last time you ordered me on assignment, I ended up being the Enlightened States' most wanted fugitive."

"Technically second," said Saan. "Jian's still much higher."

"Shut up, my lord."

"Yes, master."

She turned to leave. "Besides, I have more important responsibilities right now."

"You mean, training the boy hero? Why bother? The Khan is dead. It's over."

"Then it doesn't matter if I train him anyway," she shouted. "At the very least, I can protect him from the vultures in court."

"There is no reach too far for the court."

"I hid Jian from all of you, from the world, for over two years. Perhaps your reach is not as substantive as you imagine."

A commotion erupted outside. The unmistakable sound of blades hissing out of their sheaths followed. Taishi's hand drifted to the Swallow Dances, and she placed herself in between the duke and the doorway. Saan had instinctively reached for a weapon missing at his waist. Instead, he retreated to the back of the room where a pot of tea awaited.

"Four tea," he announced, pouring herself a cup and raising it to her lips without touching. Otherwise known as death tea. The health of the duke of Shulan was obviously paramount, and supposedly that tea was the quickest way for the one drinking to lose consciousness instantly, which would sever the connection with the duke. The concoction, however, was eventually fatal to all whose lips touched the drink. Fortunately, it didn't have to come to that.

The front double doors to the residence cut into the tree flew open. The two Mute Men who were standing guard outside flooded in first, moving to Taishi's flanks. Then the two Hansoo came in. The doors were wide enough to allow them to pass through without destroying the frame.

"What is the meaning of this?" said Saan.

Soyo lowered his head. "Apologies to you both, duke and master, but the oracle insisted."

Pei walked in last, or was it the Oracle of the Tiandi? Taishi couldn't be sure. "Ling Taishi, I bring urgent news."

"What is it, Pei?" she asked.

"The Prophesied Hero of the Tiandi is in danger. You need to go to him immediately."

Taishi's chest squeezed, and her throat closed. The constant slight quivering that sometimes vibrated up and down her good arm locked in place, almost painfully, and then the shakes returned stronger than ever. "That's not possible. He should be home."

"He is in the Bahngtown settlement in the clutches of those who seek to control him." She closed her eyes and then opened them. "He will soon be lost to you unless you hurry to his side."

Taishi was already heading out the door. She burst outside and was met by the other war artist masters waiting just outside. All three stood at alert with their hands drifting toward their weapons. They must have been attracted by the commotion.

"Urwan," her voice carried throughout the quiet settlement. "Saddle the lions. We depart immediately."

The horselord shook his head. "Impossible. The shishi traveled for over a day straight. They require more rest. You'll kill them otherwise."

"Then they die," she snapped. "They don't matter. The enemy has Jian."

Bhasani's eyes widened. "Who has him?"

"I don't know. It doesn't matter. I will save him at all costs."

"And I'm telling you we won't make it back if we ride the shishi now." Urwan rubbed his chin and considered. "Righteous lions sleep in a hibernated state. They'll be a wreck if woken prematurely and be unable to function for such a long journey, not unlike Fausan drawing the short chopstick to taking second watch in the middle of the night."

Bhasani snorted. "At least you didn't have to sleep next to him for a decade. The way he snores, no one else sleeps."

Taishi snarled. Her emotions flirted with panic as her mind struggled to find a solution. The one time she had to get to Jian immediately and she found herself in the far crack end of civilization. She snarled and walked up to the pathway railing overlooking the underground forest. She could just make out the hole in the cavern ceiling leading up to the land above. The air down here was unusually still. There was no breeze, no movement, and few sounds save for the echoes of their voices as they carried across the dead space.

There wasn't any other option. "How far can they take us before they die? Can we make it to the nearest settlement and procure new mounts?"

"It won't be that simple. We're better off just letting our lions rest those two days."

"It will be too late if your journey begins with the rise of the King," said Pei, appearing behind them at the doorway.

Taishi pointed at the girl and glared at Urwan. "You hear that? It'll be too late. So find me a solution."

Urwan shook his head. "I'm sorry, Taishi. "It's the best we can do. Trying anything else will only delay your journey."

"Take mine," said Saan, stepping outside to join them. He sauntered over to them. "Take my pride of shishi. They're well rested. They can carry you back to wherever you need to go and then back to the Red Lantern temple, Master Ling Taishi."

That stopped her in her tracks. "How long have you known?"

"Few days after you arrived with your group. I had a man watching it the entire time. Said you were accompanied by a Hansoo." Saan chuckled. "Did you seriously think, as you say the world's most wanted fugitive, that you could so easily just change your name and hide in plain sight in your *own* home?"

"Not many know where I live," she admitted. "Why didn't you arrest us?"

"Arrest you?" he scoffed. "Who do you think has been protecting you all this time?"

Saan liked to exaggerate, but it did make sense. She had been far too lucky the past few years. "Thank you, Saan, deeply." Taishi meant every word. "I will not forget this."

"Will you reconsider going to Allanto and serve as my shadow adviser?"

"Not for all the gold liang in the world." She unexpectedly offered a formal bow. "Thank you, Duke Saan, for the generous gift."

"Bah, go." Saan waved her off. "I'll collect from you when it really counts."

Taishi signaled to the others to leave and sent Urwan to prepare the duke's pride of lions. Her gaze met little Pei's. She decided to ask the thing that had been bothering her. She might not get another chance. "Why are you helping me? Isn't that rather meddlesome for an oracle? Aren't you breaking prophecy rules or something?"

"I've seen the possible paths branching out before me. The ones where Ling Taishi and Wen Jian are separated end with great devastation." It was the oracle's turn to shrug. A small smile crept onto her face. "The great unknown is always free will. Everyone has preferences, even oracles." Her eyes grew intense. "When the time comes, Ling Taishi, and that hard choice has to be made, make sure Jian chooses wisely. Do not let him deviate from expectations. Do you understand?"

"Not a clue, but I'll worry about that when the time comes." Taishi didn't care either, especially right now. She noticed Zofi standing off to the side. "Why are you still standing around? Get moving!"

CHAPTER THIRTY-SIX

STORMCHASER

Sali kicked Hampa and Daewon awake when she finally returned to the cobbler shop from the underground cave with the ritualist. The two young men had fallen asleep on the penguin rug, huddled together like cuddlebugs. "We're leaving."

Hampa awoke, mostly alert. He looked up. "Why is it always day?"

Daewon yawned. He looked over Sali's face. Disappointment soon followed. "Did you find a cure?"

"Long story." She continued back to the square, trusting them to follow her. "It's complicated. I don't want to get into it now."

"Wait," stammered the tinker, catching up. "So are you cured?"

"No." Sali shrugged. "But that's not important."

"Not important?" he sputtered. "Isn't that the only reason why we're out here in the freeze?"

"It doesn't matter, not right now."

Hampa excused himself and ran back to the caves. The lad had remembered to run back and retrieve her armor and weapons. Sali had been so distracted she left it all at the cave and was just wearing plain under-robes. Her neophyte was breathing heavily by the time he caught back up to them.

"We need to work on your conditioning, little brother."

He huffed. "You also forgot your tongue."

"I did." Misplacing a weapon was usually an unforgivable sin, but Sali was giving herself a little grace this time. Finding out that the Khan was a corrupted spirit from Hrusha that was brainwashed by the spirit shamans and coerced to conquer the entire Grass Sea was a completely outland-ish tale, one usually saved for the opera or a street clown. Yet here they were. Now that she had seen and heard the Happans' version of the Eternal Khan of Katuia, or their Warrior, she didn't know what to be-lieve. But it didn't matter. The only thing that was important was that he could not return as long as she lived. Every day she saw the dawn was one more day of keeping the Khan from hunting Nezra.

It was evening by the time they neared the lake, which meant the city was starting to die down. A small night market opened along the shore, but other than a few drinking stalls, Hrusha shut down at the fourth wind chime of the day.

"We're done here," she said. "As soon as we wrap up our business, we go home."

"I still need to pick up my order of ore."

"Do so first thing tomorrow. How much time do you need?"

"Half day?"

"I will talk to the captain. Hampa, go with him."

"Are you sure, mentor? I don't know if it's wise we separate."

Sali tended to agree. Perhaps it was wiser to travel with them, or maybe consider abandoning the ore and losing their deposit. "Whatever you need to do, I want to be on that boat sailing home by tomorrow eve-ning. Understood?"

"Yes, mentor."

They turned the corner and moved along the narrow path following the lake's curve. The docks would be closed at this hour, but it shouldn't be hard for them to sneak in, even with Daewon. They could always pre-tend to be sailors reporting back from leave.

Sali was thinking of home when she sensed a heavy, strong presence. A passing familiarity, like an old scratch of the mind. A figure in purple and black walked toward them. His light robes shifted and danced in the breeze, obfuscating his body. His face: handsome, sharp but not arrogant, more confident.

"Salminde the Viperstrike," he called in his assured, steady voice.

Sali muttered, "Get back to the *Hana Iceberg*. If I'm not back by dawn, sail home. Take care of our people."

"No," stammered Hampa. "My place is with you, mentor."

"Daewon, double whatever order you were going to make. Take care of Malinde. Hampa, stop looking at me like that. That is a command, neophyte. Lean into your natural skills, little brother."

"I will defend you to my last breath."

Sali wrapped a fist around his collar and pulled him close. "Do as your mentor instructs, neophyte, or go find another."

Hampa blanched. Tears welled in his eyes. "Yes, mentor."

Sali embraced him. "Protect the empty-headed tinker, eh?"

"I'll try."

"Now, go." Sali shoved him aside and continued forward, preparing herself for the task ahead. Her heart sped up and her body loosened even as her senses heightened.

"Salminde the Viperstrike," the man repeated, coming closer. He passed under the light of a torch. He still cut a roguish, if not more weathered, figure.

"Raydan the Stormchaser."

Raydan broke into a smile. "I wish I could say it was good to see you. It has been a lifetime since we last laid eyes on each other. We were just young warriors . . ."

"Breaking bones," she remembered.

"Breaking hearts," he finished.

"We were pretty stupid weeds then," she said. "You look like I remembered."

Raydan stared at her, his long hair and breezy robes fluttered in the wind until finally settling around his shoulders. "You've waded into deep waters, old friend. There are certain sins that not even friendship can overlook. I truly grieved, wept even, when the high spirit shaman informed me that Salminde the Viperstrike was sighted at the Grand Monastery of the Dawn Song."

She shrugged. "I had completely forgotten about you." A small lie.

Raydan approached. He was now within the range of her tongue. "Out of love and respect to my old raidsister, I offer you this. Surrender, and I promise upon my honor and sect that no harm will befall you until we reach the Black City."

"Then the spirit shamans will sacrifice me to the Altar of the Eternal," said Sali just as matter-of-factly. "Your offer is not nearly as attractive as you think it is."

The stormchaser's casual tone changed. "At least if you return, you fulfill your sacred vow to our Khan. I would have never thought under a thousand stars that Salminde the Viperstrike is an oathbreaker who is terrified of death."

Sali shot a derisive laugh. "You think that's why I didn't lay down and let those sadistic shamans drain all my blood and embalm me while I was still alive?"

Raydan's demeanor suddenly took a violent turn as his tone became thunderous. "That was your duty! To all of our people! You turned your back and betrayed us!"

"You're a flaccid fool if you know me, yet do not question what has happened. A fool or a neutered hound."

Raydan drew his weapon, Whirlwind, a famed short staff slightly taller than him with two scythes on each end facing opposite directions. Sali remembered often stopping to admire the stormchaser's beautiful and deadly artistic style as he cut through swaths of enemy in battle. The stormchaser twirled the double-ended staff in his hands before ending its rotation with an aggressive attack stance. It was certainly a flashy weapon, although he had always been a showman. The man couldn't drink water without causing a scene. Sali had always thought he was too much of a self-promoter, but there was no arguing with his results. He was a savage and balletic war artist. There were few within the Grass Sea with a greater or fiercer reputation than Sali. Raydan had both. Whether he was more skilled than her was up for debate. The outcome of this particular encounter, however, would not settle that question. Any fight between them today could only end one way.

"This fight is duty, Salminde the Viperstrike, not a choice. Honor demands it. I know you understand." Raydan changed stances two more times before Sali bothered to settle into one. The man had always been one of those who liked to pose and look in the mirror, but now he was embedding poses within poses.

Sali grasped the loops of her tongue off its holster and lowered herself into a defensive position. Her chest, already heaving from the exertion of just staying upright, began to stutter. She gripped her chest. Her heartbeat was irregular, two quick and then a single beat. She swallowed a cough and grimaced as her body spasmed. Her vision began to swim, and the ground began to feel like it was shifting beneath her feet.

"Our paths don't have to cross, Raydan. Let me continue on my way if we truly were friends once. This honor you speak of is just vanity. It's ambition, not duty."

"Why can't it be both?" Whirlwind twirled over his head once before coming to rest in his right hand. Raydan leaned forward as if preparing to pounce.

Sali settled into her stance and stayed relaxed. There was still a fair amount of distance between them. Make him come to her.

The stormchaser blinked and disappeared. One moment he was down the road, just at the edge of the range of her tongue, the next he was in her face. The sudden flash and movement, called a lightning stride, was the stormchaser's signature. These were fast, quick attacks that you could miss if you weren't alert and ready. The sect and this technique had earned the stormchasers a fierce reputation among the Grass Sea. Sali had never been that impressed, but then she also had never been on the target end of a stormchaser.

Sali was about to find out exactly how good the stormchaser was.

Raydan was quicker than she remembered. Sali avoided the first high scythe slice, Whirlwind spinning so quickly it was like a giant circular saw in the stormchaser's hands. Sparks flew as Whirlwind met the rope of the tongue curled around Sali's forearms, acting as bracers.

Sali blocked a series of high slashes, skipped away as Raydan swept low with those hissing scythe blades. Her luck was bound to run out, and it did as Raydan chained his attack with a clever little stutter spin. Sali fell for it, and the long, curved scythe blade raked her chest, cutting through her scale armor like wool. She managed to twist away and avoid the worst of it, but the blade still grazed her ribs.

More attacks came in rapid succession. Raydan lightning-strided from her left to her right, then he attacked with short staff swings before swirling the scythe blades at unexpected angles. Sali took several more cuts, on the arms and thigh, her right shoulder and left knee. Her leg nearly gave out when she tried to retaliate with an embarrassingly slow jab that struck empty air.

Raydan strode once more to her other side. Sali failed to adjust, and he swept his right foot forward, catching both of her heels and flipping her onto her back.

He looked puzzled as he strolled in a circle around her. "Who are you? You certainly cannot be Salminde the Viperstrike. She was never this slow and modest." He offered a hand.

Sali grunted and slapped it away. She didn't want him to feel her tremble. "You're lucky. You caught me on a day when I am under the weather."

He did not look convinced. "The years have not been kind to you, raidsister."

"I wish I could say the same for you." Sali picked herself up and drew her tongue. She sent a jolt through it and then lowered her guard toward Raydan. "Get this over with."

The stormchaser came at her again. This time, Whirlwind stayed at his back as he fought with his hands. The results were the same. Her reaction was slightly late, and then these late reactions piled up until Raydan slipped through her guard.

The punch felt like her spleen had burst. Her body changed direction as the sudden force blew her off her feet. She crashed so hard into the city pod ground that her body cracked several of the tempered wooden panels. Sali groaned and palmed the ground. She nearly blacked out before forcing herself to stay awake through sheer will.

"The Salminde I knew," Raydan continued, flourishing his long fingers as he orated, "once singlehandedly ambushed an entire Zhuun platoon just to save her horse. What was the name of that horse?"

Sali used up whatever strength she had left to get to one knee, and then she had to rest. A smirk broke on her face. "Ugly Brown Horse."

"That's right." Raydan pointed. "The ugliest horse I've ever seen." He shook his head. "You loved that beast."

"I did." Sali tried to rise again, and again failed. "Enough talk. Let's go."

The stormchaser raised a hand. "Take your time, Salminde. Catch your breath. You obviously need it." He flashed a smile. "Before this goes further, I ask as a friend. What ails you, raidsister? What is really wrong?"

Her chest spasmed, and it was all she could do to keep standing. She loosed a long, uneven breath, and then spat up blood from her lungs. She couldn't take many more of those blows. How humiliating. "The Khan's blessing is what happened. Like everything else the spirit shaman touches, it poisons. Having a piece of Jiamin's soul has rotted my body. It decays from the inside."

A flash of anger broke on Raydan's face. "You have only yourself to blame. You were supposed to sacrifice yourself like the rest of the Will of the Khans and Sacred Cohorts. The spirit shamans had warned the chiefs about your turn to heresy. I wouldn't have believed it until I saw it just now." Raydan looked mournful. He adjusted his flowing navy blue cloud-shaped robes. "I feel robbed that I was not able to stake my honor against the real Salminde the Viperstrike. I promise to remember you as you were, and not as the sad creature you have become."

His pity only made Sali more furious, but it wasn't like she was in a position to do something about it. Her mind raced. Fighting Raydan was a losing bid. He was an equal match for her on her best day, and today was certainly not that. He may be better than she remembered. Sali hated to admit it, but she wasn't sure if she could have beat him before she took ill. None of that mattered because she couldn't beat him now.

"Come. I promise to capture you with dignity. Salvage what little honor you have left." Raydan advanced, not bothering to lightning-stride.

She had to get away, but that was impossible in her current condition.

She was sprawled on her backside in the center of the main road. The stormchaser could easily catch her anyway.

Unless.

Sali picked up the bite of her tongue and made a show of weakly throwing it at Raydan. It fell well short and landed harmlessly at his feet. The stormchaser put a foot on the bite. "Your tongue has always been a beautiful and elegant weapon, difficult to learn but extraordinary in skilled hands. I will be honored to add it to my collection as a remembrance of my noble friend Salminde the Viperstrike before she turned from her people and trotted down the dark ways."

"You talk too much." Sali sent a jolt through her loose tongue, stiffening the shaft to its full length and launching Sali most of the way over the shore. She recoiled the tongue and held on to the looped rope tightly as she plunged into the roiling red, yellow, and pink waters of the Sun Under Lagoon.

CHAPTER THIRTY-SEVEN

NOTHING PLEASANT HAPPENS AFTER MIDNIGHT

Porla was missing from their room the next day. Estatekeeper Hari had informed Ruli that the girl had had a mishap at the concubine's tower the night before. To Qisami's chagrin, Ruli blamed *her* for not helping the girl out more.

"You should have been there for her, Kiki," she scolded. "You were in her position not too long ago. You know how those pretty bitches are with the new girls. You should have protected her!"

"You were like a big sister to her," another servant chastised.

Someone even dared poke her shoulder. "We have to look out for each other, girl."

Why was everyone blaming *her*? Qisami had no choice but to eat all of their criticisms. If they only knew what had actually happened. Still, she took her lumps, apologizing profusely for something she should have done when she was actually the one who did far worse. It was poetic in a way. She hated feeling guilty. Worse, she wasn't even sure why she felt this way, but she did, and it was deeply annoying.

That evening, after she finished her rounds with the twins at the Aki household, Qisami met with Chiafana at the cellar to hand over the satchel of notes.

"Any issues?" the minister asked.

Qisami shook her head. "Smooth service, as always."

"The messenger is dead?"

"You won't have to worry about them anymore." She did her best to brush off this topic. "Next time, give me more than a day's lead, yeah? I can't keep offering top quality service if you don't give me time to prepare."

"You will be informed when needed." Chiafana grunted. "My spy in the administration is working to assign you to the negotiation staff. Be ready for it."

"What are you talking about? I *just* joined the Aki household," Qisami sputtered. "You can't keep reassigning me. It'll raise suspicion and reflect poorly on my employment records."

"What do you care about your *employment records*?" mocked the minister.

That stumped Qisami too. Why did she?

"I need to get back," said Chiafana. "The duchess should have finished dinner with Yanso by now."

"Are they really going to get married?" Qisami blurted.

The Minister of Critical Purpose gave her a narrow side-eye before she walked away.

"That's not a no," she chortled.

Qisami waited five minutes after the minister left the cellar before she crept out. It was dusk, but crews were still coming and going. She had her shadowkill garb on under her robes this time. She would rather not be seen as Kiki at this hour. Management had strict rules about curfew for servants while on estate grounds. It was probably for their safety. Young, entitled nobles, often staying out late in packs carousing and drinking, were sloppy predators to commoners, especially women.

She departed the Fourth Palace from the second-story window directly above the cellar. The east end of the palace was heading the wrong direction, but it was the most sparsely used section of the grounds. She dropped down next to a paved landing with benches and tables and made herself small behind a stone statue of the philosopher Goramh tinged a bit green. She listened for a response, and then took off, zigzagging from darkness to darkness, skirting along the framed edges of the buildings until she reached the perimeter wall. One quick bound on top and then one more onto the curved hook of a low-hanging eave, and she was moving across the top of a row of buildings.

Qisami hung off the center spine of the steep tiled roof with one hand—it was too easy to get spotted running along the spine—and admired the horizon of buildings and walls behind the long strip. Only the Queen and Prince were out, casting the landscape in a soft turquoise hue, and the clear sky held court to an army of twinkling stars. It was a calm night.

She wondered if Porla was going to be all right. The other servants were telling her the girl was a wreck and afraid to leave her bed in the infirmary. Qisami sucked in her breath. She didn't feel any responsibility for the girl's plight. In fact, Qisami had *saved* her life! It was just a job, nothing personal. Blame should fall on the client, or in this case, Minister of Critical Purpose Chiafana. It had always been that way within the lunar court. Still, Qisami couldn't help but feel a little bad. The least she could do was try to arrange to have Porla transferred to one of the duke's country estates or one of his many flower farms.

"It's all Firstwife's fault," she huffed. In fact, Qisami considered putting a death mark on the woman. It would be an incredibly brazen, egotistical, and not to mention dangerous kill. Qisami had never met hubris she couldn't overcome, however.

It was then that she realized she hated working for that wretched woman, and by extension Duchess Sunri. This was what she got for dipping her stupid toe into politics, no matter how desperate she was. If she had only stayed in her comfort zone and killed regular rich people, she would still have been a top-ranked diamond-tiered shadowkill.

"I can't finish the job." If she was honest, she actually didn't *want* to finish the job. "You let yourself get too involved with the assignment, stupid girl. You should let the job go and disappear with your crew." It was cathartic to hear those words, even if it didn't temper her anger or fill that well of loss or heal the cut left by guilt.

She stood, balancing easily against the side of the steep roof, and remembered the words of her favorite teacher at the training pool, even if she didn't remember his name: a good job requires as much sense as tactics. If either falls short of expectations, let it go.

"It's time to abort." Qisami knew she was trying to convince herself. The rest of the cell would be furious. All of them had sunk too much time and effort into it. To walk away with nothing would be devastating. But it was obvious to her now that her instincts were telling her to walk away while they still could. The smart if not painful choice was to call it before she was asked to do something worse.

What would she do, though? Go back to running petty kill jobs? More jilted lovers and sibling lineage quarrels? Workplace politics and petty revenge? What if Qisami stayed on the estate staff?

She blew a raspberry. "Diamond-tier shadowkill to estate maiden." It was a preposterous idea, of course, but why? It was a lowbrow existence, but so what. She had many friends, a community, and an environment where she wasn't always looking over her shoulder. The work was sometimes fun. It would be a fresh start, a new life.

Qisami was still fantasizing about starting a new life and about murdering Chiafana when she noticed a figure creeping toward the corner below her on the ground. This trespasser was doing a fair attempt at staying hidden, following a row of willow trees along the edge of the pond that partitioned off the back wall of the Fourth Palace and the servant quarter streets. Then, this strange figure stepped onto the water and strode across the pond, creating small ripples with each step. Suddenly, they leaped and landed on a large boulder close to shore before disappearing.

Qisami let go of the spine, skated down to the edge of the roof, and dropped to the street. It was probably none of her business, but she was curious. Also, this stranger, a fellow nightblossom, was moving toward the Fourth Palace. An assassination attempt, perhaps? She bet thwarting it would come with a pretty heavy payout. It would certainly lessen the blow of letting a job go.

Time to collect some extra credit.

Qisami moved in pursuit, scampering to the top of the Fourth Palace walls to get a better vantage point. She dropped inside, stepped into the shadow, and emerged behind the shadow of a large branch halfway up a giant acacia tree near the Zen garden. She surveyed the area again, filtering out the white noise and the nightingales. At first, she thought the other nightblossom had eluded her, but then she caught sight of the interloper scaling a curtain of vines onto the glass roof of the passageway that led to the east wing. How did they get there so quickly?

It was time to scratch that itch again. Qisami went after them, dropping to the ground, then slipping into a shadow and out next to a pet mausoleum, across a bed of flowers, and through the pieces of a giant game of Siege. She caught her prey, still unaware that they were being followed, moving toward an open window on the third level.

Qisami's blood pumped as she stalked her prey. This was one of her favorite pastimes. Killing was fine, but the real thrill was the foreplay. She wasn't a sadist who usually allowed death to linger, but she would often stretch her pursuit so she could revel in the hunt.

The trespasser was almost within kill range. One quick step through a shadow, appearing at the right place and time, and she would get the drop on the nightblossom. Quick, quiet, and deadly. For a moment, she considered taking her prey alive, perhaps to squeeze out information or set up a ransom. Then she remembered that she was here to send a message and earn that gold liang. There was no mention of taking anyone alive. Why try to go for extra credit when there was none?

The trespasser's actions, so far, gave nothing away regarding their background or style of war arts. The figure was dressed in black with a hood and cloak over a mask and tight robes. They were certainly skilled, with fluid movements that spoke of intention, and smooth and efficient use of jing. Qisami wanted to understand who she was up against when she went for the kill. Might as well do that now. The end of her finger touched the handle of one of her black knives, and she slowly drew it from its sheath.

She was mere steps from making the kill when the figure passed behind a wooden column and disappeared. Qisami tilted her head side to side, but her prey had somehow eluded her. Qisami dropped into the shadow of a rose bush and emerged behind the column beneath the glass roof. She caught sight of the trespasser climbing into the second-floor window halfway down the palace's outer wall.

How did they get there so quickly?

She might be dealing with a teahouse. Where shadowkills used their jing to slip in and out of darkness, teahouses used their jing to move *as* shadows. Their war art was mostly annoying when it came to battle, but the damage they could do with their spying was often far more deadly than any blade.

Qisami chased after them, scaling up the columns and running along the length of glass roof. She dove headfirst into the shadowed corner of the main building and used the momentum of the fall to emerge below that third-floor window. She shot her hand out and managed a finger hold on the ledge.

Qisami stepped onto a balcony that wrapped around the inside of the palace overlooking the main hall. Three wooden bridges spanned the gap while several rafters crisscrossed near the ceiling. There were many nooks and crannies to hide a nightblossom.

Having scouted their rotations, Qisami knew that the night watch consisted of four guards on the ground level, two on the second, and two on the third. She now was sure she knew where this intruder was heading. The only place of interest or value was the duchess's quarters. These guards were easy to avoid. Chiafana had made it clear that it was critical she remain invisible and unknown to both sides.

Qisami caught sight of the intruder moving along the shadows, almost like a black spot swimming through different shades of darkness as she crept toward Sunri's door. Qisami shadowstepped once more and popped out in an adjacent darkened room, entering the hallway behind the intruder. Her black knife hissed from its sheath as she moved in for the kill.

That was when she realized her error.

In her hurry to catch up to the other nightblossom, Qisami had moved in on the intruder too aggressively. An unlucky lull in the nightingales' songs had allowed a few moments of silence, and the soft puff of air rushing to fill the space alerted anyone of her presence, if they knew what to listen for. In this case, the intruder did, turning to face Qisami and loosening a triangular throwing star as Qisami stepped into the hall-way.

Qisami ducked to the side as the star thunked into a wall beside her. The two similarly black-clad creatures of the night stared each other down. The intruder was tall and thin, dressed in tight clothes with an oversize hood and cloak draped down to their ankles. The mask beneath the hood gave nothing away save bright, nearly yellow eyes. A long, loose braid snaked over one shoulder.

Each nightblossom waited for the other to make the first move. Qisami obliged and offered a friendly wave with her knife in hand. "This is your unlucky night. You're not supposed to be here. Why don't we go somewhere private and have a chat before you get hurt?"

The intruder wisely ran the other direction, heading for the closest window. Qisami was ready for that, however, and stepped into a nearby corner only to appear in a blink, blocking the path of her fleeing prey. She brandished two knives. Now she'd see how good this intruder was. "Suit yourself. I prefer doing it this way as well."

The other nightblossoms—teahouses, silkspinners, blacklotuses, abyssalfogs—had their expertise. None of them, however, could match the sheer killing brilliance of a shadowkill. She struck at the intruder, a horizontal slash aimed at severing their head. To Qisami's surprise, the intruder ducked the slash and slid feet-first to the right. Directly into the dimmed corner, and then through it, disappearing.

Qisami gasped. "What did you—"

A heavy weight crashed on her from above, nearly snapping her neck. Qisami was fortunate the blow didn't land harder, but it was still enough to knock her flat on her back. Dazed, she looked at the intruder towering over her, crescent moon blades extended near her neck.

Qisami sputtered at the nightblossom. "Great holy hot buns. You're a me! You're a shadowkill!"

Maza Qisami stared at the opposing shadowkill standing over her. It had been years since she'd fought another of her kind, not since her training pool days. She remembered losing that mirror match; she tended to get overly creative and cute with her tactics, which would often back-fire when pitted against another experienced shadowkill.

Someone must have sent them after Sunri on an off-book kill. The Consortium would never sanction such a brazen act. Part of Qisami wanted to call a temporary no-killing timeout to ask her unlucky challenger how much bounties on dukes go for these days. She bet it was enough to fund her debt and retirement. Killing dukes didn't come cheap. Qisami would be lying if taking out Sunri for the payout hadn't crossed her mind, but that's not how things worked. This wasn't an open bounty, and she hadn't been commissioned for the mark, so she might not get paid for the job.

Instead of seizing their advantage against a downed opponent, though, the other shadowkill did an unlike-a-shadowkill thing and escaped through the open window, plunging headfirst through the fourth-floor opening as if diving into the sea. Qisami picked herself up and ran to the window. That was weird. Shadowkills never left witnesses, nor did they hesitate to kill. The other shadowkill, assuming they were one, had excellent form, however. Good, clean lines.

Qisami might not be able to earn the score by killing a duke, but she bet she could earn an even greater score saving one. Or in this case, a duchess. "You're not getting away that easily."

She leaped out the window after the shadowkill. In the back of her mind, a small voice reminded her about what happened the last time she did a job off the cuff. It catastrophically led her to this very moment. Still, it was excusable; the money had been worth it, like this jackpot would be if she saved Sunri from a shadowkill.

Qisami dropped three stories and rolled out of her fall, ending on her feet in a full sprint. The other shadowkill was already several lengths ahead. Two black throwing knives shot from Qisami's outstretched fingers, streaking true toward their head and the middle of their back. The other shadowkill spun as the two blades closed in. They ducked the first and kicked the second out of the air, then spun back and kept on going.

They moved with fluid and efficient actions; their control was complete. Qisami was impressed. Too bad this wasn't opera. Doing it pretty got you only so far. She continued her pursuit, following the other shadowkill into the orchid garden. She caught sight of them running into the shadow of a pine tree, and then reemerging on the rooftop the next building over. Qisami stopped and gawked; that was an exceedingly long shadowstep. This wasn't some cellar-dwelling gold-tier shadowkill, but a real snarling, competent bitch. This killer was diamond-tier.

Qisami's blood pumped, and she felt aroused and honestly a little jealous of her opponent's competence as she continued the pursuit following a different intercepting route. She wasn't willing to bet she could have stepped such a long distance, and getting forcibly ejected from the shadow was always an incredibly uncomfortable and sometimes fatal experience. She planned a way up the side of the nearby wall and then a jump to the lower deck. She was making her way toward the third-floor window when she looked up and saw the other shadowkill standing on the roof staring down at her. Taunting her, daring her to follow.

Qisami gritted her teeth. "I don't know if I can make this." Getting lost in the black void was probably one of the worst ways to die.

Still, she was never one to back down from a challenge. She snarled, took a breath, and hissed, and then stepped into the shadow. A rush of bubbles tickled her skin as the world turned monochromatic, bleeding away all color save black and white. Her limbs tingled as they stretched forward and backward, extending longer than humanly possible. Black static began to fall upward. Qisami's heart pounded. Her joints burned as they stretched as though she were being quartered. Reality condensed. Color returned in a splash of paint as the black-and-white-peppered static drizzled upward and away. But here she was, standing next to a chimney on the roof. The other shadowkill was gone, but at least Qisami had made the shadowstep.

"Oh, wow." She inhaled. "I made it." It took several moments to recover. The sudden compression of her limbs smooshing together as she stepped out of the shadow had been equally painful.

Qisami caught sight of the other shadowkill, running across the spines of a roof bordering the third consort palace. She loosed two more knives. This time, the other shadowkill kicked both out of the air at the same time, and then sent a knife of their own to Qisami. Qisami made a show of ignoring it as it slipped dangerously close to her neck.

Another barrage of knives followed the first. This time, the shadowkill slid down the side of the steep roof and leaped onto a gazebo.

Qisami stayed after them as best she could, bounding down from the curved eave corner of the roof into a small landscape garden filled with low manicured foliage and rock formations. This was becoming more of an exercise than she had bargained. They both took extreme pains to avoid disturbing delicate designs, which slowed them down. She wasn't the only one who had orders to be as invisible as possible.

They bounded on top of a small boulder and leaped across a narrow gap onto a cypress tree on the other side of a wall of bushes, and then continued across another palace and down to a balcony before swinging around the side of a stained-glass greenhouse. They bounded from the pathway to a small boulder and up to a tree branch. Then across to the wall of another palace on the main strip, down to a balcony, and around the side of the building. Both shadowstepped in and out of crevices, corners, and shades, playing a game of cat and mouse across the rooftops of the estate.

Qisami dug her nails into her left forearm. *Opposing shadowkill. Threat level: big freaking trouble. Heading south on short strip west side just passed the Homestead of Infinite Virginity. Every cell, close in now.* She didn't wait even a ten-count. *Where are you stupid eggs?*

Already leaving the rabble garrison, Koteuni replied.

The rest, who were merely awake on an as-needed basis, answered one by one.

I come now.

What is the situation, boss?

Then several moments later. *Whaxap pa.* That was obviously Cyyk.

She replied. *Whale shadowkill going after Sunri. Kill is the priority.*

The other shadowkill made another impressive shadowstep, skipping over a guardhouse off the main strip and into one of the kitchens. Qisami knew she couldn't make this step, and instead, took three smaller jumps to cover the same distance.

Qisami couldn't believe this person existed. She could count on her fingers and toes the number of shadowkills more skilled than she was. She regularly received blood scrawls from several of them taunting her fall. Like all war art styles, each subset had few practitioners functioning at the family's highest level, and they usually all knew one another.

Qisami was confident she belonged in that echelon. What baffled her, however, was that she could not figure out who she was going after. None of the high-end players possessed this tall, slim figure. Many of their moves reminded Qisami of her own training pool flavor. So, who were they?

Kiki, I've passed the strip on the southwest end. Which building in the servant quarters are you?

Heading in from the eastern edge, boss. Three minutes behind Koteuni.

Three minutes was a lifetime during a chase. Qisami blood-scrawled. *Close in on the consort towers.*

She jumped onto a bridge connecting two of Yanso's four concubine towers. There was an overflow complex off to the side. The duke had a well-earned reputation of enjoying variety.

Two of the three moons were prominent in the sky, the Prince bathing the nearby wall in green, robbing them of cover. The other shadowkill had slowed and appeared to be struggling to scale the building's wall. It gave Qisami the opening to throw a knife. At this distance, it was like trying to hit a fly from across the room, but Qisami was a better shot than most. She just managed to nick their leg, causing the other shadowkill to slip and crash to the ground with a heavy thud.

"I got you now, bitch!"

The shadowkill picked themselves up, impressive considering the distance they had plummeted. Qisami seized the opening and pounced on them, two black blades flashing left and right, cutting arms and legs. Her counterpart drew a pair of crescent moon knives, each with two waning crescent blades curving into each other and intersecting at both ends to form four sharpened points. It was an interesting weapon choice. It had been years since she had seen anyone wield crescent moon blades. They had fallen out of favor in the lunar court a generation ago and were now considered antique. Qisami couldn't name anyone who specialized in this weapon, let alone someone operating at the highest levels of the Consortium.

Weapons clashed, the sounds of metal striking metal clanging loudly in the night. Shadowkill fights, unlike many other war art styles, were not pretty. They were not demonstrations of beautiful violence, nor was the shadowkill fighting style a creative example of martial tactics. Shadowkill fights were a brutal display filled with quick, short strikes, with each war artist aiming for high-percentage attacks to disable and kill. Kill it until it's dead was a training pool mantra. Every attack came in combination flurries. Direct thrusts were complemented by snapping low kicks. Every blade deflection was met with an attempt to disarm the other.

The two shadowkills fought close, as if in an embrace. Qisami's knives were quicker, but the crescent moons were more dangerous. Within seconds, Qisami was bleeding like a gutted lamb in three places. She was fortunate her light padded leather had protected her from even worse injuries. She hated to admit that this shadowkill was spectacular. Even better than Qisami, which was hard to accept. But she knew when she was losing and needed to pull away until the rest of the cell arrived.

The other shadowkill would not have it, however. As soon as Qisami tried to disengage, the mark became the hunter as the other shadowkill came close. The two tussled, short elbow locks clashing with sharp punches. One wrong move and her opponent would take advantage and control. In this case, it was Qisami who made the wrong move. She got cute and tried a fancy butterfly twist move. It failed. The other shadowkill tossed her onto her back.

As she flew through the air, Qisami managed to counter her opponent's throw by torquing her body while holding on to the other shadowkill's collar, sending them both tumbling to the ground. Neither woman let up as they rolled in the dirt, grappling and throwing each other.

Unfortunately, the other shadowkill won this tussle as well, and ended up in the dominant position with a front tip of the crescent moon hovering near Qisami's exposed neck. Only her forearm kept her from having her throat slit. The tip of the crescent blade hovered dangerously close to her eye.

Qisami pushed back as best she could against the heavier, stronger enemy. The other shadowkill did not move. It took Qisami a few seconds to realize that, for some reason, the other shadowkill wasn't pressing their advantage. They could have easily forced the blade into Qisami's eye. What were they waiting for?

It didn't matter. Qisami took advantage of this. She kept her right forearm locked with the woman's, and then smacked her on the side of the head with her left hand. Her fingers curled around the long tail of the other shadowkill's hair. She yanked hard, pulling the other shadowkill off balance enough to buck her off.

The two shadowkills disengaged, rolling in opposite directions and onto their feet with their guards raised. They, in fact, were assuming the exact same fighting stance. She wasn't focused on that, however. During the scuffle, Qisami had managed to grab a fistful of the other shadowkill's mask and tore it off when they separated.

"Nice try. If you—"

It couldn't be. Qisami's brain broke. For an instant, she couldn't think. She stared, and then blinked, and then stared again with her mouth dropped all the while. Then she realized that she was still holding a very sharp and deadly weapon to the throat of none other than Duchess Sunri of Caobiu.

The duchess's beautiful face was gashed and bruised, and she was breathing heavily, but there was no mistaking who she was. Both shadowkills rose to their feet. Qisami was legitimately conflicted between killing her now or throwing herself at the woman's feet and begging for forgiveness.

The duchess, surprisingly, was the first to lower her weapon. "You're as good as advertised, Maza Qisami."

"You're a shadowkill!" Qisami blurted, still grappling with her shock. "How is this possible? You're a duchess! You are the most powerful woman in the Enlightened States." It suddenly occurred to her. "You're my employer. Why did you attack me then?"

"You attacked *me*. I was simply trying to disengage." Sunri looked equally thoughtful. "You surprised me with your skills, child."

I'm here with Zwei, Kiki. The sound of fighting stopped. Where are you?

The duchess noticed her glance down at her forearm. She looked toward the rooftops. "We can't be caught out here. The estate guards will arrive shortly, as well as your people."

"You read my blood scrawl?"

"You didn't bother hiding it. No one can know about me. Not even your cell. Meet me at my chambers in one hour. Do you understand?" The expression on the supremely confident Sunri's face looked concerned, even desperate.

Qisami was at a complete loss for words, or thoughts for that matter. Her head bobbed up and down. What choice did she have? She watched as Sunri backed away, retreating through a nearby corner and then emerging a good distance away on the far side of the field, again an impressive and masterful shadowstep. The duchess continued moving, darting from shadow to shadow with the practiced ease of a master, and then she was out of sight. The Duchess Sunri of Caobiu. A shadowkill! Never had she imagined this.

Koteuni and Zwei arrived a few moments later, armed and ready for battle. They noticed the blood and cuts on her and scanned the premises.

"What happened?" asked Zwei.

"Did the opposing shadowkill escape?" said Koteuni.

Qisami's gaze lingered on the spot she had last seen Sunri before she was swallowed by the night. She holstered her knives. "She got away, no thanks to you floating turds. Good job."

CHAPTER THIRTY-EIGHT

THE RESCUE

Taishi did her best to bottle up her emotions and bury them somewhere deep inside her so as not to corrupt her decisions. It wasn't working, not in the slightest. She could barely suppress that white-hot fury boiling just under her skin. It was a constant struggle as Taishi flitted above the lush forest canopy, the tips of her toes brushing against the tops of the trees.

It was now the deepest depth of night as the Queen was completing her journey toward the horizon, leaving the Prince and Princess free to frolic on their own during this blistering third cycle summer and blanketing the land with dark, muted mixes of blue, brown, and black.

This pocket of night was commonly known as the Grave Hours. When the Queen was with her children, her brilliant blue hue made the land sparkle like the clear sea, but that glow always died when she dipped past the horizon. The mischievous twins, when left to themselves, blended their hues to bathe the land in a muted ash gray. Not even the celestial sky provided any reprieve during the Grave Hours.

Taishi landed on the edge of an oak tree's branch, off to the side of the front gates as Bahngtown came into view. The edge of the branch dipped and bobbed under her weight. She relaxed, letting her body flow with nature. The night watch had three torches, two flanking the top of the wooden double gates and one higher up a watchtower. This was two more than what was usually used at night. Something must be up. There was never a reason to waste oil.

Taishi and the other masters had ridden all day and well into the night. Her original plan was to just ride the righteous lions straight through the main gate and barrel through the settlement like a pissed-off elephant until they located Jian. Cooler heads—Zofi in particular— eventually prevailed. The mapmaker's daughter finally convinced Taishi that crashing into the settlement in a rage would do Jian more harm than good. If these kidnappers planned to kill him, then he was already dead; then she could satiate her vengeance. If they planned to keep him alive, however, she might still have time to save him, but she would have to move cautiously as well as quickly. Taishi knew all this, having been in-volved in more than her share of prisoner swaps and kidnappings. The situation was completely different, however, when it came to her disci-ple, her ward, her *child*, and it took effort to walk away from the ledge and think rationally.

In hindsight, it was wrong to have pushed the righteous lions so hard. The poor pride was near death from exhaustion and had collapsed as soon as they reached one of Urwan's ranches just a short ways up the third Ugly Brother mountain from Bahngtown. Such a large group riding these extremely fine shishis would certainly draw attention in this tiny chatty settlement.

Urwan had to stay behind to take care of the beasts. He was con-cerned half of the pride might not survive the night. Considering the owner of these lions, it was a wise consideration. Saan always did love his pets. He had had an entire menagerie ever since he was a boy.

The group set out immediately for Bahngtown, a short hour's down-hill jaunt away.

It didn't mean Taishi, having the fastest method of transportation, was going to just meander at their pace. She swore she would not enter the settlement without them, and then sped on ahead.

Taishi windslipped along the southern side of the settlement first, windslipping through the chaotic and slippery wind currents whipping around this downhill slope filled with chest-high grass and sporadic willow trees. Of course, the Yukian River was at the bottom of this slope. The winds that roamed the massive river were legendary.

She had made two loops around the settlement before the other masters arrived. By then, she had already figured out the easiest way to jump the wall and get to the teahouse. Security definitely was more heightened than usual. There were also many more wagons and carriages inside, and not just the usual two- and four-wheeled flatbed variety commonly seen in this region. There were so many inside that the parking overflowed past the main gates. Seeing this many wagons wasn't too unusual for this time of year.

The streets were more crowded even at this late hour. Many residents in the Five Ugly Brothers mountain range often hibernate inside the protective and warmer walls during the particularly harsh third cycle winters.

Taishi took a quick headcount. Everyone insisted on coming, even Zofi. Taishi put her finger to her lips as she signaled for them to follow. She led the small group through a field of shoulder-height elephant grass between the settlement and the rushing river. Sneaking to her chosen insertion point was not difficult. The guard towers were spaced at modest intervals, but even then, only every other one was manned. She could have swept up there and killed the guard before he could open his mouth to yawn, but it wasn't necessary.

They made it to the base of the wall a third of the way down from the north main gate without much effort. Directly on the other side was the hint of a gaudy yellow roof. The cursed twins in the sky had a way of leaching the color out of the land with their somber grayness. Taishi pointed up, and both Hachi and Fausan immediately threw themselves at the wall. The two whipfingers made it look easy as they used their strong fingers to claw and grab their way up to the top and disappeared on the other side.

Bhasani crossed her arms and tapped her foot. "Everyone has a weakness, and for me,"—she shrugged—"it's walls."

Taishi didn't have time for this. She looped her arm around Zofi's waist and jumped with her onto the top of the wall, her foot tapping the tip of the pointed fence as she landed on the other side. Then she returned for Bhasani. They regrouped in a sunflower patch and picked their way across two backyards before they reached the teahouse.

Taishi nudged Fausan as they crept. "I haven't seen you move like that in years."

"Impressive, right?" he said.

"Not really."

"Never one to offer unearned praise, heh?" Fausan snorted. The night was calm save for the rustling of leaves and the occasional shout coming from the direction of the gambling hall and room salon. He added quietly, "I'm confident Jian is well. We'll get him back."

Taishi appreciated the sentiment, but she knew better. Now was not the time for her emotions to take over. That would happen after she saved him, and then Tiandi have pity on his captors because she would not.

They reached the teahouse a short while later. Taishi guided her party and cut through a row of ficus bushes before emerging at the lone rear gate of the teahouse. She knocked on it softly but insistently. It opened immediately with the tip of a needle blade pointing at her exposed neck. Taishi didn't acknowledge it. "What happened?"

Tea Master Naifun stood at the doorway dressed as if she had come out of retirement. She was covered from head to toe in black wearing a dramatic but light and fluttering cloak that snaked around her chest and shoulders in loops. It was known as a cocoon shawl, with which a skilled teahouse spook could make themselves practically invisible in any situation and place.

Naifun scowled. "Next time, use the knock password."

"I never learned it," said Taishi, walking inside. "You insist on changing it every cycle and I can't be bothered."

"One of these days, I'm not going to be here and my spooks won't let you in."

"One of these days, I'm going to remember that you sold me out to the Duke of Shulan."

"Don't be petulant, Taishi. You know I had little choice in the matter. One cannot deny a duke." Naifun pursed her lips. "Besides, I made him give me his word upon the Heart of the Tiandi Throne that he would not make an attempt on your life or freedom." Naifun lowered her voice. "What did he want from you, anyway?"

"He offered me a job."

"That's rather anticlimactic." Naifun looked disappointed. "I even vowed I would rather die than betray you. Sounds like a big waste of a life vow if you ask me." Naifun looked disappointed. Her eyes narrowed. "An employment offer using a mindseer? Must be interesting."

"It's irrelevant. I turned it down already." Taishi cut the small talk. "Where is Jian now, tea master?"

"Either above or below, but never whisper secrets on the ground. Everyone inside first. Head to the top floor where it's insulated and private." Her spooks—her apprentices—who were standing in a row against the side wall, came to life as the tea master clapped her hands and barked orders like a drill instructor. "Large table. Six chairs. Full outside sweep."

"Yes, tea master," all five responded in unison. They might have harmonized too. Now *that* was a well-trained squad. Three broke away from the wall and raced up the staircase.

If only Jian could be so sharp. No, that was unfair. That boy worked hard. It was *she* who was failing him.

"Brew the Special Reserve," called Naifun before she started following them upstairs. Naifun led the party up a wide, winding staircase.

"What do you know about Jian?" asked Taishi.

"Last my spook tracked, he was running from some ruffians and sought refuge in the newly opened Temple of the Tiandi."

"A temple? I'm going to skin that boy with ghost peppers." He obviously wasn't working hard enough.

They continued to the spiral staircase that led to the upper levels. Zofi paused and frowned when they reached the second-floor landing, and then stopped again at the third floor and stared at the blank wall.

"What is it?" asked Hachi.

She stared back down the way they had come up. "There are sizable gaps in between the floors. Why is that?" She squinted at the space between the second and third floors. "How many floors are in this building, tea master?"

"You are very observant, girl." Naifun waggled a finger on the nearby wall. "There are four floors total. Three and two halves. One half between the first and second and another above the third."

"What are those half floors used for, tea master?" asked Hachi.

Naifun kept a straight face. "Storage, of course. What else would it be used for?"

They reached the top floor and entered a plain room with four couches boxing in a small, square table in the center. Four translucent paper walls closed off the room, making it appear smaller than it actually was. A chandelier and several colored ropes hung from the ceiling. The small fire in a small hearth beneath the table provided enough light and warmth to give the room a comfortable, if not hazy, atmosphere. A pot of tea with four cups awaited them. The two young girls were waiting expectantly at the doorway with a stack of robes in their arms, each with the same flamboyant yellow-and-red patterns that Sumi and her attendants wore.

"Make yourself comfortable but not for too long. I'm brokering an assassination for breakfast and plan to sell Lawkan naval placements to a Shulan spy later over dim sum."

"You said you were retired," said Bhasani.

"I dabble to feel alive," said the tea master. "I am unfortunately exceptionally good at my job, so work keeps finding me."

"Brewing tea?" asked Hachi.

"Yes, son," said Naifun. "I make a fantastic pot of tea."

A silhouette behind the paper walls on the far side appeared, and then the door slid open, revealing Sohn. He broke into one of those grins he had whenever he was trying to bluff his way out of a losing hand. "Glad you're finally here, Taishi. We have a trivial problem. Nothing you can't fix, I'm sure."

Taishi reached for the Swallow Dances.

Naifun looked mildly annoyed. "Drawing a weapon will not be allowed in my establishment. I thought your father broke that rudeness from you as a girl."

Taishi scowled and sheathed her sword with a loud thunk.

Sohn, wide-eyed and nervous, lowered his guard. "I'm glad you're seeing reason. Now we can—"

A colorful teapot was the nearest bludgeoning object in Taishi's line of sight. She flicked her wrist and sent it cannoning off the table as if it had been launched by a ballista. As expected, given his expertise, Sohn had no problem blocking it with his forearm guard. The eternal bright light family's defense was the envy of the lunar court.

Taishi next hurled the salt shaker, a small porcelain plate, a bread knife, and then a cupcake. The last had the most impact as it splattered on his face. "You had one task. One. Stupid. Responsibility. And still, you flubbed it. I'm going to roast your pea-soup brain like a salted melon. One task! How hard could that possibly be? And yet here you are, you unsalted plain white egg!"

"Now, now, Taishi." Sohn raised his hands apologetically. "Things happen. I acknowledge my mistake. What's important right now is we need to work together and find Jian, agreed?"

"*Things happen?*" She grabbed a pair of chopsticks and crossed the room like an avenging spirit and pressed the tip into the soft flesh of his neck. "Do you think I care that you recognize the flaws in your useless jackass brain?"

The bright light fist master didn't so much as flinch. He had always been more brave than smart. Sohn put the tip of his finger on the chopsticks and pushed them aside. "You don't have enough friends left to afford to murder one. Besides, you'll need me to help rescue him."

Not smart, but clever. "Fine. You get to live for now, only because I want to make sure you suffer before I kill you."

Sohn's face brightened. "Excellent! I didn't think that was going to work. I was sure you were going to run me through with that blue blade of yours the moment you laid eyes on me. You must be getting soft, Taishi."

Or perhaps more desperate. Taishi kept her gaze trained on the eternal bright light master.

Naifun stepped in between them. "I'm billing you for this, Taishi. Now that you've burned through this childish tantrum, I'll remind you that this is a civilized establishment, not a room salon. Any more outbursts and the teahouse cuts you off. Is that understood? The White Pearls white tea is on its way up. I will not suffer any more rudeness around my table. Is that understood?"

"I don't have time for this, Naifun," said Taishi. "Jian's out there."

The tea master snorted. "You spent half the night traveling. You can afford ten minutes to rest and recover before you spend the other half fighting."

"What do you say Taishi? When was the last time we drank double whites on the house?" said Sohn. "Or say the word and my shield will lead where you point."

The man had a point and was right on every count. Taishi couldn't afford to reject his help. "Fine." She offered an apologetic nod to the tea master. "Forgive my outburst, tea master."

"For you, forgiveness is not necessary." Naifun intoned graciously. She side-eyed Sohn who was sitting next to Taishi. "With the exception of that dog dick over there."

Sohn looked wounded. "Tea master, I thought we agreed to keep this between us."

The arrival of the White Pearls white tea squelched all discussions. Known as the Nectar of the Demi-Gods, double whites was a rare and extremely expensive tea, drunk almost exclusively by the nobility and only on rare occasions. It had a reputation for curing fog in the mind, improving virility between the legs, and had the ability to keep bugs away for months after drinking a cup. The milky sweet tea was worth its weight in gold. Taishi had experienced it a handful of times. She was surprised Naifun could obtain such a thing in this remote part of the world. The other tea masters must hold the Black Night of Xing in high regard.

"What do we know about this temple he was last seen in?" asked Taishi.

"The monk came last cycle," began Naifun. "He arrived one day with a purchase marker to take residence at the former fat shop's retail space. A few weeks later, the temple opened."

"And you had no problem with them moving in like that?"

"Why would we?" said Naifun. "This is Shulan. You can't throw a stick and miss a true believer. A temple is as good as any other place as long as they paid the settlement rent. I mean, don't get me wrong, I was hoping for either an actual bookstore or a sex shop, but instead, we got a temple. What can you do?"

"Was there anything strange about it?" asked Fausan.

"Didn't look too closely," admitted Naifun. "Everyone thought it was some ambitious young monk trying to stake his monastic claim on an unclaimed territory. He was a handsome young man, as far as monks go. Broad-shouldered, with a nice smile for the girls to ogle. He was polite and kept mostly to himself. I never bothered putting eyes on him or burrowing into his past."

Taishi was still struck by learning that Jian's kidnapper was a member of the Tiandi. She had been confident in assuming that Jian's kidnappers had been bounty hunters, or at worst, one of the dukes. Those people could be bargained with; arrangements and deals could be made. The abbots of the Jade Tower of the Vigilant Spirit, on the other hand, were allergic to reason or negotiation. Religion had a way of hardening one's worldview.

Naifun closed her eyes and glanced down and off to the side for several moments. Without opening them, she took a sip of her tea. "I received word that one of my spooks was following a lead, an unmarked rickshaw leaving from the vicinity of the temple, heading to the harbor. She was tracking the movements of the rickshaw and followed it to a ship that had pulled in just before the last gate of the night. The dockmaster is in my pocket. The harbormaster is one of my magpies and my spook was able to obtain the ship's manifest. They claim to be a merchant ship but have no inventory. It was also too heavily armored for river trade. My spook believes it's a Tiandi lotus sect ship. This cannot be a coincidence."

"Which lotus sect? There're like three, right?" Taishi ticked her finger. "They have these generic names that sound straight out of a bad steamy romance. It's something generic like Sky Lotus sect, Moon Lotus sect, and the Cloud Lotus sect. Their flags all use the same variations of the same mountain and crescent symbols just turned in different directions. It's such lazy branding."

Fausan shook his head. "The lotus is unwelcome news. I don't like messing with them. It's not worth getting on their castigate list. You know, they publish that list in every capital just to publicly shame people. The monks announce it to the square and turn the people against them. It's defamation, I tell you."

"There are actually *four* lotus sects, and yes, they're all bad news," said Naifun. "The last sect, the Lotus Lotus sect, uses the upside-down symbol with the mountain on top over the crescent. It is by far the smallest and most forgotten of the four sects. They're considered a fringe group and not a serious player in their sect politics."

Sohn sniffed. "Lotus Lotus is a dumb name."

Bhasani arced an eyebrow. "Your family style is called Eternal Bright Light."

"What's wrong with it? That's a fine name."

"Sure, if you're four years old."

Naifun chuckled. "The lotus sects are fanatics and not known for their creativity, but don't let those brittle-skins hear you say as much. In any case, they're all dangerous. I hope you younger geriatrics have kept up with your practice and stayed in shape." She prodded Fausan's generous midsection with a set of long chopsticks. "You obviously haven't."

"Bah." The whipfinger slapped his belly. "I was fatter during my best years."

Lotus Lotus *was* a dumb name. Fausan also had a point. If a Lotus sect was operating here, their problems were now magnified. Their sects were dangerous and considered top-tier within the Tiandi religion's hierarchy. Their strength was nearly on par with the Hansoo, but the Lotus were far more numerous and influential. Whereas the Hansoo were called the Shield of the Tiandi, the Lotus were the bludgeoning Hammer of the Tiandi.

"How did the sect know about Jian?" asked Bhasani

"What about the other children?" asked Taishi. "Are Kaiyu and Sonaya safe? I sent a bird to Kasa but he may not receive it until morning."

"My spooks gathered the rest of your party after the boy went missing," Naifun continued. "We only retrieved two, however. The drowned fist girl is nowhere to be found." Bhasani sucked in her breath. "It doesn't mean she is in danger," added the tea master. "They all went their own directions that day. As for young Kaiyu, he's sleeping in the attic. He had an exhausting day searching for Jian, so I thought it best to let him sleep."

Taishi caught sight of a shadow lurking behind a paper screen. She flicked a finger and slid the panel open, revealing the Houtou heir hunched over caught in mid-creep. He startled and hung his head. The boy looked as if he hadn't slept in days.

Naifun sipped her cup. "You're slipping, Taishi. I heard the boy the moment he rolled out of bed."

"None of us has a spook's delicate palates and senses." Taishi beckoned to Kaiyu. "No need to cower, boy. Join us."

The boy looked despondent when he stepped out from behind the sliding door. His feet minced forward as he mumbled, staring at the floor, "I lost Jian too. I'm just as responsible."

Taishi cupped his chin and raised it. "Now you see here, Hwang Kaiyu. You failed no one. Sometimes, things that are out of your control happen. You are not to blame. What's important is what you do next."

Kaiyu looked as if he were about to burst into a fresh sob of tears. Instead, even as his eyes welled, he wiped them with his sleeve and nodded.

"Thanks for saying that, Taishi," said Sohn. "I really appreciated it."

"No, you pea-brained gopher. You, I absolutely blame!" She turned to Naifun. "Where does the teahouse stand?"

The tea master shook her head. "My spooks are scouring the settlement and harbor and will report back with any news, but this establishment does not sting."

Taishi was genuinely surprised. "Wasn't that the Black Night of the Xing's specialty?"

"It was, once, two retirements ago." Naifun loosed a long sigh. "Killing is dirty, dark work. Too many rules, too much risk, and too many grudges. I'm old, lazy, and rich now. I don't need that headache or the dirty liang. Besides, assassinations are boring. It's craftsmen's work." She placed a palm on her chest. "My teahouse has evolved. It takes a true artist to pass through undetected and leave no trace, to be nowhere yet everywhere. We pride ourselves on training spooks that move like the cool breath tickling the ear, who can hear and see all. The work we do is delicate and refined."

Taishi didn't care. "What's the name of this lotus ship in the harbor?"

"It's a river cutter named *White Ship Six Two*."

The militant sects of the Tiandi really weren't the most imaginative bunch.

Fausan frowned. "I never realized the Tiandi religion had a navy."

"Which dock is the ship anchored at?" asked Zofi. "Do you have a map of the harbor?"

"My spook has been informed that the ship is currently taking in cargo and does not plan to leave until tomorrow morning. They also hired several locals to help load the cargo."

Fausan frowned. "At this hour? That's golden time rates."

"Port manifest says the ship isn't scheduled for departure until dawn," added Naifun.

"No captain is foolish enough to sail the Yukian in the Cloud Pillars at night," added Sohn. He raised an eyebrow. "Unless it's terribly urgent."

"We need to come up with a plan," said Fausan.

Taishi pointed toward the south. "Jian is a few hundred yards that way right now. I'm going to go get him."

"What if they threaten to kill him if you attack?"

Taishi snapped. "He's the bloody Prophesied Hero of the Tiandi. Whoever took him would have either killed him by now, or would go through the soggy ends of the world to protect him. It better be the latter, for everyone's sake. If that ship sails, Jian is lost."

Naifun sipped her tea. "I've sent two more spooks to infiltrate the ship. Give them a few hours. If the boy is on board, they'll find him. It will serve you much better than going in blind and battering down the front door."

Fausan interjected. "Ships don't really have front doors."

Naifun gave him a flat stare.

"I'll shut up now," said the whipfinger master. He raised his cup. "This tea is magnificent, by the way."

Taishi didn't have time for this. "Very well. Wait here until you receive word from the teahouse spooks. You can discuss your plan to free him over breakfast, and then go through some trial runs until sometime next week. Make sure you get everything perfect. Then maybe you'll decide to finally do something." She turned and walked away.

"Where are you going?" Fausan called after her.

"I'm getting my son back."

CHAPTER THIRTY-NINE

THE RETREAT

Sali had never been a strong swimmer. To be fair, most of her people weren't, even though they lived in a place resting on a bed of water. Water was dangerous, whether from the many deadly creatures that lived beneath its surface or the many invisible deadly toxins that resided within. That was why it was a minor miracle that Sali had managed to stay afloat long enough to make it back to shore, probably due to the salt and oil that helped keep her buoyant. Nevertheless, she was able to drag her way to land and hobble along the shore to the harbor.

She avoided the morning crews working the docks and sneaked onto the *Hana Iceberg* by leaping onboard behind several stacks of cargo crates. She almost didn't make the usually short hop onto the barge and nearly plummeted back into the icy water. Her injured leg gave out the moment she landed on the barge's deck, and she collapsed onto the floor. Sali lay there for several moments, trying to catch her breath. She coughed, spitting blood on the dirty snow. Her wet clothing had frozen. Her teeth chattered, and her fingers were blue and numb. Fortunately, the paddlewheel house was close, and she managed to crawl inside to warm up next to the furnace.

Sali leaned against the wall next to the furnace and stripped her wet clothing. She massaged her numb limbs and huddled as close to the stoked furnace as possible without inflaming her skin. Her mind raced to the last image she saw when she had plunged into the water. Why didn't Raydan come after her? Maybe he thought she was done for. Maybe he didn't like getting wet. Maybe he couldn't swim. Or maybe he was—

The door to the furnace swung open, and someone charged inside swinging a utility spade. Even in her weakened state, she managed to catch the weapon mid-swing and disarm him. Fortunately for the crewman, Sali had more self-control. She tossed the spade aside. "Chef Soressa Luiga Chinna Choy, it's Salminde the Viperstrike."

"Landlady?" The head cook blinked. "I saw the trail of blood on the snow. Are you well? What are you doing here? I did not hear your chord on the pipes tonight."

She wasn't, but there was nothing to do about it now. "Is *Hana* still sailing tomorrow?"

Soressa Luiga Chinna Choy nodded. "Aye, soon as that gaggle of pilgrims get onboard and settled. We're taking them back to the Grass Tundra."

Sali covered her head with her hood and pulled the cloak around her body. "Tell no one about my return, at least not until we've pulled anchor. It's important."

"Sure thing, landlady."

"You're going to tell someone, aren't you?"

"Probably right away. But only good people, yes?"

"It'll have to do. Send for Captain Lehuangxi Thiraput Cungle."

"The captain is dining with the Masau citychief."

Of course he was. Why should Sali think he wouldn't hobnob with the enemy? "Have you seen Hampa and Daewon?"

"Your travel companions are back in your old tent. I can wrap you in a blanket and take you there if you wish. I will inform the captain upon his return."

He wrapped his otter fur suit around her shoulders—an unnecessary but appreciated gesture—and led her back to the tent. She stopped as she was about to head inside. "Hey, Chef Soressa Luiga Chinna Choy, can you get me a plate?"

"I don't know, lady. You did just try to stow aboard." He winked and broke into a smile. "I'll send a cook along shortly with a tray." He looked her over. "And the doctor as well."

"That is not necessary."

Sali stifled a groan as she ducked inside the tent. Her leg throbbed, and the makeshift tourniquet she had wrapped around her thigh was soaked and dribbling a thin line of red on the snow wherever she trod.

"Sali!" Both Hampa and Daewon rushed over to her.

It wasn't a moment too soon. As soon as the two young men helped support her weight, her strength deserted her. The two helped carry her to the cot. Daewon hurried to retrieve his satchel to get bandages and cauterizing powder. Hampa helped lay her down on the cot and began to massage her arms and legs to get her blood moving again. He stopped when he noticed the deep gash running across her chest and yelled over his shoulder, "I need needle and thread. Hurry!"

Sali pushed his hand way. "A needle won't do. Cauterize it."

Hampa's face paled. He nodded. "Get a fire burning."

"But the barge rules said—"

"I don't care what the captain says!" Hampa roared. He stomped over to the chest on the other side of the tent. His face was dark when he returned. Sali bit her lip when he doused her with powder, his gaze growing more intense as the liquid bubbled and burned her flesh.

"Do you need something to numb the pain?" Hampa dabbed it with a rag.

She nodded.

"Daewon, quickly. Poppy and antiseptic, or slumberweed. Anything. Go!"

Sali clutched the tinker's wrist as he tried to leave. "No slumberweed. Hard sorghum or zuijo. Opium if they have it. The stronger the better."

"Goldfish wine."

The thought of drinking fish alcohol kicked her gag reflex and made her wound bleed even more. "Anything but that. Please."

No sooner had Daewon left the tent, Hampa unleashed his anger. "Who is responsible for this? Did this happen after we left you?"

"Did you notice anyone beat my rump while I was with you?"

"You know what I mean! Did you send us away because of this? You're in no condition to fight. My place is always by your side, sister. No excuses!" It always amused her that she called him brother as a sign of affection, while he used sister only when he was furious.

"Do as you're told, neophyte."

He glared before finally softening his expression. "Who was it?"

"The stormchaser."

"A stormchaser? That's bad news."

"Not *a* stormchaser, Hampa. *The* stormchaser. I couldn't absorb his blows," Sali admitted, her shoulders slumping. "I'm becoming a liability. A sick, pathetic joke. I can't guard anything. I can barely stand upright. How am I supposed to lead my clan and protect the ones I love?" She looked on. "You know, back during the raid days, sometimes we'd take wounds in battle. Bad enough you can't go on. Do you know what the raid does?"

Hampa shook his head. "Carry them on a sled?"

"They left them. Every raider knows the code. The raid before all else. Neither snow, injury, nor death shall slow it down. Every raid leaves their wounded who cannot keep up with a promise to pick them up on the return. Most don't make it."

Hampa sat next to her, keeping pressure on her bleeding leg. He did a respectable job keeping her mind off the burning cauterizing. "Were you ever left behind?"

"Once. Broken leg. Raid came back for me two months later. I wasn't there. I had to abandon the spot due to a scar creep infestation in the area." She stared at nothing. "The raid had intended to abandon me, but one raidbrother refused. He offered his shares to allow himself three days to search for me. My brother found me on the night of the third day, half dead and blood inflamed from Raku poisoning. He saved my life."

"Who was he?" asked Hampa.

"Raydan the Stormchaser." Sali knocked Hampa's fussy hands away and sat up. The excruciating pain had subsided into a maddening, throb-

bing numbness. "That man may be an overbearing turd, but his righ-
teousness and loyalty always pointed true north. He's not a bad guy, he's
just on the wrong side." She mused. "Or maybe we are. I honestly don't
know anymore."

"It doesn't matter which side is right. I'm on our side," Hampa muttered as he checked the heat from Daewon's portable tinker furnace. He
stuck the flat of an iron blade into its mouth. His face was lined by anx-
iousness, and his hands were shaking. Sali reminded herself that her neophyte had probably never cauterized a wound before. There was a first
rite for everything. Might as well make it here.

"Can you still ride after the injury? We still have at least two weeks'
worth of travel before we reach Shetty Caldera."

"You might as well just leave me. I am no use to the clan." She felt
helpless and hated feeling like a burden.

Hampa stopped his triage. "Stop it, sister, I will never leave you behind. You are exactly who you need to be right now to protect the clan."

"How do you figure that? I can barely stand."

"You were Nezra's champion for many years. You were our protector
who warded us against our enemies. You may not be that shield any longer, but you now protect us against something far deadlier. Your continuing breath prevents the Eternal Khan of Katuia from the return. Your role
now is more important than ever."

Sali looked at Hampa in a new light. She felt a swell of pride. He was
ready. "Thank you, little brother. Still, it may not matter much longer if
Raydan finds me."

Hampa looked impressed. "Raydan *the* Stormchaser. They say that
he retired from campaigns a few years back. It made sense he would return to their chapter house. Were you followed?"

Sali shook her head, although she couldn't be sure. She barely had
the strength to make it here alive, let alone bother to cover her tracks. "It
may not matter. We're on a bloody island. If they close the harbor, then it
will only be a matter of time."

"We should be away from Hrusha immediately. Call the captain and
get as many leagues from Hrusha as possible. Bonus him if necessary."

Sali agreed. "Arrange it." She settled onto her cot and propped one of her injured legs up. She might as well get comfortable. She might be bed-ridden for most of the trip.

Daewon returned a while later carrying several small jars, one large gourd, a plate of sliced raw fish, and hot turtle soup. The two men con-versed quietly at the other end of the tent before returning to tend her. Hampa moved behind Sali's head and placed his hands on her shoul-ders, while Daewon fetched the cauterizing blade.

"I'm going to keep you still, mentor, all right?"

"Just get it over with." Sali took one look at the glowing crimson metal and held out her hand toward the gourd on the nearby table. "Is that al-cohol in there?"

Daewon nodded. "A little, but—"

Sali snatched it and swigged from the gourd. She gagged after a few large gulps. It *was* fish-based booze and tasted like it had been distilled through someone's soiled armor. To make matters worse, it was weak, so she had to drink the entire gourd. As soon as she drained the piss-colored contents, however, the room began to swim and a cold numbness washed over her. She lost all sensation in her limbs, and the gourd slipped through her fingers.

Her eyes became heavy. "What did I just drink?"

Daewon became very preoccupied studying his toes. "The cook didn't have anything strong enough, so we ground some slumberweed."

"I said no—"

"Blame me later," said Hampa. "I told him to add that if there was nothing else."

By this time, the slumberweed's effect was setting in, and Sali was too drowsy to argue. Her eyelids grew heavy.

She tried to focus on Daewon's face. The tinker looked positively dis-traught as he held the hot iron over her. "I'm sorry, sister-in-law."

"It's all right." Sali closed her eyes and waited for the inevitable burn-ing agony. The seconds ticked by. Nothing happened. She opened her eyes again. Hampa hadn't moved. "What are you doing?"

Daewon was sweating profusely. "I don't think I can do this."

The anticipation was beginning to annoy Sali. "Just get it over with!"

Finally, Hampa took it into his hands. "Here, give me that. Hold Sali down while I do the work."

The two men switched places with Daewon pressing on her shoulders while Hampa held the glowing hot iron. "I'm going to count to three, mentor. One . . ." Hampa pressed the blade directly on her wound.

Sali screamed, and her body bucked and folded. The smell of burning flesh filled the room. Her toes curled and her back arched. Instinct took over. Even in her weakened state, Daewon was not strong enough to keep her down. She shucked him off easily and threw him across the tent. Then she reached over and grabbed Hampa's collar, pulling him close before losing consciousness.

She didn't know how long she was out. Just that one moment both Hampa and Daewon were hovering over her; the next, something outside awoke her. Sali was alone in the tent. Both the portable furnace and lantern hanging off the center pole had been extinguished.

Most of the pain had subsided, leaving her a numb, throbbing, aching mess. She should be in a lot more pain, but that meant the slumberweed and opium were doing their jobs. She was already feeling like her old self again, which meant the pain from the beating she took was once again replaced by churning nausea, labored breathing, and the sensation of a giant clenched fist constricting her body.

Hampa came in through the tent flap a moment later, covered in a light dusting of snow. "You're up. Sorry to wake you."

Sali grimaced as she struggled to sit. Between the nausea, her slight headache, and her injuries, she wasn't in the best shape. "How long have I been out?"

"It's been a few hours." Hampa fussed over her dressings. "It's the slumberweed keeping you in bed more than shock or pain. The dressing on your chest needs to be changed. The captain says we can set sail this evening as soon as the Fushand temple pilgrims board. We don't need to offer a bribe. The barge should be ready to depart before the fourth light chimes. It will be good to be home again."

Sali agreed, although the message was bittersweet. With her decision to delay the Khan from returning for as long as possible, Sali was going home to be with her clan, but also to die, whether it was a year from now or five or twenty. At least she would be with her family and not on some faraway battlefield in a foreign land. The worst part was she knew she probably wouldn't be able to protect them if the Liqusa ever found their caves. At least she would be home to see her niece or nephew's birth. Even then Sali knew there were no guarantees in life. The Katuia could soon claim her just as quickly as the Pull of the Khan.

"Come on," said Hampa, bringing over a bucket of ice water and a bowl of honey locust mashed into a paste. "Wash yourself first, for the love of the Khan. I just repaired your armor, washed your undergarments, and scrubbed the blood off your robe. I won't have your bloodied dirty body ruin my good laundry."

"Fair enough." She accepted a rag from him and dipped it into the bucket. The water was frigid with chunks of ice still floating near the surface. She dabbed wet, dark sand from a bowl and began to scrub herself. Most of the pain from her lopsided loss had subsided, but she was discovering new aches by the hour. It was humiliating to lose to someone she once considered nearly her equal.

The icy water shocked at first, and then felt welcoming as it chilled her inflamed body. She bent over and dipped her entire head into the bucket, only to surface after a good ten breaths. The shock was pleasurable, much like a bite within a kiss.

Sali accepted a dry rag from Hampa and toweled her hair. "Where's the tinker?"

"He had to step off the barge for an hour."

"What?" Sali threw the towel at him. "Why did you let him leave the barge? We should be hunkered down until the barge pulls out of the harbor."

"He said he had to pick up his shipment of sparkstones."

That was as good a reason to risk leaving the barge as any. Sali would have done the same. The clan needed that ore more than they needed her. "You should have gone with him," she muttered. Getting the last word in was practically part of the mentor's job description. Sali peeked through the crack between the tent wall and the door flap to the daylight outside. "How much time do we have left?"

"Second chime was a little while ago." Hampa offered a neatly folded stack of her undergarments. "They're still a little damp. They wouldn't let me hang them in the furnace room. Those pilgrims aren't here yet either, and the *Hana* won't leave without them. Daewon has time."

A harmony of gongs all of a sudden rang across the barge, a message to expect business, which, in this case, was likely the arrival of the acolytes of Fushand. So much for still having time.

Sali stood up and got dressed. The undergarments were more than still damp. She took two steps toward the tent flap and then spotted her armor arranged off to the side. She should strap it on before meeting the captain. Salminde the Viperstrike struck a much more convincing figure than Salminde in her torn undergarments.

Three loud off-key bells rang. Damn, no time to dress.

"That's from the paddlewheel houses. They're leaving. Now." Sali stepped past her neophyte and left the tent. The True Freeze sky was as bright as ever, but there was an unexplained chilliness to it now as evening set. The *Hana Iceberg* was coming to life. Several of the crew were unfurling the sails. The stacks over each paddlewheel house began to stoke as they heated the furnaces.

Sali hurried toward the front of the barge, her bare feet oblivious to the biting snow, her stained and shredded undergarments flapping in the breeze. She wished she had at least run a brush through her hair. Most importantly, she wished she had put on her boots.

Captain Lehuangxi Thiraput Cungle was standing at his usual place on the platform at the bow of the ship. He threw his arms wide when he saw her approach. "My good friend. So fantastic to see you on your feet, and in such bold, fashionable garb. My cook tells me you made quite a mess bleeding and puking all over my barge. I'm afraid I have to charge a cleanup fee for that. Other than that, I trust your business here at Hrusha has concluded. We leave early just as you wish, yeah?"

"We can't leave yet," said Sali. "My tinker is still out there."

"But you are here. That was the agreement. My pilgrims are also here, and now we depart."

"Please! Give him until the fifth chime," she pleaded. That would be the middle of the night. Something was definitely wrong if he hadn't returned by then. "He'll be back soon. He's picking up a shipment of ore."

The captain made a show of checking his oil clock and compass. "Fourth chime was the promise. *Hana* pulls out at the first ring, not a moment later."

It would have to do. "Thank you, Captain Lehuangxi Thiraput Cungle."

Sali had bought Daewon a little more time. He should have no excuse not to be back by then. Hopefully, he was already riding on a wagon or rickshaw to the *Hana*. Sali considered sending Hampa to go find Daewon, but knowing their luck, she would end up finding one only to lose the other. None on Masau were aware of Daewon anyway. They should have no reason to be searching for him. The best thing to do was stay put and assume nothing was wrong.

Sali returned to her tent to get dressed, throw on her fursuit, and put on a pair of proper boots. She found herself famished again and went for food. The cook made her beg a little, but Sali walked away with a full plate of finely sliced raw fish. For some reason, she never felt full after eating this fare. She met up with Hampa afterward, and the two waited at the top of the ramp for Daewon to show. She locked her gaze on the main street entering the harbor where it curved around the edge of the lake. Daewon would come through there. The two viperstrikes needed to be ready to help get his goods on the barge when he arrived. More time passed. The slow dread of worry began to creep into Sali's thoughts.

The third chime echoed across the lake valley, and still no Daewon. At this point, ore be damned, Sali just needed Sprout's husband to show. A little while later, the starboard paddlewheel furnace kicked to life. Some of the crew began to break down the cargo ramps. A chorus of instruments began to harmonize in the night. Still Sali looked on.

"Salminde the Viperstrike," said Captain Lehuangxi Thiraput Cungle, approaching. "The fourth chime comes, friend. Where is your man?"

Sali respected the captain enough not to beg for more time. She closed her eyes. It should be an easy call. As much as she lamented her ineffectiveness, Hampa was right that Sali staying alive and keeping the

Khan from returning was crucial to her clan's survival. The spirit shamans would never tolerate exiles breaking away from the khanate. It
would only encourage other rim clans to do the same. That would be a
death knell for Chaqra's control over the horde.

Sali looked over at her neophyte leaning on the railing next to her.
"Listen, little brother, when we return to Nezra, I want you to choose a
howler to help run those teams. Wani is a good candidate."

Hampa nodded. "She's talented, but young. I can manage them well
enough, mentor."

"I have another assignment for you." She put her arms around his
shoulders. "I need you to go into the jungle and find a single piece of
blackwood, vantam preferably, and bring it back. It's time to carve your
name on the totem."

She felt his body stiffen and then tremble. He looked at her, mouth
opening and closing, but forming no words. His face contorted as he
failed to keep his eyes from watering. He finally stammered, "I'm not
worthy."

"You're ready. You earned it, Hampa the Viperstrike."

The lad broke into a fit of sobs as he buried his head into her chest, his
shoulders shaking as he fell into a fit of ugly crying.

"There's more to a viperstrike than skill," she said. "There's leadership, wisdom, and kindness. Your strengths more than make up for any
weaknesses you may have. I'm proud to be your mentor and sister and
honored to ask you to lead the next generation of viperstrikes."

"I'll never be as good as you."

"Being honest with yourself is part of what makes a good war artist,
and a leader. Congratulations, little brother."

He wept in her arms for a little while longer before finally settling into
a joyous silence. "I wish my brothers and sisters could see this," he whimpered. "They would have never believed me." His family had fallen with
Nezra during the battle with the Zhuun.

"Your ancestors are watching, or if not, they will see your name carved
onto the sect totem, and then their eternal spirits will remember."

Hampa wiped the wetness from his face. "Do vantam blackwood
trees grow this far north?"

Sali allowed herself a small smile. She had asked a similar question once upon a time. "You have to go east, toward the salt waters."

"I can't leave the clan. I can't leave you to go all the way out there to find some wood."

"Let's worry about the scheduling after we get home."

The fourth chime rang. Four long, lonely gongs that echoed throughout the valley. Night had fallen. They were out of time. Sali looked at the now deserted harbor. All the ships that would have sailed today had already left port. The rest were quiet.

Still no Daewon.

"Blasted tinker." Sali clenched her fist. The decision was a simple one, easy math. Should two viperstrikes gamble their chances to return home for the sake of one tinker? The right choice was obvious. Perhaps Daewon could figure out how to return home on his own. Who was she kidding? Abandoning him now was akin to a death sentence. It was still an easy choice. Anything less than sacrificing him to save her and Hampa was sheer idiocy. Flawed judgment and questionable priorities.

In either case, Sali had to learn of his fate before they left Hrusha. At the very least, she owed it to Mali to find out what had happened to her husband. Not knowing what happened to a loved one was often the cruelest fate, one Sali had experienced firsthand when searching for Sprout. She imagined the look on Mali's face when they returned without her husband, the love of her life, the father of her unborn child. She saw the grief wreck and scar her, forever shattering her joy. It would only get worse once Sali explained how they returned without her soulmate.

There was also the matter of the child, the girl, maybe a boy. Sali intended to be involved in their lives, as long as she breathed. Would this child learn to hate Sali once they learned that it was *she* who abandoned and sentenced their father to death or enslavement? They could never live with that.

Sali opened her eyes. She looked toward the bow platform where Captain Lehuangxi Thiraput Cungle was directing the symphony as all the stations on the barge began reporting in, ringing their respective instruments. She sprinted over, shoving a few of the crew out of the way. "Stop the barge!"

The captain turned and frowned. "What is the problem?"

"Stop the barge," she said. Her freshly cauterized wound midsection was screaming. Part of it had ripped open and was bleeding again.

"I'm afraid that's impossible, my friend."

When the *Hana Iceberg* ignored her and continued to move, Sali drew her tongue and threw out the bite until it stretched before her extended onto the platform. "I'm going to say it one last time, and then we're going to stop being friends. Stop the barge."

CHAPTER FORTY

PRISONER

Jian startled awake to the sound of muttering voices. He blinked and saw nothing at first. His face was dripping with sweat. His breath was hot and his skin itched. What happened? Where was he? As he often was wont to do in the middle of panic, Jian froze. Seconds ticked by. The conversations continued all around him from all sides, some high-pitched, others low, all males. Their voices were faint murmurs just beyond comprehension.

"... doesn't look like much."

Jian definitely heard those words.

"Are you sure we caught the right person?"

"Who's we?" said another man. "You weren't there when *we* caught him."

"You didn't do anything except hold the door open, Shumo."

"At least I was there, not back on the ship folding bedsheets."

It all came rushing back to Jian. The punch in the gut. It stunned him more than it hurt, but then came the nose-curling minty scent of slumberweed. His breath stank. He could still taste the weed's lingering coolness in the back of his throat. Sweat poured down his face, dribbled down his chin. Jian tugged gently at his wrists tied behind his back. He wondered if the kidnappers were going to torture him. He hoped not. This was his first time getting kidnapped, and he was fairly certain he would cave under torture within the first minute, which would be a little embarrassing. There were already enough rumors about him. The last thing he wanted to add to his tarnished reputation was that he folded like a paper fan in a light breeze the moment he took a little torture. Jian wasn't sure why he cared about his reputation at this point, but he did, deeply.

"Is he awake? I saw him twitch."

"Take his hood off."

"*You* take it off."

The whispers grew louder as the verbal jousting became more heated. The scattered conversations dwindled one by one until they all, inevitably, coalesced to a consensus that one particular person should do the deed and reveal Jian's face.

"Myca will do it. Myca will do anything."

"Yeah, go Myca."

"My-ca, My-ca," people chanted. Most sounded like boys his age, some even younger.

"Fine, you limp lilies." That must be Myca. "If the neophytefather finds out, it better be one of your skins, not mine."

"My-ca, My-ca," the group continued to chant.

The sound of heavy footsteps echoing on hollow floors approached from the side. Where were they holding him? Was he still in Bahngtown somewhere? Jian felt the floor move beneath him, shifting as it bobbed up and down. His center of gravity shifted as well when the swaying listed to one side. He shifted in his seat and realized that the chair he was bound to was also bolted to the floor. That was when Jian realized he was inside a boat. His heart went double-time, and his breathing became even more labored as renewed panic surged through him. How long had he been unconscious? If he was on a ship traveling the Yukian, then he could be anywhere.

The left side of his face became shadowed as someone yanked the burlap sack off his head. Jian squeezed his eyes shut as cool air blasted his face. He bit his lips and tried to swallow his rising panic. He blinked and averted his eyes from the several light sources dotting the room. Finally, he looked up, afraid of what he would see. He saw, instead, surprised fear staring back at him. Many faces full of fear, actually. A large cluster of boys had surrounded him and were gawking like quivering fawns. Most looked to be twelve, with a few of the older ones closer to Jian's age. None looked like they needed to shave yet.

They must be a gaggle of initiates by the rough look of their worn red-and-white robes, draped over each of their shoulders with slight variations. It must be rankings of some sort. The younger ones were staring at him in awe, the older ones mostly in disbelief with a drizzle of revulsion and disappointment. The disgust on some of their faces was a little insulting. By now, Jian was used to looks of disappointment. Some of the monks even fell to their knees and kowtowed. Jian's face turned crimson.

This group of the Tiandi faithful was especially confusing. Jian didn't know what their deal was. On one hand, they were worshiping him, which was neat. On the other, they had kidnapped him, so he didn't know how he should feel about all this. He was scared, but not for himself. He had accepted his fate a long time ago. He just didn't want Taishi and Zofi to worry. Taishi had been ill more often than not lately. The cold and damp weather in the Cloud Pillars was doing her health no favors. It was time they considered moving, either to the cliff-edge coasts of Lawkan or to Xing, near the Sea of Flowers.

Jian was getting ahead of himself. The first thing he had to do was escape. It could be time to lean into his celebrity and throw his weight around. "I am the Prophesied Hero . . ." He tried again and made his voice deeper. "I am the Prophesied Hero of the Tiandi. How dare you treat me this way. Free me at once."

"By the great lord of the Celestial Kingdom. It is a blessing to bask in the holy relic of our religion," prayed one of the monks on his knees, his face glowing with rapture.

That was more like it. "Many thanks to the Tian—"

"Curse you, Villain of the Tiandi!" The young monk's tone changed to one of unbelievable fury. This was not for show. "May your death find you crushed beneath the weight of the Teardrop Stones as penance for your betrayal. May the cold realm of the eighth hell freeze your shame for an eternity. May you be a warning to all sinners and betrayers until Heaven is brought forth to the Middle Kingdom."

That was quite a detailed curse. Jian wasn't sure how to respond. "That sounds unreasonably harsh." So much for trying to talk his way out. Regardless of belief or disbelief, everyone hated him.

One of the nearby monks spoke. "How do we know you're actually him? You look a little too delicate, like any old forest monkey back at home."

"Trust me, no one is more disappointed in me than me," muttered Jian.

A door in the back of the room opened, and another monk entered. His voice was familiar. "What is going on in here?"

The initiates all stood at attention and held a low bow.

Jian's eyes narrowed. "Lao, you snake, is that you?"

Brother Hu Lao, the Tiandi monk from the temple, ducked his head as he walked in. He scowled at the initiates clustered around his feet. "You've had your turn to gawk. Off with you before I have you switched."

"Yes, Big Brother Hu. Right away, Big Brother."

"My apologies," said Lao as the initiates scrambled for the door. "You were to be left alone. Do not be too hard on these curious little rodents. You are a once-in-a-lifetime event for them." He paced a circle around Jian. "The actual Villain of the Tiandi, in the flesh. Breathing the same air in the very same room, no less. It really is a lucky day."

"Lucky for you maybe," snapped Jian. "How did you find me? Why do you even care? The prophecy is dead."

"The prophecy is not dead. It was just misinterpreted." Lao oozed smugness. "Did you actually think the Tiandi faithful would have stopped searching for the Villain of the Tiandi?"

"Stop calling me that," mumbled Jian. "When did you suspect me?"

"I suspected you the day we met," said Lao. "I've been hunting you for years. I was only a week behind you when those dishonorable Kati scum broke their indentured servitude in Jiayi. By the time I got there, you were gone. I came across this rumor of a Lu Hiro who was a secret master of the war arts. Then your Longxian school burned down and your master was slain. Very suspicious. I lost your trail for a few years until finally my sect purchased a tip from a former brother about a young war artist who attacked a caravan and disrupted ducal postal service."

"*I* disrupted the postal service?"

"It took quite a bit more digging. The people in this area are notoriously difficult to bribe. It didn't take long to learn about a young man named Hiro who arrived three years ago with his aunt. He's the right age, the right size, and easily looked to have had some training. But there was so little known about him, which was strange for these remote, tight-knit communities. It was what I didn't know that drew me to you." He paused. "You really should have changed your name. That was foolish."

Taishi had said the same thing, but he had been lazy and optimistic and had forgotten to craft a new alibi by the time he had been introduced to the locals, so now he was just Hiro.

"So, all this time, you were trapping me." Jian wished he had listened to Taishi. "I trusted you!"

"Trusted me?" Lao looked offended. "We trusted *you*! You betrayed us. You were supposed to be our savior. Instead, you conspired with the devilish allies of the Khan to enslave us."

"I did not! I've never even met the guy! I've been working my butt off preparing for . . ." His voice trailed off. Now that he thought about it, what exactly *was* the point of this? The Khan was dead. "What does it matter? He's dead!"

"It's not about the Khan!"

"It's not?" That was new to Jian. "Then what are we arguing about?"

"It's about your betrayal!" the monk screamed. "We believed in you, and you shattered our trust! When word came from the abbots of this betrayal, the faithful were despondent. We have always sought you for guidance. We've sacrificed and prayed, offering our hearts and minds to use for the greater good of the Zhuun."

"What exactly," asked Jian, "do you think I did?"

"You betrayed the faithful."

"No, I got that. *How* did I betray the faithful?"

"By conspiring with the allies of the Khan of Katuia."

"I see you took the 'eternal' part out at least. You think he's dead too," said Jian. "But why would I do that?"

Lao threw the question back at him, as if that clarified anything. "Why *would* you do that? Ask yourself that, devil. I prayed to the Heavens every day for our salvation, and you turned your back on us!"

"But I haven't. I've never even met the guy. Every Katuia I've ever met tried to kill me."

"Which makes your betrayal all the more baffling and sinister!"

"I feel like we're just going in circles." Jian tried changing tactics. "Have you ever considered the possibility that maybe I haven't betrayed you?"

Lao shook his head. "The templeabbots have decreed by doctrine that you are an evil villain."

"They're wrong. Have you thought about that?" hollered Jian. He leaned forward, straining at the straps binding his wrists behind his back. "Maybe the templeabbots are lying!"

"They have never led me astray. Besides, the scriptures are infallible."

"What do you mean?" hollered Jian. "Your abbots were calling me the Hero of the Tiandi just a few years ago!"

"It was a misinterpretation!"

"Maybe the templeabbots are interpreting the scriptures wrong now!"

Lao shook his head. "It is sacrilege to question the wisdom of the templeabbots."

"That's stupidly convenient." Jian's head hurt. "Let me get this straight. The Tiandi scriptures are infallible, but you have to trust the templeabbots to interpret them correctly, but you're also not allowed to question how it's interpreted?"

Lao nodded. "Now you understand how deep and terrible your betrayal is to the Zhuun people."

"I don't. I have no idea." Jian couldn't believe it. "Maybe your templeabbots are lying!"

"The templeabbots never speak falsehoods, but of course your twisted tongue would attempt to corrupt me." The Tiandi monk stood. "I will not tolerate it, nor will I allow you to corrupt anyone else. I will post guards at the door for your sake, and for those of my brothers. May the Tiandi burn away your tainted soul, Villain of the Tiandi."

The door closed with a loud bang, finally leaving Jian alone with his thoughts. He was less terrified than he thought he would be. Mostly, he was exhausted and wanted to close his eyes and go back to sleep. He roused himself awake. He couldn't just go to sleep and wait for Taishi to rescue him. He had to do something. He had to save himself.

Jian took in his surroundings. This was no ordinary ship. He found himself sitting in a spacious mess hall with two rows of tables and benches lining the walls. There was a round fireplace in the center of the room and a bar counter at the far end. A giant wooden chandelier was directly overhead. At least he wasn't in a jail cell or a cage. Jian had expected to wake freezing in a dank, chilly, underground prison or lie on a piss-soaked straw bed while fighting off cat-sized rats trying to steal his food. At least that was the way captivity was described in Zofi's Burning Hearts romance stories. She had used those books to teach him how to read. She also claimed they were a good introduction to court politics and intrigue. Jian never realized how much of court life revolved around longing for someone and love triangles.

The architecture here was too intricate and luxurious for a warship or a merchant vessel. The wood beams that spanned overhead were covered with carvings of sea serpents and flying turtles. There was a large map of the territory surrounding the Yukian River on one wall, and a tapestry of a mountain hovering in the air over the top of a crescent lying on its back with its ends pointing upward. The chair Jian was sitting on was fine-crackled blackwood. The rest of the furnishings were equally grand. Even the long benches at the table were intricately carved by an artisan. This was a noble's ship. A familiar memory bubbled up in Jian's mind, and he found himself momentarily longing for the comforts of the Celestial Palace.

What was it doing here, so deep in the Cloud Pillars? Jian wondered if any of his friends were here. Did they capture Kaiyu too? What about Master Soa? Did Sohn even realize Jian had been kidnapped? Maybe his kidnappers took them too. Maybe they had died defending him. Each thought grew more sordid than the last. The thought of people he cared about hurt on his behalf was difficult to accept. The ship continued to sway and bob, swinging the chandelier back and forth with vigor, sending a blizzard of black snow streaking along the wall. The wood in the ceiling creaked as muffled footsteps passed overhead. A low rumble emanated from somewhere deep beneath the floor.

The room began to sway more violently, the chandelier swinging like a pendulum. The Yukian was having one of her famous tantrums. He was fortunate everything here was bolted to the ground, or he would have fallen over to be crushed by the dirty dish cart.

In any case, he was going to make these monks pay for thinking him helpless. The fact that none of the true believers in *his* religion had any faith in his abilities stung a little more than he'd like to admit. He knew he shouldn't care what these bastards thought, but he did. What hurt even more was the High Mound of Heaven, the leadership of the Tiandi religion, must have known what the dukes were planning. They must have sanctioned it. The dukes wouldn't have dared otherwise.

Jian got to work on his bindings, squirming his wrists back and forth, up and down, thrashing back and forth, and succeeded only in cutting his wrists raw. He tried to relax his arms until they were like streams of water and then slip free. Then he tried sheer primal strength. Nothing worked. If anything, the binding became even tighter. This continued for a while longer until Jian's wrists were bleeding. He finally gave up and slouched in his seat. It was even a soft cushion.

Time passed. Jian wasn't sure how long. The portholes were black, and the waves were battering the ship, pressing and rubbing the hull against the docks. Men were shouting just outside as the ceiling creaked while someone dragged something heavy across the floor on the level above. A chorus of shouts echoed through the hallways. Something about the last shipment, and then the words became a jumble. Something about wagons and loads. Why wagons? Were they going to travel over land instead of in this fine ship? Perhaps the captain had decided not to risk travel down the world's most temperamental and mean-spirited river.

More time passed.

Jian woke with a start, blinking his eyes. So much for not falling asleep and escaping on his own. Something heavy bumped against the hull, and a loud groan reverberated through the ship. He tried to sit up, wincing when the rope cut into his wrists, which forced him to relax again. There was nothing else he could do, so he dozed off again.

The sleep wasn't restful. Jian fell in and out of consciousness. His body bobbed up and down, forward and then back, with his raw and bleeding wrists a constant stinging reminder of his predicament. It was during one of those times when he leaned forward that the bindings around his wrists snapped. Jian's body pitched downward. He was unconscious when his head bounced off the floor and woke to find himself scrunched in a ball on his knees with his backside sticking up. His head throbbed. There was going to be a big knot on his head tomorrow, assuming he lived that long.

Sonaya hovered over him, her look of concern ruined by the mirth in her eyes. "That looked like it hurt. I didn't mean for you to fall like that when I cut you free, but it was funny." She sheathed her knife and offered her hand. "Come on, we have to get going." She clasped his arms as Jian struggled to his feet.

He arched his sore back. "How did you get here?"

She shrugged. "Same way I get invited to all the best court parties. I asked nicely."

"With a slather of compulsion?"

"I couldn't risk it," she admitted. "Many lotus sect monks have mental training and could sense any attempt at compulsion." She tugged at her robe. "I stole this and just walked around pretending to be a lowly initiate."

Jian began checking the doors and windows. "Can we get out the same way?"

"I *did* have to use compulsion on the guards outside. It was a small request to get them out of the way. I'm afraid they'll be back at any moment."

As if on cue, voices and footsteps could be heard outside the door. Jian's mind raced as he panicked for a way out. Even worse, Sonaya was now trapped in here too. He held up his wrists to Sonaya. "Hurry, shackle me back up! You have to hide. Get out of here. Find Taishi."

She slapped his arms away. "Don't even think about it, Five Champ. I found you first. I'm getting the glory."

"There's no glory in death."

"That's where the glory is thickest." Sonaya pulled him by the hand to the other side of the hold. The door in the corner was locked. The one next to it was a latrine. She slammed into the corner door with her shoulder and grimaced. "Any other ideas?"

The portholes were too small to fit either of them, although the two still tried. Several muffled voices could be heard outside the door. Jian's heart went double-time. Sweat poured down his brow as his breath exhaled in short, stuttering gasps. He looked frantically for an escape.

"We need to hide, in case someone comes in," Jian hissed and dragged her to the front of the room. "Here, try the pantry or closet."

"That's the first place they'll look, you cracked egg!" she hissed, yanking him the opposite direction. "We're going to have to fight through them."

"We can't fight an entire ship of monks!" Out of desperation and, frankly, with nothing else to do, Jian tried the door at the far corner again. It was still as locked as it was a few seconds earlier. Jian snatched his hand away and looked over the latrine. For some reason, Jian thought of Sohn. It took a moment for him to remember why.

Jian's eyebrows rose to the top of his forehead. He gestured to Sonaya. "Come here. I have a way out."

The drowned fist saw him standing next to the latrine and quickly ciphered his idea. She shook her head. "No way. I'd rather die fighting for glory than slide down there like a floater."

"Come on," said Jian. "It's the only way. It goes into the river. You'll be all cleaned up. And who knows, maybe we'll live. Please!"

Sonaya rolled her eyes. "Fine. You first."

Jian tore off the latrine hatch and lowered himself in. Surprisingly, the chute was fairly clean. It smelled of rosewood. He looked up and waved at Sonaya to join him. She scowled, but complied, lowering into the chute as he closed the wooden board.

"This is gross," said Sonaya, "but I'm glad we're still alive."

"Me too," he replied. Their noses were almost touching.

"I think you should squeeze past me and go down first," the drowned fist said.

"Sure." Jian wiggled his hips and shoulders to start making his way down.

"Just in case there's crocodiles."

"What crocodiles? I'm not a strong swimm—" A foot pressed onto Jian's shoulder and shoved. He began to slide down.

"Try not to drown either."

CHAPTER FORTY-ONE

THE HARBOR

Bhasani was the first one to catch up with Taishi just as she reached the bottom of the stairs at the teahouse. "You know," the drowned fist master said without a hint of sarcasm, "it's usually polite to give your compatriots a few moments to mull and digest things over before plunging headfirst into an ideological conflict."

"Don't be such a silly goose," Taishi huffed. "I'm protecting Jian."

"The Tiandi religion have changed their position on him. That makes what's happening now a conflict between opposing doctrines, which makes this a religious war."

Armed conflict and religion certainly made for an explosive concoction. Taishi had wanted to avoid that at all costs. "I don't understand why you and Fausan are always so keen to plan everything. We never planned a tenth as much back when we ran in the lunar court. We went where we needed to go, killed who we needed to kill, and conquered what had to be conquered. We turned out all right."

Bhasani cackled. "None of us have families. Most of our friends are dead. We're rotting here in this wilderness. The only thing any of us own are our fading names and our heirloom weapons, which we'll give to our disciples, because, again, we have no children to pass along our legacy." The drowned fist immediately regretted her words. "I'm sorry. I heard you had a son. That was inconsiderate." She looked away. "I had a daughter."

Taishi didn't know that. "What happened?"

Bhasani shook her head. "She hates me with the brilliance of a shooting star, so she went to live with her father. It's been fifteen years."

It was, in many ways, even worse. "I'm sorry, Bhasani."

The drowned fist looked ahead. "I don't think any of us are all right, Taishi. We're all broken one way or another."

Sohn caught up and interrupted them just as they stepped out of the teahouse. "Hey, I'm coming. Sorry. What did I miss?"

Taishi's face hardened, and then she relaxed. She was still furious with him, but anger was an injury that would quickly fester and poison if not soon dressed. She was well acquainted with his demons, but she also knew his soul, so she wasn't without sympathy. Losing Jian, however, crossed the line. There was no coming back, no forgiveness, if any harm came to her boy. However, for now, the most important thing was to rescue Jian, and to accomplish that, she needed mighty war artists. And as undependable as he was in every aspect of living, Sohn was equally supremely dependable in battle, and the one person she absolutely needed by her side if she was going to rescue Jian.

"Maybe we should pause for a moment to see if anyone else is coming," said Bhasani. "You know we could use every fighter tonight, especially since you . . ."

"Since I what?" said Taishi, approaching the thick perimeter wall surrounding the settlement.

"You know what I mean," snapped the drowned fist master. "Your pride speaks too often for you instead of your brain, Taishi. Our fires are now only embers, old friend. Taishi during her prime could take on entire garrisons, but you're not her anymore and you haven't been for a long time."

Taishi stood at the base of the thick wooden perimeter wall. She placed her palm on the large wooden post and hardened her jing, feeling the instant connection between the earth and her palm. The jing rippled from her feet, up her leg, across her body and through her arm until it exploded from her palm. The raw force of her inner strength disintegrated the pole, exploding it into a shower of splinters. Taishi gave Bhasani a pointed look and stepped through the gap in the wall.

Fausan stumbled out the back door and caught up with them a moment later. He was already panting by the time he squeezed past the wall. "You could have at least let me finish my tea before storming off. I'm never going to drink something that expensive again. I wasn't saying let's take all night and draw up battle plans. I just wanted to talk a few things over before the four of us go plunging after a ship in the middle of the night. Just an hour to plan things through. Was that so unreasonable?"

The disciples jogging after Taishi were halfway down the slope toward the harbor, where they waited for Kaiyu to change out of his sleeping clothes and into his fighting robes. Hachi and Kaiyu could take care of themselves. It wasn't them she was worried about. "Listen, Zofi, go back to the teahouse. You're not needed here. We'll send for you when this is over."

"I am coming with you whether you want me to or not," the mapmaker's daughter shot back defiantly. "Jian's my best friend."

"He's your only friend."

The mapmaker's daughter crossed her arms. "While you were busy storming off, I took the time to jot down the name of the ship and its dock number. Only *I* know it, and I'm not telling, so you're going to have to bring me along unless you intend to search every boat in the harbor. Do you even know the name of the ship holding him?"

Taishi struggled with the answer. She had been so anxious and riled up, her thoughts had been elsewhere. "*White Ship Seven* something. *White Ship Seven Two.* This isn't a game, girl. You'll be in the way!"

Hurt flashed across Zofi's face. She stopped, her eyes intense but her nose quivering. It always hurt when the obvious had to be said aloud. Her next words were dejected. "I brought the herbs for your cough, just in case."

That impudent, clever girl. Taishi's heart swelled even as her head scoffed at the ploy. She finally loosed a long sigh and cupped the girl's chin. "Just stay out of danger. I don't want to lose both my children tonight."

"I'll stay with Hachi. He'll keep me safe." The two had gotten closer over the past few weeks.

Taishi refocused her wrath next on Kaiyu. "But you! Head back to the teahouse, boy. I am not going to be responsible to your ba. You are his ward. I will not bring you into danger. Go back, scoot, boy."

Kaiyu tried to imitate Zofi's defiance but came up short. Still, it was a noble effort. He planted his feet and crossed his arms. "He's my best friend too, Master Ling. I'm going, and nothing you can say is going to change my mind."

Taishi wanted to reach out and bonk him on the head. "Since when did Jian become everyone's best friend? Whatever. I don't have time for this. Your job is to protect Zofi. That's your only job. Do you understand?"

"Yes, Master Ling. I will make my father proud. You'll see."

"Just don't die," she muttered. "I'll never hear the end of it."

"Hey, Taishi." Fausan waved her over. "We need a plan. There could be two hundred souls on a large junk ship. We can't just walk in and ask if it's all right to search their decks for your missing disciple who also is the central figure of their religion. Frankly, I don't feel like killing two hundred clergy tonight. That's going to be a big black mark on my quest to sainthood."

"Does he ever turn that off?" asked Taishi.

"Never," said Bhasani. "It's exhausting. Now you know why we ended."

"I honestly can't believe it could have ever begun, but here we are."

"To be fair," said the drowned fist master. "He also makes me laugh. Just looking at his bulbous but cute cantaloupe-shaped head puts a smile on my face. And then he completely ruins that charm by opening his mouth."

"You know I'm standing next to you," he muttered. "Anyway, Taishi, at the very least we should get off the main road."

"It's the only road to the harbor," she said. "I'm not wading through jungle brush down a brambled, muddy slope in the middle of the night when there's a perfectly good road right here for us to use. Besides, you're already breathing heavily."

"I had been preparing for a hot bath and a soft bed." He broke into a grin. "Feels like old times."

"Does it?" Taishi frowned. "Back then, battles were thrilling. Flirting with death was glorious. We were eager for war. It made our blood boil. Now,"—she shook her head—"I feel nothing but worry. There's no joy in that."

"I'm really glad I don't have kids," Fausan replied.

"That you know of," they barked in unison, momentarily transported back to when they were young and foolish. They roared and leaned on one another for support as if they were going to topple over. A moment of levity before battle often freed the jing in a body that was tense from anticipation.

Bhasani rolled her eyes. "Are you two insufferable billy goats finished?"

Taishi glanced over at Sohn, who was standing to the side probably still brooding over his mistake. He had always been a melancholy one. A war artist should carry a short memory lest the weight of experience become too heavy. Sohn, on the other hand, never let anything go. He lived with every insult, disrespect, or hurt feeling he had ever experienced, and kept replaying them in his head. That was why he was still so furious about losing his place as the head of their family to his younger brother. Taishi didn't have the heart to tell him that Soa Sohi, the Grandmaster of the Eternal Bright Light Fist Pan Family Pan lineage, had died five years ago in a kite flying accident. Sohi's son, Sohnsho, was now head of the family. Sohn had held on to so much anger against his brother for something that happened so many decades ago.

"Hey, boulderhead." She hadn't called him that in decades.

Sohn's face tensed. "What?"

"Take your old spot guarding my flank?" It was an offer of trust.

He blinked, his eyes brimming. "Your shadow will see the dawn. I won't let you down."

"Again, you mean."

"Yes, I won't let you down twice."

The jungle canopy hung low and became so thick it felt like a tunnel. She could hear rushing water up ahead. The road curved as it ran down the mountain path, edged around a cliffside, and then snaked in between two toppled pillars. Just as they rounded the bend, Taishi walked into a group of armed men manning a checkpoint.

"See—" hissed Fausan. "I told you we should have made a plan and gotten off the road."

"Shut your mouth," she hissed back.

One look at their white robes, monk spade, and moon sickle blade swords told Taishi exactly what she needed to know. There were eight or so at this checkpoint. Two held up torches. The rest, while armed, were relaxed with their weapons sheathed. The leader of this squad, an older bald monk with a square head and broad shoulders, was wielding a moon spade, or a long pole with a bladed digging spade on one end and a sharpened crescent moon on the other. He put his left palm on his chest and bowed, making a pretense of sounding friendly. "Pardon us, devout, but the harbor is off-limits tonight by the Will of the Tiandi."

Fausan cut in front of her. "Of course, holy ones. My family and I are living on a houseboat on the harbor. Surely your worthwhile and righteous blockade does not include residents of the harbor."

"No exceptions, friend." The initially friendly tone was gone. "No one enters the harbor until sunrise."

"Hey," said another monk. He held up a wanted poster of Taishi. The last round of hand-drawn pictures had been shockingly accurate. It forced Taishi to get a haircut. The monk squinted. "I think that's the Villainousness of the Tiandi! Seize her!"

"I'm the what?"

Fausan burst into gut-clutching laughter. "Oh, that's good. You're never going to live that one down."

Villainousness of the Tiandi. Now she knew how Jian felt. What a terrible title and an ignominious end to what would have been a glorious career full of mostly positive titles. There was nothing Taishi could do but embrace it. She launched herself into the low and thick forest canopy. She bounded across various levels of branches, then plunged back down through the canopy. She landed on one of the monks, flattening him to the ground.

"Do you think you're a match for the Villainousness of the Tiandi?" she hissed. Taishi was angry, but not beneath having a good chuckle at an enemy's expense.

To her dismay, her threat worked. Instead of cowing them as she expected, the monks fled. One of them even dropped his moon blade, a sickle-shaped sword that curved three quarters of a moon.

"Wait, come back!" Of course, none of the monks did. Taishi cursed. It had just been a taunt. She hadn't really meant it. "By the tattered Mosaic of the Tiandi. They can't warn the ship!"

Two metal stones leaped from Fausan's fingers. He reached his spread fingers into the two satchel bags at his sides and drew four more round bullets, two in each hand, wedged between the second, third, and fourth fingers. He flicked two more stones, which rewarded him with one cry of pain from somewhere in the thicket. Sohn lumbered into the brush in pursuit. The eternal bright light master had thick, powerful legs common to those who practice that style. However, he ran about as fast as a mule pulling a cart. Hachi was shooting his bullets while Kaiyu tangled with one of the monks. Taishi couldn't see Zofi, and prayed the girl was smart enough to stay hidden.

She caught sight of two monks trying to escape and shot through the air again, arcing like an arrow in flight. She slammed the straggler in the back with her knee and sent the young man flying headfirst into a tree trunk. Taishi would come back for him later. She caught up to the other monk, grabbed his collar, and dragged him to the ground. She towered over him with her fist chambered and stopped.

This one was even younger, barely Jian's age. The boy—no, the enemy monk—was fleeing when he craned his head back to see her and crashed headlong into a tree. He cried out and tried to scramble away, half blubbering the Holy Warrior's Last Rites chant while still trying to threaten her. "May the blessings of the Tiandi's most devout. Stay back, Villainousness! I'll gut you from navel to neck! Shine upon the paradise of the mosaic where love is eternal. You will burn in the Tenth Pit of Hell, bitch." Tears streamed down his face.

Taishi rolled her eyes and sighed. "Go. Get out of here."

The young monk paused between sniffles. "Really?"

"Before I decide to drink your blood." She spanked him on the ass with the flat of her blade and glowered as the monk scampered away and disappeared into the brush. It was true what they said about someone as they aged. "You fluffy old bitch."

Taishi stepped back and regrouped with the others. Most of them had gathered, and no one appeared worse for wear, save for Sohn and Fausan, who were huffing as if they had just run up the side of a mountain.

Bhasani returned to the road a few moments later. "I couldn't reach the last one in time but sent him a compulsion of suddenly being desperately homesick. It should wear off in an hour or so." She looked around. "Did we get all of them?"

Fausan nodded and coughed. His gruff voice feigned assuredness. "Of course."

Sohn shrugged. "I knocked two unconscious. I almost killed the last, but he fainted on me."

Taishi should have kept it to herself. Instead she was often honest to a fault. "I let mine go."

The others looked at her, their faces betraying an equal mix of incredulity and confusion. She almost felt insulted too.

Sohn whistled. "Never thought I'd see the day."

"She really *has* gone limp," said Bhasani.

"I don't want to hear it." Taishi grimaced. "I saw the damn kid's face. A farm boy initiate who didn't know his Zhingzhi, let alone how to read the mosaic. He doesn't know what he's doing out here. He didn't deserve to die." She shook her head. "Call me limp if you will. Say I lost my edge. It doesn't matter. I just couldn't do it."

Fausan raised his hands in capitulation. "I let mine go too. I intentionally missed all my marks." He drew a symbol in the air as if trying to ward off evil. "Killing clergy is just bad luck."

"By the Tiandi," snapped Bhasani. "I'm fighting alongside a band of goose down pillows."

Zofi matched the indignant drowned fist's intensity. "The ones who escaped are going to warn the ship. And you call *me* the pacifist? This is not the time to get soft, Taishi. Jian's out there. They're going to get away!"

Taishi agreed. She knew what was at stake. Why *did* she behave so foolishly? She picked up her pace down the last stretch of road before reaching the harbor.

Fausan pulled up next to her. Sweat was beading on his forehead. He looked about to keel over. "You know," he uttered in between short, sharp breaths, "not that I'm rubbing it in, but that was an unnecessary fight if we had gotten off the road."

"Isn't that exactly what rubbing it in means?" she shot back.

"I'm just wondering if we should reconsider and take a few minutes now to come up with a plan."

The forest ended, and the ground abruptly changed to sand. On the other side of a long, wide beach was the harbor, which was as unimpressive as one would expect for a tiny settlement in the middle of the jungle. There was only one wharf and two ships docked at the moment. The smaller, slim ship on the right was completely dark while the large junk on the left was lit like a night of fireflies and a hive of wasp activity.

Taishi looked over at Zofi. The mapmaker's daughter acted innocent. She pointed at the ship that looked like a sailing Lunar New Year. "I'm guessing that's *White Ship Seven Two* over there in dock one?"

"It's *White Ship Six Two*," Zofi muttered. "And that's dock two, but yes, that's the right ship."

The sounds of metal clanging rang in the air as the ship began to retract its anchor and pull up the ramp. *White Ship Six Two* was warned and now pulling out. Taishi crossed the beach in three long strides, the currents pushing her. She reached the wooden wharf and sprinted down its length as the ship pulled away. A cough crawled up her throat, but she shoved it back down to her gut, sucking in deep, forced breaths as her aching feet pedaled toward the far end where the two ships were parked. She was close enough to attempt a jump and ride a current to the stern of the ship, where she could destroy the rudder and damage the ship in the water or ground it against the riverbank. The rest of her party could catch up. At the very least, it wouldn't be able to escape with Jian.

Taishi was mere paces away from leaping off the deck with the intent to land on the stern when *White Ship Six Two* unfurled her sails. The large sails immediately caught the strong breeze and burst to full, joining the ship with the fast-moving white waters, leaving Taishi standing alone at the end of the pier as the strong third cycle gale blew the large junk ship out of reach. She could still make the jump, but that would mean fighting the entire ship on her own. Taishi was tempted to risk it anyway.

The rest of her group caught up a few moments later. They stared as the ship turned the bend and disappeared. Jian was now out of her reach, perhaps forever. She cursed and stomped her foot in frustration, snapping the planks beneath her feet. Sohn caught up with her and rested a hand on her arm before she plummeted into the drink.

"What do we do now?" asked Bhasani.

Taishi had no answer. She could only look into the darkness as the pit of her gut twisted into knots. She hadn't felt this profound a loss since the moment she realized she had survived Sanso's final test to assume the mantle of master windwhisper. Taishi fell to her knees. Agony born in the depths of her wounded heart clawed its way up her throat to manifest in a loud wail before finally ending in a fit of coughing. She buried her face in her sleeve. There were specks of blood on it when she pulled it away.

"What is this ruckus?" a voice roared from above. "Did you break the flooring? You better pay for it and not pass the blame to me."

Taishi looked up to see a man wearing a loose nightgown standing on the upper deck of the remaining ship. He was holding the lantern in one hand while clutching the railing with the other as he leaned over the side. He certainly looked in charge. Only one way to find out. "Is this your boat, handsome man?" she asked.

"Of course it is." The man puffed his chest. "Captain Tee Mun, and *Slippery Minnow* here is my shipwife. She's the quickest river cutter in all Cloud Pillars."

Taishi bounded from the wharf onto the moored ship in one leap, landing softly on the deck of the *Slippery Minnow* next to Tee Mun. She stared him down even though he was a head taller. "I'm commandeering your ship on ducal business. We depart this instant."

"B-but I still haven't received my cargo . . ."

Taishi placed her right foot on the ground, and then cracked three floorboards without moving. "You were saying?"

"I'll need a few minutes to rouse the crew, boss."

"Good. Put a plank out and get the rest of the people on board."

"Yes, ma'am." Tee Mun turned to go and then turned back to her. "Just curious. Which duke do you serve, exactly? For tax purposes, of course."

CHAPTER FORTY-TWO

JAILBREAK

The first thing Sali and Hampa did after they disembarked the *Hana Iceberg* was watch it pull out of the harbor. There was a good chance that by morning the gates would be locked. She could be banned from boarding any ship. The *Hana Iceberg* could have been her only chance to escape Hrusha.

Sali allowed a moment to watch their prospects fade before focusing on the task at hand. There was no use crying over missed spoils, as they said on the raid. She sent Hampa to fetch some supplies while she stabled the horses and looked for a cheap room, preferably with a bed. There weren't many options available this late in the day, closer to the fifth and last chime, which would mark the start of a new day.

The hostel she checked into, aptly named the Downtrodden's Sleep, was a short way up Shark Fin Way, three intersections from the main road. The slope ran alongside a sulfurous stream, so everything smelled like rotten eggs, which explained why the buildings nearby were run-down and why ruffians and thugs lined the path at all times. None paid a sick, poorly dressed woman any attention, however.

The Downtrodden's Sleep was a squat, wide building with a garish orange roof and several narrow sleep rooms facing a shared living space. Each person was allocated a sleeping barrel, which were stacked in tight columns. There was no bath, and the outhouse hung off a cliffside past the back landing. Sali had initially balked at sleeping in long, thin wooden tubes that were barely long enough to slide into, and too narrow to allow her to sit, but at least it was clean.

Hampa returned a little later walking alongside Hoisannisi Jayngnaga Marhi. The Hightop Cluster rumblerlead waved.

Sali, sitting in front of a small hearth with her feet up, only looked on. "What are you doing here?"

"Was following you the whole time," the girl quipped. Sali appreciated that. "The ritualist wants eyes on you. I was surprised you jumped off the barge right when it was leaving, so I decided to ask handsome here why you two were still moping around town." She beamed.

"We lost one of our own." Sali gestured for them to join her at the fire.

"I know, the funny looking one. Handsome here told me." She and Hampa sat across from Sali, a little closer than two strangers should.

Good for him, although he would have no idea what to do with a girl like that. "Yes, him."

"Are you talking about me?" Hampa looked puzzled.

The girl giggled.

Sali laid a throw on her lap and wrapped a travel cloak around her shoulders for the rest of the night. She sat there staying mostly to herself as Hampa and Marhi chatted up the night. It was really more Marhi doing most of the nonstop stream of thought talking, but Hampa played a good listener. It seemed to work for them, and the two seemed to enjoy each other's company, even though they came from such different worlds.

"That's the thing." Marhi's words were slurring as she waved her tenth cup delicately between her thumb and forefinger. "Hrusha has dozens of Happan clusters and fifty rumbler gangs. If we all did a team-up, like a big party, we'd have five hundred rumblers against only a hundred towerspears. We would roll over them easy."

"So why don't you?" asked Hampa. He was only nursing his third cup but drinking more out of politeness.

"Stormchasers," said Sali.

Marhi sloshed her drink, nodding at Sali. "Yep, that's it, right there. It's those bastard stormchasers. Masau is their home city, so there's always at least ten to twelve stormchasers who homestead. My guys can't do anything about them." That certainly was true. An expert war artist was easily worth a squad of spears. A master was worth ten of those.

Marhi ended up staying at the hostel overnight. She and Hampa sat on the stairs in front of the hostel and drank cheap Tsunarcos cumlange until both couldn't see straight. Sali had endured their company for as long as she was able before retreating back to the sleeping barrel. The last thing Sali saw before sleep was the two sitting side by side, staring at the stars. That boy was an oblivious donkey.

Sali woke first the next morning and crawled out of that cramped but surprisingly comfortable barrel to find the two slumbering exactly where Sali had left them the previous night, huddled side by side under a dirty white bear throw. There were broken gourds, empty pitchers, and spilled cups scattered on the ground around them. Sali kicked them awake.

Hampa shot up in an instant. He was fully dressed, at least. He blinked and then cupped the top of his head with both hands. "Ow. Everything in here hurts."

The girl just turned over and continued to sleep, snoring.

Sali hovered over him with a bowl of sardine congee. "You look worse than a dying Will of the Khan," Sali remarked, yawning as she stepped out into the cool morning.

Hampa winced. "That's a dark thing to say, sister."

"I'm allowed. How late did you stay up?"

"Marhi and I were just talking. Did you know if you look carefully, you can see the stars hiding in the shadows behind these northern days?"

"Do I look like I care? What else did you do?" She nudged him with a toe. "You just counted stars?"

He looked slightly offended. "This body will not touch man or woman until my name is carved with my brethren onto the sect totem."

Sali bonked him on the head with her pair of chopsticks. "I wouldn't have minded as long as you treated the girl well."

Hampa looked surprised. "Wouldn't that break the neophyte's vow?"

"That was the first vow I broke when I was a neophyte. Two days after I took them," she replied. "You should try it sometime."

"How could you live with yourself?"

Sali snorted. "Rules are there for a reason. Some are good, some are dumb. Know why they exist and stop following them blindly."

"Yes, mentor."

Marhi woke on her own time, just as they were finishing their congee. She looked refreshed and calm, as if she hadn't just drunk the entire night. Of course the girl could hold her drink. Hampa could not.

"Good morning, Katis." Marhi stifled a yawn as she pulled up a chair next to them. She caught herself. "I'm sorry, handsome. Good morning, Katuia. What are your plans today? I'm supposed to be following you."

The Happan women were apparently bolder and more assertive than the Katuia, and Sali was enjoying seeing Hampa squirm under the attention.

"Daewon last went to pick up his order from an ore wholesaler," said Sali. "I figure we'd start there."

Marhi pulled herself a cup of hot tea. "There're only two in the settlement. We'll start at Hootie's place. I hope your tinker went there. She's the only honest one. The Shaw brothers are lake scum."

Hampa perked up. "We? You're coming with us?"

She nodded. "The ritualist says you're important and Rich Man Yuraki told me to keep an eye on you." The Happan leaned into Hampa and gave his neck a long sniff. "I'm glad you missed your boat, handsome, and that you're sticking around a little longer."

Hampa gulped and blushed. "I'm glad . . . too?"

Marhi stood. "I'll get my satchel, then we can head out."

Sali looked disapprovingly at her neophyte as he stared at the rumbler heading back into the hostel. "Don't lead the girl on, neophyte."

"I'm not." He paused. "At least I'm not trying to. We get along and she's interesting."

"She's Happan. What are you going to do, bring her back to the Grass Sea? Don't be ridiculous."

Hampa didn't look bothered. "*Why* is that so ridiculous?"

"Because . . . ." Sali was stumped. Yes, why? The answer was simple.

The Katuia from the capital cities disapproved of their people mingling with outsiders, even some rim clans. All it meant was that Sali was an elitist snob staring fondly at the old ways and traditions. Even though it was these same traditions that ordered her to kill herself on a slab. It was these traditions that offered the survivors of Nezra to the Zhuun, and it was these same damn traditionalists who exiled their clan.

If this girl made Hampa happy, and she could tolerate living in the gut of a mountain and possibly being on the run for the rest of their lives, then who was Sali to stand in the way of true love? Hampa was a young, good-looking lad with an admittedly fine mane of hair. Several girls in the clan had chased after him, but he had always stayed true to his vow. Sali told him it was stupid, but he wouldn't budge. But just because he was celibate didn't mean he wasn't vulnerable to the charms of a pretty girl.

She nudged him. "Go slow. We can talk about it if you're both serious, and we survive this island. Our situation isn't exactly stable. I'm not sure you want to bring your Happan girl into our fugitive lifestyle. Being an exile on the run might not suit her taste."

Marhi returned with her gear a few minutes later, and the three set off to find their missing tinker. Sali feared the worst. Perhaps it was a stormchaser or Masau towerspears who had picked him up, or it could be something as straightforward as a random footpad thinking him easy prey. Hampa should have gone with him, but she understood why he didn't. A mentor was always a neophyte's priority. It was really Sali's fault for coming out so badly on the losing end of a fight.

The three departed shortly after the second chime, which meant high noon, although there had been no change in the light, nor had the sun paid the sky a visit. The second chime was nothing more than the island's inhabitants agreeing that this felt like the right time to call noon.

It ended up being a good thing Marhi had accompanied them. The business owner, Hootie, a stern, crinkled-faced woman with hard eyes, had immediately dismissed them with a wave of her hand the moment they wandered into her establishment. It was only after Hootie saw Marhi that she paid these foreigners any attention. Unfortunately, Daewon did *not* place the purchase order with Hootie, the reputable ore wholesaler.

The three quickly moved to the second wholesaler and were able to find the answers they were looking for. The chatter about the foreign tinker was the day's gossip. Hrusha was not a large establishment, so any gossip, especially something as juicy as the towerspears arresting a foreign Katuia tinker, was big news that spread rapidly, like warts.

"Yeah, lady," said a soot-stained worker shoveling piles of prickle sand into barrels. "Tinker came in the other day asking to buy bulk, which perked up a few ears." The air was a haze of blue dust as he continued working. Sali covered her mouth as he spoke. Prickle sand had a tendency, when inhaled, to grow crystals in someone's lungs. This poor lad wouldn't live long. Good thing sparkstone mining paid well, or so she heard. "Nobody buys sparkstone in that many barrels unless they're running a city or they want to blow something up. Besides, there're only twenty or so tinkers on Hrusha, and they all belong to the same family. That guy looked nothing like a big fatty Cha Chi."

Hampa and Marhi stood near the entrance with their heads together. Hampa glanced at Sali. "What's a big fatty—"

"Never mind," pressed Sali. "What happened?"

The worker stopped shoveling and stuck the spade into the sand. "You want some gossip. I have some. Cost you a chip or two copper liangs, lady."

Of course. Sali paid it anyway. "What happened?"

"The Masau folks had put up a new bulletin earlier that day. Seems there was a fracas at the big monastery with some crazed plague Kati, and the stormchasers were paying for tips on foreign Katis acting strangely. Sort of like you two. Anyway, that scrawny tinker was Kati, and he certainly was a frazzled bundle of nerves, so no doubt one of the boys here decided to earn some coin and report the tip."

Sali scanned the warehouse. There were dozens of workers in the shop. It could have been any of them. "So the tinker got sold out to the stormchasers. What happened next?"

"That'll cost you two more liang, lady."

The ore digger disappeared the coins into his dirty tunic as soon as she dropped them in his palm. He gave her a toothy grin. His teeth were stained bright blue. "When the tinker returned to collect his order, he had to wait a spell as we fulfilled it. One of the guys probably slipped out to get paid for the tip, and before you know it, one moment that tinker is falling asleep on that bench over there—" He pointed at a circular bench wrapped around a pillar of ice. "The next, the bleeding stormchaser and four towerspears pounce on him like a pack of dogs on a stray baby. Beat him up good, and then hauled him away. Called him some sort of exile."

Sali grimaced. The thought of Daewon taking a beating wasn't pleasant. The man didn't take pain well. "So the towerspears have him."

"Yes, lady, in their jailhouse adjacent to the same pod as the towerspear headquarters in the heart of Masau."

Sali signaled to Hampa she was finished. They had their next stop. "Thanks, good man." She turned to leave and hesitated, scanning the workers in the warehouse. "Do you, by chance, know which one of these dogs sold the tinker out?"

"Why I do, lady," said the worker. "Two liang."

Sali knew she shouldn't bother, but she paid it. "All right, spill."

The worker bowed like one of those pathetic Zhuun servants. "Why, that would be me, good lady. Thank you for the repeat business." He smiled and went back to work, leaving Sali standing there.

Sali very much wanted to stab the man, but she also had to respect his game. He'd played them all beautifully and had been paid by all sides. Too bad he was going to die in a few years. "Spend it well and fast," she muttered.

Hampa and Marhi fell in beside her as they left the ore shop. Marhi shook her head. "That younger Shaw was always a dirt-digging snitch."

"That's one of the owners? Why didn't you warn me?" Sali shot back, irritated.

"Why would I? Little Shaw has always been pond slime, but he's still a Happan." Marhi wagged a finger at the two of them. "And you're not. Why would you think I'm on *your* side?"

That was a fair point.

"Where next, mentor?" asked Hampa.

"To the jailhouse, young one." The three continued down Ice Dragon Tail sloping toward the lake. It was early afternoon, and the streets around the lake were filled with steady traffic.

"Do you think Little Shaw is going to sell us out?" asked Hampa.

"Oh, for sure," said Marhi.

Sali eyed the Masau city pods. "Have you ever broken anyone out of jail?"

He shook his head. "Have you?"

"Dozens of times. We used to get guys captured during raids all the time. We always broke them out or got them killed trying." She pointed at the sky. "The raid way."

"What makes a jailbreak more interesting than any other battle?" he asked.

"It's the rescuing part, and the intricate planning," she said. "That's always the most interesting part of a battle. You're not just winning and killing for something silly such as gold, honor, or a horse. You win and you save a person! It's deeply gratifying."

Hampa furrowed his brow. "I guess I'll have to experience it to understand it, mentor."

The three turned the corner to the main square with the bridge leading into Masau. It was just past a line of Happan waiting to enter the city that Sali noticed the row of stockades lining the lake. Half were currently occupied with the hands and heads of three men cuffed in a plank of wood.

Sali would have kept walking if she hadn't noticed the apron dangling off the body of one. She squinted and dragged Hampa to a stop. "I guess we don't need to break him out of jail after all." She pulled him toward Daewon in his stockade. "This will save us a lot of time."

"Sali," said Hampa, "it's the middle of the day and there are tower-spears guarding the prisoners."

"Just two. I'm weak now, but I'm not that weak."

Hampa stepped in front of her. "Mentor, we can't. We're on an island. There's no place to hide. Let's wait until the fifth chime. He'll likely still be there tonight. There will only be a few around and we'll break him out without anyone the wiser."

"Hampa is right, viperstrike," said Marhi. "There's a time and place."

Sali swallowed her annoyance. Hampa was right again. They both were. She knew that too, except her patience had slowly withered alongside her strength. An inevitable death made wasting time all the more painful.

Sali turned abruptly and walked the other way. "I've seen enough. Let's get back to the hostel and rest before tonight." Half a day of standing had already exhausted her. She exhaled. She never thought she would live long enough to leave her sides unshaven, but perhaps it was time. This was her final adventure. In a way, Sali felt she should feel blessed knowing this was her last outing. That way, she could relish it. Most have no idea about the time of their deaths, and often don't live in the moment until it's too late. Sali intended to make the most of this with Hampa, as bittersweet as this felt.

"I have a task for you after we rescue Daewon," she said as they circled back down the main street heading toward the harbor.

"What is it, Sali?"

"We need a discreet way off this island. Find a captain within the underbelly of Hrusha who would be willing to take us back to the mainland. We may not be able to escape through the port gates, so he would have to be willing to meet us outside, along the edge of the island."

"That sounds difficult to arrange," he replied.

"It has to be cheap too," she added. "Because we can't pay."

Hampa threw up his arms. "How do you expect me to pull that off?"

"I have an uncle that may help. He'll do me and the ritualist a favor." Marhi winked. "I don't come cheap, though, handsome."

Sali patted him on the back as if she were burping a fussy baby. "I have faith in you."

They had just turned from the main street when Sali noticed the two suspicious figures following them. She should have seen them sooner. She had been distracted. Sali lowered her voice. "Being followed. Two trailing in back." So of course Hampa craned his neck to look. She rapped him lightly on the head with a knuckle. "Don't give up our initiative."

Hampa nodded, his hands being very obvious as he reached for his weapons. Idiot. Sali was about to make the turn when she noticed two towerspears walking toward them, then two more walking directly toward them from farther down the path. Six enemies against two weren't terrible odds, but if she so far counted six, she was certain there must be at least twelve around.

"This was a trap," she hissed. The stormchasers knew they would come looking for Daewon. They had placed the bait in plain sight, and she had fallen for it.

"What's the plan now?" asked Hampa.

Sali yanked the two violently into a side alley and shoved them. "Run!"

CHAPTER FORTY-THREE

THE TRUTH

After Qisami sent the rest of her cell home, she returned to the Palace of the Gracious Guest, easily sneaking past those worthless guards as she crept to the cellar of the palace. It was times like this she wished this were a wine cellar instead of the pickled vegetable type, and not just because of the smell.

She sat alone in the dark, recovering from the encounter. Her mind roiled with chaotic thoughts about tonight's revelation. This was the Duchess of Caobiu, one of the five most powerful people in the Enlightened States, who also happened to be her employer. Some secrets were too big to leak, even to those she entrusted with her life, which was a pathetically brief list. It was funny and sad that the only honest people she knew were the other servants on the estate staff and possibly the hot and fierce Salminde the Viperstrike, who had actually *tried* to kill her.

What Qisami couldn't shake off, however, was how no one knew about Sunri being a shadowkill. How could the Consortium not know, or were they keeping it a closely guarded secret? There had to have been records, a registry from when she first waded into the training pools, to the commission of every contract she had ever undertaken, or if she had been severed from service. Shadowkills didn't just disappear. The Consortium relentlessly and inevitably hunted them down. They couldn't allow even one precedent to occur. If Qisami had to guess, she bet both parties were using each other somehow.

Not to mention how Sunri managed to infiltrate her way to this exalted position all while keeping this hidden all these decades? She must be, without a doubt, the greatest shadowkill in the world, in all history. Shadowkills of all generations and litters should be reading about her in books and screaming her name in worship during orgies. She was a legend!

Or Sunri *hadn't* been educated and raised in a training pool litter. It wasn't unheard of for a self-taught shadowkill to manifest, although that was exceedingly rare. In most cases of undocumented talent, it was always a rogue shadowkill home-brewing his own unauthorized tadpoles. Somehow, Qisami didn't think either was the case. Most wildlings and homeschooled could barely perform first-year tricks. Only a few of those amateurs ever became competent with shadowstepping, which was the base standard from which all shadowkills earned their titles. Sunri was not just brilliant, she moved and fought like a true master.

Qisami was still deep in reverie when there was a knock on the cellar door. Her black blades materialized in her hands, and she pressed herself against one of the shelves. This room was a dead end, and there was no talking her way out of the situation while she was dressed in a black leather tunic and cloak with enough sharp weapons on her to arm an entire squad. Whoever came into that room next was not going to walk out.

The seconds ticked by. There was no follow-up to the knocking. The heavy wooden door did not swing open, nor did any voice announce themself. Qisami's curiosity got the best of her. She crept up the short flight of stairs leading to the door and peeked through the gap underneath. There was no one there. She pressed her ear to the door and listened: still nothing.

Qisami clutched the door handle and slid it open. Her head stuck out the entrance, and her gaze swept left and then right. And then down. On the ground, folded neatly, was a string-bound parcel of clothing. She frowned, picked it up, and retreated back inside the cellar. She whipped the clothing free to reveal a set of servant's robes. Measured perfectly to her body.

A few moments later, Qisami reemerged to the world as Companion Kiki once more. She lowered her head as she passed the guards and proceeded toward the third-floor landing in the duchess's wing. Another guard questioned where she was heading but otherwise allowed her to continue onward to the duchess's suite.

Chiafana stood before the double doors, as if guarding them. "Maza Qisami. You've been busy."

"Firstwife." She waved. "I thought I was getting extra credit."

Chiafana placed a hand on her elbow as Qisami went to go inside. This time, she shook off the minister's hand. "I can walk myself." A disapproving noise crawled out of the woman's throat, but she did not press the issue.

The doors to the duchess's chambers opened to a long, dark hallway with dark marble floors, mahogany wall paneling, and a glass ceiling. The hallway opened into a luxurious square room with a sunken center that encircled a large fire pit.

Sunri was seated at a small table with her legs crossed wearing a fine but thin see-through robe, eating grapes from a bowl at a small round table. The duchess's sheer robes were distracting. Her body rippled with taut, graceful muscles simultaneously exhibiting strength and sensuality. It was a sign to Qisami that she was unarmed and had nothing to hide. Sunri was intending to parlay, and this small hole-in-the-ground was the closest they would have to privacy in the Palace of the Gracious Guest.

Then Qisami noticed that the duchess's left arm above the elbow was wrapped tightly with bandages. For a moment, she panicked. Did she actually injure the Duchess of Caobiu? Were a bunch of Mute Men about to jump out of the blinds and chop her into pieces?

Instead, the duchess looked up. "Thank you, Chiafana. You may go."

There was a pause. "Yes, Your Grace." The minister bowed and retreated from the room.

Qisami craned her head and watched Firstwife depart until the door closed with a solid thunk. "You train your pet well."

"Poor discipline comes from the very top," Sunri replied. "Goramh's twenty-seventh Tenet of War."

"Why does Goramh have forty tenets for war but only two for everything else?" asked Qisami.

"Goramh's second Tenet of Humility. The mind should starve in victory and be ravenous in defeat," recited the duchess.

"Goramh must have lost a lot of wars," Qisami quipped.

"The reality is that he got more people killed than the green plague that wiped out half of the empire."

Both shadowkills settled in and focused on each other.

"But enough about old dead frauds," said Sunri. "You look like you have questions. You may ask them."

"Are you actually a shadowkill?" she blurted. Her body tingled, and her feet tapped like an eager hare.

The ends of Sunri's lips curled. "Once, a long time ago. From the same training pool as you, actually."

What! Qisami was stunned. "You were Bo Po Mo Fo?"

"Once in the pool, always in the pool," the duchess recited with a wry smile.

Suddenly Qisami recalled an old legend the girls used to share. Every training pool had their own mythos. Most were silly fables, but there were elements of truth in others. Qisami recalled one particular bit of training pool lore. "Hold up. Are you . . . are you Sparkle Legend? Five generations before mine. You were the hotshot rising star of your pod who disappeared, never to be seen again. Am I right? Is that you? By the Tiandi it *is* you! What happened?"

Sunri snorted in a very un-duchess-like way, which Qisami appreciated. "Sparkle Legend was a terrible name back then too. As for what happened, the emperor did. Pull up a cushion, sister." Sunri's tone had changed, and she looked more relaxed now that they were alone. Qisami lowered her guard and did as asked.

"I was a young, arrogant shadowkill once, much like you are now,"

Sunri continued. "I had accepted a brazen job to murder the High Calculus, the head math scholar in the empire. I infiltrated the Celestial Court as a palacemaiden, much like you now. While I was planning the kill, I caught the eye of Xuanshing, may his greatness ever last. The emperor fancied me and elevated me to concubine, which I then leveraged to become his wife, then chief adviser, then his general, and then his empress. And now, his heir."

"What about the Consortium?" asked Qisami. "They must have known."

Sunri shrugged and beckoned for Qisami to join her at the table. Qisami obliged, and Sunri slid over the bowl of grapes. "Of course, but what were they going to do? They knew. They were furious. I was a valuable asset. But by that time the emperor had made me a concubine." She shrugged. "They tried to leverage my position in court, but I refused. I became untouchable. No shadowkill, no matter how young and promising, was worth the wrath of the Celestial Throne."

Qisami was even more impressed. "Those stories about your rise to power were true?"

"I haven't heard all the stories, but most have been accurate, yes."

"That is *wicked*." To think, someone like *her* could one day become a duchess. "And you're really from the Bo Po Mo Fo pool?"

Sunri raised her arm, torqued it inward, and fanned four of her fingers. It was their blood sign, known only to her siblings within the pool.

"I can't believe it," Qisami crowed in an excited whisper. "It's almost like having a sister who is royalty."

"Your sister *is* royalty," corrected Sunri. "Why do you think I expressly sought you for this job?"

"You did?" Qisami had rarely felt so flattered.

The duchess ticked her long, elegant fingers one by one. "You are a skilled and ruthless killer. Your earn rate is off the charts, and you are stunningly efficient. Almost as much as I was," she admitted. "From a performance and earnings standpoint, there are a few bigger sharks, but few so young. The silkspinner deal with the Central Orb was ill-advised, foolish, and full of hubris, but that is all said in hindsight. I wager any shadowkill worth their blade would have taken that job as well. I certainly would have. I also think the debt garnishment they imposed on you is rubbing salt in the wound. So, as a fellow Bo Po Mo Fo, I wanted to give you an opportunity to earn it out and cast off your chains."

Sunri obviously had deep connections with the Consortium to hold such privileged ledger information. And she used it to check up on Qisami. How neat was that? Qisami was touched, which was a rare emotion. Not everything they said about Sunri was true after all. However, she didn't believe Sunri, of all people, was doing this out of sisterhood and magnanimity. "What's in it for you? Everyone gets their cut, especially a duchess, I wager."

Sunri popped a grape into her mouth. She even ate prettily. "These are precarious times, Maza Qisami. These negotiations with Yanso, this situation, quartering here in the enemy's lair without my army and Mute Men is dangerous and volatile. A duchess bleeds as easily as a peasant. I need someone I can trust to watch my back, and who better than a pool sister? Our fight today has proved to me that you're not only a deadly war artist, but a potentially great asset, especially since we're bonded by sisterhood."

The two spent the next hour reminiscing about their time at the training pool, back when they were young and naive. They shared so many similarities. The two had joined a litter at the same age, although separated by many generations of children. Their bunks had been only three apart. Their shared quarters when they got older were one level apart from each other. They laughed about the awful communal tubs and reminisced about running wild as pool brats on the streets of Manjing, where their underground training pool resided. Both graduated at the top of their litters, and both were top earners for their generation. Qisami felt as if she was following in the duchess's footsteps. By the time their discussion wound down, her skepticism had all but disappeared. She never realized how badly she had wanted a sister until now, when one sat next to her. Especially one so powerful and rich.

"So," Qisami finally asked, "why did you try to kill me last night?"

Sunri bit into another grape. "Why did *you* try to kill *me*?"

"What? I didn't know you were you." Qisami shrugged. "I thought you were someone trying to kill me. But you obviously knew who I was."

"If I was *actually* trying to kill you," said Sunri, "we would not be sitting in my personal chambers enjoying a bowl of fruit."

It was Sunri's way of reminding Qisami that she was still the stronger war artist. It didn't bother Qisami as much as she thought it would. Just being reputed to have a connection with Sparkle Legend would make her more infamous, if that was even possible. The important thing to consider was how she could use this information to her advantage. After this job was done, of course.

"What were you doing out there?" asked Qisami. "Shouldn't you be under heavy guard?"

Sunri sniffed. "As you well know, dear sister, the common soldier, no matter how elite, is little defense against our kind."

"That's for sure." Yanso had the juiciest and sweetest grapes. Qisami ate them by the handful.

The duchess continued, "Chiafana, who heads my security, told me that the shadows came alive the moment I arrived in Allanto, but had assured me that she was handling it. Imagine my surprise when you appeared." She broke into a smirk. "And then tried to kill me."

"I was trying to *defend* you!"

"I tried to break away, dear, but you followed doggedly, as I would expect of a sister from my Bo Po Mo Fo pool, until I had no choice but to fight. Your reputation is well earned, diamond. It's a shame the Consortium threw you to the wolves to appease those orb-lickers."

Sunri had just used lunar court slang. That made Qisami adore her even more. Behind that perfectly painted face and the expensive silk robes, here in this luxurious palace was a stone-cold nightblossom killer. Qisami admired the fact that the Duchess of Caobiu was willing to get her hands bloodied. "What happens now?"

"I will need you more than ever, sister. Succession politics has always been the most brutal sort of family affair. You did me this great service by severing the leak to the Shulan," said Sunri. "Now I need you even more vigilant. There are many nightblossoms about, at least two or three teahouses, and maybe even shadowkills. I'm certain the other dukes have hired eyes as well." She paused. "I would be comforted if there was one of our kind watching over me at night, especially once Saan arrives."

"Of course, sister. Consider it done. When is the Lord of Shulan arriving?"

"My stepson, fortunately, is delayed trying to reorganize his collapsed Lawkan border, plugging the holes in his faltering lines. Shulan may have the best war artists in the Enlightened States, but he's learned a hard lesson that great warriors do not necessarily make great armies. Yanso and I are already negotiating the framework of this . . ." Sunri bristled. ". . . marriage. It would be amusing if the stakes weren't so high. I'm trying to keep my borders intact and maintain autonomy over my duchy while all he can think about is throwing the biggest wedding ceremony in the history of the Enlightened States."

Qisami startled. "He can't be serious."

"Of course he's not serious," snapped Sunri. "Yanso is no fool. He knows I'm the weak link. The longer he delays, the weaker my position. The more desperate I'll get, and the more I'll give up. Saan knows this too, which is why he's rushing here before we can come to an agreement."

Qisami frowned. "Wait. So, do you *want* this alliance to succeed? I can't tell with you nobility anymore."

"Both options are poor choices," admitted Sunri. "Unfortunately, a marriage will ensure our survival. Even now, the Xing are probing the Celu Mountains from the south, burning and looting like a plague of locusts. The Alabaster Armada has choked my supply lines from the west, and those cowardly white chickens of Gyian are always making noise and then running away. I can either keep fighting on all fronts and die, or I can get married and survive." The duchess rose to her feet, her head nearly bumping the ceiling. She was a tall woman. She offered Qisami a hand. "Sister, now that you know the truth, can I count on you to guard my shadow?"

Qisami didn't need long to consider. This news changed everything. Some bonds were too great to ignore. Besides, victory here would place her as the right-hand woman of the Duchess of Caobiu. "Sure. Anything for a royal sister."

In a less starstruck time, she would have tried to finagle a fee for the work, but this was not only a pool sister, but a duchess and the most powerful woman in the Enlightened States. Qisami was sure the reward for success at the end would be far greater than what she could wheedle out of the duchess now.

"Good, sister. I know I can count on you. Now, best you go before it gets too late and you're missed. I'll have a wagon take you back to your tower."

The rest of the visit was a blur. After their chat, the Voice of the Court appeared and escorted Qisami down the main corridors parading her in front of the staff and guards. A palacemaiden given such honor must mean special status in the eyes of the duchess. It completely validated everything Qisami was hoping before being close to the duchess. In their eyes, she was now an important person of note, and she lapped up all of the attention.

She stepped out of the front entrance to the Palace of the Gracious Guest and was delighted to find a six-wheeled yellow carriage being pulled by six righteous lions waiting for her at the driveway.

Was that beautiful carriage for *her*?

It had been a while since she last enjoyed life with this privilege. It felt like warm sunshine after a cold, chilly night. Her mind still couldn't grasp that Sunri, the Duchess of Caobiu, the Desert Lioness, was a nightblossom who had come from the same dingy ranks of the nightblossoms. Not only that, but she was also an apex predator: a shadowkill! It made her giddy just thinking about it.

"One of us, one of us!" Qisami cooed, pumping her fists in the air as the carriage pulled up.

There was so much potential here. In the lunar court, relationships mean everything. It was rarely about who you knew, but who you could talk to, and how big of a posse you could gather if it came down to throwing blades. To have such a direct line to a duke of the Enlightened States . . . the power she wielded could be seismic. Every underworld would beg to ally with her. And to think Qisami had actually been thinking about quitting the killing business just a few hours ago. What a silly thought.

"This is so fancy," she practically tittered as the coachboy laid steps for her to the carriage doors. Qisami had a thing for carriages, and this six-wheeler was easily one of the nicest she would ever ride inside. Maybe there was even good wine here. She was so sick of low-class zuijo. Always gave her headaches.

Qisami pawed the soft red cushions as she climbed inside. Ooh, so lush. She palmed the gold railings and stared lustfully at the black mahogany wooden frame. How decadent. Qisami looked up at the ceiling to admire the small gold chandelier hanging from the center tip of the roof. It swayed as the carriage pulled out of the palace grounds. No wonder the carriage needed four shishis to pull it.

She should probably find a seat soon. Qisami turned toward the back end of the long carriage and suddenly noticed, for the first time, that she had company. The Minister of Critical Purpose was sitting in the far back. Talk about ruining a nice moment.

Chiafana raised a teacup to a sharp birdlike face. "Have a seat, shadowkill."

Qisami did as she was told, dragging her feet like a pouting child. The cushions were every bit as soft and silky as she expected.

"Tea?" the minister offered.

Qisami accepted, pouring herself a hot brew.

"I don't know what you think you have going with the duchess, foolish girl, but I assure you it's less than you think." Her voice was sharp, tart even. "Your status doesn't matter, nor does your influence. What matters is that you have a job to accomplish. I have assignments for you and your people. Information gathering, some sabotage, nothing your . . . types can't handle."

Already? She hoped it didn't entail beating up another servant. The estate staff was traumatized as it was. "What is it?"

The minister rambled off several orders. It was then Qisami understood why the minister had placed her people in the positions they were currently in.

Qisami committed everything to memory. "Anything else?"

"We've found the source of the leak to Shulan. It's none other than High Lord Aki Niam himself. He's coordinating with them and negotiating behind our back. We need him neutralized."

Qisami sputtered. "Are you stupid? I can't kill a high lord."

"Don't be absurd. We would never encourage that practice among the nobility. We don't want you to kill him. We need him to be distracted and unable to perform his duties." She paused. "Lord Aki Niam is famous for being a good family man. He has a large brood. Twelve children if I am not mistaken. I hear he's particularly fond of his two youngest. Little girls, I believe. Those he can afford to lose. Kill them."

Qisami spat out her tea and ruined the nice fabric. "The twins? They're babies!"

The minister did not seem to care. "Just one will suffice, I suppose. Make it look natural. I recommend poison."

"They're four years old," she choked. "And they're rather delightful little pisses. Can't we drown his favorite concubine or something?"

Chiafana cocked her head. "Why do you think you were assigned to be their companion?"

The carriage came to a stop in front of the Tower of Blessed Servitude. Neither woman moved as they continued to fix eyes upon each other. Qisami was an equal opportunity killer and had rarely been too choosy about who she murdered. There were exceptions, though: animals—dogs specifically—and children. Both pushed the boundaries of her meager morals.

Qisami finally found her limit. "No. I'm not doing that. I'm not killing kids for you. Do that dirty work yourself."

"Are you reneging on your end of the agreement with the Duchess of Caobiu? That is a death sentence, shadowkill."

"I don't think so, minister," Qisami sneered. "The duchess and I are bonded in a way you could never understand. Besides, I signed up to protect Sunri, not to murder little children."

"Since when, ruthless shadowkill?"

"Since I started spending all this stupid time with them," she admitted. "But it doesn't matter. I'm not murdering the Aki girls."

The Minister of Critical Purpose glared. Qisami glared back. "There will be consequences for this, shadowkill."

"I'm not killing kids, you bitch!"

"Well, that's unfortunate."

Luckily, the carriage arrived at the Grand Tower of the Blessed Servitude just in time. Qisami stepped out of the carriage and slammed the door. She glared as it pulled away, its wooden wheels crunching against the rocks. That ride had drained her previous exuberance. All she had now was a sour taste in the back of her throat.

CHAPTER FORTY-FOUR

BOAT FIGHT

It took Captain Tee Mun fifteen minutes to rouse the crew aboard his river cutter, the *Slippery Minnow*. Fifteen minutes in naval time was a bad joke. It showed that either the captain was a poor one, or he had stalled for time in the hope of getting Taishi thrown off his ship and arrested.

Too bad, captain. It took another fifteen minutes to hoist their anchors and cast off, but soon they were pulling away from Bahngtown harbor, albeit nearly thirty minutes behind *White Ship Six Two*, the Tiandi religion's vessel holding Jian.

Fortunately, a river cutter was a nimble craft built for speed. It should be agile and quick enough to easily streak these chaotic waters and catch up to that much larger pregnant junk ship. Assuming, of course, the *Slippery Minnow* was as fast as her captain claimed. If the quickness with which the crew roused to their stations was any indication, they were going to be in trouble.

It didn't take long for Taishi to realize that the captain was not blowing hot air up her robes. The *Slippery Minnow* was indeed just as fast as his brags as she shot down the middle of the Yukian. Apparently, the captain was not fazed by limited visibility with the starless night and the thick blanket of mist rolling through the valley. Of course, smugglers were used to operating with low visibility. They probably preferred it.

The river carried them to the edge of the fifth Ugly Brother mountain before they finally sighted *White Ship Six Two*'s spotlights waving in the distance. The monk's junk was lumbering at a careful speed down the last stretch of the massive river before it spilled out of the Cloud Pillars and into the valley to the southeast dividing Shulan and Lawkan. Once there, *White Ship Six Two* would become lost to them. With the web of riverways, frequent Lawkan patrols, checkpoints, and blockades, their ship would stand no chance of catching the Lotus ship. The Alabaster Armada would snap them up within an hour. Not that it mattered because—

"We're not going to catch them, boss." Captain Tee Mun must have read her mind. "I'll get you within ballista range, but that's about it, and then we're out in the lowlands. We're done, and I'm clearing out. I don't care what you say. The Yukian in the plains is a woodchipper. I won't take my ship there."

"Keep going until I give the command," she retorted. "Remember, ducal orders."

"Which duke again?"

"Worry about doing the job first, captain," she snapped.

The longer they sailed, however, the clearer it became that Tee Mun hadn't been weaseling lazy lies. They weren't going to catch *White Ship Six Two* in time. The King was rising soon too. Once it became light, they would lose their element of surprise. The much heavier armed Lotus junk would blow them out of the water before they could get close enough to board.

Taishi stood at the bow of the ship as the freezing waters of the Yukian sprayed onto the deck. Common sense was telling her to call off the pursuit. Don't chase what you can't catch. Regroup and figure out their next steps. That was the smart thing to do. Taishi's heart, however, wouldn't listen. They would be close to ten ship lengths away before they ran out of river. It was too close not to try. Taishi tensed, and she hissed a labored breath through clenched teeth. If only she had insisted on going to the harbor immediately rather than drinking tea. If only she had brought Jian with her to Daleh. If only she was not so old and slow these days.

The *White Ship Six Two* was about to pass the final fork when a large object emerged from the starboard side of the ship and began to cross the river, moving toward the Lotus sect ship.

"What is that?" asked Bhasani, stepping onto the deck.

"Another ship?" said Fausan.

"Yes, but with a strange shape." Taishi squinted and shook her head. "It looks like a . . . house. It's a houseboat."

"Is someone else trying to board the same ship we're trying to board?" Sohn huffed. "That's rather rude, isn't it?"

Bhasani pondered. "Can't be a coincidence. Exactly how many people know about tonight?"

The impact came a few minutes later, to everyone's surprise. They had expected the encroaching ship to try to either sink or board the junk. Instead, whoever was captain on the other ship had crazier ideas as it plowed directly into the side of the junk with a thunderous clatter of wood and spray. The Lotus ship began listing against its injured side with the remnants of the attacking ship embedded deep into its hull. The two ships began to circle like dance partners in a third era romance.

Taishi yanked Tee Mun's sleeve and pulled him close. "See, you might earn that catch bonus I offered, after all. Try to be more positive next time, Captain. You'll never get anywhere if all you can say is 'no.'"

"You don't understand," shouted the captain. "Getting close to that ship right now would be a very bad idea. Anyone with half a rock for brains knows that. The crew is on alert and will see us coming, the ship has lost all controls, and they always blame the closest nearby ship for the sinking, and I really don't need holy heat."

"Just tell them I commandeered this ship and made you an unwilling participant," she replied.

"That's not a bad idea," said the captain.

"Of course," she added, "then that means I'm not paying you for this work."

"Hey!"

"That's what I thought. Get me alongside that ship. Let's go!"

Tee Mun cocked his head. "Which duke is reimbursing me for damages again?"

The *Slippery Minnow* neared the spinning wrecks, still caught in their lethal embrace. The main mast of *White Ship Six Two* snapped with a thunderous crack and splashed loudly into the water. Water continued to spill into the gaping wound in the side of the junk caused by Kasa's houseboat—she now clearly recognized the torn remnants of his sails fluttering in the breeze.

Taishi didn't have much time. She should have waited for the *Slippery Minnow* to pull within fifty feet or so before she attempted the leap. Taishi stepped onto a current and let it propel her forward. She almost didn't make it. The currents were chaotic tonight, and it was quickly apparent she wasn't going to make the leap between ships. At best, Taishi would slam into the hull at a high speed and break whatever she had not already broken. Fortunately, desperation offered her a deep well of strength, which Taishi was able to draw upon to almost will herself onto the deck of *White Ship Six Two*. She still came up short, but by only a few feet. She landed on the angled hull of the junk and bounced onto the deck a moment later.

Taishi landed on her feet, one hand on the hilt of the Swallow Dances, prepared to fight against overwhelming numbers. The rest of her people better get here fast. She would be hard-pressed to defeat a junk's entire crew. Even if she could defeat these numbers, she would keel over from exhaustion afterward. However, to her surprise, no one paid attention to her. A large gathering of sailors and white-clad monks was crowding the bow near where the two ships had collided. Several were waiting their turn to jump to the offending ship that had rammed *White Ship Six Two*. No one paid any attention to the master war artist standing with a drawn sword on the main deck.

Taishi looked over the other side to see Kasa standing on the roof of his houseboat with a crowd of monks swarming the deck. The old man was still impressive. No wonder it had been so easy to get close and slip aboard the *Slippery Minnow*. Kasa crashing his home into the Lotus junk not only prevented their escape, but it also distracted them long enough for Taishi to arrive and rescue Jian.

Even at his advanced age, there were few war artists who wielded the staff as elegantly as the Houtou master. His movements were poetry, and the long staff acted not only as an extension of his body, but also like a beloved partner twirling in a violent dance. His shining staff, aptly named the Summer Bow, held a glimmer of sunlight as it swung in long, looping arcs, spinning in figure eights and twirling like lotus blossoms in a lively breeze. The legendary staff flailed in every direction, bending and flexing like a striking serpent as it whipped around the Houtou master, daring any of the Lotus monks to get close. When they did give him too much berth, Kasa would bend and flex Summer Bow into a bow and make them pay with a barrage of arrows.

The old master bled in several places, his fisherman's burlap robes stained red and clinging to his body. The side of his head was damp with blood. Whether his injuries were from the collision or the fighting, she could not tell. He was surrounded, and it didn't look like he could hold the attacking monks at bay for much longer.

Taishi wasn't about to let her friend fall alone. She gripped the Swallow Dances, took two slow steps, and then shot forward like an arrow springing from a bow. The Swallow Dances hissed from its place of rest as she descended upon the group of monks with the wrath of Palantha Sow, the Goddess of Lopsided Embarrassing Victories. That, or a furious and concerned master.

Most of the ones milling about around here were young initiates, far too innocent and naive to deserve a war artist's death. The rest were just deeply devout idiots. The Swallow Dances began to slap Lotus sect monks around. Taishi used the flat of its blade in this case, sparing all their lives. In any case, Fausan wasn't wrong. Killing a bad monk here or there was perfectly fine, but it was generally frowned upon. Slaughtering an entire boatload, however, was probably a permanent, deep stain on her eternal soul.

Besides, just because she didn't use the edge of the Swallow Dances to bite didn't mean her strikes didn't hurt. Five had been knocked unconscious by the flat of her blade. About the same had been kicked off deck or swept off the ship by a wind current and into the dark drink. Whether they lived, Taishi didn't know, nor did she care. Let them drown. Her mercy extended only as far as wielding non-lethal attacks.

It didn't mean, however, she showed any mercy to those who attacked her. Taishi stepped to the side to avoid the looping swing of a monk spade and severed one of the monk's arms at the elbow. She continued moving, dodging, ducking, and weaving, flowing through the crowd of monks toward the bow like water seeking the lowest point.

Most of the enemy were wielding moon blades. They were short, heavy, deadly in the right hands, but mostly stupid. The Lotus sect had wanted a uniquely Lotus sect weapon and sometime back their vanity project produced this dumb thing. Taishi never understood the logic behind the moon blade's form. Its curved shape added unnecessary weight to the weapon while limiting its reach. Its bulbous form made it a poor weapon to slice with, as its weight and center of gravity were near the blade's base. It was also a poor weapon to chop with, not to mention chopping with the tip pointed the way it was made it especially vulnerable to getting stuck on bone. Whoever designed this weapon certainly valued form over function. And worst of all, the function looked ridiculous. Taishi scowled at the nearest monk wielding moon blades in both hands. The only thing worse than wielding a badly designed weapon was wielding two of them.

Several Lotus gawked at the angry woman who had just dropped into their midst. One managed to yell a warning before a quick sword slash severed the main artery to his heart. The Swallow Dances sliced several more times as she slipped her way toward Kasa, scribbling death with Taishi's skilled hand. The rest of the unarmed monks stood no chance, but she gave them high marks for effort as they tried to smother and drag her to the ground. Two lost limbs in one slice, and a third took such a quick, darting thrust into the gut that it took them a minute to realize they'd been stabbed. She turned and batted an arrow out of the air and sent it streaking back toward an archer on the upper deck shooting at her back. A muffled cry followed.

More monks realized that there was now a new, even deadlier threat on the broken ship, and turned their attention to her. Taishi danced with a dozen partners all at once, sweeping through them, leaving a third gasping their last breaths. Blood sprayed into the air with each new partner and then she was on the move again, barely giving any of her opponents more than a passing thought as she pressed forward. By the time she reached the bow of the ship, there was hardly anyone left standing. The last surviving monk dropped his moon blade and begged for his life. "Merciful Mosaic. You're not human," he uttered. When she took a step forward, he launched himself over the side into the dark waters below.

Taishi had planned to let him live, but this worked just as well. The ones who died here earned instant, efficient, and merciful deaths. All that remained were the group still tussling with Kasa on his houseboat, unaware that they had just lost the main ship.

"By the Tiandi, what happened here?"

Taishi looked over to see Fausan and Hachi climb on board. Bhasani followed next with Sohn. The drowned fist surveyed the carnage strewn across the main deck.

Taishi sheathed her blade with an emphatic thunk. "I guess I still have it."

"You've been stewing over that, haven't you?" Bhasani chortled, an unusually rough cackle for someone so sophisticated. Sometimes, the woman's cool demeanor would fail her to reveal her true peasant upbringing. "That's what I admire about you. Your ability to hold a grudge, no matter what."

"Do you really want to do this right now?" hissed Taishi between clenched teeth.

"Now is as good a time as any," Bhasani shot back.

Fausan pushed his way between them. "This is actually the *worst* time. The Old Monkey looks like he's in trouble."

"Get to Kasa," she yelled at Bhasani as a clatter of arrows drizzled upon the deck floor. Taishi knocked a crossbolt out of the air and turned to see a row of archers lining the upper deck. Several archers had assembled on the top deck of the stern and were plunking arrows at them. She was fortunate the choppy waters made shooting difficult. Another hail of arrows and bolts rained down upon her. This time, Sohn rushed in front of Taishi and blocked several of the arrows. His shield somehow blocked a much larger area than should have been physically possible.

The short, thick man roared; his presence suddenly felt much greater than his size. "I got this rabble. Help Kasa!"

The eternal bright light master leaped from the main deck to the stern in one bound, not making it over the railing, instead plowing through it. Sohn bludgeoned several monks with his shield, knocking them in all directions like a child's rolling pins. Very few things could stop the Boulder once he got going, and nothing could if he was angry. He seemed to have taken his mistake with Jian to heart this time. Taishi appreciated that. He was finally taking responsibility, or maybe he had suddenly become Jian's best friend like everyone else inexplicably had.

A bullet flew past her, curved around the upper railing, and struck down an archer. Two streaked by, hitting one more target. A door to the main deck slammed open, and three monks fell after taking two steps as Fausan continued to flick bullet after bullet against anyone coming on deck.

The main deck was nearly secured.

Taishi grabbed Hachi's shoulder as she stormed past. "Where's Zofi?"

The whipfinger disciple looked left and then right. "Uh, I left her on the boat with Kaiyu guarding her. Figure best way to keep them both safe."

Taishi gave Hachi an approving smile. "You have a good head on you, son."

"Hopefully." He shook his head. "Two monks attacked them by the time I climbed onto the deck. Kaiyu handled them, I think. I hope."

That approving smile dropped in a blink. "Then what are *you* doing here? You were instructed to protect them at all costs. That was your only duty."

"My master told me to guard the top of the ladder." He saw the look on her face and gulped. "I'll just go back to the boat and make sure everything is okay."

"You do that, boy."

A shrill whistle screamed into the night and was followed by a streaking snow-white light that exploded into a kaleidoscope of flowers. It was followed by another that shot even higher exploding into an even larger singular flower.

"What is that?" asked Hachi, shielding his eyes.

"It's a white signal flare." Fausan's gaze lingered at the sky. "It's white."

"What does the color matter, master?"

"It matters." Taishi understood the reference as well. She took off, catching sight of the monks who had launched the flares. They had to be neutralized before they could send another one. The Swallow Dances continued to sing as its blade moved through air and flesh with equal ease. One monk with the moon spade died while standing, the faint blue shadow fading around him. Another wielding a moon spade barely had enough time to look confused and raise his guard when she hacked with the Swallow Dances and cut through his monk spade's shaft, down through the crown of his head, past his skull, and deep into the thinking bits beneath.

A particularly ambitious and aggressive monk came from her blind spot, swinging a wide, looping slash with his moon blade. Taishi sidestepped it by a hair's breadth. He followed with the second moon blade in his other hand. He sliced and diced at her with the two curved sickle-shaped blades, drawing the typical patterns most fall back to when they wield double swords. It never worked. Taishi didn't know why people still tried.

Taishi was perfectly willing to offer him a free lesson. The young monk made a poor show of not telegraphing his moves. One quick glance at a sequence was all she required before properly reading his tell. The next time his arms rolled toward the same sequence, she sidestepped the disciple and bumped him with the pommel of her sword, right onto his elbow. The silly monk's elaborate figure eights went awry, and he ended up lopping off his own left hand at the wrist. The man, staring at his bloody stump, screamed.

Taishi turned her attention back to the houseboat and saw an exhausted Kasa struggling with two monks who had grabbed hold of Summer Bow. By now Bhasani had made it to his side and was fighting back-to-back with him. One monk wielding a monk spade stepped up to her, and then on his own lost his balance and fell into the river. The waters near Bhasani's feet were filled with many of his brothers flailing about and clinging to debris. Both ships were slowly sinking, even as they continued to float downstream.

Taishi launched herself off *White Ship Six Two* and landed on the houseboat with a crash. The Swallow Dances flowed through Blizzarding Pine Needles form and then slipped into Maiden Fans the Lake, melting away the group of Lotus monks caught unaware from behind. She cut down two more monks before coming face-to-face with a poor sap caught between her and Bhasani. The man's hands shook so badly he risked cutting off his own wrist with the moon blade.

"Allow me," said Bhasani, taking a step in front of Taishi. She fixed the monk with a look. "Go jump in the river."

The man did not look like he needed much encouragement as he immediately dove into the black rushing waters and disappeared. Bhasani looked at Taishi and shrugged. "What can I say? You are a very scary woman."

"Flattery doesn't work with me," said Taishi as they made their way to Kasa, who was hunched over on one knee, one hand on his chest, visibly in pain.

"What got you, old man?" She hurried over to help him up. Taishi's breath caught when he turned toward her, revealing the jagged splinter of a broken wooden post piercing his chest just below the right shoulder. The old Houtou master was pale. The shaft of Summer Bow was stained with deep streaks of red.

Kasa broke into a bloody grin. "That was fun. I've always wanted to crash the boat into something. How bad is it?"

Taishi's throat caught as blood leaked from the ends of his lips. Kasa wavered on his feet, and then Taishi was there to support him. "The Lotus ship? You rammed it very well."

He hacked a cough. "Not the bloody ship, girl. How bad do I look?"

"You look pretty awful." Taishi had too much respect for him to say otherwise.

Kasa offered her Summer Bow. "Just in case. You know what to do.

Elevate him. He's ready. I don't want him to think he didn't earn it. Promise me that, Taishi?"

She nodded. "I swear. Honor is the way. It will be as you decree. But let's not worry about that right now, you old rooster. We need to get you off this boat and to a doctor."

"Hah, wishful thinking. It's all right, girl. I feel like I went out with a lion's roar. Make sure they record it in song and stories. A couple of constellations named after me would be pretty sweet."

Taishi forced a chuckle. "How did you even know about the ship?"

The Houtou master grinned and wiped the blood from the ends of his lips with his sleeve. "One of Naifun's spooks paid me a visit earlier tonight. He relayed his messages to me from the Black Night of Xing herself. I learned about the monk ship escaping and thought I'd do something about it. There's only one way out of the Five Ugly Brothers by ship, so I sat at the mouth and waited."

"No one told you to crash your house into the ship!"

Kasa barked a rough laugh, which ended in a fit of labored coughs. "I was just trying to get close enough to get on board. The crashing part was a bonus." He slumped against her as they made their way to the stern of the houseboat until they were close to the side of *White Ship Six Two*.

"Father!" Kaiyu was halfway down the stairs to the lower deck when he saw Kasa. The boy rushed to his side, and together they aided the Houtou master to the main deck.

Taishi felt a rush of relief when Zofi appeared a moment later. The mapmaker's daughter gave the Houtou master a worried look before speaking with Taishi. "The junk has two levels below the main deck. Fausan and Hachi are already scouring the lowest deck, but it's slowly flooding."

Taishi watched as the water lapped into the Lotus ship. The hole wasn't too large, and the front half of the houseboat was plugging it, but it was still taking on water. This ship was fated to rest at the bottom of the Yukian within an hour, if that. Taishi handed Kasa over to the eternal bright light. "Take Kasa with you and transfer him to the river cutter. The rest of us will finish sweeping the ship and meet you there once we find Jian."

Zofi scowled. "About that, our good Captain Tee Mun abandoned us the moment everyone was off the ship. We're trapped here."

That was not unexpected. Taishi didn't blame the guy one bit. It was still annoying, considering their current situation. Whatever. Taishi didn't have time to get angry. She counted heads; everyone was accounted for. She could save herself, perhaps one or two others. No more than that. And, as far as she was concerned, that reserved spot was already taken. In any case, one thing at a time. "Split up. Find Jian."

CHAPTER FORTY-FIVE

THE ALLIANCE

"Where are we going?" yelled Hampa as they weaved through the narrow alley, around vagrants sitting with their legs sprawled out, around piles of garbage, and between vendor stalls selling anything from flavored ice on sticks to stone shoes.

"I have no idea, but just go." Sali was already panting hard.

After this many twists along their path, she had no idea which direction they were facing anymore. These narrow alleys had long awnings hanging overhead that obscured the sky and made it difficult to use some of the larger island landmarks as anchors. Dozens of colorful washed-out rugs and tapestries hung off the walls to both sides of her, perhaps to keep the buildings insulated.

There were now six towerspears behind them, fully armored with their large trademark black shields and crimson spears, knocking over people who were unfortunate enough not to get out of their way in time. Sali should be glad. Their heavy armor slowed their pursuit, which was equaled by the fact Sali could barely maintain this brisk trotting pace. She couldn't keep up this pace for much longer and was already edging toward exhaustion.

What was more pressing, however, was who was chasing them overhead. Sali had caught sight of at least two stormchasers converging on them along the rooftops. They would be the far greater threat. The longer they stayed out in the open, the likelier it was that they would get caught.

Sali yanked Marhi's sleeve. "Girl, where can we find shelter on this accursed ice cube?"

Marhi was holding Hampa's hand. She looked both ways at an intersection. "There are tunnels that run deep into the mountains. The Masau never dare go down there. If we can reach one of the cave entrances, we should be safe."

"Where's the nearest cave mouth?" asked Sali.

Marhi stopped and peered around, trying to get her bearings. "We entered Penguin Paddle, and then cut across Orca Way. That means we're—"

Another group of towerspears appeared before them, cutting them off. The two sides closed in. Hampa stepped in front of Marhi, facing the oncoming group of three towerspears, while Sali turned to meet the six coming from behind.

"Come taste the bicker of my quarrels!" Hampa roared.

Sali rolled her eyes as she focused on the advancing Masau. The towerspears closed in at a lazy pace; their large, rectangular shields and heavy spears probably made the jog up the hill unpleasant. Good. They were still loosely clustered together as they grunted uphill toward them. Sali would make them pay for that sloppiness.

Her tongue shot to its full length and darted over the shoulder of the lead towerspear, biting through the neck of the second. Sali yanked her tongue back violently, causing the corpse to topple forward, tripping his squad behind him. She sent a jolt into her stiffened tongue and then used the narrow alleyway to her advantage, thrusting with the supple tongue in sharp, quick strikes. The towerspears had formed a shield wall, which was difficult for Sali's tongue to penetrate. Instead, she swung the spear over the top of the shields, bending the shaft and causing the bite to flex and chop through a metal helm.

Sali checked in on her neophyte. Hampa was doing his usual thing, chopping wood, hammering at the shields with his mace and ax. One was already down while a second had a splintered shield. The tower-spears would be no match for the two of them, but there was a whole is-land of towerspears, and they were trapped here. They couldn't fight their way out of this. The two viperstrikes had to find a way to lose them.

A stormchaser landed behind Hampa. Wielding a shiny golden saber, he slashed at the viperstrike's back. Sali loosened the shaft of her tongue and sent it the opposite direction. The stormchaser was too far away, but the supports for the awning over his head weren't. Sali's tongue shattered the weak wooden stick holding the canvas up and collapsed it over the stormchaser.

Another stormchaser stood directly over Sali. He jumped directly on top of her. She dropped to one knee and shot her tongue upward. The stormchaser lightning-strided away before the tongue punched right through him. He materialized next to her and slashed with his saber. Sali threw herself back just in time, feeling the air from the tip of the blade scrape the scale armor along her side. She lost her balance and tumbled onto her backside. She managed to get one foot under her and push off as the second attack came, narrowly missing getting chopped a second time as the blade struck the ground. Sali's back slammed against a wall; she ducked as a third horizontal attack came, this time aiming at the soft flesh of her neck.

Sali seized her opening, slipping under the stormchaser's arm and emerging behind him. She held the relaxed rope of her tongue in her hands and slipped it behind the stormchaser's neck, and then crossed her arm and squeezed. The rope tightened. The man swung his blade and pawed at his neck, but Sali dropped, yanking him backward, and arching his body. He tried to lightning-stride away but couldn't escape her grasp. Within seconds his body went limp.

Sali shoved him toward the towerspears who were still standing just outside spear range. They couldn't keep this up for much longer. Sali re-treated until she bumped against Hampa. "We can't stay here."

"I almost bashed my way through," he yelled. He knocked a spear thrust aside with the mace and then slammed down on the towerspear's lead hand with the flat of his ax. Hampa immediately followed up, flicking the ax upward and burying it directly into the man's chin.

Sali looked up. "We can't outrun them on the ground."

"Where to then?"

"We need to go up top."

"What about Marhi? She can't follow us along the roofs. We can't leave her!"

Sali looked around. Where did the rumbler go? Did she abandon them?

By now, the stormchaser who got caught in the collapsed awning had shed the curtain. He threw the cloth aside and was about to advance on the two viperstrikes when someone came from behind a curtain hanging along the wall and bashed his head with a club.

Marhi appeared. "In here!"

Hampa shoved Sali forward first, nudging her into a needle-thin alleyway.

The Happan ran ahead while Sali followed. The passage was so narrow they had to turn their bodies and shuffle sideways to move. Fortunately, that made it even more difficult for the heavily armored towerspears to follow. Sali looked up, watching for more stormchasers. There was still a narrow sliver of sky above them, although several ropes crisscrossed over the gaps holding up lights, shades, and pieces of clothing hanging to dry.

They entered what Sali could only describe as a maze of narrow back alley passages sandwiched between the main slopes. She became even more confused as they followed Marhi, who made seemingly random turns several more times. Sali found herself lagging farther and farther behind the girl. If it wasn't for Hampa refusing to let her slow down, Sali would have fallen behind and lost sight of her.

"Wait," Sali called. She was barely staying on her feet. The last melee had lasted only a few seconds, but it had already drained her of what little strength she possessed. She was growing weaker by the hour. She stopped and hunched over, breathing heavily. Hampa was there a moment later, helping her stay upright.

"I have you, sister." He called over her shoulder. "Marhi, where are we going?"

Sali had no idea. They hurried after Marhi, passing large heaps of garbage, a small vagrant cluster, and what appeared to be a fungus garden. Finally, after more twists and turns than Sali could count, Marhi led them to a long, narrow alleyway with a white-and-blue light at the far opening. This must be the way out. Sali felt a new surge of energy as she sprinted as best she could toward the light. The tight enclosures of these alleys were deeply uncomfortable, not to mention smelly.

Sali finally caught up with Marhi, who was standing at the mouth of the alley. She stopped behind the Happan, only bumping her with her momentum. Marhi didn't seem to notice. Sali looked up and realized why.

They were back on the main street before the lake, next to the bridge leading to Masau. Not only that, but there were also many more towerspears manning the checkpoint now than there were previously.

"Now how did that happen?" Marhi mused. "I must have made a wrong turn somewhere back at Penguin . . ."

They must have appeared suspicious, catching the attention of a squad of towerspears standing at the beachhead. Four broke off and trotted toward them.

"Where to now?" asked Hampa.

Marhi took two slow steps sideways, and then broke into a run. "Follow me!"

It wasn't like they had much of a choice. Sali took one step after the Happan girl, and then was scooped up by Hampa running after her.

"I'm not that frail yet," she yelled as he ran.

"You'll just slow us down. This is faster."

Sali nodded. "Glad that caring for your injured mentor was not part of your reasoning."

Hampa was already staring ahead. "Do you think she'll come with us if I ask?"

"I think all she knows is she's known you for a few days and already is being chased by towerspears. Worry about tomorrow when you are certain there is one." Sali looked over Hampa's shoulder. The towerspears were pursuing, with more on the way.

There was no way Hampa could carry her with her armor for too long. "Put me down. I can run."

"How about I put you down when I need a breath, yeah?" Hampa was catching up with Marhi. "Besides, we need to conserve your strength for the fighting."

That was certainly true. Sali was still recovering from that beating she took the other day. Between that and the Pull of the Khan, she was a shell of her former self, but she could still summon short bursts of power to take on most here, including stormchasers. Which was good, because two appeared from the west, lightning-striding from rooftop to rooftop. They would be here any moment.

The three neared the blue roof and turned a sharp right. Sali waited as the towerspears closed in. Marhi had just reached the last turn before reaching Hightop Cluster. She stopped and waved frantically at them to hurry. Her mouth dropped in horror as she witnessed the two stormchasers lightning-striding with bright white shocks of light as they bore down on Hampa. They both reached the top of the building next to him at the same time and leaped down at him, one wielding a saber and the other a forked trident.

Sali had played limp as he carried her until the very last moment. And to think Alyna had once accused Sali of being the most frank and unsubtle war artist she had ever met. If only her own mentor could see her now, playing dead in her neophyte's arms.

"Toss me up," she growled.

Hampa obliged, throwing Sali into the air. Her foot shot out and sank into the abdomen of the nearer stormchaser, knocking her out of the air with an abrupt, strong kick. Sali twisted to face the other stormchaser and loosed her tongue, streaking it toward the chest of the stormchaser who wielded the two-handed dragon saber. That one lightning-strided away just in time, causing the bite of Sali's tongue to punch through a wall of ice.

Sali landed on her feet next to Hampa and yanked her tongue back, taking a large chunk of ice with it. She swung it overhead like a meteor hammer and smashed it at the evading stormchaser, who again strided away just in time. Either this man was quick, or Sali was too slow. It was probably the latter.

She snuck a peek at Hampa, who was engaging the other stormchaser she had kicked. Hampa had boxed the woman into a corner and hammered at her with his ax and mace. Unfortunately for him, the woman he was fighting against was wielding a double shield, which while a rare armament, was also probably the worst possible matchup for him. Winning fights often came down to matchups. Sali was tempted to call to him to switch opponents, but a long two-handed weapon would be equally problematic for her neophyte.

Sali swung the giant block of ice in wide loops, then she changed its trajectory and brought it down upon where the stormchaser had been a moment before. Her opponent stepped out of the way, lightning-strided next to her, and slashed with the dragon saber. Sali blocked the attack with the rope of her tongue, and then yanked the block arcing toward the stormchaser. The two danced their melee back and forth as they ducked and swiped, while both avoiding sword thrusts and flying blocks of ice. The ice eventually shattered as the two fought close, neither allowing the other to take advantage of the longer ranges of their weapon.

No matter how hard she tried, however, Sali couldn't break through the man's defenses. He must have sensed her slowing down. Whenever she was able to penetrate his guard, he would stride away several paces back to reset. The stormchaser was not at Sali's level, but he was younger and stronger, and her sprint of jing was nearly exhausted. She sucked in gulps of air through her uncovered mouth, expending enormous amounts of effort just to breathe. It would have been a humiliating defeat not only for Sali, the Viperstrike, but also for her sect if she had perished to an average war artist like this one.

The two of them became tangled in a knot with her tongue wrapped around the blade of his dragon saber. He clutched the handle and the blade with both hands and pressed, while Sali struggled to divert the sharp edge aside. In this particular instance, the stormchaser was stronger, and the blade inched closer and closer to her exposed neck.

Just as Sali was about to be driven to a knee, the head of a mace crashed into the side of his head, sending him collapsing unconscious. Sali loosed a long breath in relief. She felt as if it was the dawn after a midnight battle. Her body was falling to pieces.

"Come on, sister," said Hampa, hauling her to her feet. Marhi ran back to them, and the three hobbled toward the closed entrance to the Hightop Cluster.

"Open the gates!" Marhi screamed. "Get your blubbery asses up and open these gates!" She added, in a very Happan way, "Please!"

Apparently, saying please paid off, because the double wooden gates slowly creaked open. Several of Marhi's people in the arctic fox fur suits poked their head out.

"Rumblerlead Hoisannisi Jayngnaga Marhi!" one of them shouted. "We're supposed to lock down for—"

"Open the blasted gates or I'll stuff you in a vat of oil."

They obliged as the three dragged their way into the cluster.

"Close them," she ordered the moment they passed through. "I want every rumbler called up now!"

"Yes, Rumblerlead."

Marhi broke away to bark more orders, while Sali and Hampa continued limping across the courtyard. She caught back up with them a moment later. "I have to get my guys in a row. Take your mentor back to the ritualist. You remember the way to the cobbler, right? Two forks on the left. I have to go." She leaned in close as if to embrace him and stopped short of touching. She drew in a long breath. "I'll see you later, handsome."

Sali watched Rumblerlead Marhi run off. "I swear, if you end up staying on this island, I'm going to tear your spine out."

Hampa was still watching her go. He half snorted, half chuckled. "Why would I ever do that?"

The two viperstrikes had just made it to the other end of the pear-shaped courtyard, when the large wooden double gates protecting the cluster exploded into thousands of fragments peppering those closest to them with jagged shards of shattered wood. The rumblers who were behind the gate were blown into the dirt several feet back.

A plume of dust rolled in, slowly revealing a dark silhouette standing inside. The haze dissipated, revealing Raydan the Stormchaser, standing where the shattered gates once stood.

"Salminde the Viperstrike." His voice carried across the neighborhood. "Step forward and we'll spare this cluster." Raydan stepped over a body and looked around run-down buildings, many with damaged walls and windows. "Do not comply, and this neighborhood will be held in contempt for harboring exiled fugitives of Katuia. Their suffering will be upon you."

Sali slowed. This tradeoff wasn't entirely unreasonable. These Happan had shown her kindness. They'd given her knowledge. They'd offered shelter and refuge when she needed it. Now, she repaid them by bringing doom and death to their doorsteps. It was shameful. Honor screamed for her to make that sacrifice. She looked back at Raydan, who was dispatching a dozen Happans. Perhaps it was time . . .

Marhi, along with half a dozen of her fleeing rumblers, slammed into them. "Why are you two still standing here? We can't fight stormchasers. Go!" The rumblerlead wrapped her arm around Sali's waist and began shoving her toward the cobbler's shop.

Raydan strolled toward them even as the chaos erupted throughout the cluster. A few foolish rumblers charged at him, only to be dispatched quickly and violently. The blood of the courtyard ran red from the trail of bodies and debris. "Salminde! There's no escape from justice! Surrender and offer what little good you can with what short tenure you have left in this world."

The door to the cobbler's hut swung open the moment they arrived. Cobbler and Ritualist Conchitsha Abu Suriptika ushered them in quickly. "Get to the caves. Hurry!" The ritualist looked outside. "What are they doing here? How did they find us?"

He led them through his modest shop and to the back courtyard. They had just reached the entrance to the tunnel when the rear wall of the cobbler's shop exploded into another hail of fragments. Raydan stepped out from the rubble as fragments of rock, ice, and wood rained down around him. He locked eyes with Sali and stepped forward, again, and again, lightning-striding half the distance between them in a flash of light.

Hampa stared at the man approaching them like a force of nature. He looked at the temple facade, and then back at the approaching war arts master. "We're not going to make it. He'll catch up with us even if we reach the caves." He grabbed Sali and shoved her into Marhi's arms. "I'm going to buy you time. Get lost in the tunnels. Go!"

"No!" Sali reached for her neophyte, but Marhi's rumbler blocked her way and pushed her through the temple doors and into the mouth of the caves.

She shoved one of the rumblers aside and spun another to the floor as she made her way back to her neophyte. One of the rumblers threw his beefy arms around her and tried to pick her up. Sali shifted her weight and adroitly used the momentum of his slip to throw him to the ground with just a swing of her hips. She face-palmed one approaching from the side and shoved him away.

There was nothing between her and the glorious last stand of the viperstrike sect when Ritualist Conchitsha Abu Suriptika stepped directly in front of her. "We go into the mountain now or we die, and your man over there will have died for nothing. What is your choice, lady?"

Sali's chest shuddered as she labored for every breath. She hesitated, staring at the doors. It had grown silent. Her eyes watered. She could only stare, her heart torn to bits as the wooden doors slowly closed. Hampa held his ax and mace over his head, banging his right fist to his heart in a challenge. "Come on, stormchaser! If you're not a coward, come taste the bicker of my quarrels!"

Then the wooden gates closed shut, and everything went black. The sounds of muffled screams rose just outside.

CHAPTER FORTY-SIX

ESCAPE

J ian and Sonaya's plan was simple, but full of risks. They would escape the ship through the disposal chute and slip into the crocodile- and hippopotamus-infested Yukian River. Jian had initially balked at dropping down into the dark churning waters until Sonaya assured him that crocodiles and hippopotamuses were in fact *not* nocturnal, as most believed.

"It's just a superstition," she said. "Hippopotamuses and crocodiles only eat in the morning. Everyone knows that."

He frowned. "Are you sure? I'm fairly certain they hunt at night."

"It's just old mams' stories to keep you from sneaking out to swim with friends."

The drowned fist did sound *very* sure of her statement, which Jian guessed was good enough.

After they hit the water, the plan was to make their way to the west bank of the Yukian. Now, Jian wasn't a strong swimmer, but Sonaya also sounded sure of herself on this point, telling him that the waters were calm and the shore was close. The last part of the plan was still a work in progress and up for debate. Sonaya wanted to hole up in the teahouse until they could be spirited out by the masters, while Jian wanted to make his way to Kaiyu's place and head back to the temple by morning. Returning to the teahouse was risky because the kidnappers could still be around. Heading directly to Kasa's home was just as dangerous. The Cloud Pillars were not a welcoming place while under the Queen's reign. It was ten times worse during the third cycle when the very heavens and earth came alive to burn, drown, and outright slay you.

Without a doubt, there was a lot that could go wrong. In some ways, it was fortunate their escape was foiled when both Jian and Sonaya slid down the chute and stopped at an iron grate with bars as thick as his forearm. No amount of kicking and pushing or prying was going to break through it.

Jian reached his arm through to try to scoop up some water. That slumberweed had clogged his sinuses and throat full of mucus. The opening was not that low, nor was his arm remotely long enough, but he was desperate for even a few drops from the spray of the water.

Something moved in the water, and he snatched his hand back. He looked over at Sonaya, wide-eyed. "Something just moved in the water next to the ship. I think it was a hippopotamus."

"Are you sure? It's so dark out there. How can you even see—" The big blob of blubber broke the water's surface again and yawned, opening its impressively massive maw full of twisted, long teeth. It made a honking noise before sinking back into the water. The drowned fist looked at Jian, equally wide-eyed. "Wow, that thing is big. I wonder what it's doing out here. It's a good thing we have a backup plan. We have a backup plan, right?"

They had no other choice than to backtrack up part of the main chute. They found another small chute that joined with this one. This tributary chute was more gradual. The two war artists climbed their way back out of that lower chute and found themselves in the cargo hold on the lowest deck of the ship, huddling in the cold with the ship's spare parts. Jian shivered in the damp, chilly, cramped hold.

Jian's stomach was growling so loudly Sonaya heard it and offered some of her snacks. Jian had noticed pretty early in their friendship that she was always snacking. He was so famished, he took Sonaya up on her offer and tried one of the dried mushroom chips. He never could stomach mushrooms. This time was no exception as he gagged at the taste of the dry earthy slivers and spat them out, much to her chagrin.

"That was the last of my food!" Sonaya buried her head in her hands. "I'm going to die on an empty stomach. What a nightmare."

"At least we have each other," he said, after a lengthy pause.

"I really did think we were going on holiday when Mother told me to pack my bags for an extended stay."

The only way out of the bilge was a door in the ceiling that was locked on the other side. It must open to a heavily trafficked hallway, given the constant patter of footsteps passing overhead. Jian and Sonaya did not dare try opening it, so here they were, trapped, slowly freezing, and slowly starving. The two lost track of time in the darkness. Jian had lost feeling in his toes. They huddled together for warmth. Jian didn't know how it happened, but he was somehow now in a worse position than when he had been tied up. At least the room where he had been kept had light and heating.

Sonaya sniffed him. "You stink."

He shrugged. "I just went down a disposal chute. What do you expect?"

"I went down the same chute. I don't smell." Sonaya actually did, but she still smelled good.

"I was kidnapped."

She squeezed him close. "It's a good thing I rescued you."

Jian suddenly felt hot even though he was freezing down in the lower hold. Their cheeks were touching, and he was uncomfortably aware that Sonaya was staring at him. All he had to do was turn his face just a little to the left, and then their lips would meet. That short distance, however, was still too close for his anxious young quivering soul to cross.

He sighed with relief when several loud shouts from the upper levels and a thunderous stampede of footsteps broke through the tension. Both teens shielded their heads as dust and debris sprinkled over them as the wooden planks groaned and creaked. The tone from upstairs grew frantic as the shouting grew more urgent and the sounds of heavy footsteps became a hailstorm. The sounds above them crescendoed. The whistling of arrows loosing from their bows punctuated the screams and footsteps.

Someone was ringing a bell incessantly. Jian guessed that something bad was about to happen now—

Gravity shifted as the entire hold tilted violently to one side, tossing the two out of their corner perch. Jian instinctively held Sonaya close, shielding her body with his as they bounced around like corn in a hot kettle. Something sharp cracked the back of his neck and a crate bounced off his shoulder and side, and then he landed hard on his back on top of a wooden beam, but otherwise did not seem to suffer any severe injury.

Sonaya was on top of him, her head buried in his neck. She waited a few more beats to make sure they weren't going to get thrown around again, and then she raised her head to face him. "Are you all right?"

Not really. Jian hurt all over. He nodded. "Are you?"

She nodded too, and then looked around. "That was scary. What happened?"

"I think the ship hit something."

She shook her head. "No, something hit this ship."

Several of the containers in the hold were overturned, spilling their contents. Most were tools and parts. A couple barrels of what appeared to be salt and ink spilled, and then a corpse rolled out of an overturned casket. Another corpse fell out of a casket that was resting on a higher shelf. That was when Jian realized that this room was mostly filled with caskets. He was fortunate his stomach was empty, and he tried to swallow his revulsion. It wasn't that he had a queasy stomach, but dead people made him uncomfortable, and a room of them was the stuff of nightmares. Sonaya, on the other hand, did not seemed bothered that a half dozen corpses had just toppled into the cramped quarters with them.

A pool of water had gathered at the keel of the ship and was rising quickly. Whatever this ship had collided with had delivered a lethal blow. In a way, Jian was happy to see this happen. Except now they were going to drown. The pool of water was rising faster and faster. The two soon had to climb up the stairs leading out of the hold to stay above the water line.

"We have to go up now!" Sonaya began probing the hatch door.

"They'll catch us."

"Much preferable to drowning in water flavored with corpse juice."

Jian had to work hard to swallow that gag reflex. The two found the handles to the hatch and raised it just a sliver. They were in the middle of a large intersection. The ship was now listing to one side. There was also no one in sight. He could make out the unmistakable sounds of blades clashing and men screaming. The lights in the hallways were dim, some having been snuffed out. The coast seemed clear, but Jian couldn't quite muster the courage to climb out.

Water touched their feet and began to climb up their legs. Sonaya hissed in annoyance and pushed past him, throwing the hatch door open. She climbed out first, surveyed the hall, and then offered her hand. "Let's go, Five Champ."

They were a level or two below the main floor, but they could still hear the loud cracks of battle. More voices joined, with men screaming, steel ringing, and more dying. The ship was also groaning as one of the masts toppled over and splashed the waters just outside the nearby porthole.

"I don't think we should go up there." Jian had thought he was stating the obvious when Sonaya gave him a light shove.

"You're the Champion of the Five Under Heaven. Move, you wilting lily."

Sonaya liked to say that denial was the greatest compulsion, but Jian was fairly certain it was shame. His spine stiffened, and he stomped to the nearest staircase. "I'm not a lily."

She dragged him back by the elbow. "I meant for you to sneak out slowly and carefully, not pop out like a sailor's prick on shore leave."

He frowned. "I have no idea what that means."

"Never mind." She held up an arm. "Look, I'm hungry, cold, and crabby. All that rejuvenating goodness I got at that room salon over the past two days evaporated in an instant in that waterlogged morgue."

Of course. Jian shook off his jacket and offered it to her. She gave him a flat side-eyed stare. "The puppy can be trained. Better late than not at all."

"Next time, ask," he replied.

"Next time, pay attention."

Jian grabbed Sonaya's hand, and the two crept down the hallway, the swaying lanterns bringing the shadows to life dancing all around them. It would have been almost hypnotic if not so disorienting. Sonaya held up a hand and pushed him to the side. The two flattened against the wall, their fingers clenched with each other tightly, as a large group of monks passed by the next intersection. He could pick out only a few phrases.

"Can you believe it? Broadsided by a . . ."

"Can't be a coincidence."

". . . sure it's not flying monkeys?"

A figure appeared at the base of the staircase. "You five, secure main deck. You, get into the starboard armory. You three louts standing around, head to the captain's quarters and fetch the flares."

"Yes, abbot," said one of the monks. "And where will you be?"

The man looked down their hallway. Both Jian and Sonaya looked away and tried to make themselves small, hoping the shadows in the dimmed corridor provided enough cover. "I'll be guarding the Villain of the Tiandi. He's the only thing that matters."

Jian thought that was nice of the man to say. It was nice to feel important, albeit for the wrong reasons. It still felt good to matter. Wait, was that Lao? It *was* that snake! He tensed as the monk approached their hiding spot behind a stack of netted-down crates. He didn't know what they should do when Lao passed. Should Jian try to jump him, or should they hide and see if he noticed them? Of course Lao was going to see them when he walked by. This was a terrible hiding spot. It would be much smarter to not lose the element of surprise. He should attack first. Show Sonaya that he was not a wilting lily. Wait, why did that matter right now? Why should he care at all what she thought? He was definitely not a wilting lily. *She* was a wilting lily, which made no sense because she really was anything but that.

Jian was so deep in thought he nearly missed Lao walking past. Fortunately, the monk hadn't paid attention as he walked up to the door of one of the corner rooms. "Where are the brothers who should be standing guard?" he growled. "Short-sighted guppies don't see the greater . . . Hey, what happened in here?"

Sonaya nudged Jian. "Now's our chance. Let's go!"

Their apparent good fortune turned in a heartbeat. Lao sped back out of the room as quickly as he went in and spied the two still crouched behind the containers. Both men blinked in surprise at each other.

"Wen Jian, is that you?" His eyes were locked on Jian's. Relief shone on his face. "What are you doing here?"

"Trying to escape," Jian admitted.

"Well, you picked a very poor place to make that attempt." Lao held out a hand. "The ship is sinking. It's imperative you come with me and fulfill your destiny. You can be the hero again. You've been misled for so long. Come back to the Tiandi so we may guide you."

"You put a sack over my head!"

"It was for your own good, holy one! Just because you are lost does not mean you're not still a divine symbol." Lao was using that reassuring sermon voice again. Jian responded with a raised pinky.

Sonaya looked between them, confused. "Are you two friends?"

"It's a long story," Jian spat, "but he's not to be trusted."

"Isn't that because he kidnapped you?" He couldn't tell if Sonaya was saying or asking that.

"I have only been acting for your own good ever since we met, Jian," said Lao.

"You tried to have me killed after you thought I wasn't needed anymore."

"The dukes did that. The faithful only have so much reach. That's why it's important we have you, Wen Jian, to help regain glory for the Tiandi. You don't have to hide any longer, brother."

He hesitated. "I didn't do anything wrong."

"We know, brother." Lao held out his hand. "Wen Jian, listen to me. You've been gone from the guidance of the Tiandi for too long. Place your faith in the devout. We've tried to guide you to the light. Come with me willingly and be restored to the proper path."

Sonaya waved her hands. "Are you kidding me with this?"

"It was really unfair for everyone to turn on me like that."

"It's time to return to the loving bosom of the Tiandi."

"Did he just say bosom?" Sonaya snickered, and then her tone changed. "Jian, lock your mind like we practiced. He's lacing compulsion over you. Listen to my voice, Jian."

Lao drew his moon blade and pointed the flat side at her. "And who do I honor, fellow thought sister?"

"I am not your family. Our trees stand apart," retorted Sonaya. There was a sharp edge to her voice. "My war arts style is not anything like the perversions of your practice."

"Silence, faithless murmur witch. Your betters require this space."

"You can't talk to my friend like that!" Jian threw a sloppy right cross, which missed with a casual tilt of Lao's head, and then Jian felt a hard crack on the side of his knee as his legs buckled. The monk had been baiting him, waiting with that counter, and Jian fell for it. He managed to suck in one good breath before Lao squeezed Jian's neck between his biceps. Lao was surprisingly muscular. Jian didn't know the man even trained.

Having successfully neutralized him with one arm as Jian pounded against his beefy arms, Lao turned his attention to Sonaya. "On your way, girl. The matters of the Tiandi are better overseen by the gender of stronger wills."

"Is that so?" she said, taking a step forward, and then another. "Stronger than a man accustomed to barking commands and having them obeyed, eh? No communication, no sophistication, no collaboration. Just blunt narration. Do as you say, or else. You're right about one thing, though. I am a witch, one much more powerful than you."

"What womanly drivel are you speaking?" The Moon Lotus shuddered, and then recoiled, staring at his arm in confusion. "What was that? Where did that snake—"

"Hush, monk. Here's a free lesson about showing, not telling," Sonaya whispered, her words a sharp hiss. Her voice took on a more siren-like tone, strangely melodic yet piercing. "The words of the Tiandi are dead. You cling to its corpse on a bed of broken truths. All because of him." She pointed at Jian. "What do you see now, with the failed Prophesied Hero of the Tiandi standing before you? What do you feel? What do you want to tell him? Do to him? How hot is your rage at the betrayal?"

Lao's brows furled and twisted in hate. He focused his anger at Jian. His arms tightened around Jian's neck, cutting off the breath to his lips. He drew a long, curved jade dagger. Jian barely had time to open his mouth to cry out when the tip of the dagger came plunging toward his neck. Fortunately, Sonaya expected this violence and was prepared. She reached out and grabbed Lao's wrist with both hands the moment it rose and twisted her body to torque his arm into an awkward angle, forcing him to release the weapon. Then the drowned fist's leg kicked out and snapped Lao on the side of the head, and he flew like a rag doll into the wall.

She caught Jian as he fell out of Lao's grasp. She cooed, "I got you."

"You could have warned me that you were going to use me as the distraction." He looked at her, temporarily frozen. "I . . . That fight wasn't one of my better performances."

"It really wasn't," she agreed. "But things ended pretty well, so you'll get a chance to get it right next time." Sonaya liked to throw that flat playful smile at him, and he was never sure if she was being serious. Their noses touched, and their breaths mingled.

"That ability to read his thoughts is impressive." Then he realized she was focused on him now. His face flushed.

Sonaya cupped his chin with a hand. "I didn't need to use any of my skills to read what you're thinking. Any girl could. Next time, Five Champ, don't overthink it."

Someone above them coughed in that fake, patronizing way. Both Jian and Sonaya looked up to see Bhasani and Fausan glancing down at them with a bloodied metal fan hovering close to their heads.

Jian had been expecting rescue, but it still came as a startling euphoric relief. "Masters! It's you!"

"You had us worried, little lamb," said Bhasani.

Fausan looked amused. "What exactly were you two doing down on the floor? Don't you know the ship is sinking?"

"We're trying to escape," said Sonaya. "We neutralized the enemy, and are making our way to the deck to escape. I'm willing to fight through anything to protect the Champion of the Five Under Heaven." She gestured at Jian as if offering a cookie.

"This is how you escape, huh? Interesting tactic." Bhasani did not look amused.

"Is Taishi here?" asked Jian.

Fausan was grinning openly. "Everyone is, boy. You threw a big party and everyone came. Come on, I'll bring you to her."

The four made their way back toward the main passage. Bhasani was hissing heatedly into Sonaya's ear while Fausan just smirked at Jian as they turned the corner toward the stairs. The whipfinger master nudged him with an elbow, burst into a full-blown grin, and then nudged him again.

"What's so funny?" asked Jian.

"Nothing, son." Fausan leaned in. "But as a friend with experience, let me tell you beforehand about some truths when it comes to being involved with a drowned fist. For starters, you'll never win an argument again. You will never be right, and be prepared to be the dumb one, which we know you already are anyway. Take it from someone who knows." Fausan slapped Jian hard on the chest and laughed.

They didn't have to go far. No sooner had they reached the base of the stairs, Taishi blew in from the other direction, her blue sword a little more perky than usual, its aura bathing the darkened corridors a ghostly blue. At first, all Jian could think of was how angry she must be with him. He had broken sworn rules at his first opportunity and broken her trust. He must be in so much trouble. Jian fretted about the many punishments to come. Maybe Taishi would make him stand on his knees during the next thunderstorm for the next three days, again. Or maybe she would punish him by ordering him to run through forms nonstop until exhaustion. That had happened to him twice so far as well. Or maybe she would make an example of this by taking back her promise for a righteous lion. He quailed inside at the imaginary future pain. Then Jian's and Taishi's eyes locked.

His master was certainly angry with him. Her eyes were ablaze, fierce and menacing. Taishi's glare was known to knock out most men and topple towers, as he and Zofi often joked. Her mouth was pursed and the ends of her lips were flat, but he could see it. Her upper lip was twitching slightly, as if revving to snarl. A cold shiver swept through him.

Jian nearly averted his eyes, but then some small detail on her face prevented him from breaking contact. Around his master's intense eyes were deep lines: around the orbitals, her forehead, a cascade across her cheeks. She looked tired. He noticed then, the longer they held their gaze, how each of those lines gradually lifted, relaxing just a bit in an exhale of relief. She must have been so worried about him. She was shaking with concern. That or she still had that lingering cold.

Jian suddenly felt deep shame, and it made him queasy, as if having spoiled cheese in his gut. He ran forward two steps toward her and dropped to his knees. "Master, I'm so sorry. I take full responsibility for this. I beg for your forgiveness and will willingly suffer my penance."

Taishi did not look amused. "You're not dead. Good. Get up. You look ridiculous. The ship's sinking."

Jian didn't budge. "Master, I was reckless and selfish. I put you and your friends in danger. I have shamed you and the lineage. I am not worthy—"

To his surprise, his master reached over and embraced him. Her grip on him was like a vise. The quivering felt stronger than it looked. "I thought I would lose you, foolish boy."

"I won't disappoint you again." His quivering words were muffled against her shoulders.

Then she slapped him on the top of the head with the flat of her straight sword. "Never marry your name with a promise you cannot keep, disciple."

"Ow."

Bhasani cut in between them and pulled on his arm. "Come on, we *really* do have to go. The ship *actually* is sinking."

Sonaya asked, pulling up the rear, "What hit it?"

"A house." Taishi broke away and led them up the stairs. The moment was gone.

Hachi and Zofi met them once they reached the main deck. The mapmaker's daughter flew into Jian's arms and squeezed. "You soggy peanut! Why would you go shopping without me?"

"I'm sorry." He meant it to her as well. That rotten cheese was curdling inside. He briefly considered completely blaming Sohn for leading him astray when some of Xinde's words about brotherhood and snitch-ing came to mind. "We were running out of supplies so I thought I'd go."

"Did you at least buy a bundle of the butcher's seasonal smoked and sweetened jerky?"

"What? No."

"You idiot! He only makes it once a year! Why else would you go there now?"

Hachi and Jian next greeted each other like brothers who made a point to appear unconcerned.

"Hey," said Hachi.

Jian nodded. "Hey."

"You okay?"

He nodded again. "You?"

"I'm not important." Hachi shrugged. "Next time, don't get kid-napped without me, yeah?"

Jian patted his friend's shoulder. "Let's not do this again ever, yeah?"

"Yeah."

"What hit us?"

Hachi pointed down the slanted floor to the starboard side of the ship. "See for yourself."

Jian held on to the mast and made his way to the other side of the ship. He glanced over the edge and gasped. Taishi hadn't been joking. Kasa's houseboat had rammed the side of the ship. The damage to both was significant with the front of the houseboat tearing a large hole in the hull of the Moon Lotus ship. The two ships were lodged together and limping down the rushing river.

Jian looked over and saw Sohn and Kaiyu helping lift a limp Kasa from the wrecked houseboat to the deck of the Moon Lotus ship. "Is ev-eryone all right?"

"Nicks and bruises. Kasa got it the worst there when his home punched this ship. Hope he's all right."

"He'll be fine," muttered Jian. The old man always was. "Are we going to sink and drown?"

Hachi shrugged. "I'm a great swimmer. I don't know about you."

Jian was not. "Can we make it ashore?"

The whipfinger shook his head. "Fausan said the riverbanks here are too rocky and dangerous. The ship would break apart before it reached the shore. He's trying to keep us afloat long enough to reach a calmer part of the river. He spent his early years as an apprentice shipwright, so he knows his way around a boat. I think."

"He claims to know his way around a lot of things."

"I have never seen him on a boat," Hachi admitted.

The two boys watched as the connected ships swept along the winding Yukian, cutting through the thick forest and past a few more stone pillars. The river narrowed briefly as it squeezed into an underground river known by the locals as the Crack of Blind Faith. The rust-colored predawn morning blinked black as the ship passed into the mouth of the opening, through the short tunnel, and emerged on the other side a few seconds later picking up speed as it rushed away from the Cloud Pillars and into the wet plains in the lower valley.

The landscape changed very abruptly. Gone were the twisting, un-tamed trees and the haphazardly stacked stone monoliths. They were now surrounded by an open plain, with grasslands on one side and rice paddies on the other. Jian craned his head back the way they came and watched the trees and stones of the Cloud Pillars disappear into the distance.

A sudden bang like fireworks pulled his attention back toward the front of the ship. It was followed by the distant sounds of long, melodic whistling.

Sohn hurried next to them a few moments later. "Did you boys hear that?"

"Hear what?" asked Hachi.

"The whistling. Did you hear it?" The eternal bright light master peered at the horizon. He looked worried.

"I heard it. It was coming from that direction." Jian pointed straight ahead.

He noticed, for the first time in the predawn darkness, that dozens of tiny bursts of light emanated from the river farther downstream. They were followed by more faint, long whistles. Then several crashes and ex-plosions erupted to the left, deeper inland.

Sohn squinted and then cursed. "There goes the oil in our sizzle."

"What is it, Master Soa?" asked Hachi.

He raised the gourd to his lips and threw its contents back in one swig. It hovered in the air for several seconds as Sohn emptied the last remaining drops. Then he tossed the gourd out into the waters. "Jian, fetch your master. Tell her the ship is plowing straight into a pitched battle. Also fetch me another gourd of wine. Anything. I don't care if it's cooking wine. Everyone is going to need another drink."

CHAPTER FORTY-SEVEN

PALACE INTRIGUE

Qisami was still reeling from the discovery the night before that Duchess Sunri was not only a shadowkill, but the once nearly mythical Sparkle Legend. She tossed and turned even as she pretended to be asleep when Ruli woke. With Qisami so busy lately and Porla still at the infirmary, poor Ruli had been assigned to the geese crew. The odds of Porla returning to the estate staff were dwindling by the day. Rumor had it the poor girl was going to get shipped off to one of the duke's country estates. It was completely unexpected. Estatekeeper Hari did not tolerate low performers.

Qisami finally gave up trying to sleep and reluctantly rolled out of bed. Lord Aki was taking his family boating on the lake. She needed to report back to the Fourth Palace later this afternoon, but today she had a rare morning off, and she couldn't even sleep in. With a dissatisfied grunt, she rolled out of bed. Might as well get Chiafana's assignments handed out to the rest of the cell.

Qisami threw on a fresh set of plain robes and a large bonnet that covered much of her face and hurried out the door, blood scrawling as she left her room. *Cell meeting. Now. Usual breakfast place. Mandatory.*

The responses came back in delayed dribbles.

I just spent the entire night beating protesters. I'm beat. Can we make it a little later?

The choir is rehearsing my solo.

No.

I busy no friendship flower.

Qisami, irritated, cut her arm so deep it bled. *Right now, you moist, lazy cretins! Remember what you are doing here.*

In the end, she cajoled everyone into meeting right this moment except for Zwei. They could not be budged from their rehearsal, at the risk of breaking their cover. Qisami was grudgingly understanding. It still annoyed her.

She instead decided to pay Zwei a visit since the Theater of the Tethered Dreams was along the way. She walked the main servants' road toward the First Palace. She reached the long strip and walked parallel to it along the backside street until she found a curved set of stairs hugging a stone wall. She hurdled up three steps at a time to the top.

Qisami reached a grassy field where the estate's grand theater floated in the middle of a man-made pond. Yanso had the pond dug exclusively to house the venue. The theater was beautiful and spectacular, but it certainly felt like the duke was running out of creative ways to spend his vast wealth.

She found Zwei rehearsing a Gyian folksong with three others accompanying a flute. In the song, a young boy witnesses a wealthy man drop his fat coin purse bulging with gold and silver. The boy returns the purse to the wealthy man and is rewarded with a handsome silver liang for his upstanding service and honesty. The boy returns home to his impoverished family and is beaten by his father for his pride and foolishness.

Qisami listened. There were many layers to that story, but Zwei's voice was surprisingly good. They had been holding out on the cell. Qisami waited until their session broke. It would raise eyebrows if Kiki the palacemaiden barged in on the choir practicing. Artists were held in far higher esteem than the house staff.

She continued to wait for Zwei to finish their practice. She passed the time watching a group of workers struggle with the chandelier hanging from the central spire. She daydreamed of giving the wobbly scaffolding a good shove just to see it all crashing down. She sighed. Even imagining death had lost some of its luster. Her mind continued to wander, and eventually it went to the same place it often did lately: what would Qisami be doing right now if she had never become a shadowkill?

"Thanks, ba." One of these days, she was going to make good on that brood atonement: find her dear father who had sold her to the Consortium to stave off assassination, and finally collect that debt. The Consortium personally paid for that mark, and always paid well. Qisami wondered why she hadn't gone through with it yet. She hated her father for shipping her off to the Consortium, but she always found an excuse not to lance that part of her life like she'd lance a boil.

"Because he once bought you a purple pony," she grumbled. Qisami *loved* Glitter Mane. She had found out years later that her father had paid the local horselord's apprentice to dye Glitter Mane's coat every week to keep up the pretense. He had been a good father, until he wasn't. Instead of protecting her, he sacrificed her to save himself. Thinking of her father always put her in a foul mood.

Fortunately, rehearsal finally ended. Zwei approached, toweling their glistening brow and damp hair. Qisami always got a little annoyed standing next to them. They were just so tall. "What's going on, Kiki? What did you think of the performance?"

"Not bad. Better than I thought," she admitted.

"Not my favorite work, but there will be a large audience. The duke wants to put on a concert after the negotiations conclude." Zwei preened. "I think this will be my breakout."

"About to become a star, eh?" Qisami replied. Zwei must have forgotten who they really were.

"Exactly." The opera, of course, was oblivious. "What do you need, Kiki?"

"Our employer needs you to set fire to the estate main stables in the next few days."

"You said it was a little job," Zwei argued. "Setting fire to a lord's stables is *not* a small job. Especially since the duke is my patron."

"Better not get caught then. The fire just needs to be big enough so the stable hands have to relocate the horses for a few weeks."

"I did *not* sign up to this cell to be an arsonist, Kiki. Why me? The stables are all the way on the opposite end of the estate!"

"I didn't bring you on board to be the lead tenor of a choir either, but here we are. Get it done. Before your work assignment expires."

"But . . ." Zwei didn't appear happy. "Yes, boss."

Qisami honestly wasn't either. The small jobs she was handing out were fine, but the one with killing one of the twins turned her stomach. She couldn't shake off her low-key disgust. To be honest, Qisami wasn't sure what upset her more, that she had been asked to kill a child, or that she was upset about it. In any case, her stomach hurt thinking about it.

"Hey, Kiki," Zwei called as she turned to leave. Zwei's usually porcelain face flushed as they glanced at the expecting choir, who all pretended to be busy doing something else. "Speaking of an invitation, do you think you can arrange to get my ensemble to perform for Duchess Sunri, you two being so close and all?"

"Are you serious?" Qisami grimaced. "You're asking me to book you a singing gig?"

"It would mean a lot to my people, and it would really raise my profile," said Zwei. "Besides, it's not like you're paying me much, so might as well do this favor." They batted their eyes. "It'll keep me content for a little while, at least."

"Burn down the stables first," Qisami snarled. "By the way, your second soprano is off-key and can't hold a note worth a damn." She could hear the ensemble quietly tittering behind her back as she stormed toward the door. This was ridiculous. Her cell was getting cheeky. They were starting to challenge her.

Then the realization struck her, leaving her cold. Qisami no longer had a choice on this job. She was in too deep. She *had* to be fully committed to Sunri. Her cell would live and die by this job's success. Failure would likely break the cell, leaving Qisami in debt for the rest of her life.

She left the theater barge and looped back toward the Fourth Palace, this time electing to head off-strip and take the servant routes, where it was quieter and filled with fewer annoying noble kids. Much of Yanso's strip was open to the nobility. It was the center of their world. He had created an amusement park for the powerful and bought their loyalty by entertaining them. It was genius, really. The nobles lapped it up.

Qisami headed out of the south gate entrance and immediately turned back to her favorite haunt down the Night Block. It was now late morning and there were still young nobles and wealthy house sons and daughters filing out of some of the local establishments. Others, like Qisami, were heading in for other reasons.

In her case, their new usual spot, the Golden Chalice of Fantastic Earnings, converted to a congee breakfast bar by day, and the food was really good. The Chalice, as it was called, was a popular establishment and catered to eclectic groups of young people, so no one would raise any suspicion if a disparate group were to go congregate.

Burandin was there first at the same booth on the fourth floor, his regular spot. It *did* have a beautiful view of the sprawling southern face of the city. "Boss." He poured her a zuijo as she slid into her seat.

"Thanks, big guy." They touched cups and drained their first drink. "How's the play coming?"

He grunted. "Good."

"Are you being the best tree you can be?"

"Good."

"Did you kill anyone interesting lately?"

"No. Job boring." Out of the cell, Burandin stayed on his assignment the most.

Several moments of awkward silence passed. "Okay, good talk."

The silence held until Cyyk showed up. Broodbaby was shirtless under his training jerkin, which was a thin leather tunic with hay stuffed around his neck, shoulders, and joints. A large bull's-eye served as his chest piece. His bare face and forearms were a mass of welts, bruises, and cuts.

"Still enjoy being a hitting dummy?" she asked.

He sighed as he took a seat next to her. She passed him a cup. "Yanso's middle daughter thinks it's great fun whenever she draws blood."

"Where's your wife?" she asked. Burandin shrugged. *Where are you, Koteuni?*

I'm busy, Kiki. About to toss a shoe factory. I'm leading my own goon squad now. Anyone need a new pair of shoes?

Qisami struggled to mask her annoyance. *There is a suspected Shulan group working under the second finger. I need you to bring some goons and trash the place. Find me tonight and I'll give you details.*

She turned her attention to the ones present. "All right, it's just you two. Things are coming to a head. It's a particularly dangerous moment during the negotiations. I have some assignments for you . . ."

The establishment came alive as a sudden stream of children wearing boiled-egg hats flooded inside, fanning out across all floors like a plague of locusts. Almost all were estate runners, young servantborn boys and girls serving their first jobs as messengers. Several of the children spoke to the patrons in the nearby booths. To a person, everyone stopped what they were doing, leaped to their feet, and hurried out. That was peculiar. Qisami felt left out that no messenger came to claim her.

"Wait here," she ordered. Qisami joined the stream to the street level where a modest crowd was growing in size. Servants and nobles alike were clustered in groups chatting urgently. The air was charged.

Qisami found Hilao across the street with Soso, a young First Palace officer she had been having morning tea with the past few weeks. He was okay. Qisami thought her friend could do better. His war arts skill was also rather middling. Hilao saw her standing in the middle of the street and gestured furiously for her to approach.

"What's going on?" Qisami asked. "Why is everyone looking spooked? Did Saan arrive?"

"You didn't hear? Oh, Kiki, I'm so sorry. Lord Aki and his family were having breakfast on the lake. There was an accident, and their barge sank."

Qisami blinked. "Is everyone all right?"

"The whole family drowned. Even the children. I'm so sorry. Poor little Akiya and Akiana." Hilao's eyes were red and brimming as she fought back tears. She reached over and wrapped her arms around Qisami, pulling her close.

"How could this happen? It's a flat, shallow, man-made lake. You can wade across most of it!" Qisami was stunned. "You almost have to *try* to drown!"

"It's not your fault, Kiki!" Hilao sobbed. "The Tiandi will watch over them."

"Of course it's not my fault." To her mild surprise and disgust, her eyes watered as she struggled for an explanation. Could it be her fault? Did her refusal to kill one of Lord Aki's children doom their entire family? The Minister of Critical Purpose was making a point. Was she responsible for those little girls' deaths? Qisami felt a sudden strange pain in her chest. She exhaled forcefully, her mind numb yet racing time. The first time they met, Akiya gave Qisami a poisonous flower while Akiana had challenged her to a fight. Within a brief time, one ended up idolizing her while the other wanted Qisami to be her big sister. Were they dead because of her?

Qisami's breathing became labored as it took every ounce of effort not to break her cover, and still she failed. A bubble of rage burped from deep inside. She really, really needed to hurt someone right now. Qisami pushed Hilao away and fled into the nearest alley.

"Where are you going, Kiki?" called Hilao.

She ignored her friend as she gripped the top of her head with her hands. She stalked back and forth, muttering incomprehensible words, her fingers contorting into claws and digging into her scalp. Finally, she stopped as a pained and agonizing sob escaped her lips.

She wiped her eyes with her sleeve. "Fucking tears. Fuck!"

Qisami looked down at her wet sleeve and noticed the faint scars on her left forearm. Her pain hardened. Her grief took on a sharp edge. This was no accident. She knew what had happened. Qisami looked up at the sky and screamed. "You want consequences, Firstwife? You want some? Here's one for you." She jerked her right arm and shot a black blade from its sheath wrapped around her forearm into her hand. She held the blade over her skin and drew a deep cut just below the elbow. A curtain of blood began to ooze down her arm. Qisami held up her hand, and then smeared it from her forehead down to her lips. "You're death-marked now, Chiafana. I got you, today or tomorrow. You're dead, bitch."

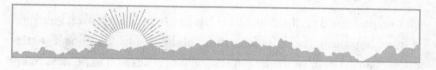

CHAPTER FORTY-EIGHT

SURRENDER

Taishi surveyed the field with mild dismay and irritation as the incapacitated *White Ship Six Two* limped down the section of the Yukian River that narrowed into the bottleneck just outside the Cloud Pillars. Sohn wasn't exaggerating. They were encroaching head-first into a siege between the Alabaster Navy arrayed on the river, against a fortified outpost of the Winged Army of the Holy Righteous on the Shulan side of the river.

The Lawkan navy, known as the Alabaster Armada, was the backbone of the duchy. Their fearsome ships controlled the vast rivers running throughout their lands. They were the only reason no army had ever successfully penetrated deep within their territory. Their ships were unbeatable by sheer number and advancements, and Lawkan sailors were the most skilled in the world. That extensive investment in the Alabaster Armada, however, was also the reason Lawkan had a laughably pitiful standing army.

At this moment, her little group had very few options. Half of Kasa's houseboat was still stuck in the hull of the Lotus ship, and they had lost all ability to steer this blasted thing. Fausan, who somewhat knew his way around boats, was on the upper deck trying to repair the broken helm and rudder, but Taishi had little faith in his abilities. The whipfinger master often claimed to have worked in several industries and to possess many skills, but all that told Taishi was that the man couldn't hold down a job. The only talents she had ever seen him be good at were talking, gambling, and fighting.

Her people were now trapped on a sinking ship they couldn't steer, moving toward not one but two enemies who wanted their heads, and—she glanced over to where Bhasani and Sonaya were tending Kasa with Kaiyu—with an injured friend who would not survive the morning. This was about the worst outcome that Taishi could imagine. It couldn't be worse unless one of the dukes showed up or the Eternal Khan suddenly galloped onto that cliffside with his endless horde of Grass Riders. That was unlikely, considering the Grass Sea was on the far side of the Enlightened States. That, and the Khan was dead.

Taishi studied the battlefield. There wasn't much to it. The medium-size armada engaged a Shulan fortification located on an elevated and advantageous mound halfway up a rocky incline. The fifteen amassed ships, a mix of arrow and siege engine junks, exchanged fire with approximately three hundred yards of beach between them.

Two alabaster ships had sunk, and the fortification's outer walls were heavily damaged and collapsed in some places. The Shulan artillery and Lawkan rainships had been going at it for quite some time. That meant the fight had started at dawn, but why? There was nothing here to defend. Why commit such a large force to an insignificant garrison? Also, why fight at night? It was Taishi's personal belief that battles at night were uncouth and inconsiderate. In a just world, battles should happen after everyone's had a good night's sleep, a hot meal, and one last gaze at the King rising in the morning.

Bhasani, standing next to her, shook her head in disbelief. "I can't believe our luck could be this bad. Isn't the God of Gamblers' supposed good luck the only reason we keep Fausan around?"

"I like him better than I like you," said Taishi as she looked for a way out of this mess. There was no way their ship was going to just slip past this armada. They couldn't get to shore without any control of the ship.

Even if they could reach one of the shores, both the White Wings and the Alabaster Navy wished them dead. Bhasani was glowering at her with disgust.

Taishi faced her. "What?" A few seconds ticked by. "Out with it, Bhasani. What's your problem?"

The drowned fist finally spoke. "They had my mam, Taishi. The Block Butchers did. They told me they'd sell her to one of the slave ships in the Ngyn. She'd be lost forever, impossible to track down, doomed to a life of slavery, even if I killed the blackmailers." Her eyes were furious. She leaned into Taishi. "What would you have done if you were in my shoes, with your beloved family's fate in your hands? Not only their death, but a long life of slavery and servitude. What choice would you have made, Taishi?"

"I would have done the exact same damn thing," Taishi said. It didn't make things right, but there was more to life's journey than being right or wrong. "Why didn't you tell us?"

"You know how extortion works. I couldn't risk it."

"Not even after it was over? Your silence made you seem guilty."

"I had no choice. The Block Brigade wanted to keep their noses clean. Told me they're always watching, you know." Bhasani's face contorted from regret to pain when she looked up at Taishi. "Do you know what hurt me, Taishi? It's certainly not your petty, casual jibes. We've been friends since we were thigh-high little girls. We battled through war arts schools and tournaments. We were partners, you and I, the Twisted Sisters. We were closer than blood, and ruled the schoolyards and the streets of Allanto. We both became notable individually, but the best part was we did it together."

"Aye, we were," Taishi admitted.

"And you bought into the insulting alibi that I betrayed all of my friends for money. After the wars and battles we've fought, that's how little you thought of me." Bhasani's tone wallowed with hurt. "That honestly hurt more than anything."

What else could Taishi say? "I'm sorry. I should have had more faith in our friendship. I misjudged you badly."

Bhasani soaked her apology in for a few beats longer than appropriate, but then she nodded. "Good. I appreciate that." The drowned fist was already moving on. "So, how do we get out of this mess? What do we do next?"

Taishi and Bhasani were still crafting inane plans when Sohn joined them. The eternal bright light was two-fisting two gourds he must have found in storage, not yet spoiled by river water. He offered one to Taishi, who did not hesitate to partake. She took a short swig, and then offered it to Bhasani.

The eternal bright light drank from his remaining gourd and pointed at the fort flying the red-and-white Shulan flags. "That outpost guards the Crack of Cracks and has been stationed here for the better part of two years. There's no strategic value, but that huge fleet came here and intentionally picked a fight with it anyway. Why?"

"To establish a landing zone for an offensive?" said Bhasani.

"Why choose a spot with an entrenched army? You find a place with light traffic so as not to give away the element of surprise."

"They were passing by. An incursion into the Cloud Pillars or just running an errand." Taishi's voice trailed off. "They were likely coming for us, weren't they?"

Sohn crackled his knuckles. "Remember when one of those filthy monks on this ship sent off a flare? I bet that's why this armada's on the move."

Sohn continued to study the fleet farther downstream. "I count a dozen ships, and is that three, no, that's one whole ship." He pulled back, stunned, and then peered at it again. "By the Tiandi, there's a six-unit serpent barge up ahead. That means there's an admiral on board."

Taishi followed the eternal bright light's gaze. At first, she couldn't make out much from the individual ships floating in the middle of the Yukian River, staying just out of range of the fort's artillery. Several of their deadly rainships manned to the gills in archers patrolled the shore in order to keep the Shulan units at bay.

Then she saw it: a long, dark, coiled ship, six large junks connected front and back like a giant snake. This particular serpent barge was larger than most, fat and wide with the hulls of six warships connected by flexible tunnels built from wooden planks and canvas to form a passageway between units. It was as impressive a beast as had ever sailed along the Yukian. Most serpent barges sailed in twos and threes, rarely fours, and were often built by the lords as a display of their wealth and power. A six-unit, however, was unheard of, and could only be ducal. Which meant, if Sohn was right about the Alabaster Armada responding to a Tiandi Religion Lotus signal . . .

"This is a problem" was all she could muster.

Sohn must have read her mind. "You're in belly deep."

Then, as if on cue, the large serpent barge facing the outpost turned until it exposed its side to them. It would be hard to slip past in *White Ship Six Two*'s condition. That was if they didn't sink first. That was also assuming the serpent ship's many artillery didn't shred their ship to splinters first. Somehow, she doubted that. If Lawkan was working with the Tiandi religion, then they would not risk sinking them if they suspected that Jian was on board. Then, as if on cue, lights along that serpent barge of six giant ships shone and spotlighted on their approaching *White Ship Six Two*.

"And Kasa's houseboat," she muttered. She said louder, "Any ideas?"

Bhasani shook her head. "We can't disembark because the Lawkan beachblades will run us down and cut us to ribbons."

Sohn said, "We can't stay on board because we're floating into the waiting arms of capture on that serpent barge."

"And," added the drowned fist, "even if we do avoid certain death from the Lawkan, who's to know the Shulan contingent wouldn't do even worse. They loathe you in Shulan."

"That feels a little strong," said Taishi.

"It's spot on. The devout are very pissed with you. You ruined their national pastime." Bhasani added, "It's fine. In time, your reputation will recover. It's healthy for you, to be honest. Ling Taishi needed to be brought down a few pegs."

Fausan looked puzzled. "So, we'll die if we stay on the ship, and we'll die if we get off. Does that sound about right?"

"And we can't steer," Bhasani added helpfully.

Sohn raised his hand. "I also can't swim."

"We can take our chances in enemy territory and go on the Lawkan side," said Bhasani. "It would be a minimally wiser decision. Smuggling *is* their national pastime. It's easy to move about there. All we need is to connect with their underworld, and poof, we are ghosts."

Taishi couldn't disagree. Besides, it would be a while before she could return to the Cloud Pillars. She had been getting too comfortable anyway. A change of scenery from a mountain to an ocean would do her some good.

Or maybe not: Taishi hated sand and was secretly deeply uncomfortable around crustaceans.

"None of this matters if we don't regain control of the ship," she said. "Can we turn this cow or what?"

"Well, actually." Fausan huffed onto the deck, breathing heavily. "I have good news. I figured out how to turn the ship. I also have some unwelcome news. I broke it as soon as I figured it out. I was testing the lever to turn the rudder when I just pushed on it and it snapped. I'm just too strong for my own good, so yeah, it's broken."

"That's just bad news then," Bhasani said.

"Don't they sort of just even out?" He frowned.

"No, not all news carries equal weight, especially if one's usefulness is dependent on the other. Who *cares* if you found controls if they don't work?"

"You're just being overly critical, again."

"And you're being an idiot again."

Sohn, arms crossed, leaned into Taishi. "One day, I'll find a love like that."

"I doubt it. Have you met you?" She shrugged. "Where's Jian?"

"Helping Hachi with something. Don't worry. I cleared the ship. Rest of the monks jumped overboard."

They could feel their center of gravity shift as the ship began lurching toward the left riverbank, taking them to the Shulan side, where an enemy army awaited them. Somehow, it appeared as if there was no end to this dire situation and things kept getting worse.

"So much for disappearing in Lawkan," she swore.

"Hey, look who we rescued," said Jian, appearing on deck. He and the rest of the children had spent the better part of the past half hour saving a small drove of donkeys who were in danger of drowning in the lower level stables instead of gathering supplies like they were asked.

Taishi rubbed her temples. "I wanted food, or medicine, or supplies. Anything. And this is what you've come back with?"

He looked only slightly dressed down. "Sure, master, but the stables were half flooded and they were thrashing about, neck-deep, all tied up. I couldn't let them drown."

That good-hearted, foolish boy. Taishi would have been disappointed in him otherwise. "The Champion of the Five Under Heaven needs to be counted on to do his duty, understood?"

"I don't regret it, master."

"Good," she said. "You have the capability and talent to accomplish both. Next time, follow orders *and* save the drowning farm animals."

Jian bowed his head. "Yes, master."

"Maybe these donkeys can swim. We can use them for flotation . . ." Her voice trailed off. That still didn't address their Shulan problem, unless . . . Taishi snapped her head up. "Fausan, how soon before we run ashore?"

"More like crash ashore." He scratched his thinning hair. "Five minutes? The thing to really worry about is if the ship will break apart once it hits something hard. My guess is she'll split in two."

Bhasani stared at Taishi. "I see that look in your eyes. You have a plan you're certain won't work but you'll try anyway."

"No time to explain. You have to trust me," she declared. "There's ten of us, three horses, and eight donkeys. Bring them all. We'll need the spare."

"And flee which direction?" asked Bhasani.

"And then where to?" asked Sohn. "We're trapped in the middle of a battlefield between two armies. We'll either get shot with artillery and arrows or run down by mounted cavalry."

Taishi didn't want to explain herself. "Just follow my lead."

Sohn pointed at the two ships closest to shore. "The moment we disembark, those rainships are going to be on us. We'll get cut to pieces by hundreds of arrows."

"Donkeys aren't exactly quick beasts," said Hachi.

A crack shuddered through the ship as the Shulan shore neared. It was followed by a low groan as the keel of the ship cut through the riverbed. One of the Lawkan rainships broke from its ranks and moved their way. A flaming streak shot into the air in a high arch and landed short of the ship. The rainship was gauging its range. Its arrows would be upon them soon.

Sohn shook his head. "They're going to pincushion us."

Fausan agreed. "He's right. We'll be riding these slow beasts out in the open with absolutely no cover."

"I'm not giving up, Jian," she muttered.

"This is madness, Taishi. This plan of yours will get us killed."

"I never promised we were all going to make it," she snapped. "But at least it gives us a chance. It gives *him* a chance."

"That is, unless someone can keep that rainship at bay," said an old, tired voice.

"Father, what are you doing on your feet?" Kaiyu rushed to his side.

The old man leaned on his adopted son. "There's a bed crossbow fixed on the bow of the ship. I'm a fairly good shot. I bet I can keep them off your backs for a bit."

"Ba, no!" Kaiyu clutched Kasa's robes.

"Hush, boy. I didn't raise you to be disrespectful to your elders." The Houtou master cuffed his son, and then pulled him close in a tight embrace. "Nor did I take you in from the streets to die needlessly under a hail of arrows."

"You can't leave me," sobbed Kaiyu. "I'm not ready to be without you."

"Don't even dream it," said Taishi automatically. "You know we don't play that tactic."

Sohn agreed. "Brothers of the lunar court do not sacrifice each other."

"Bah," snorted Kasa through painful gasps. "I'm old enough to be father to all of you. Let's be real about things. This is my last battle. I might as well grab the last of the glory before it's too late, yeah?"

Fausan intervened. "This is very touching, but if we go, we must go now."

Taishi hated making this choice. It was a circumstance that had crossed her path a few times in her lengthy career, but never with someone so close and dear. She closed her eyes. "Buy us three minutes. That's all we need."

"If I get you five, then you owe me the name of your next child." He touched his fist to his palm. "It's been a privilege, Ling Taishi. More importantly, it's been fun."

Taishi suddenly found herself biting back tears. "What do you need?"

"The Taishi I know already knows what to do. Just follow your heart." Kasa glanced briefly at Kaiyu. "Someone needs to be with him for his final test. It's supposed to be a joyous occasion. Make sure he doesn't mope too much over me. You hear?"

She nodded. "It would be my honor."

"Remember, he earned it." Kasa's voice cracked, and his eyes brimmed. "Don't you let him think otherwise."

"I will, noble friend." She bowed, deeply and formally, as if she were the disciple.

"Also," he added last, "you owe him a new house, yeah?"

"Don't push your luck."

Fausan rushed over to her. "We're about to hit land."

"What happens then?"

"Well." He shrugged. "If we're lucky, the ship just slides up all cozy to the shore, and we breeze off."

"And if we're not?"

He shrugged. "The ship breaks in two and we collapse into a death-trap to be sliced up and crushed into minced meat."

"All right." She raised her voice. "Everyone to the back of the ship, including the donkeys." Especially the donkeys, before even a few in their party, but she didn't think it was necessary for Sohn to know his place in the hierarchy.

The tired and exhausted group gathered near the back of the junk and watched in quiet apprehension as the ship rumbled and ground its way onto the riverbank. There was little left of Kasa's houseboat, it having disintegrated along the way until only a skeleton frame remained still dangling what was once Kasa's home. Taishi's focus faltered. She really was leaving Kaiyu an orphan, though he wouldn't be as long as she lived, which, admittedly, was not great collateral at the moment.

She found Jian in the back holding the reins of two donkeys and squeezed him close.

He shifted, uncertain yet still comforted in her embrace. While it might appear on the surface to be a moment of sentimentality, in reality she was preparing to spirit him off this dying wreck if things veered toward the bad luck side of Fausan's estimations. Taishi hated abandoning the others, but Jian was all that was important. The rest of them were expendable. Not being able to save Zofi would cut deep. Taishi hadn't felt that sense of loss since Sanso.

She muttered in his ear, "Stay close to me no matter what. If the ship breaks, let the donkeys go. Trust the skill of your comrades if you see them in trouble. They can take care of themselves."

"We should help them, right?" he asked.

"Yes, we should," she replied. "But not you. You stay alive."

Kasa and Kaiyu were the only ones who did not join them. The Houtou master stood next to the bed crossbow, and his son would not leave his side.

The two were embracing tightly with Kasa squeezing the boy close and speaking into his ear. He then abruptly pulled away. The Houtou master held his disciple by the shoulders, and then presented Summer Bow, the Hwang family heirloom, and relic of the Houtou style. "The staff of the Houtou is yours, my son."

Kaiyu immediately tried to give it back. Kasa shoved it into his arms and pointed at Taishi, his instructions clear. When Kaiyu refused to go, Kasa clipped him across the shoulder, scolding him loudly over the crash over the waves until the boy scurried away. Taishi caught him as he ran past and held him close. She looked over at Kasa hunched beside the crossbow. The father's eyes were in even worse shape than his son's. Taishi shared one last glance and dragged Kaiyu with her to the others.

The floor buckled, nearly throwing her off her feet. Her footing remained firm, and she held on to Jian with an iron grip. Of course the boy would forget to let go of the donkeys. Then the *White Ship Six Two* crashed into the Shulan shore of the Yukian River. As their luck had been consistent over the course of the evening, Taishi also wasn't surprised when the junk broke into three pieces. The front half, already damaged from the houseboat, completely disintegrated. The middle section caved in on itself, but fortunately the third section was spared any real damage.

Jian was still hanging on to the reins of his donkeys as the poor creatures began to slide with the tilt of the ship. Taishi tried to hold on to him, but there was no fighting the combined weight of the two asses. What was left of *White Ship Six Two* grounded to a halt and came to a quiet stop. The rest of the people, along with the donkeys, slipped into a tangle of arms, legs, and hooves. One of the donkeys bounced off the railings and flipped overboard with a panicked bray. Taishi, rather than risking plunging into that heap, tightened her grip around Jian's waist and launched them onto a fragment of the hull floating in the water, then bounded away again when the junk's mast fractured and crashed on top of them, fortunately missing the group by a few feet. Their steeds, however, were not so fortunate.

It took a minute to gather everyone. They had lost all three horses and half the donkeys, leaving only four remaining. Four for ten people were not going to get the group very far. No, not ten any longer. Nine. Taishi looked at the artillery platform. Somehow it had stayed intact. Kasa had already loosed a long rambolt from the bed crossbow and was loading another. Taishi created her final memory of her friend. She was determined to ensure that his sacrifice wasn't wasted.

Taishi took inventory. "Zofi, you and Kaiyu on that big donkey there. Sohn and I will go on foot. Fausan gets his own poor beast. Everyone else double up." It took only a few seconds to rally the group. There was surprisingly only a few serious injuries, save for Sohn, who took a splintered wooden beam through his side, and Bhasani, who suffered a bad gash to her chest and sprained her ankle. Jian was watching the eternal bright light master mount his donkey with fragments of the shattered beam sticking through him, and marveled at the master's fortitude and endurance. How could that man still be standing?

Sohn caught him staring and offered a pained smile. "The eternal bright lights never dim, boy." His smile contorted into a grimace as he slumped over his steed.

"If you are planning on hanging around, you could at least help," yelled Kasa. "Otherwise, get out of here!"

"Fausan, get everyone on an ass somehow. I'll hoof it by air."

"But where are we going?" Fausan pointed at the hills farther upstream. "We'll never make it that far, even if we weren't being chased by mounted lancers."

"We're not going that way," she replied.

"Then where?"

Taishi pointed at the Shulan army camp. "Right toward them."

He looked incredulous. "That's your plan?"

"That's my plan."

"Your plan stinks," said the whipfinger.

"I know."

The party left the beach with Taishi leading the way on a current. Jian, Kaiyu, and Zofi sat on one donkey with Jian sandwiched in the middle—Taishi insisted. Bhasani and Hachi shared another, while the two men got their own ride. That was fine by Taishi. She might have been able to make room with Sohn, but both of them were needed if they wanted to make it out of this alive. They were barely off the sand when the first drizzle of arrows from the rainship began to stab into the ground around them.

One would have killed Fausan's donkey if he hadn't caught the arrow as it fell. He shouted, "I thought you said they wanted Jian alive."

"I'm guessing the Lawkan navy has different priorities than the Tiandi religion. Better dead than Shulan for them, I wager."

The ground erupted as something significantly larger than an arrow crashed nearby. One of the donkeys reared and dumped Hachi and Sohn. The eternal bright light master was immediately on his feet, tracking the falling arrows as he helped the boy up and got him back on the spooked steed.

There was a sudden explosion as the wreckage of *White Ship Six Two* sent a geyser of water and wood in every direction, leaving just a pile of debris in its wake that slowly separated in the water.

"Ba!" Kaiyu screamed. He tried to turn their donkey around, but Zofi was having none of it.

She fought his frantic hands off as he tried to reach over her shoulder. After a brief exchange, Zofi had had enough. She turned to face Kaiyu and slapped him hard across the face. The hit temporarily stunned him, and then she threw her arms around him and squeezed him.

"He did it for you. Now keep going for him. He did it for you. Keep going for him." She repeated it over and over.

Taishi rode her current next to them as their donkey became disoriented with the many hands fighting over its reins. She would have been touched by Zofi's display of affection and support if it weren't for the fact Jian was sandwiched between the two children. Zofi was still embracing Kaiyu—and by extension Jian—when she looked up. "Pull the donkey left. Hurry!"

"Your left or mine?" Of course Jian chose incorrectly, and several arrows punched the ground perilously close to them. Taishi knocked aside an arrow that would have punched squarely into Kaiyu's back.

"Always your left," Zofi screamed. "Now right!"

Somehow, he got this wrong too.

"I'm really confused," he screamed back, as another sheet of arrows punched into the soft sand. Three dozen or so somehow missed their marks. Their recent patch of good fortune was still holding up.

The group spread out as they sprinted across the sand toward the Shulan outpost. It was farther than Taishi had hoped, but it wasn't like they had a choice. The mariner lancers had disembarked from the rainships like arrows themselves, speeding toward them at a full cavalry charge. Their stupid donkeys were going to get ripped to shreds. More arrows continued to punch into the ground around them. They weren't going to make it.

"Why are we heading for the Shulan outpost?" yelled Sohn. The master's face was pale, and he was leaking a trail of blood behind him.

"Don't they want to kill you too?" said Fausan.

"Probably," she snapped.

"Great. First the Lawkan. Now the Shulan. That's what I get for spending time with you."

It was too late to change course. The gates to the outpost swung open, and a new group of horsemen spilled out wearing the red and brown colors of Shulan. This much larger group of horsemen were now bearing down on Taishi. The ground roared with the thunderous beat of their hooves. The mariner lancers had not changed course as they closed in on Taishi's group from the direction of the river, inching closer and closer. They would broadside their donkeys a few moments before the Shulan. And then once the red and brown reached them, this entire beach would devolve into a pitched battle. This was not how Taishi had intended to keep Jian safe.

Taishi leaped away and sprinted against the wind this time as she attacked the lead mariner lancer, knocking him on the side of the head with her foot, and then planted both knees on the face of the one behind him. Both men toppled to the ground as she landed lightly on her feet. Taishi barely avoided the next lancer as he strafed by and tore through her robes. She responded by striking his horse in the side so hard it toppled over on him. Taishi watched as the falling man's saber flew through the air before plunging into the sand at her feet. She picked it up and flung it toward the nearest lancer. And then she was surrounded.

Taishi stood in the sand as the rest of the light mounted horsemen converged on her. She ducked thrusts from all directions and managed to easily pull one off his horse when he foolishly got too close. When they had slowed and surrounded her, Taishi took to the currents again, using a nearby lance as a step as she launched herself above their heads and hurtled back toward her people. It would provide her people only a few moments, but possibly enough for them to reach the Shulan first.

Bhasani, riding off to the side, screamed and would have fallen off her mount if it hadn't been for Hachi grabbing on to her.

"Master Narwani!"

The drowned fist master went limp with the shaft of an arrow sticking out of her back, nearly toppling her donkey over. Hachi held the reins in a clenched fist and managed to hold on to her body as their donkey spun in circles. A pained cry leaped from his lips.

Taishi leaped from Jian to the two drowned fists' side and helped him keep Bhasani upright on her donkey. "Keep going, boy," Taishi shouted at Jian. "Straight ahead, don't stop no matter what."

As soon as Bhasani and Hachi's donkey continued past her, Taishi had to stop. Her lungs felt shredded, and her throat burned every time she inhaled. She hunched over and sucked in several deep breaths. This was not the time. Any time but this. She swallowed the pain, summoned what little jing she still possessed, and took to the currents. She held her breath and clenched her body as she flew like a hurricane past her group and slingshotted toward the Shulan cavalry.

Taishi landed before the lead mount and fell to her knees, her head held high and her arms splayed wide. "My name is Ling Taishi, Master of the Windwhispering School of the Zhang lineage. I am a top bounty and offer my unconditional surrender to Duke Saan of Shulan. Take me to him and you will be rewarded beyond your wildest dreams!"

CHAPTER FORTY-NINE

THE SOLUTION

S ali did not know how deep they wandered into the ice caves, nor did she know how much time had passed. She, Marhi, and Suriptika hobbled down a crooked, rocky descent along with a line of Happan stragglers fleeing into the caves from all over the city. Apparently attacking Hightop Cluster was just the start. The surrounding neighborhoods, already tense with towerspears marching about and stormchasers flighting across the roofs, had erupted into protests and violence. Masau must have tried to take advantage of this situation to exterminate the problem neighborhoods in the city.

The ritualist eventually signaled a stop. He waved the torch into a side cavern where several groups of children huddled together beside several containers stacked to the ceiling. The children were quiet and well behaved, showing no sign of panic or surprise.

"Come," said Suriptika. "I have a medicine stash here. At the very least, we can calm some of your ailments."

For a while—Sali had no idea how long—they stayed in what looked like an old catacomb. Light was strongly discouraged, so they sat in darkness, listening to the songs of the caverns echoing through its canals.

Sali asked for news with every new wave of travelers coming from Hightop. There was nothing conclusive other than mass arrests and beatings. Slowly, however, a decree began filtering through to her: bring Salminde the Viperstrike of Nezra to the spirit shamans and all will be pardoned for harboring the exiled, traitorous, heretical rebel.

"Exiled, traitorous, heretical, *and* a rebel?" Marhi chuckled when she first heard it. "You covered everything, haven't you? I'm actually rather jealous."

"Work harder then, lass." Sali couldn't stop looking in the direction Hampa would have come if he had survived the fight and made his way down here.

While there was no question who won that fight, it didn't necessarily mean Hampa was killed. Most fights between war artists, in fact, did not end in death. He could have escaped, or been knocked unconscious, or taken prisoner. Maybe buried under rubble or thrown off a cliff and too much of a hassle to finish off. The last was surprisingly common in fights. For all of their many thousands of dedicated, hard hours training and honing their war arts style, war artists were often strangely lazy. Beating an opponent was fun. Having to dig him out of a collapsed building was not, and by what Sali could tell, the ice buildings on Hrusha were not exactly sturdy. The Happan stacked them like building blocks that they could remove and rearrange on a whim.

In any case, Sali held out hope that she was going to see her neophyte soon, or at least have to plan a rescue. That wouldn't be that bad an outcome, either. The settlement probably had only one jail, and she had to rescue Daewon anyway, so having to save two wasn't that much more of a hassle. The problem, of course, was Raydan. Not the towerspears, nor even the rest of the stormchasers, just the man. Sali was no match for him in her current state. The jailbreak would have to be clandestine, and Sali wasn't the stealthiest individual.

There was also the question of if she should even attempt it. The odds were impossible. Not even the Khan in his prime could take down an entire sect's home chapter, especially one as powerful as the stormchasers. Contrary to what the Zhuun believe, the Khan was still a man in every sense. In many ways, he was more humanly vulnerable than most.

"Hey, soul rot," said the ritualist, returning to her small corner of the cavern. Suriptika had been helping the jing masseuse tend the injured. The only reason the Hightop Cluster wasn't arrested was because Marhi's rumblers had thrown themselves at the Masau, buying many of the elders and the young time to make it into the caves. Many were butchered in the process, while the survivors were likely captured.

"Yes, Ritualist Conchitsha Abu Suriptika?" Sali had noticed that when the ritualist gave an order, everyone dropped what they were doing and immediately went to fulfill it.

"It's going to be dangerous here for a while. I've arranged to have you spirited away on a fishing trawler tonight. They're heading toward Tsunarcos, but at least they're leaving. The captain has agreed to pick you up on the Skull Shore just west of the gate. One of the miners will lead you through the caves to the other side. It's a long trek, so I suggest you rest, viperstrike."

The idea of abandoning Hampa and Daewon had never crossed her mind. It was not an option. If Hampa was alive, then she would not leave without both her neophyte and brother-in-law. If he was dead, then she would bring his body home.

"I'm not leaving, ritualist," she said. "I have people here."

"Don't be a fool, Salminde." Suriptika was unusually blunt. "You are in no shape to fight, let alone challenge the stormchasers. If you intend to free them, I suggest you go home and raise an army. The Masau are rounding up the Happan like cattle above our heads right now. They've been itching for an excuse, and you're it. So, while my people suffer, the least you can do is honor our sacrifice by getting to safety. That, or pick up a club and join a crew."

The ritualist was correct. Her pride was talking instead of her head. Her poor decision making had cost people's lives. So many had suffered and sacrificed and now died for her, and here she was, still being selfish during her final days. She nodded. "Apologies, Ritualist Conchitsha Abu Suriptika. Thank you for making the arrangement. I will be on that ship tonight."

Marhi appeared a while later. She looked like she hadn't slept; her face was a mix of grief and exhaustion. Her mood was grim and crestfallen. "More than half my rumblers are missing. We thought the rumblers were so tough and ready. My guys gave the towerspears hell, but the stormchasers butchered us." She wiped away a tear. "They rounded up the councils from all of the Happan neighborhoods and locked them up, including Hightop."

"Rich Man Yuraki?"

Suriptika's eyes narrowed. "That's really bad. He's the only one every neighborhood respects and listens to, and the only one who can rally and convince the Happan clusters to work together."

"We'll need to rally every rumbler squad in Hrusha if we intend to break them out of jail," Marhi said.

"They have at least a dozen stormchasers!" Suriptika snapped back.

"I'm not doing nothing, not after what they did," the girl said. "We have to do something! This dishonor cannot stand."

"You have no idea what dishonor is, lass." Suriptika got in her face. "Your *something* means an uprising, which we'll lose, just like we did the last one, and the time before, and the one before that, and every attempt to earn our freedom since the day Katuia took our island. They've been itching for an excuse to burn us out the past few years and"—he jabbed a finger at her—"she gave them one."

Marhi stared at her. "They made a demand."

"Of course," muttered Sali.

"What is it? What's the demand?" Then Suriptika got it. "Oh. Not a chance."

Sali crossed her arms. "It's a good trade."

"Hundreds of Happan have been rounded up," added Marhi. "I'm rounding up all the rumblerleads just to get organized and ready. I don't need your permission, ritualist."

"You will do no such thing, young lady." Suriptika crossed his arms. "You'll get an entire generation of our young men and women butchered by the stormchasers. Best to do what we always do and hide until the Katuia forget. And you, viperstrike!" The old, long-bearded ritualist turned on her with a sudden ferocity. "You have a boat to catch. I suggest you prepare yourself and say your goodbyes. I will send with you medicine and potions to stem the Pull of the Khan. You can live a long and full life for years, decades even. Imagine living long enough to see your family grow and prosper. Every day the sun rises will be one more day without the cursed Khan ravaging these lands.

"I assure you, if your associates are found and released, the Happan will see to their safety and arrange their return to the mainland." There was a finality to his words.

The ritualist and the rumbler had many pressing emergencies to address and left Sali to her thoughts. She sat there in the darkness, watching the Happan huddle together like refugees in their own city. Rage filled her knowing it was Katuia causing this misery, regret that she was helpless to do anything about it, and endless shame that she was running away.

If she did hide, maybe she could prevent the Khan from returning for a long time, decades, the ritualist had said. By then the spirit shamans' power over the rest of the khanate would have weakened. That would be one way to tear down Chaqra: to just live.

A true warrior did not flee battle. To be weak and passive and thankful just to have breath was not Sali's way. Viperstrikes did not run. They did not fear. They did not hide. Viperstrikes lay in wait. They struck with grace and precision. Viperstrikes seized the initiative. They stood and faced the inevitable when they were all that stood in the way of their enemies and their home. A warrior's creed and duty, however, were straightforward. For all of her vaunted reputation and credentials, Sali had never wanted to lead her clan nor be painted as a symbol to her people. At her core, Salminde the Viperstrike was a simple war artist.

Unfortunately, destiny did not care for Sali's desires. A leader did not have the luxury of such simple choices. Which battle would she choose to fight: delaying the Khan's return or the stormchasers now? Was her purpose for living to buy enough time for her clan to escape his eventual wrath, or would she sacrifice her people's future to try to save Daewon and possibly Hampa, if he was still alive? Sali did not care for either, but in the end, it came down to what was the greater for Nezra, for Mali, and her sister's unborn child. She closed her eyes. The choice was clear, but she hated making it.

"May Mali forgive me." Sali settled into a cross-legged sitting position and tried to meditate on this matter. It was a close decision, but her choice had been made. Now she had to soothe her own troubled soul and think of what she could possibly say to her sister and people when she returned without her husband and one of the leaders of the clan as well as the only other viperstrike and qualified war artist in the clan. Sali refused to think Hampa was gone until she heard news otherwise. The decision weighed heavily upon her as she struggled to find peace with her decision.

Rumblerlead Marhi and Ritualist Conchitsha Abu Suriptika found her later at some point. Sali sensed their presence as they approached. Her eyes remained closed. "Is it time to go?"

"Viperstrike Salminde." The voice was cracked and unsteady. Sali opened her eyes and saw the wetness on the girl's face. She immediately knew what this was about. "We found Hampa," the rumbler managed to choke out.

Sali allowed those words to soak into her thoughts. She had already made peace with his fate, but she still needed a moment to process the finality of it. War artists were more altruistic than most when it came to death. Hampa the Viperstrike had died in battle for an honorable cause. There wasn't more he could have wished for, except for maybe training those howlers. He did love those kids.

Sali had lost dear friends before, companions, raidsiblings. Every death hurt in its own way, and she mourned every lost life, but had also come to understand that this was the natural cycle in their chosen calling. This death was different. It had hit her in a way she never thought she would feel ever again. After all, other than Malinde, Sali had run out of family to lose. Hampa was not just a viperstrike, nor was he just her neophyte; Hampa was also the little brother she never had. He was family, and that wasn't just to her.

Everyone had their qualities. Sali was respected by the clan because of her stature and martial ability. Mali was considered the brightest. Shobansa was the wealthiest and most generous. Even Daewon dreamed big and bravely stood by his convictions, and people gravitated toward that. That was how he was able to rally the shattered clan back in Jiayi.

Hampa was different from everyone else, though. Many looked up to him—the younger children certainly did—but not because of his intelligence or wisdom, nor his competence or charm, and certainly not because of his war arts ability. Many trusted Hampa because he was always sincere, real, and honest. What he lacked in talent and skill, he more than made up for in tenacity and optimism. He also laughed, a lot. Most in the clan loved him for his affable charm and humility. Sali especially.

Sali's composure wavered but remained unchanged. She would need to mourn him at a later time. There were more critical issues at stake. "Where is he? I need to bring him home."

"At the jail with everyone else." Marhi's voice fell to a hush. "Hanging by his ankle from a lamppost in front of the towerspear headquarters. His body badly beaten."

Sali's heart fell into her gut. Her heart stopped, momentarily, and a bitter choked wail escaped her lips. The well of grief was barely contained. This news, this insult, this dishonor, this cruelty to Hampa was not something she had been prepared to tolerate. She couldn't hold back the pain any longer. "Who is responsible for this?"

"Witnesses saw stormchasers string him up."

Sali nearly cracked her teeth. "Raydan will pay. By the eternal souls of my ancestors, I will see his light extinguished and his body sunk into the waves of the abyss beneath the Grass Sea. I will grind his bones to ash and sprinkle it over the True Freeze so his eternal soul will wander for eternity. I will burn his soul to ash so that it will never find another cycle."

"Well, you can't. At least, not right now," said Suriptika matter-of-factly. "You will have to do that on your own time."

Maybe it was time to seize her destiny in her own hands. She was tired of waiting, reacting, and running, always looking for that final resting place. "Cure me. Cure me of the Pull of the Khan. I can help your people."

The ritualist looked taken back. "No, you're speaking madness, Salminde the Viperstrike of Nezra."

"Cure me," she repeated. "Attack the towerspear headquarters with your rumblers. Don't worry about the stormchasers. Cure me, and I'll take care of them." Once she killed a few stormchasers, Raydan would be sure to come.

Marhi didn't look like she believed Sali. "All of them? There're a dozen of those bastards on the island."

"That means eight, since Hampa and I already took out several of them," she replied. "Cure me and I'll take out every stormchaser while your people assault the jail."

Marhi's look was hungry and tinged with excitement. "If you're anything like the Viperstrike of reputation, we might actually have a chance. I'm putting out the call now." The rumblerlead was practically tittering with excitement as she sped off, supposedly to rally her army of wide-eyed rebels. Sali watched her go, wondering if the ritualist was right. Was Sali leading many of these young people to their deaths?

The ritualist did not seem on board with this plan, however. Suriptika clutched her shoulder and turned her around. "If I cure you of the Pull of the Khan, you release the last fragment of his soul. You know that, right? Just so you're clear, by this time next year, his banner will fly and the Eternal Khan of Katuia will ride again, and you will bear the responsibility for his return. Are you willing to accept that?"

"The safety of our people should not hinge upon my failing breath. The very act of being alive will attract every Katuia city and bounty hunter. I will become the scent that the hunters track for the rest of my life. I refuse to live like that, so cure me," she said. "And after I aid the Happan and kill Raydan, and free Hrusha of Masau and the spirit shamans, I swear upon the great cycle of my ancestors, I will kill the Khan and end this cycle once and for all."

Ritualist Conchitsha Abu Suriptika studied Sali for several moments before finally nodding. "If you wish, Salminde the Viperstrike. I warn you, though, the ritual to cure you won't take long, but it will hurt."

She shrugged. "I'm used to pain. Besides, the pain can't be worse than what I feel now."

Sali found out later that she was wrong. It *could* hurt much worse.

ACT III

CHAPTER FIFTY

NEGOTIATIONS

The drawer containing Taishi's body slab slid open with the squeak of fingernails scraping glass. She blinked and tried to shield her eyes, but her arms wouldn't obey. After a week of total darkness traveling in this corpse wagon, the glowing torchlight seared her pupils. Two wary soldiers with sabers drawn came into focus hovering nearby. She breathed deep. The cool air was refreshing after days of smelling nothing but her own body odor. It was the first breath she had taken since they stuck her with needles and put her inert body onto the slab.

An older woman with gray hair braided over one shoulder leaned over Taishi. Her pointy white hat cast her eyes in shadow. She brushed her fingers lightly across Taishi's chest, neck, and face. Her eyes were focused, yet her hands were patient. She was a different acupuncturist from the man with the awful bedside manner who had immobilized them inside this macabre transport.

The vibrating numbness she felt across her entire body ebbed as her extremities regained sensation. She tried to sit up. She must have flopped like a fish a few times before it caught the notice of one of the guards, who came to check on her.

No sooner had his hand touched her shoulder than Taishi ripped the saber from his other distracted hand and slapped his opossum-head helm with the flat of the blade, sending him rolling on the floor in pain. The acupuncturist and two younger girls in similar garb cried out and scrambled back. Only the remaining guard held his ground, but the buckler strapped to his forearm quivered so much she thought it was going to fall off. Taishi sat up and looked around. They were in an underground garage of some sort with a row of wagons and carriages lined up at one end. The other side was lined by a variety of vehicles in differing degrees of assembled and disassembled states. A dozen others were clustered against the wall being led by a more decorated officer wearing a pangolin-shaped helm.

She nodded at the familiar face. "Lord Oban."

He nodded. "It has been a long time, Master Ling. Unfortunately, I could not greet you under circumstances worthy of your exalted position."

"You mean, as a wanted criminal?"

"You've been an earthquake forming tsunamis since the last time we shared space." The lord's estate was in a far northern province in Shulan near Diyu Mountain. Northerners were eccentric people who had a flowery way with words. Oban signaled to the acupuncturist. "Continue your noble work, esteemed healer."

The master nodded to her apprentices, who resumed pulling out the next slab from the drawers of the corpse wagon and set about resuscitating the person inside. Bhasani awoke next, followed by Fausan in the far back.

The apprentice working on Bhasani looked up. "Master, this one requires medical attention."

The master approached and pulled back the drowned fist's robes. "The needles slowed the blood. Heart rate steady, but soft. She has a fever." She turned the groaning drowned fist to her side. "Arrow went clean through. Good thing the needles held and slowed the blood. She'll need to go under the knife soon, however." She looked at Oban. "My lord, this one will require immediate surgery."

"See to it." Oban offered Taishi a hand. "My lord Duke Saan is quite cross with you, but until told otherwise, you are still my respected and much-admired comrade."

"You are an honorable man, Oban the Orderly." The high lord was a high general of the Shulan armies even though he hadn't fought in a battle in his life, nor swung a sword, for that matter. Oban was a brilliant logician, however, and ran the most efficient military in the Enlightened States. Saan had chosen many of the most intelligent and educated people in his court to form his thought trust.

Taishi's thoughts had been in a haze since she surrendered to the Shulan army. The Tenth Camel Reserves. Not even to a real army, but a bunch of reservists holding down supply lines. How humiliating. It was the only Shulan army around at the time, so it wasn't like she had her pick of commanders and nobles to surrender to. The Tenth Camels had, upon reporting their capture, received orders to ship them immediately to Saan. But because they were a bare-bones unit without a substantial supply of resources, the stupid Tenth Camels decided to ship Taishi and her entire group across Shulan and into Gyian in the corpse wagons alongside the bodies of anyone of significance.

With the use of a skilled acupuncturist, they were rendered immobile with needles, their bodies slowing until they no longer required sustenance. The acupuncturist had called them delicate orchids while in this state. Unfortunately, their minds were not sent into slumber so they had to experience every moment of this excruciating trip. Worse, their sense of smell had been left intact as well. This trip rated as one of Taishi's least favorite in her long memory of lousy experiences.

The master acupuncturist and her apprentice helped Taishi swing her legs over the side of the slab. Everything ached. Being immobilized for so long had atrophied her muscles. Trying to move felt as if she was a stone statue cracking and breaking apart. The needles could do nothing for that.

Taishi placed her hand on her belly and felt the hunger burning deep. She tried to put weight on her feet and wobbled, saved only by the attentive apprentice at her side. It would have been deeply embarrassing if she had fallen. Taishi managed the next few steps across the room to a waiting bench like a newborn foal.

Sitting couldn't come soon enough. She collapsed onto a bench and immediately pawed her hand at the nearby table. "Food and drink. Anything. A bowl of rice. Dumplings. A chicken. A whole cow. As much as you have."

"You'll get broth, and plenty of it, but nothing else for at least two days, you hear?" said the master acupuncturist. "Try to take in too much too quickly, and you'll rupture your intestines and obstruct your jing."

"I don't care. Just shovel it in my mouth." Taishi swiped the bowl from an attendant and cupped the hot soup between her palms. The liquid was near scalding, and still, her angry stomach made her drink too quickly, scalding her tongue and throat, and sending burning streams down her chin and neck. Yet she continued to drink the soup in large gulps.

Taishi finished her first bowl and stopped briefly to let her breath catch up. She accepted a second bowl from the master acupuncturist. "Couldn't your man have done the job right and put us to sleep instead of keeping us conscious the entire time?"

"My apologies, madam," the master acupuncturist replied. "Budget cuts, on account of the war and all. It requires sixty needles on each of your heads to keep your minds in slumber. He probably didn't have enough for the entire group as well as to support his unit. The war effort's been a drain on everything." Her voice fell to a hush. "Besides, you were booked as prisoners, not guests."

Taishi understood the point about budgets. It didn't mean she was happy about it. Medical equipment felt like a terrible thing to cut corners on. She spilled more broth down her chin as she finished two more bowls, taking a pause only to wave Fausan over. The man immediately suffered similar burns as the attendants continued to pass the bowls of scallion egg drop bone soup around. They were soon joined by Hachi, Sonaya, Kaiyu, and then lastly, Jian. The group was silent as everyone slurped their meal.

Another group of servants entered the cavernous garage with stretchers to collect Bhasani. She hoped Oban would see to it that the others received the proper medical care like he'd promised. Sonaya stopped drinking when she saw her master on a stretcher. The drowned fist heir stood and went after her.

Taishi put her hand out but then saw Oban offer a small nod. "Go with your master."

"I'm going too." Fausan put his bowl aside and stood. Hachi moved to prop his master up. The two were still not moving well and had to mince their way behind Sonaya's procession leaving the garage.

"Why?" asked Taishi. "I could use you."

Fausan snorted and then rubbed his chin while he shook his head. "I love her, Taishi. I always thought I'd die first." He wiped his eyes with his sleeve. "If she might not make it, then, like you said, spend this time wisely. In my case, the best use of my time would be at Bhasani's side."

"Go." She nodded, giving him a slight shove. "When she wakes, tell her I forgive her."

"Really, Taishi? You mean it?"

Taishi nodded. She was too old to hold grudges anyway.

Sohn, who had just awoken, was being helped by the healers as they checked the bandages on his side. The Tenth Camel Reserve healer had pulled the wooden beam out and patched him up, but his recovery ahead would be long. He turned to face her and swiped a finger past her nose. "You didn't tell me you planned to surrender to the Shulan."

"I was making it up as I went along," she said. "So what?"

"I'm a wanted fugitive in Shulan."

"Welcome to the club. It's not very exclusive."

Sohn leaned in. "I mean it, Taishi. I'm not doing another stint in a prison mountain. At least the Lawkan prison islands have nice ocean breezes."

Taishi understood that too. "Go lay low for a bit. You still owe me."

He nodded. "I'll be close, Taishi. I won't fail you again." Sohn looked at Kaiyu sitting in the corner, his shoulders drooping as he stared at the wall.

Taishi followed his gaze. "Poor boy."

"Hey, monkey boy." Sohn tried to sound cheerful. "I could use you. Come help an old man, yeah?"

Kaiyu's expression didn't change as he joined Sohn. He continued to stare blankly at the opposite wall. Taishi's heart ached for the poor boy. The eternal bright light master sensed it too, but then Sohn had always been sensitive to grief. He went over and whispered something to the boy, who momentarily broke into his usual smile. It would be good for him to keep his mind off his father for a bit.

That left only Jian. "I'm not going anywhere, master," he quipped.

"You bet you aren't." She patted his cheek. "You are not to leave my side as long as we're under Saan's reach. Do you understand?"

"What if I have to take a piss—"

"The. Entire. Time. Do you understand?"

"Yes, master."

An attendant came for them a moment later. "Pardon, noble guests, please follow me." She looked past Taishi's shoulder.

"Just the two of us," said Taishi.

The attendant nodded. "The only two that matter, as well."

Taishi didn't like the sound of that, but she and Jian followed anyway. Her strength was returning, but she really could use a few more bowls of soup. They emerged from the underground garage and were escorted through a Zen stone garden with glowing butterflies flitting about. They crossed the rear courtyard in the back of the embassy past a slaughter-house and an infirmary, and found themselves in a much needed bath-house tucked next to a small burial plot.

The attendants were instructed to make Taishi and Jian presentable, so began a two-hour procedure to wash, style, paint their faces, and tailor them for court. Fortunately, there was a table of baked goods nearby.

Jian did not leave her sight the entire time, although it wasn't for want of trying. The first attendant tried to separate them for their fittings. Taishi politely refused. The second tried to take him away for a massage. The third attendant, a pretty young girl, tried to lead him out of the room for a bath. That was when Taishi told the little pitiful thing that she would rip the spleen out of anyone who took Jian away. No one tried again for the rest of the day.

Jian and Taishi lay on the beds as a squad of facemakers began clean-ing their skin, exfoliating their faces, and coloring their cheeks and eyes, eventually tending to every unworthy part of them that might be exposed to the duke's noble gaze. The facemakers certainly were thorough. It was rather soothing. Taishi's eyes closed, and she was flirting with the idea of another nap.

"Master?" asked Jian.

"Yes?"

"What did you mean when you told Zofi I was ready for the test?"

Damn that girl and her mixed loyalties. "I don't know what you're talking about."

"She said I should prepare to take the test soon. Why would she say that?"

"You should focus on your training, boy. Just because we're no longer home doesn't mean your education isn't important. That's all she meant."

Jian looked dubious.

Taishi was going to give Zofi a verbal thrashing the next time she saw the girl, not that it mattered. The mapmaker's daughter would dig her heels in and say she was looking out for Jian's well-being. Taishi would say it was lineage business and none of hers. The girl wasn't wrong, however. Mental preparation for the test was important, as well as the physical. Fortifying the mind for the last test took both training and meditation. That was Taishi's failing. She glanced at his powdered-white face. Not yet. Give him a little more time to grow.

The single lineage of the Zhang Family Windwhisper was both the style's greatest strength and weakness. Strength in that the entirety of the training was always focused on one student, and that the master passed their jing to their heir, keeping the lineage pure and strong. It was also the windwhispers' greatest weakness because the new master of the style no longer had a mentor. That loss of wisdom and guidance to these newly powerful war artist masters proved to be their downfall. It was the case with her grandfather, it was the case with her father, as it was with Taishi. She had hoped not to pass this weakness on to the next generation. Not if she could do anything about it.

After several hours, Taishi and Jian were done being made up and looked as good as they would ever look. Although truthfully, Taishi could hardly recognize herself when she looked in the mirror. The tailor was the last to return, presenting two sets of mahogany brown and black robes.

Jian held up the drab thing. "This is what we're wearing? I don't get it. Why did we get all made up just to wear potato sacks?"

"Because mnemonics are to be heard not seen, my boy," said Oban, walking in. He looked them over. "This will do. Come."

"Where are we going?" asked Taishi.

He didn't stop. "To see the duke, of course. Why else would anyone ever get their face painted?"

Taishi fell in step with Oban, curious about what would happen next. Knowing her former student's pride and ego, she gave herself and Jian a slim chance of making it out of this alive. She wouldn't be surprised if Saan still made her an adviser but would also not be surprised if he ordered them both imprisoned. Taishi was fairly certain her former student wouldn't have her killed, though it sometimes depended on his mood. Dukes were fickle.

"Your instructions," Oban said, "are to join Duke Saan's trust during these negotiations."

"For how long?" asked Taishi.

"Until told otherwise," the lord snapped. "Each day is about six hours."

"This is ridiculous. I'm not standing for six hours, Oban."

"What's the problem? The mnemonics stand around all the time."

"Why don't you carry your negotiations standing then?"

Oban sighed. "Saan insists on attending the negotiations in full galleria dress armor. He'll fall over from exhaustion if he stands for more than an hour."

"Why do we have to stand while he sits?" she argued.

"Because Saan's the duke of Shulan, and you're a wanted fugitive. These negotiations are where you're needed. That's how you serve Duke Saan." The lord stopped. "This isn't a request. You surrendered to *us*, remember?"

She bit her lip. "This is a terrible plan. You're sending two of the most wanted fugitives in the Enlightened States to attend negotiations among three dukes and their entire courts? Are you trying to get us caught? Might as well do it yourself and collect the reward."

"I wouldn't worry about it," said Oban. "No one is going to notice you. Do you think your faces are seared on everyone's memory just because you have a bounty on your head? There's a civil war raging throughout the states, the Kati are already beginning to chafe at the armistice terms, and we're entering a bad third cycle. Nobody cares anymore, Master Ling. You're yesterday's news. They won't recognize you."

"Hey," Jian protested. "I got kidnapped back—"

Taishi cut him off with a raised hand. There was no winning this argument. She might as well try to negotiate what she could get out of this. "Fine, but Jian stays with me."

"The bounty on him is even bigger. Why risk it? Our people can safely protect him back at the duke's guest palace, or better yet, we can embed him in the army camp. He'll be untouchable there."

"He is safest by my side. Doesn't matter if he's disguised as a mnemonic, right?" Taishi had little leverage but had to make a stand somewhere. "This is my only demand. He stays with me at all times as long as we're under the duke's service."

"Prisoner demands." Oban snorted. "Sure, fine, whatever. He can stand with you. The duke will likely want an audience with him anyway." Oban gestured to a man wearing a luxurious pine-green robe. "The Voice of the Court will check you to see if you are presentable to the duke. The meeting starts within an hour." He stopped and sniffed. "The two of you bathed, good. You all smelled like cadavers who shat over themselves."

Taishi and Jian were shuttled to another room where nine other similarly robed individuals were awaiting transport. They fell in easily enough as a sturdy but austere carriage rolled by to pick them up. A troop of Shulan winged riders provided an escort as they pulled out of the embassy.

Jian was ogling the colorful cityscape through the narrow slit of the window. Taishi understood the awe. Everyone's first visit to Allanto was a revelatory experience. This must be the most magnificent city in the world, rivaling even the Celestial Palace. Every building looked related to its neighbor in design, height, and structure. Dazzling lights assaulted his senses, demanding his immediate attention. Sparkling lanterns hung from poles at every block while sculptures, paintings, and advertisements adorned the spaces of every wall. It was all overwhelming, yet he couldn't look away. Even the people walking the streets looked as if they were mystical beings sent from the heavens. Men with long queues of hair wore expertly tailored robes and traveled alongside women with exquisitely painted faces and luxurious dresses. Large groups of passengers rode on fancy palanquins and intricately carved rickshaws. Even the magistrates and guards looked like actors in an opera.

They turned the corner and passed immense, intricately carved sculptures, spectacularly designed vector walls, and beautifully colored tiled mosaics. Jian's jaw dropped when he saw a peculiar crooked tower rising around the bend in the road like a barren tree. It must have been at least seven stories tall.

"This place is like a magical realm of heaven!" Jian spoke in a hushed voice.

"Welcome to Allanto," said Taishi.

"It's beautiful." The Gyian capital was truly as enchanting as the poems claimed.

Something smacked against the side of the carriage. Jian startled and pulled back as a small amount of fruit juice sprayed through the window slit. The next thing to hit were bits of crumbled cheese. A hail of rocks and bricks clattered against the carriage walls joined by a chorus of boos and raised pinky fingers. More good fruit and vegetables were wasted on them by the crowds as they passed.

"And welcome to Allanto," said Taishi again. "This pretty rat hole is beautiful, but it's not kind, nor nice. Just terrible people who take far too many baths."

"How can you bathe too often?"

"Do you know how much indentured servitude labor, maintenance staff, and water a city needs if each resident takes one bath a day? Why do you think they carved out that lake behind the city?"

That shocked Jian more than anything else. "One bath a day? What a bunch of indulgent peacocks! Who do they think they are?"

The Shulan contingent turned and proceeded up a slope leading to the upper rise of the city. Nearby was the tower called the One Finger of

Heavenly Defiance, which was easily the tallest of the five towers. That thing must have been ten stories! It was also the heart of the Gyian court. The carriage entered an open field at the center of the city and continued toward a giant walled structure that looked like another city *inside* this one. Jian gawked as they approached a giant set of double doors that glistened like a silver star under the King's light.

"Where are we going?" he gasped, awed.

Taishi glanced out the window. "You're about to find out what people with far too much wealth spend their money on."

They joined a steady procession of wagons and carriages passing through the massive silver gates and entered an entirely new section of the city, except the buildings here were even taller and wider, and even more beautiful and divine than any other section of the city in the lower valleys. As they continued down the wide streets, the scenery became more beautiful with each passing moment. Jian gasped when they pulled alongside a carving of a noble warrior wielding a dragon straight sword that was as tall as he. The display had to be at least two stories tall.

"Which hero is that?" he asked.

"That's supposed to be Duke Yanso."

"Does it not look like him?"

"It looks just like him," Taishi replied. "But the Yanso I knew never met a chair he didn't want to lounge in. Clever and conniving as a feral alley cat, but lazy as a lion."

"Aren't lions strong and deadly? Sunri's known as the Desert Lioness, no?"

"Lionesses are hardworking and strong. Lions are just lazy bullies."

Jian continued to gape as they passed yet another set of walls and turned into an extra wide street with fine towers and palaces flanking both sides. In the distance, at the center of a massive intersection, was a familiar building, and something he still visited often in his dreams. "Is that the Celestial Palace? How is that possible?"

"It's Yanso's First Palace, which is modeled after the Celestial Palace. Xuanshing, may his greatness ever last, had forbidden the duke from building a palace larger than the emperor's residence, so Yanso had this built exactly one foot smaller along every dimension. It's all ego and too much wealth." She gestured for Jian to pull away from the window and return to his seat. "Get some rest. It's going to be a long day."

Taishi pulled away from the window and jostled for space on the bench, earning an annoyed sniff from the man sitting next to her. He had ridden the entire time with his legs splayed. She held his gaze: one, two, three . . .

The pasty-faced middle-aged man closed his knees and leaned in the opposite direction for the rest of the way.

CHAPTER FIFTY-ONE

STAFF

Qisami stared at the procession of court wagons slogging through the outer gates and down the strip toward the First Palace. Lines of hooded, robed individuals were already in the courtyard, unloading supplies from several parked transport carriages and streaming into the Wish You a Smooth Life Amphitheater alongside lines of mnemonics, advisers, and other officials, all of them ambling up the stairs in a neat line, like ants. This was part of Saan's thought trust, by their black and brown robes. The Caobiu arriving at the east gate were in their yellow and red, while the Gyian who kept quarters at the palace would be in their usual black and white. Yanso's thought trust was by far the largest contingent of the three, and also the best dressed. The other dukes looked positively drab next to him. Allanto always did have the best tailors.

Qisami continued to watch the procession from the fifth-story window of the palace. She wasn't sure what happened next. The negotiations were finally commencing. She was anxious for this job to be concluded, especially in the aftermath of the Aki family's deaths. She never did find out what happened all those weeks ago. Chiafana did not claim credit, and it was beneath Sunri. It could be any one of several factions involved in these negotiations. Or it could simply have been an accident. Qisami didn't believe that for a second.

The Minister of Critical Purpose had disappeared since their ride in the carriage, probably for the better. She *could* be busy and preoccupied with Saan arriving at the city, or she could be avoiding Qisami, for good reason. There was no such thing as coincidence in a nightblossom's line of work. Until confirmed otherwise, Qisami was certain the deaths of the Aki family were on the minister's blood-soaked hands.

Sunri, on the other hand, had practically adopted Qisami. The duchess had summoned Qisami for tea every morning before negotiations began. The two would further bond over their shared history in the training pools, as well as discuss the latest chatter surrounding the talks and possible marriage between Sunri and Yanso. Qisami knew she was being pumped for information, but she was willing to aid a fellow training pool sister. Sunri even sounded saddened by Aki Niam's passing. While he had proved to be a difficult adversary during the talks, she appeared to have liked the man and his family.

This morning was the third day of the negotiations and the intrigue was ramping into full swing. The gossip between the servants mostly consisted of salacious stories. One of the dukes was certainly winning the hearts and minds of the audience. Yanso partook in orgies every night. Sunri murdered men and bathed in their blood to stay looking so young and beautiful. And Saan, the handsome and noble painted tiger, spent every night meditating under the blue light of the Queen in the shade of the cashew Tree of Life. He'd uprooted it from the Vauzan Temple of the Tiandi in Vauzan and transported it here to Allanto, so the great duke could pray and receive wisdom from his ancestors.

The three dukes could make an alliance in one morning if they trusted one another, but they didn't. That's why these talks had been happening for the better part of a cycle. No one trusted anyone, which made for a shaky foundation for an alliance. But would there be a wedding?

Qisami pulled away from the window and walked to the arena at the bottom of the circular amphitheater five stories down. Yanso bragged that the Wish You a Smooth Life Amphitheater had the best acoustics in the world. Qisami wasn't sure what that meant, but it was true that anything said in the pit could be easily heard up to the highest seat. The lower rows near the dukes were reserved for the guards. After them, in the ring outside the inner circle, were the dukes' advisers. Above them were the mnemonics, and then the estate staff and runners.

That arena was the heart of Wish You a Smooth Life. Down in the center was where war artists dueled for honor and glory, where operas staged grand performances, and where the noblest of executions were held. The amphitheater was now hosting its most important production with the gravest stakes. A great battle was waging along three tables forming a triangle at the center of the arena. The large circular pit also housed three grand, tented pavilions each bearing the colors of their duke. This was where the negotiations among three of the most powerful people in the world would take place. The outcome of these talks would reverberate across the Enlightened States and shape the Zhuun's destiny for generations.

As far as Qisami could tell through the excited chatter among the staff, the negotiations had so far been full of surprises. Yanso, as the wealthiest and most powerful of the three, dominated the discussions. In the first days, it was clear he had the most sophisticated court among the three. He was always better prepared and more knowledgeable than the others, thanks to his thought trust that easily dwarfed the other thought trusts combined. After the first two days, Qisami had thought the man might make a rather good emperor. Yanso knew the throne was his regardless of how these talks shook out.

Saan was also making his presence felt, throwing his weight around like an arrogant rooster. It wasn't his requests that were overwhelming, but the magnitude of them. What he lacked in Yanso's cerebral calculations Saan more than made up for in charm, quantity, and tenacity. Saan wore the others down with his persistence until they capitulated to his demands. Qisami had never met another man who could utter so many words in one breath.

The real surprise and deep disappointment so far had to be Sunri's mediocre performance. How could her beautiful, smart, and cool assassin sister perform so poorly? Qisami had expected to see the cunning and dangerous woman of legend, the great general and the beguiling siren, the bloodthirsty killer every little girl aspired to be. Instead, Sunri the duchess seemed off her game and was getting outmaneuvered in every exchange. She was slow to react, prone to small mistakes, and the two men were making her pay for every one of them. They bullied her positions and often pushed her out of trade deals, and for some reason, Sunri took it. The duchess was wilting under pressure, and it infuriated Qisami, but there was nothing she could do about that. It cut deeply to see her newfound idol not acting as competently as was expected of her. Today's meeting was crucial for these negotiations. Not that any of it mattered to Qisami. All she could do was her job, which was to protect Sunri at all costs until these negotiations concluded.

Since Qisami no longer had children to look after, Hari had reassigned her as a server for these negotiations. She was spending this morning serving drinks to a group of Gyian advisers in one of the upper balconies overlooking the arena. That was the annoying thing about the job of serving at the dukes' negotiations. They would stretch the entire day, which meant all the palacemaidens had to be present at all times. Breaks were allowed only when the dukes recessed. These were exhausting days, even for a trained assassin.

Serving these entitled peacocks was exhausting. Qisami continued working at her station when the negotiations commenced, waiting as the three dukes talked around a circular table in the center of the arena. She looked up as robed administrators began to file into their rows. Qisami went to attention next to Hilao, who happened to be the other palacemaiden assigned on this deck.

"Can you trade stations with me? Serving these lords gives me jitters," Hilao asked nervously. "Lord Mubaan's been leering at me ever since he arrived."

The taxlord, wearing a hat shaped like the bust of a decapitated man's torso, had attempted to woo Qisami to his bed two of the three nights as well, becoming more persistent with each encounter. It was only a matter of time before he tried to force the issue on one of the palacemaidens as lords oft tried with servants.

"Sure, I'll swap, no problem." Qisami had never killed a taxlord before. It sounded like fun.

The five-minute gong sounded, a deep reverberating echo.

Everyone from the advisers to the servants to the mnemonics scrambled to their assigned roles. Even the elite guards had to adjust their ranks to their proper positions. That was the way of palace life when it came to nobility. It was always a game of knowing when to put up the act of servitude and when to take breaks.

The one-minute gong sounded, this one higher pitched.

As if by some unspoken agreement, everyone took their places and froze, as if time had stopped. The seconds ticked by. Then, the three dukes entered the arena, chatting amiably among themselves as if old friends. No, more like family. Even though they were the most powerful people in the Enlightened States, their branches had all grown from the same roots. They had a shared history, and would be the ones who determined their people's future.

The second session of this day continued early into the evening. The hours passed as Qisami tended to the stupid needs of these court officials and thought trusts. The negotiation's first intermission couldn't come quickly enough. As soon as the gong struck, the spectator areas of the amphitheater came to life as advisers, mnemonics, and servants shuffled about.

Qisami was still standing on the balcony of the upper deck people watching when she smelled a hot, slightly ginseng-scented odor. She wrinkled her nose and slipped to the side before turning and bowing. "Taxlord Mubaan, I was hoping to run into you."

"Oh, it is a pleasure and surprise to see you here, palacemaiden." The lord's feigned shock made him look like he was about to pass gas. "I have been so looking forward to continuing our riveting conversation from yesterday."

That was a lie. He had ogled, pestered, and talked at her for the better part of an hour. Qisami barely got a word in as he monologued about how amazing and wealthy he was. She had managed to get away briefly, but he later stalked her during the last portion of her shift. She heard that he had gloated to his friends about having used her without paying the bill. The servants' network took care of their own and made sure word had gotten back to Qisami. It was a well-intended warning for the servants to be wary around a certain lord. In Qisami's case, however, she'd had a rough couple of days with both her real and fake jobs. She could use a diversion to blow off some steam. Worse, she had learned this morning that he was only a junior shade taxlord, not even the real thing.

Qisami bowed formally anyway, lower than necessary. Mubaan probably considered it flattering, but she was using that time to scan for potential witnesses. The only other soul within sight on this balcony was the guard standing at the doorway. Qisami caught his attention. The guard nodded and slipped out of the room. She turned and was startled to see the taxlord's face close to hers. That stink of ginger kicked her gag reflex.

"I thought about it all night," he purred. "Why don't—"

Qisami didn't bother trying to be subtle about it. Her hand flew between his many layers of robes and undergarments like a professional salon girl and found exactly what she was looking for. She gripped one of his testicles between her thumb and forefinger and applied just a touch of pressure.

"What are—?" Mubaan gasped, suddenly standing erect.

"Do I have your attention now?" she asked. "Shh, don't say a word, *Junior Shade* Taxlord Mubaan Soy, third son of an even more minor lord from a farming settlement." She tightened her grip on the grape. "You will take your disgusting hands off every girl in the good Lord Yanso's estate. Is that clear? If you don't, then know that every drink that passes your lips, every morsel that you chew, every bed that you sleep in could be flavored by the guts of plague rats."

He hunched over in nervous pain as she held the testicle between her fingers. "You dare threaten—"

Qisami squeezed until it burst. Soy squealed and collapsed in a whimpering heap on the floor. "You cunt. I'm bleeding."

"I warned you not to say a word. You touch another girl and I'll come back and burst your other ball, understood?" When he didn't answer quickly enough, she broke a rib with a swift kick. "Understood?"

"Yes, please, spare me. I promise. Don't hurt me again. I . . ." Soy curled into a fetal position. "I need a doctor. Help, I need help."

Qisami nearly hit him again, just for fun, but decided it was time to leave the crime scene. She left the room in time to see the guard return. She lowered her eyes at the guard as she passed. "The lord had an accident. He will require a healer."

"I'll send word to the infirmary." The guard nodded. There was a healthy understanding between the guards and the estate staff. Each side took care of the other. She was halfway down the hall when she heard the guard enter the room, shouting, "By the Tiandi Mosaic, what happened, my lord?"

Assaulting a nobleman was a capital offense, but Qisami wasn't worried. Most lords couldn't recognize any of the servants' faces anyway, regarding them as something akin to furniture. The Mubaan family was a minor family and he was a minor son. Soy would be laughed out of court for begging the duke to punish a servant girl for him, because he couldn't do it himself. Lastly, the dainty men in these courts placed far too much emphasis on their very delicate organ. For the taxlord to admit this injury would be like calling himself half a man. To accuse a palacemaiden of the crime would only make his mockery worse.

Qisami picked up the pace as she made her way down a servant corridor. Even if there was little reason for concern, it was never smart to be near the scene of the crime. She hurried down a stairwell to the main level and exited the amphitheater from the rear. She was crossing the small courtyard with the life-size Siege game pieces when a plain, unmarked war carriage pulled up. The door swung open.

"Get in," said a voice in the darkness.

Now, Qisami was usually not against getting into a stranger's carriage. More often than not, she came out ahead regardless of whatever happened next. She recognized the voice, and climbed inside, sitting opposite the duchess. "Your Grace."

"I need you to do something, Qisami." Sunri looked pale. There were dark rings around her eyes. "I just received word that Yanso is sending an offer to Saan. I want you to intercept the courier and take their place.

Listen to the interaction within the pavilion, and then report back to me. Take out the courier however you like. A decoy squad will clean up the mess. Just hoot."

"Hoot? Like an owl?"

Sunri nodded. She peered out the window as the carriage rolled to a stop. "Our eyes said the courier is crossing a wide loop through the north servants' passages, trying to avoid suspicion. She should be passing by the kitchen intersection soon."

Her answer was automatic. "Yes, Your Grace. I won't fail you."

"You're my sister, Qisami. Do not call yourself anything less when we are in private." To her shock, Sunri, the Duchess of Caobiu, reached over and embraced her.

Qisami blinked again. This time, she had to choke back the sudden rush of feelings. "Yes, sister. I won't fail you. I swear it."

She stepped out of the wagon and found herself outside the entrance to the kitchen, across the street from the amphitheater. Exactly where she needed to be.

"They couldn't have given me more time to prepare?" she muttered, breaking into a sprint. What if she had said no? Of course, Sunri knew she wouldn't say no. A sister wouldn't do that.

Qisami continued through the kitchen, past the head cook bellowing at his many apprentices. A line of ovens roared against one wall, and along the other, stoves belched smoke as flames flared around large metal woks. Hosting dukes was always an enormous undertaking and an extraordinarily costly affair. A lord had to be immensely wealthy if they wanted to join a duke's inner circle.

None of the cooks gave her any notice. Like the guards, the estate staff had a close working relationship with the cuisine collective. Qisami passed through the kitchen and hurried down a circular ramp that led to the lower level in the north part of the amphitheater. This was a shadowkill's natural environment. The estate workers called it the catacombs due to its dimly lit, narrow, winding passages. It reminded her of the underground labyrinths her training pool had used in Manjing for weeding out weak candidates.

Qisami scanned the area and crawled forward. She disappeared into the nearest shaded corner and emerged from the opposite end near the ceiling. As soon as she felt gravity pull her down, Qisami palmed the ceiling to form a slight connection with the shadows. That small connection coupled with her feet pressing lightly against the adjoining wall created enough pressure for her to stay hidden in the corner of the ceiling. She could hear the dukes' voices echoing through the walls of the amphitheater, their muffled words just muddled enough for her to be unable to make them out.

Several minutes ticked by. Qisami didn't mind the wait. It was like foreplay, the anticipation before the kill. Two white-clad guards passed underneath her hiding spot, chatting amiably. One carried an extra-large tower shield; the other, a long pike resting on his shoulder. They were holding hands. How cute. Infernal Twins, as these pairings were known, was one of the predominant Gyian war arts schools with hefty contracts with the army. Close working relationships often turned romantic. The next three to pass were two errand boys and a mop girl. A trio of nobles strolled from the opposite direction at a brisk pace, chatting about an orgy. Perhaps the rumors spread about Yanso weren't so slanderous.

The courier appeared shortly after, walking quietly, her pose meek. There was no reason for a courier to use these underground tunnels otherwise. She was a younger woman, pretty, with hesitant eyes, wearing the standard robes for a high court palacemaiden several ranks above Qisami. Interestingly, Qisami couldn't place the face. After half a year, she had at least a passing familiarity with most of Yanso's estate staff. A fresh new face like this serving the duke probably meant she was on the duke's private staff. Interesting, although it suited Qisami all the same. She preferred assaulting people she didn't know or like.

Qisami released her suction with the shadow and dropped silently on the palacemaiden. The shadowkill's sleeves fluttered loosely as she descended upon her mark and settled around the palacemaiden's neck like a scarf on a winter's day. As soon as she found her grip, she cinched into a tight squeeze. The girl was already unconscious by the time Qisami's feet touched the floor. She released her hold and let the palacemaiden slump over. The girl was going to wake with a nasty sore throat but should be no worse off.

Qisami looked over her shoulder and saw the orgy-chatting nobles standing directly behind her and sank into a defensive posture. So much for doing this quietly. A new figure emerged from behind them and came to the forefront. Qisami's decoy.

Qisami hesitated. "Hoot?"

"We'll take care of the body," said one of the nobles.

"She's still alive," said Qisami.

"For now."

Another picked up the wooden chest that the palacemaiden had dropped and offered it to her. "They're expecting you."

Qisami accepted the package without another word and proceeded toward Duke Saan's pavilion.

CHAPTER FIFTY-TWO

EYE OF THE STORM

Jian awoke to a sharp elbow in his ribs. He squeaked and then inhaled. The sound of wind sucking into his nose carried across several aisles of mnemonic officials standing in their thought trust. It earned him a smattering of dirty looks again. He had barely made it through the first two rounds on his feet, but the third had destroyed him. Six hours of standing about in abject boredom during the negotiations between the three dukes was a fresh torture.

Jian had come to the Wish You a Smooth Life Amphitheater with grand expectations. These negotiations had been the talk of the city ever since the Caobiu came last cycle. The gossip frenzy had now reached new heights with the Shulan's arrival. People were excited and terrified at the same time. Even more dramatic, it was being held in Yanso's private amphitheater, which Jian found strange. What was the point in building a large amphitheater just for yourself? In any case, he was looking forward to the entertainment. There should be battle, drama, defeat, and jubilation. Jian had wanted to see blood in these talks, metaphorically or physically, he didn't care.

Instead of the anticipated fireworks, Jian got three people sitting across from one another at a triangular table bantering on for hours and hours, and they were so far away he couldn't see anything anyway. He was pleasantly surprised by how well the sound carried, however.

His patience had worn thin and then his attention waned, as did his focus. There was nothing to do but stand there, and his feet were aching. Taishi insisted he stay within arm's reach and wouldn't let him venture more than a few steps away, not even to relieve himself. He ended up falling asleep on his feet in his hot, sweaty, and rather itchy robe. If the man who made this was Saan's tailor, then the duke had either deplorable taste or the tailor was taking him for some sort of long con. At least their robes looked the part of mnemonic monks.

The first session centered around whom would be tasked as the military leader of their unified army. Yanso thought it should be him because he was the head of the alliance. Sunri thought it should be her because she was the best field commander. And Saan thought it should be him because he was the most popular among the people.

The affair had been fascinating for the first fifteen minutes, and then it became repetitive and dull. Thankfully, he was able to understand much of what they were talking about, due to Master Soa. Sohn's timely lessons about the court had been particularly useful. It almost made up for him putting Jian in this position in the first place.

Jian immediately rescinded that thought. It was one of Master Narwani's lessons: when it comes to oneself, always be honest with the truth.

"Time to own your stench," he grumbled. Jian could have refused to come. He could have avoided the temple, as ordered. He could have stayed in his cot the entire time knowing there were people on the lookout for him. Sohn might have been the master in charge of the household, but Jian *knew* better. The responsibility of not acting upon those truths was on him.

Throughout the back-and-forth, mnemonics and advisers continually left their stations to deliver handwritten notes to the advisers, who would then confer among themselves before drawing up a recommendation for Oban to present to Saan. The duke then would have the final say. Yanso's thought trust was the most active, almost frenetic as the large contingent of advisers, officials, and mnemonics scrambled up and down the stairs and across the aisles like ants over discarded slop.

The only way to distinguish the individuals in the thought trust was with the variety of creatively shaped hats worn to mark each person's role. The dolphin-head hats were the mnemonics storing information about maritime commerce, while the dolphin-tail hats kept an eye over the Grass Tundra and the True Freeze. The weeping willow hat recorded the census and demographics, while the hat that looked like the silhouette of a fat man was in charge of roads and trade. The head-on-a-spike and sunflower hat mnemonics often worked together. One was responsible for the military coordination while the other dealt with supply chains. Ironically, the chicken-head hat predicted the weather while the cloud-shaped hats managed the duchy's supply of chickens.

The system had been designed by Yanso as a method to manage the information that was eventually fed to the emperor. The idea of having a knowledgeable and well-informed court soon became as valuable as an army in the field. A powerful thought trust with access to an extensive whisper network is most lords' favorite preferred method of warfare. This was one advantage Yanso had always possessed. His thought collective was easily twice the size of the others. Sohn had mentioned several times during their lessons that the real alliance that should terrify the nobles was if Yanso's thought trust made an alliance with Dongshi's spy network and his secret police. It was a good thing the two men hated each other with the passion of all three moons.

The second session ended after six long hours with each of the dukes retreating to their pavilions. They would then consult with their advisers before changing and refreshing themselves for dinner and then were entertained with a performance by the esteemed Songgua Academy dance troupe.

As soon as the end gong sounded, the mnemonics slumped into their seats. Standing and thinking intensely was exhausting. Jian wouldn't know. Most of his thoughts rarely lasted longer than a minute.

Taishi hadn't moved the entire time. He nudged her. "Should we find a place to sit too? I'm hungry again. Do you think—"

Her eyes were narrow, staring in the direction of the duchess. "What is that woman doing? That was the sloppiest negotiation I've ever seen from a duke, let alone from Sunri. Yanso is swindling her while Saan is stealing her lunch. She should be shoring up her holdings and staying firm on leadership over the military. She has the most generals, for Tiandi's sake. Instead, she's giving Gyian everything and setting Caobiu up as a vassal state." Taishi pursed her lips, and her eyes widened. "She's playing them. She has to be." Taishi grabbed the sleeve of the nearest mnemonic. "You, I need to get a message to the duke. How does this note passing thing you do work?"

The man wearing a blue hat shaped like a cucumber tried to pull away. "Session's over. We're recessed."

"I don't care. I need to get a message to him right now."

The man squinted. "Wait, who are you? I've never seen you before."

Taishi reached out and yanked the pudgy, button-nosed man closer with such force he nearly fainted. "You will go jot down a note telling him that his newest advisers require a word with him right now. Do you understand, or do I need to rip your spine from the gaping hole of your decapitated head?"

This time he actually did faint.

"Mnemonic Roha," a voice said. "You are summoned."

Jian and Taishi glanced up to see a courier standing at the end of the aisle.

"Us?" asked Jian.

"Her," the man said.

"He's with me, my lord, as my auxiliary."

"Follow." The man did not look like he believed her, nor did he look like he cared. "Duke Saan waits only on the Tiandi."

"He's the nice one, right?" Jian whispered to Taishi as they fell in behind the courier and walked down the long flight of stairs toward the pit.

"'Nice' is an overly broad, very relative term," she replied.

"Sort of like when you say I'm almost ready," he blurted. Since she'd told him one night that he was ready for the test, it had completely taken over his thoughts. "You don't mean I'm ready, right?"

"What are you going off on, boy? Focus on the task at hand."

Jian bristled at being shut down again. Why did Taishi keep avoiding this conversation? Lineage was one of the most important matters for any war art style. It should be especially important to the Prophesied Hero of the Tiandi.

He stayed in her shadow as they continued down the long flight of stairs, into the belly of the amphitheater. They entered a loading area bustling with funny-shaped-hatted officials before entering a series of rooms beneath the amphitheater and finally reaching the arena floor. They passed through several ranks of Shulan soldiers standing at attention before finally reaching the Shulan Pavilion. Oban, who was now wearing a black hat with two long antennae sticking from his head with googly eyes at the ends, was waiting for them. It was one of the more ridiculous hats in court, but it also signified Oban as the Shulan high counselor.

"You got promoted since last we spoke," Taishi mused.

"I didn't want to brag," he replied. "Come in. Keep your voices down. The pavilion blocks out most sounds, but you never know whose spies are listening in."

The two were led past an array of guards, these being the ducal display guards. Not nearly as skilled or deadly as Mute Men but also not as terrifying to lay eyes upon. These were the protective detail Saan used in public outings to not frighten children during parades. Duke Saan was famous for his parades. Jian still regularly had nightmares about his last night at the Celestial Palace when the Mute Men had slain Uncle Faaru.

Saan was huddled with a group of his closest advisers when they entered. He held up a hand, silencing the room. Then he stood and snapped his head side to side, whipping his wild mane of hair around. The duke had smoky painted eyes, a square jaw, and bulging muscles. He was wearing a bold uniform that could best be described as a metal bikini with spikes. It looked impractical, but Saan did cut an imposing figure.

Jian lapped it all up. The way Saan dressed and carried himself, how he sauntered with those beefy hips, his confident smile, and his slow, relaxed drawl. There was just something so raw and cool about the man. Jian had a new idol. He wanted to be just like the legendary Painted Tiger when he grew up.

Saan crossed the room and poured plum wine for himself. He downed the cup in one gulp, poured himself another, and then returned to the back of the pavilion where a smaller version of the Heart of the Tiandi Throne sat. He finished his second cup before he took his seat.

"Duke Saan," the Hype of the Court intoned. "May one thousand bards sing one thousand songs to your great victories."

"May one thousand bards sing one thousand songs to one thousand fair maidens to your one thousand great victories," the pavilion chanted.

"May his many glories earn him favor with the Celestial Kingdom."

The group echoed that too. This continued for several more verses, each more outlandish than the last. Jian sneaked a peek at the hype standing on a dais off to the side. The Shulan court should have paid for better talent. The man had a booming voice and a smooth delivery, but his prose was awful. Now that Jian thought about it, the furniture in this pavilion was ugly as well, not to mention those hideous red-and-brown soldier uniforms. Every administrative aspect of Shulan flirted with bad taste, so maybe all of this came from the very top.

Taishi approached the duke on the throne and bowed. "You summoned, my lord. How may I serve?"

"*Now* you want to serve your lord," the duke snorted, his tone mocking but good-natured. "First you turn me down when I ask for a favor from a former student. Then you turn me down when I ask as your friend, and even as your lord. Now you're all, 'how may I serve?'"

"That's sort of how unconditional surrenders work, my lord."

Taishi met Saan's eyes. The two held their stare for several moments, with Jian still standing next to her, awkward and uncomfortable. Even Oban began to fidget.

"Something on your mind, Taishi?" said Saan. "Speak freely. Out with it."

"You look fat."

The duke didn't blink an eye. "And you look cantankerous, master."

"I'm sick and old and I'm a fugitive. What's your excuse?"

"I'm tired and foolish, and I am losing a war."

She put a hand on her waist. "Are you here to listen to my advice or to hang me?"

"I haven't decided yet." Saan held the stern look for several moments before breaking into a grin. "It's good to finally see you in person, master."

"Can't say the same for you, boy. How did you let it come to this? You should have taken obligations for Jian the moment the Khan croaked. Avoided this whole mess."

"Like I said at the time, the price was too high." The duke shrugged and looked Jian's way. Saan beckoned for him to approach. "Now I get him for free. Free's better."

Jian shuffled next to Taishi and bowed, hanging his head low. "My lord."

Saan sprang from his throne, moving fluidly, his hips shaking in an exaggerated motion. The man patted both of Jian's shoulders with his strong hands. "The impossible has happened. Two students of the Zhang lineage, actually alive."

"You technically never made it far enough to have your name written on the lineage rolls," Taishi added. "Your Grace."

"Thanks for the reminder, master," said Saan, unfazed. "My scouting reports painted you as a fine young man, and I see they are not mistaken." The duke looked him over. "Stout frame. Strong jing in the gut. Look at those muscles." Saan suddenly attacked, and Jian instinctively countered. Rolling Hammer met Song Dancing on the Breeze, followed by Two Dummies countered by Three Dummies. These were all classic and basic windwhisper techniques.

The duke burst into a grin and swung his arms around Jian's neck in a playful headlock. "Look at that! See . . . my little brother!"

"Yes, brothers!" Jian's face went numb. Did the Duke of Shulan just call him his brother? Then he realized his error too late. "I mean, Your Grace!"

"Nonsense." He turned to Taishi and jabbed Jian in the cheek with his finger. "This one is a good egg. I can tell."

She snorted and clutched her left shoulder with her right hand, her way of crossing her arms.

Saan clasped Jian's shoulders and looked him in the eye. "Listen, Wen Jian, little brother. How do you feel about coming with me and living at my palace after these negotiations? I will adopt you, and you will become an heir of the state. You will be under my ducal protection. You will be untouchable. That is a far greater shield than any army or city walls."

Jian was stunned. What was he supposed to say?

"But Master Ling..."

"Taishi of course must stay with me as well. How else could you continue your training to become a master windwhisper? Be something I could never achieve." His voice was sincere. "The Zhuun will need you at your most prepared in the event the prophecy requires fulfillment. Otherwise, I see potential in you, Wen Jian. Who knows, perhaps you may even take my name one day. I do not have an heir."

"I...I..." Jian was dumbfounded. He looked at Taishi, who was no help. She was giving Saan a flat, annoyed glare. He only managed, "Are you sure?"

"Think it over, but quickly." Saan's teeth were very white. "I need an answer before these negotiations conclude, and that may be tonight."

Taishi immediately honed in on that point. "Tonight? What do you mean?"

"Did you spectate today's sessions?" he said. "We're already near the final stretch. We can wrap this up early."

She shook her head. "I think you're overly optimistic. Tread carefully, Saan."

"Bah, Sunri's finished." Saan picked up his chalice with one hand and the pitcher with the other as he strutted around the pavilion. He placed the pitcher back on a side table and drank deeply from his silver chalice. He drained it in one long throw of his head back. "That's the way of negotiations. Once something is on the table, there is no way to take it back, under imperial law. My stepmother had already expended most of her resources and assets. She has nothing left to deal with."

Taishi's gaze didn't lift. "Are you drunk?"

"I'm celebrating, Taishi." He chortled. "Her position in the south is crumbling. Once she loses those border farms and manufacturing smithies in the west, she will have no manufacturing or production other than the war arts schools in Jiayi, and the capital has nothing. She will no longer be able to house, arm, or pay her soldiers. Sunri will have to feed her soldiers their horses and arm them with pitchforks, and once you miss payroll even once, that's the end. Total capitulation. My stepmother has erred and gave Yanso too much power while distancing herself in third position in this alliance. If she allies with Yanso, she'll be nothing but a vassal, and a bored one at that. Her only real choice is to join her wonderful stepson"—he pointed at his handsome visage—"in second position. She knows that. I know that. Even Yanso knows that." He preened. "I must be a better negotiator than you give me credit for."

The duke's analysis of the situation was close enough to Taishi's, although his assessment was far more optimistic. "Consider the possibility," she spoke carefully, "that Sunri's positions aren't crumbling, but that she is merely luring you in with unearned spoils."

"Oh, it's very earned, I'd say," said Saan, gesticulating about. "My stepmother needs an alliance the most, and everyone knows Yanso's a cheat, an abusive ally, and a terrible lay."

"I wouldn't take anything at face value, Your Grace," said Taishi. "That's how traps are sprung."

"If she is laying a trap, then she forgot to spring it."

An attendant appeared at the entrance. "Duke Saan, a messenger from the Gyian delegation is here. She is carrying an offer of alliance from Duke Yanso."

Saan dumped his drink and threw up his arms. "Or even better, we push her out entirely. What did I tell you, master? This is a victory with complete capitulation. Better start packing, gentlemen. We need to head back as soon as possible to sink some Lawkan toys." He turned to Oban. "Send the courier in."

Taishi shook her head with disgust and scowled when she caught Jian grinning like an opera chou clown, but he couldn't stop smiling around the magnetic duke. Jian could see why people gravitated to Saan. His cheerful demeanor, casual charm, and ability to instantly connect with people were downright infectious. There was something about him that lured Jian in. He was just so cool. Jian would follow Saan into battle right now if called.

Now Jian had the opportunity to become the duke's ward, live by his side, and maybe even be adopted. He couldn't believe it. A real family and a real surname! He could become Saan's heir! Jian was so jittery with excitement that he almost pissed himself. Noticing Taishi's glare, he tempered his exuberance somewhat, smothering it into a pursed smile that threatened to break free into a smirk.

Taishi tapped Jian on the back and guided him to the side of the pavilion. The other four advisers in the room were Saan's right-hand man, Oban; a general; a purselord; and a woman who looked like she might be the Wisdom of the Court, which was a position reserved for the smartest person in the room. When a duke received an audience, the honored visitor always stood alone. Jian was surprised by how many minute details he retained from Saan's court instructions.

A tall palacemaiden in red and brown escorted a diminutive palacemaiden in Gyian blue through the pavilion's front entrance. The courier carried an oversize scroll half as tall as she was in her arms with the ends of the rod displaying the imperial phoenix. The palacemaiden gracefully lowered herself to her knees, raised the scroll in her outstretched arms, and bowed her head. She was very graceful for a servant, especially for one so young. Something about her face felt familiar, and that familiarity made him feel . . . uneasy.

Saan exchanged words with the general and purselord. All three men chuckled. Saan next spoke to Oban and the wisdom, before finally approaching the palacemaiden. "What do you have for me, little one?"

"An offer from my gracious lord, Your Grace." The palacemaiden spoke in a soft and properly submissive tone.

Jian received another nudge from Taishi. His eyes were supposed to stay on the ground when in the presence of but not the focus of the duke. He lowered his gaze and saw a praying mantis skitter along the branches of a twisted heart tree near his feet. Jian fixed his eyes on it as it scrambled next to his feet. He had learned from Fausan's entomology lessons that praying mantises tasted like shrimp when cooked. The mantis had just caught a leafhopper and was in the process of tearing apart the poor insect's wings and legs as it helped itself to a meal.

Jian was focused on watching the mantis feeding when he heard a soft pop, and a sudden gurgled cry of surprise. A shadow streaked past the corner of his vision and then was followed by another soft popping sound. Jian looked around and saw Saan, more surprised than in pain, clutching his neck. Blood was pumping out of a gash in his throat with every labored heave of the duke's chest, seeping between his fingers and down his chest and forearm. He staggered in place as he pawed the black handle of a knife rammed into the soft flesh of his neck. More blood spilled from his mouth, spewing onto the Gyian palacemaiden, who looked more startled and puzzled than shocked and horrified. Duke Saan of Shulan fell to his knees and crashed to the ground. The palace-maiden fell to her knees and looked on in stunned silence as blood splat-tered across her face.

Jian noticed the stricken expression on Taishi's face. The bond be-tween master and student may fray over time but rarely does it break. She took a step toward the duke. For some reason, Jian heard Bhasani's voice in his head as he somehow managed to stay calm amidst crowds of ar-mored men flooding into the pavilion trampling over everything and knocking over furniture. Then he heard Zofi's voice screaming at him inside his head, yelling, "Stop Taishi!"

Jian did just that, blocking her from taking another step. He held on to her and hissed in her ear, "Taishi, there are three armies in this city. Someone just tried to kill a duke. We can't be here."

Oban was the next to recover from his shock as he rushed to the fallen duke's side. His voice carried across the amphitheater. "Assassin! Assassin! There has been an attempt on Duke Saan!"

"Seize that woman!" another cried out.

Jian remembered seeing the surprise on the poor palacemaiden's face before the guards rushed in and buried her under a pile of bodies. Pandemonium erupted as advisers and generals barked a flurry of orders, some demanding the room be cleared while others screamed for healers while still a flood of soldiers entered the room.

A cold gauntleted hand batted Jian across the head and shoved him aside. "You, stand at the back with everyone else. Do not . . ." The soldier squinted at Jian. "You look familiar. Where have I seen you before, boy? What's your name?" When Jian didn't respond quickly enough, the sol-dier grabbed him by the front of his robes and stuck an armored gauntlet around his throat. Jian smelled garlic and sweat as his throat constricted in the display guard's grasp. The pain lasted for only a brief moment before the man fell to the ground, either unconscious or dead, Jian wasn't sure.

Taishi didn't appreciate the way the guard treated her student. "Only I get to smack my disciple like that!" She dragged Jian farther into the pavilion until they reached the heavy canvas wall. A quick slice of her finger tore a gash in the thick fabric. When he moved too slowly for her taste, she grabbed Jian by the collar and shoved him through the gap. "The entire city is about to become the scene of the largest battle in Zhuun history. We need to head past the city walls and away from Allanto within the hour."

"What about the others?" he asked.

Taishi grimaced, and closed her eyes. "Leave them."

CHAPTER FIFTY-THREE

BAIT

Qisami knelt in the center of the Shulan pavilion as a burly ducal guard cranked her arms behind her back. She liked rough play as much as the next girl, but this was rude. At least give her a little foreplay first. Another guard appeared and pressed a short, stubby blade against her neck. Saan was still lying at her feet with several of his advisers trying to slow the bleeding. She was confused. What just happened? Did someone just kill the Duke of Shulan?

The man wearing the hat with insect antennae jabbed a finger and screamed into her face to be heard over the chaos. "What did you do, you koi fish wench?"

They thought she had killed him. Qisami kept her head down and demeanor submissive. What else could she do? "I have done nothing, my lord. I am just a courier, I swear it!"

The truth was, Qisami had no idea what had just happened. One moment, she was presenting the scroll in a formal bowing style suitable for a duke, and the next, the duke was drowning in his own blood at her feet and there was a gaping hole in his neck.

Qisami ran over events in her mind. The duke had just accepted the scroll from her when a strange dark stain in the air appeared to leak . . .

from Qisami's robes. No, not *from* her, but *beneath* her, somehow. The pool of blood had reached her knees and was now staining her blue formal servant robes.

Qisami shifted her weight as a doctor shoved her aside to check on the duke. Not like that was going to do any good. The duke was obviously very dead, with a blank stare and half-decapitated neck. One of the guards cuffed her across the head for moving. Another yanked her off her knees to her feet and patted her down for weapons. Qisami was glad she hadn't packed a knife. It had been too risky to carry during these ducal negotiations.

She did her best to comply and stay submissive, letting the understandably rough Shulan guards do what they would. Their lord had just died on their watch, in the middle of them. Their lives were forfeit. Under their plain, stoic faces, these pincushion soldiers must be panicked.

Qisami kept her head down and her presence small as they manhandled her to the ground. She watched a flurry of shadows move about as people scurried around the room. Her attention became focused on a walking lord passing by with his shadow chasing after him. Qisami's head shot up. It must have been the other shadowkill team.

A female guard walking alongside Qisami smacked her ear, knocking her off balance. Qisami lashed out instinctively and was about to end the egg hatcher's existence when she restrained herself and pulled back. Fight one guard, and you fight every guard, as the shadowkill mantra went. They already suspected she was the killer. No need to give them more evidence. Sunri should be here soon anyway. The duchess would get her out of this mess.

Whoever pulled off the kill was superb, smooth and silky, some real sexy nightblossom work. They must have hidden within Qisami's shadow when she entered the pavilion. Then they leaped out and slit Saan before escaping. It was some of the fastest and most impressive shadowstepping Qisami had ever witnessed. This was an extremely rare ability known as parasiting that few shadowkills could pull off. It required masterful control, technique, and stamina. She had read about it only in their teaching scrolls. It made sense, however, that it would be a true master shadowkill who would take on the job of killing a duke. Qisami wasn't sure when her passenger had sneaked on board, although there had been ample opportunity inside the underbelly of the amphitheater.

Oban took control of the room with his presence. His soft, flowery voice was now a storm's bellow as he barked out orders, blowing away all other chatter until only his voice remained. "Shulan ranks, close in. Display guards, maintain a perimeter. Summon the imperial hospital staff and the duke's personal acupuncturist. Get an astrologer in here this instant! I want to know exactly what just happened." He turned to the general. "Get a message to the army. Devise a plan to fight our way out of the city." He swept his finger across the room. "Detain everyone who was in this pavilion until we get to the bottom of this."

The Shulan leaped into action, moving with the precision of an army of ants. Qisami and the servants were escorted under heavy guard out of the pavilion, herded away from the arena and toward what she assumed would be a jail. Again. She hunched down and tried to make herself small. The air crackled with nervous energy, causing tension and anxiety to spread through the amphitheater like poison. The signs of impending violence were everywhere. Soldiers were forming squads. Personal retinues were closing around their lords. Even the guards were trading in their long spears for sabers and shields.

"Why do I always overstay my welcome?" she muttered.

She scanned for an escape and noticed a young man wearing mnemonic robes keeping pace with her some distance away. He was staring. Rude. She offered a slow but friendly finger wave. She appreciated the attention, but he didn't have a chance. He wasn't her type. For one thing, the boy was too young. She liked some grizzle in her men. He was also too average for her taste. She liked her fetishes really tall or really short. She was also far too good-looking for that doe-eyed llama. Who ogles someone while they're being taken to jail anyway?

Her gaze continued past the young man to the woman standing next to him. Qisami almost choked on her own spit. She wiped her chin with her shoulder and blinked. There was no mistaking that cold, haughty, worn-down side profile. Ling Taishi, the grandmaster windwhisper hag, was here. Then that could mean . . . The realization smacked her like a club to the face. By the Tiandi. It was him. Standing right next to her!

"I'm going to be soooo rich," she tittered.

Taishi caught Qisami sneaking glances. The windwhisper's eyes widened with recognition. "Shadowkill, it *is* you. Do you know what you've done, you ignorant brat? You've destroyed the Enlightened States."

"I didn't do it! I swear," Qisami hissed. "Do you think I would be so amateurish as to stick around after I killed a duke! Do I look like I have pudding for brains?"

Their conversation was cut short when both Yanso and Sunri emerged from their pavilions. Each walked with a heavily armed contingent as they converged toward the Shulan pavilion. Anxious armed guards crowded the space. The amphitheater fell silent as Yanso and Sunri stopped at the pavilion's entrance, each flanked by their own guards. Qisami pushed her way through the crowd until she was in view of the duchess. Sunri's gaze swept past her without a hint of recognition.

It was not lost on anyone that the duchess wore Blood Dancer at her hip. She drew her famed blade with a loud hiss. "A duke of the Zhuun has been slain, cowardly assassinated while under the protection of the Duke of Gyian. Justice demands accountability for this treachery."

"How dare you!" Yanso shot back. "This was not my doing. I stand to gain nothing with his death. Everyone knows you've cratered during these negotiations. Perhaps this is your way of trying to escape the poor terms you've set. It is not unsurprising that the Duchess of Caobiu is looking for a way out."

"The last thing the Zhuun need is a cowardly lord who takes no accountability and shields himself with wealth."

"Or a whore who slept her way to the Heart of the Tiandi Throne."

Muttering passed through the crowd. They were hanging on every word. Qisami slowed to a stop and craned her neck. The two dukes were performing to the masses, not to each other or their respective factions, but to the Shulan who now no longer had a lord. With the death of their duke, all lives were forfeit. That was unless honor found a reason to spare them. Honor, like everything else, was like any other commodity that can be bought and sold.

"What is a fact, however," said Sunri, "is that the prime suspect for this murder is a Gyian servant."

All eyes turned on Qisami. She was suddenly very seen, and very naked. The heat from the rage of hundreds of Shulan burned her skin. The guards surrounding her suddenly looked like protectors as the crowds pressed closer.

Yanso declared loudly, "I don't know what you're talking about. I never sent anyone to meet with Saan."

Someone shoved Qisami forward. Sunri leveled her finger at Qisami. "Is this not one of your staff?"

For that, the Duke of Gyian had no defense. "Yes, but not by my order."

"Again, the lack of accountability."

An astrologer emerged from the pavilion while the dukes were going back and forth. Both turned to him. "Well?" they said together.

"What did you find?" added Yanso. "Spit it out."

The astrologer, a frail bald man wearing a pointed hat and a cape shaped like butterfly wings, bowed. "It was murder, my lord. Nightblossom work."

"A professional then." Sunri stepped forward. "Bring the palace-maiden forward."

Rough hands grabbed Qisami by the shoulder and shoved her forward. What was Sunri doing? Why was she intentionally drawing so much attention to Qisami?

"Palacemaiden Kiki has been in the Gyian estate household since before these negotiations began. Now I know why the Gyian insisted I take her on as part of the liaison servant staff. He was trying to kill me as well. Isn't that right, Yanso?" Sunri had effectively trapped him. He had been honor bound to keep the peace, and Kiki technically was under his employ. The Shulan contingent's outrage was reaching a boiling point.

"That girl is just a servant," said Yanso. "What makes you think she could pull off killing the Painted Tiger? The real killer is a master assassin." He pointed at Qisami. "Because I assure you, this scrawny kitten isn't."

Was this jerk trying to be mean to her? Qisami intentionally whimpered. "Duchess, I have no idea what you mean." Qisami's bow nearly touched her knees. She wished she had been briefed on Sunri's plan. This was confusing.

"Seize her and carve the sign of the grand Mosaic of Tiandi on her forehead."

"What?" Qisami blinked. It would be nice if Sunri clued her in on what was happening. "You have to be kidding me."

"If she is the assassin, as you claim," Yanso declared, "she will have answers. Question her under the slow drip. I will bore the answers out of her."

"No one here hatched yesterday, my dear Yanso. Everyone knows how much you enjoy hurting little girls." Sunri turned to the Shulan contingent. Her beautiful visage was contorted with rage. Tears streamed down her face. "Saan was my son. We had our differences, but he was family. He was the only link I had to my beloved husband, Emperor Xuanshing, may his greatness ever last."

"May his greatness ever last," the Shulan and Caobiu people intoned. Invoking the popular late emperor's name was always a crowd pleaser.

Even Qisami found herself repeating the phrase. The last emperor's reign had been before her time, but like most in the Enlightened States, she had been raised to revere the throne. There was no greater fondness for their former divine ruler than in Caobiu, which formerly occupied the empire's seat of power.

"My dear son, your duke, has been slain," Sunri declared in a strident voice, now fully monologuing. "There is no punishment on earth or in the heavens that can match such a crime, yet the once-noble Duke Yanso, who pledged his hospitality on his honor, now attempts to cover up the crime." The duchess was winning the Shulan over.

"You have no proof it was the palacemaiden!" Yanso roared. "Does the diminutive peasant doll look like someone who could slay the mighty Painted Tiger? She looks more like a wench you put on your lap than a deadly assassin."

"No need to get personal," grumbled Qisami. That was when she realized the trap had been sprung, and she had been the bait. "Oh, pig feet."

"Only one way to find out." The duchess came closer, Blood Dancer waving in her hand. "Carve the Mosaic of the Tiandi on her forehead."

"Are you serious?" Qisami squeaked.

Apparently, Sunri was, or at least the guard standing next to Qisami thought she was. He grabbed her by the back of the collar and lifted her. Qisami felt her feet leave the floor, and then her shirt tightened around her neck as the guard twisted the fabric into a noose. Qisami kicked the air and squirmed like a worm on a hook. Why was Sunri forcing her to blow her cover? Should she fight, or faint? She hated fainting. What did her pool sister want her to do?

Her vision dimmed as her consciousness ebbed. What if this dumb turtle egg killed her? What had been a foreign and outrageous idea minutes ago now felt like a very real possibility. This lowly trash soldier was going to kill Qisami, and—she lolled her head to the side—it did not seem like Sunri had any intention of stopping him.

"There's only one way to find out, isn't there." Sunri's blade arm stiffened as she touched its tip to Qisami's forehead. "Prove you are just a peasant girl palacemaiden emptying piss basins and washing soiled clothing."

Qisami had run out of options. Her consciousness was about to fade. Just as it dissolved, her instincts took over. She relied on the one thing that had never failed her. Maza Qisami fed her desire to kill. There was another old shadowkill mantra: death solved all problems.

Qisami was an enthusiastic believer in that. She was unarmed, but she was never *truly* unarmed. Her mind stayed calm and razor-sharp even as her body went limp, squeezing the last ounces of life out of her. The opening came a blink later as the guard readjusted his grip to get better leverage. That was all she needed.

Qisami had one good burst left, which she leveraged to fall into the shadow his body cast from the nearby torchlight. She almost didn't fit inside and wouldn't normally have risked the attempt. Death had a way of making one do stupid things.

She shadowstepped into the tight crevice of the guard's shade. The space rejected her but phasing into the shadow made her body intangible. For an instant, grabbing her was like trying to hold on to water. This trick was an unintended discovery of shadowstepping, a dangerous and often risky side effect of the technique. In a losing fight, however, there was no such thing as too risky.

Qisami evaded the guard's grasp and swung her leg around in a wide, looping kick that cracked him along the side of the face. Both fell. Qisami, unfortunately with her hands still tied behind her back, smashed into the ground face-first. She rose immediately with a bloodied nose and likely a black eye and a cut cheek, but who cared? Pain was always the point.

Before anyone could catch her, she took off and dove headfirst between the feet of a cloaked nobleman wearing puffy robes. She came out next in the shade of the pavilion with a loud pop and then kicked up sand as she ran and shadowstepped through several clusters of soldiers. She ducked grasping hands and slid under a swinging ax, then shadowstepped once more and emerged at the tunnel entrance leading to the underbelly of the amphitheater.

Qisami stopped to catch her breath once she reached a long, safe patch of darkness. Her chest heaved, and she fell to a knee. That escape attempt had nearly decapitated her, and the last sequence of jumps had almost finished her off. She glanced in the direction she had come from. Fortunately, everyone was focused on the chaos unfolding on the arena floor.

Down in the arena pit, Sunri's voice carried across the space. "There is your proof! A shadowkill in the employ of the Duke of Gyian. Sons and daughters of Shulan, you have been betrayed! To all who are loyal to the true emperor of the Enlightened States, to Xuanshing and Xuansaan, and all under heaven, join the Caobiu in avenging your beloved lord of this terrible crime. I, Xuan Sunri, humbly accept your allegiance and pledge to unite our people and destroy the enemies of all those found both inside and outside our kingdom. What say you?" Sunri received her answer in the sounds of battle erupting as blades hissed from their sheaths, the echoes of metal ringing, and people screaming.

Qisami looked back one last time. "I'm going to get you, bitch, if it's the last thing I do."

Not today, however.

She turned toward the safety of the dark underground tunnels and fled for her life.

CHAPTER FIFTY-FOUR

THE CURE

It was long after midnight. The fifth chime had failed to ring hours ago, although keeping time was probably the least of anyone's worries. Civil order had broken down across Hrusha, and the towerspears were out in force rounding up many of the Happan community leaders, jailing suspected seditionists—which felt like the entire city—and arresting those they believed to be harboring fugitives.

It was quite obvious who they meant by fugitive. The entire island was soon locked down with a curfew in place from sundown to sunup—which made little sense since the sun technically never set, and the fact that no one knew the time. The harbor chains rose to prevent any ship from leaving, effectively making Hrusha an open-air prison.

Marhi had departed the underground caves to speak and rally the rumblers from the other neighborhoods, while the rest of her people were preparing for a fight, scrounging pieces of makeshift armor and passing out long batons roughly the length of a person's arm.

It was forbidden for Happans to possess weapons, so they'd evolved their own style of fighting with these long sticks, sometimes called arnisma, or Armor for the People. Sali had passed the time watching many of them practice and came away suitably impressed.

Ritualist Conchitsha Abu Suriptika woke Sali sometime during the night and led her to a small catacomb deep within the caves. This place was old, the rocks worn and smooth, and the air felt stale and ancient. He stopped at the far corner of the room and pointed at a round pit just large enough for one person filled with a mustard-colored translucent sludge with thousands of tiny sparkling bursts of light glittering under its surface.

"Get in." Suriptika began lighting candles scattered all over the cave.

She stared at the strange substance. "What is it?" she asked.

"Does it matter?" The ritualist unrolled a long cloth tool roll, revealing several tools, jars of incense, and a curvy serrated blade. "If it doesn't, get in."

Sali didn't like following orders blindly, but she didn't have many options. The colored mud was surprisingly warm and soothing, and the thousands of tiny sparkling lights were like bubbles tickling and massaging her aching body. A contented sigh escaped her as she submerged into the strange vat of liquid to her neck. It was rather sensuous. The ritualist walked around her hole, chanting strange words while swinging an urn and burning incense that was dangling off a rope. It smelled like burnt sugar and lavender, which made the experience all the more pleasant. This continued for nearly an hour. Sali wouldn't have minded if she spent a couple more hours here.

At some point, Sali grew too relaxed, and then bored. Her eyelids drooped as Suriptika's calm and soothing chanting eased her toward slumber. The ritualist had a strong set of pipes to chant for so long. Sali drifted off into a thankful nothingness with her pain melting away and her woes and concerns fleeing her anxious mind.

Just as she was lulled into complacency, something from within Sali smacked her so hard she vomited. Her eyes bulged so intensely several blood vessels burst. An endless wail clawed its way out of her throat, muffled by the goopy yellow muck that covered her mouth. Pain tore through Sali from deep within her chest, a tiger with razor-sharp claws tearing through the cage of her ribs. Blood began to leak from her pores, from her eyes, ears, and nose, down to her fingernails, mouth, and little sister.

Sali spasmed, alternating between her every muscle tightening one moment, to complete loss of control the next. Several of the contractions were so excruciating she wondered if she had broken a bone. The pain reached a level she didn't know possible, and then it continued to worsen.

Unfortunately, that was the easy part.

A high fever followed. Sali burned to the touch yet felt as though freezing winds were flaying her. For the next several hours, her body shook and quivered as it expunged a black and brown viscous oily substance from every other part of her flesh. It dribbled out of her eyes, her mouth, and her nose. It broke through her skin. It seeped from under her fingernails and just about every pore. The yellow vat in the tub slowly turned dark gray until it matched the granite around her. At some point, she blissfully passed out, only to be awoken a few breaths later as fresh bouts of pain surged across her body.

Ritualist Conchitsha Abu Suriptika did not seem worried. He came by a few times to check up on her. He touched her forehead and shook his head. "It would have hurt much less if you hadn't waited so long."

"You should have advertised a cure," she huffed, barely able to push the words out.

"The rot of a long-dead soul can fester like poison in a body," the ritualist explained. "You've been linked to the Khan for most of your life. It will take some time before you adjust to the sudden loss of this parasite."

The constant agony was so much Sali had to clamp down her teeth to prevent them from chattering and chipping. "Is it almost over?"

He shrugged. "I have no idea. I've never cured anyone before. In fact, no ritualist has attempted this in centuries. I'm a little giddy to be the first if you must know."

That wasn't reassuring. "But it will work, right?"

"We'll find out soon enough." Suriptika beamed. "I'll be back in a few hours."

"If I go through all this for nothing," she hollered after him, "I'm going to rip your spleen out." She really meant it.

"Then who will make the medicine to make you feel better?" he called back.

"I really hate you right now." Sali meant that too.

She settled back into the pit and lolled her head against the side, waiting for the agony to subside. Suriptika wasn't wrong and had brought up some interesting points. How would her body react afterward? What if the cure shattered her? What was the point of going through all this, unleashing the Khan into the world, if she was left helpless to defend her clan against him? Sali had become a Will of the Khan at the age of eighteen. She had lived longer as part of the Sacred Cohort than she had without. What if Sali had been the viperstrike *because* she was linked to the Eternal Khan of Katuia? What if this ritual destroyed her war arts skills, and she became an ordinary person absent any skill or ability? What if she could no longer channel her jing? Her people would end up worse off than if she hadn't been cured. The Khan would be loose upon the world, and there would be no one to stop him. All these worries plagued Sali and ran circles in her mind. They weren't a welcome distraction from the constant body-wracking pain.

Blissful numbness eventually swept over Sali. She never thought she would be so happy to go into shock. The numbness continued to spread, starting at her fingers and toes, and then creeping up her limbs. Sali blinked and noticed the stalactites hanging from the ceiling. She began to count them, making it all the way past three hundred before she finally drifted off into sleep.

Sali was surprised when Ritualist Conchitsha Abu Suriptika woke her later. "It's finished." There was a pause, as if he was waiting for a response. When none came, he continued. "I think it worked."

That wasn't reassuring. "You think?"

Sali, however, knew the answer the moment she opened her mouth. She took in a breath. Her lungs didn't try to throw it back out. She moved her arm. Her joints didn't creak back. She closed her eyes, and felt . . . nothing. The sweet bliss of just being pain free was a greater euphoria than she could possibly imagine. Sali stuttered. "By the blades of my ancestors, I feel amazing. I haven't felt this good since . . . I have never felt this great."

Suriptika nodded. "Of course. The bond with the Sacred Cohort feeds the Khan. He's a parasite to those to whom he is closest. As long as you lived, your essence, your jing, nourished him. What you feel now is your strength returning to you. That part of his soul in you is now dead, and that was what poisoned your body. For the first time, you are yourself again, Salminde the Viperstrike."

Sali sucked in a long breath, greater than she had ever breathed before. A surge of power and renewed vigor resonated through her body, tingling her fingers. She could feel an immense well of jing, deeper than she ever thought possible. It was like finally rising to the surface after being shackled at the bottom of the ocean. This terrible pressure that had engulfed her for so many years had now dissipated. Sali felt like she could break through walls and tear trees apart with her bare hands. The feeling of release and boundless energy was overwhelming.

"I am more powerful than I have ever been. Let's go kill the storm-chaser." Sali stood and nearly blacked out. The surge of blood that rushed into her head made her vision go gray. She staggered forward a few steps and then promptly fell forward, ending up flat on her face.

Ritualist Conchitsha Abu Suriptika appeared next to her. "It might take a bit to get used to the new Khan-less you. Go easy."

CHAPTER FIFTY-FIVE

OLD FRIENDS

Escaping the arena was surprisingly easy. Taishi held on to Jian's wrist in a death grip as she dragged him down the narrow, enclosed passages, keeping their heads down and their hoods covering them as the Shulan soldiers in red and brown fought alongside the Caobiu soldiers in yellow and red against the Gyian soldiers in blue. None of the warring soldiers paid attention to anyone else wearing any other colors, especially those wearing mnemonic robes.

The roar of battle and clashing metal echoed through the arena, filling her ears with the constant buzz that threatened to overwhelm her other senses. Jian began lagging behind, but Taishi refused to let him slow, forcing him to keep pace. This place was already a bloodbath and would turn into a massacre by evening. Enclosed interior battles such as in an arena or a palace were easily Taishi's least favorite battle conditions. It tended to devolve into butchery with masses of amped-up, smelly soldiers trying to squeeze through narrow spaces. It also got hot and sweaty with the stink of battle and death hanging in the air, especially with bloodied bodies lying about that became a tripping and slipping hazard. It wasn't a fun way to fight.

The Shulan and Caobiu should sit down and figure that whole color mess out one of these days, although that may be a moot point now if Sunri took over. Sunri had managed to rally the Shulan to her. That turn of events was a seismic and unwelcome shift in Sunri's favor. But then, if the Shulan had sided with Yanso and the Gyian won, that would be bad as well. Sometimes—most of the time, really—there was no such thing as a good outcome.

Right now, none of that mattered. Taishi and Jian had to get out of the arena, escape the ducal estate, and be away from Allanto before the ten hells broke loose and consumed the city with flame and blood. Jian had to be taken to safety. That was all that mattered. If Taishi got them through this, they could disappear and start over, perhaps hide in Lawkan along the Waterfall Coast. That would be nice. She had always loved that part of the world. Jian was almost ready to stand on his own. She needed a little more time to season him and soak wisdom into his maturing mind before they reached that inevitable point when he ascended as the new master of the Zhang family style.

Taishi found the nearest door leading outside and took it, shouldering it open and feeling the relief of a rush of cool wind. They stepped into a gardened area and onto a large circular checkered Siege board with stacks of life-size wooden units lined up on all four sides.

"Where are we?" asked Jian.

"One of Yanso's many play areas. This one is called the Duke's Meditation of Airy Thoughts."

"What's an airy thought?"

"Come, we'll take to the pagodas on the right, next to the lake, and ride over the wall on the far end."

They came across the aftermath of a hard-fought skirmish. Blue Gyians in larger numbers had overwhelmed a group of yellow Caobiu. She looked farther down the garden path. The victors didn't make it too far, however, since the rest were chewed up a few moments later by an even larger Shulan force. Similar casualties would likely continue and spread like wildfire throughout the city and well into the countryside. The Enlightened States very well could be down two dukes by nightfall. It certainly made for exciting times.

"Wait," said Jian as she was about to step onto a current. "We can't leave yet. Our friends at the Shulan embassy. We need to get them out too. Some are hurt."

Taishi didn't slow down. "You're what matters right now, Jian. The others can take care of themselves."

"You left your sword there."

This time, she hesitated. That reminder cut Taishi deeper than she would admit. The Swallow Dances was her prize possession, her oldest companion, and the comrade that had never let her down. The sword was a part of her identity and legend, and their adventures were intermingled in songs and stories over the last quarter century. The Swallow Dances was the only object in Taishi's life that she ever truly treasured. Losing it hurt her soul.

She continued walking and pried a two-handed dragon straight sword from a fallen soldier. "No need to go all the way back. I'll just use this one."

"But, master!"

"Now, damn it, boy!" she replied with equal force.

They proceeded past the oversize game board and continued into the infamous Garden Maze of Wandering Intellect, which was the venue for Yanso's many rumored sex orgies. Yes, the duke definitely still held those. Taishi herself had attended one some fifteen years ago, mostly as an observer. Mostly. She had been on a job to hunt a serial poisoner and met a very handsome man there, who later proved to be good only at being pretty to look at.

They had nearly reached the outer south gate of the estate when a Caobiu unit stumbled upon them. If there had been any other faction around, the soldiers would have likely ignored them. Unfortunately, that wasn't the case.

"Hey, you candle huffers. Where do you think you're going?" barked a sergeant wearing a hat shaped like an avocado.

Taishi made a show of appearing nervous, fumbling and dropping the dragon sword on her foot. She threw out her hand. "Apologies, Caobiu friends. We are simple court mnemonics fleeing to safety. Our place is not on the battlefield." Her attempt at groveling was not convincing.

The sergeant wasn't buying it either. "No one in and no one out of the estate. That's the order. Seize them."

That certainly was not going to happen. The last time anyone laid a finger on Taishi against her will, she had not yet reached womanhood. The moment the unfortunate soldier, a boy really, whose face had not yet touched a razor, grabbed her shoulder, she flipped the dragon straight sword from her foot up to her hand and then she rang his helmet like a bell with the flat of her blade, sending him to the ground on his backside.

"Seize them," the sergeant barked.

The group of soldiers formed a semicircle and closed in, their spears inching closer. This was a well-trained unit, but of course, Sunri would place her best troops for this attack on the ducal estate. Several of the spear tassels were already caked with blood. It was probably a better decision to let them search her, but Taishi didn't care. No one, especially a man, would ever put a hand on her without her consent.

"We probably should have approached that a little differently," Jian muttered. He began to raise his arms into a fighting stance.

Taishi immediately slapped his guard down. "You're an unskilled mnemonic, Hiro. You'll just get in the way," she hissed so only he could hear. "Stay unknown."

"There're twenty of them!"

She shrugged and raised her blade. "Does it matter how many after ten?"

"Doesn't it?"

"Not really."

Dragon straight swords looked like the longer and larger two-handed cousins of the traditional straight sword, although their movements differed drastically in their application. Taishi hadn't practiced with one in decades on account of having use of only one arm. Between wielding a less-than-optimal weapon and this group of dressed-up dolls, this was shaping up to be a dangerous encounter.

"What is the meaning of this?" An even more dressed-up soldier stormed into view. He wore a helm that had horns curving from the sides upward and a hideous mocking mask that dropped halfway down his face, indicating he was an officer of rank. If she thought the Caobiu uniforms were gaudy, the officer ones were actually painful. The officer carried a small, rectangular buckler that spanned the length of his forearm. A long weighted club hung off one side of his waist and a straight sword off his other. Slung across his back was a three-sectional staff, which was unusual. This man either knew his war arts or enjoyed looking like a human weapon rack. In any case, his armor and uniform were freshly polished and clean.

The sergeant snapped to attention while the rest of the soldiers held their position against Taishi. "Suspicious individuals trying to flee, Captain."

Taishi snorted.

The captain trained his demon-masked eyes on her. "They're Shulan mnemonics. They're on our side."

"The old woman attacked my men."

"We're fighting alongside them, you balloon-brained pinky finger!" the captain roared. He continued to rail at his subordinate. Taishi felt it was a little over the top. "Do you think it's a *good* or *bad* idea to butcher a member of our new ally's thought trust?"

"Yes? My orders were to bar anyone from . . ." The sergeant snapped to attention. "No, sir!"

"Exactly." The captain pointed toward the sounds of battle. "Now, go find some Gyian to kill. I better escort our new allies to safety before any other of you fish-egg brains decides to rile up our new relationship."

Jian, staying close to Taishi, perked up and took a step forward.

"Where do you think you're going?" she hissed.

He looked confused. "With the captain to escort us out, no?"

"Since when did you start following everyone's directions?" She scanned the nearby walls. "As soon as the soldiers are out of sight, we take to the roofs. Kill the captain if he tries to stop us."

Jian's gaze lingered on the captain. "Something is telling me we should follow him."

She stared at her disciple as if he had just turned purple. "Absolutely not. Remember who he serves."

Her heir turned and looked Taishi in the eye. "Trust me on this one, yeah? Just a hunch."

Taishi was about to cut her disciple down when she stopped herself. If she wanted to season him, this was the way to do it. This was the reason she needed to stay with him longer. Besides, she needed him to know she trusted him, which she did. Sort of. "Fine. Be on your guard."

The man in the bright yellow armor eyed them with his affectless mask as they approached. His hands were clutched in front of him. His posture betrayed agitation, although from excitement or concern she could not tell. Taishi kept the dragon straight sword dragging behind her and out of view as they passed through the gates and escaped the estate grounds.

No sooner had they walked out of the palace grounds together than the captain turned on them. "Jian, what are you doing here?"

"I knew it," Taishi muttered. The sword came to life in her hand as she arced it from a low angle to mask her attack and hit him from the man's blind side.

To her mild surprise, Jian was ready for it. He stepped in front of Taishi and clutched her wrist. "No, wait."

The captain took his helmet and mask off, revealing a handsome if not more weathered face from the last time Taishi had seen him.

"Xinde!" Jian and his former Longxian senior leaped into each other's arms. There was much laughing and patting and a little more jumping than she would expect as the two friends reacquainted.

After their initial rush of puppy affection subsided, Xinde turned and bowed to Taishi formally. "Master Ling Taishi. It's good to see you again."

Always such a nice boy. That was why he would never get anywhere in life. "I should ask the same of you, young Xinde. What are you doing here playing dress-up as a Caobiu captain?"

"Because I *am* a Caobiu captain," he replied. "I lead the duchess's Stone Watchers long-eyes unit."

"Why join the army at all?" asked Jian. His next words were more guarded. "You never cared for, um, fighting."

"That's the thing about the army," replied the former Longxian senior. "When you're high enough rank, you don't have to fight. You tell everyone else to do it. That's also one of the reasons I chose the reconnaissance track."

"Have you seen Meehae? How is she?"

Xinde shook his head. "Last I heard, she managed to beg Doctor Kui to return to her apprenticeship. I then traveled with Pahm to Stone Blossom Monastery. I haven't spoken with her since."

"How's the big teddy bear Hansoo doing?"

Pain flashed across his face. "Let's catch up later when we're safely away."

Jian missed that small flash of pain. Taishi noticed it, however. She asked, "Why fight for Sunri at all?"

"Because she's my liege, Master Ling. It's also a job since Master Guanshi died and the Longxian school closed down. No one else was hiring after the war broke out. Besides, you automatically obtain the rank of officer if you're a skilled war artist." He shrugged. "I'm surprisingly good at playing soldier."

"You're good at everything," Jian gushed.

Taishi snorted. The boy obviously missed his old friend and mentor, but this fawning was embarrassing and beneath the dignity of the Prophesied Hero of the Tiandi. Her eyes narrowed. Xinde *was* wearing a Caobiu uniform, and sometimes friendship was not enough. "This is a coincidence. How did you find us?"

"Spy in the Shulan embassy," he admitted. "She swore she saw you firsthand and brought you soup. I was supposed to pass it to Lady Chiafana but decided to see for myself first. I had your wagon followed this morning but then lost track of you when you joined the thought trust. I've been searching for you all day." He broke into an ear-to-ear grin. "I can't believe it's really you. Here of all places."

"You mean, the worst place in the world to meet before this city melts into an urban battlefield?" She loosed a long sigh. "Can you help get us out?"

"Not from the Caobiu side. I can escort you to the south gates." Xinde nodded. "The Gyian still controls the rest of the outer entrances along the perimeter." He loosed a long breath and rolled his eyes. "There are *so* many stupid, pointless gates in this city."

Jian glanced toward the main city. "Can you take us to Embassy Row? We have friends in the Shulan estate."

"What did I say?" said Taishi. "You are the priority. Your life is what matters. Everyone else is expendable, so stop wasting time. Xinde, get us out of here."

"Both Masters Bhasani and Sohn are injured. We need to get them out of the city, and we have a Caobiu captain now to clear the way," Jian pleaded.

Taishi ignored him. "Straight to the south gate, Xinde."

Jian planted his feet and crossed his arms. "We need to help our friends, Taishi. You've always said I can't do this alone. I need allies, master, people I trust and can rely on if I am to fulfill the prophecy. How can I depend on anyone if they can't depend on me?"

The boy had a point. "This is not the time to argue, Wen Jian. This city is about to burn."

"There's never a good time when it comes to my life," he replied. "People are always going to want to use me, or kill me. If I can't stand up for people I care about during their hardest times, then what does that say about me as a savior of the Zhuun?" He looked at the ground. "Maybe I *am* the Villain of the Tiandi."

"Oh, shut it." Taishi threw up her good hand. "Fine, we'll head to the Shulan embassy."

"You can retrieve the Swallow Dances too."

Taishi didn't answer as she mulled over his words. The young, delusional fool she had met was now wising up at the worst possible time.

A loud crash reverberated throughout the city and drew her attention to the south wall as a column of smoke filled the sky: siege weapons were now in play. Taishi looked to see an artillery tower explode in a shower of rock and dust. The Caobiu army of course had been ready and waiting to launch the first strike.

Xinde was staring at the same thing. "Whatever you want to do, master, I advise you do it quickly."

"Then we better start moving. Head to the Shulan embassy."

CHAPTER FIFTY-SIX

FIRES OF FREEDOM

Sali watched from the second floor above the fish market facing the Sun Under Lagoon. She was experimenting sucking air through her nose one moment, and then trying it through her opened mouth or clenched teeth. She had been experimenting with taking in long, slow breaths all day, marveling at the beauty of unobstructed breathing. Everything felt so clean and pure, effortless. It had never occurred to her how difficult even drawing breath had been in her previously cursed body. Since the ritual, the world had become newly strange, wonderful, and vibrant. Now that she was cured of the Pull of the Khan, she felt like a new person, literally. It was as if she had finally stopped wearing heavy cavalry armor that was two sizes too small.

Ritualist Conchitsha Abu Suriptika had insisted she spend a few days recovering from the ordeal of the cure, and truthfully she could have used much more time to heal. The Happan rebellion was afoot, and the longer they waited, the longer they risked Masau uncovering their efforts to break their people out of jail.

Sali stuck her tongue out and waggled it, then blew a raspberry with her lips.

"Are you all right, viperstrike?" said Marhi, coming up next to her. "You look a little off today."

"I've never been so *on* in my life." She turned to face the rumbler, jerking her neck too quickly in the process, giving her a little crick. There was still some getting used to her body. The ritualist had warned her to take it easy and let her acclimate. Unfortunately, there was no time for that. "I feel great. Amazing, in fact, like I just broke the world's worst fever. Have you ever woken from a long slumber and . . ." Sali stopped. She never realized how many colors there were in the lights emanating from the volcano beneath Hrusha island.

The rumbler shot her a side-eye, and then continued. "The crews are ready. My runner says there's a stormchaser and a squad of towerspears manning the checkpoint, but we have two hundred and twenty-nine rumblers at our backs ready to go."

"I thought you said five hundred."

The rumblerlead shrugged as if it made no difference. "You know how it goes. All my gossip channels have been disrupted, so it's been hard to get the call out. I may have also possibly overestimated the rumbler ranks. Five hundred is a very good event if we make flyers and offer boozy refreshments. Still, two hundred twenty-nine isn't bad, right? We still outnumber those towerspears."

Five to one odds were much stronger than two to one, especially with this untrained rabble against elite towerspears. Not to mention tossing stormchasers into the mix. But the girl was right. It didn't matter. They were going to attack no matter what. The rumbler fell in next to Sali as they continued down the stairs.

A dozen rumblerleads from other crews followed in a procession, two lines snaking around the corner, through the hallway, and along the wall of the stairs. These Happan might be formed of different independent crews, but they had all grown up together. Several acknowledged Sali with a nod as she passed, but most just looked on with suspicion. Word had spread among the Happan that a mighty Katuia was fighting with them. Even then, she was still Katuia, so they automatically hated her. She passed by two sisters who were obviously twins. The one with the lush black hair gawked at Sali in awe while her bald sister looked as if she wanted nothing more than to slit Sali's throat.

Sali and Marhi left the room and went down the narrow staircase, followed by half a dozen rumblerleads and their seconds. There was a packed crowd on the bottom floor, with many rumblers wearing many different kinds of fur suits conversing in whispers. The entire fish market looked like a rumbler gathering. It was amazing the towerspears hadn't shown up and arrested everyone already. Masau must be confident in its authority here.

The chatter died as they descended the stairs. They stared, some with hatred, and others in awe, but all with suspicion. She didn't blame them. They probably couldn't believe a high-standing Kati would fight alongside them against her own people. Many of them were probably wondering if she was leading them into a trap. With the poor two-to-one odds and an entire war arts sect thrown in, maybe she was.

"Marhi," one large brute wearing only a striped leathery fur suit and loincloth called out. "Yo, Marhi, we've been waiting all morning. I woke up early. Is this happening or what?"

"Oh, it's happening, Wezama. Get your tigersharks ready," she shot back.

"Finally!" The rumblerlead pumped his fist to a small rally of cheers.

Sali observed the sea of rumblers disperse from the main floor, presumably off to rally their crews. Those young optimists; idealistic fools. That was often the case with revolutions and rebellions. It fell upon the young and passionate, and often, the naive. How many of these youths would still draw breath by the end of the day? Hampa would have fit in perfectly in this sea of potential. How many of their deaths would be because of her? The thought of her neophyte filled her with a fresh bout of grief and clarified her objective.

Recover Hampa's body.

Help the Happan break the shackles of their oppressors.

Make Raydan pay for his crime.

"Listen up, rumblers." Sali used her war voice. The room instantly went silent. "Tell your crews to avoid the stormchasers. You leave those to me. The rest of you focus on breaking your people out of prison, understood?"

"You against the whole lot of them? That's suicide, Kati," a rumbler wearing a white-and-brown seal fur suit said.

"Guess we'll find out. Either way a 'Kati' dies, so what's it to you? Enjoy the jailbreak. There's always something special about your first one." Sali caught some of the Happan nodding, at least. She wasn't going to win any hearts and minds, but she certainly could earn their respect.

Marhi added, "Spread the word. Avoid the stormchasers. We're going now, lads."

Sali and Marhi joined the light throng leaving the fish market. The intersection was packed with weird fur suits stomping about blocking the roads and cluttering up the walkways. This whole operation felt very roughshod, which was worrying. Sali didn't like fighting alongside amateurs.

The growing procession continued down three blocks running alongside the shore toward the harbor until they reached the checkpoint, where they found about a hundred yards of loose soil between where they stood and the first barricade. Sali's eyes narrowed. "You said one squad?"

"And a stormchaser," added the rumbler.

"There're at least three squads manning the checkpoint."

Marhi frowned. "Isn't a squad whenever they all get together?"

This was fifteen heavily armored soldiers clustered at the foot of the bridge behind two rows of spiked barricades. Not to mention the purple-and-black-clad stormchaser too. Sali scowled. No, there were two stormchasers there. Not to mention an archery nest and a ballista on the nearby lancer pod. All this to defend a thin stretch of bridge. The outlook was growing uglier by the moment.

"What's the plan?" she asked Marhi as they walked to the end of the block.

That was a new concept to the girl. "I thought we'd just bum rush them."

"That's the plan?" A bunch of unarmed kids charging a hundred-yard stretch of exposed loose sand against a heavily fortified position with armored guards wielding tall shields and long spears. Sali wanted to smack her forehead, but that probably would have sent the wrong message. It was going to be a massacre. Unless she did something about it.

"Listen good, lass. I will create a diversion. Just long enough to disperse the defenders a little. Wait for the signal. Once you hit the checkpoint, keep moving across the bridge. Don't stop, or those archers and ballista are going to tear your people to shreds."

"What's the signal?" asked Marhi.

Sali had no idea. Making bird noises wasn't going to cut it. "You'll know it when you see it."

She broke away from Marhi's arctic foxes and proceeded to a less trafficked part of the beach just off the side of the bridge checkpoint. She threw her hood back and let the ribbon seal fur suit slip off her arms and fall to the ground. Sali's voice cracked like thunder. "Raydan!"

No one noticed at first, the crowds too busy and loud. The chaos of the city was thickest here.

"Raydan!" Her voice boomed across Hrusha. People noticed the second time, and then the third, and fourth. The city around them quieted, bit by bit. "Raydan! Stormchaser!"

Sali certainly had the attention of the checkpoint. The two stormchasers and a squad of the towerspears broke off and jogged her way. Sali noticed Marhi and her crowd of rumblers beginning to make their move, this slow mass of humanity rolling forward like ocean waves over shore. "Too soon, fools," she muttered, but what could she do? She pointed at the approaching towerspears. "Not yet! Slow down, you diseased arctic foxes!"

To her amusement, her nonsense worked. Marhi's procession of rumblers was the first to slow and then stop. Sali turned her attention back toward the oncoming towerspears. A squad of five flanked her sides and rear while two stormchasers, a young man and woman, confronted her. Both were wielding freshly polished, curved sabers, the staple of their sect.

"You must be Salminde the Viperstrike," said the tall, stern-faced woman with long brown hair. She wrapped her fist over her chest armor and bowed deeply. "It is an honor to meet you. You have always been someone I looked up to as a sprout. It is a heavy burden knowing I must stand opposite you on this field today. Know I harbor no ill will toward your blood and future generations."

"Get on with it," muttered Sali. Did she actually think this was a formal surrender?

The male towerspear, on the other hand, was not as respectful. He banged his closed fist against his chest in a challenge. "Drop the tongue and hands up, you traitorous, faded star. Chief says to bring you in. Didn't say in what condition. Know that my name is Harruu the stormchaser. Son of—"

Sali flipped her arm toward him, loosing the tongue in a quick blur. The bite punched through the back of his hand, through his chest, and out the other side. She recoiled it just as quickly, bringing it back into her waiting hand. Someone would have missed the attack entirely if they hadn't been paying attention. The young man had only a moment to blink in surprise and open his mouth. No sounds came out as a fountain of blood gushed from his chest. The towerspears cried out. Several stumbled back, offering her a wider berth and a bit more respect, their spears trained forward. The male stormchaser managed to stay on his feet for another breath or two, still wearing a look of shock and puzzlement, before finally toppling over.

The female stormchaser was the first to act. She spread her arms and drew two short spears from a holster on her back and lunged forward. The stormchaser made three quick feints—two too many, in Sali's opinion—and then lightning-strided just to the edge of Sali's line of sight. Sali slipped a thrust that would have slicked her neck. She parried the next jab with a kick, and then Sali dipped low and swept the woman's feet with the tongue's rope.

The stormchaser kipped back up to her feet and lightning-strided directly above Sali, hovering momentarily in the air before dropping directly down on her with a short spear in each hand stabbing downward. It was a clever technique that may have worked on most war artists. It was unfortunate for the lass that the viperstrike was unlike any other.

Sali dodged the two downward thrusts of the spears and stepped behind the woman as she landed, snaking an arm around her throat. She squeezed, holding the woman upright as she choked the breath out of her. The stormchaser was tough, however, pawing at Sali's arms and punching at her face. She threw elbows and stomped and squirmed, striking her several times and nearly succeeding in loosening the choke.

Sali glanced over to the side and noticed Marhi and the rumblers still standing there, gawking. "What are you slow-plodding furs waiting for? Go!"

Her roar woke the squad of towerspears as well. The bravest of the bunch charged her from the side. Sali, still with an iron grip on the stormchaser, sidestepped his spear and connected her shin to the side of his face, sending him spinning into the sand. Sali kicked the spear out of the hands of one towerspear and shoulder-checked another as she broke through several ranks of these armored soldiers, all while yanking the weakening stormchaser along.

Still another came from behind. Sali turned to face him in time to use the stormchaser's body as a shield. Fortunately for the lass, the towerspear pulled back, barely avoiding having his side skewered. The remaining three towerspears closed in and surrounded Sali.

At the same time, a large group of rumblers plowed into them. The five towerspears were immediately swallowed up as rumblers with batons began smashing them.

Sali dropped the now unconscious stormchaser onto the ground and joined the rest of the attack. She hurried to the checkpoint where the remaining towerspears hid behind the fortifications trying to fend off the Happan. Sali leaped over the barricades and landed in their midst. She yanked several towerspears off the line and knocked down another, quickly disrupting the Masau defenses and allowing the rumblers to overrun the checkpoint.

That was where Marhi caught up with her.

"Why did you wait so long?" Sali snapped at the girl.

"I was waiting for the signal!"

"Killing a stormchaser wasn't signal enough?"

"Next time be more specific! I'm going to lead—" A shower of arrows rained on their position. A few found their marks, striking the Happan who were defenseless without shields. A trio of arrows came at them. Sali knocked one out of the air and caught the second. The third, however, found its mark on the rumblerlead and punctured her shoulder.

Sali caught Marhi and dragged her behind an overturned table near the back of the checkpoint. "Are you all right, lass?"

"I can't feel my arm." Marhi's breath was labored and heavy. "I've never been shot with an arrow before."

"It sucks." Sali checked the wound. "Arrow went clean through. Don't pull it out, you hear? Keep it in there until you get to a healer. Now, get back to safety. Your day is done."

"What, no! I just got here!"

"Sorry. You get shot, you're done. That is the rule."

"But I have to lead my people."

"Lead your people by not being a liability." More arrows rained down, striking more unlucky Happans. "Do you have bowmen?"

Marhi's face had grown pale. She shook her head. "We're forbidden to possess bows. Instead, we use slings and rocks."

Several of the Happan fired back at the Katuia archers, but they were ineffectual against a fortified enemy nest on much higher ground. More arrows landed in the soft earth, cutting down more Happans nearby. At the same time, another group of towerspears was forming up at the other end of the stairs. The Happans were already wavering. These weren't trained soldiers. They were just idealistic young men and women who had no idea what they'd gotten themselves into, and now they were dying for it.

And Sali was responsible. She had to do something to stem the tide.

After the next wave of arrows, Sali took off from her hiding place and sprinted down the length of the bridge. Arrows fell around her feet as she ducked and weaved and knocked them out of the air as best she could. She dumped one unlucky towerspear into the lake and then reached the point on the bridge closest to the archer's nest. She was about to jump when an arrow grazed her shoulder. Her scale armor absorbed most of the impact, but it still wasn't a pleasant hit to absorb. It would certainly leave a mark by morning.

Strangely, Sali didn't mind the pain. In a way, she relished it. It had been so long since she had felt the full breadth of human sensations. She felt alive, no longer muffled. That constant hurt, coming in a myriad of ugly sensations, had blanketed her for too long. Even now, the sharp injuries of battle almost felt sensuous.

Sali reached the closest point between the lancer pod and the bridge and leaped off, skipping once on the lake surface before slamming into the pod's hull. She clung to a small porthole and then swung over to the next one. These water city pods weren't that different from their land-bound cousins. They were massive pontoons on water with two huge tubes on either end, which wasn't unlike the tanked tracks of the Grass Sea cities. The sub-levels below were used to maintain the buildings above.

She found a ventilation exhaust and was able to cut a mesh grating to get inside the pod. There were few people down in the narrow metal passages. Most looked like busy tinkers. A few glanced her way, but none bothered to confront her. She continued past them and found a stairway leading to the surface.

Sali was sighted the moment she stepped onto the main deck. The archer's nest was only a few feet higher, and they trained their bows on her. She evaded them, dancing around their streaking arrows, dodging and juking closer until she was within range. Sali leaped over the railing and into the midst of the archers.

Swatting archers didn't take much effort and was actually great fun. They were rarely well armed or well armored, and didn't tend to be an agile bunch. For a master war artist, it was like knocking over toddlers. Her tongue stayed busy as she used the stiffened shaft to smack two, then three archers out of the nest at a time. The drop was just high enough to ensure no one escaped without injury.

After she cleared the nest, Sali waved at the Happan to charge across. She spied the big-haired girl and her bald twin making their way across. Big-hair raised her stick and howled. Sali nodded and raised her spear in answer. To her surprise, the bald girl raised her sticks as well. The gesture began to rippled across the Happan ranks as more people followed those girls' lead until an entire wave rippled across the masses.

There were certainly more than two hundred and twenty-nine in the battle now. Many of the locals must have joined. Several more people mirrored the twins, saluting Sali with their raised sticks, and now shovels and picks, as they moved across the bridge.

A crash caught Sali's attention. The towerspears had erected another barricade at the end of the bridge into Masau. The lines were moving back and forth as people fell off the bridge. By sheer numbers, however, the Happan were slowly inching forward.

Sali was watching the ebb and flow of the battle when she noticed another flurry of purple: another stormchaser. She holstered her tongue and picked her way across the length of the pod toward the heart of Masau. Her detour to take out the archer's nest could prove costly. A lone stormchaser could break those passionate but fragile rumblers. Many of them would learn that their experience fighting street brawls would not be relevant when they were matched against professional killers.

Two towerspears appeared and tried to obstruct her way. Sali split the pair's spear thrusts, and shoved both aside, sending one falling flat onto her back and the other into the bright, colorful, but also freezing arctic lake. She hoped he could take his armor off before he drowned. Actually, she didn't care. She crossed to the next city pod and rushed past a growing crowd of curious spectators and concerned spirit shamans. Sali fought the urge to dump all of them into the lake as well, though it was always more important to protect your allies than to hurt your enemies, especially inconsequential ones.

Sali reached the end of the pod and leaped, taking one quick bound off the water's surface before reaching the main city pod where the fighting was thickest. There were already four or five bodies lying around a stormchaser who was wielding a long willow club with a heavy mace chain-linked to the end of its bending shaft. The stormchaser was batting any unfortunate Happan who stepped too close to his looping swings, and when they retreated out of his range, he would lightning-stride close to continue hammering them with the heavy weapon.

The stormchaser screamed with bloodthirst, reveling in violence as he bashed through Happans. "Die, Happan scum! You ungrateful here-tics! You will return as pigs next cycle for your treachery!"

The stick fighters were valiantly fighting back, hammering at the stormchaser's armor and weapons. The two sides were so entrenched they didn't see Sali approaching, and she wasn't inclined to offer the stormchaser respect. Honor is given when honor is shown.

The stormchaser caught sight of her descending on him at the last moment. He tried to bring his willow club around. Sali snatched it from his arcing hand and twirled it twice and then brought it down upon his head, cracking his helm in half. To his credit, the stormchaser stayed on his feet, dazed, then attempted to flee, lightning-striding a short distance to the edge of the pod. Sali chased after him, catching up in three bounds, and then planted her sole into the middle of his back, sending him plummeting into the lake.

She turned her attention back to the battle and was rewarded with seeing the Happan overrunning the second checkpoint. They were now inside Masau and spreading throughout the city pods. Now was the hard part. Sali never cared for sacking cities.

"Viperstrike lady," said a lad in an otter fur suit. "Marhi sent me to tell you that there's another stormchaser at the Masau chief building."

"What is that girl still doing up?" Sali recoiled her tongue and hol-stered it. "I'll be right there."

For the next hour, the battle across Masau waged as the Happan fought street-to-street across Masau's city pods, slowly making their way to the heart of the city where the main buildings were located. Sali ran all over Masau intercepting stormchasers dispersed throughout the city's defense. Fortunately they were disbursed in ones and twos; Sali could not have defeated all of them together.

Sali was locked in an intense melee with a frantic double-chain whip stormchaser when she noticed another flutter of purple waving amidst a sea of fur suits. As if they shared a connection, her target cut down a Hap-pan with his double scythe weapons, and then slowly turned toward her.

Their eyes locked. One of them would not survive this day.

Sali ducked the swinging chain whips, and then jumped in between the man's guards. An uppercut to his gut doubled him over. She yanked one of her daggers out of its sheath and rammed it into the base of the stormchaser's neck all the way to the hilt, then yanked the blade out and proceeded to move toward Raydan the Stormchaser.

Sali shoved the dead stormchaser away and ventured forth to meet her fate.

CHAPTER FIFTY-SEVEN

DECOY

Abort the job! Everyone out now! Full extraction. Screw exit narratives. This city is about to make the Great Sacking of Xusan look like a lover's quarrel.

Qisami continued to blood scrawl instructions as she sprinted and shadowstepped through narrow tunnels beneath the arena. The responses came delayed and confused, one at a time. She was still preoccupied with the chaotic melee that had erupted throughout the arena as the Gyian forces suddenly found themselves fighting both their newly allied Caobiu and Shulan counterparts.

Qisami ducked into a side passage as she barely avoided an enraged Shulan contingent crashing into a confused Gyian one. The amphitheater had erupted into a chaotic brawl. She ducked behind a side passage as violence spilled into the main hall. Big battles were never events anyone should willingly partake in. There were too many risks. Too many things could go wrong.

The savvy thing to do was to bug out of the situation as quickly as possible. No one was going to fault the servants fleeing the estate. It wouldn't surprise her if Allanto came under siege by nightfall by both Shulan and Caobiu armies.

Her cell could disappear in the chaos. Once night fell, they would be impossible to track. There would be no bounty or reward, but at least they would be alive. That was worth something, just not what Sunri promised her. Qisami seethed. The duchess was going to die by her hand; she swore it. Her hands shook just thinking about it. She had nearly made it out of the amphitheater when the scar on her forearm, just below the elbow, became more pronounced, burning as if it was on fire. She looked down and realized Chiafana was close by. The death mark throbbed, pulling her toward its true calling. She didn't realize she was squeezing the hilts of her knives until one of her fingers bled.

She blood scrawled. *I have to kill someone first. Rest of you gather just outside east gate next to that fish restaurant. Otherwise meet in South Pengnin in two days.*

Boss, when you say abort, do you mean now or can we wait until tonight? We're having our big debut tonight.

That made Qisami trip and stumble. *I am going to punch you in the larynx. There won't be a production tonight.*

Who needs killing, Kiki?

I'm going to get that firstwife cunt once and for all.

That's not being smart, Kiki, and you know it.

Koteuni had a point. This was not the time for revenge. But her second-in-command wasn't aware of the death mark. They were serious declarations in the lunar court, especially for shadowkills, since theirs was honored with a pact sealed with blood. Qisami might never get this close ever again.

Need backup, boss?

Do as you're told, Broodbaby. She was proud of him, though. He actually formed a coherent scrawl. He must be practicing.

Where? As always, Burandin was a step behind.

Boo is right. Where at, Kiki? You will need backup if you intend to take down a court minister. She will have protection.

What was wrong with everyone today? No one was listening. Whatever. Fine. Koteuni also wasn't wrong again either. Sunri was in the middle of conducting a coup. The Minister of Critical Purpose would have a security detail with her. *Fine. Head toward the north end of the amphitheater connecting to the palace.*

Qisami backtracked the way she came and let the pull of the mark guide her. That terrible death mark bond between hunter and prey cut both ways. It pointed her toward her mark, but it also pulled at her like hunger.

She was able to easily avoid most of the fights clashing throughout the amphitheater. The men and women in armor running through the hallways were looking for other people in similarly fortified garb, not a small woman wearing servant robes.

Qisami slipped into a back kitchen to avoid the rampaging crowds and slipped past small clusters of servants and cooks hiding in the back rooms frozen in abject terror. Now that she had lived as estate staff, Qisami couldn't help herself from warning them. "Run, fools! Don't bundle up like pill bugs. Save your lives!" She emphasized her words by kicking the nearest young man in the leg as she passed.

As she left the kitchen and entered a pantry followed by a long costume closet, Qisami couldn't help but wonder if this was her last day living in estate servitude. She hated to admit it, but she was going to miss this life. Working as a Gyian estate servant had always been a charade, an improvisational play that she had become too complacent and comfortable performing.

These servants didn't know the real her. They weren't her family no matter how much it felt like that sometimes. Relationships were forged from blood and collective trauma, not mediocrity and complacency. A person can't just go out and choose a family. That's now how it worked. The true Maza Qisami, not Kiki, was a heartless stone-cut killer. Her cell was her family, not these weak estate servant sheep, bleating away their wasted existence. Besides, she was responsible for that motley crew of cracked eggs. They would be lost without her.

Qisami continued moving through the side tunnels. Firstwife must be somewhere on the north end of the amphitheater, which was where all the garages, large props, and Tenth Day Prayer and other Tiandi decorations were stored. Once she reached the prop room, it was a straight shot to the garage, where the pull was strongest. The rest of the way was smooth, darting quick as a cat, skipping through shadows, and slipping behind the soldiers. Qisami had to kill only one unlucky guard who stepped in her way. She was still unarmed, and he was bamboo armored, not that it mattered. She made it quick and clean, no messes or playing around, and then she hid his body under some paint tarps.

The industrial storage garage was a cavernous chamber sandwiched between the north end of Wish you a Smooth Life Amphitheater to its south and the Grand Imperial Palace of Bountiful Wisdom to its north. It served as the underground holding area for many of Yanso's larger and more expensive toys.

This was Qisami's first time in this forbidden area. The duke had always fancied himself a collector of beautiful and interesting things, which showed in his exotic assemblage of carriages, sleds, rickshaws, and other assorted strange vehicles. There was a magnificent ten-wheel serpent carriage lined up on one side, and a giant one-wheel chariot next to it. Several carriages of all shapes and sizes, from two-story luxury coaches to a hunting cart to a large artillery war wagon with two portable trebuchets. There was even some Kati war gear.

The most interesting thing about this large room, however, was Chiafana standing in the middle of a large crowd of Caobiu soldiers. They must have found a way to sneak down here to this little-used garage and hide inside these vehicles. Qisami shadowstepped aboard what appeared to be a boat with wheels, or perhaps it was a carriage that could float. In either case, the lookout nest on the short mast provided an excellent vantage point.

The minister was poring over what appeared to be a map and blueprints of the estate and sending squads on assignments. Every time she pointed at a different part of the map and barked orders, squads would break away and depart on their assignments. The numbers in the room dwindled as the minutes ticked by. Qisami had to wait as their numbers whittled down before she struck.

One strike, one death, as the saying went.

She didn't necessarily subscribe to that motto, but a little prudence often led to greater rewards. Sometimes, an inexperienced assassin could become too focused on waiting for the perfect moment and end up missing it altogether. Her patience was eventually rewarded when the crowd in the garage thinned to only four soldiers. Chiafana's work had concluded. She gave some final instructions outside of earshot, and then began to walk away toward the other end of the garage. This was Qisami's chance. She hunted them, moving silently from cover to cover, into and out of shadow, stalking those Caobiu like a lioness. Qisami hummed off-key as she crept beneath a bath buggy, and then behind a two-story statue of the late emperor Xuanshing, may his greatness ever last. Then it was through an open window of the serpent carriage and out its tail door. She zigzagged through the shade of the looming three-decker carriage on one side of a lane and a finely painted battle wagon that had never seen battle.

She shadowstepped from the second-story window of the carriage to behind the rear spoke of the wagon. Then she skitted across the belly of the wagon and shadowstepped behind the front spoke. By now, she was only a few steps behind her blood mark. The urge was so strong she could smell it. Like sweet honey.

Qisami hit the rear guard first. She launched herself from behind a pile of rickshaw frames. The distance was a bit farther than she was comfortable with, but just like that dated one-shot, one-kill motto, waiting for the perfect moment often led to missing the moment entirely. Besides, Qisami always had an abundance of confidence.

The first soldier felt only a breeze tickle the back of his neck before he died. Qisami slid feetfirst into the darkness under a wedding pontoon and came out from behind a rolling tool cabinet and cut the back heel of the second guard. The guard managed to cry as he fell. A black blade stabbed into his ear a moment later.

Chiafana and the remaining two guards turned to see what the cry was, only to lose another soldier just as quickly and suddenly. Qisami had climbed out of the man's shadow and stabbed him in the groin. She got behind the last guard's head and had his neck cranked on one side, exposing it to her black knife. Qisami waited until she had Chiafana's attention. The moment the Minister of Critical Purpose's eyes widened with recognition, Qisami jammed the knife into his neck all the way to the hilt. She let the body fall and stepped over it toward Firstwife.

She gestured at the sword hanging from the woman's hips. "You know how to use that thing?" Of course she didn't. Good administrators were rarely good war artists, as was true the other way around. And as much as Qisami hated to admit it, the Minister of Critical Purpose was skilled at her position.

"Don't be absurd. I am a high minister of the Caobiu Court." Chiafana did not look amused. "Do you have such low regard for your life you would waste it coming after me?"

"Yeah, about that," said Qisami, walking closer, swaying side-to-side. "The Aki family. You did it, didn't you? The whole family. I mean, I don't give a piss about the family, but those little girls were under my care!" She composed herself again. "Just admit you did it and tell me who you used to do the dirty work."

"Their deaths are no concern of yours, as tragic and necessary as they were," said Chiafana. "If only someone had not refused their orders, more lives may have been saved. Now, enough of this petulance. You know who will be the one standing at the end of this coup. Beg to return to service now or start running."

Qisami flourished her knives and rolled them around her palms and fingers as if they were dancing fans. "Give me the names. I promise you a swift death. I am not one to torture. I mean, I play with my food every once in a while, but it's not the same thing."

Chiafana whipped out her needle-straight sword. That dangling, flexible thin blade was a favorite among the courts. It was more of a fencing blade often used in duels. Qisami called it the lazy person's sword.

The minister, apparently, was somewhat skilled with the weapon. Their first exchange was quick and sharp, her needle jab lunging forward to take advantage of its longer range. Qisami parried with both knife blades and skimmed toward the hilt. Chiafana retreated and spun, slashing horizontally. Qisami slapped the blade out of the way with her knuckles.

"Tell me who. Might as well do something positive with the last of your life."

"I will have your head for this." Belligerent all the way to the very end. Chiafana was struggling now, stumbling backward. She felt Qisami's jing. She thrust anyway, poking and slashing to keep her at bay. Qisami continued to press forward, ducking and weaving around the clumsy attacks as she did. Like she had said earlier: a good administrator was rarely a good war artist. The Minister of Critical Purpose was no exception.

Qisami cut her elbow with a deep swipe, causing her to drop her needle. Another poke on the shoulder with the tip of the other knife sent her falling. She spider-crawled and then scrambled to her feet to flee.

Chiafana made it only a few steps when Zwei stepped in front of her. She turned to both sides, only to find Koteuni and Burandin blocking her way. Qisami moved behind Firstwife until she was surrounded. Instead of begging for her life, however, Chiafana continued her bravado. It would have been hilarious if it wasn't so pathetic. "This is your last chance, shadowkill."

"*My* last chance," she mimicked. "A saleswoman to the end, this one. Your people suck. No wonder you need outside professionals."

Chiafana pursed her lips and stared defiantly. "Very well. Don't say I wasn't gracious."

The crack came across the back of her head. Qisami's world turned black and then she blinked back to consciousness pitching forward, falling. She tried to recover from the fall only to take a hard blow to the back of her legs. She fell to her knees and felt the edge of a blade press against her neck. She blinked as a hundred tiny stars obscured her vision.

It was the minister's turn to look down at her. "Do you really want to know who killed Lord Aki Niam's family? Well, you don't have to look any further than your own shadowkill cell."

The fist clenched in her hair yanked Qisami to her feet. She could feel the tip of a blade sticking into the back of her neck. Qisami twisted to see her assailant. The blood drained from her face. "You! You killed those girls?"

"Sorry, Kiki." Koteuni didn't sound sorry at all. "It's not personal, boss. The rest of the cell, well, we discussed it and reached a consensus.

This arrangement isn't working for us anymore. It's not that we don't love you."

Zwei raised a fist. "You're my best friend, Kiki!"

Burandin banged his chest plate. "Love you."

". . . but professionally," continued Koteuni. She bobbed her head side-to-side. "We think it's time for a change of direction."

"The rest of your cell was happy to complete the job you refused," said Chiafana. "With the same arrangement, of course. They'll be free of their Consortium debt tonight."

"You better kill me now if you don't want to look over your shoulder for the rest of your life," Qisami spat. So that's why she was still alive. The cell's funds would die with her.

"Come on, Kiki," said Koteuni. "Release our shares with the Consortium and let's walk away. We don't need to fight over money. We're family."

Qisami barked a laugh. The release was incredulous, but also cathartic. "Oh, you stupid woman, you picked the wrong night to try to overthrow me, because I'm *dying* for a fight. Thanks for volunteering."

"Don't be like that, boss," said Zwei. "It doesn't have to be so acrimonious. We don't need to fight. You have to admit things have been going salty for quite some time. The pay's dried up and we're wasting our prime earning years. Just pay us the funds from the cell's account and we'll be on our way. Think about the great adventures we had together. We can still be friends."

"We can hug it out in the afterlife." Qisami seized a very narrow opening during a tiny lull in Koteuni's grip. She threw a quick, satisfying elbow to her former best friend's face and slipped out of her grip. Unfortunately, she was surrounded, and there was not enough darkness nearby for her to shadowstep. The rest of her cell closed in around her. She assumed a wider stance and loosened her arms. "Let's dance, kitty litters."

Koteuni drew her saber, while Burandin drew double axes. Zwei had their emei daggers spinning in both hands. Two to one was a tough enough fight against Koteuni and Burandin. It depended on Cyyk. At least he wasn't here right now. For all the grief she plastered on him, the broodbaby could fight.

It was a good thing Zwei was terrible. They couldn't fight their way out of a paper lantern. Zwei was so inconsequential Qisami wrote them off as a rounding error.

As she anticipated, Zwei came at her first. The opera had tried to play relaxed and nonchalant, leaning against the side of a parked chariot. That was the first clue. Zwei played the role convincingly, appearing chill and carefree. They sold it too, except for the fact that everyone in this depot knew this was not the right time to be chill. As soon as Qisami turned away, the predictable shadowkill took the bait and seized their opening.

Qisami sidestepped the first killing blow of Zwei's twirling emei daggers, metal rods with sharpened ends on both sides set to a detachable ring worn on the middle finger. The first slash came at Qisami's throat. The next came low, to disembowel her. As usual, Zwei was too rushed to fight effectively against a skilled opponent. A war artist was patient. She sought openings and counters, and she didn't telegraph her moves. Qisami could time Zwei's frenetic attempts almost to a song. The third attack was a downward stab aimed at Qisami's face. She sidestepped, trapped Zwei's wrist, and tore the emei dagger out of the opera's hand, ripping out their entire finger in the process. Zwei's scream was ear-piercing. Qisami shut them up by breaking their jaw with a downward elbow that mussed up their pretty face. The crunch was satisfying.

Burandin reached her next, an ax in one hand swinging in looping arcs while the ax in the other was held closer to the head. Koteuni's husband was a moron, but he was a highly skilled moron who was an expert with a variety of weapons. That was his main contribution to the team. That and he was a fairly decent lay, albeit too hairy. The important thing to consider right now was that he was a weapons expert and double axes were his flavor of the cycle.

"Hey," she growled. "I gave you those axes for your birthday. You're going to try to kill me with the gift I gave you?"

He shrugged. "They are my favorite. Thank you, by the way."

"You're welcome, but that is still very rude."

"Sorry." Burandin then tried to split her head open.

A wide-looping slash of his ax with one hand was followed with a quick sharp, close jab of the ax in his other hand. Burandin weaved dual-handed weapons like few others. It was the only time anyone would ever consider him graceful. Qisami sidestepped and ducked, and then the two shared a flurry of desperate arm locking, but to no avail. He was too strong and too aware of her tricks. One of his left-handed ax thrusts nicked her shoulder. The follow-up right-hand looping swing sliced her cheek, sending a wall of red streaming down her face.

Then Koteuni joined them, her saber hacking in quick, short bites. Still unarmed, Qisami retreated, spinning away from the weapons and finding cover behind chairs and tables. The two senior members of her former cell were placing immense pressure on her. Fortunately, Zwei joining the fracas only made it more difficult for the other two shadowkills. The opera wedged their way past Burandin and launched at Qisami, forcing the ax-wielding master to pull back his attack. That silly puppy. One of Goramh's more popular quotes was "a bad ally is worse than having no ally."

Qisami blocked and dodged these overplayed aggressive attacks, and then smashed Zwei in the face again. In the other eye this time. She turned to see both Burandin and Koteuni closing in. "Can someone lend me a weapon?" she asked.

They appeared to have lost their sense of humor as well. "Losers," she grumbled, and then took off. Qisami shadowstepped onto the top of a carriage and then jumped onto the adjacent wagon. She sprang across a pile of rickshaws and scrambled up a catapult parked in the corner. The married couple stayed a step behind. Saber thrusts came from one direction, ax thrusts from the other. She pulled away, stepping into the shadow of the war sleigh, and came out behind a rolling siege tower. Burandin and Koteuni followed, continually nipping at her like dogs.

It was then that Qisami pulled off the classic portal attack. It was something Koteuni fell for more often than she should. Qisami had leaped through a shadow right in front of Koteuni only to come out of another shadow directly behind her. The forward momentum of her jump carried her barreling shoulder first into Koteuni's back. They crashed to the ground. Qisami was on her feet in an instant, her new mortal enemy less quickly. Qisami yanked two jade-marked green knives from the other shadowkill's holsters—they were Koteuni's personal brand—and then plunged one toward the little rotten traitor's face. Her former second-in-command managed to avoid getting stabbed only by shielding herself and having it sink through her forearm.

No sooner had Qisami stood than Burandin crashed into her, pressing his attack and eating up space. This time, however, Qisami had something in her hands. Her blades parried each of Burandin's heavy attacks and responded in kind with three or four sharp cuts, along the forearm, the face, the knee. So many cuts and then she was gone, retreating into the darkness. It wasn't long before a dozen, two dozen, shallow but painful gashes wore on him. Burandin thrashed and swung wildly, his vision obscured by curtains of blood dripping down his brow. Qisami continued to play with him, slicing, dicing, drawing with the tip of the blade, until he fell to his knees and stayed there, waiting for her sweet kiss of death.

Qisami kicked him in the face, sending him sprawling. She spat blood and roared. "And you thought you bunch of crumbs were ready to take me on? You knock-kneed ponies weren't pulling my wagon. I was pushing *you*!" Qisami marched to Koteuni, flipped a broadsword lying nearby into her hand with her foot, and then jabbed its tip into her chest, instantly drawing blood. "I carried your sad sack for years! What idiot planted the stupid idea that any of you useless muttonchops should have a run at me?"

"That would be *this* idiot," a strident and now familiar voice spoke.

Qisami whipped her head around and saw Sunri walk into the depot alone, Blood Dancer sheathed at her back and her two crescent blades hanging off each hip. The tips of her weapons dripped a trail of blood across the floor.

Qisami's rage burned white-hot. "You . . . over-the-hill, saggy-tit bitch! You betrayed me. Your own pool sister! Why?"

"Wait, what?" Zwei caught that first. "What did you just say about Sunri?"

Sunri's words finally settled in Qisami's mind. She whirled on Koteuni. "You . . . cunty awful friend. You set me up and sold me out."

Koteuni didn't look apologetic. "It's just business, Kiki. Everyone knew there was little chance you would take the breakup like an adult, and I knew we couldn't beat you. This was a good deal for all sides. You should have taken it."

"Don't be so modest. Your cell practically begged to betray you, pool sister," Sunri purred, strolling up to Qisami. She tsked. "You poor, foolish thing. So perfect for the job. Deadly, efficient, versatile, and with a contract success record as good as any diamond-tier shadowkill, but also gullible, with unfulfilled abandonment issues, and desperate. So very desperate. Desperate for money but even more desperate for acceptance, understanding, and a connection. You pitiful, sad creature." The duchess touched her chest with the edge of her blade. "I just gave you a little attention, and you gave me everything."

It was true, all true. Deep down inside, she knew. She had always known. Still, it crushed her. For the first time in years, she had given her trust to someone, and this was what happened. Sunri might as well have stabbed Qisami right there. Her heart certainly felt like it stopped. She just stood there, glaring. It was all she could do to not burst into tears. They almost leaked, but it took Qisami every ounce of grit she could summon to stop them from leaking out. Like with her father, she would never give them the satisfaction of seeing her break.

Instead Qisami seethed. "Did you plan this all along?"

"From the very beginning, dear sister." Sunri smirked. "You came to my attention with your truly impressive demotion. Chiafana look into you, and we concocted several variations of this plan once the negotiations were set, and simply guided you along toward a satisfactory conclusion. We ended up with one of the better endgames. Well done, Maza Qisami. You have my thanks." Sunri lightly clapped three times. "You're lucky you didn't kill that Gyian palacemaiden. The girl you choked out is one of Chiafana's favorite disciples who also happens to be her niece. She would have demanded a week's torture before sending you to your fate."

"You used me to kill Saan." Qisami found herself short of breath. She had never thought she would become someone's stooge in a thousand years. Yet, here she was about to take the fall for killing a bloody duke! Those words sunk in. She was not only a dead woman, she was a cursed one. The name Maza Qisami would become a household curse uttered by hideous, mean mothers to scare their messy, fat babies.

Sunri clapped her hands. "And you surpassed my expectations, little one. I couldn't have done it without you." Her face appeared reptilian in the partial light shining through the high windows. "You were the perfect alibi to cover up my deeds. I am in your debt, pool sister."

Knives flashed in Qisami's hands. "This is a debt you can't afford to pay."

Sunri looked amused as she drew her double crescent blades from behind her back. She twirled them until they slid neatly into her palms. She crossed her arms waving the crescent blades in a symmetrical pattern. "I had to work so hard last time to not hurt you because I needed you. This time, your usefulness has ended." She brandished her crescent blades in her hands in a lazy but intricate pattern before falling into her guard position, a modified Mesquite Tree Stands Tall stance with her crescent blades held wide.

Betrayal this great cut deeper than any wound. Qisami roared and lunged at Sunri, sprinting at an angle toward the duchess, leading with her head as she juked sideways into a shadow at the base of a ballista wagon and came out behind the duchess, her black knives reverse-gripped in her fists like a snake's fang clamping down on prey.

The tips of her blades were about to taste ducal flesh when something blasted Qisami from the side, sending her crashing into a wooden climbing obstacle. Her body shattered the boards and went through them. She landed hard, rolling several times before skidding to a stop. She groaned and clutched her injured ribs. At least two had been broken. Qisami sucked in a shallow breath and tried to rise, unsuccessfully.

A black boot stepped on her hand as she struggled to push herself up. She looked up and saw a Mute Woman towering over her. A male version of her came into view, followed by two more. Qisami tried to speak but succeeded only in spitting blood. Two shadowkills appeared on both sides. One kicked her in the belly while the other rolled her over and tied her wrists behind her back. They hauled her roughly to her feet. Sunri walked up to her wearing a faint smirk.

Qisami spat blood on Sunri's cheeks. "I'll kill you one day, you old used-up rag. You eggless turtle. You cooked black hen!"

The Mute Woman holding Qisami by the elbow delivered a hard, short uppercut that found and broke one of Qisami's few intact ribs. Her vision fluttered as she sagged forward, gasping in pain.

Sunri leaned forward and raised Qisami's chin with the end of her long, delicate forefinger. "Did you think you were worthy of fighting Sparkle Legend, the Duchess of Caobiu? Wretched shadow. Do you really think you're worthy of killing the first Empress of the Enlightened States?"

"You cheated," mumbled Qisami. "No Mute Men allowed."

Sunri retorted with a mocking, trilling chuckle. "Oh, dear, I broke the rules while executing my coup."

"I could have taken you." It was getting harder for Qisami to breathe, let alone speak.

"I'm sure you could have, dear sister. Unfortunately, we'll never find out." The duchess pulled away. "You gave me the Enlightened States, pool sister. I will not forget this. However, you *did* kill a duke, so I will have to make an example of you. Worry not. I am magnanimous and will not have you killed. Maybe sent to a distant prison labor camp up north, in the Grass Tundra. I hope you appreciate the cold. But fear not, I'll return this favor and pardon you in ten years as a sign of the empress's good heart." The duchess bared her teeth like the predator she was. "How does that sound, dear sister?"

There was a commotion, and Cyyk suddenly ran into the depot, panting and out of breath. "Hey, sorry I'm late. It's like a pitched battle throughout the entire estates." He raised his head. His eyes widened. "What's going on here?"

"You too?" Qisami snarled.

Burandin stepped next to Broodbaby and leveled him with a blow to the back of the head that sent him crumpling in a heap to the ground.

Okay, maybe Cyyk wasn't in on this. She would spare him then.

"Is that General Quan Sah's youngest boy?" Sunri looked at the grunt, puzzled, as the Mute Men trussed up Cyyk too. "Any other surprises?"

A soldier came in and spoke into Chiafana's ear. The Minister of Critical Purpose stepped forward. "Your Grace."

Sunri looked over, the playfulness in her voice gone. "What is it, minister?"

"The majority of the Shulan generals are with us. We expect to have control of their army by nightfall. Yanso has escaped the amphitheater and barricaded himself in the Second Palace."

Sunri nodded. "I want his headless body presented to me by dawn."

"There's one more thing. One of your captains recognized a young man in the Shulan thought trust. He may be of interest to you." Chiafana whispered something to Sunri.

The duchess's eyes widened. "I'll see to it personally." She turned to leave. "Take care of this mess."

Chiafana bowed and kept her head down as Sunri left the room with the Mute Men trailing after.

The Minister of Critical Purpose stepped forward. "Take the boy. The empress does not need to give the general of her armies a reason to hold a grudge. As for you, assassin, we need to keep you close but out of sight in case the empress ever needs to publicly bring Duke Saan's murderer to justice."

Chiafana drew her needle sword and approached. "Now you'll know how well I can use this blade." She raised her arm and cracked Qisami hard across the temple with the hilt of the sword, pitching her world into darkness.

CHAPTER FIFTY-EIGHT

THE DUEL

Salminde the Viperstrike and Raydan the Stormchaser stood at opposite ends of Masau's main square with the Grand Monastery of the Dawn Song dominating one side of the city pod, and the Stormchaser chapter house the other. The battle continued to sing around them. The Happan still appeared to have the numbers, but many were lying unmoving on the ground. The towerspears were not nearly as numerous, but their bodies were also far more scattered than the Happan. There were certainly more than one hundred towerspears manning the garrison. Easily double that number. The Happan were fortunate that the rest of the city had risen up with them, or they would have been slaughtered. Even now the outcome was in doubt. It was an ugly back-and-forth; an untrained army fighting an undermanned one.

Still, at that moment, Sali stopped keeping tabs. Only one thing mattered at that moment: Raydan. Her chest grew hot just seeing him. She was rarely the type to fall into a berserking frenzy, but she had her moments, and this was one of them. Her eyes locked on him, and the world blurred and faded. The dull roar of battle sounded like ocean waves. Sali was the storm. She was vengeance. She was death.

Sali rushed him in a few quick bounds and slammed her tongue down where he was standing. He lightning-strided away, and the impact cracked several rows of the pod's wooden floorboards. Sali chased him, moving without a care for tactics or technique.

Raydan skipped ahead, lightning-striding in rapid succession, making it seem like he was in three places at once. His flowing robes only further muddled his movements. The three images coalesced into one standing right next to her. She could feel his exhale on her skin, the glint in his eyes. Raydan cracked her side with Whirlwind and then spin-kicked her midsection, sending her skidding along the ground, almost tipping her off her feet. Almost, but not quite. Sali could withstand his blows now.

The man had improved dramatically since their days together.

The stormchaser was more elusive than she remembered, moving at a speed that none she'd yet fought could match. His positioning was immaculate, always knowing when to duck for a quick shot before escaping to safety. His attacks came from every direction, spinning and striking with Whirlwind from awkward and unusual angles. Sali barely avoided getting her head lopped off as she continued pressing, chasing him around the square.

It had been years since Sali last fought another master of such high caliber. Raydan's movements were sharp and precise. The other stormchasers looked like poor imitations in comparison. It was easy to lose track of him as he lightning-strided around her. One mistake was all it would take to lose any advantage.

That mistake came a moment later when the stormchaser feinted to her left and then lightning-strided to her right. Sali was out of position, and her weight was shifted too far to the right to react properly, bringing her in range of Whirlwind's deadly arc. The scythe blurred across her side. Scale mail bits exploded off her armor. The impact sent her spinning through the air and then crashing to the ground. She grunted and sucked in several deep breaths. She was lucky her guts weren't spilling out onto the sidewalk. Hampa always kept her armor in good condition and had just recently repaired it on the barge. It was another debt she owed her loyal friend.

The stormchaser approached, his demeanor calm and relaxed as if out on a stroll. "I am pleased to see that you are looking more like yourself again, Salminde. This is the ferocity and skill that I have come to expect from the mighty viperstrike of Nezra."

Skilled war artists trained to never show effort, however. Strain fed the enemy, as the saying went. Still, she could tell his breath was heavy.

"Sorry to disappoint you," she replied.

"Nonsense," he retorted. "It would have been a terrible shame if my last memory of you was that weak, pathetic thing I thrashed the other day. Today has already proven to be a much better showing, although as a point of advice, you are coming in a bit hot."

Sali wanted to stuff his smug head down his throat. He wasn't wrong, though. That was a wild exchange. She wasn't thinking straight. Sali had to get a handle on herself. Her aggressiveness was going to cost her.

On top of that, her body still wasn't following her thoughts as closely as she needed. Adapting to her new state required a period of adjustment. She couldn't put her finger on it. Her rejuvenated body, while strong and fresh, also felt foreign. She never realized the numbing effect from the Pull of the Khan until she had excised it from her body. Now she felt every small sensation—many she didn't know even existed—and it was overwhelming. Her ears rang, and her reactions were sometimes too fast, and other times too slow. A slow creeping headache was growing and throbbing between her ears. She also ached in ways she didn't expect with her knees feeling wobbly and fatigued. The ritualist had warned it could be some time before she returned to her full strength. Whether that meant months or years, he couldn't say. Sali was looking forward to that day—that was if she lived that long.

The two master war artists were about to go another round when a large group of Happan appeared, crossing a bridge. At the same time, several squads of towerspears appeared on the ramp from the opposite end of the pod. Both sides saw each other and charged, crashing into each other where Sali and Raydan were fighting.

Bodies flew past them as battle cries and people screaming and weapons clashing filled the air around them. A towerspear stabbed a woman in the gut right in front of Sali while only to, in turn, get clubbed and battered down by three Happans with sticks. Sali was tempted to join the general melee, but she still had the stormchaser standing on the other side to kill first.

Some of the Happan and towerspears were wise enough to avoid both war artists. Others, unfortunately, weren't. It began with a young Happan who probably wasn't paying attention to whom he was attacking.

Raydan looked on with utter contempt as the lad charged him. The stormchaser smacked him so hard the boy stiffened as he fell and then began convulsing. At the same time, a towerspear tried to stick Sali from behind. She sidestepped and threw a back elbow, flipping him onto his belly. Neither fool got up after that.

She looked around the chaotic battlefield. "Perhaps we should move to higher ground."

The stormchaser swiveled his head side to side. "What's the matter, Salminde? Is a little light traffic throwing off your focus?"

Another towerspear charged Sali. She maintained a flat expression as she grabbed the towerspear by the collar and yanked him closer before slipping her arm around his neck, pulling him into a chokehold. She pulled out a dagger with her other hand and rammed it into the towerspear's neck. "Do I look bothered by them?"

"Good, then we finish here."

The two met in the center of the pod again. This time, Sali did her best to push her emotions aside. She wielded her tongue like a staff, meeting Raydan blow for blow. Diving Hawk into Tall Grass met Tornado Raven. The West Wind Rides the Twilight slammed against Big Wheel Block. Raydan lightning-strided out of sight, and then hit her from her blind spot. Sali went low and cracked back, flicking both ends of the staff in rapid succession. Back and forth their furious exchange continued.

Sali tried to maintain her focus on the fight, but she found her mind wandering. She had always had an abundance of reasons to wage battle. She fought for glory and riches. She fought for honor and adventure, brotherhood and prestige, and sometimes even love. With Hampa, however, it was deeper than that. Losing him had struck a chord in her she didn't know she had, and it hurt in a way she had never experienced. Hampa embodied everything she fought for, and more. He was someone no one else in the world could be. His goodness was a bright light in the world. He was joy and kindness, loyalty and justice, with a pure mind and pure heart. His death robbed the world of all the potential change he could have done.

Hampa was also her legacy; he was her future. He was the goodness and wisdom she had hoped to leave behind after she passed. It was through Hampa she had hoped to keep her name alive, to keep the Viperstrike sect alive. And now, he was gone, and the ache hurt her in a way no physical pain could. If remaining cursed with the Pull of the Khan could have ensured he lived, Sali would not have hesitated.

It was a miracle Sali's wandering mind didn't get her into more trouble during this fight, but her luck was bound to end sooner or later. It happened sooner as Sali missed Raydan's feint and kissed an upward vertical slash across the side of her face. Blood dribbled over her eye, obscuring her vision as she staggered back, and then she ate another hard shot into the midsection. Sali fell onto her backside, and then immediately had to roll to avoid the bloodied edge of the scythe coming in for a second taste.

She rolled and then somersaulted into a crabwalk, scampering out of reach of the curved blades spinning and cutting downward in looping circles. Her already tattered fur suit was now thoroughly shredded and oozing a strange green oil. She managed to put enough distance between her and Raydan's blades and scampered back to her feet.

"I used to wonder," said Raydan, "who among our merry raid of spoiled rich kids would become the greatest warrior. I had it between you, me, and Pangu."

"Pangu?" Sali nearly spat blood from a burst of laughter. "Are you serious? I mean, he was all right. He talked a mighty game and mostly backed it up, but he was mediocre in just about every other way, except for that mean right hook."

"One Punch Pangu." Raydan nodded. He approached and offered her a hand.

Sali slapped it away as she stood. "We do not get to be civil anymore. That is a privilege denied to you for the rest of your short life."

"There's no need to be rude, Salminde. We are honorable people."

"You murdered my neophyte, Raydan." Sali spoke quietly, but somehow her words carried over the roar of fighting.

"You have slain half of my sect here today." He shrugged. "I believe we are more than equal in that regard."

She fought the urge to lunge at the man. "You didn't have to kill him. We could have dueled. I would have honored it. You didn't have to go down this dark path."

"It was certainly necessary," he replied. "I needed a reason to keep you on Hrusha. Honor demands you avenge your neophyte and guaranteed our meeting today. You came here to die. Regardless of the outcome, whether I capture or kill you, the spirit shamans will recover the part of the Khan's soul that you have stolen. My stormchaser brothers and sisters who perished today would have wanted nothing less."

Sali wouldn't give him the satisfaction of knowing that she had already fulfilled the dirty deed of releasing the Khan's soul. "The Raydan I knew went back for his wounded. He cared about his raidbrothers and sister."

"That Raydan found a higher calling joining the Stormchasers and serving the Eternal Khan, like you should have."

"I never betrayed Jiamin, Raydan. You know that in your bones," Sali snapped. "He was my heartbrother."

"Yet you denied his place in the next cycle. You had a *duty*, Salminde!" Raydan thundered, the conviction of fanaticism resonating with every word. "I didn't believe any of those stories about you. They were impossible. Not Salminde. Not the viperstrike. They say her Katuia blood burned purer than anyone's. There was no chance the heroic Salminde the Viperstrike could be this crazed lunatic who broke her sacred vow, spat on the wisdom of the spirit shamans, and turned her back on her people. Not only that, but her actions also resulted in her clan's exile. This couldn't be Salminde, my raidsister, but here we are."

"Here we are," she repeated.

"And now you're allied with these filthy Happan. Against your own people! It's disgusting. You are beyond redemption." He banged a fist to his heart, signifying a mortal wound. The gravest insult.

"In that case"—Sali banged her chest—"let's stop wasting time and just kill each other."

They clashed, a choreographed dance of extending and retracting, of parallel and intercepting footwork. Their bodies weaved and flowed like finely spun yarn. They looked almost in love, if it weren't for the fact they were both trying to end each other. She wasn't here out of a hatred for Raydan, though. She was here out of her love for Hampa, her little brother, a fellow viperstrike. The fact he never got the chance to carve his name on the sect totem pained her soul in the most physical manner. It wasn't fair. He should have lived a long life. Sali should have been the one to die. Now was her chance to make things right. She had to stop tapping into that burning anger and infuse her actions with cold, calm justice.

Their weapons clashed, ringing so often that it almost sounded like one continuous note. The world slowed. Sali had a heartbeat to read the enemy and anticipate his moves. King Cobra Lurches met Dazzling Skin Shine. Top Down Light Strike countered Serpent Sinks in Venom. This time, Sali was focused. Bit by bit, Sali read two to three moves ahead, and predicted how to punch through an opening in the storm-chaser's elusive guard.

She finally found the opportunity in a trade. He was going to slice her guts open, giving her the opening to stab him in the heart. Raydan feinted high and then slashed low. Another row of scale mail blew off her chest, this time, taking a deep gash into Sali's midsection. She had been ready for it, otherwise she might have fainted from the pain. At the same time, she stabbed with the full force of her tongue, sending it straight toward the stormchaser's chest.

Sali lost sight of him as she keeled over and her head pitched forward, smashing face-first into the ground. She nearly gave herself a concussion—definitely a black eye, maybe a broken nose—but she managed to stay conscious and blinked away her blurry vision almost instantly.

She clutched her ruptured belly, desperately hoping her intestines weren't going to spill out. Blood seeped out like a waterfall between her fingers as she pushed herself into a sitting position. She bit her lip and counted her heartbeats with each ragged breath as she tried to focus and push past the excruciating pain. A scream clawed its way up her throat and died there. Her nerves felt like they were covered in acid. Sali was leaking a thimble of blood with every breath as she pawed at a pouch of cauterizing powder in her waist pack. She glanced up and was disappointed to see that her aim had been errant.

The stormchaser had managed to block her thrust with his knee. That was the bad news. The good news was it looked like she had shattered his kneecap, which for a war artist—a stormchaser, especially—was a rather important limb. Raydan's lips were curled in pain as he tried to get back onto his feet. The moment he put weight on his left leg, however, it hobbled and gave out. He landed with a thud, and the two war artists sat opposite each other, shooting glares like arrows as they each attempted to finish their triage.

Sali bit down and ripped the drawstring off the pouch as she drizzled the burning powder on her bleeding gut. The new wound almost connected with the one from a few days ago. Twice, Whirlwind had come close to cutting her in two. The brown-and-green powder sizzled the moment it touched blood, and the pain shot straight up her spine to the crown of her skull as well as down her backside through her legs until her toes clenched.

Raydan wasn't faring much better as he clutched his injured leg. He managed to splint it with two knife sheaths bound together by rags. He finished first and hobbled to his feet like a weak lamb. Sali was only a breath behind him as she finished wrapping her waist with torn pieces of her fur suit.

The two war artists picked themselves up one more time, Raydan favoring his right, while Sali couldn't stand straight lest she tear her wounds open again.

"It's not too late to surrender, Sali."

"Very well, I accept."

"At least you still have a sense of humor."

Suddenly the large circular window set high in the face of the Grand

Monastery of the Dawn Song exploded as a giant ballista bolt smashed into it.

Raydan gaped. "Your boneheaded Happan have seized control of the ballistae and are shooting the holy city!"

Sali made a face. "I'm not that happy about this development either." The two had to dive apart when an errant bolt crashed into the ground where they stood. Another followed, hitting the Stormchaser sect house, exploding part of its roof. Two more struck the monastery, collapsing its front facade.

"This is all your doing!" Raydan, furious, crashed down on her. Whirlwind missed and cut clean through the ground, sending a spider-web of cracks spreading in all directions. He yanked it out and chased her. This time, *he* was the one who was coming in too hot. She bided her time, waited, set up feints and openings, and then at the right time she parried the stormchaser's heavy attack, reversed it, and then brought her tongue down on him. The two weapons' shafts touched, strength against strength, pressure against pressure, Sali's will against Raydan's.

The stormchaser's injured knee gave first, but then the city pod's ground gave as well. The accumulated abuse it had received from their duel and the ballista bolts must have weakened it enough to finally collapse. First, a wooden support broke and then, a large sinkhole opened, sending both war artists crashing into the depths of the lower deck.

The two plummeted one story to the lower deck, and then to the deck below that. The world went black, and then Sali slammed against the top of what appeared to be a large furnace. She tumbled off its side to the ground with a heavy crunch. One of those blows must have knocked her unconscious. She woke up a few moments later with her eyes stinging and her throat choking amidst a cloud of dust and debris.

Sali rose to her feet and winced as she limped across what appeared to be an engine room. She may have twisted an ankle, or worse, broken it, in that fall. It was a miracle her injuries hadn't been worse. A row of six large engines was lined up on one end while metal tubes and strangely shaped apparatuses were on the other. In the center, a large pile of debris was stacked chest-high with sharp fragments sticking out like a porcupine's quills. Lying at the top of the pile was Raydan's broken body, with three metal rods protruding from his chest. His left leg had been sheared off at the knee and blood flowed freely from the ends of his lips.

His eyes were alert and moving, however. He tried to raise an arm toward her as she approached. "Salminde." He coughed. "That was a good scrap. You did not disappoint."

"It was," she acknowledged.

He reached for Whirlwind. His famed weapon was sticking out of the rubble, now covered in blood and dust. "I have a nephew . . . Please . . . His name is Saidon, a Bullcrash neophyte. Can you see . . ."

Sali resented having to accept last demands. Hampa's screams were still fresh on her mind. However, she was many things, but she was never intentionally cruel. More importantly, honor mattered, even when no one saw it, a lesson she'd learned from Hampa, who was wiser than his years. She picked up the blade and placed Raydan's in his palm, wrapping his fingers around it. "Whirlwind will have no master until it is returned to your family."

Raydan struggled to sit up, but the metal rods impaling him held him in place. "Will you honor me with a warrior's sendoff?"

Again, Sali had to suppress the urge to let her thirst for vengeance consume her thoughts. She drew her dagger and approached, placing the point over his heart. "Until the next cycle, stormchaser. You were a good raidbrother, a great warrior, and . . ." She dug deep. "You were devout."

"Honor is the way." His voice and breath were weakening. "For what it's worth, I regret how things ended between us."

"I don't." Sali plunged the blade into his heart.

Raydan the Stormchaser's body trembled, and then went limp, his eyes staring toward the blue sky past the hole in the deck above. Whirlwind tumbled from his fingers and slid down to the floor. Sali brushed her fingers over his eyelids, closing them forever, and then she went to pick up the famed weapon. "Saidon the Bullcrash from Sheetan, I will honor my word."

The fighting had subsided by the time Sali returned topside. By now, the Happan had taken over the majority of the city pods. The spirit shamans were forced to retract the ramps connecting the pods still under their control, and the two sides were now in talks, negotiating for a peaceful conclusion to the violence.

Sali found most of the Happan clustered around the towerspear chapter house. During the melee, it had been broken into and all of the prisoners freed. She found Marhi standing next to Rich Man Yuraki as she directed her people to help the prisoners.

Rich Man saw her before she saw him. He looked no worse for wear from his stint in jail other than his now-filthy puffin fur suit. "Salminde, are you all right? You look pale and . . ." He noticed her lower half drenched with blood. "Marhi, get over here! The viperstrike is injured!"

Sali was immediately surrounded by Happan as several answered the call. She lay on the ground and Ritualist Conchitsha Abu Suriptika was summoned to tend her. It wasn't a moment too soon, because Sali was starting to get dizzy.

"We've won," said Marhi, clutching her hand. "Thanks to you, Salminde. You not only defeated the stormchasers, but you also inspired all of Hrusha to rise up and shake the yoke of the spirit shamans."

"How are your casualties?" A good leader always prioritized their people first.

"Many heroes sacrificed their lives today, but Hrusha stands strong and more united than ever." Marhi beamed with pride even as her face glistened with tears and sweat. "I've never seen my people rise up as one so united before."

"What about the remaining spirit shamans and towerspears?"

"I'm part of the delegation who will be meeting with Masau's chief. The spirit shamans are trying to negotiate a way to leave Hrusha in peace. Half of the Happan leaders want to execute them for their crimes, while the other half want to imprison them."

"Let them go," said Sali. "If you kill or imprison them, Chaqra will demand retaliation. If you let them leave in peace, there may be a peaceful compromise." She doubted it, but they had to try.

Yuraki nodded. "There is wisdom in that. I will see to it." Rich Man walked off, likely looking for the spirit shamans to offer terms.

Sali doubted Chaqra would be so magnanimous, but it was the right thing to do. Sali's anger during the fight with Raydan had nearly consumed her. Executing the spirit shamans would be an evil deed, a sin that could not be cleansed. Letting them return to the Grass Sea was the righteous decision.

"Thank you, Hampa," she said.

"Excuse me," said Marhi, now looking lost in thought.

"What is it, lass?"

"What happens now that we've won?"

That stumped Sali. "What do you mean, girl? You've defeated your oppressors and earned your freedom. Now it is upon the Happan of Hrusha to defend that freedom and forge your own destiny."

The girl looked troubled. "I thought we were all going to die today. It happens every generation. Our young people rise up and get crushed, and then our people are beaten down until the next generation forgets. I never dared to wonder what would happen after we won because it's never happened." She hesitated. "Did we actually win?"

Sali didn't want to ruin the moment, but she was never one to speak lightly of the truth. "That depends on your definition of winning. Chaqra must answer. Hrusha is far too important to them to allow your rebellion to go unanswered. Many of the other rim clans may be inspired to do the same. So no, you may have won the battle, but the fight is just beginning. Winning your freedom is hard. Keeping it will be even more difficult."

"What should we do?"

"You prepare to fight," Sali replied. "Freedom is rarely given freely. It must be guarded."

"The spirit shamans will never leave us alone, will they?"

"Aye. That's why you haven't won yet, and why you must keep fighting. For now, stop looking so far ahead. Worry about tomorrow when you are sure there is one. Today is the only thing that matters."

Ritualist Conchitsha Abu Suriptika brought over several wraps and began to work on Sali's wounds. He made several disgusted sounds as he tried to stem the bleeding. After a while, he sat back. "I don't think you'll die. That's the good news."

"And the bad?"

"Are you now really going to kill the Khan?"

Sali shrugged. "One of us is probably going to kill the other. I'd rather he be the one dying."

"The Happan can help. We want the Warrior returned to our people and cleansed of the Kati taint. If you help us do that, we'll help you."

Sali considered. She wasn't in the position to negotiate an alliance, especially now since she was at risk of bleeding out. It sounded like a promising alliance, however. "There is always strength with friends."

"Sali!"

She looked over as Rich Man Yuraki returned with Daewon. The tinker looked no worse than he looked after he was out all night tinkering. He rushed up to her, pulling up short. His eyes widened as he took in her condition. "Are you all right?"

She reached up and pulled him close. "I am now that you're here, brother of my sister's heart."

"I'm sorry I got arrested. Did we miss the boat?"

She nodded. "We'll have to find another way home. You shouldn't have gotten arrested."

"I couldn't leave the ore purchase. I mean, we really—"

Sali put a hand over his lips. His tendency to babble when excited was not something she wanted to deal with right now. "It's all right. You're alive and well. That's what matters. As for the ore and a ship home . . ." She turned to the ritualist. "Can Nezra's new allies help?"

Yuraki raised an eyebrow but said nothing.

Daewon, on the other hand, looked indignant. "I was only in jail for two days. How did you already make an alliance?" The tinker scanned the crowded area. "Hey, where's Hampa?"

Sali closed her eyes. "A lot has happened over the past few days. Help me up. We have much to discuss before we can go home."

CHAPTER FIFTY-NINE

ESCAPE

The streets between the ducal estates to the upper two of the five fingers were a mess of fighting and looting and random buffoonery by the young nobility and their personal guards. Taishi ignored them. It was always the same story with every city that got sacked.

The Gyian, it appeared, weren't as caught by surprise as she expected. Many of their army divisions in their stylish and menacing blue uniforms had already established defensive checkpoints at key intersections, repelling both Caobiu and Shulan units.

Taishi and the other two then took to the tops of buildings, the wind-whispers riding currents to the roofs while Xinde scampered along with his Longxian technique. The three bounded from building to building, running along the spines of the long rows of buildings and skipping across alleyways and streets.

Masses of Caobiu yellow charged groups of Gyian blue as the chaos consumed each finger of the city. Most of the Shulan red, however, were crowded around the ducal estate. She didn't blame them. Their lord had been slain. That's what she would do too—she glanced at Jian—if she didn't have a higher calling.

Between Xinde's Caobiu captain's colors and Taishi's mnemonic robes, the three war artists were left relatively un-harassed during the jaunt toward the Finger of the Splendid Luck. They ran into several Gyian patrols and magistrates along the way, but they cared only about large groups of the enemy, not piddling numbers of twos and threes. The residents of the city, at least in the upper hill, did not seem particularly worried about what was happening outside their walls. If anything, they were curious and chatting excitedly. That was the thing with the rich and noble. Wealth and power were their own shield against change and up-heaval.

The three made it to the Shulan embassy after a long, meandering journey through several blocks of buildings. They had avoided several fights, including a few groups of war artists vying for rooftop supremacy. Several of the soldiers eyed Xinde warily, but Taishi's thunderous glare instantly cowed them. They knew who she was by now. Secrets never keep in any army, and gossip that Ling Taishi was alive and here had likely already spread through the ranks. Saan was a fool to think he could bring her here and keep it private. The embassy was in the process of building fortifications, with piles of crates and furniture getting pushed against one of its many, many doors.

After questioning a passing servant, they were directed to the infir-mary tucked in the far corner of the estate. Sonaya and Fausan were hunched over a game of Siege when Taishi burst through the front door. She gazed over the two, both wearing silky bathrobes. Bhasani and Sohn were resting on beds off to the side. At least she assumed they were still alive. She noticed the dozens of needles on their arms a moment later. Taishi noticed the Swallow Dances resting on a table with the rest of their belongings. Regardless of her earlier bravado, she was secretly pleased to be reunited with her treasured heirloom.

"Get dressed. Pack up. We're leaving now." Taishi took charge of the room. "Get Bhasani and Sohn ready to move. Hachi, find some wheels."

"Yes, master." Hachi emerged from the back room and left just as quickly.

Sonaya was eying Xinde, who had just taken off his helmet. Her eyes widened. "Who is this perfect specimen of a man?"

Taishi made a quick, dismissive introduction. "This is Xinde. Don't let the Caobiu uniform fool you. Xinde, that's Ras Sonaya, heir to the drowned fist, and Noon Fausan, master of the whipfinger."

Xinde's eyes were wide. "Were you named after the God of Gamblers?"

Fausan snorted. "There is no substitute for the real thing."

"Pleased to meet you," Sonaya purred and extended Xinde a hand.

He barely noticed. All of his attention was focused on the whipfinger master. "You even look like your statue." He looked as excited as a child. "I can't believe you're real. This is amazing."

Taishi snorted. "This is embarrassing."

"I *am* pretty amazing," said Fausan. "But you're wrong about the statues. I don't look like them; they look like me, okay, kid? Get that right." He turned to Taishi. "What's going on out there?"

"Full outbreak. Saan is dead. Caobiu has allied with Shulan, Yanso is outnumbered but this is his home territory."

The God of Gamblers was in disbelief. "The Duke of Shulan is dead?"

"You're joking," gasped Sonaya.

"We need to get out of the city while we still have a chance." Taishi's head swung to the side and glared at Hachi, who stood in the corner. "Didn't I tell you to find transportation?"

"Yes, master. I found a hitched empty cadaver—"

"How about finding transportation meant for the living?" Taishi had had her fill of traveling in morgues. "No more corpse wagons. No more hiding with dead people. Get me something with cushions."

"There aren't many options, but I'll see what I can do." Hachi turned to head back the way he had come. "There is a two-row rickshaw back there. I guess we can use that."

"Hachi," Jian barked. "Get the cadaver wagon. It's fine." He gave Taishi a pointed look. "It's fine, master. Let's just make it work for now, yeah? We just need to make it out of the city, and Masters Sohn and Bhasani need to stay on their backs anyway."

"Fine," she groused. Her disciple was choosing the worst time to find his own authority and make good points.

"I'll get Kaiyu. He's grieving next to the koi pond," said Sonaya. "What about supplies?"

"Raid the kitchen," she ordered. "Jian, make yourself useful and go with her. Grab meats, duck especially if they have any, fruit too. Peaches if possible, and none of that disgusting blended meat meant for dogs and foreign workers."

"I'll speak with the lord of the embassy," said Fausan. "He'll get us what we need. He's a fan."

"Everyone hurry back." Taishi watched as everyone scattered to set about their tasks, leaving her alone in the infirmary. She checked on the two unconscious masters first. Both were being kept under with acupuncture and glass jar cupping. Their injuries had been rewrapped, and both appeared to be comfortably unconscious. She put a hand lightly over Bhasani's chest and mouth, feeling the drowned fist's breath pass through her fingers and the cadence of her chest. She checked Sohn next, and then helped herself to the infirmary's supplies, packing alcohol, wraps, and herbs. Taishi's medical knowledge was minimal, but anyone who spent a lifetime in battle picked up some basic skills over the years.

She emptied the shelves of bottles and jars, first taking supplies she needed and knew how to use, then the blankets, and then everything else that looked useful or valuable that they could sell or barter later. She did not know when she would have the opportunity to return to the Diyu Temple to retrieve her stash of liang hidden in a false floor in her bedchamber.

Taishi was still rummaging through the medicine drawers when Hachi returned a few moments later sprinting at full speed. His face was white, and he looked spooked. "Taishi, someone's coming. They look like Mute Men."

Taishi hurried by his side and peered out the door. She clutched his elbow. "Hachi, listen carefully. Find Jian. Now, go!"

"I'll fetch him immediately!"

Her fingers became claws that dug into his arm. "No," she said, her gaze still trained on the four approaching black-garbed figures. "No. Find Jian, and then run. Both of you." She looked at the whipfinger disciple. "Get him as far away from this city as you can. Protect him."

"But . . ." He nodded. "Yes, master."

Taishi didn't watch him leave. Her attention remained solely on the four dark-clad figures. They entered the infirmary's small courtyard, which was fenced off by two waist-high dividing walls and the side of the adjacent slaughterhouse. She studied them as they approached. The two in front and the one trailing in the rear were undoubtedly Mute Men with their black armor and comically short cloaks. The one in the middle, however . . . Taishi couldn't place the extravagant armor and many-pointed helm that fanned like a sun, giving off a menacing silhouette.

And then Taishi realized. "Oh, what a bitch's tit."

"Ling Taishi," purred Sunri. "Thank you for coming to my coronation as the new and rightful Empress of the Enlightened Empire. Having the Champion of the Five Under Heaven under my care will only solidify my claim to the Heart of the Tiandi Throne, for which you will be handsomely rewarded," she added. "Assuming you hand him over. I'd even consider canceling the bounty on your head."

"That's a generous offer," said Taishi. She picked up the Swallow Dances from where it lay and strolled out to the courtyard to meet the four. "Here's my counteroffer. Forget the Prophesied Hero of the Tiandi. Go back to Yanso's estate and complete your slaughter. Be the empress of war and blood and enjoy the fruits of your conniving, cruel nature. Leave the boy alone, and I will leave you alone."

The duchess smiled as two crescent blades appeared in her hands. That was a surprising and interesting choice. Duchess Sunri of Caobiu had always been paired with the straight sword Blood Dancer. For Sunri to choose to wield a pair of crescent blades instead of that legendary straight sword was a rather odd choice.

They had been wiped clean but traces of red could be seen along the edges. "You misunderstood my intention, Taishi. I want not only the boy but also the notoriety of being the woman who slays Ling Taishi."

"Killing for acclaim is low class," Taishi replied. "I shouldn't expect too much from someone who leverages the death of her family for political gain."

"Calling Saan family is a stretch," Sunri scoffed. "His mother, the secondwife, tried to have me strangled in my sleep, but I'm used to my dear husband's blood being my greatest threat."

"That's where you're mistaken, Your Grace." Taishi drew the Swallow Dances from its sheath. The blue blade shimmered under the light of the King. "Last chance, girl. Leave and enjoy your victory."

Sunri's eyes flashed, and her smile grew larger and more sinister. "Owning the Prophesied Hero of the Tiandi will effectively give me control of the Tiandi religion. However, singlehandedly defeating Ling Taishi would make me a legend."

"Singlehandedly." Taishi sneered. "I love your optimism."

The two women, possibly the most powerful in the Enlightened States, stood at opposite ends of the courtyard, both assuming formal dueling stances. Taishi, as the esteemed elder, waited. Sunri, as the much higher-ranked noble, waited as well.

The three mute people, technically two women and one man, spread out along the edge of the space, two to the sides of Taishi and one behind her. Whether they would honor the terms of single combat was still unknown. Taishi would have to prepare for that.

The light of the King was just beginning to turn orange, casting long shadows across the rapidly dusking courtyard. A lone servant carrying a basket of de-feathered chickens emerged from the adjacent building. He looked at the group of armed combatants and immediately retreated back inside, locking himself in the coop. Smart man. The seconds continued to tick by as each woman waited for the other to initiate the first move.

To her surprise, a visibly annoyed Sunri capitulated first. Her well of patience was certainly much smaller than her need to follow decorum. "Honor is the way," she spat.

"Honor is the only way." Taishi allowed a small smirk to grow on her face, which only infuriated the duchess more. She bared her teeth.

No sooner had the formality ended than the duchess launched herself at Taishi with a speed that was nearly supernatural. Sunri covered the distance between them in two steps, thrusting low with one crescent blade while simultaneously swinging high with the other.

Taishi learned much about the duchess in those first moves. Duchess Sunri's fighting style and footwork painted a fascinating story. Every social class contained favored styles of war arts, even concubines. In many cases, those women needed it more than most. Concubines and many who worked in salons and brothels commonly practiced a war art known as Singing Spring, which was a style that fought with short, quick arm movements, joint locking, and grappling, and was favored by many women because it allowed them to fight in short, confined spaces while turning a stronger opponent's strength against them.

The nobility, on the other hand, tended to favor flowery and graceful war art styles, with wide, looping moves, beautiful aesthetics, complex combinations, and jumps that emphasized extravagant strikes that drew a spectator's eye. In their case, looking good was as important, if not more so, as actually being good.

Sunri, however, had studied neither branch of war arts. The duchess moved with the grace and efficiency of someone highly trained who kept herself in elite conditioning. Her stance work was surprisingly lunar court in flavor with short, stuttering steps and tight, rapid strikes. Instead of standing tall, she leaned and stalked Taishi like a night predator. Her guard was small, and her attacks were short and sudden. They minced along the ground hypnotically almost like a poisonous centipede. The woman was definitely a nightblossom, which for the Duchess of Caobiu should be patently absurd.

That or patently impressive.

Taishi had a newfound respect for Sunri just as the duchess was in the midst of trying to slice her belly open with the jagged tips of her crescent blades. They could have been friends or allies in another life. The duchess was good, surprisingly so. Her crisp movements were far sharper than one would expect from a woman of her height and long limbs, especially for someone with the burden of government on her shoulders. Most rulers did not make great war artists. The burden of leadership made it impossible. There simply wasn't enough time in the day to dedicate to the rule and the art. That was why she had always taken it easy on Saan. That and the man simply wasn't that talented. Sunri, on the other hand, *was* that talented and seemed to have kept up with her training.

The Swallow Dances earned its name today as its sharpened tip cal-
ligraphied the air, parrying and warding against Sunri's crescent blades
while also probing and scratching for weaknesses in the duchess's elaborate armor, which, surprisingly, were very few. Taishi imagined someone
as vain as Sunri would prioritize aesthetics over function, but that was not
the case. The duchess's armor was as stout as they came. While light, it
had been expertly considered.

It was challenging to mount an offensive against Sunri, but Taishi
stayed aggressive. The Swallow Dances ran two variations of Diving Falcon Catches Fish while her feet mud walked and then joined in the attack with sneaky heel hook sweeps and the footwork of Big Belly Big
Brain Stomps Their Feet. Sunri saw through the feints. The duchess
countered with several classic foundational attacks found in several
nightblossom styles but then moved into more elaborate maneuvers. Taishi felt as if she had seen some of it before with the flow of the melee
between them feeling strangely familiar. She couldn't remember the last
time she had fought a nightblossom, however.

One thing was blatantly clear after their first three sequences of exchanges, however: Taishi was more skilled and *should* win the fight. This
should be obvious to Sunri as well. Most fights between masters could be
determined within the first few moves, barring any mistakes, which masters tended not to make unless that mistake was forced upon them. Sunri
knew she was being bested, slowly, bit by bit. The firm lines on her pretty
face deepened and contorted with each exchange. The duchess was not
accustomed to fighting a superior opponent.

Sunri's defense with her two crescent blades, however, was strong,
and it would take some battering and whittling down the woman's tricky
guard to break her. Fights between masters were rarely dramatic. They
were battles of attrition, of wearing their opponents down until someone
made a mistake.

Taishi used light pushes of air to slide side-to-side and hit the duchess
at odd and weak angles. That was the extent of her use of jing. As the superior war artist, she had little need to overextend. Keep it simple to min-
imize her enemy's opportunities and openings, and fight patiently until
an opening presented itself where she could overwhelm Sunri with a

fatal attack. She kept increasing the pressure, driving the duchess backward until she almost touched the nearby corner where the slaughter-
house met the infirmary, neatly boxing Sunri in. The end would come for
her soon, which meant Taishi needed to be aware of the mute people if
they decided to jump to their duchess's defense.

The Emperor's Mighty Cleave met Fireflies Rake the Night followed
by Evil Twins Cheat at Dice countered by Baby Goat, the Dumb Jerk.
Taishi was impressed, not only with Sunri's skill, but several of her
stances and techniques were dated and had long fallen out of favor.
Which meant she was a student of the craft.

"We really could have been friends in another life," she muttered.

"What was that?" Sunri huffed, her chest heaving and the calm facade on her face cracking.

"Nothing. I didn't realize you were so talented. I regret having to kill
you."

"Kill me? I'm Sunri, the Duchess of Caobiu," she proclaimed. She
double-slashed from side to side and then spun into a butterfly kick into a
front sweep until finally ending in a double jab. She struck only air but did
come close a few times. "Your death will elevate my myth. I will be the
greatest woman in Zhuun history."

Taishi ducked left and skipped out of that sequence. She countered
with a deceptively hard swing that sent Sunri skidding back several feet.
"You know, you could have already been the greatest woman in our people's history if you weren't such a murderous bitch. And maybe stop pillaging so much?"

"It's easy to criticize without having to bear the mantle of responsibility. You may be a great warrior, but I am the Duchess of Caobiu."

"Is that your answer to everything?" Taishi then sprung the feint, her
high attack darting low and then flicking beneath her guard in an upward
flick that gashed Sunri's arm just below the armpit. The duchess expelled
an involuntary gritted cry and dropped to a knee. The Swallow Dances
twirled out of Taishi's grasp and flipped as she launched herself into the
air. Sword and hand met again at the zenith of her jump as she reverse-
gripped her straight sword and plunged it down toward Sunri's exposed

flesh where the shoulder met neck. The Swallow Dances was an instant from biting its prey when it struck smoke, then stone, and then shattered the tile floor.

"What the—" Taishi looked to the side and barely pulled up her guard in time to parry a crescent blade that nearly took her head off. Both women bounced back and reset. Taishi's mouth dropped. Few things surprised her anymore, but this did. "That's a neat trick. I was right. You're actually a nightblossom. Not only that, but the Duchess of Cao-biu is a shadowkill." She was almost in awe. "Now I *really* wish we were friends . . ."

Taishi's words trailed off as the three Mute Men stepped forward. Two barred her way while the third helped Sunri to her feet. The duchess's arm was badly injured, with blood soaking her left side.

"This fight is not over yet," snarled Sunri, trying to shake her Mute Woman loose. The Mute Woman, however, was not having it with Sunri's tantrum. Apparently, they were tasked with protecting the duchess from herself. She picked up the duchess by the waist and dragged her away. The Mute Woman signaled to the other two, who then stepped in between Taishi and the departing Sunri.

"That's a forfeit, by the way. You would have lost anyway," Taishi called. She turned to face the two mute people and muttered to herself, "Well, you always did want to see how you'd match up against them."

Mute Men. The dukes' personal war sects. Fanatically loyal and specially trained since birth, they were the most feared entity throughout the Enlightened States. The Silent Death were the demons and devils that parents told their children about at bedtime to frighten them to sleep. They were the personal extension of the duke's will and might.

Taishi had always been morbidly curious about matching hands with them. "It's time to find out if they're worth the children's nightmares." She sprung first, the Swallow Dances nipping again at their black garb that seemed to shimmer, spreading like ink before turning into smoke and drifting away. The air felt muddled and chilled, and she felt a deadening pull toward them. When her sword struck the Mute Woman's body on a hack to the thigh, it felt like she had just sliced a lump of clay or wet sand. The blade stuck momentarily before Taishi could pry it out. A blow like that with the Swallow Dances usually cut all the way to the bone. Whether it was an armored skirt or an alchemical concoction, Taishi didn't have time to analyze these mysterious war artists.

The man was wielding an almost comically large two-handed saber, commonly called a big saber, though some big sabers were obviously bigger than others. He swung competently, however, several times coming close to loping off one of Taishi's limbs. She managed to find a clean opening and plunge the Swallow Dances through the right side of his chest. If an unnaturally sharp blade slicing through his lungs hurt, he didn't show it as he tried to return the favor with the big saber. She watched in fascination and mild horror as he continued his attack even as blood gushed from the open wound after she yanked the blade out and tore up more of his flesh.

The Mute Woman, on the other hand, was fighting with double chain whips. She was an aggressive one, that girl, swinging each whip with resounding aggression, and then letting it wrap around her fist, forming a cutting and hard metal knuckle to use in close combat. Just like the man, pain did not appear to touch her. She bled from several places where Taishi had cut her, but nothing slowed her down. Their relentless aggression was exhausting, and Taishi soon found herself running out of areas of retreat.

Not only that, but the mute people were fast. Their attacks were coordinated, fighting like a cohesive unit. The man kept Taishi's attention while the woman harried Taishi from her blind side. One would dart in and then the other. Their attacks spilled dribbles of the black intangible ink-like substance that evaporated from their bodies. Their movements were two speeds of high aggression, always pressing and brutal, constantly probing for a killing blow. These mute people did not bother with nuance or setup.

Lastly, these mute people were strong. Taishi could feel her energy sap with each deflection. If every blow was a killing one, then Taishi could not make any mistakes. Every block, every deflection and parry, hit her with such strength and force, they slowly wore her down. It was a struggle to create space and catch her breath.

She now understood what made these mute people so deadly. They were strong, but not unbelievably so. They were skilled, but not more deadly than any expert practitioner. Their tactics were effective, but not more so than any high-level school. No, what made them effective was that they seemed impervious to pain, or worse, even to injury. Taishi's kick to the Mute Woman's chest should have shattered several ribs. That blow would have brought a Hansoo to their knees. Instead, the woman walked right through it. Strikes on them felt like punching sandbags. Their bodies did not register impact. Their faces did not show pain. It didn't even slow them down.

That changed the dynamic of the fight, with both mute people pushing into her space, forcing Taishi to constantly give ground and fight on her heels, which was a position she absolutely detested. Even though her skill level was far greater than theirs, they kept her busy and backtracking for the duration of their exchanges. Finally, with her desperation rising, Taishi latched on to a current that carried her to the other end of the courtyard. She caught two quick breaths to recover. The longer she kept their attention, the farther Jian could travel. He better be running away. She was going to smack him to next cycle if he decided to show up.

Eventually, one of the attacks got through, nicking Taishi along the side of her head, nearly taking off a piece of her ear. Fresh crimson leaked from her wound as burning pain immediately shocked and numbed half her face. Poison. Taishi pushed through the sensation, smothering and swallowing it. She torqued her body in a sharp pivot and punched her arm out, plunging the Swallow Dances through his heart.

Her blow finally caught the attention of the Mute Man this time. He stopped abruptly, looking confused, and then down at his chest. He took a step forward, and then another, his body sliding along the blade closer to the hilt. Then the Mute Man spasmed, and he fell to the side, sliding off the sword. Apparently, Mute Men weren't invulnerable after all.

Taishi pulled to the side, narrowly dodging a heavy swing of the chain whip that bit the ground, slicing and kicking up debris from the stone tiles. It was followed by a second vertical slash, and then two quick horizontal swings as the Mute Woman closed the distance between them, her chain whips recoiling shorter and shorter around her fist.

Sparks burst between them as the Mute Woman's chained fists clashed repeatedly with Taishi's straight sword. The woman had a tendency to skillfully throw double punches from different angles. Taishi wasn't sure why. All were relatively easy to block, with the sword on one punch and either Taishi's forearm or raised knee to block the other. The sharp metal corners of the links of the chain whip that were wrapped around her fists, however, cut with every punch. Taishi's robes were shredded, and then bruises appeared on her arms and legs, soon followed by blood.

Taishi was still giving better than she received, however. The Mute Woman was bleeding in a dozen places. Since she couldn't feel any pain or sense her injuries, Taishi wouldn't be surprised if the Mute Woman continued to fight until she literally bled out. Still, they fought a slow war of attrition between the two women. Which would drop first? The poisoned one, or the one with the blood loss?

Taishi slammed the Mute Woman in the face with a blast of air and then sliced with all her strength at the Mute Woman's arms below the elbow. She tried to pull away, and instead, the sword sliced against the chain whip once more. The Swallow Dances this time struck a link of the chain whip, and the piece unraveled. This was the opening she needed. Taishi flitted to the right almost like a hummingbird and began the swing that would decapitate the Mute Woman. That was when a fit of coughs overtook her. Taishi's chest spasmed, and her thrust went awry.

The Mute Woman seized the opening and countered, punching Taishi across the side of the face, sending her reeling and skidding across the courtyard. She miraculously somehow stayed on her feet. The burning from the poison returned, raking across her face and cutting at her nerves. Taishi's legs gave, and she fell to one knee, her head growing heavy.

"Cheater . . ." she uttered through long, laborious breaths. Taishi tried to rise to her feet, but her knees were shaking. She crashed down to one knee again. The Mute Woman offered a formal bow and then raised her fist to strike the killing blow.

A high-pitched yell pierced the air, and then a silhouette crashed into the Mute Woman, knocking her to the side. A pair of worn brown rubber shoes stepped between Taishi and the Mute Woman. Taishi's body continued to spasm as she struggled to her feet.

Jian put a hand on her shoulder. "Stay back, master. This one is mine."

CHAPTER SIXTY

THE STAND

J ian never thought he would ever—in a hundred lifetimes—need to
cross fists with the Quiet Death, so no, contrary to what he had just
told Taishi, he definitely did *not* have this. These Mute Men, these
creatures—whatever they were—were unkillable, practically immortal.
There was no way he was ever going to beat one in singular combat. He
hoped he made a respectable showing and did not embarrass Taishi too
much.

He suddenly wondered. Why should he worry about Taishi's approval when he was the one about to get torn apart?

"Don't be a concrete head," Taishi panted, trying to stand. "Escape
while you still can. You're never going to beat a Mute Woman, and I'm in
no shape to escape, so let's both do the right thing, boy. Get out of here!"

He voiced under his breath, "Or how about, 'Yay, Jian! You can do it!
Don't give up!'"

"Would that actually motivate you?" she asked.

"Not really," he admitted.

"So, we're just wasting time here. Is that what you're doing?"

"No, I mean, proper motivation matters." Jian looked to change the subject. "Hachi!"

"What is it, Jian?" said the whipfinger, appearing out of the infirmary. His eyes widened. "Oh, damn, it really is a Mute Man. I thought you were being paranoid."

"Take Taishi back to the garage and help Sonaya load the injured onto the wagons. I'll take care of this one."

The Mute Man just stood there with a deadpan expression.

"Jian, you can't fight a Mute Man by yourself."

"Then hurry back and help! I'll stall him as long as I can."

Hachi hesitated. "Right. Come, Master Ling."

She smacked him on the shoulder. "You were supposed to run away from trouble, not toward it, you seedless oaf. That was the whole point of the exercise."

"Sorry, master," said Hachi. "Jian insisted."

"Yes, I did." Jian and the remaining Mute Man continued to eye each other.

"And you obeyed *him* over *me*?"

Hachi hesitated. "Now that you put it that way."

Jian turned his attention back to the Mute Man. He tried a little bravado first. "You already lost one. Why don't you quit while you're ahead, Mute Man."

"Mute Woman," yelled Taishi, her voice growing hoarse as Hachi dragged her away from the battlefield. "Also, watch her left. She drops it like a bad habit."

Now Jian was all alone with the Mute Man—sorry, Mute Woman—and he was terrified.

The Mute Woman's face was shaking, spasming and contorting in strange ways. At first Jian wondered if she was having a stroke, and then he realized she was laughing at him. She adjusted the chains looped around her fists, and then raised her arms, keeping her left elbow intentionally close to her body. She had obviously heard Taishi's critique as well.

Not that any of this mattered. This fight was not going to end well.

Jian was going to die in a very brutal and ugly manner. He hadn't thought this through at all. He had just seen Taishi injured and acted instinctively. Now there was no backing out. He might as well make it a good fight worthy of his sacrifice. There was no way he was going to beat her, but he didn't have to in order to win. Buying time for his master and friends to escape was a good enough win.

As the Prophesied Hero of the Tiandi, that was probably idiocy, but right now Jian didn't care. He was, in all likelihood, a bigger target for her than Taishi. Perhaps the Mute Woman would lose interest in the others after she was done with him.

Well, no choice now but to see what happened. Jian rolled his shoulders and squared up against the Mute Woman. Any attempt at confidence was betrayed by his shaky hands and wobbly stance. Fighting one of the Quiet Death was like having a childhood nightmare come to life. What made it even more humiliating was the Mute Woman wasn't even paying attention to him. She was looking over his shoulder off to the side at where Hachi and Taishi had retreated into the building.

That was when he realized the flaw in his plan.

The Mute Woman had no idea who he was. She probably assumed he was just some soft egg attempting death by Mute Men, which actually was a popular undertaking among many older war artists nearing the end of their lives. One last chance to go in a fiery blaze of glory. Right now was certainly not one of those cases.

Should he tell her?

Jian felt pretentious, and his cheeks turned red even thinking of the phrase. He stuttered as he belted it out. "Do you know who I am? I'm the Champion of the Five Under Heaven."

It was technically the Four Under Heaven now.

Jian stepped in front of her as she stalked in the direction toward Taishi. The Mute Woman, eyes still intent on her target, was dismissive and threw a lazy backhand to knock him out of the way. Both were mildly surprised when he successfully blocked it, probably Jian a little more so. Her lazy swipe hurt. Even swung casually, the force of the swing knocked him backward and nearly off his feet. Nearly.

Jian shook his aching forearms, which had taken the brunt of the blow. "Hey, that wasn't too bad—"

The Mute Woman surged forward with a straight punch. Jian saw it coming. He just managed to cover up. The straight punch hit him in the forearms, and this time the impact sent him skidding flat on his back. It felt like someone had just run him over with a wagon. The hit to his forearms was so hard he felt the pain from his shoulders down to his lower back. He groaned and lifted his head.

The Mute Woman had already forgotten him and was almost to the door where his friends were being loaded onto the wagon inside the garage. Jian grunted his way back to his feet and grabbed a shovel lying against the wall. He held on to the end and rushed behind the Mute Woman, swinging it with all his force. The shovel struck the Mute Woman across the side of the head and splintered into fragments. This finally caught her attention.

The blow knocked her sideways, and she stumbled a few steps. The Mute Woman turned to face Jian, as if actually seeing him for the first time. She looked surprised, curious, and definitely angry. Then she tried to murder him.

The Mute Woman pounced, throwing heavy punches in rapid succession. Each would have knocked him out if they had connected. Jian ducked the first two and blocked the third, which again knocked him off his feet. How could anyone be so strong or hit so hard?

She followed up with three more killing blows, making zero attempt to feint or set up her attacks. Jian backpedaled as he defended himself. He couldn't take too many of her heavy hits so instead worked on maintaining odd angles and deflecting her strikes to the side. He found far more success working this way once he was able to gauge her speed. The fight began to slow down for him as he was able to better read and predict her movements. Jian even managed a counterattack, kicking her once in the thigh and connecting a punch to the side of her head, although he was pretty certain he did more damage to his hand than he did to her head.

The Mute Woman continued to move forward and apply more intense pressure, throwing combinations and flurries, and several long, sweeping kicks. Her attacks chained together and came at different angles, each thrown with the full power of her jing. Jian did his best to anticipate her cadence and avoided taking severe damage, and then attempted to hit back.

Jian was honestly shocked how well he was doing so far. The woman was strong and fast, but not nearly as powerful as Taishi. Jian had trained with the best; everyone else felt like a shadow in comparison. He couldn't believe he was standing toe-to-toe with her. She wasn't quicker or smarter or more skilled. His confidence soared. Maybe he *could* beat her!

Jian blocked a particularly sneaky sequence when the Mute Woman tried to trip him. It didn't work. He saw it coming. Jian stepped back and grinned. "Hah! Do you even know who I am? Maybe now you should—"

She snapped a straight hard kick down the middle, connecting with his chest and sending him tumbling and rolling on the dirt until he came to a stop with his head bumping against the garage's wooden wall.

The world blinked momentarily. He groaned, sitting up. "Ow. That one hurt."

The Mute Woman advanced. Her movements were more deliberate now. She was actually taking him seriously now.

He scrambled back to his feet and assumed a defensive Wind Flower stance, his arms out, lilting like a tree swaying in the wind. Then he changed his mind and switched to a Sunken Turtle and then once more to something he had invented a few months back, and then once more to Shrieking Dragonfly. Nothing felt right.

The Mute Woman didn't seem to care what tactics he was employing as they met again at the edge of the courtyard, hands matching in a complex exchange. They exchanged elbow strikes and kicks, sweeps and flying knees. Jian certainly felt outmatched but not too outclassed, not enough that he didn't get a few solid hits in as well. Still nothing fazed the Mute Woman. Maybe they actually *were* immortal.

The melee continued with neither giving ground, but the injuries accumulated were decidedly one-sided. After several exchanges, the Mute Woman looked as fresh as if she had just woken up from a nap and was going through morning stretches. Jian on the other hand was battered blue and purple all over, and leaking like a stuck pig.

Her chained punches were tenderizing his guard until finally his arms decided they were done with this fight. The next time he tried to raise his guard, his arms refused to cooperate. He just managed to duck a swing that would likely have taken his head clean off.

Jian had to get away. He wasn't going to last much longer. He tried to take to the air and whisk away on a current. The Mute Woman wasn't allowing any of that, however. The chains wrapped around her wrists and fists unraveled, and she whipped him hard across the back with them as he tried to flee, knocking him off the current and sending him pitching headfirst back to the hard stone ground. The jaunt into darkness lasted longer this time.

She walked over and grabbed his ankle with one hand, and picked him up, hanging him upside down as if he were a child. She swung him around in a looping circle to pick up speed and tossed him, sending him flying and crashing into and through the garage's wooden walls.

He landed just inside the garage under a plume of dust half buried by debris. He raised his hand weakly as the Mute Woman stepped through the freshly made entrance. One of the chains wrapped around her wrist slowly unraveled. The Mute Woman was like a terra cotta warrior, unrelenting and unstoppable. He barely slowed her down.

Jian's vision was still blurred as he tried to stand, but this time his legs gave. He tried to crawl away, but she was on top of him once more, picking him up by the neck. He screamed and punched her a few times in the face, but succeeded only in breaking two of his fingers.

The Mute Woman wrapped one of the chains around his neck and tightened it, cutting the sharp metal edges into his flesh. Jian kicked out once, twice, and then his legs went limp. She continued to eye him with an intense, unblinking stare. This time, there was nothing dismissive about her gaze. He had earned her respect, and she was treating him like a peer. She rotated her wrist, which caused the chain to twist, causing the sharp links to close off his breathing even more. He managed to take in a few shallow gulps of air, but there was not much else he could do.

The world began to dim a third time, possibly permanently.

Something struck the Mute Woman on the side of the head, snapping it violently to the side. She stumbled and then spasmed again as two more metal bullets punctured her body.

"Get up, Jian," Hachi called.

Jian fell onto all fours, coughing and retching. "About time you got here," he squeaked.

"No, really, you should get up," a voice tickled his ear. Sonaya appeared next to Hachi at the infirmary door. "What in the Tiandi is going on, you inflated strutting fool? I'm gone ten minutes and you pick a fight with a Mute Man? Are you *trying* to get yourself killed?"

"Woman," he mumbled, more out of reflex. "Mute Woman."

There was a pause before the drowned fist next spoke. "I find you very deeply attractive right now, Wen Jian."

"I do have a sparkling—"

"Hush. Don't ruin it by talking, Five Champ. Now get up and help."

The Mute Woman was terribly angry with Hachi, running him down as the whipfinger retreated. Whipfingers specialized in fighting at range and avoidance. Every time she closed in on him, Hachi skipped backward and flicked bullets at her. The shots would usually kill a person from the sheer force of the impact, but the Mute Woman was wincing only slightly as each blow thudded into her dense flesh.

Sonaya joined to assist Hachi, using her compulsion to distract the woman. The Mute Woman was having none of that, however, and tuned her out. Sonaya was having some effect, however. The Quiet Death's jaws were clenched, and she continually shot annoyed looks at the drowned fist. Jian tried to do his part by staying between the Mute Woman and the others, but he was worn down and had little energy left, managing only to slow the Mute Woman a little as she knocked him down and ran him over on her way to attack his friends. He grabbed on to an ankle and held on tight as she stepped over and dragged him along the ground.

This certainly was an embarrassing scene, to witness the Prophesied Hero of the Tiandi being dragged along the dirt like an unruly child, but he didn't care. This monster was trying to hurt his friends. The Mute

Woman shucked him off after she was halfway across the courtyard chasing Hachi, and then shuddered as an arrow struck her chest. Another sank into her shoulder. Jian glanced up and saw Kaiyu squatting at the edge of the slaughterhouse roof. He carried his father's staff as a bow. Kaiyu loosed two more arrows and then slid down the roof. He leaped off, flipped in the air, and came down with Summer Bow in its staff form, slamming it onto the ground where the Quiet Death had stood moments before, cracking a row of stone tiles. This entire courtyard would have to be repaved at this rate.

The boy's youthful demeanor was gone. "People like her killed my ba, didn't they?"

"Sort of" was the best Jian could muster without blatantly lying.

The Houtou disciple was still in shock and grieving over his father. Kaiyu snarled, sounding feral as he twirled Summer Bow over his head and attacked the Mute Woman.

The Mute Woman responded to the new threat by promptly forgetting Jian. He actually felt a little neglected. She unleashed a single whip chain this time to meet Kaiyu's bendy and tricky staff. Xinde charged in next, wielding his three-sectional staff. Sonaya and Hachi joined in, and soon the three were giving the Quiet Death more than she could manage.

Jian tried to pick himself up and help, but Zofi was there, grabbing him by the waist and pulling him away from the fight.

He was too weak to even struggle against her. "Let me go. I need to—"

"You already filled your quota of getting beaten up, Five Champ. You're done for the day."

"Not you too," he mumbled.

Zofi dragged him next to Taishi, who was slumped beside the cadaver wagon again. His master's face was pale, and her robes were soaked with sweat. She covered her mouth with her sleeve and coughed. Flecks of red stained the fabric there. His master wrapped her hand around his neck and pulled him close.

"Why do you keep changing your guard during the fight? Take what the enemy gives you and adapt. Stances aren't just there to look good."

Taishi fell into sharp coughs and hacks and leaned against him for support. "By the way, you're telegraphing too much with that five-frame combination sequence. You're changing levels too often. Stick with one for longer and lull them into complacency. Also, slip through her guard like an eel, not an oiled-up baboon. Also, I keep pointing out that thing you do with the positioning of your lead foot. For the thousandth time, can you not embarrass me with such basic mistakes?"

Taishi spent the next minute breaking down each of his errors in that fight, which was a surprising number given he had lasted only two minutes with the Mute Woman. It made Jian wonder how he had survived. Of course, he wouldn't have without his friends. It was another good reason to have come back for them. Taishi's analysis was sound, and her advice was invaluable, however.

Eventually, the combined effort of those four war artists was too much even for a Mute Woman. Xinde and Kaiyu kept her occupied. The Mute Woman slumped to a knee after Xinde struck her with the end of his three-sectional staff. When she tried to get away, Sonaya disoriented her, preventing her escape, and then Hachi followed with a killing shot to her temple. The Mute Woman collapsed to the ground with the rest of their winded group standing over her.

"Killing her will cause problems," said Hachi. "There will be investigations. Neither the nobility nor the broods take the death of Mute Men lightly."

Sonaya pointed at the dead Mute Man that Taishi had slain. "We already have one dead Mute Man. What does it matter if we add another?"

Jian watched from the sidelines as they congratulated one another and celebrated their hard-earned kill. Hachi was giving Sonaya a piggyback ride because she had hurt her foot. Kaiyu and Xinde were both beaten up but wore wide, weary smiles. The former Longxian senior and now Caobiu captain said something to Kaiyu, and the boy giggled. Go figure: the two people who were everyone's friend instantly became friends with each other. Few things forged quicker and stronger bonds than battle.

It was a good thing his friends were here. They had to save him from his own hubris. Everyone had had to clean up his messes lately. Jian once again felt like an outsider looking in as they stood together and basked in their victory. He couldn't help but grimace; he should be used to this by now.

Jian swallowed his bitterness and waved as they approached. "Great job, everyone."

"Jian," said Xinde, coming forth to clutch his shoulders. "By the Tiandi, I only caught glimpses of your fight with the Mute Man, but you were mighty! I can't believe this was the same boy who showed up one night death-touched and mostly dead. You've come such a long way."

"I have?" Jian blinked. He certainly didn't think so.

"You held your own with her for quite a long time." Xinde nodded. "I know when I have been surpassed by one of my former students, and it fills me with pride."

"That was good work," said Hachi. "You bought me enough time to fetch the others."

"I totally did, right?" Jian replied. It never dawned on him how his actions could have helped his friends. "I may have even weakened the Mute Woman, right?"

Neither Xinde nor Hachi responded to that.

Sonaya walked up to him and dug her nails into his sore ribs, making him scrunch his body like a pill bug. "Don't ever try to fight a Mute Man without me, you silly duckling."

As his face wavered closer, she reached over and planted a hungry, yearning kiss. Her soft lips pressed against his. Their tongues touched, and every ache and pain and screaming discomfort momentarily faded. She let go of him a few moments later, and he promptly fell to the floor.

Sonaya smirked and helped him up. "Come on, Five Champ. We're not safe yet."

The door to the infirmary slammed open, and Fausan appeared accompanied by a well-dressed court official wearing a windmill hat. "Fortuitous news, children." His face wore a smile. "I, the God of Gamblers, once again caught the golden rabbit of luck and cooked its ears for a hearty meal! My good friend here, Lord Hoosoh, the embassylord, and truly a wonderful man who happens to be one of my biggest fans, has graciously granted you the loan of his household carriage as long as we promise to keep quiet, stay out of trouble, and don't go excessively committing any crimes that could be linked back to him . . ." His boisterousness turned to confusion as he noticed, for the first time, the gaping hole in the garage wall. "What happened?"

The embassylord, a plump and stout older man with a red button nose, who looked fond of wine, gawked at the extensive damage to his garage, and then his mouth dropped when his gaze trained on the black-clad body lying in the middle. "Is that a dead Caobiu Mute Man on embassy grounds?"

"Mute Woman," Jian muttered absently.

CHAPTER SIXTY-ONE

HOMECOMING

Malinde the master tinker, sectchief of the Nezra chapter—
albeit uncertified by the Head Tinker Main Branch for obvious reasons—member of the Nezra Council, interim leader
of the Nezra clan, and the head of the Nezra City Reclamation project,
woke with an upset stomach that caused her to spend a good hour in
front of a piss basin retching the contents from last night's dinner.

"Are you all right?" asked Kara, her apprentice, Mali's fourth this
year.

"Tea, bland." She retched. "And make it hot. Scalding."

"I'm sorry, mentor, but Supplychief Shobansa threatened to cut off
my hands if he caught me stealing from the store room again."

Mali raised her fist. "You tell that coin-sniffing bastard that the master
tinker can't start her day without a kettle of hot tea." She leaned forward
and threw up again. After several more dry heaves and heavy panting, she
raised her head and stared forlornly at the puddle of yesterday's banana-
wrapped rice balls floating in the basin. What a waste. The clan was already working on half rations, though Mali suspected the mothers and
great mothers were sneaking her extra meals.

Mali sat back after it felt like her stomach had nothing left. She stuck her tongue out, miserable. She was fatigued and cranky. Her feet were swollen. She felt the intense need to pee but knew that nothing would come out. She was also hungry again. Mali really wished Daewon was here to read poetry and rub her feet. Most of all, however, she just wanted some hot tea.

"How long until breakfast?" she asked.

Kara checked a little drip clock. "It's the middle of the night, mentor."

Mali cursed. "Well, that should make it easier for you to steal some sparkstones from storage to brew some tea."

"I'm sorry, mentor, but I like having hands."

"Then don't get caught. Go!"

Mali watched as her neophyte scuttled away. Sho really wasn't going to cut off the girl's hands. At least, Mali didn't think so. The lass was one of dozens of clan orphans who had lost both parents during the destruction of Nezra, and Nezra did not abandon their own. The lass had sneaked into Mali's quarters one night looking for something to steal or eat. She had come across Mali's tinker books and became so fascinated with them that Mali had woken up the next morning to Kara still flipping through them. What was more impressive was that the girl already understood many of the basic tinker concepts just by studying the pictures. Mali had made the lass her apprentice on the spot.

Mali had high hopes for the girl. Good talent was hard to come by these days, especially for their ragtag clan of refugees. Kara was only twelve, young for an apprentice, but the clan would need their best and brightest if they were to survive their exile. The girl was a little socially awkward and could become so focused on a task that she forgot everything else, but she was inquisitive and possessed a tinker's mind. In many ways, the precocious lass reminded Mali of herself at that age.

Mali checked the drip clock again. It was still early, though she had long lost any sense of time down here in the caves. While most Nezrans found time to spend on the surface, at least once every few days, Mali had been too busy excavating the city pods to bother. The last time she had laid eyes on the sun was when she saw Daewon and Sali depart for the True Freeze nearly an entire cycle ago, or it felt that way.

Mali blew a raspberry and stood. If she wasn't going to sleep, she might as well make herself useful and head to the dig site. The work had gone better than she had hoped, for the most part. Fourteen city pods had been dug up or chipped out of the ice with at least double that number still waiting to be excavated. The problem now was sourcing the materials for repairs and to power these beauties. The clan was low on just about everything, including food, drinking water, and most basic necessities.

To make matters worse, their luck, as expected, had run out. A few weeks ago, a Liqusa patrol—by dumb luck—ran into a group of howlers and chased the children within a half day's trek to Shetty. Now the enemy Katuia clan had moved into the immediate region with regular patrols passing within sight of the mountain. This made hunting and foraging risky, and the clan's meager stores were suffering and nearly dry. The howler leaders, all children, were not seasoned or skilled enough to reorganize and stay safe. The council had decided that the children's lives were not worth the risk. They would need to wait until Hampa returned. The howlers were an important part of the clan now. They could use a permanent leader, or at least a custodian.

Mali hurried out of her quarters and made her way through the small maze of tunnels toward the dig site. She wasn't showing yet, but it comforted her to place her hand over the small life growing inside her. Daewon hoped for a boy, while Sali wanted a girl. Mali just wanted a healthy baby who would have a real chance at a normal life. The odds of that happening were growing dimmer by the day, but Mali was never going to lose hope.

"Don't you worry about a thing, Little Sprocket," she cooed. That was her nickname for the baby until they settled on a name. Daewon had volunteered several names so far, and Sali for sure would have her own list to offer. Mali hadn't admitted it yet, but the main reason why she hadn't settled on a name yet was because she was waiting to see what happened to Salminde. If it was a girl, and Sali didn't make it . . .

Mali reached the dig site and, as expected, was the only one there. She took her usual place at the workbench and continued taking apart the giant pistons of a war pod tank track. She had worked on similar things before back on Nezra, but the designs appeared to have come from an entirely different engineering tree. Mali would be content spending the rest of her life working on these contraptions, which might be the case.

To her disappointment, these didn't appear to be war pods. Their tracks were thinner and longer than the ones typically used in the modern cities, yet the links appeared more tightly integrated, which would make these machineries more efficient and quicker. The technology was far older, yet also more advanced. It made Mali ponder what other fantastic technologies had been lost over time.

For the next several hours, she hummed as she worked, wielding a scalpel like a painter while brushing dirt from the dismantled pieces like a loving mother. Work like this was joyful, when she could forget the troubles and miseries of the world and just bask in the lyrical puzzles that all these gears and parts made. Kara stopped by at some point to serve lukewarm tea. It would have to do, although Mali did take a torch to her cup to heat it up more when no one was around.

Mali was deep into her work, whistling an off-key tune her parents used to sing. They would belt it out poorly, but proudly. Mali had a theory her parents' bad singing was the reason Sali always talked like she was annoyed and shouting. Mali had been thinking a lot about her mother lately, for obvious reasons. She was cursing herself for not remembering the lullabies. How was she going to pass the tradition back to baby Sprocket?

She was nearly done with it when a small indentation along the side of the metal piece caught her eye. She squinted and brought the lantern closer. There it was: the curved dome over a line, and then to the right two pointers up. It was a city marking!

Excitement filled Mali so instantly she nearly threw up again. She rolled off her seat and hurried to her shelf of books, where she pulled a gray-bound notebook detailing the old capital cities that roamed the Grass Sea. She rummaged through the pages, searching to match that symbol. Mali found it near the end, in the golden age legendary section. Not a war city, but nearly as good. Her fingers trembled as she matched the curved dome over a line, and two pointers sticking upward, the symbol of a hare.

These pods must belong to Kahun the Elusive, the speed city, lost six centuries ago when it was ambushed by the Happan Horde. Mali skimmed the description, most of which validated what she had unearthed so far. Known as the Elusive, Kahun was the smallest and the least armed of the legendary capital cities. It was also the fastest and widely considered the most versatile. Its material hailed from the White Ghost—

A commotion pulled Mali out of her book. She saw two of her tinkers run past the site entrance. "Hey, Rha, what's going on?" And they were gone.

Then the dull ringing of the cowbells in the distance became more pronounced: the general alarm. That could usually mean one of several things, but none of them good. It was most likely a cave-in or a collapsed wall, or perhaps water had leaked into some of the chambers. Mali hoped it wasn't that stupid giant lizard again. The children had taken to calling him Sludgy, and he had proved a terrible nuisance. The thing left a trail of corrosive slime everywhere it went, and none of the hunters so far had managed to slay it.

Just in case, Mali slid off her seat and tossed her apron on the table. She lifted her repeating crossbow off its perch, grabbed her ammo pouch, and joined the throng of Nezra heading toward the camp's entrance. Mali found Supplychief Shobansa directing traffic at one of the main corridors. "What's going on, Sho?"

"Intruders in the main tunnel heading for the clan," said Shobansa. "Howler couldn't get a good look in the dark."

An urge of hope swelled in her. "Could it be Daewon?"

"There were at least ten in this group," he shouted. "No! Put that oil drum back. No tar. We can always burn that for heat when we run out of everything else."

"Won't the fumes just kill us in these caves?" said Mali.

He shrugged. "Pick your poison: freeze or fumes."

One of the older great mothers who over-mothered her pregnancy stormed up to the supply chief. "Mali has to go back to bed. She's with child. You can't expect her to fight."

Sho opened his mouth as if to reply and then turned to Mali. "Lua has a point. Maybe you should sit back."

"Every child of Nezra defends her home," Mali replied.

"Think of the child, Malinde. Not this one," sputtered Lua, jabbing her forehead, and then touching her belly. "This one."

Mali pulled out a tall, thin, rectangular clip of bolts from her ammo pouch and slammed the entire box through the loading chamber. She loaded the crossbow with a quick jerk of the loading lever and then stared down both Lua and Shobansa. "Let's go."

And that was that.

Mali joined about fifty warriors manning a loose barricade made by their travel wagons, crates, and other packed supplies. That was another reason Shobansa refused to allow anything flammable in the caves unless necessary. About an equal number of their regular clan folks had shown up as well to provide auxiliary backup. Some were too old, and others too weak, but mostly because they didn't have enough weapons to go around.

Mali took position at a sliver in between two boarded-up window frames serving as murder holes. The barricade fell silent as those manning it snuffed their torches and closed their lanterns. For the next ten minutes, they heard nothing save for the usual cave noises: dripping water, creeks gurgling, and the static of small rocks shifting. Then, she heard the sound of muffled footsteps. They were soft, but grew louder and more plentiful with each passing minute until it became an entire chorus of echoing footsteps.

A spark of torchlight appeared in the distance. Mali, who was resting against a stack of chicken crates, signaled to those around her to rouse as they focused on those approaching. The low chatter spread as men and women settled back into their places. Someone accidentally kicked his shin on a board and cursed.

The procession in the distance continued to grow. There must be at least ten with mounts, so it couldn't be Daewon and Sali. Mali signaled to Shobansa. "If it's a patrol, we can't let any survivors report back to the city." The supply chief nodded and spoke to the next man down the line. The torches grew closer and footsteps louder as the procession finally came to a stop about twenty yards from the barricade gates.

"Stop right there." Shobansa opened a lantern, spotlighting the lead person in the group. "Who are you? What do you want?"

One cloaked figure stepped forward with his hands raised. "Sorry, it's the middle of the night. I was trying not to wake anyone."

Mali recognized that nasally voice anywhere. She jumped up, excited. "Daewon!" She squeezed through the murder hole and dropped to the ground, flinging herself into the arms of her husband. "You're still breathing!" She sobbed as he held her close. She noticed the strange people wearing strange animal skins behind him. Who were they?

"I'm over here, Sprout." Mali looked back toward the barricade gate and saw Sali leaning against it, grinning. "I went ahead and have been waiting here for someone to notice me for five minutes." Sali swept her up as Mali rushed into her big sister's arms. The tears were coming freely. All this excitement really made her want to throw up again.

"I wasn't sure if I would ever see you again."

"Of course we'd come back," said Sali, her voice muffled by Mali's shoulder.

That wasn't what Mali had meant, considering their depleted stores, but that was a worry for later.

The rest of the Nezrans poured out from the barricades to join them. By now, word had spread and every man, woman, and child who had come to defend their clan stayed to see the viperstrike's return. There were several minutes of hugs and greetings, back-slaps and clasped forearms. Mali couldn't stop the waterworks, nor could she release Daewon's hands.

Shobansa, of course, kept the reunion brief as he immediately moved past pleasantries. "Salminde, who are your friends?"

Sali looked up from speaking with a few of the warriors. "Nezra now has allies, and they sent help. This is Marhi, the Arctic Fox Rumblerlead and Ambassador of Hrusha."

A hard-looking girl with a handsome face wearing a white fur coat stepped forward. "The people of Hrusha welcome our new allies in our mutual fight against the Katuia. To aid your efforts, we brought with us six crates of ore, fabrication machinery, and ten bolts of fur. We also offer the services of a metalsmith, two sparksmiths, four Arnisma fighting masters, three furweavers, a doctor, and an accountant."

Mali had no idea what the last one was, but Shobansa's eyes certainly lit up at the mention of the person.

"What about you, sister? Did you find a cure for the Pull of the Khan?" Mali already knew the answer to that, however. Seeing Sali up close, embracing her, she felt her sister's strength. Even her hair seemed to have revived, being richer and fuller.

"Yes, I'm cured." Sali took a long deep breath, almost a sad sigh.

"That's amazing, no?"

"There's good and bad. It's complicated."

Mali couldn't care less about what these complications were. They would figure them out when the time came. What was important was that Sali was alive and healthy. She hadn't believed there was a cure and had more recently accepted the inevitable that Salminde, the last of her family and protector of Nezra, was not long for this world. Sprocket was going to know their aunt. Mali's eyes watered.

Mali looked around. There was a missing face. "Where's Hampa?" Sali's and Daewon's answering expressions told her everything she needed to know. "I'm so sorry, sister."

"I wouldn't be here if it wasn't for him," said Sali. "He saved my life. With the spirit shaman's dogs bearing down on us, he barred their way and bought me enough time to escape and return back to you. He died a hero." Sali's eyes intensified but betrayed no other emotion. Her warrior's mask had always been strong.

It was then Mali made her choice. Her hand drifted to her belly. "You can tell young Hampa all about his namesake when he is of age."

Of course Shobansa had to ruin the nice moment. "What is this complication you speak of, Salminde? Will it affect Nezra?"

"Yes, you could say that," Sali replied slowly, apparently picking her words carefully. "Me being alive and sick from the Khan's curse was the only thing that prevented the Eternal Khan of Katuia from returning to this world. There's this being called a Xoangiagu . . . it's a long story. I'll explain later. How goes the excavation, Master Tinker?"

The recent discovery Mali had made leaped into her mind. "It's going well. Our new home is an old home. I found markings this morning revealing that this site is the final resting place of Kahun."

Daewon startled. "The legendary speed city?"

Mali nodded. "She's recoverable, as long as we have the resources to revive her."

"Hrusha will ensure that you do," said Marhi, stepping forward.

"Nezra has returned." For as long as Mali had been alive, she had never seen her sister's tears. Now, they flowed freely. The famed viperstrike's chest heaved, and her voice cracked. "We have a home. We finally have a home again."

"What did you mean the Khan will return sooner?" asked Shobansa. "What does that mean for Nezra?"

"It means there will be battle and bloodshed in our future." Sali's expression of joyous elation quickly turned grim. She broke away from Mali's embrace and spoke directly to her people. "For far too long, the spirit shamans have used the Eternal Khan to control and hold dominion over our people. I say no more! There can be no peace as long as the Khan walks our world. We must destroy his cycle and return him back to his birthplace in the depths of the Sun Under Lagoon. It is time to shatter the spirit shamans' hold over our people and free all Katuia once and for all. We fight for our freedom and the freedom for future generations!"

The clan raised their fists. Scattered cheers of "Viperstrike" and "Nezra lives forever" echoed throughout the caves.

Sali's eyes grew intense and hard. "My brothers and sisters of Nezra. It is time to prepare for war!"

CHAPTER SIXTY-TWO

THE TEST

Jian sat hunched on the bench behind the temple tulip garden called the Field of Bottom Smiling Faces. The Temple of the Tiandi he was currently hiding in was nice and picturesque. The early fall season of the first cycle of the new year in Vauzan was utterly enchanting and splendid. Having grown up in the Celestial Palace and then at the Diyu Temple, Jian had been used to dry, scorching summers or frigid, wet winters. Vauzan was the first place he'd been where the weather was perfect and comfortable. According to some of the initiate monks here, what they gained in the warm seasons they would pay for during the cold ones. Supposedly the freeze crawled this far south regularly during the third cycle winters.

Zofi appeared a moment later. She sat next to him and leaned in. "Is Taishi awake? Have you seen her? Where is everyone else?"

He shrugged, feeling annoyed and on edge. "It looks like we were the only ones she summoned."

"That's good, no? What's the matter?"

"Sonaya just admitted that Taishi had awoken three days ago." He failed to hide his frustration. "Why didn't they fetch us sooner?"

"Maybe she needed time to recover first."

"She's my master. What if she had died? I wouldn't..." Jian clenched his fists. "... I wouldn't have had the chance to say goodbye."

Zofi patted his thigh. "Well, she lived. She didn't die, so don't go looking for trouble. Enough bad things happen as it is."

Their escape from Allanto five weeks ago had been surprisingly clean and uneventful, except for the minor stumble with Fausan having to kill Lord Hoosoh when the embassylord reneged on his offer to let them use the carriage. Instead, the God of Gamblers' biggest fan tried to have them seized and arrested. They had managed to rumble their way out of the embassy, through the city, and past the city gates ahead of both the Cao-biu and Shulan magistrates and soldiers. From there, it was a straight shot west along Ryli Road to Vauzan, the capital of Shulan. For a reason that still eluded Jian, Taishi had insisted they head there, to the Temple of the Tiandi, before she lost consciousness.

The door slid open, and Templeabbot Lee Mori walked out. He nodded. "Good, children, it's just you two. That's all she wants to see."

The templeabbot had not even blinked when the group of ragtag refugees and fugitives rolled up in a cadaver wagon filled with a group of injured war artists, three of whom had rather large bounties on their heads. He had immediately summoned his temple healers to try to save Taishi, and she had been in an induced coma ever since. Until now. Technically, three days ago.

"Why didn't you summon me the moment she woke?" The question still burned in him.

Lee Mori wasn't fazed. "Better she explains it than me, but don't be so dense to think Ling Taishi wouldn't have called for her disciple earlier if she could have."

"I..." Jian scratched the back of his head. His ears felt a bit warm.

The group had rested at the temple for the past two weeks, which included the end of spring and the entire summer of the first cycle, basking in the perfect temperate weather, while the temple healers cared for Taishi. Mori was kind enough to give them a small, abandoned house at the edge of the temple grounds. Though they had used assumed names, the templeabbot immediately recognized Jian and declared that their secret was safe with him. Taishi had claimed to trust him completely, and that was good enough for Jian. The two must have shared some sort of old bond because Taishi trusted no one, not even Jian, most of the time.

"Come in." Mori stopped Zofi after Jian passed. "Taishi asked to speak to Jian first if that's all right."

Jian walked tentatively into the house as if fearful that any noise he made would aggravate his master's injuries. It was stuffy in here and smelled like medicine and sickness. A row of incense sticks in small vases lined one wall. In the back was a faded Mosaic of the Tiandi. Hanging on the opposite wall was the Unabridged Wisdoms of Goramh stitched on lambskin, notably chronicling his heavier drinking years. Three healers who frequently tended Taishi were mashing herbs at a small table in the middle of the room. All three stopped what they were doing and stared.

The hair on the back of Jian's neck rose. He recognized the frantically devout. The mood of the air was strange. Over the past few weeks, since they fled Allanto, Jian had begun to effortlessly sense the air currents instead of having to study them. They almost felt alive, brushing against his skin with moods and personalities of their own. In a way, the currents now felt more present yet invisible all at once.

One of the healers stood from her chair and bowed. She would have fallen to her knee had Jian not stopped her. "That's not necessary, Master Healer."

"This way then, prophesied hero," she said. The healer was a little older than Jian, likely an apprentice, but the way she looked at him made him deeply uncomfortable, as if she were about to either worship him or try to marry him. Sonaya would probably dare him to do something about it.

The healer led him to the adjacent room, where Taishi was sitting on a heated marble bed with the sheets pulled up to her chest eating noodles from a plate of food on her lap. It was even hotter here than it had been in the last room. Taishi's face glistened with sweat, and she looked pale. Her cheeks were sunken, and she was losing chunks of hair. His master looked over at him. "About time."

Jian ran to her bedside. "Master, I thought you were—"

She bounced a chopstick off the crown of his head. "Don't start that idiocy again. I thought I had beaten those silly habits out of you."

He rubbed his smarting head. At least her demeanor had returned. "Is there anything you need? You should rest, Taishi."

"I'll rest when I'm dead," said Taishi. "Tell me, disciple. How's your Grand Supreme Punch?"

He was taken aback. "The Grand Supreme Punch? I know it's fine, I guess. It's impossible to land in a fight. It's a worthless technique."

Taishi fell into a fit of coughs, which then set off a chain reaction of more coughs as her body jerked about violently. Another healer, an herbalist this time, entered the room carrying a tray of a steaming drink. Eventually, the episode ended, and Taishi sounded like herself again. She continued. "It has one use, which you will now need."

"I don't understand, master."

His master sighed, her shoulders slumped. "The Grand Supreme Punch is a death touch, the only one in our lineage. You are wrong that it is a worthless technique, Jian. It has one specific use. It's the engine and tool for the Zhang windwhisper final test."

"What?" Jian felt ill. He shook his head. "No, no, that's impossible. I'm not ready."

"You're ready, son. You have to be." She then added, "I'm dying, Jian."

"What?" This time he could think of no other words. "That's not possible. It's just an injury. The temple healers will take care of you." Hot, frantic rage engulfed him as he rounded on the three healers working in the other room. "What are you doing standing there? Do something!"

"There's nothing for them to do," said Taishi. "I've felt my bond to the heavens tighten every day for a while now."

This time, Jian did fall to his knees, not giving a whit what she thought about that. It was difficult to find the words he needed. "How long do you have, master?"

She shrugged. "Two days. Two months. Two years. Who knows."

He folded his arms. "Then what's the rush? I'm not ready yet. We can revisit this in two years."

She cupped his chin. "You are ready, Jian, and you have been for a while, physically." She touched his head. "Now you are ready here as well."

"I still have much to learn," Jian pressed. "With your guidance, I can grow even stronger and smarter."

"You do still have much to learn, but we're out of time, my son." She held up her scarred and blemished arm. There was a faint tremor in her hand. "I've been sick for a while, Jian. The Mute Woman's tainted blade has only hastened it. I can feel the poison disrupting the jing flowing through my body." She drew in a breath and squeezed his hand. "Between my sickness and this poison . . . That's why you have to do the test now, while I am still able to transfer the power of the Zhang lineage before it's lost forever."

"No, no, no," he sobbed. Jian had never wanted this. "I don't want to lose you too."

Taishi looked annoyed. "Stop crying. I'm not spending the last few hours of my life dealing with you crying over me."

"But please, master . . ."

"And I will certainly not tolerate my disciple questioning my instructions. Do not shame me, disciple."

Jian squeezed his eyes shut and swallowed the blubbery sobs threatening to escape him. The door creaked open and slammed shut, and then Zofi stormed into the room. "That's your plan? You're going to make him pass the test? You're going to death-by-disciple right when he needs you most? What sort of a selfish bitch are you?"

"These are holy grounds!" Mori shouted as he stomped in behind her.

"How did you overhear us?" asked Taishi.

"I was spying on you outside the window," said the mapmaker's daughter. "Stop trying to change the subject. What sort of idiotic mule-brained shit-stomping egg white idea is it for Jian to kill you?"

"That's enough!" snapped Taishi. "I don't plan on spending my last hours in a spitting argument, either."

Zofi jabbed a finger at Jian. "You think he has a chance right now against the Eternal Khan? That's laughable."

"He will have no chance if he doesn't pass the final test. The continuation of our generational jing is vital to the power of the master windwhisper. Otherwise, his final power will never reach the celestial greatness that is required to fulfill the prophecy. If I die before he uses the Grand Supreme Punch on me, then it will be lost forever."

"Still . . ." Zofi was at a loss for words. Her eyes brimmed. "It's too soon!"

"Any time is the right time when it is time," said Taishi. "Now, I need to prepare. Leave me and summon the others. I don't want to make a big deal out of this."

Jian stood, numb. His feet refused to move. "Master, there has to be another way."

"This is what you signed up for when you became my disciple." Her tone grew stern. "How did you think this was going to end?"

"I . . ." The truth was Jian had pushed it out of his mind. Heck, had he known the Grand Supreme Punch was the technique used in the final windwhisper test, he would not have bothered to learn it at all. He fell to his knees. "Please, master, don't make me do this."

Zofi sank beside him as well. "Please, Taishi. We need you."

"Enough groveling," she snapped. "I've made up my mind. Inform the others. I'll say my goodbyes, and then we perform the ceremony in the private garden behind the Pagoda of Sacrifice. It's fitting, I guess, my final sacrifice will be a gift to you and the people of Zhuun."

Jian's mind raced, but he was in too great a panic to think clearly. "I don't think I can do it, Taishi. I know I can't. Just give me a little more time. A few years, months, anything!"

"Groveling is beneath the Prophesied Hero of the Tiandi." Taishi visibly kept back tears as she lectured him in that particularly stiff tone of hers. She touched his face with her hand and lifted his cheeks. "Straighten up, boy. Don't embarrass me."

"I can't do it without you," he blubbered.

She cupped his chin. "You can, and you will."

"He really can't," Zofi echoed.

"I can't," he wailed. By now, Jian had completely lost it, but he didn't care.

"Enough!" Taishi overturned her tray of food. "My mind is made up. Now get out. We begin the test in four hours. Prepare yourself, Jian." She looked over at Zofi. "Pull yourself together, girl. I expect more from you." Taishi turned her attention back to Jian. She blinked, and a single tear escaped her eye and rolled down her cheek. "By tonight, you will assume the mantle as the new master of the Windwhispering School of the Zhang lineage, but now of the Wen family style."

CHAPTER SIXTY-THREE

THE RESULTS

Wen Jian walked outside the small house alongside Lee Mori and stopped in front of the small gathering of people. The masters were all there. Both Sohn and Bhasani were still recovering from their injuries. Bhasani would require several more months before she fully recovered. All the students were there too. Zofi was sitting next to Hachi, crying on his shoulder. Sonaya had immediately gotten up and hugged Jian as soon as he emerged, while Kaiyu sat alone a little ways off to the side. The boy, and new master of the Houtou style Third Lin lineage, was still grieving over his father.

The last of the group was Xinde, who was now officially a deserter of the Caobiu army. The former Longxian senior had discarded his uniform and was now plainly garbed in traditional basic war artist robes, which blended in well within the lunar court. He looked far more at ease dressed like that than in armor.

The other attendees were the three temple healers and a Hansoo, who Mori had vouched was trustworthy. The war monk was staring at Jian with a quiet intensity. He looked as if he was about to either prostrate himself at Jian's feet or attack him.

Jian's face was pale and stoic when he spoke. He appeared in shock, uncertain, scared. "It's done."

"All hail the new Master Windwhisper of the Zhang lineage, first in the Wen family style," intoned Templeabbot Lee Mori.

Zofi and Sonaya were holding each other, with Zofi burying her head in the drowned fist's shoulder. Occasionally Zofi would peek at Jian, furious. Surprisingly, Fausan was sobbing openly as well, the large man letting it all out and not bothering to hide his grief. He was histrionic, to say the least. It was a surprise he hadn't started rending his clothes. Sohn, sitting next to him, was clutching his hands together with his head hanging low, no doubt wracked with guilt for being the catalyst that led to all this. It served him right.

Jian looked solemn, almost dignified. Then he opened his mouth, and his voice cracked. "Ling Taishi was one of the greatest war artists of not one, but three generations. She was admired by people of honor, feared by villains, and scorned by lovers. She stood as an unequaled warrior in skill and legend. The lunar court will sing her praise for eight by eight generations." He closed his eyes and took another breath. "Ling Taishi also was the only one who ever cared about me. She saw the truth when others wove lies. She saw potential when they only saw failure. She was my shield when the world stood against me. Taishi took me under her roof when no one else would. She was the only family I ever had. She was my master, my friend, and my parent. Taishi sacrificed herself for the greater good, for all our people. It's now up to me, to us, if you will, to finish what she began and see that the prophecy is fulfilled to its rightful conclusion. It is the greatest honor we can bestow upon her. I intend to make her proud." An awkward silence passed. Jian was at a loss for words. He closed his eyes and buried his head in his hands. Sonaya rose from where she was sitting and went to embrace him. He rested his head on her shoulder.

Eventually, Jian recovered and continued his eulogy, although his words were muffled and drowned by the song of several nightingales.

After he was done, Sohn stood, using crutches, and reminisced about the one time he saved Taishi's life and the nine times she saved his. The eternal bright light master could be eloquent when he tried, although he was exaggerating some of the key details. Bhasani stood next and said that Taishi was the closest thing she ever had to a sister and a mortal enemy, and Bhasani was going to miss her terribly. Fausan tried to say a few words but fell apart and ugly cried, crumbling into a blubbering, slobbery mess. It was very unlike the man.

Mori spoke last, standing before the group and placing his hand on Jian's shoulder. "I may not be battle brethren with Taishi like most of you, but I have held her in high esteem for most of my life. She was the most capable, fiercely competent, and dynamic woman I've ever met. The world is a darker place now with her light gone. May the Tiandi shine her star brightly in the heavens." He pointed at the large vase filled with fragrant incense sticks. "Please join me in prayer to the Mosaic of the Tiandi."

The group stood one by one, each drawing one of the long white burning sticks, and joined Mori in prayer and kneeling and kowtowing to the great Mosaic so that Taishi could find her way to the celestial heavens. The templeabbot kept the ceremony simple, sincere, and honest. He also kept it brief and to the point, which was appreciated by all, and how Taishi would have preferred it.

After that, it was over.

"Hey," Hachi called to Jian as the group dispersed. "What will you do now?"

"I'm not sure," he replied. "Fulfill the prophecy, I guess."

"You guess?"

Jian shrugged. "Want to help?"

The whipfinger nodded. "Sure, man. I'm in. We'll make a name for ourselves, yeah?"

He nodded. "Yeah."

"What did you two just decide to do?" demanded Sonaya. "Without consulting me first?"

Jian looked confused. "Was I supposed to?"

Xinde came up to him from behind and put his arm around Jian's shoulders. "It would be the best way to honor your master's legacy, little brother. Mine too; Master Guanshi's honor still cries for justice."

There was more small talk and raising their fists in gestures of solidar-

ity. Everyone touched fists because they could not touch cups. The Vauzan Temple of the Tiandi had strict rules about drinking.

Jian was the last one in the yard before he went to the small house in
the far corner of the temple grounds. He closed the door behind him and
pressed against it before taking several long breaths: inhale, exhale, inhale, and then exhale. Jian looked up. "What do you think?"

Taishi, wearing a fuzzy, hooded bathrobe, sat behind the colored
glass window. "Your acting is atrocious, and the eulogy was a solid if
rather underwhelming effort."

"I'm sorry I haven't had much time for opera training lately. I'm sorry
I also didn't have time to write a speech because you sort of sprang this on
me last minute."

"It was fine," said Taishi. "You did fine. Whatever, just fine."

His eyes narrowed. One of her tells was being blandly agreeable.
"What's the matter, master? You're annoyed. Did you not like your memorial?"

She grimaced. "I thought it would be funnier, to be honest. Everyone
was so solemn. That's not how war artists eulogize their companions. I
thought they would lighten up after my death."

"Maybe you mean much more to them than just a companion," he
replied.

"Let's not get all sappy here. It's only my funeral." She studied him.
"It's not too late to go through with the Test of the Lineage. You're making a big mistake, but I can't force you. You have to want it." She'd tried;
she'd really tried. Taishi had ordered and commanded and screamed and
demanded and pleaded with Jian to follow through with the Grand Supreme Punch and the final Test of the Lineage, but he had refused and
wouldn't move from his decision.

"I'm sure, master. There was no way I would ever have gone through
with this." Jian shook his head. "You're more valuable to me as a mentor
than becoming the master of the lineage. I don't know how many days
you have left, but I will treasure them and learn from you until that last
day."

Taishi blinked. By the Tiandi, the boy really was ready. Ready to become his own man, and ready to assume the role of the Champion of the

Five Under Heaven. He was going to be pulverized when he fought the Eternal Khan, but hopefully, they would find a solution to that when it came time to address it. Until then, Wen Jian was ready to fulfill the prophecy.

"Are you sure we can't tell anyone?" asked Jian.

Taishi shook her head. "If you don't have my power and the full might of the Zhang windwhisper, then your allies and enemies must believe you do. They must assume you speak from a position of great power. I can no longer be there to protect you. My jing is deteriorating. Your aura of being the master windwhisper must now serve as your shield, Jian. All I can do is advise and train, but only in the shadows. No one must know of me outside of you and Mori. Is that clear, Jian?"

Jian looked unsure. "No one knows you're supposed to be dead."

"Of course they do." Taishi snorted. "You don't think of the temple gossips? Word will have leaked by now that over the past month, someone of significance had been sick in the back temple grounds. Mori posting security served only as a flame for curious moths. Now, today, we held a memorial. By the end of this cycle, word will have spread throughout the lunar court that Ling Taishi is dead and Wen Jian, the Prophesied Hero of the Tiandi and Champion of the Five Under Heaven, is the Zhang Master Windwhisper of the Wen family style. By the end of next cycle, the entire world will know. That's the beauty of this plan. We had to attempt to hide this knowledge in order to make it valuable. It's the subtle and badly hidden secrets like this that will spill across the land like wildfire."

"Every day after today is a blessing, master. We'll make it count."

"Now you're just being embarrassing." Taishi snorted. "Cut it out. Your platitudes and devotion, while well-intentioned, will get you no closer to fulfilling the prophecy. You have your work cut out for you, my son."

"What will you do next?"

"I don't know. I never retired before." Taishi shrugged. "I may take a long vacation. Rent out a villa along the Sea of Flowers and enjoy the weather. The herbalist says clement weather will help with my sickness. Maybe I . . ." Jian, however, was already not paying attention. Her former disciple was staring out the window. "Barely retired five minutes," she grumbled.

Jian's face was scrunched together. "Master, are you expecting company?"

"No, I'm dead, remember? No one knows I'm here," she replied. "And I'm not the master anymore. You're the master windwhisper now. You better get comfortable with that title."

"There's someone coming to the door." Jian squinted through the crack in the curtains. He reached for a saber leaning against the wall next to the door. Taishi hadn't officially offered him the Swallow Dances yet. That was probably the last step, and the one that would hit closest to home. It would be real then. She would not be the master windwhisper any longer.

There was a polite knock on the door, and then Mori walked in. The templeabbot's eyes were wide and his flesh pale. The bewilderment on his face was so unsettling that Taishi had initially thought someone was holding a blade into his back.

"Taishi," he panted. "I have the glorious honor of—"

The child oracle shoved Mori aside and stomped toward Taishi, high-kneeing every step of the way. Deep lines etched into her face as her mouth and eyes contorted in sharp and violent ways. Taishi must be dealing with Pei right now, because this little girl was *pissed*. "Taishi! What have you done?"

"Oracle," Taishi acknowledged with a slight tilt of her head. "Can we keep it down? I'm supposed to be dead."

"Do the right thing! That's all you had to do. Do the right thing, and everything had the best chance of turning out right. Do the right thing. That's all I asked." She actually raised her rag doll and hurled it at Taishi. The precocious little oracle was melting into a full-on tantrum. Floppy, her little pet red fox, joined in, slinking between the girl's ankles and hissing at Taishi like an ill-tempered cat. It was all rather adorable. Jian covered his mouth while he chuckled. No need to be rude about it. Her rage was something to behold. There was more to it, though, something else: fear.

Taishi looked unaffected by the outburst. She swirled the spoon in her cup of tea. "Hello, Pei. We believe we did exactly that."

"No," the oracle snapped. "You did exactly what *you* wanted to do."

"Why not both?"

"How convenient!" Pei jabbed a tiny finger in Taishi's face. "One thing, Taishi, the right thing, that was it, and you couldn't help but muddle that up! The only constant in your life is that you always make bad choices! Why even bother working to become one of the greatest war artists of your generation if you're going to ignore your responsibilities and screw with fate like a spoiled goober!"

Now Pei was getting a little personal. Jian raised his hand. "What do you mean, the right thing?"

The oracle turned her little wrath on Jian, and it was indeed furious. "And you! You rock brain. You discount dummy. You were *supposed* to kill her and take her power! That was the whole point of the entire exercise. That was everything. This terrible path is the best one we have left, and you just messed it up. Only on this path with Wen Jian assuming the mantle of the windwhisper lineage could anyone have become strong enough to kill the last of the Xoangiagu."

"The what?" he asked.

"We were almost there." Pei held up her forefinger and thumb. "See this? That was how much further you had to go and we would have stood a chance.

"That's the worst part," the oracle hissed. "You gave up all that just for a brief while longer with *her*?" The not-so-nice girl now shot an accusing finger at Taishi. "She's already dying!"

Jian shrugged, sticking his chin out at her, his eyes fierce and blazing. "You're never going to make me feel guilty for sparing my master's life."

The tiny prophet screamed. "No you hairless peanut! It's not about you, you monkey scrotum. I've seen the how the vision shifts." Pei's tone changed too. It became hushed, fearful. "Everyone now will die."

ACKNOWLEDGMENTS

You would think, after having written twelve books and twelve acknowledgments, that I would eventually run out of people to thank, but that's the thing with publishing. It really does take a village.

The Art of Destiny was an extra-tough project to crack. Part of it was wrangling this increasingly complex story. Part of it was the dreaded second-book-in-a-trilogy transition. And part of it was because the characters often had a mind of their own. Just like failed prophecies, free will often does not care about your outline.

Oh, and we also welcomed baby River to the world during the throes of the pandemic. Let me tell ya; having two young boys locked in the house with you was a special experience. One thing for sure, I needed the entire village while working on this book, and thankfully everyone showed up.

So here goes:

To my wife, Paula, I couldn't have asked for a better life partner. There were ups and downs and a bunch of sideways, but I couldn't have reached that light at the end of the tunnel without you pushing, dragging, and sometimes kicking me along the way.

To my boys, Hunter and River, nothing is more important to me than seeing you two grow to become such brilliant sparks of joy. You are my 42.

To my parents, Mike and Yukie, for always being there when we needed the grandparents. To my siblings, Stephen and Amy, for just being my life's anchors.

To my agent, Russ, who guided me to make the right decisions despite myself.

To my wonderful editor, Tricia, whose sharp instincts yet gentle hand helped hone this book into focus. You are my book whisperer.

To Sarah, part cheerleader, part savage, you kept this book on the right path.

To the team at Del Rey, the best in publishing: Keith Clayton, Scott Shannon, Alex Larned, Bree Gary, Ayesha Shibli, Ashleigh Heaton, Tori Henson, Sabrina Shen, David Moench, Ada Maduka, Cassie Gonzales, Jo Anne Metsch, Nancy Delia, Samuel Wetzler. This gorgeous book is the product of your hard work, talent, and dedication.

To Tran Nguyen, whose talent continues to amaze. The War Arts Saga is blessed to have your artwork grace its covers.

As always, thank you readers for continuing this journey alongside Taishi, Jian, Sali, and even Qisami. You are the reason I get to keep telling more stories. I hope we get to continue adventuring together for a long time.

ABOUT THE AUTHOR

WESLEY CHU is the #1 *New York Times* bestselling author of thirteen published novels, including *The Art of Prophecy, Time Salvager, The Rise of Io,* and *The Walking Dead: Typhoon.* He won the Astounding Award for Best New Writer. His debut, *The Lives of Tao,* won the Young Adult Library Services Association Alex Award. Chu is an accomplished martial artist and a former member of the Screen Actors Guild. He has acted in film and television, worked as a model and stuntman, and summited Kilimanjaro. He currently resides in Los Angeles with his wife, Paula, and two boys, Hunter and River.

wesleychu.com
Twitter: @wes_chu
Instagram: @wesleychu1

ABOUT THE TYPE

This book was set in Electra, a typeface designed for Linotype by
W. A. Dwiggins, the renowned type designer (1880–1956). Electra
is a fluid typeface, avoiding the contrasts of thick and thin strokes
that are prevalent in most modern typefaces.